READER'S DIGEST

CONDENSED BOOKS

FIRST EDITION

THE READER'S DIGEST ASSOCIATION LIMITED
25 Berkeley Square, London W1X 6AB

**THE READER'S DIGEST ASSOCIATION
SOUTH AFRICA (PTY) LTD**
Nedbank Centre, Strand Street, Cape Town

Printed in Great Britain by Petty & Sons Ltd, Leeds

Original cover design by Jeffery Matthews F.S.I.A.D.

For information as to ownership
of copyright in the material in this book see last page

ISBN 0 340 27254 6

Reader's Digest
CONDENSED BOOKS

THE LORD GOD MADE THEM ALL
James Herriot

LICENCE RENEWED
John Gardner

THE CRADLE WILL FALL
Mary Higgins Clark

A VERY PRIVATE WAR
Jon Cleary

COLLECTOR'S LIBRARY
EDITION

In this Volume:

The Lord God Made Them All
by James Herriot (p. 9)

Here is the latest of James Herriot's much-loved books about life as a Yorkshire vet. The war is over, and James returns from the RAF to his old friends in Darrowby and to the new joys and anxieties of fatherhood.

In the practice, methods are changing. But though one day James can be performing his first caesarean operation on a cow, or seeing the miraculous effect of penicillin, the next he finds the old ways are still the right ones, and that a sick animal needs the same care and kindness as it always has.

by John Gardner (p.111)

That most dashing secret agent of them all, James Bond, returns to the fray to pit his wits and skill against an enemy every bit as evil as Goldfinger or Blofeld.

In a remote Highland castle, the Laird of Murcaldy is plotting to hold the world to ransom. When James Bond learns of the laird's plan to entrap the major Western powers, even Bond's ingenuity is taxed to the limit as he battles single-handed to outwit his manic adversary.

THE CRADLE WILL FALL

by Mary Higgins Clark (p.257)

The injuries she had sustained in a car accident were slight, but Katie DeMaio was still feeling dizzy as she stared out of the hospital window. Through drifting sleet she saw a man lowering an unwieldy bundle into the boot of a car. Was she dreaming? Briefly the wind lifted the covering of the bundle. Katie muffled the scream that tore at her throat. The man looked up. At that moment she became an unacceptable risk. The author of *A Stranger is Watching* has written yet another electrifying thriller.

A VERY PRIVATE WAR

by Jon Cleary   *(p. 395)*

It is 1942, and in the South Pacific Allied forces are trying desperately to secure Guadalcanal and the Solomon Islands. To help the cause, expatriate American Con Mullane volunteers for an almost impossible job. He must slip through miles of enemy-infested jungle to spy on Japanese installations. The trek seems a madness, but Con Mullane has his own private reasons for hating the Japanese. For him this is an opportunity not only for heroism—but for revenge.

The Lord God Made Them All

A CONDENSATION OF THE BOOK BY
JAMES HERRIOT

ILLUSTRATED BY BRIAN SANDERS
PUBLISHED BY MICHAEL JOSEPH

When James Herriot returns to Yorkshire after war-time service in the RAF, he finds many changes in veterinary practice. New drugs and new surgical techniques make huge differences in the treatment of sick animals, saving lives where there has been no hope before. But Herriot finds too that the most important things are unchanged: the peace and beauty of the Dales, the rugged Yorkshire farmers, the animals themselves and their ailments. Helen is, as ever, a tower of strength to her husband, Siegfried Farnon is still his partner, and Tristan still erupts at intervals into their lives. And two little Herriots are added to the family, giving their parents much joy and amusement. This delightful book is a worthy successor to James Herriot's earlier books of reminiscence. Warmly human and sometimes very funny, it will charm all old admirers and make the author many new friends.

Chapter One

The high moorland road was unfenced and my car wheels ran easily from the strip of tarmac onto the turf, cropped to a velvet closeness by the sheep. I stopped the engine, got out and looked around me.

The road cut cleanly through the grass and heather before dipping into the valley beyond. This was one of the good places where I could see into two dales, the one I had left and the one in front. The whole land was spread beneath me; the soft fields in the valley floors, the grazing cattle, and the rivers thickly fringed with trees. The brilliant green of the walled pastures pushed up the sides of the fells until the heather and the harsh moor grass began, and only the endless pattern of walls was left climbing to the mottled summits, disappearing over the bare ridges which marked the beginning of the wild country.

I leaned back against the car and the wind blew the cold sweet air around me. I had been only a few weeks back in civilian life, and during my time in RAF blue I had thought constantly of Yorkshire, but I had forgotten how beautiful it was. Just thinking from afar could not evoke the peace, the solitude, the sense of the nearness of the wild which makes the Dales thrilling and comforting at the same time. Among the crowds, the drabness and stale air of the towns, I could not really imagine a place where I could be quite alone on the wide green roof of England, where every breath was filled with the grass scent.

I had had a disturbing morning. Everywhere I had gone I was

reminded that I had come back to a world of change, and I did not like it. One old farmer saying, "It's all t'needle now, Mr. Herriot," as I injected his cow, had made me look down almost with surprise at the syringe in my hand, realizing suddenly that this indeed was what I was doing most of the time.

Only a few years ago I would have been more likely to have "drenched" his cow: grabbed it by the nose and poured a pint of medicine down its throat. We still carried a special drenching bottle around with us, an empty wine bottle with no shoulders which allowed the liquid to run easily. Often we would mix the medicine with black treacle from the barrel which stood in the corner of most cow byres. But all this was disappearing and the farmer's remark brought it home to me that things were never going to be the same again.

A revolution had begun in agriculture and in veterinary practice. Farming had become more scientific and concepts cherished for generations were being abandoned, while in the veterinary world the first new advances were being seen. Previously undreamed of surgical procedures were being carried out, the sulpha drugs were going full blast, and, most exciting of all, the war, with its urgent need for better treatment of wounds, had given a tremendous impetus to the development of penicillin. This was not yet in the hands of the profession, but it was the advance guard of the therapeutic army which was to sweep our old treatments into oblivion.

There were signs, too, that the small farmer was on the way out. These men, some with only six cows and a few pigs and poultry, still made up most of our practice, but they were beginning to wonder if they could make a living. Doggedly they did the things they had always done for the sole reason that they had always done them. They were the men I cherished, the truly rich characters living by the ancient values, speaking the old Yorkshire dialect which television and radio have now almost extinguished.

I took a last long breath, then got into my car and drove back to Skeldale House. All was new here, too. My partner Siegfried had married and was living a few miles outside Darrowby, and Helen and I with our little son, Jimmy, were installed in the practice headquarters. When I got out of the car I gazed up at the ivy climbing over the mellow brick to the little rooms which looked out from under the tiles to the hills. Helen and I had started our married life in those rooms, but now we had the run of the whole house. It was too big for us, of course, but we both loved the old place with its spaciousness and its Georgian elegance.

Helen and I slept in the big room which I had occupied in my bachelor days, and Jimmy was in the dressing room where Siegfried's student brother, Tristan, used to rest his head. Tristan, alas, had left us. When the war ended he was Captain Farnon of the Royal Army Veterinary Corps; he married and joined the Ministry of Agriculture as an Infertility Investigation Officer. He left a sad gap in our lives, but fortunately we still saw him and his wife regularly.

I opened the front door and in the passage the fragrance of pulv aromat was strong. It was the aromatic powder which we mixed with our medicaments and it always had an excitement for me. It was the smell of our trade.

Halfway along the passage I passed the doorway to the long, high-walled garden and turned into the dispensary. This was a room whose significance was already on the wane. The rows of beautifully-shaped glass bottles with their latin titles engraved on them looked down at me: Spiritus Aetheris Nitrosi, Liquor Ammonii Acetatis Fortis, Potassii Nitras. Noble names. My head was stuffed with hundreds of them, their properties, actions and uses, and their dosage in horse, ox, sheep, pig, dog and cat. But soon I would have to concern myself only with how much of the latest antibiotic to administer.

As I left the dispensary I almost bumped into Siegfried. He was storming along the passage and he grabbed my arm in an agitated manner. "Ah, James, just the man I was looking for! I've had the most ghastly time this morning. I knocked the exhaust off my car going up that awful track to High Liston and now I'm without transport. They've sent for a new exhaust but until they get it fitted I'm stuck. It's maddening!"

"That's all right, Siegfried. I'll do your calls."

"No, no, James, it's kind of you, but don't you see, this sort of thing is going to happen again and again. That's what I wanted to

11

talk to you about. We need a spare car, something to fall back upon at a time like this. As a matter of fact I rang Hammond at the garage to bring round something suitable for us to look at. I think I can hear him outside now."

I followed my partner to the front door. Mr. Hammond was there with a 1933 Morris Oxford, and Siegfried trotted down the steps towards it.

"A hundred pounds, you said, eh, Mr. Hammond?" He walked around the car a couple of times, picking off pieces of rust from the black paintwork, opening the doors and peering at the upholstery. "Ah well, it's seen better days, but the appearance doesn't matter as long as it goes all right."

"It's a sound little job, Mr. Farnon," the garage proprietor said. "New battery and a good bit o' tread on the tyres." He adjusted the spectacles on his long nose and adopted a business-like expression.

"How about the brakes? Important in this hilly country."

"They're champion, Mr. Farnon. First rate."

"Good, good. You don't mind if I drive her round the block?"

"Nay, nay, of course not," Mr. Hammond replied. "Give 'er any trial you like." He was a man who prided himself on his imperturbability and he dropped confidently into the passenger seat as Siegfried took the wheel.

"Hop in the back, James!" my partner cried. I opened the rear door and took my place behind Mr. Hammond in the musty interior.

Siegfried took off abruptly with a roaring and creaking from the old vehicle, and despite the garage man's outward calm I saw the back of his shirt collar rise a couple of inches above his jacket as we shot along Trengate. The collar subsided a little when Siegfried slowed down at the church to make a left turn, but reappeared spasmodically as we negotiated a series of sharp and narrow bends at top speed.

When we reached the end of the long straight lane which runs parallel to Trengate, Siegfried came almost to a halt as he turned left.

"I think we'll test the brakes, Mr. Hammond," he said cheerfully, and hurled the car suddenly along the home straight for Trengate.

12

The roar of the ancient engine rose to a scream and the street approached with frightening rapidity. When Siegfried stood on the brakes the car slewed violently to the right and, as we catapulted crabwise into Trengate, Mr. Hammond's head was jammed against the roof. When we came to a halt he slid slowly back into his seat. At no time had he spoken or shown any emotion.

At the front door of the surgery we got out and my colleague rubbed his chin doubtfully. "She does pull a little to the right on braking, Mr. Hammond. I think we'd need to have that rectified, or perhaps you have another vehicle available?"

The garage man did not answer for a few moments. His spectacles were askew and he was very pale.

"Aye . . . aye . . ." he said shakily. "I 'ave another little job might suit you."

"Capital!" Siegfried rubbed his hands. "Perhaps you'd bring it along after lunch and we can have a spin round to try it."

Mr. Hammond swallowed a few times. "I'm goin' to be busy this afternoon, Mr. Farnon. I'll send one of me men."

We bade him goodbye and went back into the house. Walking along the passage my partner put an arm across my shoulders. "Well, James, another step towards increasing the efficiency of the practice. Anyway," he smiled, and whistled a few cheerful bars, "I rather enjoy these little interludes."

Suddenly I began to feel good. So many things were new and different, but the Dales hadn't changed, and Siegfried hadn't changed either.

Chapter Two

"Hello! Hello!" I bellowed.

"Hello! Hello!" little Jimmy piped just behind me.

I turned and looked at my son. He was four years old now and had been coming on my rounds with me for over a year. It was clear that he considered himself a veteran of the farmyards, an old hand versed in all aspects of agricultural lore.

This shouting was a common habit of mine. When a vet arrived on

13

a farm it was often surprisingly difficult to find the farmer. He might be a dot on a tractor half a mile across the fields, on rare occasions he might be in the house, but I usually hoped to find him among the buildings and relied on a few brisk shouts to locate him. Certain farms were distinctive in that you could never find anybody around. The house door would be locked and we would scour the barns, cowhouses and fold yards while our cries echoed back at us from the unheeding walls. What Siegfried and I used to call the "no finding" places were responsible for a lot of wasted time.

Jimmy had caught on to the problem quite early and there was no doubt he enjoyed the opportunity to exercise his lungs a bit. I watched him now as he strutted importantly over the cobbles, giving tongue every few seconds. He was also making an unnecessary amount of noise by clattering on the rough stones with his new boots.

Those boots were his pride, the final recognition of his status as veterinary assistant. When I first began to take him round with me his reaction was the simple joy of a child at being able to see animals of all kinds, particularly the young ones—there was the thrill of discovery when he came upon a huddle of kittens in the straw or found a bitch with pups in a loosebox. Before long, however, he wanted to get into the action. The contents of my car boot were soon as familiar to him as his toy box at home, and he delighted in handing out the tins of stomach powder, the white lotion and the long cartons of Universal Cattle Medicine. Finally he began to forestall me by rushing back to the car for calcium and flutter valve as soon as he saw a recumbent cow. He had become a diagnostician as well.

I think the thing he enjoyed most was accompanying me on an evening call, if Helen would allow him to postpone his bedtime. He was in heaven driving into the country in the darkness, training my torch on a cow's teat while I stitched it.

The farmers were kind, as they always are with young people. Even the most uncommunicative would grunt, "Ah see you've got t'apprentice with ye," as we got out of the car.

But those farmers had something which Jimmy coveted: their big hobnailed boots. He had a great admiration for farmers in general;

strong, hardy men who spent their lives in the open and who pushed fearlessly among plunging packs of cattle and slapped the rumps of massive cart horses. I could see he was deeply impressed as he watched them mounting granary steps with twelve or sixteen stone sacks on their shoulders, or hanging on effortlessly to the noses of huge bullocks, their boots slithering over the floor. Sturdy and unyielding, those boots seemed to symbolize for Jimmy the characters of the men who wore them.

Matters came to a head one day when we were conversing in the car. Or rather my son was doing the conversing in the form of a barrage of questions which I did my best to fend off while trying to think about my cases. These questions followed a well-tried formula.

"What is the fastest train—the Blue Peter or the Flying Scotsman?"

"Well now . . . I really don't know. I should say the Blue Peter."

Then, getting into deeper water. "Is a giant train faster than a phantom racing car?"

"That's a difficult one. Let's see now . . . maybe the phantom racer."

Jimmy changed his tack suddenly. "That was a big man at the last farm, wasn't he?"

"He certainly was."

"Was he bigger than Mr. Robinson?"

We were launching into his favourite "big man" game and I knew how it would end, but I played my part. "Oh yes, he was."

"Was he bigger than Mr. Leeming?"

"Certainly."

Jimmy gave me a sidelong glance and I knew he was about to play his two trump cards. "Was he bigger than the gas man?"

The towering gentleman who came to read the gas meters at Skeldale House had always fascinated my son and I had to think very carefully over my reply. "Well, you know, I really think he was."

"Ah, but . . ." The corner of Jimmy's mouth twitched up craftily. "Was he bigger than Mr. Thackray?"

That was the killer punch. Nobody was bigger than Mr. Thackray,

15

who looked down on the other inhabitants of Darrowby from six feet seven inches.

I shrugged my shoulders in defeat. "No, I have to admit it. He wasn't as big as Mr. Thackray."

Jimmy smiled and nodded, well satisfied. This put him in such high good humour that he broached something which must have been on his mind for some time. "Daddy," he said, "can I have some boots?"

"Boots? But you've got some already, haven't you?" I pointed down at the little wellingtons in which Helen always rigged him before he set out for the farms.

He gazed at his feet sadly before replying. "Yes, I know, but I want proper boots like the farmers."

This was a facer. "But Jim, little boys like you don't have boots like that. Maybe when you're bigger . . . ."

"Oh, I want proper boots now," he moaned in anguished tones.

At first I thought it was a passing whim but he kept up his campaign. As Helen drew on the wellingtons each morning, disgusted looks and a listless slouching conveyed the message that his footwear was entirely unsuitable for a man. Finally Helen and I talked it over one night.

"They surely don't have farm boots in his size, do they?" I asked.

Helen shook her head. "I wouldn't have thought so, but I'll look around in any case."

And it seemed that Jimmy wasn't the only little boy to have this idea because within a week my wife returned flushed with success and bearing the smallest pair of farm boots I had ever seen. I couldn't help laughing. They were so tiny, yet so perfect: thick, hobnailed soles, chunky uppers and a long row of lace-holes with metal loops at the top.

Jimmy didn't laugh when he saw them. He handled them with awe and once he had got them on his demeanour changed. He was naturally square set and jaunty, but to see him striding round a farmyard in corduroy leggings and those boots you would think he owned the place. He clumped and stamped, held himself very upright, and his cries of "Hello! Hello!" took on a new authority.

He was never what I would call naughty—certainly never

16

destructive or cruel—but he had that bit of devil which I suppose all boys need to have. He liked to assert himself and he was not above taking advantage of me in awkward situations. There was one afternoon when Mr. Garrett brought his sheepdog in. The animal was very lame, and as I hoisted him onto the table in the consulting room a small head appeared for a moment at the window which overlooked the sunlit garden.

I didn't mind that. Jimmy often watched me dealing with our small animal patients and I half expected him to come into the room for a closer look.

It is often difficult to locate the source of a dog's lameness but in this case I found it immediately. When I gently squeezed the outside pad on his left foot he winced and a tiny bead of serum appeared on the black surface. "He's got something in there, Mr. Garrett," I said. "Probably a thorn. I'll have to give him a shot of local anaesthetic and open up his pad."

It was when I was filling the syringe that a knee came into view at the corner of the window. I felt a pang of annoyance; Jimmy surely couldn't be climbing up the wisteria. It was dangerous and I had expressly forbidden it. The branches of the beautiful creeper curled all over the back of the house, and though they were as thick as a man's leg near ground level, they became quite slender as they made their way up to the roof.

I decided that I was mistaken and began to infiltrate the pad. The modern anaesthetics worked very quickly and within a minute or two I reached for the scalpel. "Hold his leg up and keep it as steady as you can," I said.

Mr. Garrett nodded and pursed his lips. He was a serious-faced man at any time, and obviously deeply concerned about his dog. His eyes narrowed in apprehension as I poised my knife.

With the point of my blade I made a careful nick in the tough tissue of the pad—and at that moment a shadow crossed the window. I glanced up. It was Jimmy, all right. The little blighter *was* on the wisteria, but there was nothing I could do about it then, except to give him a quick glare.

I cut a little deeper and squeezed, but still nothing showed in the wound. I didn't want to make a big hole but it was clear that I had to make a cross-shaped incision to see further down. I was drawing the scalpel across at right angles to my first cut when from the corner of my eye I spotted two feet dangling just below the top of the window. The feet swung and kicked repeatedly, obviously for my benefit. At last they disappeared, which could only mean that their owner was ascending to the dangerous regions. I dug down a little deeper and swabbed with cotton wool.

Ah yes, I could see something now, but it was very deep, probably the tip of a thorn which had broken off well below the surface. I reached for forceps and just then Jimmy's head showed itself, upside down this time: he was hanging by his feet from the branches and the face was positively leering. I had been trying to ignore the by-play from outside but this was too much. I shook my fist violently. My fury must have startled the performer because the face vanished instantly and I could hear faint sounds of feet scrambling upwards.

I forced myself back to my task. "Sorry, Mr. Garrett," I said. "Will you hold the leg up again, please."

He replied with a thin smile and I pushed my forceps into the depths. They grated on something hard. I gripped, pulled gently, and, oh lovely, out came the pointed, glistening head of a thorn. I had done it. It was one of the tiny triumphs which lighten vets' lives, and I was beaming at my client and patting his dog's head when I heard the crack from above. It was followed by a long howl of terror as a small form hurtled past the window and thudded with horrid force into the garden.

I threw down the forceps and shot out of the room, through the side door into the garden. Jimmy was already sitting up among the wallflowers and I was too relieved to be angry.

"Have you hurt yourself?" I gasped, and he shook his head.

I lifted him to his feet and felt him over carefully. There appeared to be no damage. "Go along and see mummy," I said, and returned to the consulting room.

I must have been deathly pale when I entered because Mr. Garrett looked startled. "Is he all right?" he asked.

"Yes, yes, I think so. But I do apologize for rushing out like that. It was really too bad of me to . . ."

Mr. Garrett laid his hand on my shoulder. "Say no more, Mr. Herriot, I have children of my own." And then he spoke the words which have become engraved on my heart. "You need nerves of steel to be a parent."

Later at tea I watched my son demolishing a poached egg on toast. I thanked heaven he was no worse for his fall, but I still had to remonstrate with him. "Look, young man," I said. "That was a very naughty thing you did out there. I've told you again and again not to climb the wisteria."

Jimmy bit into his toast and regarded me impassively. I could see that whatever I was going to say he wasn't going to take it too seriously.

"If you're going to behave like this," I went on, "I'm not going to take you round the farms with me. I'll just have to find another little boy to help me with my cases."

His chewing slowed down and I looked for some reaction in this morsel of humanity who was later to become a far better veterinary surgeon than I could ever be. "Another little boy?" Jimmy inquired.

"That's right. I'll have to find somebody else."

Jimmy thought this over for a minute or so, and then he shrugged and appeared to accept the situation philosophically. He started to slap jam on a slice of bread.

Then in a flash his sangfroid evaporated. He looked up at me in wide-eyed alarm and his voice came out in a high quaver. "Would he have my boots?"

Chapter Three

"It was Hemingway who said that, wasn't it?"

Norman Beaumont shook his head. "No, Scott Fitzgerald."

I didn't argue because Norman usually knew. In fact it was one of the attractive things about him.

I enjoyed having veterinary students seeing practice with us. They helped with fetching and carrying, they opened gates and they were company on our lonely rounds. In return they absorbed a lot of knowledge from our discussions, and it was priceless experience for them to be involved in the practical side of veterinary work.

Since the war, however, my relationship with these young men had undergone a distinct change. I found I was learning from them just about as much as they were learning from me. The reason, of course, was that veterinary teaching had taken a leap forward. The vast new field of small animal work was opening up dramatically; advanced surgical procedures were being carried out on farm animals, too, and the students had the great advantage of being able to see such things done in the new veterinary schools with their modern clinics and operating theatres.

New specialist textbooks were being written which made my own well-thumbed volumes seem like museum pieces. I was still a young man, but all the knowledge which I had nurtured so proudly was becoming irrelevant. Quittor, fistulous withers, poll evil, bog spavin, stringhalt—they didn't seem to matter much any more.

Norman Beaumont was in his final year and was a deep well of information at which I drank greedily. But apart from the veterinary side we had a common love of reading. When we weren't talking shop the conversation was usually on literary lines.

Norman was immensely likeable with a personality that was formal and dignified beyond his twenty-two years. He was a solid citizen in the making if ever I saw one, and this impression was strengthened by his slightly pear-shaped physique and the fact that he was determinedly trying to cultivate a pipe. I could see him plainly twenty years from now, definitely tubby, sitting at the fireside with his wife and children, puffing at that pipe which he had finally subjugated: an upright, dependable family man with a prosperous practice.

As the dry-stone walls rolled past the car windows I changed the topic to new operations. "And you say they are actually doing caesareans on cows in the college clinics?"

"Good Lord, yes." Norman made an expansive gesture. "It's a regular thing."

"Gosh, you don't know how lucky you are," I said. "The number of hours I've slaved on byre floors calving cows, knocking my guts out trying to bring heads round or reach feet. I think I must have shortened my life. And if only I'd known how, I could have saved

21

myself the trouble with a nice straightforward operation. What sort of a job is it, anyway?"

The student gave me a superior smile. "Nothing much to it, really." He lit his pipe, tamped the tobacco down and winced as he burned his finger. "Takes about an hour, and no hard labour."

"Sounds marvellous." I shook my head wistfully. "I'm beginning to think I was born too soon. I suppose it's the same with ewes?"

"Oh, yes indeed," Norman murmured airily. "Ewes, cows, sows—they're in and out of the place every day. No problem at all."

"Ah well, you young lads are lucky. It's so much easier to tackle these jobs when you've seen a lot of them done."

"True, true. But of course most bovine parturitions don't need a caesarean and I'm always glad to have a calving for my casebook."

I nodded in agreement. Norman's casebook was a heavily bound volume with every scrap of interesting material meticulously entered under headings in red ink. The examiners always wanted to see these books and this one would be worth a few extra marks to Norman in his finals.

I dropped the student at his digs in the late afternoon and went back to Skeldale House for tea. I had just finished when Helen got up to answer the phone. "It's Mr. Bushell of Sycamore House," she said. "He has a cow calving."

"Oh damn," I said as I put down my cup. It was August Bank Holiday and I'd hoped for a quiet evening at home. "Tell him I'll be right out, Helen, will you? One thing, Norman will be pleased. He was just saying he wanted something for his casebook."

I was right. The young man rubbed his hands in glee when I called for him and he was in excellent humour as we drove to the farm.

"I was reading some poetry when you rang the bell," he said. "You can always find something there to apply to life. How about now, when I'm expecting something interesting: 'Hope springs eternal in the human breast.' "

"Alexander Pope, Essay on Man," I grunted. I wasn't feeling so enthusiastic as we drove through the farm gateway into the yard. "What about 'Abandon hope all ye who enter here.' "

"Dante, of course, The Inferno. But don't be so pessimistic."

Norman patted me on the shoulder as I put on my wellingtons.

The farmer led us into the byre, and in a stall opposite the window a small cow looked up at us anxiously from her straw bed. Above her head, her name, Bella, was chalked on a board.

"She isn't very big, Mr. Bushell," I shouted, remembering that he was hard of hearing.

The farmer shrugged. "Aye. Had a rough time with her first calvin' but she milked well enough after it."

I looked thoughtfully at the cow as I stripped off my shirt and soaped my arms. I didn't like the look of that narrow pelvis and I breathed a silent prayer that there might be a tiny calf inside.

The farmer poked at the rump with his foot and shouted at the animal to make her rise. "She won't budge, Mr. Herriot," he said. "She's been painin' all day."

I didn't like the sound of that either. There was always something wrong when a cow strained for a long time without result. And the little animal did look utterly spent. Her head hung down and her eyelids drooped wearily.

If she wouldn't get up I had to get down. With my bare chest in contact with the ground, I thought that cobbles didn't get any softer with the passage of the years. But when I slid my hand into the vagina I forgot about my discomfort. The pelvic opening was villainously narrow, and beyond was something which froze my blood: two enormous hooves and a huge expanse of muzzle with twitching nostrils, squeezing into the small space like a cork in a bottle. As I withdrew my hand the rough surface of the calf's tongue flicked briefly against my palm.

I sat back on my heels and looked up at the farmer. "There's an elephant in there, Mr. Bushell. A tremendous calf, and no room for it to come out."

"Well, that's a beggar," Mr. Bushell said. "She's a good little milker. Ah don't want to send 'er to the butcher."

Neither did I. I hated the very thought of it. In a great moment of decision I turned to the student. "This is it, Norman! The ideal indication for a caesar. What a good job I've got you with me." I was slightly breathless with excitement and I hardly noticed the flicker of anxiety in the young man's eyes.

I got to my feet and seized the farmer's arm. "Mr. Bushell, I'd like to do a caesarean operation on your cow—open her up and remove the calf surgically."

"Tek it out o' the side, d'ye mean? Like they do wi' women?"

"That's right."

"Well, that's a rum'un." The farmer's eyebrows went up. "I never knew you could do that wi' cows. I reckon she'd die if you made a bloody great 'ole in her like that. Maybe she'd be better goin' for slaughter."

I could see my big moment slipping away from me. "But she's only a thin little thing. She wouldn't be worth much for meat and with a bit of luck we might get a live calf out of her."

I was going against one of my steadfast rules—never to talk a farmer into doing something—but I was seized by a kind of madness. Mr. Bushell looked at me for a long time, then without changing expression he nodded.

"Awright. What do you want?"

"Two buckets of warm water, soap, towels," I replied. "And I'll bring some instruments into the house to boil if I may."

When the farmer had departed I thumped Norman on the shoulder. "This is just right. Plenty of light, a live calf to aim for, and if we keep our voices down I'll be able to ask you things as we go along."

Norman didn't say anything. I told him to set up some straw bales for our equipment while I boiled the instruments in a pan in the farm kitchen. Soon syringes, suture materials, scalpels, scissors, local anaesthetic and cotton wool were laid in a row on a clean towel draped over one of the bales. I added some antiseptic to the water and addressed the farmer. "We'll roll her over and you can hold the head down, Mr. Bushell."

Norman and I pushed at the shoulder and Bella flopped on her side without resistance. The farmer put his knee against her neck and the long area of the left flank was exposed for our attention. I nudged the student. "Where do I make the incision?" I whispered.

"Well, er, it's about . . ." Norman pointed vaguely.

I nodded. "Around the rumenotomy site, eh? But a bit lower I suppose." I began to clip away the hair from a foot long strip. It

24

would need a big opening for that calf to come through. Then I quickly infiltrated the area with local anaesthetic. I cut through skin, muscle layers and peritoneum and was confronted by a protruding pink and white mass of tissue.

I poked at it with my finger. There was something hard inside. "What's that?" I hissed. "Is it the rumen or the uterus? It's pretty low down for the first stomach, it could be the uterus."

The student swallowed a couple of times. "Yes . . . yes . . . that's the uterus all right."

"Good." I smiled in relief and made a bold incision. A great gout of grass welled out followed by an outflow of dirty brown fluid.

"Oh God!" I gasped. "It's the rumen. Look at all that mess!" I groaned aloud as the filthy tide surged away down and out of sight into the abdominal cavity. "What the hell are you playing at, Norman?"

I could feel the young man's body trembling against mine.

"Don't just sit there!" I shouted. "Thread me one of those needles. Quick! Quick!"

Norman bounded to his feet, rushed over to the bale and returned with a trailing length of catgut. Dry-mouthed, I stitched the gash I had made in the cow's stomach. Then the two of us made frantic attempts to swab away the escaped rumenal contents with cotton wool and antiseptic but much of it was beyond our reach. The contamination would be massive.

When we had done what we could, I sat back and looked at the student. My voice was a hoarse growl. "I thought you knew all about these operations. How many caesareans have you seen?"

Norman looked at me with frightened eyes. "Well . . . er . . . one, actually."

"One! To hear you speak I thought you were an expert! Even if you'd seen only one you should know a little bit about it."

He shuffled his knees around on the cobbles. "The thing is . . . I was right at the back of the class. I couldn't see very well."

"Well, you're a stupid young fool!" I said in a vicious whisper. "Dishing out your confident instructions when you know damn all. You realize you've killed this good cow. With all that contamination she'll certainly develop peritonitis and die. All we can hope for now is to get the calf out alive." I turned my gaze from his stricken face. "Anyway, let's get on with it."

Apart from my first shouts of panic the entire interchange had been carried out pianissimo and Mr. Bushell kept shooting inquiring glances at us. I gave him what I hoped was a reassuring smile and returned to the attack. Plunging my arm deep below what I now knew was the rumen I encountered a smooth and mighty organ lying on the abdominal floor, containing an enormous bulk with the hardness and immobility of a sack of coal. I felt my way along the surface and came upon the unmistakable contours of a hock pushing against the slippery wall. That was the calf all right, but it was far, far away.

I withdrew my arm and started on Norman again. "From your position at the back of the class," I inquired bitingly, "did you happen to notice what they did next?"

"Next? Ah yes." He licked his lips. "You are supposed to exteriorize the uterus—bring it up to the wound."

"Good God!" I said. "King Kong couldn't lift up that uterus. In fact I can't move it an inch. Have a feel."

The student, who was stripped and soaped like myself, introduced his arm and for a few moments I watched his eyes pop and his face redden. Then he nodded sheepishly. "You're right. It won't move."

"Only one thing to do." I picked up a scalpel. "I'll have to cut into the uterus and grab that hock. There's nothing else to get hold of."

It was very nasty fiddling about down in the dark unknown, my arm buried to the shoulder in the cow. I was terrified I might slash into something vital but in fact it was my own fingers that I cut, several times, before I was able to draw the scalpel across the bulge made by the hock. A second later I had my hand round the hairy leg.

Gingerly I enlarged the incision, inch by inch. I hoped fervently I had made it big enough as I seized the leg and tried to lift it, and immediately I knew it was going to take tremendous strength to bring the calf into the light of day. Nowadays when I do a caesar I take care to have a big strong farm lad ready to help me. "Come on, Norman," I panted. "Give me a hand."

26

We reached down together and began to pull. Grunting with effort, we hauled upwards till at last I was able to grasp the other hind leg. Even then, with a foot apiece in our hands, nothing wanted to move. I wished with all my heart and soul that I had never started this ghastly job. If only I had followed Mr. Bushell's suggestion to send the cow for slaughter I would now be driving peacefully on my rounds. Instead, here I was, killing myself, and I hadn't the slightest idea what was going to happen next.

But the calf was gradually coming through. The tail appeared, then an unbelievably massive rib cage and finally, with a rush, the shoulders and head. Norman and I sat down with a bump, the calf rolling over our knees. And like a gleam of light in the darkness I saw that he was snorting and shaking his head.

"By gaw, he's a big 'un!" exclaimed the farmer.

I nodded. "Yes, he's huge. One of the biggest I've ever seen." I felt between the hind legs. "A bull, as I thought. He'd never have come out the proper way."

My attention was whisked back to the cow. Where was the uterus? It had vanished. Again I started my frantic groping inside. My hand became entangled with yards of placenta; I pulled it out and dropped it on the floor but I still couldn't find the uterus. I wondered what would happen if I never did locate it, and then my fingers came upon the ragged edge of my incision.

I pulled as much as possible of the organ up to the light and I noticed with sinking disquiet that the opening had been enlarged by the passage of that enormous calf, and that there was a long tear disappearing out of sight towards the cervix.

"Sutures." I held my hand out and Norman gave me a fresh needle. "Hold the lips of the wound," I said and began to stitch.

I worked as quickly as I could and was doing fine until the tear ran out of sight. The rest was a kind of martyrdom. Norman hung on grimly while I stabbed around at the invisible tissue far below. And to my dismay a further complication had arisen: the calf was now on his feet, blundering unsteadily around.

The speed with which newly-born animals get onto their legs has always fascinated me but at this moment it was an unmitigated nuisance. The calf, looking for the udder with that instinct which

27

nobody can explain, kept pushing his nose at the cow's flank and at times went toppling head first into the gaping hole in her side.

"Reckon 'e wants back in again," Mr. Bushell said with a grin. "By 'eck he is a wick 'un."

"Wick" is Yorkshire for lively and the word was never more aptly applied. As I worked I had to keep nudging the wet muzzle away with my elbow, but as fast as I pushed him back the calf charged in again and with sick resignation I saw that every time he nosed his way into the cavity he spread straw and dirt from the floor over the abdominal contents. "Look at that," I moaned. "As if there wasn't enough muck in there."

Norman didn't reply. His mouth was hanging open and the sweat ran down his blood-streaked face as he grappled with that unseen wound. And in his fixed stare I seemed to read a growing doubt as to his wisdom in deciding to be a veterinary surgeon.

I would rather not go into any more painful details. Sufficient to say that after an eternity I got as far down the uterine tear as I could, and then cleared away a lot of rubbish from the cow's abdomen and covered everything with antiseptic dusting powder. I stitched up the muscle and skin layers with the calf trying all the time to get in on the act, and at last the thing was finished.

Norman and I got to our feet very slowly, like two old, old men. Then, since we were both plastered with caked blood and filth, we began the slow process of scrubbing and scraping ourselves clean.

Mr. Bushell left his position by the head and looked at the row of skin stitches. "Nice neat job," he said. "And a grand calf, too."

Yes, that was something. The little creature was a beauty, his body swaying on unsteady legs, his wide-set eyes filled with gentle curiosity. But that "neat job" hid things I didn't dare think about, and I knew there was no hope for the cow. More as a gesture than anything else I left the farmer some sulphanilamide powders to give her three times a day. Then I got off the farm as quickly as I could.

We drove away in silence. I rounded a couple of corners, and then stopped the car under a tree and sank my head against the steering wheel.

"Oh hell," I groaned. "What a mess. Did you ever see such a performance? All that straw and muck in among that poor cow's bowels. It made me think about the story of that surgeon who left his hat inside his patient. It was as bad as that."

"I know." Norman spoke in a strangled undertone. "And it was all my fault."

"Oh no, it wasn't," I replied. "I made a right rollocks of the whole thing and I tried to blame you because I got in a panic. I owe you an apology. I am supposed to be a qualified veterinary surgeon and I did nearly everything wrong."

"You didn't, really you didn't . . . I . . . ."

"Anyway, Norman," I broke in. "I'm going to thank you now. You worked like a trojan and I'd have got nowhere at all without you. Let's go and have a pint."

With the early evening sunshine filtering into the bar parlour of the village inn, we dropped into a quiet corner and pulled deeply at our beer glasses. We were both hot and weary.

"Do you think that cow has any chance?" Norman asked.

I examined the cuts and punctures of my fingers for a moment. "No, Norman. Peritonitis is inevitable and I'm pretty sure I've left a good sized hole in her uterus." I shuddered at the memory.

I was sure I would never see Bella alive again, but next morning a morbid curiosity made me lift the phone to find out if she had survived so far. The "buzz-buzz" at the other end seemed to last a long time before Mr. Bushell answered.

"Oh, it's Mr. Herriot. Cow's up and eatin'."

It was several seconds before I was able to absorb his words. "Doesn't she look a bit dull or uncomfortable?" I asked huskily.

"Nay, nay, she's bright as a cricket. Finished off a rackful of hay and I got a couple o' gallons of milk from 'er. When'll you take them stitches out?"

"Stitches . . . ? Oh yes." I gave myself a shake. "In a fortnight, Mr. Bushell, in a fortnight."

After the horrors of the first visit I was glad Norman was with me when I removed the sutures. There was no swelling round the wound and Bella chewed her cud happily as I snipped away. In a pen nearby the calf gambolled and kicked his feet in the air.

I couldn't help asking, "Has she shown any symptoms at all, Mr. Bushell?"

"Nay." The farmer shook his head slowly. "You wouldn't know owt had happened to 'er."

That was the way it was at my first caesarean. Over the years Bella went on to have eight more calves normally and unaided, a miracle which I can still hardly believe.

As Norman and I drove away we felt an elation which was all the sweeter for being unexpected. I looked at the young man's smiling face. "Well, Norman," I said. "That's veterinary practice for you. You get a lot of nasty shocks but some lovely surprises, too. I've often heard of the wonderful resistance of the bovine peritoneum and thank heavens it's true."

"The whole thing's marvellous, isn't it," he murmured dreamily. "I can't describe the way I feel. My head seems to be full of quotations like: 'Out of this nettle, danger, we pluck this flower, safety.'"

"Splendid, splendid," I replied. "Shakespeare, Henry the Fifth."

"No, Henry the Fourth."

I opened my mouth to argue but Norman held up a confident hand. "It's no good, I'm right. And this time I *do* know what I'm talking about."

Chapter Four

The farm man moved between the cows to take hold of my patient's tail, and when I saw his haircut I knew immediately that Josh Anderson had been on the job again. It was a Sunday morning and everything fitted into place. I really didn't have to ask.

"Were you in the Hare and Pheasant last night?" I inquired carelessly as I inserted my thermometer.

He ran a hand ruefully over his head. "Aye, ye can see straight off, can't ye? T'missus has been playin' 'ell with me ever since."

"I suppose Josh had had one too many, eh?"

"Aye he had. I should've known better, pickin' a Saturday night. It's me own fault."

Josh Anderson was one of the local barbers. He was devoted to his job, even to the extent of taking his scissors and clippers to the pub with him every night. For the price of a pint he would give anybody a quick trim in the gents' lavatory.

Habitués of the Hare and Pheasant were never surprised to find one of the customers sitting impassively on the toilet seat with Josh snip-snipping round his head. With beer at sixpence a pint it was good value, but Josh's clients knew they were taking a chance. If the barber's intake had been moderate they would escape relatively unscathed, but if he had imbibed beyond a certain point terrible things could happen. Josh had not as yet been known to cut off anybody's ear, but if you strolled around the town on Sundays you were liable to come across some very strange coiffures.

I looked again at the farm man's head. From my experience I judged that Josh would have been around the ten pint mark when he did that one. The upper half seemed to have been delved into at random, leaving bare patches in some parts and long dangling wisps in others. I couldn't see the back but I had no doubt that there could be a pigtail or anything lurking behind there.

I always played safe, and when my hair needed cutting I went to Josh's shop, where he operated in a state of strict sobriety. I was sitting there a few days later waiting my turn, with my beagle, Sam, under my seat, and I watched the barber at work. There was a burly man in the chair and his red face, reflected in the mirror, was contorted every few seconds with spasms of pain. The simple fact was that Josh didn't cut hair, he pulled it out. He did this not only because his equipment was antiquated and needed sharpening, but because he had perfected a certain flick of the wrist with his hand clippers which wrenched the hairs from their follicles at the end of each stroke.

The wonder was that anybody went to Josh for a haircut, because there was another barber in the town. My own opinion was that it was because everybody liked him.

He was a tiny man in his fifties with a gentle smile which never seemed to leave his face, and a bald head which made a mockery of the hair restorer on his shelves. As his client rose from the chair, patently relieved that his ordeal was over, Josh fussed around him, brushing him down, patting his back and chattering gaily. You could see his obvious love of his fellow men.

Next to the big farmer, Josh looked smaller than ever, and I marvelled at how he managed to accommodate all that beer. Even now, after forty years in Yorkshire, I cannot compete; after two or three pints discomfort sets in. Yet Josh would swallow around eight pints every night of the week except Saturday, when he stepped up his intake to between ten and fourteen, and he never looked much different. His professional skill suffered, but that was all.

He was turning to me now. "Well, Mr. Herriot, it's good to see you again. Are you very well?"

"I'm fine, thank you, Mr. Anderson," I replied as he ushered me to the chair. "And how are you?"

"Nicely, sir, nicely." He began to tuck the sheet under my chin and laughed delightedly as my little dog trotted in under the folds. "By gum, Mr. Herriot, Sam's a faithful friend. Never lets you out of 'is sight if he can help it."

"That's right," I said. "And I don't like to go anywhere without him." I screwed round in my chair. "By the way, didn't I see you with a dog the other day?"

Josh paused, scissors in hand. "You did an' all. A little stray bitch—got 'er from the Cat and Dog Home at York. Now that our kids have all left home t'missus and I fancied gettin' a dog and we think the world of her. I tell ye, she's a grand 'un."

"What breed is she?"

"Eee, nobbut a mongrel, I reckon. Hang on a minute and I'll bring 'er down."

He clumped upstairs to where he lived above the shop and returned with a little bitch in his arms. "There you are, Mr. Herriot. What d'you think of that?" He stood her on the floor for my inspection.

The little animal was a light grey in colour with very long crinkled hair. In fact at a quick glance she looked like a miniature Wensleydale sheep. Definitely a hound of baffling lineage, but the panting mouth and swishing tail bore witness to her good nature.

"I like her," I said. "I think you've picked a winner there."

"That's what we think." He stooped and fondled his new pet. "We've called her Venus, because she's so beautiful," he said seriously.

32

"Ah yes," I said. "I see."

He washed his hands, took up his scissors again and grasped a few strands of my hair. It wasn't too bad with the scissors—it was when he reached for the clippers that I gripped the arms of the chair as though I were at the dentist. That jerk at the end, plucking the last tuft from its roots set my face grimacing at me in the mirror; once or twice an involuntary "Ooh!" or "Aah!" escaped me.

Though he was the least arrogant or conceited of men, Josh did consider himself a gifted hairdresser. Even now as he gave me a final combing I could see the pride shining from his face. Head on one side, he made a finicky snip here and there before holding up the hand mirror for my inspection. "All right, Mr. Herriot?"

"Lovely, Mr. Anderson, just fine." Relief added warmth to my voice.

"Aye, you know, it's easy enough to cut hair off. The secret is knowin' what to leave on."

I had heard him say it a hundred times before but I laughed dutifully as he whisked his brush over the back of my coat.

Before I paid my next visit to the barber he arrived on my front door step, carrying Venus in his arms. She was a vastly different creature from the placid little animal I had seen in his shop. She was bubbling saliva, retching and pawing frantically at her face.

"Has she swallowed something, Mr. Anderson?"

"Aye, she's 'ad a chicken bone." Josh looked distraught. "We'd had a bird for our dinner and she pinched the frame out of the dustbin, the little beggar. She had a good crunch at it afore I spotted 'er and now she's goin' to choke!" He was on the verge of tears.

"Now just calm down," I said. "I don't think Venus is choking. By the way she's pawing I should say there's something stuck in her mouth."

I grabbed the little animal's jaws with finger and thumb and forced them apart. And I saw with a surge of relief the sight familiar to all vets—a long bone jammed tightly between the back molars and forming a bar across the roof of the mouth. It is a common occurrence in practice and a happy one because it is easily relieved by a flick of the forceps. Recovery is instantaneous, skill minimal, and the kudos most warming.

I put my hand on the barber's shoulder. "You can stop worrying, Mr. Anderson, it's just a bone stuck in her teeth. Come through to the consulting room and I'll have it out in a jiffy."

I could see the man relaxing as we walked along to the back of the house. "Oh, thank God for that, Mr. Herriot. I thought she'd had it, and we've grown right fond of the little thing. I couldn't bear to lose 'er."

I put the dog on the table and reached for a strong pair of forceps. "No question of that, I assure you. This won't take a minute."

Jimmy had left his tea and trailed after us. Even at his age he had seen this sort of thing many a time and it wasn't very exciting, but you never knew in veterinary practice; it was worth hanging around because funny things could happen. He put his hands in his pockets and rocked back and forth on his heels, whistling softly as he watched me.

Usually it is simply a matter of opening the mouth, clamping the forceps on the bone and removing it. But Venus recoiled in terror from the gleaming metal and so did the barber. I tried to be soothing. "This is nothing, Mr. Anderson. I'm not going to hurt her in the least, but you'll just have to hold her head firmly for a moment."

The little man took a deep breath, grasped the dog's neck, and screwed his eyes tight shut. Venus struggled violently, pawing at my hand, to the accompaniment of strange moaning sounds from her owner. When I did get the forceps into her mouth she locked her front teeth on the instrument and hung on fiercely, and as I began to grapple with her Mr. Anderson could stand it no longer and let go. The little dog leaped to the floor.

I looked at the barber more in sorrow than anger. This was just not his thing. He was as manually ham-fisted as his hairdressing proved and he seemed quite incapable of holding a wriggling dog.

"Let's have another go," I said cheerfully. "We'll try it on the floor this time. Maybe she's frightened of the table."

But each time the little man reached for her she slithered away from him until he slipped face down onto the tiles. Jimmy giggled. Things were looking up.

I helped the barber to his feet. "I tell you what, Mr. Anderson, I'll give her a short-acting anaesthetic. That will cut out all this fighting and struggling."

Josh's face paled. "An anaesthetic? Put her to sleep, you mean?" He glanced pitifully at his pet. "Will she be all right?"

"Of course, of course. Just leave her to me and come back for her in about an hour. She'll be able to walk then." I began to steer him through the door into the passage. "We'll only upset her if we go on this way."

"Very well, then, I'll go along to me brother's for an hour."

"Splendid." I waited till I heard the front door close behind him and then quickly made up a dose of pentothal.

Dogs do not put on such a tough front when their owners are not present and I scooped Venus easily from the floor onto the table. I gripped her leg above the elbow and clipped an area from the raised radial vein. I slid the needle in, depressed the plunger and within seconds her fighting pose relaxed and her whole body sagged onto the table. She was fast asleep.

"No trouble now, Jimmy lad," I said. I pushed the teeth apart effortlessly, gripped the bone with the forceps and lifted it from the mouth. "Nothing left in there—all done. Yes, that's the professional way to do it, my boy. No undignified scrambling."

My son nodded briefly. Things had gone dull again. He had been hoping for great things when Mr. Anderson draped himself along the surgery floor, but this was tame stuff. He had stopped smiling.

My own satisfied smile, however, had become a little fixed. Venus wasn't breathing. I tried to ignore the lurch in my stomach because I have always been a nervous anaesthetist, and I told myself as always that there was no danger. She had received the correct dose and you often did get this with pentothal, but just the same I wished to God she would start breathing.

The heart was still going all right. I depressed the ribs a few times—nothing. I touched the eyeball—no corneal reflex. I began to stare closely at the little animal and I could see that Jimmy was watching me just as keenly. His deep interest in veterinary practice was given extra colour by the fact that he never knew when his father might do something funny. The unpredictable mishaps of the daily round were all good for a laugh and my son with his unerring

35

instinct had a feeling that something of the sort was going to happen now.

His hunch was proved right when I suddenly lifted Venus from the table, shook her vainly a few times above my head, and then set off at full gallop along the passage. I could hear the eager shuffle of the little slippers just behind me. I threw open the side door and shot into the back garden, continuing my headlong rush till I reached the big lawn. The little dog's ribs were not moving and the eyes stared sightlessly ahead.

Oh, this just couldn't happen! I seized Venus by a hind leg in either hand and began to whirl her round and round my head, attaining a remarkable speed as I put all my strength into the swing. This method of resuscitation seems to have gone out of fashion now, but it was very much in vogue then. It certainly met with the full approval of my son. He laughed so much that he fell down. When I stopped and glared at the still immobile ribs he cried, "Again, daddy, again," until daddy was in full action once more with Venus swooping through the air like a bird on the wing.

It exceeded all Jimmy's expectations. He probably had wondered about leaving his jam sandwiches to see the old man perform, but how gloriously he had been rewarded. To this day the whole scene is vivid; my tension and misery lest my patient should die, and in the background the helpless, high-pitched laughter of my son.

I don't know how many times I stopped, then recommenced my whirling, but at last the chest wall gave a heave and the eyes blinked. With a gasp of relief I collapsed face down on the cool turf and peered through the green blades as the breathing became regular and Venus began to lick her lips and look around her.

Jimmy was disappointed. "Aren't you going to do any more, daddy?"

"No, son, no." I sat up, the old brick walls of the garden still dancing around me, and dragged Venus onto my lap. "It's all over now."

"Well, that was funny. Why did you do it?"

"To make the dog breathe."

"Do you always do that to make them breathe?"

"No, thank heaven, not often." I got slowly to my feet and carried the little animal back to the consulting room. By the time Josh Anderson arrived his pet was looking almost normal.

"She's still a little unsteady from the anaesthetic," I said. "But that won't last long."

"Eee, isn't that grand. And that nasty bone, is it . . . ?"

"All gone, Mr. Anderson." I opened the mouth. "You see? Not a thing."

He smiled happily. "Did ye have any bother with her?"

I swallowed. "Not a bit, Mr. Anderson. A quite uneventful operation." To tell him that his dog had been almost dead for a considerable time would not cheer him nor would it bolster his faith in me. It was the whitest of lies, but it nearly choked me and the aftertaste of guilt was strong.

"Wonderful, wonderful. I am grateful, Mr. Herriot." He bent over the dog and stroked her long hair. "Have ye been floatin' through the air, Venus?" he murmured absently.

The back of my neck prickled. "What . . . what makes you say that?"

"Well . . . I reckon she'd think she was floatin' while she was asleep. Just a funny feeling I had."

"Ah, yes, well, er . . . right." I had a very funny feeling myself. "You'd better take her home now and keep her quiet for the rest of the day."

I was very thoughtful as I finished my tea. Floating . . . floating.

A fortnight later I was again seated in Josh's barber's chair, bracing myself for the ordeal. To my alarm he started straight in with the dread clippers, and in an attempt to alleviate the pain I began to chatter with an edge of hysteria in my voice. "How is—ouch—Venus going on?"

"Oh, fine, fine." Josh smiled at me tenderly in the mirror as he whipped out another tuft with that inimitable flick of his. "It's a grand thing to 'ave faith in your vet, Mr. Herriot. I knew our little pet was in good 'ands."

"Well, thank you very much, Mr. Anderson, it's—aaah—very nice to hear that." I was gratified, but that guilty feeling was still there.

I tried to concentrate on something else. It is a trick I adopt at the dentist's and as the little man tugged away I thought as hard as I could about my garden. The lawns really did want mowing and there were all those weeds to get at when I had a minute to spare. I had got round to considering whether it was time to put some fertilizer on my tomatoes when the barber's voice pulled me back to reality.

"Mr. Herriot." He was twiddling away at a wisp of my hair with his fingers. "I like gardening, too."

I almost jumped from the chair. "That's remarkable. I was just thinking about my garden."

"Aye, ah know." There was a faraway look in his eyes as he rolled the strand with finger and thumb. "It comes through the hair, ye know. Your thoughts come through to me. Them hairs go right down into your head and they catch summat from your brain and send it up to me."

"Oh really, you're kidding me." I gave a hollow laugh.

Josh shook his head. "I'm not jokin' nor jestin', Mr. Herriot. I've been at this game for nearly forty years and it keeps happenin' to me. You'd be flabbergasted if I told ye some of the thoughts that's come up. Couldn't repeat 'em, I tell ye."

I slumped lower in my white sheet. Absolute rubbish, of course, but I made a firm resolve never to think of Venus's anaesthetic during a haircut.

Chapter Five

"This is Biggins 'ere."

I gripped the telephone tightly. Mr. Biggins's vacillations always tried me sorely. He regarded calling out the vet as a final desperate measure and it was always sheer torture for him to make up his mind to do so. On top of that he was extremely pig-headed about taking my advice whenever I did manage to fight my way onto his farm.

"What's the trouble, Mr. Biggins?"

"Well . . . I 'ave a heifer badly."

"Right, I'll have a look at her this morning."

"Haud on, just a minute. Are you sure she needs seein'?"

"Well, I don't know. What is she doing?"

There was a long pause. "Just laid out, like."

"Laid out?" I said. "That sounds rather serious to me. I'll be along as soon as possible."

"Now then, she 'asn't allus been laid out, just this last couple o' days. She's been off her grub for a week and now she's gone down."

I took a long breath. "So she's been ill for a week, and now she's collapsed you've decided to call me? I'll be with you very soon."

"Ah, but . . . but . . . are ye sure there's any need . . . ?"

I put down the receiver. I knew from hard experience that this conversation could go on for a long time. I also knew that I was probably visiting a hopeless case.

I was on the farm within ten minutes and Mr. Biggins met me with his typical attitude. Hands in pockets, shoulders hunched, eyes regarding me suspiciously from under a thick fringe of greying eyebrows. "Ye're ower late," he grunted.

I stopped with one foot out of the car. "You mean she's dead?"

"Nay, but just about. Ye're too late to do owt about it now."

I gritted my teeth. This animal had been ill for a week, I had arrived in ten minutes, but the farmer's tone was unequivocal: if it died it would be my fault. I had come ower late.

"Ah well," I said, trying to relax. "If she's dying there's nothing I can do." I began to get back into the car.

Mr. Biggins kicked at a cobblestone with a massive boot. "Are ye not going to look at 'er while you're 'ere? You're the vitnery."

"Right, if that's what you want." I climbed out again.

He hesitated. "Will ye charge me extra?"

"No, I won't. I've made the journey to your farm and, if I can't do anything more, that's all you'll pay for."

The skinny young beast lying in a dark corner of the fold yard was a sadly familiar sight. The eyes, sunken and glazed, moved every few seconds with the slow oscillation of approaching death. Her temperature was 99°.

"Yes, you're right, Mr. Biggins," I said. "She's dying." I put my thermometer away and began to leave. "I'm truly sorry about your heifer, Mr. Biggins, but she's beyond human aid."

"So you're just goin' to walk away without doin' owt?" He gave me a truculent stare.

"But she's dying. You said so yourself. She could go any minute."

"Aye, but I've allus heard that where there's life there's hope. Aren't you goin' to give her a chance?"

"Well . . . if you like I can try giving her a stimulant injection." I trailed out to the car for the syringe.

The heifer, in a deep coma, knew nothing as I slipped the needle into the jugular vein. As I depressed the plunger Mr. Biggins gave tongue again. "Expensive things, them injections. How much is this goin' to cost me, then?"

"I honestly don't know." My brain was beginning to reel.

"You'll know awright when you get t'pen in your 'and to send me that big bill, won't ye?"

I didn't answer. As the last drop of fluid trickled into the vein the heifer extended her fore limbs, stared sightlessly ahead for a second then stopped breathing. I put my hand over her heart. "I'm afraid she's dead, Mr. Biggins."

He bent quickly. "Have ye killed 'er?"

"No, no, of course not. She was just ready to go."

The farmer rubbed his chin. "It wasn't much of a bloody stimulant, was it? You've wasted ma money with that injection."

I had no answer to that one and began to put my syringe away, increasingly anxious to get off this farm as quickly as possible. I was on the way to the car when Mr. Biggins caught at my arm.

"Well, what was t'matter with 'er?"

"I don't know."

"You don't know? Vets are supposed to know, aren't they?"

"Yes, Mr. Biggins, they are. But in this case you would need a post mortem examination to find out the cause of death."

The farmer began to pluck excitedly at his coat. "Well, this is a funny carry on. I 'ave a dead beast here and nobody knows what killed her. Could be anything, couldn't it? Could be anthrax!"

"Oh no, Mr. Biggins. Anthrax is very sudden and you say this heifer was ill for over a week."

"Nay, nay, not right ill. Just a bit off it, then she went down like a shot at t'end. And Fred Bramley along t'road had a beast wi' anthrax last month—the *Darrowby and Houlton Times* was on about it and they said all sudden deaths should be examined for anthrax because it was right dangerous and fatal to people." Mr. Biggins stuck his jaw out. "I want ma heifer examined!"

"OK," I replied wearily. "If you say so. As it happens, I have my microscope with me."

"Microscope? That sounds a costly job. How much will that be?"

"That's all right, the ministry pays me," I said, and began to walk towards the house. "I've got to use your phone to report to the ministry and get permission. I'll pay for the call," I added hastily.

Mr. Biggins stood by me as I spoke to the ministry clerk, fidgeting impatiently as I asked him for the proper name of the farm and the breed of the heifer. "Didn't know ah'd have to go through all this," he mumbled.

I went out and got my post mortem knife from the car, made a nick at the root of the heifer's tail and smeared a film of blood onto a glass slide. I took this, along with the microscope into the farmhouse kitchen. The sink was full of dirty dishes which the farmer removed with groans of protest while I fixed the blood film by drawing it through the flames in the hearth. Then I moved to the sink and poured methylene blue over the slide. In the process a small blue pool formed in the white sink bottom.

"Look at the bloody mess you've made!" Mr. Biggins exclaimed. "The missus'll play 'ell when she gets home this afternoon."

I forced a smile. "Don't worry, it will come off quite easily."

I dried the slide off, rigged up the microscope on the table and peered through the eyepiece. As I expected I found only the usual pattern of red and white corpuscles: not an anthrax bacillus in sight.

"Well, there's nothing there," I said. "You can call the knacker man quite safely."

Mr. Biggins blew out his cheeks and made a long-suffering gesture with one hand. "All that fuss for nothin'," he sighed.

As I drove away I felt, not for the first time, that you just couldn't win with Mr. Biggins, and a month later the conviction was strengthened when he came into the surgery one market day.

"One of me cows has wooden tongue," he announced. "I want some iodine to paint on."

Siegfried looked up from the day book where he was checking the visits. "Oh, you're a bit out of date, Mr. Biggins," he said, smiling. "We've got far better medicine than that now."

The farmer took up his usual stance, head down, glowering under his eyebrows. "Ah want the stuff I've allus used."

"But Mr. Biggins," Siegfried was at his most reasonable, "painting the tongue with iodine went out years ago. Since then we've used intravenous injections of sodium iodide, but now even that has been replaced by sulphanilamide."

"Big words, Mr. Farnon, big fancy words," grunted the farmer. "Are you goin' to give me the iodine or not?"

"No, I am not," Siegfried replied, his smile fading. "I wouldn't be a competent veterinary surgeon if I prescribed something as totally outdated as that." He turned to me. "James, would you slip through to the stockroom and bring a pound packet of the sulphanilamide."

There was plenty of sulphanilamide in the stockroom because at that time this drug bulked very large in our veterinary life as a striking improvement on our old remedies. It was useful in many kinds of bacterial diseases, it was an excellent dusting powder for wounds and, as Siegfried had said, it cleared up actinobacillosis, or wooden tongue, quite rapidly. I grabbed one of the square packets tied with string from the shelf and returned at a trot, listening to the two voices echoing along the passage.

The argument was still raging when I came back to the office and I could see that Siegfried's patience was running out. He seized the packet from me and began to write the instructions on the label.

"You give three tablespoonsful in a pint of water to start with, then you follow with one tablespoonful three times daily . . ."

"But ah tell you ah don't want . . ."

". . . and after you've used the packet let us know and we'll give you another supply if necessary."

The farmer glared at my partner. "That stuff'll do no good."

"Mr. Biggins," Siegfried said with ominous calm, "it will cure your cow." He brought his hand down on the desk with a thud. "Take this, and if it doesn't do the trick I won't charge you, all right?"

Mr. Biggins narrowed his eyes and I could see that the idea of something for nothing had an irresistible appeal. Slowly he stretched out his hand and took the sulphanilamide.

"Splendid!" Siegfried jumped up. "Now you get in touch with us when you've used it. I bet you anything your cow will soon be much better."

It was about ten days after this interview that Siegfried and I had to pass through Mr. Biggins's village. Siegfried slowed down when he saw the farmhouse, square faced and massive with the front garden full of potato plants. Mr. Biggins did not believe in wasting money on ornamentation.

"Tell you what, James," my partner murmured. "We'll just drop in there. We haven't heard from our old friend about the sulphanilamide. Doesn't want to lose face, I suspect." He laughed softly and drove round to the yard at the back of the house.

Outside the kitchen door Siegfried raised his hand to knock, and then he gripped my arm. "Look at that, James!" he said in an urgent whisper, pointing to the kitchen window. There on the sill was our square white packet, virgin and unopened, the string binding undisturbed.

My partner clenched his fist. "The cussed old blighter! He wouldn't try it—out of sheer spite."

At that moment the farmer opened the door and Siegfried greeted him cheerfully. "Ah, good morning to you, Mr. Biggins. We were just passing and thought we'd check on how your cow was progressing. No charge, I give you my word. This is just for our own interest."

The eyes under the shaggy brows registered sudden alarm. "But . . . but . . . I've got me slippers on. There's no need for ye to . . ."

But Siegfried was already striding towards the cow byre. The patient was easy to pick out. Her skin was stretched tightly over the jutting ribs and pelvic bones, saliva drooled from her lips and a long swelling bulged from under her jaw. She was a scarecrow among her sleek neighbours.

Siegfried moved quickly to her head, seized the nose and pulled it towards him. With his other hand he prised open the mouth and fingered the tongue. "Feel that, James," he said softly.

I ran my hand over the knobbly hard surface which for centuries had given actinobacillosis its evocative name of "wooden tongue". "This is awful. It's a wonder she can eat at all."

At that moment the byre door burst open and Mr. Biggins hurried in, panting slightly. My partner looked at him sadly along the cow's back. "Well, it seems you were right: our medicine hasn't done a bit of good. And your poor cow is a mess, I'm afraid. Almost starving to death. I do apologize."

The farmer's face was a study. "Aye, well . . . that's right . . . she's done no good . . . I reckon she'll . . ."

Siegfried broke in. "Look here," he said. "I feel responsible for this. My medicine has failed so it's up to me to get her right. I have an injection in the car which I think will do the trick."

"Now then, wait a minute . . . I don't know . . ." But the farmer's words went unheeded as my colleague hurried out to the yard.

He was back very quickly holding a bottle which I couldn't recognize. He held it up and began to fill a 20 cc syringe, watching the rising level intently and whistling tunelessly under his breath. "Hold the tail, will you, James," he said, and poised the needle over the cow's rump. With his hand held high he looked across at Mr. Biggins. "This is an excellent injection but it's a good job you've been using our medicine. On its own it could have serious effects on the animal."

"You mean . . . could kill 'er?"

"Just possible," Siegfried murmured. "But you've nothing to worry about. She's had the sulphanilamide." He was about to plunge the needle in when Mr. Biggins gave tongue.

"Hey, hey, haud on. Don't do that! There's maybe been a bit of a misunderstandin'." Conflicting emotions chased across the farmer's face. "Ye see, it's like this—ah don't think she's been gettin' enough of your stuff."

Siegfried lowered his arm. "You mean you've been under-dosing? I wrote the instructions on the packet if you remember."

"That's right. But ah must have got a bit mixed up."

"Oh, that doesn't matter. As long as you put her back to full dosage all will be well." Siegfried inserted the needle and, ignoring Mr. Biggins's yelp of alarm, he injected the full contents.

As he put the syringe back in its case he sighed with satisfaction.

"Well, I'm sure that will put everything right. But remember you must start again with the full three tablespoonsful and continue till you've finished the packet."

As we drove away I stared at my colleague. "What the devil was that injection?"

"Oh, mixed vitamins. It'll help the poor thing's condition but it had nothing to do with the wooden tongue. Just part of my plan." He smiled gleefully. "Now he's *got* to use the sulphanilamide. It will be interesting to see what happens."

It was indeed interesting. Within a week Mr. Biggins was back in the surgery, looking sheepish.

"Can I have some more o' that stuff?" he muttered.

"By all means." Siegfried extended his arm in an expansive gesture. "As much as you like. I suppose the cow is looking better?"

"Aye."

"Stopped slavering? Putting on flesh, is she?"

"Aye, aye, she is." Mr. Biggins lowered his head as though he didn't want to answer any more questions. Siegfried gave him another packet.

Through the surgery window we watched him cross the street and my partner thumped me on the shoulder.

"Well, James. That was a little victory. At last we've managed to beat Mr. Biggins."

I laughed. But when I look back over the years I realize it was the only time we did beat him.

Chapter Six

"Just look at that," the farmer said.

"At what?" I was "cleansing" a cow (removing the afterbirth) and my arm was buried deep in the cow's uterus. I turned my head to see him pointing beneath my patient. I saw four white jets of milk spurting onto the byre floor from the animal's udder.

He grinned. "That's a funny thing, isn't it?"

"It isn't really," I said. "It's a reflex action caused by my hand twiddling the uterus about. This acts on a gland in the brain which causes the milk to flow. I often see cows letting their milk down like that when I'm cleansing them."

"Well, that's a rum 'un." The farmer laughed. "Any road, you'd better get finished quick or you'll have a few pints of milk to knock off your bill."

That was in 1947, the year of the great snow. I have never known snow like that before or since, and the odd thing was that it took such a long time to get started. Nothing happened in November and we had a green Christmas, but then it began to get colder and colder. All through January a northeast wind blew, apparently straight from the Arctic, and then, borne on the wind, very fine flakes began to appear over the last few days of the month. They were the forerunners of the real thing; at the beginning of February big, fat flakes started a steady relentless descent on our countryside.

For weeks and weeks the snow fell, sometimes in a gentle, almost lazy curtain which remorselessly obliterated the familiar landmarks, at others in fierce blizzards. In between, the frost took over and transformed the roads into glassy tracks of flattened snow over which we drove at fifteen miles an hour.

The long garden at Skeldale House disappeared under a white blanket. There was a single deep channel by the wall-side where I fought my way daily to my car in the yard at the top; the yard itself had to be dug out every day and the opening of its big double doors was a backbreaking job.

To get to our cases we did a lot of walking since so many of the farm tracks were blocked wall to wall. On the very high country there were some farms which we couldn't reach at all, and there was no doubt that many animals died for lack of veterinary help. It was around the middle of March when helicopters were dropping food on these isolated spots that Bert Kealey telephoned me. He was one of those who was out of reach on a high moor which was bleak even in summertime.

"I thought your phone wires would be down, Bert," I said, surprised.

"Naw, they've survived, God knows how." The young farmer's voice was cheerful as always. He ran a small herd of cows on the high tops and was one of the many who scratched a living from the unfriendly soil. "But ah'm in trouble," he went on. "Polly's just had a litter and she hasn't a drop of milk."

"Oh dear, that's unfortunate," I said. Polly was the only pig on the Kealey farm.

"Aye, it's a beggar. Bad enough losin' the litter—there's twelve smashin' little pigs—but it's Tess I'm bothered about."

"Yes . . . yes . . ." I was thinking of Tess, too. She was Bert's eight-year-old daughter and she had a thing about little pigs. She had persuaded her father to buy her a sow so that she could have a litter of her own. I could remember Tess's excitement when she showed me her birthday gift a few days after its arrival.

"That's Polly Pig," she said, pointing to the sow nuzzling the straw in its pen. "She's mine. My dad gave her to me."

I leaned over the pen. "You're a lucky girl. She looks a fine pig."

"Oh, she is, she is." The little girl's eyes shone with pleasure. "I feed her every day and she lets me stroke her. She's nice. And do you know something else?" Tess's voice took on a conspiratorial tone. "She's going to have babies in March."

"Well I never!" I said. "Is that so? You'll have a whole lot of little pink pigs to look after." I held my hands a few inches apart. "Just about this size."

She was so thrilled at the thought that she was lost for words.

All this came back to me as I listened to Bert Kealey's voice on the phone. "Do you think she's got mastitis, Bert?" I asked. "Is the udder red and swollen?"

"No, nowt like that. Her udder's not a bit inflamed."

"Well, then, she needs a shot of pituitrin to bring down the milk, but how the heck is she going to get it? Your district's been cut off for weeks now."

It takes a lot to make a Yorkshire farmer admit that his farm is inaccessible because of the weather but Bert had to agree. "I know," he said. "Ah've tried diggin' me road out, but it fills up as fast as I clear it. Anyway, top road's blocked for two miles so I'm wastin' me time."

I thought for a moment. "Have you tried getting some cow's milk into the piglets? An egg mixed with a quart of milk and a teaspoonful of glucose isn't a bad substitute."

"I've tried 'em with that but they wouldn't look at it," Bert replied. "If only they could have a good suck at their mother and get summat into their bellies, it would start them off and then they'd maybe have a go at t'substitute."

He was right. There was nothing to compare with that first suck. And if they didn't get it, those tiny creatures could start dying at an alarming rate. Little Tess would be heartbroken.

An idea was forming in my mind. "There's just one possibility," I said. "I know I can get to the top of Dennor Bank because the road is open to there. After that it's all flat going to your place. I could maybe get there on skis. I've been using them a bit lately. I can't be sure that I'll make it as far as your farm but I'll try."

"By 'eck, I'd be very grateful if you would, Mr. Herriot. It's t'little lass ah'm thinkin' of."

"Same here, Bert. Anyway, I'll have a go. I'll leave now."

On the summit of Dennor Bank I manoeuvred my car as close as possible to the tall white walls which the snow ploughs had thrown up, got out and buckled on my skis. One bonus of the long spell of snow and frost was that some nice little slopes had become available, and I had found that gliding down in the frosty air was one of the most exhilarating things I had ever known.

All I needed was the bottle of pituitrin and a syringe, and I put them in my pocket.

To get to the Kealey farm in normal conditions you drove a couple of miles along a very straight road and turned right. Bert's farm lay in an isolated position about halfway along this second road. But that day, although I had travelled the region a hundred times, I might have been in a strange country; the stone walls had been deeply engulfed so there were no fields, no roads, nothing but a yawning white expanse with the tops of telegraph poles sticking up here and there. It was uncanny.

I felt a twinge of misgiving, but I had promised to try. Anyway, I would be able to travel cross-country, cutting off two sides of a triangle, and I was pretty sure the farm lay in one of the hollows just below the dark skyline.

I am afraid that this is not a glorious episode in my history. I had slithered amateurishly for about half a mile when the snow started

49

again. A swirling screen of flakes cut me off completely from my surroundings. There was no point in going on because I had lost all sense of direction. I was scared. If the snow didn't stop I could blunder for miles in that empty wilderness without coming upon a house.

The flurry stopped as suddenly as it had begun. My heart thumped as I stared around me, and the dark smudge of my car roof in the white distance was a sweet sight. I headed back to it with a speed worthy of an Olympic skier. Relief flowed through me as I threw my skis into the back and started the engine, and I was well on the way to Darrowby before my pulse rate returned to normal.

"Bert," I said on the phone. "I'm terribly sorry but I just couldn't make it. I got caught by a snow shower and had to turn back."

"Well, ah'm glad ye did turn. Fellers have got lost and died in the snow up here. I shouldn't have let you try." He paused for a moment then said wistfully. "If only there was some other way to make Polly let 'er milk down."

As he spoke, the picture flashed into my mind of that cow I had been cleansing and the white jets striking the byre floor. When I was doing uterine examinations on sows, the same thing had happened.

"Maybe there is a way," I blurted out. "Bert, have you ever had your hand inside a sow?"

"Eh? You mean . . . in 'er pig bed? Ah leave that to you chaps."

"Well, I want you to start now. Get some warm water and soap and . . ."

"Hey, hang on, Mr. Herriot. I'm sure there's no pigs left in 'er."

"I don't suppose there are, Bert, but do as I say. Soap your arm well and use any household antiseptic you have. Then feel your way into the vagina till you come to the cervix. Put a finger inside and waggle the pig bed around a bit."

"Oh 'eck, I don't fancy this. What's it all about?"

"It often brings the milk down, that's what it's about."

I put down the phone and went through to have lunch. Helen kept glancing at me during the meal; she knew something was on my mind and I don't suppose she was surprised when I leaped to my feet at the sound of the phone ringing.

It was Bert, breathless but triumphant. "It worked, Mr. Herriot! I 'ad a good waggle round like you said, then I tried the udder. I could draw milk out of every tit and there wasn't a drop there before. It was like magic."

"Are the piglets feeding?"

"Not half! They're all laid quiet in a row, suckin' hard. It's lovely to see them."

"Well, that's great," I said. "The piglets have had that vital first feed but Polly will probably dry up again by tomorrow or even tonight. You'll have to get your hand in once more."

"Oh crumbs." A lot of the enthusiasm went out of Bert's voice. "I thought I'd finished wi' that."

The poor man did indeed have to perform his unusual task several times and Polly never did come fully to her milk, but the piglets were kept going until they were able to drink the milk substitute.

The great snow of 1947 was followed by the most glorious summer I can remember, though in late April in the high country the white streaks still lay behind the walls, standing out against the green moorland like the ribs of a great beast. But the roads were clear and my journey to see one of Bert Kealey's heifers had none of the drama of the last time. When I had finished my job, young Tess took me through to see her beloved Polly and family.

"They're pretty, aren't they?" she said as we looked into the pen at the twelve chunky little pigs playing around their mother.

"They certainly are, Tess," I replied. "Your first attempt at pig breeding has been a big success but I really think you have to thank your father for it. He did a wonderful job."

Bert screwed up his face at the memory. "Aye, maybe so, and I reckon it was worth it. But I'll tell ye, ah didn't enjoy it."

Chapter Seven

"Are you all right, Helen?"

I looked round anxiously as my wife fidgeted in her seat. We were in the one and ninepennies in the La Scala cinema in Brawton and I had a strong conviction that we had no right to be there.

I had voiced my doubts that morning. "I know it's our half day, Helen, but with the baby due any time don't you think it would be safer to stay around Darrowby?"

"No, of course not." Helen laughed incredulously at the very idea of missing our outing, that oasis of relaxation in our busy lives. For me it was an escape from the telephone and the mud and the wellington boots, and for my wife it meant a rest from her own hard slog.

"But what if the thing comes on quickly?" I said. "We don't want our second child to be born in the back of a car."

The whole business had me worried. It wasn't as bad as when Jimmy was on his way; I had been in the RAF then and had lost two stones in weight, going into a sort of decline which wasn't all due to the hard training. There was something about having babies which really got through to me, and lately I had spent a lot of time flapping around watching Helen's every move, much to her amusement. I just couldn't be calm, and over the last two days the tension had built up.

But Helen had been adamant this morning. She wasn't going to be done out of her half day, and now here we were in the La Scala with Humphrey Bogart competing vainly for my attention as my wife squirmed around and occasionally ran a thoughtful hand over her swollen abdomen. As I scrutinized her keenly from the corner of my eye she gave a convulsive jerk and her lips parted in a soft moan. A dew of perspiration had already sprung out all over me before she turned and whispered, "I think we'd better go now, Jim."

Stumbling over the outstretched legs in the darkness I guided her up the sloping aisle, and such was my panic that I felt sure the crisis would be upon us before we reached the street and our little car. As we set off I seemed to notice the rattles and bumping of the old springs for the first time. It was the only time in my life that I wished I had a Rolls Royce.

The twenty-five miles to Darrowby seemed to take an eternity. Helen sat very quiet by my side, occasionally closing her eyes and catching her breath while my heart beat a tattoo against my ribs. When we reached our little town I turned the car towards the market place.

Helen looked at me in surprise. "Where are you going?"

"Well, to Nurse Brown's of course."

"Oh, don't be so silly," Helen laughed. "It's not time for that yet. I've had a baby before, remember? Come on, let's go home."

Heavy with misgiving, I drove to Skeldale House, marvelling at Helen's composure. When we got into bed she lay patiently, and there was about her a calm acceptance of the inevitable which I could not share.

I suppose I kept dropping into what is termed a fitful slumber because it was 6:00 am when she nudged my arm.

"Time to go, Jim." Her tone was very matter of fact.

I shot from the bed like a jack-in-the-box, threw on my clothes and shouted across the landing to Auntie Lucy who was staying with us for the occasion. "We're off!"

A faint reply came through the door. "All right, I'll see to Jimmy."

Helen was dressing methodically. "Get that suitcase out of the cupboard, Jim," she said. "It's got everything I'll need. Go on, bring it out."

Suppressing a groan I carried the case out and stood waiting. I had missed all this last time because of the war and had often regretted it, but at that moment I wasn't at all sure whether I wouldn't rather be elsewhere. Outside it was a glorious May morning, the air limpid with the new day freshness which had soothed the irritation of many an early call, but it was all lost on me as I drove across the empty market place.

We had only about half a mile to go and I was pulling up outside Greenside Nursing Home within minutes. There was a touch of grandeur about the name, but in fact it was just the small dwelling house of Nurse Brown. Upstairs there were a couple of bedrooms which for many years had seen the arrival of the local children.

I knocked at the door and pushed it open. Nurse Brown gave me a quick smile, put her arm round Helen's shoulders and led her upstairs. I was left in the kitchen feeling helpless.

"Now then, Jim, it's a grand mornin'."

Cliff, Nurse Brown's husband, was sitting in the kitchen eating his breakfast and he spoke to me casually as though we had encountered each other in the street. He wore the broad grin which never seemed to leave his face and he continued to work his way phlegmatically through the stack of bacon, eggs, sausage and tomatoes on his plate. I realized that over the years he must have seen hundreds of quivering husbands standing in that kitchen. It was old stuff to him.

"Yes, Cliff . . . yes . . ." I replied. "I think it will turn out hot later." I cringed inwardly at the creaking sounds from the floorboards above. What was happening in that bedroom?

As he chewed, Cliff seemed to notice that I was perhaps one of the more distraught type of husbands because he turned his big kind smile on me. He spoke gently. "Don't worry, lad," he said. "It'll be right."

His words were mildly soothing and I fled. In those days it was unheard of for the husband to be present at the birth and though it is now the in thing to observe it all, I marvel at the fortitude of these young men. I know beyond all doubt that I would be carried away unconscious at some time during the proceedings. Back at our surgery, I found that expectant fathers really did pace the floor for long periods, and I varied this by trying to read the newspaper upside down.

It was around eleven o'clock when the long awaited telephone call came from my doctor and good friend, Harry Allinson. Harry always spoke in a sort of cheerful shout and this morning the booming voice was like the sweetest music. "A sister for Jimmy!" His words were followed by a burst of laughter.

"Oh great, Harry. Thank you, thank you. That's marvellous news." I put the receiver down, then lay back in my chair until my nerves had stopped vibrating.

I am a fairly sensible man, but with a propensity for doing daft things, and on an impulse I decided that I had to go round to the nursing home immediately. At that time a husband was not welcome straight after the birth. I knew it because I had gone to see Jimmy too soon and had not been well received. But still, I went.

When I burst into her establishment, Nurse Brown's usual smile was absent. "You've done it again, haven't you?" she said with some asperity. "I told you with Jimmy that you should have given us time to get the baby washed but it seems you took no notice."

I hung my head sheepishly and she relented. "Oh well, now you're here you might as well come upstairs."

Helen had the same tired, flushed look that I remembered before. I kissed her thankfully. We didn't say anything, just smiled at each other. Then I had a look in the cot by the bed.

Nurse Brown regarded me with tight lips and narrowed eyes as I peered down. Last time I had been so aghast at Jimmy's appearance that I had mortally offended her by asking if there was anything wrong with him, and heaven help me I felt the same now. The new little girl's face was all squashed and red and bloated and the sense of shock hit me as it had done before.

I looked up at the nurse and it was only too clear from her threatening scowl that she was waiting for me to say something derogatory. One wrong word from me and she would have kicked me on the shins—I was sure of that.

"Gorgeous," I said weakly. "Really gorgeous."

"All right, out you go." Nurse Brown ushered me downstairs and as she opened the outside door she fixed me with a piercing eye, speaking slowly and deliberately as though addressing a person of limited intelligence.

"That . . . is . . . a . . . lovely . . . healthy . . . baby . . . ." she said, and closed the door in my face.

As I drove away I knew she must be right. And now, all these years later, when I look at my handsome son and my beautiful daughter I can hardly believe my own stupidity.

When I returned to the surgery there was one visit waiting for me, high in the hills, and the journey up there was like a happy dream. My worry was over and it seemed that all nature was rejoicing with me. The sun blazed and soft breezes swirled into the car, carrying their spring fragrance from the fells around, an elusive breath of the bluebells, primroses and violets scattered on the grass and among the shadows of the trees.

After I had seen my patient I took a walk along a favourite path on the hill's edge with Sam trotting at my heels. I looked away over the rolling patchwork of the plain, and at the young bracken on the hillside springing straight and green from last year's dead brown stalks. Everywhere new life was calling out its exultant message—

with my new little daughter lying down there in Darrowby.

We had decided to call her Rosemary. It is such a pretty name but it didn't last long. It became Rosie at a very early stage and has remained so: she is now Doctor Rosie in our community.

When I got back to Skeldale House I began to telephone my glad news all over the country. It was received rapturously by all, but it was Tristan who grasped the essential of the situation.

"We've got to wet this baby's head, Jim," he said crisply. "I'll come over at seven."

TRISTAN WAS CONCERNED about the venue of the celebration. There were four of us in the sitting room at Skeldale House—Siegfried, Tristan, Alex Taylor and myself. Alex was my oldest friend—we had started school together in Glasgow at the age of four—and when he came out of the army after five years in the western desert and Italy he had come to spend a few weeks with Helen and me in Darrowby. It wasn't long before he had fallen under the spell of country life and now he was starting a new career in farming and estate agency. It was good that he should be with me tonight.

Tristan's fingers drummed on the arm of his chair as he thought aloud, his expression fixed and grave. "We'd normally go to the Drovers but they've got that big party on tonight, so that's no good," he muttered. "Let's see now, there's the George and Dragon—splendid Tetley's beer, but I've known them a bit careless with their pipes and I've had the odd sour mouthful."

"Just a minute, Tris," I broke in. "I went round to Nurse Brown's this evening to see Helen, and Cliff asked if he could come with us. Don't you think it would be rather nice to go to his favourite pub since the baby was born in his house? It's the Black Horse."

"Ah yes, ye-es." Tristan looked at me thoughtfully and put his fingertips together. "Russell and Rangham's. A good little brewery, that. I've had some first rate pints in the Black Horse though I have noticed a slight loss of nuttiness under very warm conditions."

"Oh for heaven's sake!" Siegfried leaped to his feet. "You sound like an analytical chemist. It's only beer you're talking about, after all."

Tristan looked at him in shocked silence, but Siegfried turned to me briskly. "I think that's a pleasant idea of yours, James. Let's go with Cliff to the Black Horse. It's a quiet little place."

And indeed as we dropped onto the chairs in the bar parlour I felt we had chosen the ideal spot. The evening sunshine sent long golden shafts over the pitted oak tables and the high-backed settees where a few farm men sat with their glasses. There was nothing smart about this little inn, but the furniture which hadn't been changed for a hundred years gave it an air of tranquillity. It was just right.

The diminutive landlord, Reg Wilkey, charged our glasses from his tall white jug, and Siegfried raised his pint. "James, may I be the first to wish a long life, health and happiness to Rosemary."

"Thank you, Siegfried," I said, feeling suddenly very much among friends as the others said "hear, hear" and began to drink.

Cliff lowered the level in his glass by half and then turned to the landlord. "It gets better, Reg," he said reverently. "I've said for years that me two best friends are Mr. Russell and Mr. Rangham. I think the world of 'em."

After a couple of pints Siegfried patted me on the shoulder. "I'm off to watch the shop, James. Have a good time. Can't tell you how pleased I am."

This was my night; my anxieties were over, and it was one of those cosy evenings when everything seemed perfect. Alex and I recalled our childhood in Glasgow, Tristan came up with some splendid memories of Skeldale House in the bachelor days, and over everything, like a beneficent moon, hung the huge smile of Cliff Brown. A great love of my fellow men mounted in me and I kept buying drinks for the local people around us. Finally I grew tired of fumbling for money and handed my wallet to the landlord. It was stuffed with notes because I had made a special visit to the bank that afternoon.

"Here, Reg," I said. "Just keep taking the drinks out of that."

"Aye, right, Mr. Herriot," he replied, without changing expression. "It'll mek it easier."

It did make it a lot easier. Men whom I hardly knew raised their glasses and toasted my new daughter repeatedly, and when closing time was announced it didn't seem possible that it was all coming to an end. As the little pub emptied I approached the landlord. "We can't go home yet, Reg. This is a special night."

He looked at me quizzically. "Well, ye know the law, Mr. Herriot." He hesitated for a moment. "Tell ye what. I'll lock up, and then we could go down and 'ave one or two in the cellar."

I put my arm round his shoulders. "Reg, what a delightful idea. Let's go down there."

We descended into the pub cellar, switched on the light and pulled the trap door closed after us. As we disposed ourselves among the barrels and crates I looked around the company; we original four were now augmented by two young farmers, one of the local grocers and an official from the Darrowby Water Board. We were a warmly-knit little group.

"Still plenty in the wallet, Reg?" I shouted.

"Aye, there's plenty 'ere, don't worry. Help yourselves."

It was much easier down there. We just went to a barrel and turned the tap, and the party never flagged. It must have been past midnight when we heard the thumping on the outside door.

Reg went upstairs. When he returned he was preceded through the trap door by the long blue legs, tunic, cadaverous face and helmet of Police Constable Hubert Goole. A silence fell on the merry gathering as the constable's melancholy gaze passed slowly over us.

"Drinkin' a bit late, aren't ye?" he inquired tonelessly.

"Ah well." Tristan gave a gay little laugh. "It's a special occasion, you see, Mr. Goole. Mr. Herriot's wife gave birth to a daughter this morning."

"Oh aye?" The Old Testament countenance looked down on my friend. "I don't remember Mr. Wilkey applyin' for an extended licence for tonight."

P.C. Goole was known in the town as a stern and unbending man, one who went by the book. It was no good riding a bike at night without lights when P.C. Goole was around; he was particularly merciless on this offence. He sang in the church choir, he was active in community work, and his morals were impeccable.

Tristan bounced back. "But of course this was a totally impromptu thing, spur of the moment, you know."

"Ye can call it what ye like, but you're breakin' the law and you know it." The big man unbuttoned his breast pocket and flipped open his notebook. "I'll have to 'ave your names."

What an end to the happy evening. Nothing much happened in the town and this would make headlines in the *Darrowby and Houlton Times*. All my friends were involved, as well as poor little Reg standing sheepishly in the background. He would really get it in the neck, and it was all my fault.

Tristan, however, was not beaten yet. "Mr. Goole," he said coldly, "I'm disappointed in you. I'd have expected you to show a different attitude on an occasion like this."

The constable was unmoved. He poised his pencil. "I'm a policeman, Mr. Farnon, and I 'ave my duty to do. What's your address, now?"

"It seems to me," said Tristan, ignoring the question, "that you have forgotten all about little Julie."

"What about Julie?" The long face showed a certain animation for the first time. Tristan's mention of P.C. Goole's beloved Yorkshire Terrier had found a tender spot.

"Well, as I recall," Tristan went on, "Mr. Herriot sat up for several hours during the night with Julie when she was having pups. In fact if it hadn't been for him you might have lost the pups and Julie, too. Surely you could have a drink with us when Mr. Herriot has just become a father for the second time. It's the same thing in a way."

P.C. Goole paused, his face softened. "Julie's still goin' strong."

"Yes, I know," I said. "Wonderful little thing for her age."

"And I still have one of them pups."

"Of course. You've had him in to see me a few times."

"Aye . . . aye . . ." P.C. Goole delved in his trouser pocket, brought out a large watch and studied it thoughtfully. "Well, I'm off duty about now. Suppose I could have a drink with ye. I'll just phone in to the office first."

When the constable returned from the phone he raised his glass solemnly. "Here's wishin' t'little lass all the best," he said.

"Thank you, Mr. Goole," I replied. "You're very kind. Please have another."

It was surprising how soon he seemed to forget all about his notebook. The party picked up again rapidly and joy reigned.

"It's bloody 'ot down 'ere," P.C. Goole remarked after some time, and removed his tunic. With this symbolic gesture the last barrier went down. And yet, over the next two hours, nobody got really plastered. Nobody, that is, except P.C. Goole, who passed through all the phases on the road to profound inebriation. The first was when he insisted on Christian names, and then he became almost tearfully affectionate as he rhapsodized on the wonders of birth, human and canine. His last phase was more aggressive.

"You're 'avin' another, Jim." It was a statement rather than an inquiry as the tall, shirt-sleeved figure bent over the barrel.

"No thanks, Hubert," I replied. "I've had enough—I started long before you, and anyway, it's half past two. I really ought to go."

"Goin'?" Hubert glared at me belligerently. "Whassa matter with you? The night's young yet." He slurped down another mouthful of beer indignantly. "You ask a feller to 'ave a drink with you and next minute ye say we're goin'. Itsh not right."

"Now, now, Hubert," said little Reg Wilkey, sidling up to him and radiating the bonhomie which came from thirty years' practice at easing reluctant clients from his premises. "Be a good lad, now. We've all 'ad a grand time, but everybody's settin' off 'ome. Now where's your jacket?"

The constable muttered and grumbled as we helped him into his tunic and allowed us to lead him up the steps into the darkness of the pub. Outside I installed him in the back of my car with Tristan and Alex on either side; Cliff sat with me in front. Before we left, the landlord passed my wallet through the window. It had slimmed down to the point of emaciation.

I drove through the sleeping town and turned down the narrow street towards the market place. As we approached I could see that the cobbled square was deserted except for two figures, and with a twinge of alarm I recognized Inspector Bowles and Sergeant Rostron, our two head policemen. They were standing, very erect and trim-looking, glancing around them keenly. They looked as though they wouldn't miss any misdemeanours in their vicinity.

A sudden scream from the back seat almost sent me through a

shop window. Hubert had seen them too. "It's that bugger Rostron!" he yelled. "I 'ate 'im! He's 'ad it in for me for years and I'm goin' to tell 'im what I think about 'im!"

There was a thrashing of arms in the back as he wound down the window, and for the second time that night I felt an icy dread that something awful was going to happen because of me. "Quell him!" I shouted. "For God's sake, quell him!"

However, my friends in the rear had anticipated me. Hubert's cries were suddenly switched off as Tristan and Alex bundled him to the floor and fell on top of him. Tristan was actually sitting on his head when we came up to the two policemen and only muffled sounds came from below. As we passed, the inspector nodded and smiled and the sergeant gave me a friendly salute. It was not difficult to read their minds: Mr. Herriot was returning from yet another night call. A dedicated vet, that young man.

With their colleague writhing on the floor behind me I could not relax until we had turned off the square out of sight and sound. Hubert, when allowed to get up, seemed to have lost a lot of his belligerence, and when we reached his home he walked quietly and fairly steadily up his garden path.

Back in Skeldale House I went up to our bedroom. The big room with the double bed was eerily empty without Helen. I opened the door to the long narrow apartment which had been Tristan's room. Now it was Jimmy's and his bed stood in exactly the same place as my old friend's.

I looked down on my sleeping son, and then glanced at the other end of the room where a cot stood to receive Rosie. Soon, I thought, I would have two in here. I was becoming rich.

Chapter Eight

"This is Amber," Sister Rose said. "The one I wanted you to examine."

I looked at the pale, almost honey-coloured shading of the hair on the dog's ears and flanks. "I can see why you've given her that name. I bet she'd really glow in the sunshine."

The nurse laughed. "Yes, funnily enough it was sunny when I first saw her and the name just jumped into my mind." She gave me a sideways glance. "I'm good at names, as you know."

"Oh yes, without a doubt," I said, smiling. Sister Rose had to be good at christening the endless stream of unwanted animals which passed through the little dog sanctuary which she ran and maintained by organizing small shows and jumble sales. Not only did she give her own money, but she gave her precious time. As a nursing sister she led a full life of service to the human race, and still found the time to fight for the animals, too.

"Where did this one come from?" I asked.

Sister Rose shrugged. "Oh, found wandering in the streets of Hebbleton. Obviously abandoned."

I felt the old tightening of anger in my throat. "How could anyone do this to such a beautiful dog?"

"Oh, people like that have some astonishing reasons. In this case I think it's because Amber has a little skin disease. Perhaps it frightened them."

"They could at least have taken her to a vet," I grunted as I opened the door of the pen. I noticed some bare patches around the toes and as I knelt and examined the feet, Amber nuzzled my cheek and wagged her tail. I looked up at her, at the flopping ears, the pronounced jowls and the trusting eyes which had been betrayed.

"It's a hound's face," I said. "But how about the rest of her?"

Sister Rose laughed. "Oh, she's a puzzle." Her body, dappled with patches of brown, black and white, was the wrong shape for a hound. She had very large feet, a long thin tail in constant motion and everywhere on her coat was the delicate sheen of gold.

"Well," I said. "Whatever she is, she's a bonny one, and good-natured, too." I opened the mouth and looked at the rows of untainted teeth. "I'd say she's nine or ten months old—she's just a big pup."

"That's what I thought. She'll be really large when she reaches full size, but we'll have no difficulty in finding a home for her. She's the perfect pet."

As if to prove the sister's words, the young bitch reared up and planted her forefeet on my chest. I looked again at the laughing mouth and those eyes. "Amber," I said. "I really like you."

"Oh, I'm so glad," Sister Rose said. "We must get this skin trouble cleared up as quickly as possible and then I can start finding her a home. It's just a bit of eczema, isn't it?"

"Probably . . . I see there's some bareness around the eyes and cheeks, too." Skin diseases in dogs, as in humans, are tricky things, often baffling in origin and difficult to cure. I fingered the hairless areas; the skin was dry and sound; but I didn't like the combination of feet and face. I banished to the back of my mind a spectre which appeared for a brief instant.

"Yes, probably eczema," I said briskly. "Rub on this ointment night and morning." I handed over a box of zinc oxide and lanoline, hoping it would do the trick in combination with the nurse's good feeding.

When two weeks passed without news of Amber I was relieved, but I was brought back to reality with a bump when Sister Rose phoned one morning.

"Mr. Herriot, those bare patches aren't any better. In fact they're spreading up her legs and on the face."

The spectre leaped up again. Oh not that, please. "I'll come right out, Sister," I said, and on my way to the car I picked up the microscope.

Amber greeted me as she had before, with dancing eyes and lashing tail, but I felt sick when I saw the ragged denudation of the face and legs. I got hold of the young animal and held her close, sniffing at the hairless areas.

Sister Rose looked at me in surprise. "What are you doing?"

"Trying to detect a mousy smell. And it's there. It's mange."

"Oh dear." The nurse put a hand to her mouth. "That's rather nasty, isn't it." Then she put her shoulders back in a characteristic gesture. "Well, I can tackle it with sulphur baths, but there's such a danger of infection to the other dogs. It really is a worry."

I put Amber down and stood up, feeling suddenly weary. "You're thinking of sarcoptic mange, Sister. I'm afraid this is something rather worse. The whole look of the thing suggests demodectic mange. It's very often incurable."

"Goodness me, I had no idea. She wasn't scratching much, so I didn't worry."

"Yes, that's just it," I said wryly. "Dogs scratch almost non-stop with sarcoptic mange and we can cure it, but they often show only mild discomfort with demodectic, which usually defeats us."

I lifted the microscope from the back of the car. "Anyway, I may be jumping the gun. This is the only way to find out."

There was a patch on Amber's left leg which I squeezed and scraped with a scalpel blade. I deposited the debris and serum on a glass slide, added a few drops of potassium hydroxide and put a cover-slip on top. I rigged up the microscope and looked down the eyepiece. My stomach tightened as I saw what I didn't want to see—the dread mite, *demodex canis:* the head, the eight stumpy legs and the long, cigar-shaped body. The whole microscopic field was teeming with them.

"Well, there's no doubt about it, Sister," I said. "I'm very sorry."

The corners of her mouth drooped. "Isn't there anything we can do?"

"Oh yes, we can try. And we're going to try like anything, because I've taken a fancy to Amber. I've cured a few demodex cases in my time, always by using the same stuff." I went to the car and fished around in the boot. "Here it is—Odylen." I held up the can in front of her. "I'll show you how to apply it."

It was difficult to rub the lotion into the affected patches as Amber wagged and licked but I finished at last.

"Now do that every day," I said, "and let me know in about a week. Sometimes that Odylen really does work."

Sister Rose stuck out her jaw with the determination which had saved so many animals. "I assure you I'll do it most carefully. But how about my other dogs? Won't they become infected?"

I shook my head. "Demodex very rarely spreads to another animal."

"That's something, anyway."

I heard from Sister Rose within a week: she had been applying the Odylen religiously but the disease was spreading further up the legs. I hurried out there and my fears were confirmed when I saw Amber's face, disfigured by increasing hairlessness. When I thought of the beauty which had captivated me on my first visit the sight was like a blow. Her tail-wagging cheerfulness was undiminished and that seemed to make the whole thing worse.

I had to try something else, and I started her on a course of Fowler's solution of arsenic which at that time was popular in the treatment of skin conditions. When ten days passed I had begun to hope, and it was a bitter disappointment when Sister Rose telephoned just after breakfast.

Her voice trembled as she spoke. "Mr. Herriot, she really is deteriorating all the time, and . . ."

I cut her off in mid sentence. "All right, I'll be out there within an hour. Don't give up hope yet. These cases sometimes take months to recover."

I knew as I drove to the sanctuary that my words had no real substance. But I had tried to say something comforting because there was nothing Sister Rose hated more than putting a dog to sleep. Of all the hundreds of animals which had passed through her hands I could remember only a handful which had defeated her: very old dogs with chronic kidney or heart conditions, or young ones with distemper. With all the others she had battled until they were fit to go to their new homes. And I myself recoiled from the idea of doing such a thing to Amber. There was something about that dog which had taken hold of me.

When I arrived I still had no idea what I was going to do and was half surprised at what I said. "Sister, I've come to take Amber home with me. You've got enough to do, looking after your other dogs. I know you have done everything possible but I'm going to take on this job myself."

"But . . . you are a busy man. How will you find the time?"

"I can treat her in the evenings and any other spare moments. This way I'll be able to check on her progress all the time. I'm determined to get her right."

And, driving back to the surgery, I was surprised at the depth of my feeling. Throughout my career I have often had a compulsive desire to cure an animal, but never stronger than with Amber. The young bitch was delighted to be in the car with me; she capered around, licking my ear, resting her paws on the dashboard and

66

peering through the windscreen. I looked at her happy face, scarred by the disease, and thumped my hand on the wheel. Demodectic mange was hell, but this was one case which was going to get better.

It was the beginning of a strangely vivid episode in my life, as fresh now as it was then, more than thirty years ago. We had no facilities for boarding dogs, but I made up a comfortable billet for her in the old stable in the yard, penning off one of the stalls with a sheet of plywood and putting down a bed of straw. She would be snug in there.

Veterinary surgeons would never last in their profession if they became too involved with their patients, but before I knew what was happening I became involved with Amber.

I fed her myself, changed her bedding and carried out the treatment. It was late November, darkness came in soon after four o'clock, and when I came home I always drove round to the yard at the back of Skeldale House and trained my headlights on the stable. When I threw open the door Amber was always there, waiting to welcome me, her long yellow ears gleaming in the bright beam. That is my picture of her to this day. Her temperament never altered and her tail swished the straw unceasingly as I did uncomfortable things to her; rubbing the tender skin with the lotion, taking further skin scrapings to check progress.

As the days and the weeks went by and I saw no improvement I became a little desperate. I gave her sulphur baths and derris baths; I also began to go through all the quack "cures". I lost count of the shampoos and washes I swilled over the young animal in the hope that there might be some magic element in them. These nightly sessions under the headlights became part of my life, until one very dark evening when I seemed to see the young dog for the first time.

The condition had spread over the entire body, leaving only tufts and straggling wisps of hair. The long ears were golden no longer: they were almost bald, as was the rest of her face and head. Everywhere her skin was thickened and wrinkled, and when I squeezed it a slow ooze of serum came up around my fingers.

I flopped back and sat down in the straw while Amber leaped around me, licking and wagging. Despite her terrible state, her nature was unchanged. But I knew now that she and I had come to the end of the road.

It took me until the following lunchtime to summon the will to telephone Sister Rose. In my effort to be matter-of-fact I fear I was almost brusque. "Sister," I said, "I'm afraid it's all over with Amber. I've tried everything and she has got worse. I do think it would be the kindest thing to put her to sleep."

Shock was evident in her voice. "But . . . it's just a skin disease."

"I know, but this one can ruin an animal's life. Amber must be very uncomfortable now and soon she is going to be in pain."

"Oh . . . well, I trust in your judgment, Mr. Herriot. I know you wouldn't do anything that wasn't necessary." There was a long pause and I knew she was trying to control her voice. "I think I would like to come out and see her when I can get away from the hospital."

"Please, Sister," I said gently. "I'd much rather you didn't."

Again the pause, and then, "Very well, Mr. Herriot. I leave everything to you."

I had an urgent visit immediately afterwards and a rush of work kept me going all afternoon. It was pitch dark when I drove into the yard and opened the garage doors. And it was like all the other times. Amber was there in the beam, paws on the plywood, mouth open and panting with delight, welcoming me.

I put the barbiturate and syringe into my pocket before climbing into the pen. For a long time I made a fuss of her, patting her and talking to her. Then I filled the syringe.

"Sit, girl," I said, and she flopped obediently onto her hindquarters. I gripped her right leg above the elbow and Amber looked at me interestedly, wondering what new game this might be as I slipped the needle into the radial vein. I realized that there was no need to say the things I always said. "She won't know a thing . . . This is just an overdose of anaesthetic," or "It's an easy way out for her." There was no sorrowing owner to hear me. There were just the two of us.

But as I murmured, "Good girl, Amber, good lass," as she sank down on the straw I had the conviction that those comforting words would have been true. She didn't know a thing between her playfulness and oblivion, and it was indeed an easy way out from that prison which would soon become a torture chamber.

I stepped from the pen and switched off the car lights and in the cold darkness the yard had never seemed so empty. After the weeks of struggle the sense of loss and of failure was overpowering, and I feel some of it now after all these years.

At the present time we can cure most cases of demodectic mange by a long course of organo-phosphates and antibiotics. I know several fine dogs in Darrowby who have survived and when I see them in the streets, healthy and glossy-coated, the picture of Amber comes back into my mind. It is always dark, and she is always in the headlight's beam.

Chapter Nine

The bull with the bowler hat.

That was one of the irreverent terms for artificial insemination when it first arrived on the post-war scene. Of course AI was a wonderful advance. Up till then many farmers had used any available male bovine to get their cows in calf. A cow had to produce a calf before it would give milk and it was milk that was the goal of the dairy farmers, but unfortunately the progeny of these "scrub" bulls were often low grade and weakly.

But AI was a great improvement. To use a high class, pedigree bull to inseminate large numbers of cows for farmers who could never afford to own such an animal was and is a splendid idea. Over the years I have seen thousands of superior cattle populate the farms of Britain and I have rejoiced.

I am speaking theoretically. My own practical experience of artificial insemination was brief and unhappy.

When the thing began, most practitioners thought they would be doing a lot of insemination on their own account and Siegfried and I could hardly wait to get started. We purchased an artificial vagina, which was a tube of hard vulcanized rubber about eighteen inches long with a lining of latex. There was a little tap on the tube and warm water was run into the liner to simulate the temperature of a genuine cow. On one end of the AV was a latex cone terminating in a glass tube in which the semen was collected. Apart from its use in insemination this instrument provided an excellent means of testing the farmers' own bulls for fertility. It was in this context that I had my first experience.

Wally Hartley had bought a young Ayrshire bull from one of the big dairy farmers and he wanted the animal's fertility tested by the new method. He rang me to ask if I would do the job and I was elated at the chance to try out our new acquisition.

At the farm I filled the liner with water just nicely at blood heat and fastened on the cone and glass tube. I was ready and eager for action. The required cow in oestrus was in a large loosebox off the yard and the farmer led the bull towards it. "He's nobbut a little 'un," Mr. Hartley said, "but I wouldn't trust 'im. He's a cheeky young bugger—never served a cow yet, but keen as mustard."

I eyed the bull. Certainly he wasn't large, but he had mean eyes and the sharp curving horns of the typical Ayrshire. Anyway, this job shouldn't be much trouble. I had flipped through a pamphlet on the subject and it seemed simple enough: all you did was wait till the bull started to mount, then you directed the penis into the AV. Apparently then, the bull, with surprising gullibility, thrust happily into the cylinder and ejaculated into the tube. I had been told repeatedly that there was nothing to it.

I went into the box. "Let him in, Wally," I said, and the farmer opened the half door. The bull trotted inside and the cow submitted calmly as he sniffed around her. He seemed to like what he saw because he finally stationed himself behind her with eager anticipation. This was the moment. Take up position on the right side of the bull, the pamphlet had said, and the rest would be easy.

With surprising speed the young animal threw his forelegs on the cow's rump and surged forward. I had to move quickly and as the penis emerged from the sheath I grabbed it and poised the AV for action. But I didn't get the chance: the bull dismounted immediately and swung round on me with an affronted glare. He looked me carefully up and down as though he didn't quite believe what he saw, and there was not an ounce of friendliness in his expression. Then he turned his attention to the cow again.

He leaped up, I grabbed, and once more he suspended his activities abruptly and brought his forefeet thudding to the ground. This time there was anger in his eyes. He snorted, shook the needle-sharp horns in my direction and dragged a little straw along the floor with a hoof before fixing me with a long stare. His message was unequivocal: just try that once more, chum, and you've had it.

At length the bull, with a final warning glance at me, decided to resume his business and reared up on the cow once more. I gulped, bent quickly and as his slim red organ shot forth I grasped it and tried to bring the AV down on it.

This time the bull didn't mess about. He sprang away from the cow, put his head down and came at me like a bullet. In that fleeting instant I realized what a fool I had been to stand with the animals between me and the door. I was trapped.

Fortunately the AV was dangling from my right hand and as the bull charged I was able to catch him an upward blow on the snout. If I had hit him on the top of the head he would never have felt it and one or both of those nasty horns would inevitably have started to explore my interior. But as it was, the hard rubber cylinder thumping against his nose brought him to a slithering halt and while he was making up his mind about having a second go, I rained blows on him with a frenzy born of terror.

I have often wondered if I am the only veterinary surgeon to have used an artificial vagina as a defensive weapon. It certainly was not built for the purpose, because it soon began to disintegrate under my onslaught: first the glass tube hurtled past the ear of the startled farmer who was watching, wide-eyed, from the doorway, then the cone spun away against the flank of the cow who had started to chew her cud placidly, oblivious of the drama.

I alternated my swipes with thrusts and lunges worthy of a fencing master but I still couldn't jockey my way out of that corner. I obviously had the bull puzzled but I knew he was out to get me, and I was wondering how it would feel to receive a cornada when he took a step back and came in again full tilt, head down. I met him with a back-handed slash and that was what saved me: the elastic holding the latex lining came off and the warm water from within fountained into the bull's eyes.

He stopped suddenly and it was then I think he just decided to give up. In his experience of humans I was something new to him. I had taken intimate liberties with him in the pursuit of his lawful duty, I had belaboured him with a rubber instrument and finally squirted water in his face. He had plainly had enough.

During his pause for thought I dodged past him and escaped into the yard. The farmer looked at me as I fought for breath. "By gaw, Mr. Herriot, it's a 'ell of a job, this AI, isn't it?"

"Yes, Wally," I replied shakily. "It is, rather."

"Is it allus like that?"

"No, Wally, no . . ." I looked sadly at my bedraggled AV. "This is an exceptional case. I . . . I think we'd better get a specialist in to collect a sample from this bull."

The farmer rubbed his ear where the tube had clipped it in passing. "Awright, then, Mr. Herriot. It'll be another bit of excitement to look forward to."

His words did nothing to ease the feeling of abject failure as I crept away from the farm. Vets were taking semen samples every day now with no trouble at all. What was the matter with me?

Back in the surgery I phoned the advisory service. Yes, they said, they would send out one of their sterility advisory officers. He would meet me on the farm at ten o'clock the next morning.

When I arrived there on the following day the officer was already in the yard and I thought there was something familiar about the back of the jaunty figure strolling over the cobbles and blowing out clouds of cigarette smoke. When he turned round I saw with a gush of relief that it was Tristan. I hadn't been looking forward to recounting my shameful performance to a stranger.

His broad grin was like a tonic. "Hello, Jim, how are things?"

"Fine," I replied. "Except for this semen collection. I know you're doing it all the time but I had a shambolic experience yesterday." We stepped inside the loosebox, and I began my tale.

I hadn't got far before Tristan's jaw dropped. "You mean you just let the bull in here on his own, without any restraint? You're lucky to be here. In the first place this job should always be done out in the open, and secondly the bull should always be held by a halter through the nose ring. I like to have two or three blokes helping me." As I proceeded with my story his expression began to change. His mouth twitched, his chin trembled and little giggles burst from him. "Are you trying to tell me that you grabbed him by his old man? Jim, lad, you are supposed to handle only the sheath to do the directing. Oh dear, oh dear!"

I gave a wry smile. "Oh, I know that now. I read the pamphlet again last night and realized I had made a lot of mistakes."

"Well, never mind," he said. "Carry on with your story."

The next few minutes had a devastating effect on my ex-colleague. As I described the bull's attack on me he slumped, shouting, against the door and by the time I had finished tears were coursing down his cheeks.

"You were . . . you were in that corner, fighting the bull off with the AV . . ." He reached for his handkerchief. "For God's sake don't tell me any more, Jim. You'll do me an injury." He wiped his eyes and straightened up as he heard the farmer's footsteps in the yard. "Ah, good morning, Mr. Hartley," he said. "We can get started now."

Tristan was very business-like as he directed operations. Yesterday's cow was still in oestrus and within minutes she was tied to a gatepost in the yard with a man on either side. "That's to stop her swinging round when the bull mounts," he explained to me.

He turned to the farmer and handed him the AV. "Will you fill this with warm water, please and screw the stopper on tightly."

The farmer trotted into the house and as he returned another of his men led out the bull. This time my antagonist of yesterday was securely held by a halter through his ring: Tristan had certainly got everything arranged in an orderly fashion.

The bull was indeed "keen as mustard": he took one look at the cow and started towards her, a picture of urgent lust. Tristan scarcely had time to get the AV into his hand before the bull was clambering eagerly aboard his quarry, and I had to admit that Tristan was lightning fast as he stooped, seized the sheath, and sent the penis plunging into the AV. So that was how it was done, I thought wistfully. So very easy.

My feeling of shame was building up when the bull pushed out his tongue and emitted a long-drawn, deafening bellow of rage. And he had scarcely entered the AV when he withdrew with a backward leap and began to caper around on the end of his halter, filling the air with disapproving bawls.

"What the hell . . . ?" Tristan stared at the animal in bewilderment, then he poked his finger into the AV. "Good God!" he cried. "The water in here is damned hot!"

Wally Hartley nodded. "Aye well, the kettle had just come to the boil when I went into t'house, so ah just poured it straight in."

Tristan clutched his brow and groaned. "Oh, damn it! I always check the temperature, but what with talking to you and that young beggar going into action so fast, I clean forgot. Boiling water! No wonder the poor beast got out quick."

Meanwhile the bull had stopped his noise and was circling the cow, sniffing her over and regarding her with a mixture of disbelief and respect. "What a woman!" was clearly the dominant thought in his mind.

"Anyway, let's have another try." Tristan made for the farmhouse. "I'll fill the thing myself this time."

Soon the stage was set once more: Tristan standing at the ready, and the bull, apparently undeterred by his recent experience, patently eager to join battle yet again. By his attitude now he looked as though, come hell or high water, he was going to serve that cow.

My impression was confirmed when he made a sudden rush at her. Tristan, slightly pop-eyed, managed to jam on the AV, but as he did so the velocity of the charge caused the animal to lose his footing so that the bull slid on his back clean underneath the cow. The AV was jerked from Tristan's grasp and soared high into the air. It described a graceful parabola before landing on a pile of straw at the other end of the yard.

As the bull scrambled to his feet Tristan strolled unhurriedly towards the straw. The glass tube was still attached to the cylinder, and my friend held it up at eye level. "Ah, yes," he murmured. "A nice 3 cc sample."

The farmer came puffing up. "You've got what you wanted, 'ave you? By 'ell, it's a complicated sort o' business, isn't it?"

"It can be just a little, at times," Tristan replied airily. "Anyway, I'll get my microscope from the car and examine the sample."

It didn't take long and soon afterwards we were all having a cup of tea in the kitchen. "That's a fine fertile bull you have there, Mr. Hartley," said Tristan as he reached for a scone.

"Eee, that's champion." The farmer rubbed his hands. "I paid a fair bit o' brass for 'im and it's grand to know he's up to scratch." He looked at the young man with undisguised admiration. "You've done a grand job and I'm right grateful to you."

As I sipped my tea, the thought occurred to me that despite the passage of the years things hadn't changed. Just as that glass tube had landed on a soft bed of straw, Tristan always landed on his feet.

Chapter Ten

"I let my heart fall into careless hands." Little Rosie's voice piped in my ear as I guided my car over a stretch of rutted road. I was on my way to dress a wound on a cow's back and it was nice to have the singing to cheer the hours of driving. But it was beginning to dawn on me that something better still was happening: I was starting all over again with another child. When Jimmy went to school I missed his company in the car, the childish chatter which never palled, and the intense pleasure of seeing his growing wonder at the things of the countryside. Now the whole thing was going to begin again with Rosie.

The singing had originated in the purchase of a radiogram. Music has always meant a lot to me and hi-fi outfits hadn't been heard of at that time, nor stereo, nor any of the other things which have revolutionized the world of listening. The best the music lover could do was to get a good radiogram. After much agonizing, I made my choice: it had to be the Murphy. A handsome piece of furniture with a louvred front and graceful legs, it bellowed out the full volume of the Philharmonia Orchestra without a trace of muzziness. I was enchanted with it, but it cost over ninety pounds and that was an awful lot of money in 1950.

"Helen," I said when we had installed it in the sitting room. "We've got to look after this thing. We must keep the kids away from it."

Foolish words. The very next day as I came in the front door the passage was echoing with "Yippee ay ooooh, yippee ay aaaay, ghost riders in the skyyy!" It was Bing Crosby's back-up choir belting out the other side of the "Careless Hands" record and the Murphy was giving it full value.

I peeped round the sitting room door. "Ghost Riders" had come to an end and with her chubby little hands Rosie removed the record, placed it in its cover and marched to the record cabinet. She selected another disc and was halfway across the floor when I waylaid her. "Which one is that?" I asked.

" 'The Little Ginger Bread Man'," she replied, even though the array of children's records looked exactly the same and Rosie at the age of three could not read. She fitted the disc expertly on the turntable and set it going.

I had an hour to spare and Rosie gave me a recital. We went through "Uncle Mac's Nursery Rhymes", "The Happy Prince", "Peter and the Wolf", and many of the immortal Bing to whom I was and am devoted. I was intrigued to find that Rosie's favourite Crosby record was "Careless Hands". This one had something special for her.

At the end of the session I decided that it was fruitless to try to keep Rosie and the Murphy apart. Whenever she was not out with me she played with it. She did my precious acquisition no harm and when she came with me on my rounds she sang the songs she had played so often and which were word perfect in her mind. And I really loved that singing: "Careless Hands" soon became my favourite, too.

There were three gates on the road to the farm we were visiting and as we came bumping up to the first one the singing stopped abruptly. This was one of my daughter's big moments. When I drew up she jumped from the car, strutted proudly to the gate and opened it. She took this duty very seriously and her small face was grave as I drove through. When she returned to take her place on the passenger seat, I patted her knee. "Thank you, sweetheart," I said. "You're such a big help to me."

She didn't say anything but blushed and seemed to swell with importance. She knew I meant it because opening gates is a chore.

We negotiated the other two gates in similar manner and drove into the farmyard. The farmer, Mr. Binns, had shut the cow up in a ramshackle pen with a passage which stretched from a dead end to the outside. I saw with some apprehension that the animal was a Galloway—black and shaggy with a fringe of hair hanging over bad-tempered eyes. She lowered her head and swished her tail as she watched me.

"Couldn't you have got her tied up, Mr. Binns?" I asked.

The farmer shook his head. "Nay, I'm short o' room and this 'un spends most of 'er time on the moors."

I could believe it. There was nothing domesticated about this animal. I looked down at my daughter. Usually I lifted her into a hay rack while I worked but I didn't want her anywhere near the Galloway. "It's no place for you in there, Rosie," I said. "Go and stand at the end of the passage well out of the way."

We went into the pen and I was pleasantly surprised when the farmer managed to drop a halter over the cow's head. He backed into a corner and held tightly to the shank.

I looked at him doubtfully. "Can you hold her?"

"I think so," Mr. Binns replied, a little breathlessly. "You'll find t'place at the end of her back, there."

It was a big discharging abscess near the root of the tail, and that tail was whipping perpetually from side to side—a sure sign of ill nature in a bovine. Gently I passed my fingers over the swelling and like a natural reflex the hind foot lashed out, catching me a glancing blow on the thigh. I had expected this and I got on with my exploration.

"How long has she had this?"

The farmer dug his heels in and leaned back on the rope. "Oh, 'bout two months. It keeps bustin' and fillin' up over and over again. What's cause of it?"

"I don't know, Mr. Binns. She must have had a wound there at some time and it's become infected. On the back, drainage is poor, and there's a lot of dead tissue which I'll have to clear away before the thing heals."

I leaned from the pen. "Rosie, will you bring me my scissors, the cotton wool and that bottle of peroxide."

The farmer watched wonderingly as the tiny figure trotted to the car. "By gaw, t'little lass knows 'er way around."

"Oh yes," I said, smiling. "I'm not saying she knows where everything is, but she's an expert on the things I use regularly."

Rosie handed me my requirements as I reached over the door. Then she retreated to her place at the end of the passage, and I began my work on the abscess. Since the tissue was dead the cow couldn't feel anything as I snipped and swabbed, but that didn't stop the hind leg from pistoning out every few seconds. Some animals cannot tolerate any kind of interference and this was one of them.

I finished at last with a nice wide clean area onto which I trickled the hydrogen peroxide. I had a lot of faith in this old remedy as a penetrative antiseptic and I watched contentedly as it bubbled on the skin surface. The cow, however, did not seem to enjoy the sensation because she made a sudden leap into the air, tore the rope from the farmer's hands, brushed me to one side and made for the door. The hairy, black monster went straight through it with a splintering crash, shot into the passage and began to thunder down towards the dead end where my little daughter was standing.

It was one of the worst moments of my life. As I dashed towards the broken door I heard a small voice say "Mama". There was no scream of terror, just that one quiet word. Rosie was standing with her back against the end wall of the passage and the cow was stationary, looking at her from a distance of two feet.

The animal turned when she heard my footsteps, and then whipped round and galloped past me into the yard. I was shaking when I lifted Rosie into my arms. She could easily have been killed and a jumble of thoughts whirled in my brain. Why had she been apparently unafraid? I didn't known the answers. All I felt was an overwhelming thankfulness.

Driving away I remembered that something very like this had happened when Jimmy was out with me. It was not so horrific because he was playing in a passage with an open end, and was not trapped when the cow I was working on broke loose and hurtled towards him. I could see nothing but I heard a piercing yell of AAAAGH!" before I rounded the corner. To my intense relief Jimmy was streaking across the field to where my car was standing and the cow was trotting away in another direction. This reaction was typical because Jimmy was always the noisy one of the family. Under any form of stress he believed in making his feelings known in the form of loud cries.

Rosie solemnly opened the three gates on the way back and then looked up at me expectantly. I knew what it was—she wanted to play one of her games. She loved being quizzed just as Jimmy had loved to quiz me.

I took my cue and began. "Give me the names of six blue flowers."

She coloured quickly in satisfaction because of course she knew. "Field Scabious, Harebell, Forget-me-not, Bluebell, Speedwell, Meadow Cranesbill."

"Clever girl," I said. "Now, let's see—how about the names of six birds?"

Again the blush and the quick reply. "Magpie, Curlew, Thrush, Plover, Yellowhammer, Rook."

"Very good indeed. Now name me six red flowers." And so it went on, day after day, with infinite variations. I only half realized at the time how lucky I was: I had a demanding, round-the-clock job and yet I had the company of my children at the same time. So many men work so hard to keep the home going that they lose touch with the families who are at the heart of it.

With Rosie, as her schooldays approached, her attitude, always solicitous, became distinctly maternal. She really couldn't see how I was going to get by without her and by the time she was five she was definitely worried. "Daddy," she would say seriously, "how are you going to manage when I'm at school? All those gates to open and having to get everything out of the boot by yourself. It's going to be awful for you."

I used to try to reassure her, patting her head as she looked up at me in the car. "I know, Rosie, I know. I'm going to miss you, but I'll get along somehow."

Her response was always the same: a relieved smile and then the comforting words, "but never mind, Daddy, I'll be with you every Saturday and Sunday. You'll be all right then."

I suppose it was a natural result of my children seeing veterinary practice from early childhood and witnessing my own pleasure in my work, that they never thought of being anything else but veterinary surgeons. There was no problem with Jimmy: he was a tough little fellow and well able to stand the buffets of our job, but somehow I couldn't bear the idea of my daughter being kicked and trodden on and knocked down and covered with muck. Practice was so much rougher in those days. There were no metal crushes to hold the big struggling beasts, there were still quite a number of farm horses around and they were the ones which regularly put the vets in hospital with broken legs and ribs. I have always believed that children should follow their inclinations, but as Rosie entered her teens I dropped a long series of broad hints, and perhaps played unfairly by showing her as many grisly, dirty jobs as possible. Rosie finally decided to specialize in human medicine and is now a happy and successful doctor.

However, all that was far in the future as I drove home from Mr. Binns with my three-year-old daughter by my side. She had started to sing again and was just finishing the first verse of her great favourite: *"Careless hands don't care when dreams slip through."*

Chapter Eleven

In the semi-darkness of the surgery passage I thought it was a hideous growth dangling from the side of the dog's face, but as he came closer I saw that it was only a condensed milk can. Not that condensed milk cans are commonly found sprouting from dogs' cheeks—this was only normal when I was dealing with Brandy.

I hoisted him onto the table. "Brandy, you've been at the dustbin again."

The big golden labrador gave me an apologetic grin and did his best to lick my face. He couldn't manage it since his tongue was jammed in the can, but he made up for it by furious tail wagging.

"Oh, Mr. Herriot, I am sorry to trouble you again." Mrs. Westby, his attractive young mistress, smiled ruefully. "He just won't keep out of that dustbin. Sometimes the children and I can get the cans off ourselves, but this one has trapped his tongue under the lid."

"Yes . . . yes . . ." I eased my finger along the jagged edge of the metal. "It's a bit tricky, isn't it? We don't want to cut his mouth."

As I reached for a pair of forceps I thought of the many other occasions when I had done something like this for Brandy. He was a huge, lolloping, slightly goofy animal, and this dustbin raiding was becoming an obsession. He liked to fish out a can and lick out the tasty remnants, but his licking was carried out with such dedication that he often got stuck. Again and again he had been freed by his family or myself from fruit salad cans, corned beef cans, baked bean cans, soup cans; there didn't seem to be anything he didn't like.

I gripped the edge of the lid with my forceps and gently bent it back along its length until I was able to lift it away from the tongue. An instant later that tongue was slobbering all over my cheek in delight and thanks. "Get back, you daft dog!" I said, laughing, as I held the panting face away from me.

"Yes, come down, Brandy." Mrs. Westby spoke sharply. "You're becoming a nuisance with this business. It will have to stop."

The scolding had no effect on the lashing tail and I saw that his mistress was smiling. You just couldn't help liking Brandy, because he was a great ball of affection without an ounce of malice in him. I had seen the Westby children—there were three girls and a boy—carrying him around upside down, or pushing him in a pram dressed in baby clothes. Those youngsters played all sorts of games with him, but he suffered them all with good humour.

Brandy had other idiosyncrasies apart from his fondness for dustbins. I was attending the Westby cat at their home one afternoon when I noticed the dog acting strangely. Mrs. Westby was sitting knitting in an armchair, and when I was searching my pockets for my thermometer I noticed Brandy slinking into the room. He moved furtively across the carpet and sat down with studied carelessness in front of his mistress. After a few moments he began to work his rear end gradually up the front of the chair towards her knees; absently she took a hand away from her knitting and pushed him down but he immediately restarted his extraordinary backward ascent, hips moving in a very slow rumba rhythm as he elevated them inch by inch, and all the time the golden face blank and innocent as though nothing at all was happening.

I watched, fascinated. Mrs. Westby was absorbed in an intricate part of her knitting and didn't seem to notice that Brandy's bottom was now firmly parked on her shapely knees which were clad in blue jeans. The dog paused as though acknowledging that phase one had been successfully completed, and then he began to consolidate his position, pushing his way up the front of the chair with his fore limbs until he was almost standing on his head. Just when one final backward heave would have seen the great dog ensconced on her lap, Mrs. Westby looked up.

"Oh, really, Brandy, you are silly!" She put a hand on his rump and sent him slithering disconsolately to the carpet.

"What was all that about?" I asked.

Mrs. Westby laughed. "Oh, it's these old blue jeans. When Brandy first came here as a tiny puppy I spent hours nursing him on my knee and I used to wear the jeans a lot then. Ever since the very sight of the things makes him try to get on my knee. He's tried jumping up and got ticked off—he knows perfectly well I can't have a fully-grown labrador in my lap."

"So now it's the stealthy approach, eh?"

She giggled. "That's right. When I'm preoccupied sometimes he manages to get nearly all the way up, and if he's been playing in the mud he makes an awful mess and I have to go and change. That's when he really does receive a scolding."

A patient like Brandy added colour to my daily round. When I was walking my own dog I often saw him playing in the fields by the river, and while other dogs would take to the water sedately, Brandy's approach was unique: he would launch himself outwards, legs splayed in a sort of swallow dive, and hang for a moment in the air rather like a flying fox before splashing thunderously into the depths. To me it was the action of a completely happy extrovert.

One day in those same fields I witnessed something even more extraordinary in the children's playground: Brandy was disporting himself on the slide. For this activity he had assumed an uncharacteristic gravity of expression, and stood calmly in the queue of children. When his turn came he mounted the steps, slid down the metal slope, all dignity and importance, then took a staid walk round to rejoin the queue. I could have watched him all day.

I often smiled to myself when I thought of Brandy's antics but I didn't smile when Mrs. Westby brought him into the surgery a few months later. His bounding ebullience had disappeared and he had to drag himself along the passage to the consulting room.

As I lifted him onto the table I noticed that he had lost a lot of weight. "What is the trouble, Mrs. Westby?" I asked.

She looked at me worriedly. "He's been off colour for a few days now, listless and coughing and not eating very well, but this morning he seems quite ill and you can see he's starting to pant."

"Yes . . . yes . . ." As I inserted the thermometer I watched the rapid rise and fall of the rib cage and noted the gaping mouth and anxious eyes. "He does look very sorry for himself." His temperature was 104°. I took out my stethoscope and listened to his lungs. I have heard of an old Scottish doctor describing a patient's chest as sounding like a "kist o' whustles" and that just about described Brandy's. Wheezes, squeaks and bubblings—they were all there against a background of laboured respiration.

I put the stethoscope back in my pocket. "He's got pneumonia."

"Oh dear. That's bad, isn't it?"

"Yes, I'm afraid so."

"But . . ." Mrs. Westby gave me an appealing glance. "I understand it isn't so fatal since the new drugs came out."

I hesitated. "Yes, that's quite right. In humans and most animals the sulpha drugs and now penicillin have changed the picture completely, but dogs are still very difficult to cure."

Thirty years later it is still the same. Even with all the armoury of antibiotics which followed penicillin—streptomycin, the tetracyclines, and the new steroids—I still hate to see pneumonia in a dog.

"But Brandy is young and strong," I went on. "He must stand a fair chance. I wonder what started this off?"

"He had a swim in the river about a week ago, Mr. Herriot. I try to keep him out of the water in this cold weather, but if he sees a stick floating he just takes a dive into the middle."

"Was he shivery afterwards?"

"He was. I walked him straight home but it was a freezing cold day. I could feel him trembling as I dried him down."

I nodded. "That would be the cause, all right. Anyway, I'm going to give him this injection of penicillin and I'll call at your house tomorrow to repeat it. He's not well enough to come to the surgery. Also, I want you to make him what we call a pneumonia jacket: cut two holes in an old blanket for his forelegs and stitch him into it along his back—he must have his chest warmly covered. Only let him out in the garden for necessities."

I called and repeated the injection on the following day. There wasn't much change. I injected him for four more days and the realization came to me sadly that Brandy wasn't responding. The temperature did drop a little but he ate hardly anything and grew gradually thinner.

As the days passed and he continued to sink deeper into a blank-eyed lethargy, I was forced more and more to a conclusion which, a few weeks before, would have seemed impossible: this happy, bounding animal was going to die.

Brandy didn't die. He survived, but you couldn't put it any higher than that. His temperature came down and his appetite improved, and he climbed onto a plateau of twilight existence where he seemed content to stay.

"He isn't Brandy any more," Mrs. Westby said a few weeks later when I called in. Her eyes filled with tears as she spoke.

I shook my head. "No, I'm afraid he isn't. He has recovered from a really virulent pneumonia, but it's left him with a chronic pleurisy, adhesions and probably other kinds of lung damage."

She dabbed at her eyes. "It breaks my heart to see him like this. He's only five, but he's like an old, old dog." She sniffed and blew her nose. "When I think of how I used to scold him for getting into the dustbins and muddying up my jeans, I wish he would do some of his funny old tricks. Now he doesn't even want to go for a walk."

As I watched, Brandy rose and pottered slowly over to the fire. He stood there for a moment, gaunt and dead-eyed before he coughed, groaned and flopped down on the hearth rug.

"Do you think he'll always be like this?" Mrs. Westby asked.

I shrugged. "We can only hope."

But as I got into my car and drove away I really didn't have much hope. I had seen calves with lung damage after bad pneumonias. They recovered but were called "bad doers" because they remained thin and listless for the rest of their lives. Doctors, too, had plenty of "chesty" people on their books who were more or less in the same predicament.

Months went by, and the only time I saw the labrador was when Mrs. Westby was walking him on his lead; he seemed reluctant to move and his mistress had to stroll along very slowly so that he could keep up with her. I sadly thought of the lolloping Brandy of old, but I told myself that I could do no more for him now, and I made a determined effort to push him out of my mind.

I managed to forget Brandy fairly well until one afternoon in February. On the previous night I had treated a colicky horse until 4:00 am and was crawling into bed when I was called to a calving. I managed to produce a large live calf from a small heifer, but the effort drained the last of my strength, and when I got home it was too late to return to bed. Ploughing through the morning round I was so tired that I felt disembodied, and at lunch Helen watched me anxiously as my head nodded over my food.

There were a few dogs in the waiting room at two o'clock and I dealt with them mechanically, peering through half-closed eyelids. By the time I reached my last patient I had the feeling that I wasn't there at all.

"Next, please," I mumbled, as I pushed open the waiting room door and stood back waiting for the usual sight of a dog being led out to the passage.

But this time there was a big difference. There was a man in the doorway all right and he had a little poodle with him, but the thing that made my eyes snap wide open was that the dog was walking upright on his hind limbs. Surely I wasn't seeing things? I stared down at the dog; the little creature strutted through the doorway, chest out, head up, as erect as a soldier.

"Follow me, please," I said hoarsely. The man must have seen the bewilderment in my face because he burst into a roar of laughter.

"Don't worry, Mr. Herriot," he said. "This little dog was circus-trained before I got him as a pet. I like to show off his little tricks. This one really startles people."

"You can say that again," I said breathlessly. "It nearly gave me heart failure."

The poodle wasn't ill; he just wanted his nails clipped. I hoisted him onto the table and began to ply the clippers, but by the time I had finished the old lassitude had taken over again, and I felt ready to fall down as I showed man and dog to the front door.

I watched the little animal trotting away down the street—in the orthodox manner this time—and it came to me suddenly that it had been a long time since I had seen a dog doing something unusual and amusing—like the things Brandy used to do. A wave of gentle memories flowed through me as I leaned wearily against the door post and closed my eyes.

When I opened them I saw Brandy coming round the corner of the street with Mrs. Westby. His nose was entirely obscured by a large, red, tomato soup can, and he strained madly at the leash and whipped his tail when he saw me.

It was certainly a hallucination this time. I really ought to go to bed immediately. But I was still rooted to the door post when the labrador bounded up the steps, made an abortive attempt to lick my face and contented himself with cocking a convivial leg against the bottom step.

I stared into Mrs. Westby's radiant face. "What . . . what . . . ?"

With her sparkling eyes and wide smile she looked more attractive than ever. "Look, Mr. Herriot, look! He's better, he's better!"

"And I . . . I suppose you'll want me to get that can off him?"

"Oh yes, yes, please!"

In an instant I was wide awake, but it took all my strength to lift him onto the table. He was heavier now than before his illness. I reached for the forceps and began to turn the jagged edges of the can outwards from the nose and mouth. Tomato soup must have been one of his favourites because he was really deeply embedded and it took some time before I was able to slide the can from his face.

I fought off his slobbering attack. "He's back in the dustbins, I see."

"Yes, he is, quite regularly. And he goes sliding with the children, too." She smiled happily.

Thoughtfully I took my stethoscope and listened to his lungs. They were wonderfully clear: a slight roughness here and there, but the old cacophony had gone. I looked at the great dog with a mixture of thankfulness and incredulity. He was as before, boisterous and full of the joy of living. His tongue lolled in a happy grin and the sun glinted through the surgery window on his sleek golden coat.

"But Mr. Herriot," Mrs. Westby's eyes were wide. "How on earth has this happened? How has he got better?"

"*Vis medicatrix naturae*," I replied in tones of deep respect. "The healing power of nature—something no veterinary surgeon can compete with when it decides to act."

For a few seconds we were silent as we stroked the dog's head and ears and flanks.

"Oh, by the way," I said. "Has he shown any renewed interest in the blue jeans?"

"Oh my word, yes! They're in the sink at this very moment, absolutely covered in mud. Isn't it marvellous!"

I COULD FIND SOMETHING attractive in nearly all my canine patients, but I had to make an exception in the cases of Ruffles and Muffles Whithorn. Try as I might I could find no lovable traits, only unpleasant ones—like their unvarying method of welcoming me into their home.

"Down! Down!" I yelped, as I always did. The two little animals—West Highland Whites—were standing on their hind limbs clawing furiously at my trouser legs with their front paws and the effect was agonizing.

As I backed away on tiptoe like a ballet dancer going into reverse, the room resounded to Mr. and Mrs. Whithorn's delighted laughter. They found this unfailingly amusing.

"Aren't they little pets!" Mr. Whithorn gasped between paroxysms. "Don't they give you a lovely greeting, bless them!"

I wasn't so sure about that. The dogs were glaring up at me balefully, teeth chattering in a characteristic manner. It wasn't exactly a snarl, but it wasn't friendly either.

"Come, my darlings." The man gathered the dogs into his arms and kissed them both fondly. He was still giggling.

"You know, Mr. Herriot, isn't it priceless that they welcome you into our house so lovingly and then try to stop you from leaving."

I didn't say anything, but massaged my trousers in silence. The truth was that these animals invariably clawed me on my entry then did their best to bite my ankles on the way out. In between, they molested me in whatever ways they could devise. The strange thing was that they were both old—Ruffles fourteen and Muffles twelve—and one might have expected some mellowness in their characters.

"Well," I said, after reassuring myself that my wounds were superficial. "I understand Ruffles is lame."

"Yes." Mrs. Whithorn took the dog and placed him on the table where she had spread some newspapers. "It's his left front paw. He's in agony, poor dear."

Gingerly I took hold of the foot then whipped my hand away as the teeth snapped shut less than an inch from my fingers.

"Oh, my precious!" Mrs. Whithorn exclaimed. "It's so painful. Do be careful, Mr. Herriot, I think you're hurting him."

I breathed deeply. This dog should have had a tape muzzle

applied right at the start, but I had previously caused shock to the Whithorns by suggesting such a thing so I had to manage as best I could. Anyway, I wasn't a novice. It would take a very smart biter to catch me.

I curled my forefinger round the leg and had another look and I was able to see what I wanted to see in the fleeting instant before the next snap. A reddish swelling pouting from between the toes.

An interdigital cyst! How ridiculous that a vet should be making a house call for such a trivial ailment. But the Whithorns had always firmly refused to bring their dogs to surgery. It frightened the darlings, they said.

I stood back from the table. "This is just a harmless cyst, but it is painful so I'd advise you to bathe it in hot water until it bursts. That will relieve the pain. Many dogs burst these things themselves by nibbling at them but you can hasten the process." I drew some antibiotic into a syringe. "I'll give him this shot in case of infection."

I achieved the injection by holding the little animal by the scruff of the neck. Then Mrs. Whithorn lifted the other dog onto the table.

"You'd better give him a check-up while you're here," she said.

I palpated the snarling bundle of white hair and went over him with stethoscope and thermometer. He had most of the afflictions which beset old dogs—arthritis, nephritis, and a heart murmur which was difficult to hear among the bad-tempered rumblings which echoed round his thorax.

My examination completed, I replenished his various medicaments and prepared to leave. This was when the exit phase of my visit started. The ritual never changed. As their owners tittered gleefully the two little dogs stationed themselves in the doorway, effectively barring my way out. Their lips were drawn back from their teeth. They were the very picture of venom. To draw them away from their posts I feinted to the right then made a rush for the door but with my fingers on the handle I had to turn and fend off the hungry jaws snapping at my ankles.

But I escaped, crashing the door thankfully behind me.

I was regaining my breath when Doug Watson, the milkman, drew up in his blue van. "Mornin', Mr. Herriot." He gestured towards the house. "You been in to see them dogs?"

"Yes."

"Proper little sods, aren't they? I've got to watch them myself when I deliver t'milk. If that door happens to be open they're straight for me feet. Sometimes I feel a right Charlie, jumpin' about like a daft thing in front of everybody."

I nodded. "I know exactly how you feel."

"But ah'll tell tha summat and maybe ye won't believe me. Them dogs used to be real nice little things."

"What!"

"I'm not joking. When they fust came here they were as friendly as any dogs I've seen."

"Well, that's remarkable," I said. "I wonder what happened."

Doug shrugged his shoulders. "God knows, but each one of 'em turned nasty after a few months and they've got wuss and wuss ever since."

Doug's words stayed with me until I got back to the surgery. I was puzzled. Westies, in my experience, were a particularly amiable breed.

Siegfried was in the dispensary, writing directions on a bottle of colic mixture. I mentioned the situation to him. "Yes," he said. "I've heard the same thing. I've been to the Whithorns a couple of times and I know why those dogs are so objectionable. Their owners never correct them and they slobber over them all the time."

"You could be right," I said. "All that kissing and cuddling is a bit sickening."

"Quite. Too much of that is bad for a dog. And those two animals are the bosses in that home. A dog likes to obey. It gives him security. Believe me, Ruffles and Muffles would be happy and good-tempered if they had been controlled from the start."

The months passed, I had a few more visits to the Whithorns and went through the usual dancing routine, then, oddly, both the old dogs died peacefully within a few weeks of each other.

It was like a chapter in my life closing, but shortly afterwards Mr. Whithorn rang me. "Mr. Herriot," he said. "We have acquired another pair of Westies and I wonder if you would call and give them their distemper inoculations."

It was a delightful change to go into the room and be met by two

90

tail-wagging puppies. They were twelve weeks old and they looked up at me with benevolent eyes.

"They're beautiful," I said. "What have you called them?"

"Ruffles and Muffles," Mr. Whithorn replied.

"Same again, eh?"

"Yes, we wanted to keep the memory of our other darlings alive."

After the inoculations, it was nearly a year before I saw the little dogs again, for a check-up. When I went into the sitting room, Ruffles and Muffles Mark 2 were seated side by side on the sofa. There was an odd immobility in their attitude. As I approached they stared at me coldly and as if responding to a signal they bared their teeth and growled softly but menacingly.

A chill ran through me. It couldn't be happening all over again. But as Mr. Whithorn lifted Ruffles onto the table and I took the auroscope from its box, I quickly realized that fate had turned the clock back. The little animal regarded me with a bristling mistrust.

"Hold his head, will you, please," I said. "I want to examine his ears first." I took the ear between finger and thumb and gently inserted the auroscope. I applied my eye to the instrument and was inspecting the external meatus when the dog exploded into action. I heard a vicious snarl and as I jerked my head back the draught of the crunching teeth fanned my face.

Mr. Whithorn leaned back and abandoned himself to mirth. "Oh, isn't he a little monkey! Ha-ha-ha, he just won't stand any nonsense."

I stared at the man. The fact that he might easily have been confronted by a noseless veterinary surgeon did not seem to weigh with him. I looked, too, at his wife standing behind him. She was laughing just as merrily. What was the use of trying to instil reason into these people?

"Mr. Whithorn," I said tautly. "Will you please hold him again, and this time take a tight grip with your hands on either side of his neck."

He looked at me anxiously. "But won't it hurt the little pet?"

"No, no, of course not."

"All right." He placed his cheek against the dog's face and whispered lovingly. "Daddy promises to be gentle, my angel."

He grasped the loose skin of the neck as I directed and I warily recommenced operations. Peering at the interior of the ear, listening to Mr. Whithorn's murmured endearments, I was tensed in readiness for another explosion. But when it came with a ferocious yap I found I was in no danger because Ruffles had turned his attention elsewhere.

As I dropped the auroscope and jumped back I saw that the dog had sunk his teeth into the ball of his master's thumb. And it wasn't an ordinary bite. He was hanging on, grinding deeply into the flesh.

Mr. Whithorn emitted a piercing yell of agony before shaking himself free.

"*You rotten little bugger!*" he screamed, dancing around the room, holding the stricken hand. He looked at the blood pouring from the two deep holes then glared at Ruffles. "*Oh, you bloody little swine!*"

I thought of Siegfried's wish that these people might take a more sensible view of their dogs. Well, this could be a start.

Chapter Twelve

Mr. Garrett's words about parents needing nerves of steel have come back to me many times over the years. One notable occasion was the annual recital given by Miss Livingstone's piano class.

Miss Livingstone was a soft-voiced, charming lady in her fifties who gave the local children piano lessons, and once a year she held a concert in the Methodist Hall for her pupils to show their paces. They ranged from six-year-olds to teenagers, and the room was packed with their proud parents. Jimmy was nine at the time and had been practising without much enthusiasm for the big day.

Everybody knows everybody else in a small town like Darrowby, and as the place filled up there was much nodding and smiling as people recognized each other. I found myself on the centre aisle with Helen on my right and just across the few feet of space I saw Jeff Ward, old Willie Richardson's cowman, sitting very upright, hands on knees. He was dressed in his Sunday best, and the dark serge was stretched tightly across his muscular frame. His red, strong-boned face shone with intensive scrubbing and his normally wayward thatch of hair was plastered down with brilliantine.

"Hello, Jeff," I said. "One of your youngsters performing today?"

He turned and grinned. "Aye, Mr. Herriot, it's our Margaret. She's been comin' on right well at t'piano and I just hope she does herself justice this afternoon."

"Of course she will, Jeff. Miss Livingstone is an excellent teacher. She'll do fine."

He nodded and turned to the front as the concert commenced. The first few performers who mounted the platform were very small boys in shorts and socks or tiny girls in frilly dresses, and their feet dangled far above the pedals as they sat at the keyboard. Miss Livingstone hovered nearby to prompt them but their little mistakes were greeted with indulgent smiles from the assembly, and at the conclusion of each piece there was thunderous applause.

I noticed, however, that as the children grew bigger and the pieces became more difficult a certain tension began to build up in the hall. When little Jenny Newcombe, the fruiterer's daughter, halted a couple of times the silence in the room was charged with anxiety. When Jenny successfully restarted and I relaxed with all the others, the realization burst upon me that we were not just a roomful of parents watching our children perform, we were a band of brothers and sisters suffering together.

When little Margaret Ward climbed up to the platform her father stiffened perceptibly in his seat. From the corner of my eye I could see Jeff's big, work-roughened fingers clutching tightly at his knees. Margaret went on very nicely till she came to a rather complicated chord which jarred with harsh dissonance; she knew she had got the notes wrong and tried again . . . and again . . . and again, each time jerking her head with the effort.

I glanced round at Jeff. It was impossible for anybody with his complexion to turn pale, but his face had assumed a hideously mottled appearance and his legs were twitching convulsively.

As Margaret fought for the right notes a total silence settled on the packed hall. It seemed an eternity before the little girl got it right and galloped away over the rest of the piece, and everybody applauded with relief as much as approval.

After a succession of children went up and did their thing without incident it was Jimmy's turn. Most of the performers and parents were suffering from nerves, but my son almost whistled as he trotted up the steps and there was a hint of swagger in his walk up to the piano. This, he clearly thought, was going to be a doddle. In marked contrast I went into a sort of rigor as soon as he appeared, and my palms broke out in an instant sweat. I told myself that this was utterly ridiculous, but it was no good. It was how I felt.

Jimmy's piece was called The Miller's Dance, a title which is burned on my brain till the day I die. It was a rollicking little melody which of course by now I knew down to the last semiquaver. Jimmy started off in great style, throwing his hands about and tossing his head like Arthur Rubinstein in full flow.

Around the middle of The Miller's Dance there is a pause in the quick tempo where the music goes from a brisk *ta-rum-tum-tiddle-iddle-om-pom-pom* to a lingering *taa-rum, taa-rum, taa-rum*, before starting off again at top speed. It was a clever little ploy which gave a touch of variety to the whole thing. Jimmy dashed up to this point with flailing arms till he slowed down at the familiar *taa-rum, taa-rum, taa-rum*. I waited for him to take off again but nothing happened; he stopped and looked down fixedly at the keys for a few seconds, then played the slow bit again and halted once more.

My heart gave a great thud. Come on, lad, you know the next part—I've heard you play it a hundred times. My voiceless plea was born of desperation, but Jimmy didn't seem troubled at all as Miss Livingstone's gentle voice came over the quivering silence. "Perhaps you'd better start at the beginning again, Jimmy."

"OK." My son's tone was perky as he plunged confidently into the melody again and I closed my eyes as he approached the fateful bars. *Ta-rum-tum-tiddle-iddle-om-pom-pom, taa-rum, taa-rum, taa-rum*—then nothing. This time he put his hands on his knees and bent closely over the keyboard as though the strips of ivory were trying to hide something from him. He showed no sign of panic, only a faint curiosity.

In the almost palpable hush of that room I was sure that the hammering of my heart must be audible. I could feel Helen's leg trembling against mine, and I knew we couldn't take much more.

Miss Livingstone's voice was soft as a zephyr. "Jimmy, dear, shall we try it once more from the beginning?"

"Yes, yes, right." Away he went again like a hurricane, all fire and fury. It was unbelievable that there could ever be a flaw in such virtuosity.

The whole room was in agony. By now the other parents had come to know The Miller's Dance almost as well as I did, and we waited together for the dread passage. Jimmy came up to it at breakneck speed. *Ta-rum-tum-tiddle-iddle-om-pom-pom, taa-rum, taa-rum, taa-rum . . .* and silence.

I stole an anxious glance at Helen's face. She was pale, but she didn't look ready to faint just yet. Something had to break soon and once more it was Miss Livingstone's voice which cut into the terrible atmosphere.

"All right, Jimmy dear," she said. "Never mind. Perhaps you'd better go and sit down now."

My son rose from the stool and rejoined his fellow pupils in the first few rows. I slumped back in my seat. Ah well, that was the final indignity. The poor little lad had blown it. And though he didn't seem troubled I was sure he must feel a sense of shame.

A wave of misery enveloped me, and though many of the other parents directed sickly smiles of sympathy at Helen and me it didn't help. I hardly heard the rest of the concert, which was a pity because the musical standard rose to remarkable heights.

At the end, Miss Livingstone came to the front of the platform. "Thank you, ladies and gentlemen, for the kind reception you have given my pupils. I do hope you have enjoyed it as much as we have."

There was more clapping, and as the chairs started to push back I rose to my feet, feeling slightly sick. But Miss Livingstone wasn't finished yet.

"Just one thing more." She raised a hand. "There is a young man here who, I know, can do much better. I wouldn't be happy going home now without giving him another opportunity." She beckoned towards the second row. "Jimmy, I wonder . . . I wonder if you would like to have one more try."

As Helen and I exchanged horrified glances there was an

immediate response from the front. Our son's voice rang out, chirpy and confident. "Aye, aye, I'll have a go!"

I couldn't believe it. From a great distance I heard, "Jimmy will play The Miller's Dance."

As though in the middle of a bad dream I resumed my seat. A few seconds earlier I had been conscious only of a great weariness, but now I was gripped by a fiercer tension than I had known all afternoon. As Jimmy poised his hands over the keys a vibrant sense of strain lapped around the silent room.

The little lad started off as though he hadn't a care in the world, and I began a series of long shuddering breaths designed to carry me past the moment which was fast approaching. Because I knew that he would stop again. And I knew, just as surely, that when he did I would topple senseless to the floor.

I didn't dare look round at anybody. In fact when we reached the crucial bars I closed my eyes tightly. But I could still hear the music—so very clearly. *Ta-rum-tum-tiddle-iddle-om-pom-pom, taa-rum, taa-rum, taa-rum* . . . There was a pause of unbearable length then, *tiddle-iddle-om-pom*, Jimmy was blissfully on his way again. He raced through the second half of the piece but I kept my eyes closed as relief flooded through me, opening them only when he came to the finale which I knew so well. Jimmy was making a real meal of it, head down, fingers thumping, and at the last crashing chord he held up one hand in a flourish a foot above the keyboard before letting it fall by his side in the true manner of the concert pianist.

I doubt if the Methodist Hall has ever heard a noise like the great cheer which followed. The place erupted in a storm of clapping and shouting and Jimmy was not the man to ignore such an accolade. All the other children had walked impassively from the stage at the end of their efforts, but not so my son.

To my astonishment, he strode from the stool to the front of the platform, placed one arm across his abdomen and the other behind his back, extended one foot and bowed to one side of the audience with the grace of an eighteenth-century courtier. He then reversed arms and pushed out the other foot before repeating his bow to the other side of the hall.

I drove back to Skeldale House very slowly. I was still in a weak condition and I felt it dangerous to exceed twenty-five miles an hour. The colour had returned to Helen's face but there were lines of exhaustion round her mouth and eyes as she stared ahead through the windscreen.

Jimmy, in the back, was lying full length along the seat, kicking his legs in the air and whistling some of the tunes which had been played that afternoon. "Mum! Dad!" he exclaimed in the staccato manner which was so typical of him. "I like music."

I glanced at him in the driving mirror. "That's good, son, that's good. So do we."

Suddenly he rolled off the back seat and thrust his head between us. "Do you know why I like music so much?"

I shook my head.

"I've just found out," he cried delightedly. "It's because it's so soothing."

Chapter Thirteen

When Walt Barnett asked me to see his cat I was surprised. He had always employed other veterinary surgeons ever since Siegfried had mortally offended him by charging him ten pounds for castrating a horse, and that had been a long time ago. I was surprised, too, that a man like him should concern himself with the ailments of a cat.

A lot of people said Walt Barnett was the richest man in Darrowby. He was mainly a scrap merchant, but he had a haulage business too, and was a dealer in second-hand cars, furniture, anything, in fact, that came his way. I knew he kept some livestock and horses around his big house outside the town, but there was money in these things and money was the ruling passion of his life. There was no profit in cat keeping, and another thing which puzzled me as I drove to his office was that owning a pet indicated some warmth of character, a vein of sentiment, however small. It just didn't fit in with his nature.

I picked my way through the litter of the scrapyard to the wooden shed in the corner from which the empire was run. Walt Barnett was sitting behind a cheap desk, exactly as I remembered him, the massive body stretching the seams of the shiny blue suit, the cigarette dangling from his lips, the brown trilby hat perched on the back of his head. Unchanged, too, was the beefy red face with its arrogant expression and hostile eyes.

"Over there," he said, glowering at me and poking a finger at a black and white cat sitting among the papers on the desk. It was a typical greeting.

I reached across the desk and tickled the animal's cheek, and was rewarded by a rich purring and an arching of the back against my hand. He was a big tom, long-haired and attractively marked with a white breast and white paws, and I took an immediate liking to him. He exuded friendliness. "Nice cat," I said. "What's the trouble?"

"It's 'is leg, that 'un there. Must've cut 'isself."

I felt among the fluffy hair and the little creature flinched as I reached a point halfway up the limb. I took out my scissors and clipped a clear area. I could see a transverse wound, quite deep, discharging a thin serous fluid. "Yes . . . this could be a cut, but there's something unusual about it. I can't see how he's done it. Does he go out in the yard much?"

The big man nodded. "Aye, wanders around a bit."

"Ah well, he may have caught it on some sharp object. I'll give him a penicillin injection and leave you a tube of ointment to squeeze into the wound night and morning."

Some cats object strongly to hypodermics but this one never moved as I inserted the needle. "He really is good-natured," I said. "What do you call him?"

"Fred." Walt Barnett looked at me expressionlessly, his face discouraging further comment.

I produced the ointment from my bag and placed it on the desk. "Right, let me know if he doesn't improve."

I received no reply, neither acknowledgment nor goodbye, and I took my leave feeling the same prickle of resentment as when I first encountered his boorishness. But as I walked across the yard I forgot my annoyance in my preoccupation with the case. There was something very peculiar about that wound. It didn't look accidental; it was neat and deep as though somebody had drawn a razor blade across the flesh. An inner voice told me that things were not as they seemed.

A touch on my arm brought me out of my musings. One of the men who had been working among the scrap was looking at me conspiratorially. "You've been in to see t'big boss? Funny thing t'awd bugger botherin' about a cat, eh?"

"I suppose so. How long has he had it?"

"Oh, about two years now. It was a stray. Ran into 'is office one day and I thought he'd 'ave booted it straight out, but 'e didn't. Ah can't reckon it up. It sits there all day on 'is desk."

"He must like it," I said.

"Him? He doesn't like anythin' or anybody. He's a . . ."

"Hey, you! Get on with your bloody work!" The bellow from the office doorway cut him short, and the man, after one terrified glance, scuttled away. This was how Walt Barnett lived—surrounded by fear and hate.

I heard his voice on the phone two days later. "Get out 'ere sharpish and see that cat."

"Isn't the wound any better?"

"Naw, it's wuss, so don't be long."

Fred was in his usual place on the desk and he purred as I went up and stroked him, but the leg was certainly more painful. What really baffled me was that the wound was bigger instead of smaller. The narrow slit in the skin had undoubtedly lengthened. It was as though it was trying to creep its way round the leg.

I had brought some extra instruments with me and I passed a metal probe gently into the depths of the cut. I could feel something down there, something which caught the end of the probe and sprang away. I gripped the unknown object with long forceps, and when I brought it to the surface and saw the narrow brown strand all became suddenly clear. "He's got an elastic band round his leg," I said. I snipped it through, withdrew it and dropped it on the desk. "There it is. He'll be all right now."

Walt Barnett jerked himself upright in his chair. "Elastic band! Why the 'ell didn't you find it fust time?"

"I'm sorry, Mr. Barnett," I said. "The elastic was embedded in the flesh, out of sight." It was true, but I didn't feel proud.

He puffed rapidly at the ever present cigarette. "And 'ow did it get there?"

"Somebody put it on his leg, without a doubt. I've heard of cases like this—there are some cruel folk around."

"One o' them fellers in the yard, ah'll wager."

"Not necessarily. Fred goes out in the street, doesn't he?"

"Oh aye, often."

"Well, it could have been anybody."

There was a long silence as the big man sat scowling, his eyes half closed. I wondered if he was going over the list of his enemies. That would take some time.

"Anyway," I said. "The leg will heal very quickly now. That's the main thing."

Walt Barnett reached across the desk and slowly rubbed the cat's side with a sausage-like forefinger. I had seen him do this during my previous visit. It was an odd gesture, but probably the nearest he could get to a caress.

Walt Barnett was on the phone three weeks later and I felt a twinge of apprehension at the sound of the familiar voice. "Is his leg still troubling him?" I asked.

"Naw, that's 'ealed up. There's summat matter with 'is head. 'E keeps cockin' it from side to side. Come and see 'im."

This sounded to me like canker, but when I saw the cat the ears were clean and painless. He seemed to like being examined and the purring rose to a crescendo as I made a close inspection of his teeth, mouth, eyes and nostrils. Nothing; yet something up there was causing a lot of discomfort.

I began to work my way through the black hair and suddenly the purring was interrupted by a sharp "miaow" as my fingers came upon a painful spot on his neck. I took out my scissors and began to clip. And as the hair fell away and the skin showed through, a wave of disbelief swept through me. I was looking down at a neat little transverse slit, the identical twin of the one I had seen before. My God, surely not on the neck . . .

I went into the wound with probe and forceps and within seconds I had brought the familiar brown band to the surface. A quick snip and I pulled it clear. "More elastic," I said dully.

"Round 'is neck."

"Afraid so. Somebody really meant business this time."

Walt Barnett drew his enormous forefinger along the furry flank and the cat rubbed delightedly against him. "Who's doin' this?"

I shrugged. "No way of telling. The police are always on the look out for cruelty, but they would have to catch a person actually in the act."

I knew he was wondering when the next attempt would come, and so was I, but there were no more elastic bands for Fred. The neck healed rapidly and I didn't see the cat for nearly a year, until one morning Helen met me as I was coming in from my round.

"Mr. Barnett's just been on the phone, Jim. Would you please go at once—he thinks his cat has been poisoned."

When I hurried into Walt Barnett's office the cat was not on his old place on the desk but was crouched on the floor among a litter of newspapers, and as I went over to him he retched and vomited a yellow fluid onto the paper. More vomit lay around among yellowish pools of diarrhoea.

Walt Barnett spoke past his dangling cigarette. "He's poisoned, isn't 'e? Somebody's given 'im sommat."

"It's possible . . ." I watched the cat move slowly to a saucer of milk and sit over it in the same crouching attitude. There was a sad familiarity in the little animal's appearance. This could be something worse even than poison.

"I'm not sure," I said. I took the cat's temperature. It was 105°, and he was sunk in a profound lethargy. I palpated the abdomen, feeling the lack of muscular tone.

"Well, if it's not that, what is it?"

"It's feline enteritis. I'm nearly certain."

He looked at me blankly. "There's an outbreak in Darrowby just now," I explained. "I've seen several cases lately and Fred's symptoms are typical."

The big man heaved his bulk from behind the desk, went over to the cat and rubbed his forefinger along the unheeding back. "Well, can you cure 'im?"

"I'll do my best, Mr. Barnett, but I'm afraid the mortality rate is very high—most cases die."

"How can that be? I thought you fellers had all them wonderful new medicines now."

"Yes, but this is a virus and viruses are resistant to antibiotics."

"Awright, then." Wheezing, he drew himself upright and returned to his chair. "What are you goin' to do?"

"I'm going to start right now," I said. I injected electrolytic fluid to combat the dehydration. I gave antibiotics against the secondary bacteria, and finished with a sedative to control the vomiting. But I knew that everything I had done was merely supportive. I had never had much luck with feline enteritis.

I visited Fred each morning and the very sight of him made me unhappy. He was either hunched over the saucer or he was curled up on the desk in a little basket. He had no interest in the world around him. On the fourth morning I could see that he was sinking rapidly.

"I'll call in tomorrow," I said, and Walt Barnett nodded without speaking. He had shown no emotion throughout the cat's illness.

Next day when I entered the office I found the usual scene: the huge figure in his chair, the cat in the basket on the desk. Fred was very still and as I approached I saw with a dull feeling of inevitability that he was not breathing. I put my stethoscope over his heart for a few moments, and then looked up.

"I'm afraid he's dead, Mr. Barnett."

The big man did not change expression. He reached slowly across and rubbed his forefinger against the dark fur in that familiar gesture. Then he put his elbows on the desk and covered his face with his hands. I watched helplessly as his shoulders began to shake and tears welled between the thick fingers. He stayed like that for some time and then he spoke. "He was my friend."

I could find no words, and the silence was heavy in the room until he suddenly pulled his hands from his face and glared at me defiantly. "Aye, ah know what you're thinkin'. This is that big tough bugger, Walt Barnett, cryin' his eyes out over a cat. What a joke! I reckon you'll have a bloody good laugh later on."

Evidently he was sure that what he considered a display of weakness would lower my opinion of him; yet he was so wrong. I have liked him better ever since.

Chapter Fourteen

It was a Sunday morning in June and I was washing my hands in the sink in Matt Clarke's kitchen. The sun was bright and there was a brisk wind scouring the fell-sides, so that through the window I could see every cleft and gully lying sharp and clear on the green flanks as the cloud shadows drove across them.

I glanced back beyond the stone flags at the white head of Grandma Clarke bent over her knitting. The radio on the dresser was tuned to the morning service and, as I watched, the old lady looked up from her work and listened intently to the sermon for a few moments before starting her needles clicking again.

In that brief time I had a profound impression of serenity and unquestioning faith which has remained with me to this day. Whenever I hear discussions and arguments on the varying religious beliefs and doctrines, there still rises before me the seamed old face and calm eyes of Grandma Clarke. She knew, and was secure. Goodness seemed to flow from her.

She was in her late eighties and always dressed in black with a little black neckband. She had come through the hard times of farming and could look back on a long life of toil, in the fields as well as in the home.

As I reached for the towel, the farmer led Rosie into the kitchen.

"Mr. Clarke's been showing me some baby chicks, Daddy," she said.

Grandma looked up again. "Is that your little lass, Mr. Herriot?"

"Yes, Mrs. Clarke," I replied. "This is Rosie."

"Aye, of course. I've seen her before, many a time." The old lady put down her knitting and rose stiffly from her chair. She shuffled over to a cupboard, brought out a gaily coloured tin and extracted a bar of chocolate. "How old are ye now, Rosie?" she asked as she presented the chocolate.

"Thank you. I'm six," my daughter replied.

Grandma looked down at the smiling face, at the sturdy tanned legs in their blue shorts. "Well, you're a grand little lass." For a moment she rested her work-roughened hand against the little girl's

103

cheek, and then returned to her chair. They didn't make much of a fuss, those old Yorkshire folk, but to me the gesture was like a benediction.

The old lady picked up her knitting again. "Six, eh. . . . ?" For a few seconds her thoughts seemed far away as she plied her needles. Then she looked at me again. "Maybe ye don't know it, Mr. Herriot, but this is the best time of your life. When your children are young and growin' up around ye—that's when it's best. A lot o' folk don't know it and a lot find out when it's too late. It doesn't last long, you know."

"I believe I've always realized that, Mrs. Clarke, without thinking about it very much."

"Reckon you have, young man." She gave me a sideways smile. "You allus seem to have one or t'other of your bairns with you on your calls."

As I drove away from the farm the old lady's words stayed in my mind, and they are still in my mind, all these years later, when Helen and I are about to celebrate forty years of marriage. Life has been good to us, and is still good to us—but I think we both agree that Grandma Clarke was right about the very best time of all.

When I got back to Skeldale House that summer morning I found Siegfried replenishing the store of drugs in his car boot. His children, Alan and Janet, were helping. Like me, he usually took his family around with him.

He banged down the lid of the boot. "Right, that's that for another few days." He glanced at me and smiled. "There are no more calls at the moment, James. Let's have a walk down the back."

With the children running ahead of us we went through the house and out into the long garden. Here the sunshine was imprisoned between the high old walls, with the wind banished to the upper air and ruffling the top leaves of the apple trees. Siegfried flopped on the turf and rested on his elbow, pulling a piece of grass to chew as I sat down by his side.

"Pity about the acacia," he murmured contemplatively.

I looked at him in surprise. It was many years since the beautiful tree which had once soared from the middle of the lawn had blown down in a gale.

"Yes, it is," I said. "It was magnificent." I paused for a moment.

104

"Remember I fell asleep against it the day I came here to apply for a job? We first met right on this spot."

Siegfried laughed. "I do remember." He looked around him at the mellow brick and stone copings of the walls, at the rockery and rose bed, the children playing in the old henhouse at the far end. "My word, James, when you think about it, we've come through a few things together since then. A lot of water has flowed under the bridge."

We were both silent for a while and my thoughts went back over the struggles and the laughter of those years. Almost unconsciously I lay back on the grass and closed my eyes, feeling the sun warm on my face, hearing the hum of the bees among the flowers, the croaking of the rooks in the great elms which overhung the yard.

My colleague's voice seemed to come from afar. "Hey, you're not going to do the same trick again, are you? Going to sleep in front of me?"

I sat up, blinking. "Gosh, I'm sorry, Siegfried, I nearly did. I was

out at a farrowing at five o'clock this morning and it's just catching up with me."

"Ah, well," he said, smiling. "You won't need to count sheep tonight."

"No," I laughed, rolling on to my side. "By the way, I was at Matt Clarke's this morning." I told him what Grandma had said.

Siegfried selected a fresh piece of grass and resumed his chewing. "Well, she's a wise old lady and she's seen it all. And you know, James, I'm convinced that the same thing applies to our job. We're going through the best time there, too. Look at all the new advances since the war—we can look after our animals in a way that would have been impossible a few years ago and the farmers realize this. You've seen them crowding into the surgery on market day to ask advice—they've gained a new respect for the profession and they know it pays to call in the vet now."

"That's true," I said. "We're certainly busier than we've ever been, with the ministry work going full blast, too."

"Yes, everything is buzzing. In fact, James, I'd like to bet that these present years are the high noon of country practice."

I thought for a moment. "You could be right. But if we are on the top now does it mean that our lives will decline later?"

"No, no, of course not. They'll be different, that's all. I sometimes think we've only touched the fringe of so many other things, like small animal work." Siegfried brandished his gnawed piece of grass at me and his eyes shone with the enthusiasm which always uplifted me.

"I tell you this, James. There are great days ahead!"

James Herriot

In spite of the fame and fortune which James Herriot's books have brought him, his life remains essentially unchanged. First and foremost he is still a country vet, absorbed by his practice in Yorkshire. The animals he cares for have top priority, and though the real Darrowby has been identified by many of the vet's admirers and forty to fifty fans turn up every day on his doorstep, the animals in the surgery are tended first. After that, James Herriot goes out to meet his reading public, to have a chat with them, to pose for their clicking cameras, and to autograph copies of his books.

James and Helen now live in a village outside Darrowby, and the practice has increased in size. Siegfried and James have been joined in the partnership by Jimmy, and besides three veterinary assistants, they have the help of Jimmy's own four-year-old son, Nicholas. In true Herriot tradition he loves to accompany his father on his rounds. James is delighted with his three grandchildren: Nicholas has a baby sister, Zoe, and Rosie, a doctor in a neighbouring group practice, has a six-year-old daughter, Emma.

In the past James Herriot travelled widely, in connection with veterinary work and to publicize his books, but he prefers to stay at home now. When a new book comes out he tours the British Isles for signing sessions and much enjoys meeting his readers, but his and Helen's idea of a perfect holiday is to tuck themselves away in a remote little cottage they have in the Dales.

Though James Herriot has been in practice since before the war, he has not begun to think of retirement. "I just can't imagine what it would be like never to go through that surgery door again," he says.

A CONDENSATION OF THE BOOK BY

John Gardner

ILLUSTRATED BY KEVIN TWEDDELL

PUBLISHED BY CAPE AND HODDER & STOUGHTON

James Bond is back—a little older, but just as suave and brilliant as ever. John Gardner, a talented author in his own right, here recreates Fleming's immortal hero to dazzling effect.

A series of clandestine meetings between an international terrorist known as Franco and the discredited nuclear physicist Anton Murik, Laird of Murcaldy, alerts Her Majesty's Secret Service to an ominous situation. The incredible project that master agent James Bond then uncovers at the laird's Highland castle threatens to reduce large areas of the world to a radioactive wasteland if certain demands are not met.

So with the aid of the laird's beautiful ward, Lavender Peacock, Bond pits his nerve and cunning against his deranged opponent with an awesome goal in mind: to save the Western world from annihilation.

Passenger for Flight 154

The man who entered the airport washroom had light hair, cut neatly to collar length. Stocky, and around five feet three inches in height, he wore crumpled jeans, a T-shirt and sneakers. A trained observer would have particularly noted the piercing light-blue eyes, above which thin brows arched in long curves that almost met above the slim nose.

The man's face was thin in comparison with his body, and the complexion a shade dark in contrast to the colour of the hair. He carried a small brown suitcase, and, on entering the washroom, walked straight towards one of the cubicles, stepping carefully past a dungareed cleaner who was mopping the floor without enthusiasm.

Once inside, the man slid the bolt and placed the suitcase on the lavatory seat, opening it to remove a mirror which he hung on the door hook before stripping as far as his underpants. Before removing the T-shirt, he slid his fingers expertly below the hairline at his temples, peeling back the wig to reveal his own close-cropped hair underneath. With a finger and thumb he grasped the corner of his left eyebrow and pulled, as a nurse will quickly rip sticking plaster from a cut. The slim eyebrows disappeared, leaving black, untrimmed lines of natural hair in their place.

The man worked like a professional—with care and speed. From the suitcase he took a canvas corset, wrapping it around his waist, pulling tightly at the lacing, giving the immediate twin effect of slimming the waistline and an illusion of more height. Carefully folding the jeans and T-shirt, the man pushed his socks into his abandoned sneakers, and pulled on a new pair of dark-grey socks, followed by well-cut charcoal-grey trousers and black slip-on shoes, into which were built what actors call "lifts", adding a good two inches to his normal stature.

Adjusting the mirror on the door, he now donned a white silk shirt, and knotted a pearl-grey tie into place, before taking an oblong plastic box from the suitcase. The box contained new components for the man's face. First, dark contact lenses changed those distinctive light-blue eyes to almost jet black. Next, small foam-rubber pads inserted into the cheeks fattened the face. The pièce de résistance was a short beard and moustache, sculptured from real hair onto an invisible, adhesive, latex frame which, even at very close range, gave the impression of complete reality.

The man smiled at the unfamiliar face now looking back at him from the mirror, completing the new picture with a pair of steel-framed spectacles.

Now he closed the oblong box, removed a jacket from the case, and filled his pockets with an assortment of items—wallet, passport, travel documents and loose change. He then packed everything with extreme care, clipped a gold digital watch around his left wrist and removed a final item from a pocket in the case—a tightly fitting cover, which, when slipped into place over the suitcase, gave it an outer skin, changing the colour from brown to glossy black. He slid the new skin around the case, and spun the numbered safety locks.

Taking a final look around, the man left the cubicle. He walked straight out, across the concourse, to the check-in desk.

Inside the washroom, the man who had been swabbing the floor leaned his mop against the wall and left. He also headed across the concourse to a door marked Private, which he unlocked with a personal key. Inside the small room there was a table, chair and telephone. As the man with a new face was preparing to board Aer Lingus flight EI 154 from Dublin to London, Heathrow, the insignificant-looking cleaner was speaking rapidly into the telephone. The time was shortly before 8:45 am.

Thoughts in a Surrey Lane

James Bond changed down into third gear, drifted the Saab 900 Turbo into a tight left-hand turn, then put on a fraction more power to bring the car out of the bend. He was driving through a complicated series of country lanes, following a short cut through the rolling fields and cathedral arches of trees threading the byways of Surrey. The route would, finally, take him onto the Guildford bypass and a straight run into London.

Bond was travelling much too fast. A glance at the display of digital instruments told him the machine was touching seventy miles per hour. Gently common sense took over, and Bond applied a touch to the brakes, reducing speed to a more realistic pace. He still, however, remained hot and angry.

Already that day he had made the same journey, in the opposite direction, to his recently acquired and newly decorated country cottage. Now on this beautiful Friday evening in early June, he was driving at breakneck speed back to London.

The weekend had been arranged for some time. Furthermore, he had planned to spend it with a girlfriend of long standing—an agile, superbly nubile blonde he had known "on and off" for years. The fact that she lived only six miles or so from the cottage had greatly influenced Bond's purchase. Earlier he had completed a mound of paperwork in record time, so that he could get out of the hot chaos of London traffic in good time before the normal Friday evening snarl-up.

The countryside had been at its best; the mixed fragrance of a perfect summer filtering into the car, bringing with it a sense of well-being and contentment—something rare for Bond these days.

On reaching the cottage, he had put a bottle of Dom Perignon '55 on ice, knowing that it would either be magnificent or the most expensive wine vinegar he had ever tasted. Discarding his somewhat conservative business suit, he showered, first under a scalding spray, then with ice-cold needles of water. After drying himself with a rough towel, Bond put on a pair of lightweight navy slacks and a white Sea Island cotton shirt. He slipped into soft leather sandals and was just clipping the old and valued gold Rolex Oyster Perpetual onto his wrist when the telephone rang.

The red phone. His heart sank. Both here and in his London flat off the King's Road, James Bond was required to have two telephones: one for normal use, though unlisted; and a second, red instrument, without dial or number punches. Called, in his trade, a "wiretap trap", this unbuggable phone was linked directly to the building overlooking Regent's Park, known as the headquarters of Transworld Export Ltd.

Before he had even put a hand to the phone, Bond experienced his first flash of mild annoyance. The only reason for a call from headquarters on a Friday evening would be some kind of emergency—and, of late, many emergencies had meant sitting in a control or communications room for days at a time. Times had changed, and Bond did not like some of the political restraints placed on the Secret Service, for which he had worked with fidelity for longer than he cared to remember. He picked up the red phone.

"James?" As Bond expected, it was Bill Tanner, M's chief-of-staff. Bond grunted a surly affirmative.

"M wants you here," Tanner said, in a voice as flat as a billiards table.

"Now?" Bond saw an idyllic weekend filtering away.

"He indicated that sooner than now would be more acceptable."

"On a Friday evening?"

"Now," repeated the chief-of-staff, closing the line.

As he reached the Guildford bypass, Bond remembered the sound of disappointment in his girlfriend's voice when he had telephoned to say the weekend was off. He supposed that should be some consolation—not that there was much to console Bond these days.

"Changing world, changing times, James," M had said to him a couple of years ago, when breaking the news that the élite Double-O status—which meant being licensed to kill in the line of duty—was being abolished. "Fools of politicians have no idea of our requirements. Have us punching time clocks before long." This was during the so-called Realignment Purge, in which many faithful members of the service had been dismissed, literally overnight.

"Trying to draw our fangs, James," M had continued on that depressing day. Then, with one of those rare smiles which seemed to light up the deep-grey eyes, M grunted that Whitehall had taken on the wrong man while he was still in charge. "As far as I'm concerned, 007, you will remain 007. There are moments when this country needs a trouble-shooter—a blunt instrument—and by heaven it's going to have one. The Double-O section will simply become the Special Section, and *you* are it. Understand, 007?"

"Of course, sir." Bond remembered smiling. In spite of M's brusque and often uncompromising attitude, Bond loved him as a father. To 007, M *was* the service, and the service was Bond's life. After all, what M suggested was exactly what the Russians had done with his old enemies SMERSH—*Smyert Shpionam*, Death to Spies. They still existed, the dark core at the heart of the KGB, having gone through a whole gamut of metamorphoses to become Department Viktor. Yet their work remained the same—kidnap; sabotage; assassination; the quick disposal of enemy agents.

Bond had left M's office on that occasion in an elated mood. Yet since then he had performed only four missions in which his Double-O prefix had played any part. Killing was not a facet of his work which he enjoyed. It was the active life that Bond missed; the continual challenge of a new problem, a difficult decision in the field, the sense of purpose and of serving his country.

He still kept in the peak of condition: each morning going through a rigorous workout of press-ups, leg-raising, and breathing exercises. There was a "refresher" on combat and silent kills once a month, and twice a year he disappeared for a fortnight to the SAS headquarters in Herefordshire. Bond had even managed to alter his lifestyle, adapting to the changing pressures of the 1980s: drastically cutting back—for most of the time—on his alcohol intake, and arranging with Morelands of Grosvenor Street for a new special blend of low-tar cigarettes.

For the rest, the last few years for Bond had been the grind of an executive officer to M: interrogating, de-briefing, bugging operations and dirty tricks, with a fair share of duty-officer watches. His only extra joys during this period had come from the purchase of the cottage and the new car.

He had fancied a small country retreat for some time, and found the right place five miles out of Haslemere. It fitted Bond's requirements perfectly and was bought within twenty-four hours of first viewing.

The car was a different matter. With fuel costs inevitably rising, Bond had allowed the beloved old Mark II Continental Bentley to go the way of its predecessor, the 4.5-litre Bentley. Some eyebrows were raised at his choice of a foreign car, but Bond pointed out that it was a British firm which carried out the sophisticated personalization—such as the head-up digital instrument display, the cruise control system, and several other pieces of magic. He did not mention that the car had been taken over for a month by the multinational Communication Control Systems (CCS) company, who had added refinements that would make Q Branch's mouths water. It was now commonplace for him to catch members of Q Branch—the "gee-whizz" technicians of the service—taking a close look. None of them ever mentioned the things they could not fail to notice—such as the bullet-proof glass, steel-reinforced ram bumpers and heavy-duty tyres, self-sealing even after being hit by bullets. There were other niceties, though, which nobody in Q Branch could detect without specialist gear.

The Saab now suited Bond's purposes. The consumption was low in relation to speed; while the turbo gave that extra dynamic thrust always needed in a tricky situation.

The Saab was in the underground garage of the headquarters building before seven thirty. As the lift sped him silently to the ninth floor where M's suite of offices was located, Bond would have put money on M having some inane and boring job waiting for him.

Miss Moneypenny, M's PA, looked up with a worried smile as Bond entered the outer office. This was the first sign that something important might be on the cards. "Hallo, Penny," Bond greeted her breezily, shrugging off his irritation over the lost weekend. "Not out with one of your young men? It's wicked Friday night, you know."

Miss Moneypenny cocked her head towards the door of M's office as she spoke. "And he's been wickedly waiting for you. Keeping me here into the bargain." She smiled. "Besides, the only man who could lure me out on the town seemed to be otherwise engaged."

Bond grinned. "Oh Penny, if only . . ."

"Tell Commander Bond to come straight in," M's voice snapped from the intercom box on Miss Moneypenny's desk.

Bond lifted a quizzical eyebrow and moved towards the door. Lowering his voice, he said, "Anyone ever tell you that Janet Reger started her business with you in mind, Penny?"

Miss Moneypenny was still blushing as Bond disappeared into M's office. She stared into space for a moment, her head filled with the after-image of the man who had just entered M's inner sanctum: the bronzed good-looking face, with dark eyebrows above the wide, level blue eyes; the three-inch scar which just showed down his right cheek; the long straight nose, the firm jaw and the fine, though cruel, mouth. Minute flecks of grey had just started to show in the dark hair, which still retained its boyish black comma above the right eye. It was the face of an attractive buccaneer, Miss Moneypenny thought, shaking herself out of a slightly improper reverie.

As BOND OPENED the door to M's office, another door was opening some five hundred miles to the north of London. The man who had left Dublin so skilfully disguised early that morning looked up, rising from his chair and extending a hand in greeting. The room in which he had been waiting was familiar to him now, after so many visits: book-lined, with a large military desk, comfortable leather chairs, the cabinet containing priceless antique weapons. The whole place had that air of solidity which comes with what is known as "old money"

The person who entered the room was its owner. The two men shook hands, almost gravely, the guest waiting in silence while his host moved to the large chair behind the desk. He did not speak until he was seated. "It's good to see you again, Franco."

"Good also to see you. But then I enjoy working for you." The man called Franco paused, searching for words. "You know, after all this time, I never know how to address you—your title, or scientific . . . ?" He made a gesture with his hands.

The other man chuckled, his bulldog face creasing into a smile. "Why not Warlock?"

117

They both laughed. "Appropriate," Franco nodded. "Operation Meltdown, with you—its creative force—Warlock."

"So be it." The man behind the desk nodded his head in a quick, birdlike manner. "You had no trouble?"

"None at all. The chopper was on time; there were no tails."

"Good." The birdlike pecking nod again. "Then I trust, my friend, that this will be your last visit here."

Franco gave a quirky little grin. "Perhaps. But maybe not quite my last. There is the question of payment."

The man opened his hands, fingers splayed. "I mean, of course, your last visit until after Meltdown is completed. Yes, of course there is the question of picking up your share. But first, location and detail. We have much to discuss; you will be here for a slightly longer period this time, Franco."

"Naturally." Franco's voice took on a cold edge.

"Europe, I presume, is completely arranged? And the States?"

"Ready and waiting for the final instructions."

"The men . . . ?"

Franco leaned forward. "These *people* are the least of my worries. Each of them is dedicated, ready to give his or her life for his separate cause. To all purposes, they consider themselves martyrs already. But the various organizations that have provided the personnel for your operation are anxious. They want assurances that they will receive their share of the money."

"Which, I trust, you have given them, Franco." The bulldog face had ceased to beam. "Our commitment was clear—we spoke of this at great length over a year ago. I provide the plan and arrange the means. You are the go-between, the contact man. Now, we have more interesting things to talk about."

The Opposition

Bond became more alert when he reached the far side of M's door. He was prepared for his old chief to be seated in his usual concentrated position behind the large glass-topped desk; but he was not expecting to find two extra men in the room.

"Come in, Bond." M addressed him with a small, economic, movement of the hand. "Gentlemen," he glanced towards his visitors, "allow me to introduce Commander James Bond. I think he's the man to fit the bill."

Bond warily acknowledged the other men. He knew who they were, though it would not do to show it openly.

M allowed the pause to lie for a moment before completing the introductions. "Commander, this is Sir Richard Duggan, Director-General of MI5; and Deputy Assistant Commissioner David Ross, head of the Special Branch of the Metropolitan Police."

It was certainly a puzzling situation. MI5, and its executive arm, the Special Branch, constituted what was known officially as the British Security Service—responsible for counter-espionage and anti-terrorist activities on British sovereign territory. To Bond's service they were always jokingly known as "the Opposition", and there had always been a keen rivalry between the two organizations: a rivalry which had sometimes led to grave misunderstandings.

M motioned Bond into a leather chair. "Our friends from MI5 have a small problem, Commander," he began. "It is an interesting situation, and I feel you might be able to help; especially as it has all the marks of moving out of MI5's jurisdiction and into our own area." He tapped his pipe into an ashtray on the desk. For the first time, Bond noticed his chief had a file lying directly in front of him, marked with red MOST SECRET: CLASSIFIED tags. Two small circles on the top righthand corner denoted that the file concerned both European and Middle East connections.

"I think," M said, looking at the director-general of MI5, "it would be best if the two of you put Commander Bond in the picture."

Sir Richard Duggan nodded and leaned down to open his briefcase, removing a file and placing a matt, ten-by-eight photograph on the desk in front of Bond. "Know the face?" he asked.

Bond nodded. "Franco—to the Press, public, and most of us. Code Foxtrot to those in the field. International terrorist. Wanted in most European countries and some in the Middle East. There is a request for him to be held in the United States; though, as far as we know, he has not operated from, or in, that country. His full name is

Franco Oliveiro Quesocriado; born Madrid 1948 of mixed parentage—Spanish father and an English mother. I believe her name was something quite ordinary, like Jones, Smith or Evans . . ."

"Leonard actually," said Ross quietly. "Mary Leonard."

"Sorry," Bond smiled at him, and the policeman returned the smile. He had the look of a modern copper, Bond thought. Quiet, with a watchfulness buried deep in his eyes, and the sense of a coiled spring held back by the retaining pin of caution. A very tough baby if roused, was Bond's instant assessment. He turned back to Sir Richard Duggan, asking if they wanted him to continue.

"Naturally." Richard Duggan was a very different breed, and Bond already knew his pedigree. Duggan was old-school Home Office. Eton and Oxford, then a short career in politics, before the Home Office snapped him up. Tall, slim and good-looking, with thick, light-coloured hair, Duggan looked authoritative and in control.

As the head of MI5 had drawled, "Naturally," Bond's eyes met those of M, and caught the tiny stir of humour. Sir Richard Duggan was not one of M's favourite people.

Bond shrugged. "Franco," he continued, "first came to our attention in connection with a hijacking of two BOAC passenger jets in the late 1960s. He appears to have no direct political affiliations, and has operated as a planner who sometimes takes part in terrorist actions. He has links with the PLO, IRA, Red Army Faction and a whole network of terrorist groups. He would, I think, be best described as an anti-capitalist." Bond gave a small quick smile. "The paradox has always been that, for an anti-capitalist, he appears to be exceptionally well-off. There is evidence that he has personally provided arms for a number of terrorist acts. A very dangerous man, Sir Richard."

Both Duggan and Ross nodded in harmony. Duggan delved into his briefcase again, bringing out five more matt photographs, which he placed in a row on M's desk. Each photograph carried a small sticker attached to the bottom righthand corner. Each sticker bore a date.

Bond immediately noted that the most recent date was today's. The other four were marked April 4th and 23rd; May 12th and 25th.

The man portrayed was shown differently in each photograph—plump, with long hair and a moustache; clean-shaven, with shoulder-length blond hair; grey-haired and gaunt in loud check, hung around with cameras, and clutching an American passport; clean-shaven again, but with dark hair, fashionably cut. Today's photograph showed him with close-cropped hair, neat beard and spectacles. The disguises were all excellent, yet Bond had no hesitation. "Franco," he said aloud.

"Of course." Duggan sounded a little patronizing, pointing out that all the photographs had been taken at Heathrow.

"Five times in the past three months, and he hasn't been picked up?" Bond's brow creased.

Deputy Assistant Commissioner David Ross took over the explanation. At a meeting earlier in the year it had been decided that certain "most wanted" terrorists like Franco should be kept under close surveillance if they arrived in the country. "When the surveillance teams at Heathrow spotted him in April—the first time—there was, naturally, a full-scale alert."

"Naturally." Bond did a fair imitation of Sir Richard Duggan's condescending drawl. M busied himself loading his pipe, keeping his eyes well down.

Ross looked a little shamefaced. "Afraid we lost him in London the first time. We checked all his possible contacts, and waited. He wasn't detected leaving the country. But as you can see, he was back at Heathrow later in the month. That time we established that he moved straight out of London, almost certainly heading north."

"You lost him again," Bond stated. Ross gave a sharp affirmative before saying they had better luck during the first May visit.

"Followed him as far as Glasgow. And on the last trip we kept him in our sights all the way. He ended up in a village called Murcaldy, at the foot of the northwest Highlands."

"And we're sure who it was he visited there," Duggan smiled. "Just as we're certain he's gone to the same place this time. I have two officers breathing down his neck—he came in from Dublin this morning, and he'll have reached his destination by now. We expect further reports any time."

A silence fell over the four men, broken only by the scraping of

M's match as he lit his pipe. Bond was the first to speak. "And he's visiting . . . ?" The question hung in the air like M's pipe smoke.

Duggan cleared his throat. "Most of the land, including the village of Murcaldy, is owned by one family—the Muriks. It's almost a feudal set-up. There is Murik Castle, which dates back to the sixteenth century, and the Murik estate—farms, hunting and fishing rights. The present laird is also a celebrity in other fields—Dr. Anton Murik, director of many companies, and a nuclear physicist of both renown and eccentricity."

"Recently resigned, under some sort of cloud, from the International Atomic Energy Research Commission," added Ross. "And there's doubt regarding his claim to be the Laird of Murcaldy."

Bond chuckled. "Well, Anton isn't exactly a well-known Scottish name. But where do I come in?"

There was none of the usual smoothness about Duggan as he spoke again. "Franco has now almost certainly made four visits to Dr. Murik. This will be his fifth. An international terrorist and a nuclear physicist of some eminence: put those together and you have a rather alarming situation. On each occasion Franco has left the country again, and our hands are tied the moment he leaves Britain. Our visit today is to ask the help of your service in tracing his movements outside this country."

"And you want me to dash off up to Scotland, make contact, and follow him out?"

Duggan deferred to M. "Only if that is—ah—convenient. But I don't think there's much time left on this trip. Murik owns a string of race horses. Two are running at Ascot this coming week—one in the Gold Cup. Racing is his one passion, apart from nuclear physics. Franco will either be gone by the middle of the week, or up at the castle awaiting Murik's return from Ascot."

Duggan was now on his feet. "I've passed on all information to M." He indicated the file on the desk. "We have come to you for assistance, in the interests of the country. It is time to work in harness, and I must now leave the final decision here with you."

M puffed on his pipe. "I'll brief Commander Bond about everything," he said pleasantly. "Be in touch with you later, Duggan. We'll do all we can—in *everybody's* interests."

122

The two officers took leave of M and Bond, and, as soon as the door closed behind them, M spoke. "What do you think, 007?"

James Bond's heart leaped. It was a long time since M had addressed him as 007, and he could almost smell the possibilities. He lit a cigarette and looked up at the ceiling before he spoke. "Not a healthy mix—an international terrorist and a renowned nuclear physicist. Been one of the nightmares for some time, hasn't it, sir? That some group would get hold of not only the materials but the means to construct a really lethal nuclear device?"

"Easiest thing in the world to construct a crude device," M snorted. "If a terrorist organization wanted to use some bomb to blackmail a government, they could do so. But for a man like Franco to be consorting with an old devil such as the Laird of Murcaldy—well, that could mean one of two things."

"Yes . . . ?" Bond leaned forward.

M jammed his pipe into the corner of his mouth. "First, it could mean that Franco is setting up a very sophisticated operation, and is soliciting Anton Murik's specialist knowledge. Second"—the fingers moved—"it could be the other way round: that Dr. Anton Murik is seeking Franco's aid on a little adventure of his own."

"And Anton Murik is capable of either of these things?" Bond's brow furrowed. He could read absolutely nothing in M's weather-beaten face, and that was always a danger signal.

"Not only capable of it, but also a likely candidate." M opened a drawer in his desk and dropped another file on top of the one provided by MI5. "We've had our eye on Dr. Anton Murik for some time now. What Ross told you is a slight understatement—about Murik resigning from the International Atomic Energy Commission under some sort of cloud. *They* don't have all the facts. We do. Murik resigned under a damned great storm. In fact, the man was kicked out."

M took the pipe from his mouth, looking Bond straight in the eyes. "Even his title—Laird of Murcaldy—is more than highly suspect, as Ross mentioned. No, I don't intend to send you scooting off to Scotland, 007. I want to get you as close to Murik as possible, on the inside; and before we get to that, there's a great deal you should know about the so-called Laird of Murcaldy."

Dossier on a Laird

It was obviously going to be a long evening, and Bond thought he should not surprise May, his able and devoted housekeeper, by returning suddenly and late to his flat off the King's Road. So before M could launch into details, he asked permission to make a telephone call.

Bond dialled his own number on Miss Moneypenny's extension. May had given up trying to fathom her employer's working hours long ago, and merely asked if he fancied anything special to eat when he did get in. Bond said he would not be averse to a nice pair of Arbroath Smokies—should she have some tucked away. "I'll see what I can do, Mr. James," May said, "but mind you don't get back too late." She had a habit of treating Bond as a nanny will treat her small charges.

M had refilled his pipe and was poring over the dossiers when Bond returned. "The Murik family is an ancient line," he began. "There was a Laird of Murcaldy at Culloden Moor. However, it is possible that the true line died out with the present laird's grandfather. It has yet to be proven, but it is a matter which greatly disturbs the Lord Lyon King of Arms." He shuffled through the first dossier. "Anton Murik's grandfather was an adventurer—a traveller. In the year 1890 he was missing for more than three months in Europe—searching, it is said, for his brother who had been disinherited for some offence. Their parents were dead, and the village folk believed that Angus Murik—that was his name—planned to return with his brother, shepherding the black sheep back into the fold. But when he did return it was with a wife: a foreign woman, who was expecting a child. There are written documents suggesting that the child, who became Anton's father, was born out of wedlock, for there is no record of a marriage."

Bond grunted, "But surely that would only weaken the line, not destroy it altogether."

"Normally, yes," M continued. "But Anton was also born in strange circumstances. His father was a wild lad who also travelled, but he did not return at all. There is a letter, extant, saying that he had married an English woman of good family in Palermo. Shortly after that a pregnant woman arrived at Murik Castle, saying that her husband, the heir to the title, had been killed by bandits during an expedition in Sicily."

"When was this?" It sounded a confused and odd story to Bond.

"Nineteen-twenty," M replied. "And there *are* newspaper reports of some 'English' gentleman having been killed in Sicily. The newspapers, however, claim that this gentleman's wife also perished at the hands of the bandits; though the young woman insisted it was her maid who died. Diaries say that the girl who presented herself as widow of the laird-presumptive was far from being a lady of good breeding. It's difficult to sort out fact from fiction, but what is certain is that some of the older people on the Murik estate maintain Anton is not the true laird—though, knowing which side their bread is buttered, they only whisper it privately."

"I presume he is a bona fide nuclear scientist? We have to take that part seriously?"

"We take him very seriously indeed," M looked grave. "There is no doubt at all that Anton Murik is a man of great intellect and influence. Just take a glance at the background précis." He passed a sheet of paper to Bond, who took it in with a quick sweep of the eyes:

Anton Angus Murik. Born Murik Castle, Murcaldy, Ross and Cromarty, Scotland, December 18th, 1920. Educated Harrow and St. John's College, Cambridge. First Class Honours in Physics followed by a Doctorate and a Fellowship. Worked under Lord Cherwell—scientific adviser to Winston Churchill; also worked on Manhattan Project (the making of the first atomic bomb); Committee for the Peaceful use of Atomic Energy; International Atomic Energy Research Commission . . . .

Murik had resigned from this last position just two years ago. There followed a lengthy and impressive list of companies with which Murik was associated. Among other things, Anton Murik was chairman of Eldon Electronics Ltd., Micro Sea Scale Ltd. and Aldan Aerospace, Inc. In addition he sat on countless boards, all of

125

which had some direct application to nuclear power or electronics.

"You spot the odd man out?" M asked from behind a cloud of pipe smoke.

Bond looked down the list again. Yes, there tucked away among all the electronics, nuclear companies and aerospace conglomerates, was a strange entry, Roussillon Fashions. Bond read it out.

"Yes. Damned dressmaking firm," M snorted.

James Bond smiled. "I think a little more than just a dressmaker, sir. Roussillon is one of the world's top fashion houses."

M grunted, "Well, Anton Murik has a majority holding in that firm."

"He must be a multi-millionaire," Bond said, almost to himself. Dr. Anton Murik obviously wielded considerable power. "How in heaven's name did he manage to get thrown out of the International Atomic Energy Research Commission, sir?"

M did not hesitate. "For one thing he's unscrupulous in business matters. At least two of the chairmanships were gained by stepping, literally, over the bodies of other men."

"Most good businessmen are inclined to be ruthless . . ." Bond began; but M held up a hand.

"There was another matter," he said. "Anton Murik is a bit of a fanatic. He mounted a campaign against the use of nuclear power and the dangers of the major types of nuclear reactor already in service. You see, 007, the man claims to have designed the ultimate in reactors—one which not only provides the power but safely disposes of the waste, and cannot go wrong. Calls it the Murik Ultra-Safe Nuclear Reactor."

"And his colleagues didn't buy it?"

" 'Didn't buy' is an understatement. His colleagues say there are grave flaws in the Ultra-Safe design. Some even claim the whole thing is potentially a hundred times more dangerous than current reactors. Murik wanted funds from the commission to build his own reactor and prove them wrong, so they cut off the money."

Bond laughed. "Murik's a multi-millionaire. Surely he could go out and build his own in his back garden—it seems big enough."

M sighed. "We're talking in billions of pounds, James. In any event, Anton Murik made a terrific row, and there were suggestions that the man's far from stable." He touched his forehead. "That's really why this contact with a fellow like Franco worries me. It is also why I will not allow you to go charging into the field without preparation. I want to establish you within the Murik entourage: and to that end I think you'd better meet Anton Murik and his household." He drew several photographs from the file.

"You're going to deny Duggan's request, then?" Bond was completely concentrated on the job in hand. Whatever plot was being hatched—either by Franco or Dr. Anton Murik—Bond would not rest until every end was tied up.

M grunted. "Duggan's got two good people in the field. I have confidence that they'll discover Franco's port of exit this time. We'll put a tail on him when the right moment comes. Your job's too important . . ." He saw the quizzical look on Bond's face. "I know that I'm putting you in on MI5's territory, but my bones tell me it won't be for long. The action's going to move out of Scotland as soon as whatever it is they're cooking comes to the boil. Now for the pretty pictures—and first, the doctor himself."

The photograph showed a pugnacious face. The line of the mouth was hard, uncompromising; the eyes were cold; and the ears lay very flat against the head. Photographs can be deceptive—Bond knew that well enough—but this bulldog of a man could have been a son of the Manse. He had that slightly puritanical look about him—a stickler for discipline, and one who would have his own way, no matter what lay in his path.

The next print showed a woman, probably in her early forties, very fine-looking, with sharp, classic features and dark, upswept hair. Her eyes were large, but not—Bond thought—innocent. The mouth was generous, the edges of the lips tilting slightly upwards to soften the features.

"Miss Mary-Jane Mashkin," said M, as though it explained everything. Bond gave his chief a look of query, the comma of hair connecting with his right eyebrow as though to form a question mark.

"His *éminence grise*, some say." M puffed at his pipe, as though slightly embarrassed. "Certainly Murik's mistress, strong right arm and personal adviser. She's a trained physicist. Cambridge University, the same as the laird. Acts as hostess for him; lives at Murik Castle." M pushed a third photograph towards Bond. This time it was another woman, much younger, and certainly, if the picture was really accurate, a stunning girl. Thick blonde hair fell smoothly around the sides of her face; she had high cheek bones, smoulder in the dark eyes, and a mouth made striking by the sensuality of her lower lip. Bond allowed himself to relax in a low whistle.

M cut short this reflex reaction. "Anton Murik's ward, Miss Lavender Peacock. The relationship is not known—daughter of some second cousin. Father and mother both killed in an air crash. There's a little money—several thousand—which comes to her when she reaches her twenty-seventh birthday. That is next year."

Bond observed that Lavender Peacock was quite a girl, and that he somehow thought he recognized her.

"Possible, 007. The girl's kept on a tight rein, though. Private tutors when she was a kid, trips abroad only when accompanied by Murik and trusted watchdogs. From time to time the laird allows her to model—you may have seen her picture in connection with that dressmaking business—but only at very special functions, and always with the watchdogs around."

"Watchdogs?" Bond picked on the expression.

M rose and strode to the window, looking out across the park, now hazy as the sun dropped slowly and the lights began to come on over the city. "Oh yes, Murik always has a few young Scottish toughs around, bodyguards not just for the ward, but the whole family. There's one in particular: sort of chief heavy. We haven't got a photograph of him, but I've had a description and that certainly matches his name. He's called Caber."

There was a long silence. At last Bond took a deep breath. "So you want me to ingratiate myself with that little lot? Find out why Franco's paying so much attention, and generally make myself indispensable?"

M turned from the window. "We have to play the game long, 007. I have great reservations about Dr. Anton Murik. He'd kill without a second thought if it meant the success of some plan; and he's obsessed, at this moment, with his Ultra-Safe Nuclear Reactor. Maybe there's some harebrained scheme of investing in one of

128

Franco's endeavours, and raking in a rich profit: enough money to prove the Atomic Energy Research Commission wrong. Who knows? It'll be your job to find out, James."

"Suggestions on how to do it would be welcome," Bond began, but, as M was about to reply, the red telephone purred on his desk. For a few minutes Bond sat listening to M's side of a conversation with Sir Richard Duggan.

When the call was completed, M sat back with a thin smile. "That's settled it. I've told MI5 that you're ready to move in and follow up any information they care to give."

"And Franco?"

"Is definitely at Murik Castle. They've confirmed. Don't worry, James, if he leaves suddenly I'll put someone on his back to cover you with MI5."

"Talking of cover . . ." Bond started.

"I was coming to that. How you get into the family circle, eh? You heard what Ross said about Murik's second passion in life—racing. Well, as you know, he's got horses running at Royal Ascot next week: this should give us the opportunity. Unless there's any sudden change of plan, I think you should be able to make contact on Gold Cup day. That'll give us time to see you're well briefed and properly equipped, eh?"

The Road to Ascot

Apart from the great golf tournaments, James Bond did not care much for those events which still constitute what the gossip columnists call "the Season". He was not naturally drawn to the Henley Regatta, or, indeed, to Royal Ascot. The fact that Bond was a staunch monarchist did not prevent the misgivings he felt when turning the Saab in the direction of Ascot on Gold Cup day.

Life had been very full since the Friday evening of the previous week. In fact, Bond had worked full seventeen-hour days during this time of preparation. To begin with, there were long briefings where M quietly took Bond through all the possibilities of the situation ahead: revealing the extent to which Anton Murik had recently invested in businesses all connected, one way or another, with nuclear energy; together with his worst private fears about possible plots now being hatched by the Laird of Murcaldy.

"The devil of it is, James," M told him, "this fellow Murik has a finger in a dozen market places—in Europe, the Middle East, and even America."

Primarily, the idea was to put Bond into the Murik ménage as a walking listening device. It was natural, then, for him to spend time with Q Branch, the technology experts. In the past, he had often found himself bored by the earnest young men of Q Branch; but times were changing. Within the last year, everyone at headquarters had been delighted by the appearance of a new face among the senior executives of Q Branch: a tall, elegant young woman with shining straw-coloured hair which she wore in an immaculate French pleat.

Within a week of her arrival, Q Branch had accorded its new executive the nickname of Q'ute, for even in so short a time she had become the target of many seduction attempts by unmarried officers of all ages. Now 007 found himself working close to the girl, for she had been detailed to arrange the equipment he would take into the field, and brief him on its uses.

Throughout this period, James Bond remained professionally distant. Q'ute was a desirable girl, but, like so many of the ladies working within the security services these days, she remained friendly yet at pains to make it clear that she was her own woman.

At forty-eight hours' notice, Q'ute's team had put together a set of what she called "personalized matching luggage". This consisted of a leather suitcase together with a steel-strengthened briefcase. Both contained cunningly devised compartments, secret and well-nigh undetectable, housing a whole range of electronic sound-stealing equipment; some sabotage gear, and a few useful survival items. These included a highly sophisticated bugging and listening device; a counter-surveillance receiver; and a pen alarm. If triggered, the alarm would provide Bond with instant signal communication to headquarters, in order to summon help. As a back-up, there was a small ultrasonic transmitter; while, among the sabotage material, Bond was to carry an exact replica of his own Dunhill cigarette lighter—the facsimile having special properties of its own; and—almost as an afterthought—Q'ute made him sign for a pair of T.H.70 Nitefinder goggles. Bond did not think it wise to mention that these lightweight goggles were part of the standard fittings Communication Control Systems had provided for the Saab.

As well as the time spent with M and Q'ute, Bond found himself discussing weaponry for long hours with Major Boothroyd, the service armourer. On M's instructions, 007 was to go armed—something not undertaken lightly these days. They had been through the basic arguments a thousand times already: a revolver is always more reliable than an automatic pistol, simply because there is less to go wrong. The revolver, however, has the drawback of taking longer to reload, usually carrying only six rounds of ammunition in its cylinder. Also—unless you go for the bigger, bulky weapon which is far too heavy and difficult to use in covert field operations—muzzle velocity is lower.

Eventually it was Bond who had the last word, with a few grumbles from Major Boothroyd—settling on an old, but well-tried and true friend: the early Browning 9mm. In spite of its age this Browning has accurate stopping power. For Bond, the appeal lay in its reliability and size—eight inches overall and with a barrel length of five inches. A flat, lethal weapon, the early Browning weighs about thirty-two ounces. Bond was happy with the weapon, knew its limitations, and had no hesitation in putting aside thoughts of more exotic, modern hand guns. Naturally, he did not disclose the fact that he carried an unauthorized Ruger Super Blackhawk .44 Magnum in a secret compartment in the Saab.

Unused weapons of all makes, types and sizes, were contained in the armourer's amazing treasure trove of a store; and he produced one of the old Brownings, still in its original box. No mean feat, as this particular gun has long since ceased to be manufactured.

The armourer knew 007 well enough not to have the pistol touched by any member of his staff; and late one afternoon he called Bond down to the gunsmith's room, so that the weapon could be cleaned off, stripped, checked and thoroughly tested on the range by the man who was to use it. It took Bond nearly an hour, and six extra magazines, before he was completely happy with the Browning. When he had finished on the range, he went back to the gunsmith's room and stripped the gun down for cleaning, an exacting chore upon which his life might one day depend.

ON THE MORNING of the Gold Cup, Bond was awake before six thirty. He exercised, and took a hot bath, followed by a cold shower, shaved, dressed and was in his dining room when the faithful May came in with his copy of *The Times* and his normal breakfast—two large cups of black coffee, without sugar; a single "perfectly boiled" brown egg (Bond still held the opinion that three and one-third minutes constitutes the perfect boiling time); then two slices of wholewheat toast and Cooper's Vintage Oxford Marmalade. Governments could come and go, crises could erupt, inflation might spiral, but—when in London—Bond's breakfast routine rarely changed. In this he was the worst thing a man in his profession could be: a man of habit, who enjoyed the day starting in one particular manner, eating from the dark-blue Minton eggcup.

Bond had hardly taken any time off during the preparation for what he now thought of as an assignation with Anton Murik at Ascot. On most evenings he had gone straight back to his flat and avidly read a book that he had come across in Paris several years before. Written at the turn of the century by a man using the pseudonym Cutpurse, it was a treatise on the ancient arts of the pickpocket and body-thief.

Using furniture, old coats—even a standard lamp—Bond practised various moves in which he was already well skilled. During discussions with M as to how he should introduce himself to the Laird of Murcaldy and his entourage, they had formulated a plan that called for the cleverest possible tricks. Bond knew that to practise some of these dodges, it was necessary to keep in constant trim.

Slowly he worked up his skill to the most difficult move in the book—the "necklace flimp". Towards the end of the period Bond was spending several hours a night perfecting this move. All he could hope for was that M's briefing would prove accurate.

Now a signpost read "Ascot 4 miles", and Bond joined a queue of Bentleys, Rolls-Royces and Daimlers, all heading towards the racecourse. He sat calmly at the wheel; his Browning in its holster, locked away in the glove compartment; Q'ute's personalized luggage in the boot of the car, and himself in shirtsleeves, the grey morning coat neatly folded on the rear seat, with the top hat beside it. He looked like any other man out to cut a dash in the Royal Enclosure. In fact his mind was focused on one thing only—Dr. Anton Murik, Laird of Murcaldy.

As he approached the racecourse, Bond felt slightly elated, though a small twist in his guts told him the scent of danger, maybe even disaster, was in the air.

Pearls before Swine

There was only one part of any racecourse that James Bond really enjoyed—the public area. Alongside the track itself, life was colourful. The characters always appeared more alive and real: there were the day-trip couples out for a quick flutter, tipsters with their sharp patter, the tick-tack sign language being passed across the heads of the punters. Here there was laughter, enjoyment and the buzz of pleasure.

For the first couple of races that day, Bond strolled in the public area, as though reluctant to take his place in the Royal Enclosure, for which the pass was pinned to the lapel of his morning coat. He even stayed down near the rails to watch the arrival of Her Majesty, Prince Philip and the Queen Mother—stirred by the inspiring sight of tradition as the members of the Royal Family were conveyed down the course in open carriages, with liveried coachmen and postilions.

His first action, on arrival, had been to check the position of Anton Murik's box in the Grandstand (a fact gleaned from one of M's expert sources). Leaning against the rails, Bond scanned the tiered boxes with the powerful binoculars provided by Q Branch. The Murik box, on the second tier, was as yet empty.

Dr. Anton Murik's entry in the Gold Cup did not stand much chance, yet Bond felt an overwhelming desire to have a wager on his target's horse. The Queen's horse was favourite, with Lester Piggott up; and odds at only five-to-four on. Other contenders were very well-tried four-year-olds. In particular, Francis's Folly, Desmond's Delight and Soft Centre were being heavily tipped. The other ten runners seemed to be there merely for the ride; Bond's race card showed that the Laird of Murcaldy's China Blue had achieved only one placing in his last three outings.

The harsh facts were borne out by the odds, which stood at twenty-five-to-one. Bond gave a sardonic smile, knowing that M would be furious when he put in his expenses. If you're going to plunge rashly with the firm's money, he thought, do it with style. He approached a bookmaker whose board showed him to be Honest Tone Snare, and placed a bet of one hundred and ten pounds to win on China Blue.

"You got money to burn, Guv?" Honest Tone gave Bond a toothy grin.

"One hundred and ten to win," Bond repeated placidly.

"Well, you know yer own mind, Guv; you must know something the rest of us don't." Honest Tone took the money in return for a ticket that, if China Blue should win, would yield Bond something in the region of two and a half thousand pounds.

Once in the Royal Enclosure, Bond felt his dislike for this side of the race meeting descend on him like a dark, depressing cloud. As much as he liked the female form, he was repelled by the idea of so many women parading in fashionable dresses and outlandish hats to attract the attention of the gossip columnists. That was not what racing was about, he considered. To quell these depressing thoughts, Bond headed for the main bar where he consumed two rounds of smoked salmon sandwiches and a small bottle of Dom Perignon.

Casually he strolled around the Enclosure, finally settling himself under the shade of the trees which surrounded the paddock. On M's instructions, he had come into the Enclosure unarmed; in case of trouble, Bond carried only the pen emergency contact device. Safe in his pocket was a well-forged owner's pass that would get him inside the paddock, close to the target. He did not have to wait long. The horses were already entering the paddock, and within a few minutes Bond identified China Blue.

The horse looked unpromising by any standards. The coat was dull and the animal had about him a lack-lustre look—as though it would take dynamite rather than a jockey to make him perform anything more than a canter on this warm, cloudless afternoon. Yet looking at the horse being led round by the stable boy, Bond had one of those sudden instincts that he would win his money. How? He had no idea. Frauds on racecourses in England are rare these days. Anton Murik would certainly not resort to unsophisticated risks like doping or substitution when competing in the Ascot Gold Cup. Yet Bond knew at that moment that China Blue would win.

Suddenly the short hairs on the back of his neck tingled, and he experienced a shiver of suspense. A man and two women were approaching China Blue—the trainer turning towards them, with a deferential smile of welcome on his face. Bond was getting his first view of Dr. Anton Murik.

He shifted position, moving closer to the paddock entrance. It *was* the man he had seen in the photograph. What the pictures had not included was the high mane of white hair sweeping back from the bulldog face. Also, no still photograph could ever capture the walk or manner. The Laird of Murcaldy was barely five feet tall, and walked in a series of darting steps. His movements—hands, head, fingers and neck—were of the same quick precision. Dr. Anton Murik had the movements of a grounded bird. However, even at this distance, the man clearly had a power that overrode physical peculiarities or eccentricities.

The two women with Murik were easily recognizable, dressed in similar classic, knitted, bouclé dresses. Over the dress each wore a short, sleeveless gilet. The elder of the women—obviously Mary-Jane Mashkin—wore the ensemble in navy, with white trimmings, and a neat, short-brimmed hat. The ward, Lavender Peacock, was taller, more slender, and just as stunning as her photograph. Her identical clothes were in white, with navy trimmings and hat. Bond wondered if their outfits were originals from Murik's Roussillon Fashions.

The younger girl was laughing, turning towards Murik. Bond could see why she was kept on what M referred to as a tight rein: Lavender Peacock looked like a spirited and healthy girl. To Bond's experienced eye, she also had the nervous tension of a young woman unused and straining at the leash.

Bond narrowed his eyes, never taking them off the girl as she talked animatedly. He was looking for something essential to the whole scheme of insinuating himself into the Laird of Murcaldy's immediate circle—and it was there, clearly visible around Lavender's neck: £500,000 worth of *mohar* pearls, strung on three short ropes, all held by a decorated box clasp and safety chain at the back of the neck.

The pearls had been kept in trust for Lavender until her twenty-first birthday, having originally been a wedding present from her father to her mother. Lavender—M had told Bond—wore them on every possible occasion, against Murik's advice.

Bond thought they could not be round a prettier neck; if he had been taken with the photograph of the girl, he was dazzled by the real thing. Murik had turned to talk to the two women, while the trainer leaned close to the jockey, giving him last instructions. China Blue looked as docile as ever: as spirited as a wooden rocking horse.

It was time for Bond to move. The entrance to the paddock was busy with people, and within the next few minutes Anton Murik and his party would be passing through this entrance—which doubled as the main exit—on their way to the Grandstand. The whole operation depended upon timing and skill. With the binocular case over his right shoulder, race card held open in his left hand, Bond made his way into the paddock, flicking the owner's pass quickly in front of an official. Horses were being mounted, and two had already begun to walk towards the exit that would take them down onto the course. Bond circled China Blue and the group around him; seeming to keep his eyes on another horse.

At last, with a final call of good luck from the assembled party, China Blue's jockey swung into the saddle looking relaxed and confident. Murik's party began to move slowly towards the exit through which Bond had just come. It was now becoming crowded with owners and friends leaving to view the race.

Carefully Bond stepped close to Murik's party. The laird was talking to his trainer, with Mary-Jane Mashkin standing to one side.

Lavender Peacock was to their rear. Bond sidled over and pushed himself in just behind her. They were five or six paces from the exit, now jammed with people trying to get through as quickly and politely as possible. Bond was directly behind the girl, his eyes fixed on the box clasp and safety chain at the back of her neck. It was clearly visible, and, as he was pushed even closer, hemmed in by the crowd, Bond was well screened. Allowing himself to be jostled slightly, he now pushed his shoulders forward for added protection, and bumped full into Lavender Peacock's back.

The next complicated moves took only a fraction of a second. Keeping the left hand, which was clutching the open race card, low down by his side, Bond's right hand moved upwards to the nape of the girl's neck. His first and second fingers grasped the box clasp which held the pearls, lifting them away, so that no strain would be felt by their owner. At the same time, his thumb passed through the safety chain, breaking it off with a deft twist. Now the box clasp fell into position, held tightly by the thumb and forefinger. He pressed hard, tilting, and felt the clasp give way.

The box clasp is constructed as two metal boxes which contain an added safety feature, a small hook, which slips around a bar in the outer box. Using thumb and first two fingers, Bond slipped the hook from its bar. He then withdrew his hand, glancing down and dropping his race card. Silently the pearls fell to the turf. His aim and timing were perfect. The race card followed the pearls, falling flat and open on top of them. Lavender Peacock did not feel a thing, though Bond caused a minor clogging of the exit as he bent to retrieve his card, lifting the pearls with it.

Relaxed now, and holding the pearls securely inside the card, Bond followed Anton Murik's party towards the Grandstand. Lavender had caught up with them, and Bond prayed she would not discover her loss before reaching the box.

Murik's party disappeared into the stand. About two minutes later Bond entered the side door, and climbed the stairs to the second tier, and advanced on the Laird of Murcaldy's box.

They all had their backs to him as he knocked and stepped inside. Nobody noticed, for they seemed intent upon watching the runners canter down to the starting line.

Bond coughed. "Excuse me," he said. The group turned.

Anton Murik seemed a little put out. The women looked interested. Bond smiled and held out the pearls. "I believe someone has been casting pearls before this particular swine," he said, calmly. "I found these on the floor outside. Looks like the chain's broken. Do they belong to . . . ?"

With a little cry, Lavender Peacock's hand flew to her throat. "Oh my God," she breathed, the voice low and full of melody, even in this moment of stress.

" 'My God' is right." Murik's voice was low, and there was barely a hint of any Scottish accent. "Thank you very much. I've told my ward often enough that she should not wear such precious baubles in public. Now, perhaps, she'll believe me."

Lavender had gone chalk white and was fumbling towards the pearls. "I don't know how to—" she began.

Murik broke in. "The least we can do, sir, is to ask you to stay and watch the race from here." Bond was looking into dark slate eyes, the colour of cooling lava, and with as much life. "Let me introduce you. I am Anton Murik; my ward, Lavender Peacock, and an old friend, Mary-Jane Mashkin."

Bond shook hands. "My name is Bond," he said. "James Bond."

Only one thing surprised him. When she spoke, Mary-Jane Mashkin betrayed in her accent that she was undoubtedly American—something that had not appeared on any of the files in M's office.

"You'll stay for the race, then?" Murik asked.

"Oh yes. Please do." Lavender appeared to have recovered her poise.

Mary-Jane Mashkin smiled warmly. "You must stay. Anton has a horse running."

"Thank you." Bond moved closer within the box. "May I ask which horse?"

Murik had his glasses up, scanning the course, peering towards the starting gate. "China Blue." He lowered his glasses, and for a second there was movement within the lava-flow eyes. "He'll win, Mr. Bond."

"I sincerely hope so. What a coincidence," Bond laughed,

reaching for his own binocular case. "I have a small bet on your horse. Didn't notice who owned him."

"Really?" There was a faint trace of appreciation in Murik's voice. Then he gave a small smile. "Your money's safe. I shall have repaid you in part for finding Lavender's pearls. What made you choose China Blue?"

"Like the name." Bond tried to look ingenuous. "Had an aunt with a cat by that name once. Pedigree Siamese."

"They're under starter's orders." Lavender sounded breathless. They turned their glasses towards the far distance, and the start of the Ascot Gold Cup. A roar went up from the crowd below them. The horses were off.

Within half a mile a pattern seemed to emerge. The Queen's horse was bunched with the other favourites—Francis's Folly and Desmond's Delight, with Soft Centre clinging to the group, way out in front of three other horses which stood back a good ten lengths; while the rest of the field straggled out behind. Bond kept his glasses trained on the three horses behind the little bunch of four leaders. Among this trio was the distinctive yellow and black of Murik's colours on China Blue.

There was a strange tension in the box. The pace was being kept up hard; and the leading bunch did not appear to be drawing away from the three horses behind them. The Queen's horse was ahead, but almost at the halfway mark Desmond's Delight began to challenge, taking the lead so that these two horses, almost imperceptibly, started to pull away.

As the field passed the halfway mark, Bond was aware of Anton Murik muttering something under his breath. China Blue was suddenly being hard ridden, closing the distance between himself and the third and fourth runners.

"Blue! Come on, Blue," Lavender called softly. Glancing along the box rail, Bond saw Mary-Jane Mashkin standing with her hands clenched, watching as China Blue came up, very fast, on the outside.

The racing China Blue could have been a different animal from the horse Bond had watched in the paddock. He moved in a steady striding gallop; and now he was reaching a speed far in excess of any of the lead horses. By the time they reached the final three furlongs, China Blue was gaining on Desmond's Delight, who had again taken second place to the Queen's horse. A great burst of sound swept like a wind over the course as China Blue suddenly leaped forward in a tremendous surge of speed, to come home a good length in front of the pair who had made the running from the start.

Lavender was jumping up and down, excitedly clapping her hands. "He did it, Uncle Anton, he did it."

Mary-Jane Mashkin laughed—a deep, throaty sound—but Dr. Anton Murik merely smiled. "Of course he did it." Bond saw that Murik's smile did not light up his eyes. "Well, Mr. Bond, my horse has won for you. I'm pleased."

"Not as pleased as I am," said Bond, quickly, as though blurting out something he would rather have kept hidden. It was just enough to give the hint of a man rather in need of hard cash.

"Ah," the Laird of Murcaldy nodded. "Well, perhaps we'll meet again." He fumbled in his waistcoat pocket, producing a business card. "If you're ever in Scotland, look me up. I'd be glad to provide some hospitality."

Bond looked down at the card and feigned surprise. "Another coincidence," he said, smoothly. "I leave for Scotland tonight. I'll be in your area in a couple of days."

"Really?" The slate eyes grew even cooler. "Business or pleasure?"

"Pleasure mostly. But I'm always open for business." He tried to make it sound desperate.

"What kind of business, Mr. Bond?"

Bond hesitated slightly. "The contracting business."

"And what do you contract?"

Bond looked at him levelly. "Myself as a rule. I'm a soldier. A mercenary—up to the highest bidder. There, that'll be the end of our acquaintance, I expect. We're a dying breed." He gave a short laugh at his grim little joke. "People don't take too kindly to mercenaries these days."

Anton Murik's hand closed around Bond's forearm, pulling him to one side. "I am not averse to your profession, Mr. Bond. Who knows, I may even have a place for a man like yourself. Come to

Murik Castle. On Monday we have a little annual fun. Most of the land and the village—Murcaldy—is mine. So each year we hold our own version of the Highland Games. You know the kind of thing—the caber, the hammer, a little dancing, wrestling. You will enjoy it." This last sentence was almost an order.

Bond nodded, as Murik turned towards the ladies. "We must go down and accept our just rewards. Mary-Jane, Lavender, you will be seeing Mr. Bond again soon. He's kindly consented to come and stay—for the Games."

"Thank you again for the pearls, Mr. Bond," Lavender said. "I look forward to seeing you soon." There was something odd about the way she phrased the parting sentence, as though she meant what she said but was hinting some warning. Lavender, Bond thought, appeared to have some hidden fear below the charming, easy and poised exterior.

Bond stood, looking after them for a moment, wondering about Murik's personal version of the Highland Games. Then he went to collect his winnings from a suitably impressed Honest Tone Snare, before making a telephone call to Bill Tanner, M's chief-of-staff; and another to the Central Hotel in Glasgow, booking himself a room for the following morning. The Laird of Murcaldy would doubtless be flying his party back to Scotland. Bond did not want to be far behind them.

Slipping the leather strap of his glasses' case over one shoulder, James Bond walked casually towards the car park.

King of the Castle

During the furious night drive north Bond had plenty of time to puzzle over Anton Murik's win with China Blue. How had that horse romped home at Ascot? The only possible explanation lay in the old trick of having China Blue pulled back by his jockey in earlier races—not displaying his true form until the strategic moment. But perhaps the real answer would be found, with the others he sought, at Murik Castle.

The journey to Glasgow was without incident. Bond settled into his room at the Central Hotel, and was eating a breakfast of porridge, scrambled eggs, toast and coffee, by nine in the morning. He then hung out the "Do not disturb" sign and slept until seven that evening.

After studying the maps to plan his route, Bond dined in the hotel's restaurant, choosing a simple fillet steak with a green salad. He was determined to do most of the journey by night, and was on the road again by ten thirty that night, heading north. Early on the following morning, Bond stopped for a day's rest at a village just short of Loch Garry—having switched to the road that would eventually lead him as far as the coastal lochs on the western seaboard.

He reached a wooded area just to the east of Loch Carron early the next morning, and having parked the Saab well out of sight, rested through the day until dusk set in. The village of Murcaldy would only be a matter of seventy or eighty minutes' drive away. He had brought pies and some fruit, together with Perrier water, not wanting to chance anything stronger at this stage of the operation. Now he lay back, adjusted the driving seat and dozed and ate as the sun slid across the sky and began to settle behind the hills.

While there was still light, Bond began to make his preparations, transferring a packet of cigarettes from Q Branch's briefcase to his pocket. Only six of the cigarettes were of any use to a smoker, the remainder being cut short to hide a compartment into which four pre-set electronic microbugs nestled comfortably. The small receiver for these bugs—complete with tape and minute headset— remained in one of Q'ute's ingenious hiding places in the luggage. Bond also made certain that the pen alarm was still in his pocket, and that the fake Dunhill lighter—dangerous to the point of immobilizing any grown man for the best part of an hour—was well separated from his own, real lighter.

The rest of his weaponry remained locked away in the safety compartments of the car. The only other tools he required were to hand—the field glasses and the strap-on Nitefinder headset.

As the last traces of daylight vanished, Bond started the Saab, turning the car in the direction of Murcaldy. Seventy minutes later he was crossing the small bridge which led directly into the one village street with its quaint, neat rows of cottages, inn and kirk. Murcaldy was situated on a small river at one end of a wide glen. Ahead, at the far end of the glen and above the deserted village, the castle stood against the sky like a large outcrop of rock.

At the end of the street, near the kirk, the narrow road divided, a signpost pointing its two fingers in a V. Murik Castle lay directly ahead, up the glen; the other sign showed an equally narrow track leading back towards the road to Shieldaig. The track thus marked would have to follow the line of the glen to the east, so would probably lead him to a vantage point from which he could gain a view of the castle.

Bond slipped the infra-red Nitefinder kit over his head so that the little protruding glasses sat comfortably on his nose. Immediately the moonlit night became as clear as day, making the drive along the dry track a simple matter. He switched off the headlights and began to move steadily forward. The track dipped behind the eastern side of the glen, but the upper storeys of the castle were still visible above the skyline. Both village and castle had been built with an eye to strategy, and Bond had little doubt that his passage through Murcaldy had already been noted.

At last Bond reached a point parallel to the castle. He stopped the Saab and picked up the binoculars and, with the Nitefinder headset still in place, got out and surveyed the area. To his right he could clearly see low mounds of earth, just off the track, as though somebody had been doing some fresh digging. He paused, thinking he should investigate, but decided the castle must be his first concern. Turning left, Bond walked off the track and made his way towards the rolling eastern slope of the glen.

The air was sweet with night scents and clear air. Bond moved as quietly as possible, almost knee-deep in bracken and heather. Far away a dog barked, and there came the call of some predatory night bird beginning its long dark hunt. From the top of the rise, Bond could see clearly down the glen to the village, but it was impossible to gain any vantage point above the castle, which lay about a mile away on a wide plateau.

Taking up the binoculars, Bond began to focus on the castle. He

144

could see that halfway along the glen the track from the village became a metalled road, which ended at a pair of wide gates. These appeared to be the only means of access to the castle, which otherwise was surrounded by high granite walls. To the rear Bond could just make out what could well be the ruins of the original keep; but the remainder looked more like a great Gothic-style heap, beloved of Victorians—all gables and turrets.

Three cars stood in front of the main door—a wide structure with a pillared portico. The castle was set in the midst of large formal gardens, and the whole aspect produced a half-sinister, half-Disneyland quality. Craning forward, Bond could just make out the edge of a vast lawn and the corner of a marquee. For tomorrow's Games, he presumed.

Bond was just about to return to the car, drive back and present himself at King Murik's court, when he realized, too late, that he was not alone.

They had come upon him with the craft of professional hunters, materializing from the ground like spirits of the night. But these were not spirits—particularly their leader who now loomed huge above him. "Spyin' on Murik Castle, eh?" the giant accused him in a broad Scots accent.

"Now wait a minute . . ." Bond began, raising a hand to remove the Nitefinder kit; but, as he moved, so two hands, the size of large hams, grasped him by the lapels and lifted him bodily into the air.

"Ye'll come quiet wi' us. Right?" the giant said.

Bond was in no mood for going quietly with anybody. He brought his head down hard, catching the big man on the forward part of his nose bridge. The man grunted and let go of Bond. A trickle of blood had begun to flow from his nostrils. "I'll kill ye for—"

He was stopped by a voice from behind them. "Caber? Hamish? Malcolm? What is it?"

Bond instantly recognized the slight nasal twang of Mary-Jane Mashkin. "It's Bond," he shouted. "You remember, Miss Mashkin. We met at Ascot. James Bond."

"My God, Mr. Bond, what're you doing here?" She peered at the giant. "And what's happened to *you*, Caber?"

"Yon man gied me a butt to the neb," he muttered surlily.

145

Mary-Jane Mashkin laughed. "A brave man, doing something like that to Caber."

"I fear your man thought I was a poacher. He—well, he became generally aggressive. I'm sorry. Am I trespassing?"

Caber muttered something which sounded belligerent, as Mary-Jane Mashkin spoke again, "Not really. This track is a right-of-way through the laird's land. We've been doing a little night hunting, and looking at the digging." She inclined her head towards the other side of the track. "We've just started working on a new drainage system. Just as well you didn't wander that way. You could've stumbled into a pretty deep pit." She paused, coming closer to him so that he caught the scent of Madame Rochas in his nostrils. "You didn't say why you were here, Mr. Bond."

"Lost," Bond raised his hands in a gesture of innocence, slipping the Nitefinder set from his head as though it was the most natural thing to be wearing. "Lost and looking for the castle."

She put a hand on his arm. "Then I think you'd better take a closer look. I presume you were coming to visit."

"Quite," Bond nodded.

"I'll guide Mr. Bond down and you follow in the Land-Rover," Mary-Jane told Caber, who had calmly relieved Bond of the Nitefinder set.

The Land-Rover was close behind as the Saab swept up to the gates. A figure appeared to open up for them, and Mary-Jane Mashkin told Bond they kept the gates locked at night. "You can never tell. Even in an out-of-the-way place like this . . . . Anyhow, it's nice to know we have a guest like yourself, Mr. Bond—or can I call you James?"

"No need for formality here, I suppose," said Bond, as they came up to the main door with its great pillared porchway. He carefully locked the door of the Saab as Caber and the men called Hamish and Malcolm were climbing down from the Land-Rover behind them.

Just then the small, birdlike figure of Dr. Anton Murik emerged from the castle. He peered forward for a moment. Then his face lit up. "Why, it's Mr. Bond. You've come as promised. Good heavens, what happened to your nose, Caber?"

146

The big man was still dabbing blood away with his handkerchief. "My fault, I'm afraid," said Bond. "Sorry, Caber, but you were a little over-enthusiastic."

"I thocht yon man was some kind o' spy, or a poacher. I didna ken he was a visitor. Mind, he acted strange."

"Get him to bring your luggage in, Mr. Bond," Murik smiled, and Bond replied that it could wait. He had no desire for Caber to be messing about with the car.

"Fine," beamed Murik. "We'll collect the bags later. Come in and have a dram." With a sharp order to Caber to look after the Saab, he ushered Bond across the threshold.

Bond had expected the Victorian Gothic gloom of the porchway to be reflected in the interior of Murik Castle—Landseer and deer antlers. He was, therefore, greatly surprised by the dazzling sight that met his eyes. From the brooding exterior he was suddenly transported into another world. The hall, with its vast circular staircase and surrounding gallery, was decorated in shimmering white, the doors being picked out in black, and the matching white carpet underfoot giving Bond the impression that he was sinking into a soft, well-kept lawn. The walls were decorated, with elegant sparseness, by a series of highly polished halberds, *ronchas*, war forks and other thrusting weapons of the fifteenth and sixteenth centuries.

Murik spread out an arm. "The raw materials of war," he said. "I'm a bit of a collector, though the best pieces are kept in other parts of the house—except, possibly, these." He pointed to a gilded console table on which rested a glass case covering an open pistol box containing a pair of duelling pistols. "Last known English duel," Murik said proudly. "Monro and Fawcett, 1843." He indicated the nearest pistol. "Monro's weapon. Did the killing."

Bond stepped back to view the hallway again. Modern pictures hung higher up the walls. He recognized a Matisse and at least two from Picasso's Blue Period.

"Come now, Mr. Bond. You would like a drink." Mary-Jane Mashkin appeared as though on cue at the top of the stairs. "Had to do a quick change," she smiled, making a regal descent and extending a hand which appeared to drip with expensive rings.

147

"Nice to see you, Mr. Bond. It was kind of dark outside." She raised her voice. "Lavender, where are you? We have a guest. The nice Mr. Bond is here."

"You will excuse me." Murik gave his birdlike nod. "I must talk to Caber. I hope he did not treat you too roughly; though you seem to have given him good measure."

"Come." Mary-Jane Mashkin ushered Bond towards the drawing room, in the doorway of which Lavender Peacock now stood.

"Mr. Bond, how nice." Lavender's eyes shone with undisguised pleasure. Both women were dressed in evening clothes, Mary-Jane having changed into a sombre black, while Lavender glowed in flowing white. They motioned him towards the room.

"After you, ladies." As they turned, Bond detected a tiny noise from the gallery above them. Glancing up quickly, he was just in time to see a figure slipping into a doorway on the landing. It was only a fleeting glimpse, but there was little doubt in Bond's mind that Franco was still at Murik Castle.

The room in which Bond now found himself was long and wide, with a high, ornate ceiling. The walls were a delicate shell-pink, the furnishings designed for comfort. The wall opposite the doorway had been transformed into one huge picture window. Even in this light, Bond recognized the tint of the glass. One would be able to see out of this huge window; but, from the outside, the eye would only be able to note light, without detail. It was undoubtedly bulletproof.

"Well now, a drink, Mr. Bond." Mary-Jane stood by a glass cabinet. "What will you take after all your exertions?"

Bond chose Talisker. "When in Scotland . . ." he explained.

Mary-Jane Mashkin smiled, opening the cabinet and taking out the fine malt whisky. "There." She held out the glass of amber liquid which glowed like a precious stone in the light.

Lavender had seated herself on a deep leather sofa. "Well, it's certainly nice to have someone else staying here, Mr. Bond. Especially for the Games." She looked him straight in the eyes as she said it; as though trying to pass a message. Yet, as he looked quizzically at her, Bond saw the steady look faltering, and her gaze shifted over his shoulder.

"They're looking after you, then, Mr. Bond?" Murik had come silently into the room, and Bond turned to acknowledge his presence. "I have chastised Caber," the laird continued. "He has no right to manhandle people." The dangerous grey lava lurked in Anton Murik's eyes, and Bond saw that he was holding out the Nitefinder headset. "An interesting toy, Mr. Bond."

"In my profession we use interesting toys," Bond smiled. "I have to admit to carrying out a reconnaissance of the castle. You invited me; but my training . . ."

Murik smiled. "I understand, Mr. Bond. I rather like your style. If you'll let one of my men have your car keys, I'll see your luggage is taken to the guest room."

Bond did not like the idea, but he knew the only way to gain Anton Murik's confidence was to appear unruffled. After all, they would need a great deal of time to discover the secrets of both the car and baggage. He felt in his pockets and handed the keys to Murik. Almost at the same moment a burly man, whose tailcoat and demeanour proclaimed him as the butler, entered. Anton Murik addressed him as Donal, telling him to get "one of the lads to take Mr. Bond's luggage to the east guest room and then park the car."

Donal acknowledged the instructions without a word, and departed with the car keys.

"There now, Mr. Bond." Anton Murik gestured to one of the comfortable leather chairs. "Sit down. Rest yourself. As you see, we're old-fashioned enough here to dress for dinner. But, as you've arrived late, and unprepared, we'll forgive you."

"If the ladies don't mind." Bond turned to smile at Mary-Jane Mashkin and Lavender Peacock. The Mashkin woman returned his smile; Lavender gave him a broad grin.

"Not at all, Mr. Bond," said Mary-Jane, and Lavender followed with a quick, "Just this once, Mr. Bond."

James Bond nodded his thanks and took a seat. In the back of his mind, Lavender Peacock caused niggling concern. She was beautiful, obviously intelligent, and at ease when Dr. Anton Murik was absent; but in her guardian's presence Lavender had about her a certain wariness that he could not readily define.

Murik helped himself to a drink, and they chatted amiably about

Bond's journey north until Donal reappeared to confirm that Mr. Bond's luggage had been taken to his room. With a look of distinct disapproval at Bond's apparel, he announced that dinner was served.

Bond was led across the hall into the long dining room, which was decorated in more traditional style. They sat at a fine long mahogany table, polished and kept in magnificent condition, and ate with Georgian silver from an exquisite gold-rimmed dinner service. Murik's food matched the outer show: a fine lobster cocktail, a light consommé followed by rare rib of beef which almost dissolved on the tongue; and, before the cheese board was circulated, there was one of Bond's favourite Scottish puddings, the delicious cream-crowdie—toasted oatmeal folded into whipped cream.

When the port arrived, the ladies withdrew. The two muscular young men waiting at table under Donal's eye withdrew also; as did the butler himself, after placing cigars within the laird's reach. Bond refused a cigar, asking permission to smoke his own cigarettes. As he drew out the old and faithful gunmetal case, James Bond's thumb felt the rough section around the middle, where it had been skilfully repaired. The thought flashed through his head that this very case had once saved his life, by stopping a SMERSH assassin's bullet.

"So, you took up my offer, Mr. Bond?" The eyes were grey and menacing as Anton Murik faced Bond across the table.

"To visit you, yes."

Murik expelled a cloud of cigar smoke. "Oh, I didn't just mean the visit." He gave a chuckle. "I know men, Bond. I can scent them. You are a man who lives for danger. I smelled that the moment I met you. I also felt you have a similar facility for scenting out possible dangers. Yes?"

Bond shrugged. It was no time to commit himself to anything.

"You must be good," Murik continued. "Only good mercenaries stay alive. You were right to reconnoitre my estate; there may well be a job for you. We shall see. Tomorrow I may give you a small test."

There was a moment's pause, and then Bond asked levelly, "How did you win the Gold Cup with China Blue?" He did not smile.

Murik arched his eyebrows in surprise. "I have a good trainer.

How else would I win such a prestigious race? And I had the right horse."

"How?" Bond asked again. "China Blue's form made him the biggest outsider in the race. He even looked like a loser. You had him pulled in his other races?"

The Laird of Murcaldy shook his head. "There was no need for that. China Blue won. Fair and square." Then, as though suddenly making up his mind, he rose from the table. "Come, I'll show you something." He led the way to a door on the far side of the room, took out a bunch of keys, and unlocked the door.

They went down a well-lit passage which terminated at another door which Murik unlocked. A moment later they stood in a large book-lined room. There were three leather chairs facing a wide military desk and a cabinet containing exquisite pieces of antique weaponry.

Murik moved behind the desk and motioned Bond into one of the chairs facing him.

"My inner sanctum," he commented. "You are honoured to be here. This is where I work."

Bond drew the chair nearer to the desk as Murik removed a buff folder from a drawer and passed two photographs to him. "Tell me about these photographs, Mr. Bond."

Bond said they were pictures of China Blue.

"Almost correct." Murik made a deep, secretive smirk. "They are twin brothers. You see, just over four years ago I had a mare in foal, here on the estate. I was in at the birth of two absolutely identical foals. Happily I have a vet who knows how to keep his mouth closed; and it was obvious to the vet and myself that the second would always be the weaker of the two."

He paused. "I registered one only. There is one China Blue—the one you saw running at Ascot—with tremendous stamina and a natural aptitude for racing. The other? Well, he races, but has no speed and little stamina. Now, I've entrusted a secret to you. But if it ever leaks out, you are a dead man."

"Nobody's going to hear it from me." As he spoke, Bond moved his chair closer, taking out his gunmetal cigarette case and the packet of cigarettes provided by Q'ute. Murik had just answered a prize question: the man was a cheat and a fraud. Franco was in the house, and, for Bond, that was enough.

Quickly he removed a couple of the cigarettes from the packet and placed them in his case. At the same time he pressed on the side of the packet, expelling one of the electronic microbugs into his hand. As Murik leaned down to return the photographs to the drawer, Bond slid his hand under the foot-well of the desk, pressing the bug hard against the woodwork. Now the Laird of Murcaldy's inner sanctum was wired for sound.

Murik snapped the drawer closed and stood up. "Now, Mr. Bond, I suggest you say goodnight to the ladies and retire. Tomorrow we must take part in the Games. After that you may wish to stay; and I may wish to make you a proposition. It depends on many things."

In the drawing room, Mary-Jane Mashkin and Lavender Peacock sat listening to Mozart through hidden speakers. Bond thought he glimpsed a look of friendly conspiracy on Lavender's face as they entered the room. He felt that she was trying to warn him of something as they shook hands, bidding each other goodnight.

The silent Donal had appeared to show him to his room. Bond followed him up the stairs, anxious to set up the receiver in his case so that any business in Murik's inner sanctum could be recorded.

Donal opened the door, intoning, "The east guest room, sir," and Bond stepped into an Aladdin's cave for the passing visitor.

All Mod Cons

The room was decorated almost entirely in black, with soft lighting high up behind pelmets. Half of the bedroom walls and a large section of the ceiling was made of mirror, which gave the illusion of more space; it also had the unnerving effect of disorientation.

"You did not leave the keys to your luggage, sir," Donal said. "Otherwise I would have had your clothes unpacked and pressed. Perhaps tomorrow?"

"Yes, certainly." Bond turned his back, speaking sharply. "Goodnight Donal."

"Goodnight, sir." The butler withdrew, and Bond heard a solid click as the door closed. He tried the handle, immediately realizing that the door was fitted with a remote-controlled electronic lock. He was virtually a prisoner. At least, he thought, setting the briefcase on a table, he would not be secretly watched or overheard.

Unlocking the briefcase, he pressed down hard on the catches, which lifted on small hinges and revealed the real locking devices underneath: three wheels of numbers on each side. Bond spun the dials, and the briefcase opened. With this one they had made little effort to hide the equipment inside, the top of the case being a simple tray in which his toilet gear rested. Lifting out the tray, Bond uncovered the few pieces of hardware beneath.

The largest item was the one Bond required, the counter-surveillance receiver, which looked something like a chunky walky-talky, but with headphones and a hand-held probe. Bond plugged in the headset and probe, slipped the shoulder instrument's strap around his neck, and switched on. For the next ten minutes he carefully ran the probe over the entire room. The built-in verifier would quickly determine any type of bug, and even lead him to any television cameras hidden behind the large expanses of glass. Nothing showed.

Returning the counter-surveillance unit to its hiding place, he pulled out the larger piece of luggage. Once more he used his keys to open the lid, throwing the clothes out in a manner that would have made the fastidious Donal wince. When the case was empty, Bond returned to the locks, turning the keys a further three times; at the final click of the right lock, a panel slid back in the far left-hand corner of the case bottom, revealing a small numbered dial.

Bond spun the dial. Another click and he was able to slide a larger portion of the case bottom to one side, disclosing some of Q Branch's special hardware. Removing the tiny receiver/recorder—complete with a tape cassette and minute headset—Bond switched on and saw a small light glow like a red-hot pinhead. The bug placed in Murik's study was now active. He put the apparatus carefully on the dressing table and started to unpack, first sliding the hidden compartment in the case back to its locked position.

In less than five minutes Bond had shirts, underwear and other necessities packed neatly in the drawers of the long dressing table, and his other clothes hung in the built-in closets. Only then did he allow himself an examination of the room, which had the makings of an expensive movie set. The centrepiece of the main room was a vast bed, made up with white silk sheets and pillows. The visible edges of the bed glowed with light, and the whole was partially enclosed by two high, padded semi-circular panels. Bond slid onto the bed. The insides of the panels were softly lit; a large console took up the whole of one section to his left, while a television screen was set into one of the panelled sections which made up the semi-circle at the bed's foot.

After a few experiments with the console, Bond found that each section of the two semi-circles could be moved by remote control, and the bed raised or lowered. The console also had a telephone and facilities for quadrophonic sound, television and video-recording. Behind him, in a rack sunk into the black padding of the panel, was a whole range of music and video cassettes, plus a pair of headphones.

Bond recognized the bed as an exclusive Sleepcentre, made with modifications, probably on Murik's own instructions. It took a lot of will-power for him to leave it and investigate the bathroom, which also had several intriguing gadgets, including a sunken whirlpool bath, and even a blood-warm lavatory seat. "All mod cons," he said aloud.

With a short chuckle, Bond returned to the bedroom. As he headed towards the bed, a glance at the receiver on the dressing table showed the tape revolve for a second and then stop. The bug placed in Murik's study was picking up noises. Grabbing the receiver and headset, Bond dived into the Sleepcentre, slipping the phones over his ears.

Someone was in Murik's study. He heard a distinctive cough, then Murik's voice: "Come in, the door's open. Close it and shoot the bolt. We don't want to be disturbed." The sounds came clearly through the headphones: the door closing, then a rustle as someone sat down.

"I'm sorry about dinner," Anton Murik said. "I didn't think it wise for you to show yourself to my visitor."

154

"The message was understood. Who is the man?" The other voice was heavily accented. Franco, Bond thought.

"A mercenary out for hire. Could be useful—I can always do with a little intelligent muscle. We met by accident at Ascot . . ."

"You have him checked out?"

"You think I'm that much of a fool? He says his name's Bond. I have the number and details of the car—it'll give us an address and by tomorrow night I shall know everything I need about Mr. James Bond."

Bond smiled, knowing that M had him well covered. Any inquiries coming from passport number, car registration, or other means, would be blocked off: all Murik could learn would come from the cover dossier—the service record of one Major James Bond, a Guards officer who had performed certain dubious duties since leaving the armed forces—under a slight cloud—six years previously.

"I smell the need for money," Murik went on. "Mercenaries are good earners, if they live, yet they all have that tendency to spend as though tomorrow did not exist. But, my dear Franco, you're leaving shortly, and I want to get things finalized."

"Everything is clear as day. You know me well now, Warlock. The teams are ready in England, France and Germany. There is only America, and I'll be there by tomorrow afternoon."

There was a long pause before Murik spoke again. "You're quite certain of your American people? Are they willing to expend themselves in the cause?"

"Absolutely. They expect death. This is good psychology, yes?"

"I agree. Though as long as they do exactly as they're told, there'll be no risk of that. First, we only need to place four men in each station—they will secure themselves within the control rooms, and take orders from *me* alone. Second, they will have no contact with anyone outside. Third, I will make it plain to the governments concerned that they have twenty-four hours only, from the moment of takeover. The twenty-four hours runs out . . . then *boom*: England, France, Germany and the United States have big problems on their hands for many years to come—problems that will not be confined to those four countries. The death toll and

155

damage could cover almost half of the world. This is the one time that governments will have to give in to blackmail."

"Unless they do not believe you."

"Oh, they'll believe me," Murik chuckled. "Now, your Americans. How long will it take to brief them?"

"Twenty-four hours at the most."

"For both Indian Point Unit Three, and San Onofre Unit One?"

"Both. No problems."

"It's the San Onofre that will scare the wits out of them."

"Yes, I've studied papers. Still active, even though the authorities know how close it is to a seismic fault."

"Yes. America will press Europe. They just won't be able to take the risk. I see no reason why Meltdown cannot go ahead at twelve noon British Summer Time on Thursday, as planned."

"There's one thing . . ."

"Yes?" Murik's voice, sharp.

"How will you pass on the instructions without detection?"

A slight chuckle, subdued and humourless. "Your people have the receivers. You have a receiver, Franco. Just use them, and let me worry about the rest."

"But with radio signals of that strength—covering Europe and the United States—they'll pinpoint you faster than you can do your *Times* crossword; which is fast."

"I told you, Franco. Let me worry. Nobody'll have the slightest idea where any instructions are coming from. Now, we are on schedule for Thursday. If you can finish everything in America within twenty-four hours, you will be able to carry out the other assignment on Wednesday night. You think you can make that location?"

"There is time enough. Better I should do it than . . ."

Bond was suddenly distracted by a click from the door. His head whipped round, and he saw the handle turn a fraction. In one movement he grabbed the phones from his head, stuffing the receiver under the pillow before launching himself towards the door. His hand shot out, grasping the door and pulling it sharply towards him.

"It's OK," whispered Mary-Jane Mashkin, "only me." She slipped

156

inside, the door swung to heavily, and the locks thudded into place again. Mary-Jane Mashkin was dressed a shade too obviously in a heavy silk nightdress and wrap, her dark hair hanging round her face, her cheeks flushed. "I thought I should come and see that you're comfortable," she murmured coyly.

Bond indicated the door. "How do you get through that locking system? It's electronic, isn't it?" he asked.

She pushed herself towards him, smiling in a faraway manner. "The doors can be opened from the outside; and all *you* have to do is dial the switchboard on the phone. They'll open it up for you. If Anton agrees, of course."

Bond backed away. "And that's what you'll do? To get out, I mean."

"Oh, James. Are you telling me to leave?" She slid her arms around his neck. "I thought you needed company up here."

Bond's mind scrabbled around for the right actions and words. There was something decidedly wrong in a carefully orchestrated seduction scene by the mistress of Anton Murik, who was almost certainly in on whatever villainy was being planned.

"James," she whispered, "wouldn't you like me to stay for a while?" Mary-Jane Mashkin, fully dressed and made-up, had seemed a handsome woman. Now, close to, with her make-up cleaned off, she was a very different person.

"Look, Mary-Jane. It's a nice thought, but . . ." He wrenched himself free. "Isn't this risky? What about the laird? After all, you're his . . . trusted confidante."

"And I thought you were a man who was used to taking risks. James, don't make me humiliate myself . . . ."

She was a good actress, Bond would say that for her. But the whole thing smelled of a set-up. Had Anton Murik not talked earlier about testing him? The situation was delicate. A false move now might undo all the good work which had got him into Murik Castle. "Mary-Jane, don't think I'm not appreciative, but . . ."

Her expression changed into one of acid hardness. A lip curled. "I've made a fool of myself. Men used to flock . . ."

"It isn't like that. I'm Anton Murik's guest. A man can't abuse hospitality like . . ."

She laughed in a derisive single note. "Since when did a man like you stand on that kind of ceremony?" She stood up. "No, I just misread the signals. A woman can always tell when a man finds her—well, I guess, unattractive."

"I told you. It's not like that."

"Well, I know it is. Just like that." Mary-Jane was at the door now, turning in anger. "I could've saved you an awful lot of hassle, James. You may regret the last few minutes. You'll see, my friend." Her hand reached out to the door.

"Shouldn't I ring the switchboard?" Bond asked, trying to sound suitably subdued. He was becoming convinced that this unsophisticated attempt to seduce him was an act designed for some other purpose.

"No need." From the folds of her robe she produced a small oblong piece of metal the size of a credit card and slipped it into a tiny slot that Bond had not noticed, to the right of the lock. The bolts shot back, and Mary-Jane opened the door. "I'm sorry to have troubled you," she said, and was gone in a rustle of black silk.

Bond sat down on the bed. The whole business had been so bizarre that he found it difficult to take seriously. Then he remembered Murik.

The cassette was not turning when he retrieved the apparatus from under the pillow. He put the headphones over his ears and rewound the tape. The voices were as clear as though the two men were with him in the room.

"We are on schedule for Thursday," Murik was saying. "If you can really finish everything in America within twenty-four hours, you will be able to carry out the other assignment on Wednesday night. You think you can make that location?"

"There is time enough. Better I should do it than somebody else."

"It would give me greater confidence to know that it is you. What I need to know is how you will do it. Will she suffer?"

"No suffering, Warlock, I promise you. She feels nothing; and the onlookers, they imagine she has fainted. The weapon will be an air rifle, and the projectile, it has a gelatine coating. She feels a little pinprick but . . ."

There was a thud in the earphones, and the conversation became blurred. Either the adhesive on the microbug under Murik's desk had given way or one of the men had dislodged it with his knee. Gently Bond rewound the tape, but he could pick up only a few words. It was not even possible to separate the voices of the two men. ". . . very fast . . . catwalk . . . neck . . . steps . . . palace . . . Majorca . . . coma . . . death . . . two hours . . ." and so on. It meant little, except the obvious fact that someone—a woman—was being set up to be killed, just before this operation that Murik referred to as Meltdown.

This was no ordinary little plan but a deadly worldwide conspiracy: Bond knew that M's worst fears were realized. As for the contract killing, he could not even start to think how that fitted in. The weapon would be an air rifle, undoubtedly firing a capsule of quick-acting poison. As for the place and target, the word palace had been mentioned, and the victim was a woman. Bond immediately thought of royalty. The Queen, even. He would have to pass this on to M as soon as possible.

Then Bond's mind went into overdrive. Quite suddenly he had recognized two of the things overheard in Murik's conversation with Franco: two names that were familiar—Indian Point Unit Three and San Onofre Unit One. He knew that the possibilities of Murik's involvement with them carried things into a nightmare world.

Dilly-Dilly

Bond was just placing the headset in the closet, packed away in the case, when he heard the click of the door bolts again. His stomach turned over. Surely Mary-Jane would not have the nerve to return? The handle was turning, and for the second time that night Bond moved quickly to the door and yanked it open.

There was a little squeal as Lavender Peacock half fell into the room. She quickly recovered, snatching at the door, but was too late to stop it closing behind her with its ominous electronic click. "Blast," she said, shaking out her long sheeny hair. "Now I'm locked in with you."

"I can think of worse fates," Bond said, smiling, for Lavender was also dressed in her night clothes, making a distinctly more desirable picture than Mary-Jane Mashkin. "Anyway," he asked, "haven't you got one of those little metal things to open the door?"

She pulled her wrap around her, one hand brushing back her hair. "How do you know about those? Oh Lord, has Mary-Jane been up here? I can smell her scent."

"Miss Mashkin did play a scene of some ardour, but I fear she didn't go away contented."

Lavender shook her head. "I hoped I might get here before they started to play tricks with you. Anton has a warped sense of humour. I've seen him put her on offer before now, just to test people." She sighed. "I haven't the privilege of being allowed to carry electronic keys. I'm usually just as much a prisoner here as yourself." She gave a little smile. "Don't doubt that you're a prisoner, Mr. Bond."

"James."

"OK, James."

Bond gestured towards the bed. "Make yourself comfortable now you're here, Lavender."

She headed instead for one of the armchairs. "I think I'd better sit over here. That bed's too much for me. Oh, and call me Dilly, would you?"

"Dilly?"

"Silly old song—'Lavender's blue, dilly-dilly'—but I prefer it to Lavender."

Bond settled himself on the Sleepcentre, where he had a good view of his latest visitor. "You haven't told me why you're here, Dilly." He did not doubt that this might be yet another test.

She paused for a moment. "Well, I suppose I'm taking a chance trusting you, James. But I've got to talk to someone."

"Talk away."

"There's something very strange going on here. My guardian is not like other men: but you must know that already. I should ask you what you know about him, I suppose."

Bond told her that he gathered Anton Murik was a rich nuclear physicist of some note, who had half promised him a job.

"I should be careful about the job." She smiled—a knowing, foxy smile. "Anton Murik hires people to do his dirty work. But when he fires them, he does it in a literal sense." She lifted her hand, pointing the fingers like a gun. "Bang!"

Bond looked straight into her eyes. "You sure you wouldn't be more comfortable over here?" There was a challenge in her eyes, and Bond detected that familiar charge of static pass across the room between them.

"Probably *too* comfortable. No, James, I came to give you some advice. I said something strange is going on. It's more than that. It could even be disastrous."

"Yes? What sort of thing?"

"All I can gather is that it has something to do with the laird's plans for building a new kind of nuclear reactor. He left the International Atomic Energy Research Commission because they wouldn't fund his idea—he calls it an Ultra-Safe Reactor. There's a mountain of money needed, and I think he plans to use you in some way. But first he's going to put you at risk. Tomorrow. I heard him talking to Mary-Jane."

"Tomorrow? But he has his Games tomorrow."

"Quite. It probably has something to do with the Games."

"I might get hurt then. It wouldn't be the first time." Bond went over to her and kissed her lightly on the forehead.

She drew back fractionally. "That wasn't what I came for, James."

"No?"

Firmly she moved her head. "No. People've already got into a lot of trouble because of me. I just came as a kind of Cassandra, uttering warnings."

"Just uttering warnings? You said that you were virtually a prisoner like me. I wonder if you came hoping that I'd get you away."

"That's not on, I'm afraid. But I think you should get out, and I'm willing to help you."

"I can't go yet, Dilly. You've whetted my appetite about what's going on here. If I find that it's something really dangerous, or even criminal, then I'll take you up on your offer. I'll let you give me a hand. If it comes to that, will you come with me for help?"

Once more she slowly shook her head. "I was brought up here. It's all I know. Prisoner or not, there are certain responsibilities . . . ."

If I ran away now and something went wrong, things could be very bad for me. At least you can get out now, while the going's good. For your sake, I hope you find out something quickly."

Lavender rose, went over to the door, realized there was no way out, and turned to walk back to her chair. "It'll break this week, I'm certain. We're off to do a fashion show and that could be perfect cover for him."

Bond tried to sound surprised at the mention of the fashion show, and Lavender explained what he already knew, that Anton Murik owned the controlling interest in a leading fashion house. "Roussillon. I am lent out to them for major shows as a clothes' horse—but I can tell you, those shows are the high spots of my year."

"You slip the leash, eh?"

She almost blushed, and Bond slid from the bed, walked over to her chair and put an arm across her shoulders. She looked up at him, her eyes cold. "James. No. I only cause trouble."

"What kind of trouble?"

"The kind I wouldn't want to bring on you." She hesitated, indecisive for a moment. "OK. The first time was years ago, with a boy who worked here on the estate. I was about sixteen. Mary-Jane caught us and sent for Anton. The boy—David—disappeared, and his family were moved. I'm pretty certain Anton had him killed.

"David was just the first. Anton was once forced to buy someone off, in Rome—on a modelling jaunt. The man was from a wealthy Italian family. One day things were fine, the next I had a letter saying he had to go away. A year later I heard my guardian talking to Mary-Jane. He said it had cost a quarter of a million dollars, but it was money well spent."

Bond bent down and kissed her on the lips. "I'm willing to chance it, Dilly. You're . . ."

She pulled away. "I mean it, James." Then she smiled, putting a hand up to his cheek. "Not that I . . . Well, perhaps I'm being selfish. If something sinister *is* going on here, you're my one hope. I'll get you out, and you can bring in the stormtroopers: rescue the damsel in distress."

Bond laughed. "How do you get out of this room, then? Or are we forced to spend the night together in separate corners?"

Lavender said she would have to stay until early morning, when Bond could ring down and get the locks taken off. "You can say you want to go for a walk or something, when it's light. They'll let you do that because they can keep an eye on you then." She giggled: "We could bundle."

"Aye, we could do that an' all." Bond laughed, thinking of the old custom of courtship by sharing a bed, fully dressed, with a bolster to separate the couple. They made do with pillows, and Bond found it a frustrating experience, being so near and yet so far from this delightful girl. When they were settled, Bond asked if he was the only stranger in the castle, trying to make it sound like an afterthought.

She did not hesitate. "There's someone else here, but he's become a regular visitor. Anton calls him Franco. When you turned up he was pushed out of sight; but I think he's leaving in the morning."

"You think he's got something to do with what's going on?"

"I'm certain of it. He spends a lot of time closeted with Anton when he's here."

"How does he come and go?"

"In the helicopter. My guardian has a helicopter pad tucked away behind the old part of the castle."

"Thank you, Dilly. You just hang on and we'll sort it out; and thanks for the warning." He reached over the pillows and squeezed her hand.

"If we get out of here, James . . ."

"Yes?"

"Oh, nothing. Sleep, eh?"

For a few moments Bond's mind was in a turmoil of anger, the eye of his personal hurricane centred on Anton Murik: cheat, fraud; a man ruthless enough to kill his ward's lovers, like some Victorian millionaire martinet. Slowly Bond pushed down the anger. Coolness would be the only way to deal with Murik. With this in mind, Bond set his own mental alarm and drifted into restful sleep, waking accurately at five in the morning.

He roused Lavender and asked about the electronic locks. She told him they were made up of three cylindrical bolts, activated by an electro-magnet. When the locks went on, the bolts slid into tightly-fitting housings. At the end of each housing the bolt completed an electric circuit, activating an "on" light in the switchboard room. They would probably not notice the light flickering, Lavender said. They had experienced momentary malfunction before. She also told him that the inside keys were held only by certain people, and that it was impossible to get hold of them.

Bond went into the bathroom and changed into slacks and a sweatshirt, then dialled the switchboard. A voice asked why he wanted to leave his room, and he said it was his habit to exercise each morning. The voice told him to wait for a moment.

Within a minute they heard the locks fall back. Bond tried the door, and it opened easily. He kissed Lavender on the cheek, and to his surprise she reached up and kissed him firmly on the mouth. Then she was gone.

He quickly checked the room to make certain nothing incriminating was lying around, then with a final cautious look, he left. The first hint of dawn was touching the sides of the glen as James Bond went down the stairs and out into the castle grounds. As he emerged, the sound of a helicopter came throbbing in from the west. He waited until the machine turned and slowly dropped out of sight behind what had once been the keep of the old castle.

Hunching his shoulders, Bond began to jog towards the wide lawns where, only last night, he thought he had glimpsed a marquee set up for the day's Games. He wanted to give his body the best possible work-out. He knew all his reserves of stamina would be needed that day.

The Slingshot Syndrome

Later Bond was to learn that the four acres of beautifully-kept grass which ran down the far side of Murik Castle had been known as the Great Lawn for at least two centuries. Even at this early hour the estate workmen were out and about, putting the finishing touches to two large marquees, a number of small tents and an oblong arena the size of a small landing strip.

As he jogged past, Bond reflected on the numerous problems he had to resolve. It was obvious, from what he had overheard of the conversation between Murik and Franco, that they planned at least five terrorist attacks, codenamed Meltdown, in Europe and the United States. The two in America, he knew from the names, were connected with nuclear power stations. Logically, the ones in Europe would be similar targets. If his suspicions were correct, Meltdown could mean only one terrifying thing.

Jogging around the castle, Bond slowly made up his mind. In spite of what he had said to Lavender, there were two clear choices. Either he could get out now and alert M with the information already in his possession, or stay, face the test and glean the full details of the plot. If he could make a good showing, it was possible that Murik would put more trust in him; maybe even reveal everything. That this latter course of action was dangerous, Bond did not doubt; yet it was the path he had to take.

Again he thought about Murik's conversation with Franco the night before. Meltdown, the laird had said, would begin at twelve noon British Summer Time on Thursday. The operation was to be held strictly to twenty-four hours, and it involved the blackmailing of governments. For the time being, he put the contract killing by Franco aside. In time all things would be made clear.

After eleven circuits Bond returned to the castle. There appeared now to be a stirring throughout the building: the morning noises of a house coming alive. As he opened the door to his room, he sensed that someone else had been there during his absence.

Quickly he checked the cases. They had been moved, but the locks showed no sign of having been forced. Murik was checking him out—on the spot as well as through his outside sources. Bond made a mental note to look at the Saab at the earliest opportunity— not that anyone would easily be able to penetrate its secrets. The car had certainly looked all right as he had jogged past it, parked between Murik's gleaming Rolls and a wicked black BMW M1, which was probably Mary-Jane Mashkin's.

Returning to his toning up, Bond ran through his usual morning press-ups, sit-ups and leg raising. By the time he had completed the exercises, Bond's body was soaked in perspiration. He stripped off, padded through to the bathroom and showered—first under scalding water, then with an ice-cold spray.

After a good rub down and shave, he changed into lightweight slacks with a matching beige shirt and cord anorak. He filled the gunmetal cigarette case and put it in the jacket, together with his Dunhill lighter. The pen alarm was clipped into the inside of the jacket, while Q'ute's version of the Dunhill was deposited in his righthand trouser pocket.

Quietly he left the room. Passing through the hall, Bond heard voices from the dining room. Breakfast was obviously in progress, but first he had to take a quick look at the Saab.

The car was locked. Perhaps they had not got around to running a full check on it. Certainly, once he was inside, he saw that nothing seemed to have been moved or touched. Slipping his spare key into the ignition, Bond started the motor. It fired straightaway, and he allowed it to idle for a few seconds. When he switched off, Bond found Donal standing beside the car.

Removing the keys, he put on the wheel lock and activated a switch under the dashboard, then climbed out with a curt "Yes?"

The butler's face showed no emotion. "Breakfast is being served in the dining room, Mr. Bond." Bond replied that he was just going in. He locked the driver's door and stalked into the house.

Lavender and Mary-Jane were both seated at the table when he entered the room, where a sideboard almost groaned with dishes reflecting the old-style life lived by the laird. Bond bypassed the eggs, bacon, kippers, kedgeree and other delights, choosing only two pieces of toast and a cup of black coffee. Breakfast was his favourite meal, but on this occasion he knew it would be unwise to fill his stomach.

Both Mary-Jane and Lavender greeted him with seeming pleasure, and Bond had only just seated himself when Anton Murik came in, dressed, as befitted a Scottish laird, in kilt and tweed jacket, his pugnacious face all smiles. All three appeared to be excited about the Games, Murik himself particularly full of good humour, "It's my favourite day of the year, Mr. Bond. I think your breath may be taken away by the Games. It's quite a show."

"Quite a show," echoed Mary-Jane, smiling. She appeared unable to take her eyes off Bond, which he found disconcerting. There was no hint of the malice she had shown the previous night.

Murik then launched into a lengthy account of events that would take place throughout the day. "I must get going. After all, the laird is the host." He turned at the door. "Oh, Mr. Bond, I would particularly like to see you at the wrestling. My man Caber is Champion of Glen Murcaldy—a singular honour. He takes challengers at noon sharp. Please be there."

Bond had no time to answer, for the man was gone, almost with a hop, skip and jump. So that was it: a bout with the giant Caber. Bond turned gallantly to the ladies, asking if he could be their escort. Lavender said yes, of course; but Mary-Jane gave her enigmatic smile, remarking that she would have to accompany the laird. Lavender rose and asked Bond if he would wait for her to get ready.

"I wonder—do you have a library?" Bond asked Mary-Jane when Lavender had left the room. "I realized last night that I came without any reading matter."

"Of course. I'll take you there before I go out to join the laird. But what a pity that you won't allow other things to occupy your nights. No hard feelings about *last* night, by the way."

"None for my part," said Bond, puzzled by her friendliness.

"Pity," she giggled. Then her expression changed. "For my part there are a lot of feelings. You could have avoided trouble, but you refused, James, and you'll be sorry. I have suggested a small test at the Games. Anton agrees. You will be matched with Caber at the wrestling, and given his head, he'd kill you." Another laugh. "And just for giving him a bloody nose. How vain men are. But come, I'll show you the library."

The library backed onto the drawing room, and was decorated in light colours. Three of the high walls were covered with books, the fourth contained three large bay windows. It took Bond a few moments to get his bearings and work out how the books were catalogued—moving the high library steps along each wall until he found what he wanted. First, he chose a novel to cover his story— one of his old favourites, Eric Ambler's *The Mask of Dimitrios*. Then he made for his real quarry: a beautifully-bound copy of

Webster's Dictionary, which he dragged out and placed on a large lectern.

Thumbing the volume to the letter W, Bond scanned the lines of words until he came to Warlock. The entry gave the usual definition, 1: "One given to black magic: Sorcerer, wizard. 2: conjurer." Then Bond's eyes slid up to the derivations, and his heart skipped a beat. "Old English—*wærloga*: one that breaks faith, scoundrel, the Devil."

One that breaks faith? Bond wondered. Was Murik having his own joke in choosing Warlock as his codename? Was he, in turn, scheming to break faith with the terrorists he had hired through Franco?

He was replacing the copy of *Webster* when a sound made him whirl round. Lavender stood just inside the library door, wearing a pink creation which gave her a cool, poised look. As Bond approached, he saw she was pale under the smoothly applied make-up. She put her finger to her lips. "James, he's putting you up against Caber in the wrestling."

Bond grinned. "I know, the Mashkin told me with great relish."

"It's not funny. Caber's after you. Did you actually nearly break his nose?"

"Gave it a butt in the right place. Made it bleed a bit."

"He'll pound all hell out of you, James. Making Caber look stupid could drive him wild with anger."

"Let me worry about Caber, Dilly darling." Bond took hold of her hand and squeezed it. "Can you come to my room tonight with a way to let me through the main gates?"

"You're going to run?"

"Only if I've got the full story, and it's bad enough to take some definite action. If not, we'll just have to do some more bundling."

"You'll be lucky if you're not just a bundle yourself by the end of the morning."

"I told you— just work out a way for me to get through the gates, and leave Caber to me. OK?"

She replied with a worried nod; and he could feel her trembling as they went out through the hall and into the sunlight. A band was playing on the Great Lawn and already the Games were in full swing. Murik did not stint his guests on this occasion: there was food and drink for all, and plenty of entertainment. Bond wondered what price the local people had to pay in service—and silence—to the laird for this one day of blatantly feudal fun.

Groups of men and women in Highland costume were preparing to dance, while brawny young men were at the far end of the arena tossing the caber and hammer throwing. Several people respectfully doffed their bonnets to Lavender, and Bond also noticed that they glanced at him with undisguised suspicion. He tried to pick out the more dangerous of the laird's private army—the big young men with watchful eyes. Of one thing he was sure: there were a lot of them. For the next couple of hours he watched with interest the sports and dancing.

Eventually a crowd started to gather around an area at the castle end of the arena, and Bond allowed himself to be led towards it by Lavender, who whispered that this was where her guardian wanted him. Mats had been laid down, and he saw the little figure of Murik talking to a group of men on the far side. He spotted Bond and waved cheerfully before making his way towards the pair. "Well, Mr. Bond. My champion is almost ready to take on all comers. Do you feel like facing up to him?"

Bond smiled, pretending the laird was joking. "I mean it, Bond." The deadly lava was back, deep in the eyes. "And if you do well, there may be much in it for you. Can I announce you as the first competitor?"

Now Bond laughed aloud. "I hardly think I'm his weight, Laird. He'd lay me out with one finger."

Murik's face was grim as a tombstone. "That's not the point, Bond. I want to see what stuff you're made of. It's not a question of beating the man, but standing up to him. Guts, Mr. Bond, that's what I'm looking for. Guts."

Bond smiled once more. "Oh, well," he spoke casually, "that puts a different complexion on it. Yes, Laird, I'll take a bout with your champion."

He heard Lavender's sudden quick intake of breath as Murik gave a tough little grin and walked towards the centre of the mats, holding up his arms for silence. A hush came over the crowd.

"Friends," he shouted. "As you all know, it's time for the Champion of Murcaldy to offer himself to anyone who wishes to challenge his right. Give your hands to Caber, my champion."

Bond had only really caught a glimpse of Caber on the previous night. Now, as he emerged from the crowd, he seemed even larger and more formidable—his chest the size of a barrel, and his biceps standing out like miniature rugby footballs. Yet, like many big men in peak condition, the Scot moved with a sure-footed grace, nodding his head in answer to the appreciative applause.

The laird was motioning for silence. "Friends, there is one who has come to take up the challenge," he announced. Then, after a dramatic pause, "One from over the border."

A hostile buzz went around the crowd. Bond felt in his righthand trouser pocket to be certain that what he needed was there. Then he quickly slipped out of his anorak, handing it to Lavender.

"Look after this please, Dilly," he said, grinning.

"James, take care," she whispered.

"From over the border. A Mr. James Bond."

Bond sprang forward onto the mats, holding up his hands against the now angry mutterings of the crowd. "I take up the challenge, Caber."

"Well done!" The laird thrust his head forward in his birdlike manner. "Well done, James Bond."

Bond, well-built and tall as he was, felt like a pygmy next to Caber. He knew there was only one way to deal with the situation—to keep away from those hands for as long as possible; stop Caber from getting a deadly lock on him, and then move at just the right moment. The two men squared up, and the laird asked if they were ready. Bond nodded and Caber said, "Aye, it'll no tak' long."

"Then . . . wrestle," Murik shouted, at the same time ducking out of the way.

Caber came straight at Bond, who sidestepped, attempting a trip with his ankle as he did so; but the huge Caber was very quick. Before he knew what was happening, Bond was being lifted into the air and thrown, hitting the mats square on his back. Caber made a dive for him, but this time Bond beat him to it, rolling clear so that

Caber was forced to handspring back to his feet. He rounded on Bond, coming in fast. Bond weaved, but it was no good; Caber performed a quick cross-ankle pick-up, sending Bond sprawling again.

This time there was no rolling free, for Caber had one arm and a good deal of weight on Bond's right shoulder. At the same time, the giant of a man drew back his right arm, his fist balled and ready to strike hard into Bond's face. Bond's left arm was free, and he just managed to roll his head to one side as Caber's blow came hurtling towards him. The fist grazed his ear and thudded hard, and painfully, into the matting beside his head.

Caber was slightly off-balance, but still holding down Bond's right shoulder. Time to use the left arm; and use it on the area of greatest weakness in all men—even a wrestler as strong as Caber. Bond brought the left hand up, fingers pointed, in a sharp jab at Caber's groin. As he heard the big man grunt with pain, he followed up by another, slightly stronger attack at the same target.

Caber grunted again, and Bond felt his shoulder freed as the Scot fell forward, rolling as he did so. Bond backed away. It was the moment for him to be most alert. Like a wounded animal, Caber was now enraged, and it was clear to Bond that the big man would kill if he had to.

Bond let his right hand drop to the level of his trouser pocket, and, as Caber came in for the attack, Bond launched himself forward in a leg drive, the movement covering his right hand, which slid quickly in and out of the pocket.

He hit Caber's legs, though it was like diving into a wall. But now Bond had Q'ute's special Dunhill firmly clasped in his hand. He twisted, trying to bring Caber down, but the man just laughed and kicked hard, stretching his arms out and diving for Bond again. This time Bond's right hand came up as though to ward off the certain pinioning by the giant. As Caber's tree-trunk arms caught his shoulders, so Bond readied the Dunhill.

Q Branch's version of the Dunhill lighter was cunning and efficient. It was loaded, under pressure, with a liquid containing a high base of the anaesthetic Halothane. One burst of Halothane near the mouth or nose would produce the desired effect, for the drug is quick-acting, highly potent, and yet produces no nausea. "They won't know what hit 'em—before, during or after," Q'ute had said.

Bond's hand was in exactly the right place to deliver the burst, Caber's mouth and nose being less than two inches from the hidden Dunhill as he flicked the flip-top. As he moved his fingers, so Bond prepared to roll clear. He did not particularly want to get a whiff of the Halothane himself.

Caber simply kept on coming, like an aircraft landing heavily with its undercarriage down. Bond was just able to glimpse the look of surprise, then the glazing of the big Scot's eyes as he collapsed. As Bond rolled clear he grabbed at Caber's now inert arm and delivered two swift blows to the jaw: to the crowd, the whole thing would look like a clever jab to the face.

As he sprang back and away, Bond returned Q'ute's useful little toy to his pocket.

A hush had come over the crowd. Then Murik, looking shaken, was by his side, and two men were leaning over the prostrate Caber. One of them—Malcolm this time—looked up at the laird. "Yon's oot cold, Laird. Oot cold."

Murik glanced uncertainly at Bond, who smiled pleasantly and said, "I think I'm your new champion."

There was a pause lasting only a few seconds. Then the Laird of Murcaldy gave a watery smirk, and announced, "Ladies. Gentlemen. Friends. We have a new champion and you'll treat him with the respect and honour always afforded to our champions. I give you the Champion of Murcaldy—Mr. James Bond."

There was an uncertain silence, then the cheers began, and Bond was lifted shoulder-high around the Great Lawn with drums beating and the pipes skirling. He had successfully played David to Caber's Goliath, Bond thought, and Q'ute had provided him with the ultimate in the slingshot syndrome.

Through the crowd he saw Lavender Peacock looking at him with warm admiration in her eyes. Well, if he worked on Murik with speed, Bond might even have all the information he needed, to get away before the next morning. Then, once M was alerted, there could even be time to get to know Dilly Peacock really well.

172

A Contract, Mr Bond

Though Anton Murik had presented the major trophies for the Murcaldy Games, people seemed reluctant to leave. It was now just past six in the evening, and after a speech amidst much applause and cheers, the laird had set off in the direction of the castle, motioning to Bond to follow him. Lavender was left with Mary-Jane Mashkin.

Murik led Bond through the hall, past the main staircase, pushing open a set of swing doors that led to a corridor. The laird stopped halfway down the corridor, bringing out the ever-present keys—this time from his sporran—to unlock a solid oak door strengthened with steel grilles. Bond followed him down a flight of stone stairs. Tiny guide lights gleamed, throwing vague shadows in the darkness. Halfway down, Murik turned towards him. When he spoke, the laird's voice echoed eerily. "You've already seen my inner sanctum. We're going to the most interesting part of the castle this time. The oldest relic of my heritage. Now you are my champion, Mr. Bond, you should know of it."

The air smelled dank, and the stone stairs seemed endless, descending to a flagged open space, deep underground. Murik reached out to a switch on the wall and the place was suddenly flooded with light. Huge arches supported the vaulted ceiling and there were two more doors, one on each side of the flagged space. Ahead of them another narrower passage continued. Murik nodded, "That way leads to the old dungeons." His jowl moved in a twitching smile. "They are occasionally useful. To our right, a room which I do not like using. The old torture chamber." He pushed open the door and Bond followed him in.

At one end of the room Bond identified a rack, a flogging frame, and all the old sinister instruments—from branding irons to gouges. Bond shuddered. In his time he had suffered much physical torture, and its instruments were not unknown to him. Yet when he looked towards the far end of the room his blood ran cold. The walls there were tiled in white, and in the centre was an operating table. He guessed that the cabinets along the far wall would contain more

173

terrifying instruments than the brutal weapons of pain: there would be drugs to send the mind reeling to the very edge of madness, and possibly even the means of inflicting agony through electrodes attached to the most sensitive areas of the body. Few men would keep secrets for long in the more sophisticated part of this, Murik Castle's chamber of horrors.

"Occasionally this room is put to use, Mr. Bond. Have care. All who serve me are given a guided tour. You defeated Caber, so you automatically serve me. Let your glimpse of this place act as a warning. I demand complete loyalty."

Murik led the way out and across the flagged area to another door. He turned, smiling, "My operations room."

The contrast was overwhelming. They were in a long, low-vaulted chamber. Its grey walls were covered with weapons, ranging from artistic and obviously valuable rapiers, dirks and knives, through crossbows decorated with inset stones, to modern rifles, carbines, and automatic weapons.

Bond could not resist one gibe. "No thermonuclear devices to bring it right up to date?"

The laird's face darkened. "We have no need. The world provides them. They are all around us, ready and waiting to wreak disaster."

Bond's gaze moved beyond this collection of weapons to the far end of the vault which housed a long console desk, computer monitors and radio equipment. Murik motioned him to the console table, gesturing to one of the comfortable leather swivel chairs behind it. He took the other chair himself and gave a throaty laugh. "From here, Mr. Bond, I control the destiny of the world."

Bond, uncertain whether Murik was joking or not, laughed with him. There was an uneasy silence for a moment, giving Bond the opportunity to glance up at a large map of the world. Indian Point Unit Three and San Onofre Unit One were both plainly marked in red. It took all his willpower to drag his eyes back to the laird. Don't seem too eager, he told himself, willing his brain to relax.

"You know who I am?" Anton Murik asked. "I am probably the greatest nuclear physicist who has ever lived."

Nothing like modesty, Bond thought. Aloud he tried to say "Really?" with a convincing gasp.

"Let me tell you . . ." Murik launched into a description of his brilliant career. In Murik's version, however, he had resigned from the International Commission out of protest. "Those who fight for the abolition of nuclear power stations in their present form are right." His voice was slowly rising in agitation. "Note, Mr. Bond, I say in *their present form*. They are unsafe. Governments are keeping the truth from the general public. They have tried, again and again, to muzzle people like me. Now they deserve a lesson. They say that the only way out of the energy crisis is to use nuclear power. They are right: but that power must be made safe."

"You mean the problem of radioactive waste?"

"No. I'm talking about unavoidable accident. There have already been incidents galore. If you're an intelligent man you must know that. 1952, Chalk River, Ontario; 1955, Idaho Falls; 1957, Windscale, England; '61, Idaho Falls; '71, Minnesota. Need I go on? One day, with the kind of reactors we have at the moment, there will be catastrophe. The Carter Administration almost admitted it . . ." He rummaged among some papers. "There, 1977— 'Between now and the year 2000 there *will* be a serious core meltdown of a nuclear reactor; but with proper siting such accidents can be contained'. Do you realize what a core meltdown means, Mr. Bond?"

"Is that what they call the China Syndrome?" Bond played the innocent.

Anton Murik nodded. "A nuclear reactor produces the enormous heat needed to turn power generators from a core—a controlled chain reaction, and as long as it's controlled all is well. However, if there is a failure in the cooling system—that's it. The core is just left to generate more and more heat; create more and more radioactivity . . ."

"Until it goes off like a bomb?"

Murik shook his head. "No, not quite like the big bang, but the results are fairly spectacular. There would be a kind of tremor, with the earth moving, and one hell of a lot of radioactive particles being released. The core itself would become so hot that nothing could stop it going right through the earth—nothing could stand in its way. Right through to China, Mr. Bond; it could happen in any one of the nuclear reactors operating in the world today. And *I* could make it safe for them." He gave a long, slow smile, then a shrug. "But, of course, as usual, the money men won't play." He paused again, looking hard at Bond. "I'm going to demonstrate how unsafe the present systems are and at the same time show them just how safe they could be. Can you blame me, Mr. Bond?"

Bond shook his head. "Not if your system *is* as safe as you say."

For a second he thought the Laird of Murcaldy was going to lash out at him. "What do you mean?" Murik screamed. "*If* my system is as safe as *I* say? I'm telling you, I have the only one hundred per cent safe nuclear reactor system; and because of contracts and profits, because of self-seeking politicians, they've tried to make a laughing stock of me." He drew back into his chair.

Bond had managed to steal two more glances at the large map, identifying the English and French locations: Heysham One and Saint-Laurent-des-Eaux Two. What was this man going to do? Was he prepared to send suicide terrorists into nuclear reactor sites to manufacture disaster that might affect the entire world? Meltdown—of course.

Murik was speaking again. "I have prepared a master plan." He gestured towards the map, giving Bond the opportunity to take another look, his eyes moving to Germany. His heart sank when he identified the two targets marked in the German area, one in the Federal Republic, the other in the East. So, even the Eastern Bloc had not been left out of Anton Murik's plans. The job would be to lead Murik on to reveal the bulk of his Operation Meltdown; though, even without further information, Bond considered the mission complete. If he could get out that night, MI5 would be able to track down Murik and with luck collar Franco through the American security agencies. Meltdown could be blown.

"My plan will alert the world to the horrific danger that exists through the nuclear plants already working." Murik gave another of his throaty chuckles. "It will also provide me with the necessary capital to build my own safe plant, and demonstrate to those cretins that it is possible to use nuclear energy without putting the human race at risk."

"How?" Bond asked.

"It's a complicated business," Murik hedged. "But you will play your part, Mr. Bond."

"What sort of part?" Bond dropped his voice, sounding wary.

"There is one essential piece of the operation: to ensure that nobody ever knows I have had a part in what will happen. Your job is to kill one man. A contract, Mr. Bond—that's the right terminology, I believe? According to my information you need around £20,000 quite soon. I'm offering £50,000, which I'm certain is more than your usual basic fee. It should also serve to keep you silent."

"I don't know what you mean," Bond said flatly. Secretly, he was elated that Murik had been fed the entire cover story. "I mean, you know nothing about me . . . ."

"No?" Murik's eyes clouded. "I think you will find I know more than is comfortable for you, Mr. Bond. *Major* Bond. You were in the Guards, like your father before you, the late Colonel Archie Bond? Correct?"

Bond nodded, allowing his face to take on a puzzled expression.

"You see, James Bond, I know about your career. I also know about the great courage you displayed while assigned to the SAS . . . ."

"That's confidential information," Bond blurted out.

Murik nodded, unconcerned. "But *I* know. Just as I am up to date with your failures: how they allowed you to resign after that unfortunate business with the Mess funds; how you have lived by your wits and skill ever since. I also have a record of the unpleasant gambling gentlemen who would like to get their hands on either you or the £20,000 you owe them."

Bond allowed his shoulders to slump forward.

"Apart from the mercenary engagements," Murik went on, "I can make an informed guess concerning the contract killings you've performed."

M had certainly placed the information well. Bond sat up, his face impassive. "OK," he said softly, "I won't deny any of it. Nor am I going to deny that I'm good at my job. How's Caber?" There was a tinge of malice in his voice.

The Laird of Murcaldy was not smiling. "Bewildered," he said coldly. "Nobody's ever really beaten him until today. Yes, you are

177

good, Mr. Bond. If you were not, I wouldn't be offering you a contract killing now."

"Who's the lucky client?" Bond assumed a professional manner.

"A man called Franco Oliveiro Quesocriado. You'll have heard of him. Hijackings, bombings, hostage-taking; his name is often in the papers. He is said to be the most wanted terrorist on the books."

"Ah." Bond allowed a flicker of recognition to cross his face. "*That* Franco. How do I find him?"

"By staying close to me. I shall point you in the right direction. All you have to do is remove him—but not until you're told. Franco must di appear. Vanish, leaving no trace."

"For that money I might even throw in his birth certificate."

Murik shook his head. In a chilling voice he said, "That has already been taken care of. *You* will be his death certificate." Both men were silent for a moment. Then Bond looked Murik straight in the eye.

"And the money? How shall I receive it?"

"You will be free to collect £50,000 in bank notes of any currency of your choosing a week from today at my bank in Zurich." Murik stood up and began to walk calmly down the long room. "I think we should get ready for dinner now, Mr. Bond. Then I would suggest a good rest. It is likely to be an active and taxing week." There was no suggestion that Bond might like to consider the proposal. Murik had already assumed that the contract was sealed.

Bond started to follow Murik towards the door and as he did so, caught sight of one of the weapons on display. On a small shelf, among some grenades, stood a cutaway German S-Mine, from the Second World War. Bond knew the type well. An unlucky foot touching the trigger activated the deadly mine, which then leaped into the air before exploding to scatter fragments of its steel casing, together with ball bearings loaded into the sides of the mine. A pile of these small steel balls lay beside the weapon. They looked just the right size for Bond's purpose. Loudly he asked—"You're tied up with this Franco fellow? In this scheme of yours?"

Before Murik had time to reply, Bond had quietly slipped three of the ball bearings into his pocket. Murik stood by the exit as Bond caught up with him. "Yes, friend Franco has provided me with six suicide squads to infiltrate half-a-dozen major nuclear power stations. They are terrorists, fanatics: willing to die for their respective causes if need be. For them, if my plan works, it will mean vast sums of money set at the disposal of their organizations, and if it does not work, it is of no consequence—to the suicide squads, at least." He gave another of his unpleasant chuckles before continuing.

"All these men are willing to sit in nuclear control rooms and, if necessary, produce what you have called the China Syndrome. They have been trained so they can carry out destructive actions at my command. I personally do not think it will happen—but that is up to me. At the end of the day there will be a huge ransom. Franco is to get half of the final ransom money, which he will split with the groups according to his prior arrangements. It is up to Franco to come to me in order to collect his share." They were now back in the main flagged hall, where Murik closed the door to the armoury.

"You will understand, Mr. Bond, that I do not intend Franco to collect anything. For one thing, he is the only living person who would be able to tie me into this operation. For the other"—he shrugged lightly—"I need all the money myself in order to build my own reactor. It is all·for the benefit of mankind."

Bond fought down the desire to point out the terrible risk that Murik would be taking. However strongly Anton Murik felt about the ultimate threat, the situation might well be out of his control once the terrorist squads were in place.

More than ever, Bond realized that he must make a bid for freedom. They made their way slowly, side by side, to the foot of the stone stairway. "There is one thing," Bond said calmly, hands clasped behind his back.

"Go on," Murik encouraged him. The two men might have been discussing new staffing arrangements at a respectable City company.

"If you want Franco removed," Bond continued politely, "to—ah—protect your little secret and to save on expenses, why should I suppose you'll not have Caber and his men similarly dispose of me as soon as I've done the job?"

Murik stopped in mid-stride and turned to beam at Bond. "Very good, Mr. Bond. You are right to question my trustworthiness. It would be all too easy for me to arrange matters as you prognosticate—one false move would certainly bring about Caber's longed-for revenge. You have only my word for good faith. But remember, much greater risks lie on my side of the contract."

Murik flicked the switch and the vault was plunged into gloom. They mounted the stairs in silence.

Nightride

The names of the six nuclear power stations were in the forefront of Bond's mind for the rest of the evening, running like a looped tape in his head. His knowledge of nuclear power, and the location of reactors throughout the world, was sketchy, though he had done a short course on the security of such power plants.

At least he had the names, and the knowledge that they were subject to terrorist squad takeover on Thursday. Get out, Bond's experience told him. Get the information to M and leave the rest to the experts. Sir Richard Duggan's boys from MI5 almost certainly had Murik Castle under surveillance, and it would not take long for troops to move in. If they were on the ball, Franco would already be in the FBI's sights in the United States. It should not take much to pull him.

Bond did not have time to start thinking of the intricacies of Murik's plan. Already there was enough on his mind, and it was essential for him to appear completely relaxed in front of Murik, Mary-Jane Mashkin and Lavender Peacock. At dinner he drew the talk around to his favourite subject of golf, launching into a highly-embellished account of a game he had recently played. He was so caught up in the telling of the tale that he had to pull himself from the half-fantasy when the ladies withdrew, coming down to earth as he faced Anton Murik alone over the table.

Little passed between the two men, except an explicit warning from the laird, who obviously felt he had already told Bond too much about his plans. As they finally rose, he placed a hand on Bond's arm and said, "Stay alert. We shall probably be leaving here

180

in a day or two, and I shall want you on hand before you go and earn your money. You understand?"

Bond knew that if Murik was going to break faith with Franco, there would be little likelihood, had Bond really been a contract mercenary, of any money coming his way. Franco's death would undoubtedly be followed quickly by Bond's own demise. As he said goodnight to Murik and the ladies, Bond took heart from Lavender's quick, conspiratorial look, guessing that she would come to his room as soon as the castle was quiet.

Back in the east guest room, Bond heard the telltale thud as the electronic lock went on after the door was closed. He moved with speed, packing only the essential hardware and clothes into the larger case, then laying out other necessary items on the bed: the fake Dunhill, the pen alarm and a small flat object that looked like a television remote control. This last he placed next to the car keys. When the moment came, speed would be essential.

Last of all, Bond laid out a pair of dark slacks and a black roll-neck sweater. Then, after placing the three steel ball bearings near the door, he showered, changed into the dark clothing, stretched out on the Sleepcentre, and lit a cigarette. Near his right hand lay the last piece of equipment, a wide strip of thick plastic, one of many odds and ends provided by Q'ute.

Time passed slowly, and Bond occupied himself by working on the remaining pieces of the Meltdown puzzle. Six nuclear power stations were to be taken over by small suicide squads. Murik had stressed that the squads would occupy the control rooms. If Meltdown did happen, even if troops were brought onto the six sites, it would take time to break into those vault-like control rooms. Besides, the authorities would be loath to precipitate matters, particularly if they knew the terrorists were prepared to die—and take a lot of people with them—by cutting off the cooling systems to the nuclear cores. Whatever the governments of countries like Britain, the United States, France and Germany had said about never giving in to terrorist blackmail, Meltdown would present them with the gravest dilemma any country had yet faced.

With hostages, aircraft, embassies and the like, governments could afford to sit it out—establish a dialogue and find a way to stall

181

matters. Yet if this situation arose, the governments would be left with no option. The hostages would consist of millions of people— all caught in a devastating pollution that could alter the whole course of the world for decades to come.

Anton Murik was thorough. He would have worked out every move, down to the smallest detail. Yet there was still one factor for which he had not accounted: the circumstances Bond had considered earlier—the trigger-happy, death-wish uncertainty of any terrorist group under pressure. This thought—above anything else—strengthened Bond's determination to get back to M as quickly as possible.

It was almost one in the morning before he heard the click of the electronic lock. Bond sprang like a cat from the bed, the strip of plastic in one hand, the other scooping up the ball bearings. Gently he pulled back on the door, allowing Lavender to enter the room. Raising a hand, he signalled silence, then slipped one ball bearing into each of the three circular bolt housings. If Bond's thinking was accurate, the "on" lights would be activated in the castle switchboard room when the bearings made contact at the bottom of the housings. If luck was with them, the flicker as Lavender unlocked the door would have gone unnoticed.

Bond then inserted the thick plastic strip over the bolt heads to prevent them locking back into place, and partially closed the door.

Lavender was still in the dress she had worn at dinner. In one hand she carried what looked like a pocket calculator, and in the other a duelling pistol, which Bond recognized as coming from the valuable set in the hall.

"Sorry I'm late," she whispered. "They've only just gone to bed. A lot's been happening. Caber came up to the house with some of the men. The laird's been giving them instructions, Lord knows what about. Have you any idea what's going on?"

"A fair amount, Dilly: enough to call in help. Yes, it *is* serious. While I'm away, I want you to keep to yourself as much as possible—and would you please not point that thing in my direction?" He took the duelling pistol from her.

She told him it was safe: the hammer was down. "I thought you should have some kind of weapon."

182

"Just hope it doesn't blow up in my hand if I have to use it." Bond looked with some misgivings at the piece.

"The laird tests them regularly—about once a year. That one's Monro's pistol, by the way. The one that won."

Bond nodded, asking about the main doors, and the best way out. Lavender told him there was a red button high up on the main door. "You'll find a small switch just beneath it in the down position. Move it up, and the alarm system'll be disconnected. Then just press the button, and the main door locks will come off. They'll know in the switchboard room straightaway, so you won't have much time."

"And that?" Bond pointed to the flat black object.

"For the main gates," she told him. "Both Anton and Mary-Jane carry these in their cars. If you press the button marked Open at around fifty yards from the gates they'll unlock and swing back of their own accord. That's about all the help I can give you."

"It's more than enough, Dilly darling. Now you must get back to your room, before I start. If everything goes to plan, I'll have help here, and there'll be some unmasking to do. I fear your guardian could end up in the slammer for a long time."

"Just take care, James. Dear James." She put her arms round his neck and he kissed her. "Take care," she whispered again, and he opened the door—holding the plastic strip in place—wide enough for her to get out.

Bond slipped the remote control for the gates into a hip pocket, then slid the hard barrel of the duelling pistol into his waistband, making sure the hammer was right down. Next he picked up his car keys and the flat box of his own. This was also a remote operator with which he could turn on the ignition and have the motor running almost before he was out of the main castle doors.

Taking several deep breaths, Bond clutched the car keys, remote ignition control, and the suitcase in his left hand, leaving the right free. Opening the door, he allowed the thick plastic to fall and pulled the door closed behind him. The bolts shot home, and for a few seconds Bond stood in the darkness of the corridor, letting his eyes adjust. Then, slowly, he moved towards the gallery.

Quietly Bond made his way down the staircase and across the hall to the door. He could see the small panel with the red button and switch quite plainly. Reaching up he flicked off the alarm and pressed the button. The heavy bolt on the main door clunked back like a pistol shot. In the night silence of the house it was enough noise to waken the dead, he thought. At that very moment, as the door began swinging back, the lights went on and a voice told him to put his hands up.

It was Donal. Bond recognized the voice, and judged the butler to be somewhere just to the left of the stair bottom. He grasped the duelling pistol, cocking the hammer as he drew it from his waistband, and whirling round as the end of the barrel came clear.

It was a risky shot, and the pistol made far more noise than he had bargained for. But Bond's senses had been accurate. Donal was just where his ears had placed him. A pistol of some kind clattered over the floor as the butler wheeled in a complete circle, clutching his shattered shoulder where the ball had struck.

Bond was already out of the main door, pressing his own remote ignition control and dropping the duelling pistol so that he could grasp the car keys. He saw lights coming on and the shadows of figures running towards the Saab as its motor sprang to life.

Bond sprinted to the car. The motor was ticking over gently as he turned the key in the lock and pulled at the door. Throwing the case into the rear, he slid behind the wheel, slamming the door and flicking down the lock almost at the same moment as one of the shadowy figures closed on the car. It was time to test Communication Control Systems's special fitments. Working quickly, Bond unlocked the two hidden compartments, threw the Browning onto the ledge above the instrument panel and grasped the spare set of Nitefinder goggles.

There were at least five men around the car now, two of them carrying machine pistols. Someone was shouting for him to get out of the car. It was then that Bond hit the tear gas button.

One of CCS's safety devices consists of tear gas ducts placed near all four wheels. Pulling on the Nitefinder set, Bond heard the hiss of the canisters opening up. Then he saw the effects as the five men began to reel away and the angry white cloud rose around the windows of the car.

He snapped on the seatbelt, slammed the machine into gear, took off the handbrake, and pressed hard on the accelerator. The car shot forward, skidding wildly on the gravel as Bond drove at breakneck speed away from the castle. Through the rearview mirror he could see the men coughing and reeling about, shielding their eyes, and one huge figure—it could only be Caber—lunging into their midst, as though reaching out for a weapon.

He did not see the flashes; only felt the heavy bumps as a burst of automatic fire hit the rear of the Saab. Best not to be concerned about that: there was enough armour plating and bullet-proof glass around him to stop most weapons. Bond changed up, still with his foot hard on the accelerator. There were two more heavy thuds. One of the tyres, he thought. No problem there: Dunlop Denovos—puncture and split-proof.

He could see the gates in the distance, and one hand went to the gunport just below the dash. Bond removed the unauthorized Ruger Super Blackhawk .44 Magnum, pushing it into a spot where he could easily grab the butt.

The gates were coming up fast, and Bond's hand now went to the remote control given him by Lavender. After the experience with Donal and the waiting men in front of the castle, Bond had begun to doubt Lavender and her instructions, and it was with some relief that he saw the gates start to move as he pressed the control button.

Then, from the right, he caught sight of a figure running towards the gates, one arm raised. A small yellow flash, followed by a thud; then another. The gatekeeper was firing at him. Bond went for the Blackhawk and thrust the muzzle through the gunport.

The gates, still opening, came up with alarming speed as Bond let off three shots in quick succession, the noise and smell of powder filling the car and battering at his eardrums. The figure of the gatekeeper was now out of sight, but the slowly opening gates were on him. He felt both sides of the Saab scrape against the metal, then he was free, changing up again, and hurtling along the metalled road away from the castle. The speedometer showed well in excess of 85 mph; in a moment the Saab would be onto the wide track leading to the village. Time, Bond thought, to give M some warning. He reached for the pen alarm.

At first he imagined it had merely slipped inside his pocket, so often had he checked it. As the stark fact that it was missing penetrated Bond's mind, he glimpsed the lights of another car, far back towards the castle. Mary-Jane's BMW, he would guess, crammed with Caber and the boys.

Bond had to make up his mind in a matter of seconds. The village would have been alerted by this time. He reasoned that the most dangerous path lay straight ahead. The answer would be to take the Saab back along the track which ran parallel to the castle—the way he had come to reconnoitre the previous night. Without lights, the Saab would be difficult to follow and he reckoned that it would not take long to make the road to Shieldaig. A telephone call to the Regent's Park building would bring all hell down upon Murik Castle in a very short time.

Keep the speed up, he thought. Hold her straight, and try for a feint at the village, which was now visible and appeared uncannily close. Bond tried to picture the junction near the kirk. Watch for the signpost and drag the car around.

Without warning a light came on, then another: twin spots from near the kirk; the reception committee. The spots wavered, then homed in on the Saab. Bond started to pump the brakes, changing down. Slow just enough to let them think you're going to run straight through. Make them think the spots are affecting vision. That was the godsend about the Nitefinder.

Bond took in a gulp of air as he saw the first flicker of automatic fire from near the kirk. Then the slow, coloured balls curved towards him—tracer, lazy but deadly. Once again he shoved the Blackhawk through the gunport, stood on the brakes and wrenched at the wheel, slewing the car to one side and blasting off two more rounds as he did so. Then one more shot. That was the Blackhawk empty. He reached for the Browning, clawing it from the shelf as he saw, with some elation, that one of the spots had gone out.

The remaining spot lost him, then caught the Saab again as a second burst of tracer began its arc towards him. Bond squeezed the Browning's trigger in two bursts of two. For a second the firing ceased, and he realized he was driving flat-out towards the village, ears bursting with the noise and the car filled with the acrid reek of cordite. Get in as near as you can, then skid turn onto the other road. At speed it was a dangerous confidence trick. One misjudged action and he could easily run right out of road, or spin the car over onto its back.

He saw the little wooden signpost almost too late. There were figures of people running, as though afraid he would smash into them. Wrenching the wheel and doing an intricate dance between brake and accelerator, Bond went into the violent skid turn. The world seemed to dip and move out of control as the Saab started to slew round, and then he felt a judder as the tyres took hold again. He spun the wheel to the right, put on full power, and began to slide, broadside on, towards the signpost.

The car must have torn the post straight out of the ground. There was a teeth-jarring bump as the nearside door hit the sign. For a second Bond knew he was at a standstill; then he had his foot down again, heaving the wheel to the left. The Saab shuddered, then smoothly picked up speed. Briefly, in the midst of the noise, Bond thought he heard another engine running in time with his own.

He sighed with relief. He was now moving fast up the track which he had followed with such caution the night before. There was no sign of the following lights, which he had assumed to be the BMW. He changed up, feeling confidence grow with every second.

For reassurance he felt down, touching the butt of the Browning and at the same time glancing towards the panel: with the lights off and instruments dimmed, the head-up display was not as clear as normal. When he looked up again he immediately knew he was in trouble. A shape showed through the Nitefinder goggles, above and just ahead. Then the shape moved, splaying a great beam of light across his path, and he heard the engine noise he thought he had imagined back at the turn. The helicopter. He had not counted on that. But there it was, backing away slowly like some animal gently retreating, uncertain of its prey.

Well, if he hit the damned thing it was too bad. Bond did not slow down. The helicopter was dangerously low, yet remained directly in front, still backing away. Then, without warning, it lifted and retreated fast. From directly in front of the Saab came a massive flash and boom. The Saab shook, and Bond felt the inertia-reel harness clamp hold of him. He slammed a foot onto the brake as he felt, with the intuition of experience, that another grenade would follow the first. Certainly the helicopter was coming on.

It came just as he expected—the same manoeuvre, a dipping of the nose, a fast slide up and back. Bond swung the wheel to the right, changed into second, and went off the track to the right as the second large "flash-bang" exploded. His mind was just starting to grapple with the strategy he would need to use against the chopper, when the Saab began to lift its nose.

With the horrific clarity of a dream over which one has no power, Bond realized what had happened. He had been fool enough to do exactly as the helicopter had wanted. The machine was a lure. They had wanted him to go to the right, and at speed. Had not Mary-Jane Mashkin told him about the digging? A new drainage system?

All this flashed through Bond's head as he applied the car's brakes too late. The nose of the Saab reared up, the wheels clawing at empty air. Then the car began to drop forward, bouncing and bumping in a horrible crunching somersault.

In the final moments Bond was buffeted around in his harness, and something, possibly the Blackhawk, caught him on the side of the head. He felt numbness as the red mist came in, with ink in its wake, carrying him floating off into a black impenetrable sea.

"Got him," said Anton Murik with a smile, as the helicopter slowly settled on the heather.

The pilot removed the Nitefinder goggles taken from Bond the previous night. "They work well, these," he said. "Clear as sunlight up to over five hundred feet."

High Frequency

There was a blinding white light. For a moment James Bond imagined that he was still in the Saab, rolling into the ditch. He screwed up his eyes and looked at the woman now coming into focus. It was Mary-Jane Mashkin, standing above him.

"Nothing much wrong with you, James. Just a little bruising."

He tried to get up, but a harness held him tightly. Turning his

head, he saw where he was: in the white-tiled torture chamber.

They had him strapped down on the operating table, and Mary-Jane Mashkin stood beside him wearing a white coat. She smiled comfortably. Behind her were a couple of the laird's heavies.

"Well," Bond tried to sound bright. "I don't feel too bad. If you say I'm OK, why don't you let me get up?"

Anton Murik's voice came soft, and close, in his ear. "I think you have some explaining to do, Mr. Bond. Don't you?"

Bond closed his eyes. "It's getting so a man can't even go out for a night drive without people shooting at him."

"Very witty." Murik sounded anything but amused. "You killed two of my men, Mr. Bond. Making off in secret, with the knowledge you have about my current project, is not the way to keep me as a friend and protector. All previous contracts made with you are cancelled. More to the point, I would like to know your real profession."

Bond's head was almost clear now. He felt some bruising on his body and a dull ache up the right side of his head. Memory flooded back; start concentrating, Bond thought, realizing he would require all possible reserves of physical and mental strength. Aloud, he said, "You know who I am. Bond, James. 259057. Major, retired."

"So," Murik purred, "you accept work from me, and then try to blast yourself out of Murik Castle and the glen. It does not add up, Major Bond. If you *are* Major Bond."

"Got windy," Bond said, trying to sound tired and casual. In fact he was fully aware now, his mind getting sharper every minute.

"Windy?" Murik sneered.

"Fear is not an unknown failing in men. I just thought I would slip away until it was all over."

"I think we should have the truth," Murik snapped. "There is so little time left."

Mary-Jane stepped closer to the table. "I'm a trained psychiatrist," she drawled. "And I have one or two other specialities."

"Proper little Jill-of-all-trades," Bond muttered.

"Don't be frivolous, Bond. She can make it very unpleasant for you." Murik leered at him. "And you should know that we've been through your luggage. You carry very sophisticated devices for a

190

mercenary." He nodded towards Mary-Jane Mashkin, who rolled up Bond's sleeve. In panic, he began to move against the restraining straps, trying to remember the rules for a situation like this.

It was no good. Bond felt the swab being dabbed on his arm: damp, cool, the hint of its smell reaching his nostrils. The panic died, Bond conquering the immediate fear of what would come. Focus. Bond, James. 259057. Major, retired. Now what should he keep in the forefront of his consciousness? Nuclear power: Murik's own subject. Bond concentrated on the reading M had made him do before going on this mission. Just see the book with its diagrams and text. He had to remain alert. There were mental counter-measures to interrogation by drugs, and 007 had been through the whole unpleasant course at what they called the Sadist School.

"A little Mozart, I think," Murik's voice called, away from the table. Mary-Jane Mashkin moved, and Bond winced as he felt the hypodermic needle slide into his arm.

Bond felt his whole body slowly become independent of his mind. The book. See the pages. Far away an orchestra played. Violins, strings and woodwinds, a pleasant sound with a military rhythm to it; then a piano—all far away.

Walking in the park on a summer Sunday, with the band playing. Lavender was there. Holding hands. Children laughing; the ducks and other water fowl. People.

Bond heaved his mind back. Bond, James. What was the next bit? The band played on, and he could smell Lavender's scent as she held his hand tightly. No. No. Bond, James. Major, retired. The book. Nuclear power plants derive their energy from the splitting—or fission—of the uranium isotope U-235. Then Lavender was asking the questions. "James, what do you really do for a living?"

"Bond, James. 259057. Major, retired." He knew that he should not have trusted her.

"Oh, not that rubbish, James, darling. What do you *really* get up to? You've got something to do with nuclear power, haven't you? Are you from the Atomic Research Commission?"

Think, James. Be determined. Beat it. "Nuclear power is a very expensive way to boil water." Do everything they taught you.

"Come on, who are you really?" asked Lavender.

"My name . . ." It wasn't Lavender. The other one was asking the questions. What was her name? Mary-Jane? That was it, Mary-Jane Mashkin. Maybe Dilly was straight after all.

In a drowning pall of dark smoke, Bond fought hard. "Bond, James. 259057. Major, retired," he shouted. "That what you want to know, Mary-Jane?"

Another voice cut through. "He's resisting. Increase the dosage."

"You'll kill him. Try rewards."

Bond's body seemed to slide down an invisible slope, gathering speed. Then something was pressed against his ears. Headphones. Music poured in on him. Beautiful liquid sounds that slowed up his descent. Lord, he was tired. Sleep? Why not? The voice again. "What are your duties?"

"I am . . ." No, James, fight, you silly idiot. "I am 259057 . . . Major, retired . . ."

The voice snapped back, "I want the truth, not that rubbish. When you don't speak the truth, this will happen——"

Bond screamed aloud as noise filled his head. The terrifying blinding noise, the screech and wail. NO . . . No . . . No . . . As suddenly as it started, the horrific, bursting blaze of sound stopped. The soft music returned, then the voice again. "You were sent on a mission, weren't you, Bond?"

"I came here. You invited me." His body started to slip away, the mind floating.

"You made sure I invited you. Who sent you here?"

Slipping. Watch it, James. Then the agony, the screech of noise filling his head, bursting the brain, red in his eyes and the pain sweeping between his ears. His brain would burst; the soundwaves rising higher and higher. Then silence, with only the echoes of pain leaving his head the size of a giant balloon.

"Who sent you here, and what were your instructions?" Sharp. Orders, like the crack of a whip.

No, James. Concentrate. Fight. The book. Bond knew what he was saying, but could not hear it. "A nuclear plant's reactor core is suspended inside a steel vessel with thick walls like a giant pod . . ."

The white noise came in—a flood that swept away his cranium: whining, clawing, scratching, screaming into his very soul. When it

192

finally stopped, Bond was still screaming, teetering on the precipice of sanity.

"Who sent you, Bond? What were you supposed to do?"

"The twelve-foot-long fuel rods are inside the core . . ."

The madness covered him again, then stopped. The drug was now ineffective; for the pain had taken over, and all Bond knew was the terrible aftermath of the noise.

"Damn you, Murik," Bond shouted.

"No." He heard Mary-Jane shout close to his ear. "You'll get nothing now."

"Then we'll take him along for the ride. Dispose of him after the girl."

Bond found it hard to understand what they were saying. The words were there, clear enough, but he was incapable of sorting out the meaning.

"Quite extraordinary," came from the woman. "His mental discipline is amazing. He's either for real—an adventurer of some kind who got frightened—or a very tough professional."

"Get Caber. I want Bond kept safe and well away from the girl. Does she suspect anything?"

Mary-Jane Mashkin was answering, "I don't think so. I think the silly bitch imagines she's in love with him."

"Love! What's love?" spat Murik. "Get him out."

"I'd like tae do it fur permanent." It was Caber's voice, and they were Caber's tree-like arms that picked Bond from the table. Then the weakness came, and he felt the world zoom away from him.

The next time Bond opened his eyes, it was impossible to know for how long he had slept. He was in the east guest room, but it had been changed greatly. Everything movable had been taken out—tables, chairs, even the fitments in the Sleepcentre had gone.

There was a clunk of the electronic locks coming off, and Caber's bulk filled the doorway. "The laird's seen fit tae feed ye." He moved back, allowing Hamish to enter with a tray of cold meats and salads.

"Very good of him," Bond smiled. "Recovered, have we, Caber?"

"It'll be a gey long time afore ye recover, Bond."

"Might I ask a question?"

"Ye may ask; whether I answer'll be up tae me."

"What day is it?"

"Tuesday. Now tak your food. Ye'll no' be bothered agin this night." Caber gave him a look of unconcealed hatred. "But we'll all be off early in the morn." The door closed, and the locks thudded into place.

Bond suddenly realized he was very hungry. He began to tear into the meal. Tuesday, he thought; and they were leaving in the morning—Wednesday. That meant something. Yes, on Wednesday Franco had a date with someone who was to die. Catwalk . . . palace . . . Majorca . . . high-powered air rifle. The pieces of the Meltdown puzzle floated around in his head until dawn.

HIGH UP IN THE BUILDING overlooking Regent's Park, M sat at his desk, looking grave. Bill Tanner was in the room, and "the Opposition" had come calling again in the shape of Sir Richard Duggan. "When was this?" M had just asked.

"Last night—or early this morning, really. About one thirty according to our people." Duggan reported a car chase and a couple of explosions near Murik Castle. "They say your man's car was taken back to the castle this afternoon, and that it looked like a write-off."

"And Franco?"

"FBI lost him yesterday in New York. Gone to ground."

M got up and went to the window, looking down on the evening scene as dusk closed in around them.

"Your man was supposed to be in touch with my people. I hope you're not letting him operate on our patch, M."

"You're absolutely certain he didn't follow Franco?"

"Pretty sure."

"Well, that can only mean he's being detained against his will." 007 knew the score. He would make contact as soon as it was humanly possible.

"Do you think Special Branch should go in with a warrant?"

M whirled around. "On what grounds? That an officer of my service is missing? That he was sent to take a look at what was going on between the Laird of Murcaldy and an international terrorist? That's no way. If Anton Murik is involved in something shady, then it'll come to light soon enough. I would suggest that you try to keep

194

your own teams on watch. I have a lot of confidence in the man I've
sent in and I can assure you that if he does start to operate, it will
either be to warn your surveillance team or take action out of the
country."

When Duggan had gone, M turned to his chief-of-staff. "Didn't
like the sound of the car being smashed up."

"007's smashed up cars before, sir. All we can do is wait. I'm sure
he'll come up with something."

"Well, he's taking his time about it," M snorted. "Just hope he's
not loafing around enjoying himself, that's all."

Gone Away

As he was sitting towards the rear of the aircraft, it was impossible
for Bond to follow the flight path. Most of the time they had been
above layers of cloud; though he was fairly certain that he had
caught a glimpse of Paris through a wide gap among the cumulus
about an hour after takeoff.

Now, hunched between two of Murik's muscular young men, he
watched the executive jet's wing tilt. Craning forward, Bond tried to
get a better view from the small window: the horizon tipping over,
and the sight of a coastline far away. A flat plain, circled by
mountains; beaches, and a string of white buildings; then, inland,
knots of houses, a sprawl of marshy-looking land and, for a second
only, a larger, old town. Memories flicked through the card index of
his mind. He knew that view. He had been here before. Where?
They were losing altitude, turning against the mountains, inland.

Lavender sat at a window, forward, hemmed in by one of Murik's
private army. Caber's bulk seemed to fill the aisle as he bent
forward, taking instructions from Murik, who sat with Mary-Jane in
a comfortable office area just behind the flight-deck door. As for
Lavender, Bond had been allowed no contact with her, though she
had looked at him with eyes that seemed to cry out for help, or beg
forgiveness. Bond could not make up his mind which.

The journey had started on the dot of eight o'clock, when Caber
and his men arrived at the east guest room. They led Bond through

195

the servants' quarters to the rear door, where he was handcuffed and shackled between two men. Outside what was obviously the tradesman's entrance a small man loitered near a van. Faded gold lettering along the sides proclaimed that it belonged to Eric MacKenzie, Baker and Confectioner, Murcaldy. The baker's van; it was the ideal way to remove Bond without drawing any attention.

He was dragged quickly to the rear of the van. Caber was the last of Bond's guards to climb in, pulling the doors behind him and locking the catch from the inside. The giant of a man gave a quick order for Bond to stay silent, and the van started up.

It was not difficult to detect that they were making a straight-forward journey from the castle to the village, for the direction was plain, and the changes in road surface could be felt in the bumping of the van. Finally it started to slow down, then made a painful right-hand turn as though negotiating a difficult entrance. The van crawled to a stop and the doors were opened. The telltale smell of freshly baked bread pervaded the atmosphere outside. They were in MacKenzie's yard.

Parked beside them was a dark-blue truck with the words Security International stencilled in white on both sides. It looked solid and most secure, with its grilled windows, thick doors, and reinforced bumpers.

Bond was now bundled into the back of the security truck. This time Caber did not get in. The doors closed with a heavy thud, and one of the men to whom Bond was handcuffed operated the bolts on the inside.

There were uncomfortable wooden benches battened to either side of the interior, and Bond was forced onto one of these, still flanked by his guards. There were no windows.

The slow, uncomfortable journey lasted for almost six hours and it was nearly three in the afternoon when the doors of the truck were unbolted and opened. A sharp breeze cut into the truck, and Bond felt they were probably on an area of open ground. Again it was impossible to tell, for the rear of the truck had been backed up to a small concrete building, only a pace or so from a pair of open doors, now fully extended.

Inside the building they led him along a narrow passage

with, he noted, a slight downward slope. Then into a windowless room where, at last, the handcuffs were removed. Food was brought—sandwiches and coffee—and one of the guards remained with him, still impassive, but with his jacket drawn back from time to time so the butt of a snub-nosed Smith & Wesson .38 was visible.

From the moment of departure from the castle, Bond's mind hardly left the subject of a possible breakaway. This, however, was no time to try anything—locked away in a solidly built bunker, in an unknown location, kept close with armed men. Bond had been heartened by one item of his clothing they had returned to him— his thick leather belt, the secrets of which had not been discovered.

At around four o'clock there were noises from above—a helicopter very low over the building, chopping down for a landing. Then, a few minutes later, Caber entered with the other guards. "Ye'll be joining the laird now," he ordered Bond. "It's only a wee walk, so ye'll not be needing the irons. But I warn ye: any funny business, and ye'll be scattered to the four winds." Caber sounded as if he would be more than happy to do the scattering personally.

Bond was marched up the passage and through the door. The security truck had gone, and they were standing on the edge of a small airfield. A couple of Piper Cubs and an Aztec stood nearby.

To the left Bond saw the helicopter, which he presumed was from Murik Castle. In front of them, at the end of a runway, a sleek executive jet shivered as if in anticipation of flight, its motors running on idle. It looked like a very expensive toy in its glossy cream livery with gold lettering, which read Aldan Aerospace, Inc. Bond recalled the company's name in the dossier on Anton Murik which M had shown him.

Caber nodded them towards the jet and, as they walked the few yards, Bond turned his head. The board on the control tower read Aldan Aerospace, Inc. Flying Club: PRIVATE.

Anton Murik and Mary-Jane Mashkin were already seated, as was Lavender with her minder, when they climbed into the jet. The first pair did not even turn around to look at their captive, who was placed with a guard on either side, as before. A steward passed down the aisle, checking seatbelts, and it was at this point that Lavender turned to lock eyes with Bond. During the flight she repeated the action several times, on two occasions adding a wan smile.

They had hardly settled down when the door was slammed shut. Seconds later the aircraft began to roll, rocketing off the runway like a single-seater fighter and climbing rapidly into cloud.

Now they were reaching the end of the journey, with the sun low on the horizon. Bond still peered out, trying to place their location. Then, suddenly, he recognized the long, flat breast of the mountain to their left. The Canigou. No wonder he recognized it, having spent many happy holidays in the area. Roussillon—that plain circled with mountains, and bordering on the sea. They were in France, and the old town he had spotted was Perpignan, the ancient seat of the Kings of Majorca. He should have spotted the towers of the vast fortress which had once been the palace.

Roussillon? Roussillon Fashions. The blurred and sporadic conversation, overheard after the bug had been dislodged from Murik's desk, came back to Bond. It was down there, at the mediaeval palace of the Kings of Majorca, that Franco was to administer death through a high-powered air rifle on Wednesday night—tonight— the day before Operation Meltdown. The target? Bond knew with fair certainty who the target would be. Whatever the risk, he must take the first chance to get free.

They were on the final approach to Perpignan airport, only three or four miles from the town itself. The engines flamed out and the little jet bustled along the main runway, turning to taxi out towards the perimeter of the airfield. When the aircraft finally came to a halt, the guard next to Bond placed a firm restraining hand on his arm. The top brass were obviously going to disembark first.

As Murik came level with Bond his bulldog face split into a grin. "I hope you enjoyed the flight, Mr. Bond. We thought it better to have you with us, where we can keep an eye on you during this important phase. You will be well looked after."

Bond did not smile. "A hearty breakfast for the condemned man?" he asked.

"Something like that, Mr. Bond. We shall see you anon, then," said Murik, and he was off, with Mary-Jane following.

For the first time Bond was one hundred per cent certain about

198

Lavender. He looked up, giving her a broad, encouraging grin as she passed down the aircraft, her escort's hand clamped hard onto her arm. A flicker of nervousness showed in her eyes, then the warmth returned, as though Bond was willing courage and strength into the girl.

They were parked alongside a huge hangar, with adjacent office buildings, topped by a neon sign that read Aldan Aerospace (France), Inc. The guards acted like sheepdogs, closing in around Bond, trying to make the walk from the aircraft look as natural as possible. The hangar and offices were no more than a few yards from the perimeter fence of the airport, where several ancient Britannias rested, each with the legend European Air Services running above the long row of windows. The fence was low, and broken in a couple of places. Beyond, a railway track with overhead wiring ran straight past; behind that, a major road slashed with cars moving fast.

At full stretch he could be away and through that fence in a matter of thirty seconds. Thirty seconds. The muscular Scots would be prompt in their reaction. Yet Bond was almost hypnotized by the idea of escaping, should the opportunity present itself.

It was to happen sooner than he expected. They were within a few paces of the office doors when, from around the corner, in a flurry of conversation and laughter, there appeared a small group of men in uniform. They were close enough for Bond to make out the letters EAS entwined in gold on their caps: European Air Services. A fragment of English floated from the conversation as the group strolled lazily towards the Britannias.

Murik and Mary-Jane were almost at the office door, accompanied by one of the guards; behind them, Lavender was being led firmly by her minder, and Caber walked alone between her and Bond, still flanked by his two men.

It would be one of his biggest gambles. But if Murik's men could be shocked into holding fire or chase, even for a few seconds, he might just do it. Bond weighed the chances. Would Murik wish to call attention to himself and his party? Would they risk other people being hurt, killed even? It was a matter of audacity and nerve.

Later, Bond thought the train probably made up his mind; the sound of a horn in the distance, and the sight of a long train snaking its way along the tracks, about a mile off. He slowed, dropping back a couple of paces, causing one of the guards to nudge him on. Angrily, Bond shoved the man. "You can stop that," he said very loudly. "I'm not interested in your bloody meeting." Then, looking towards the group of aircrew, he raised his voice and shouted, "Good grief," already taking one step away from the nearest guard.

Bond was quick, moving in long strides towards the group of uniformed men. "Johnny," he shouted. "Johnny Manderson: what the hell are you doing here?" The uniformed men paused, turning towards him. One smiled broadly; the others looked puzzled.

Bond heard Murik hiss, "Get him. For God's sake. Take care." But, by this time, Bond had reached the group, his hand stretched out to one of the aircrew, who in turn put out his hand in a reflex action of cordiality, beginning to say something about a mistake.

"It's good to see you, Johnny." Bond pumped his hand wildly, spinning around to put the man, as a shield, between Murik's people and himself. Caber and two of the guards were advancing warily, hands inside their jackets and, doubtless, on the butts of their weapons.

Bond dropped his voice. "Terribly sorry," he said, grinning. "A little problem about non-payment of dues. Watch out for those blokes. Hoods, the lot of them. Must dash."

Using the group of uniformed men for cover, he was off, going flat out in a low crouch towards one of the jagged gaps in the fence. There were shouts from behind him, but no shots. Only the sound of pounding feet, and an argument of sorts between Caber's men and the aircrew. Bond dived through the gap, sliding down the small embankment onto the railway track—the train now bearing down on him, its roar shaking the gravel. If there was going to be shooting, it would happen in the next few seconds, before the train reached them.

There was no time for further reflection. It was now or never, in front of the train looming above him. Bond chanced it, leaping in two long strides across the track, and doubling his body into a ball, rolling as he reached the far side. The engine almost brushed his back as it passed with a great *parp* of its horn.

In an instant Bond was on his feet running down the far bank towards the Route Nationale, his thumb already up in the hitch-hiker's position. Luck was still with him. As he reached the edge of the road he saw a small, battered pick-up truck pulled into the side. Two men who looked like farm workers were being dropped off, and there were four others in the back, shouting farewells to their comrades.

"Going into Perpignan?" Bond shouted in French.

The driver, a cigarette stuck unlit in the corner of his mouth, nodded from the window.

"A lift?" Bond asked. The driver shrugged, and one of the men in the back called for him to jump up. Within seconds they were edging into traffic, Bond thanking providence for his good fortune. He sneaked a peep towards the airport but there was no sign of Caber or the others.

No, Bond thought, they would be running for cars—Murik would be well organized here. His men would already be taking short cuts into Perpignan to head him off.

Bond asked the time, and one of the workmen told him it was four minutes past nine. "We'll have to move if we're going to see the fun," the man said.

Fun? Bond explained he had just come in on a flight. He was very late, and had to meet a man in Perpignan.

"All men are in Perpignan tonight. If you can find them," laughed one of the workers. "It's the fête."

"*Vieux Saint Jean*," said another.

A third gave a bellow, lifting his arms histrionically, "*La Flamme arrive en Perpignan.*"

They all laughed. Bond suddenly remembered that he had been here before for the fête. Every town in the Mediterranean had its own rituals, its battle of flowers, carnivals. In Perpignan it was the great feast of St. John, when the whole town was crammed to the gills and there was dancing in the streets, singing, fireworks, spectacle—the festivities started when bonfires were lit by a flame brought by runners from the Canigou mountain. He could not have arrived at a better time. There would be crowd cover until the early hours: and with luck, enough breathing space to find a way of making contact with M.

Fête and Fate

They dropped him off on the corner of the Place de la Résistance, which was already full of people standing shoulder to shoulder, pushing along the pavements. Bond stepped back into the crowd. It was some years since he had been here, and first he had to get his bearings. Directly in front of him there were three great bonfires ready to be lit. To the left he saw a bridge spanning the well-kept canal, banked here by green lawns and flowers.

A platform had been built over the bridge and was even now crowded with musicians. A master of ceremonies spoke into an uncertain microphone, telling the crowds about the next *sardana* they would be playing, keeping things going until the flame arrived to ignite both bonfires and excitement. The musicians burst into music: the steady bray of pipe, drum and brass to which the *sardana* is danced. The dancers, some in traditional costume, others in suits or jeans and shirts, formed their circles, clasping hands held high, and launched into the light, intricate foot movements: a dance of peace and joy.

The crowds began to thicken, and the music thumped on, the circles of dancers growing wider, or forming into smaller groups— young and old, impeccable in their timing, and dancing as though in a trance.

Bond took a deep breath and began to move through the crowd. He had to move fast to telephone London, and for that he would need money. Above all else, he had to be watchful, for Murik's men could be already among the crowds, their eyes peeled for him; and if they saw him, Bond knew what he could expect. Most likely they would use dirks, sliding the instruments of death through his ribs, covered by the crowd. There was no point in going to the police— not on a night like this, without identification. They would simply lock him up and perhaps tomorrow, when it was too late, telephone the British Consul.

He had just started to move when a large black Mercedes swept into the Place, only to be halted by a gendarme, who signalled that the road was about to be closed. The driver spoke to the policeman in French, then turned to the occupants of the car. Bond's heart missed a beat. Next to the driver sat Caber, while the three other big Scotsmen were crammed into the rear.

Caber got out, three of the men joining him, while the gendarme made noises suggesting they get the car out of the way. Bond tried to shrink back into the crowd as he watched Caber giving orders. The men dispersed—Caber and two of them crossing the Place, the last diving into the crowd a little to Bond's right. Bond moved slowly along the fringe of the laughing, chattering crowd.

He kept looking back and then scanning the way ahead and across the road, slowly making his way towards the towering Castillet—the old city gateway. He was looking for a street he recalled from previous visits, near an ancient Place almost entirely covered by tables from the cafés. He reached the Castillet and saw another bonfire waiting to be lit. A great circle of dancers around it was going through the intricate patterns, slightly out of time to the music, which was distorted on the night air. On the far side of the circle he spotted one of Caber's men searching faces in the throng.

Bond held back, waiting until he was certain the man was looking away from him; then he dodged nimbly through the crowd until he found a clear path through the archway of the Castillet itself. He was about to cross the road on the far side when he had to leap into a shop doorway. There, walking slowly, scanning both sides of the street, was the giant Caber. Bond shrank back into the doorway, holding his breath, willing the Scot not to see him.

After what seemed an age, the giant walked on, still scanning faces constantly. Bond edged out of the doorway and continued up the street. Crossing over through the thinning crowd, Bond arrived at his goal—Perpignan's Loge de Mer, once the great financial centre of the town. The old Bourse with its grey stone walls, high arched windows and intricate carving had now been given over to a different kind of financial transaction, for it was a café. The old marble pavement was a litter of tables and chairs and people taking refreshment before joining in the festivities.

Bond walked straight into the corner Bar Tabac and asked for the *toilette.* The bartender, busy filling orders, nodded to the back of the bar. The room was empty, and Bond went into the first *cabinet*, locking the door behind him and starting work almost before the bolt slid home.

Quickly his hands moved to his belt clasp—a solid, wide U-shaped buckle with a single thick brass spike, normal enough until you twisted hard. Six turns released the spike, revealing a small steel knife blade within. Bond removed the blade, handling it with care, and inserted the cutting edge into an almost invisible crack in the buckle. With hard downwards pressure the buckle came apart, opening on a pair of tiny hinges set at the points where it joined the leather. This was also a casing for a tiny handle, into which the blade could be screwed. Equipped with this weapon, Bond pulled the belt from his waistband and began to measure the length. Each section of the double-stitched leather contained a small amount of emergency European currency in notes. In the fourth section was what Bond needed: French francs.

The small blade went through the stitching like a hot knife through butter, opening up the two-inch section to reveal a couple of thousand francs—just under two hundred pounds sterling, the way the market was running—in various denominations.

He dismantled the knife, fitted it away again, and thrust the money into his pocket. In the bar he bought a packet of Disque Bleu for change; then sauntered out into the Place. His target was the post office: a fast alert to M, then on with the other business as quickly as possible.

He continued to mingle with the crowd, keeping to the right of the circling *sardana* dancers. He crouched slightly, for Murik's man was still in place, his head and eyes roving, pausing from time to time. Bond prepared to push himself into the middle of a group heading in his direction. Then, suddenly, the music stopped. The crowd stilled in anticipation, and the amplifier system crackled into life. "My friends"—the announcer could not disguise his emotion—"the flame, carried by the brave young people of Perpignan, has arrived."

There was a great cheer as a group of young girls in short white skirts came running, the crowds parting at their approach. About eight of them, each with an unlit brand held aloft, flanked the girl who carried a great blazing torch. The girls waited until the torch was set to a spot in the middle of the bonfire. The tinder took hold, and flames began to shoot from the fire. The girls lowered their own torches to take flame from the fire before jogging away in the direction of the Castillet entrance.

The crowd started to move, backing off to get a better view. Bond moved with them. It was only a matter of turning to his left and he would be at the post office within minutes.

The bonfires in the Place went up, other groups of girls having jogged down the far side of the canal to do their work. Another roar from the crowd, and the band started up again. Before he knew what was happening, Bond was seized by both hands, a girl clinging to each, giggling and laughing at him. In a second, Bond was locked into part of the large circle of *sardana* dancers. Desperately, he tried to follow the steps so as not to draw attention to himself, now an easy target for Caber and his men.

Then, just as suddenly as it started, the *sardana* stopped, all eyes turning towards the Castillet, where the girls, with their blazing brands held high, occupied the spaces on the battlements. A rocket sped into the air, showering the sky with clusters of brilliant fire. There followed three more muted explosions, and a great flood of light appeared to rise from the battlements. The effect was as though the whole of the Castillet was on fire, gouts of crimson smoke rising from the turrets and battlements.

Bond at last freed himself from the two girls, looked around carefully, and set off again, pushing and shoving through the wall of people whose eyes could not leave the dazzling spectacle. Soon he was walking fast towards the less-populated streets and in the direction he remembered the post office to be.

The noise, music and fireworks were behind him now. Within a few minutes he recognized the landmark of the Place Arago with its palm trees, shops and attractive bars. The post office was only a minute away, in a street straight ahead to the left of the canal. At last Bond saw the line of open telephone booths, each dimly lit and empty—a row of grey electronic sentries. He counted out one-franc pieces from the change in his pocket: just enough to make the call, if the duty officer allowed him to speak without interruption.

Swiftly he inserted a coin into the slot and dialled the

number of the Regent's Park building. In the far distance he was still aware of the whoosh and crackle of the fireworks. Almost holding his breath, Bond heard the ringing tone and the receiver being lifted.

"Duty watchman. Transworld Exports," came the voice.

"007 for M . . ." Bond began, then stopped as he felt the hard steel against his ribs, and a voice say quietly, "Oot fast, or I'll put a bullet into ye."

It was the watcher who he had seen standing near the Castillet. Bond sighed.

"Fast," the voice repeated. "Put down yon telephone." The man was standing very close, pushed up behind Bond.

Primary rule: never approach a man too close with a pistol. Bond felt a twinge of regret for the man as he first turned slowly, his right hand lowering the telephone receiver, then fast, swinging around to the left as he brought the handset smashing into the Scot's face. Murik's man actually had time to get one shot away before he went down. The bullet tore through Bond's jacket before ricochetting its way through the telephone booths.

Bond's right foot connected hard with his attacker's face as the man fell. There was a groan, then silence from the figure spread-eagled on the pavement outside the open booth. The handset was wrecked. Bond swore as he rammed it back onto the rests. He bent over the unconscious figure to pick up the weapon. Cheeky devil, he thought. The gun was Bond's own Browning, obviously retrieved from the Saab.

Bond pushed the Browning into his waistband, and set off at a brisk walk, crossing the road and returning in the direction from which he had come.

At the Place Arago he stopped for traffic, looking across the road at an elegant poster prominently displayed on a wall. ROUSSILLON HAUTE COUTURE. GRAND SHOW OF THE NEW ROUSSILLON COLLECTION ON THE NIGHT OF THE FESTIVAL OF OLD ST. JOHN. PALACE OF THE KINGS OF MAJORCA. ELEVEN P.M. Eleven o'clock tonight. He gazed wildly around him. A clock over a jeweller's shop showed it was five minutes past eleven already.

Franco . . . the catwalk . . . air rifle . . . death with a gelatine capsule . . . Now. M would have to wait. Bond took a deep breath and started to run, trying to recall from his previous visits the quickest way to the ancient Palace. If he was right, the girl would die very soon. If he was right; and if he did not get there in time to prevent it.

Death in Many Fashions

The Palais des Rois de Majorque stands on the higher ground in the southern part of Perpignan. The original palace was built on a vast knoll in the eleventh century and was later walled in with the citadel, which rises to a height of almost three hundred feet.

Bond had visited the palace several times before and knew that the approach is made up of flights of zig-zagging steps leading to the main entrance and a large cobbled courtyard. Above the entrance is the King's Gallery, while to the left are apartments closed to sightseers. On the right stands the great Throne Hall, while opposite the entrance runs a cloister with a gallery above it. Behind the cloister stands the lower Queen's Chapel, and above that, off the gallery, is situated the magnificent Royal Chapel.

Above the two chapels the keep climbs upwards to a small bell-tower. This is the extent of the palace usually on view to the public. Bond knew, however, that there was a further courtyard behind the keep. This area was used as a depot for military vehicles and the surrounding buildings as billets for some of the local garrison; the bulk of whom lived below the citadel, in the Caserne Maréchal Joffre.

During his last visit to the area—on a skiing holiday in the nearby mountains some three years before—Bond had fallen in with a French army captain from the garrison. One night the captain had suggested drinks in his quarters, which lay within the second courtyard of the palace. They had driven to Perpignan, and the Frenchman had shown Bond how easy it was to penetrate the barracks by entering through a narrow alley off the Rue Waldeck-Rousseau and from there following the transport road which climbed steeply to the top of the citadel. It was then possible to enter the rear courtyard through a tiny gap in the long terrace of living quarters forming the rear side of the courtyard.

So it was to the palace that he was now running as if the plague was at his heels. He knew there was little chance of gaining admittance to the main courtyard by the normal route. Concerts were held there, and he had few doubts that this was where the fashion show was being staged, with the audience seated in the cobbled yard, or occupying the galleries.

It took nearly fifteen minutes for Bond to find the dusty transport track. He forced himself to start the gruelling climb. Above he could see the burst of light from the main courtyard, while music and applause floated sporadically down on the still air. The fashion show was in full swing.

At last he reached the rear of the buildings that formed the very far end of the second courtyard. Far away fireworks still lit up the night in great starbursts of colour, shooting comets of blue, gold and red against the clear sky. It took a few minutes to find the gap which he squeezed through, hoping that the bulk of the garrison would be down in the town celebrating with the locals.

At last Bond stood inside the dimly-lit courtyard. The large gateway was to his left, with a row of six heavy military trucks standing in line to its right. Facing the gates in single file were four armoured troop carriers as though in a readiness position. Few lights came from the barrack blocks which made up three sides of the yard. But Bond did not doubt that the carrier crews would be in duty rooms nearby.

Keeping to the shadow of the walls, he moved quickly to the archway which led to the main palace. As he stepped into the passage he was able to see up the wide tunnel, the darkness giving way to a picture of colour and activity. If his memory was correct, a small doorway lay to the right of the tunnel, which would take him up a flight of steps and out onto the gallery in front of the Royal Chapel. He was amazed at the lack of security so far, and could only suppose that Murik's men were still in the town searching for him.

Within seconds he had found the doorway and the short flight of steps leading to the gallery. It was lined with people who had obviously paid well for the privilege of viewing the fashion show from this vantage point. People stood at the high arched windows of the Throne Hall to his left and at those of the former royal apartments on the right of the courtyard. Across the yard, the King's Gallery was also crowded; and below, in the great yard itself, the show was in full swing. The main entrance led to a scaffold of carpeted steps, arranged to accommodate a small orchestra. A similarly carpeted catwalk stretched out from directly below where Bond stood, probably starting at the edge of the cloister in front of the Queen's Chapel. It ran the length of the courtyard, to end only a short distance from the orchestra, and was flanked by rows of those small gilt chairs so beloved by the organizers of major fashion shows the world over.

Murik's organization had certainly drawn a full house, well-heeled and immaculately dressed. Bond caught sight of Murik himself in the first row to the left of the catwalk, sitting, resplendent in a white dinner jacket and maroon bow tie. Next to him was Mary-Jane Mashkin, swathed in white silk, a necklace sparkling at her throat.

The setting for the Roussillon show was undoubtedly magnificent. But it had an ambience that did not match others Bond had attended. It was a minute or so before he realized that the difference lay in the music. Looking closer, he saw that the musicians were using copies of early, probably fifteenth or six-teenth-century instruments—lutes, viols, citterns, early flutes, pipes and tambours. The noise they produced was pleasing enough: simple, dance-like, romantic, with a strong melody. To judge from the appearance of the models following each other on and off the catwalk, this year's collection had undoubtedly been created to reflect mediaeval costume and patterns, and the music was pro-vided to match the dress designs.

The materials were silks, brocades and chiffons, and the designs ranged from long-waisted dresses with wide drooping sleeves to elaborate costumes incorporating trains and surcoats. The colours were dazzling, the shapes enchanting, as they flared, rustled and floated around the models. Bond reflected that these clothes were, like so many collections of *haute couture*, the stuff that dreams were made of, rather than the clothing of everyday life.

Lavender was just leaving the catwalk, clad in a loose gold creation of multi-layered chiffon, with a short embroidered surcoat dropping ecclesiastically in front and behind. Bond had to use a surge of willpower to drag himself from his reverie. It must be well after eleven thirty by now. Somewhere Franco was waiting with a pellet of death, which he intended to use before the fashion show had ended.

Bond's eyes moved carefully over the crowds up to the roofs. There seemed to be no place for a man to hide. Unless . . . the answer came to him, and he glanced upwards, towards the gallery ceiling. Directly behind him lay the Royal Chapel. Above that, the keep rose, topped with the small bell-tower. Above the keep, he knew, there was a loft that had once served as the ringing chamber. This ringing chamber had at least three unglazed windows, all of which looked straight down into the courtyard.

The door to the keep was set into the wall, to the right of the Royal Chapel door, not more than a dozen paces from where he stood. Bond whirled round and strode towards the door, with its great ring latch. He tried the ring and it moved smoothly, soundless and well oiled. Gently he pulled the door open and stepped through. Bond started to climb a narrow stone spiral of stairs, as quietly and quickly as he dared in the darkness. His thigh muscles felt weak after the exertions of the last half hour or so; but he plodded on silently, cheered by occasional shafts of light on the landings in the keep. As he neared the top of the climb, Bond felt sweat trickling from his hairline and down the insides of his arms. Slowly he took out the Browning and slipped off the safety catch.

Holding his breath, Bond reached the topmost steps, his head just below the wooden-planked floor of the ringing chamber. Putting all his weight on the right foot, Bond slowly lifted his body so that his eyes came just above floor level.

Franco was at right angles to him, lying in the classic prone position of a marksman. The killer's concentration seemed to be centred completely on the scene below, his eyes close to a sniperscope fitted on top of the powerful Anschütz .22 air rifle, his finger on the trigger, ready to fire. Bond leaped up the remaining steps, calling out softly but sharply, "Franco! Don't shoot!"

The marksman's head swivelled round as Bond heard the dull plop from the air rifle. In the same second, Bond flung himself onto the prone figure of Franco, landing with a crash across the marksman's shoulders. In a flash, lying spread-eagled, James Bond took in the scene below, looking from Franco's viewpoint.

Lavender Peacock was alone in the centre of the catwalk, pirouetting in magnificent scarlet which drooped in long folds, like a crimson waterfall, around her body. Slightly to her left and behind her, Anton Murik sat partly turned in his chair, frozen for a moment, looking towards Mary-Jane Mashkin who had half-risen, one hand at her throat, the other like a claw to her chest. Almost exactly in line with Lavender, she was doubling forward, and, in what seemed like slow motion, she teetered, hovered, and then pitched headlong among the chairs.

Underneath Bond, Franco was struggling to free himself from 007's grip. "*Merda!* I hit the wrong one. You'll . . ." His voice evaporated in a hiss of air as he let his muscles relax, then arched his back and jerked his legs to dislodge his assailant. Bond was taken by surprise and was thrown off, his shoulder thudding against the wall on the far side of the chamber. Franco was on his feet in a second, his hand dropping to his hip and coming away with a small revolver. Bond, winded from the throw, levered himself from the wall and kicked wildly at the terrorist's hand, loosening his hold on the gun. It was enough to send Franco weaving and ducking down the narrow spiral stairs.

The staircase would be a deathtrap for either of them, and no place for a shooting match. Bond started after the terrorist, glancing quickly down into the courtyard as he went. A small huddle of people were gathered around where he had seen Mary-Jane fall. Lavender had come off the catwalk, and one of Murik's guard stood very close to her. Caber was also there, with Murik apparently shouting orders to him.

Bond waited at the top of the stairs until he was certain Franco had passed the first landing. Then he began the difficult descent, the Browning held in front of him, at the ready.

Franco was being just as careful. Bond could hear him pausing at each landing, before quickly negotiating the next spiral. At last

Bond heard the door close below, and took the last section of stairs in a dangerous rush, grabbing at the door, pushing the Browning out of sight and stepping out into the gallery, where people were craning over into the courtyard. Franco was just ahead, making for the small flight of steps that would bring him into the archway through which Bond had entered the palace. Bond went after his quarry, but by the time he reached the archway, there was no one to be seen.

There was silence in the rear courtyard; Bond could see the shapes of the heavy trucks lined up along the wall near the gate to his far right. Franco was there, though; Bond could almost smell him, lurking in the shadows, or behind the line of troop carriers.

Slowly, Bond began to crab his way along the wall to his right, deciding that Franco would most likely have made for the cover of the vehicles. Now he must out-think Franco. This man was clever, a terrorist who, in his career, had passed through whole dragnets. Eventually he would have to run a long way, for his contract had gone awry in the most deadly manner. A gelatine capsule, Bond thought. That had been the missile, whose thin coating had burst on impact, injecting something into the victim's bloodstream. It would have to be very fast-acting, for Mary-Jane had collapsed within seconds.

It had been meant for Lavender. Bond had no doubt about that. Now Franco would know that the full might of Murik's private forces would be out to hunt him down.

He was getting close to the first truck. If Franco was hidden there he would certainly keep his nerve, holding back a natural desire to be rid of his pursuer by chancing a shot which could only call attention to his position.

But Bond had misread the hunted man. The shot came directly from beside the rearmost troop carrier, a single round, passing like an angry hornet past Bond's ear. Dropping to the ground, Bond rolled towards the trucks parked against the wall, coming to a stop beside the great, heavy rear offside wheel of the first truck. He had the Browning up, pointing towards the flash from the shot.

Once more Bond set himself the task of out-thinking his enemy. What would he do in that situation? The trucks were at right angles to the little line of armoured troop carriers facing the gate. Bond thought he would have moved down to the second carrier, protected by its armour, and then skipped across the gap to the truck behind which Bond was sheltering. If he was right Franco should at this moment be coming around this very truck and trying to take Bond from the rear.

Crouched low, Bond silently crossed the few yards' gap between his truck and the rear troop carriers. Whirling around, he dropped onto one knee and waited for Franco's figure to emerge from the cover which he had just relinquished.

This time his thinking was right. Bond heard nothing but saw the shape of the hunted man as he carefully felt his way around the bonnet of the big truck, hoping to come upon his opponent from behind. Bond remained like a statue, the Browning an extension of his arms, held in a vice with both hands, and pointing directly towards the shadow that was Franco. Bond was staking his life on his own stillness, yet the terrorist detected something. With a sudden move, the man dived to the ground, firing twice as he did so.

Bond held his ground. Franco's shots had gone wide, and the target remained in line with the Browning's barrel. Bond fired with steady care: four shots in quick succession.

There was no cry or moan. Franco simply reared up, the head and trunk of his body arching into a bow from the ground. The force of the shots slewed him in a complete circle, then pushed him back along the ground as though wrenched by an invisible wire.

Bond could smell the death—in his head rather than nostrils. Then he became aware of lights coming on, running feet, shouts and activity. He sprinted towards the minute gap between the far buildings, and so down the dusty track to the Caserne Maréchal Joffre. When he reached the Caserne, Bond slowed down. Always walk with purpose, as though it was your right to be where you were. He stepped with a smile into the Rue Waldeck-Rousseau. He was home and dry: the street was empty.

Bond had walked four paces when the piercing whistle came from nearby. For a second he thought it was a police whistle. Then he recognized it as a human sound, the kind of noise made to call in hounds, dogs, or other beasts. Now it brought in the Mercedes, lights blazing. A pair of steel-like hands took him from the rear, pinioning his arms to his sides and pressing so that pain shot down to his fingers. The Browning dropped to the pavement.

"I suppose ye got Franco, then. But it'll do ye nae bluddy guid for yersel, Bond," Caber whispered in his ear. "The laird's mor'n a mite upset—and wi' good reason. I doubt he has some grand plans for ye."

The car came alongside and Caber propelled Bond into the back seat as soon as the door was opened.

A Watched Plot

M sat grey-faced, listening to the tape for the sixth time. "It's him all right." He looked up and Bill Tanner nodded. M turned to the duty officer. "And the number?" he asked.

The telephone equipment at the Regent's Park Building was the most sophisticated in the country. Not only were all incoming calls monitored and taped, but a printout including both the words spoken and the number from which the call had been dialled, was available almost immediately.

The duty officer shifted in his chair. "It's French. We're sure of that because of the code." He was a young man, in his first year of duty. He sighed. "As to its origin . . . well . . ."

"Well?" M's eyes flashed angrily.

"They're cooperating, of course, but at this time of night . . ."

"I know," Bill Tanner cut in. "It *is* tricky, sir. But I'll go off, with your permission, and try to ginger them up."

"You do that, Tanner." M's grey eyes showed no emotion as he picked up his red telephone. "It's time Duggan's people did something positive. Time for them to go into that damned castle. It's safe enough now."

"I SHOULDA FINISHED yon man off long ago, Laird." Caber spoke softly. Everyone around the Laird of Murcaldy had become quiet, almost reverent. A death in the family, Bond thought grimly.

Anton Murik looked shaken—if anything a shade shrunken in

214

height. "I think not." He looked hard at the huge Scot. "A quick breaking of the neck or an accurate bullet's really too good for him now, Caber. When the time comes . . ." He gave a thin smile.

They were in a comfortable room, fitted simply with stripped pine desk, table and chairs. Bond sat shackled by wrists and ankles. He knew they were inside the Aldan Aerospace offices at the airport, but there were no windows to this room.

The laird dismissed Caber and sat, looking at Bond, for a long time. Then he passed a hand over his forehead wearily. "You must forgive me, Mr. Bond. I have been at the hospital, and with the police for some time."

"The Franco business?" Bond asked.

"In a way." Murik gave a bitter little laugh and repeated, "In a way. You did it then, Bond. Finished off Franco."

"There was no option. Even though you had cancelled my contract."

"Yes." The laird gave a small sigh, almost of regret. "Unhappily you have not only interfered a little early, but caused me great grief. Franco's death is, I gather, being treated simply as some gangland vendetta. They have yet to identify him." He sighed again. "The common flatworm," he muttered. *"Leptoplana tremellaris.* It seems strange that my dear Mary-Jane has perished at the hands of a worm. We had spent many years together, Mr. Bond. Now you have been the cause of her death."

Bond asked coolly if Murik would have mourned greatly had the death been that of his intended victim.

"Not in the least," Murik flared. "She is a useless little strumpet. Mary-Jane was a brilliant scientist . . ." He lapsed into silence. Then he repeated, "The common flatworm. There's no getting away from it, Franco was a clever devil; an organizer of ingenuity and a killer of even greater skill. He explained it to me, Bond. A very small amount of an extract removed from the flatworm's skin will bring on a heart attack in a matter of seconds."

Bond asked if the authorities suspected anything. No, not a thing Murik told him. As far as everyone was concerned, Mary-Jane Mashkin had suffered cardiac arrest. "We shall bury her when Meltdown is complete." As he said it, the laird's mood changed, as

215

though he had become his old self again. "She was a soldier, killed in action for my cause. It would be wrong to mourn. Now, there are more important things to be done. Really, Mr. Bond, I have to admit some admiration for you. The play-acting at the airport was worthy of a professional. But, then, it appears that you are a professional of some kind, aren't you?"

"If you say so," Bond was tight-lipped. It must now be well after one in the morning. Less than twelve hours to go before the sinister laird's Meltdown project went into action.

Murik leaned forward with one of his little pecking movements. "The man whose face you smashed up in the telephone booth, Mr. Bond." Murik smiled again. "He heard the words you used. Who is M?"

Bond shook his head. "Haven't the foggiest."

"Well, I have." The Laird of Murcaldy leaned further across the desk. "In my time as a nuclear physicist, I too have signed the Official Secrets Act. I have been privy to what the novelists call the secret world. M, if I am correct, is the designation used for the head of the British Secret Service."

"Really?" Bond raised his eyebrows. Put your mind into overdrive, he told himself; knowing that, at the very least, the London headquarters would be able eventually to identify the general locality of his telephone call.

Murik was speaking again, and Bond had to pull his attention back to the little man's words. ". . . not much of a message to M, was it? I don't think we can expect too much trouble from that source." He gave a little cough, clearing his throat. "In any case, there's no chance of stopping Meltdown now. My demands will go out the moment I receive information that certain nuclear power stations are in the hands of our late, unlamented Franco's terrorists."

"Six nuclear reactors, I believe," Bond said smoothly. He must do everything possible to ruffle Murik's confidence. "Six: one in England, one here in France, one in the Federal Republic of Germany, one in East Germany and two in the United States."

The bulldog face broke into a radiant smile. "Clever, James Bond. So you know the locations; just as I know you cannot have passed them on to anyone who matters." The wretched man refused to be rattled. "Yes, by the time we leave here, just before one o'clock local time—noon in England—Franco's suicide squads will be preparing their individual assaults . . ."

"Which could go wrong. The security on those places just about precludes any serious terrorist activity." The conversation had become bizarre. Like a pair of war-gamers discussing moves.

"From within?" Murik asked with mock surprise. "My dear Bond, you don't think something as important as this has been left to chance?" He slapped the pine desk with the flat of his hand. "The targets were infiltrated about a year ago. We've had to be very patient, but patience pays off. There are four of Franco's contacts working at each of the targets; four trusted people, there now, at each reactor. Each person is known to the security men; and each one has been most successful in smuggling in the equipment necessary for the task."

"Weapons can sometimes backfire." Bond tried hard not to crease his brow with the worry now nagging at him.

"The weapons are only small things." Murik's eyes stirred like deadly molten lava. "The weapons are needed for one moment only. The men and women, all twenty-four of them, will be on duty in their various plants at the required moment. Weapons will be used as a last resort only—possibly as a threat. The takeover of the control rooms should be quite bloodless."

"How do you know?"

Murik looked up with surprise. "Franco instructed the teams. Nothing has been left to chance. You see, the initial moves in the control rooms will be elementary precautions only. For one thing, the remote switches will be cut: this means that no master control can scram the plants."

"Scram?"

"It is a word we use. Scram means the sudden shutdown of a fission reactor by remote control." His smile was as unpleasant, and nerve-twitching, as the lava look in his eyes. "It would defeat our purpose if the squads did not have complete control over their destinies."

Bond's muscles had gone as rigid as his tightened lips. Tension built steadily through his body. "And the other thing?"

"Oh," Murik pecked his head forward. "The most obvious one, of course. As they separate themselves from the master control, they will also cut all communication lines to the outside world."

"No contact at all?"

"They won't need contact. That can lead only to a dangerous lack of concentration. They have their orders; the times and details." He gave his humourless smile once more. "They have one, and only one, method of communication. That lies with me, and it will be used most sparingly.

"Each group is equipped with a small but immensely high-powered transceiver. Once they're in and completely isolated, each team will signal one code word, together with an identification. Only one person in the entire world will be able to receive those messages." Smugly he tapped his chest. "Myself. In turn, the groups will be the only people able to receive my message—another code word of course—to inform them to abort their mission. That instruction will be given only when my demands are met in full. If they do not receive my abort signal within twenty-four hours of the takeovers . . ." He gave a sad little gesture with his hands. "If they do not receive it, they'll go ahead—on the dot—and cut off the cooling systems to each of their reactors."

Bond's face was set like stone, his eyes locking with those of Anton Murik. "And if they do that, millions of lives will be lost, large parts of the world will be rendered uninhabitable for a long time, there will be pollution . . ."

Murik nodded like a Buddha. "Yes, Mr. Bond, that is why the governments concerned will not allow it to happen. My demands will be met; of that I am a hundred per cent sure."

"And how will the world know of your demands?"

"You will see, Bond, you will see. You'll have a ringside seat from start to finish." He chuckled. "And after it is all over . . . ." He spread his hands in a gesture meant to convey an inevitability. "I feel it a little dishonourable withholding your fee. After all, you did achieve success of a sort, even if not in the way I would have wished. However, I cannot allow you to remain in possession of the facts."

"So you'll kill me?"

"Something like that. I had a nice idea originally, but since Mary-Jane's death, I think you deserve a longer agony."

"And Lavender?"

He hit the table hard, with a balled fist, "She should already be dead, instead of my Mary-Jane. But don't worry, Bond, she'll be with you—right up to the very end." A throaty chuckle. "Or right down to the very end."

"You bastard." James Bond spoke quietly, in control of his emotions. "Your own ward . . ."

"Who has been a thorn in my side for many years." Murik also spoke with no trace of emotion.

"Why?" Bond stabbed in the dark. "Why? Because she is the rightful heir to your title, estate and money?"

Anton Murik raised his eyebrows. "Most astute," he said, sharply. "There's no harm, I suppose, in your knowing, for there is very little to prove it. Yes, she is the rightful heir. I came to my own position by devious means, you see . . ."

"You mean the business with your grandfather? And then the doubts about your own mother being the rightful wife to your late lamented father?"

For the first time in the whole conversation, Murik looked bewildered, then angry. "How do you know this?"

Bond took his mind back to the moment M had explained the chequered history of the Muriks.

"The business in Sicily?" he said. "The graves of your father and your mother's maid? The facts about that are well documented. After all, the Lord Lyon King of Arms has been carrying out a lengthy investigation . . ."

Murik's face twitched, then the smile came back. "Ah, maybe. But nothing can be proved."

"Oh, I don't know. Your own mother was your father's maid, wasn't she?"

Murik nodded. "But I was *his* son."

Once more, Bond stabbed in the dark: "But you had a brother—a half-brother anyway. By your father and his true wife. A brother born at the time of the bandit episode in Sicily. What did he do? Come back to haunt you?"

219

"He came back with a wife, child, and every possible legal document," snapped Murik.

"And died, with his wife, in an air disaster."

Murik chuckled. "Oh, most certainly. He was what you might call intrepid: a man of many parts. Or at least he was when he died." A further chuckle. "The Sicilians have faults, but they love children. The bandits kept him, made him one of their own, and then told him the truth. Like myself, he was good at waiting. But not so good at judging character. I told him I would relinquish Murcaldy and Murik Castle to him. He believed me. Such a pity." Murik's eyes took on a distant look. "He had bought a new aeroplane. I encouraged him to buy it. After all, he was inheriting the money. He actually flew it into the glen. His wife was with him, but the child wasn't; taken ill with colic, as I remember it. I was not there, of course. I had to go to Edinburgh to see the lawyers about relinquishing my title. They said it was terrible. You know, he avoided crashing into the castle by a matter of feet. Very brave. They both died instantly, and everybody said the infant had had a lucky escape."

Bond nodded. "You had to get back quickly, so the lawyers never saw the documents?"

Murik shook his head, in mock sadness. "No, they did not see them. Nobody's seen them. They lie safe in the castle, where nobody will find them." His hand reached for a button by the telephone. "We all need a little rest. Tomorrow will be quite a day—or today, I should say, for it is almost three in the morning. I'm afraid our facilities here are cramped. You'll have to share the one secure room with my ward."

Just before Caber came in to lead him away, Bond asked the final question. "You said we would be leaving here, and that I'd have a ringside seat. Where?"

Murik pecked forward. "Of course, you don't know. I mentioned the transceivers we'll be using; well, tomorrow my company here will be conducting tests with just such equipment—on another frequency, of course. My associates here have developed high-frequency transceivers which have a safety-screened beam; this means their signals *cannot* be monitored. We have a large aircraft," he gave another little chuckle, "provided, incidentally, by the United States. It is our flying testbed, and not only can it carry all the equipment we need, but also stay aloft for more than twenty-four hours. That's where you'll get your ringside seat."

Caber and one of the other men arrived and led Bond away. They handled him roughly, but Caber undid the shackles once they reached what he referred to as "the secure room".

"Ye'll no be gettin' oot o' here," Caber sneered. Bond could not fault Caber's confidence, for the place was simply a narrow cell with no windows and only a tiny ventilation grille set into the wall. The door was of eight-inch steel, with no handles on the inside, and so hung that it became part of the wall when closed. There were two beds and one small light, which burned behind thick glass and a mesh cover, flush with the ceiling.

Lavender had been dozing on one of the beds, but woke with a start as soon as they shoved Bond into the cell. As soon as she realized it was Bond, she was in his arms.

"Oh James! They caught you. I hoped that you, at least, had got away. Terrible things are going on . . . . Did you know Mary-Jane is dead . . . ?"

He stopped her with a kiss. She was a tough young girl, under that soft exterior, and Bond felt she should know the truth. "Listen, Dilly," he began, and then with tact told her the real facts of Mary-Jane Mashkin's heart attack, and how it had been meant for her. He also briefly outlined Murik's plans for the morning.

She was silent for a time. Speaking at last with a voice that was calm and almost resigned, she said, "Then it looks as though we've had it. I should imagine that he has something very nasty planned for us."

Bond put a finger to her lips. "It hasn't happened yet." He tried to make light of things, saying that there was still time for help to arrive. "Anyway, Dilly, at least we'll be together."

She bit her lip and nodded bravely, then pulled his head down to hers. To Bond it felt as though they had both escaped from time and trouble and were floating with increasing joy towards a whirlpool of earthly delights.

Later, they fell asleep, entwined on the small bed.

IT WAS ALMOST six in the morning before Bill Tanner returned to M's office with the bad news that they had not yet received a trace on the number from which James Bond had dialled.

"They'll have it for you before nine o'clock," he said wearily.

M looked washed out, his skin like parchment and deep creases of worry around discoloured eyes. "Nobody seems to know the meaning of urgency any more," he growled. Deep inside, M had a feeling that they were close to something catastrophic. "Duggan's the same," he snorted. "Got shirty with me when I reversed my views about him going into Murik Castle. Anyway, they've all buzzed off like a swarm of daft bees—Duggan, his men, and a load of Special Branch to lead the way." He gave a sigh. "Even so, they won't be able to do anything much before nine either."

Bill Tanner, worried as he was, tried to make light of it. "Should've sent a gunboat in the first place, sir."

M grunted. "Send some coffee, more likely. Get some up now, Chief-of-Staff. Black, hot, sweet and strong. I've got a feeling it's going to be a long, hard day."

Ultimatum

They came armed, and in strength. Caber and three of the hoods; Caber carrying an automatic pistol, two of the hoods with trays. "It's a special breakfast the laird's been pleased to order for ye. He said ye'd understand." As the trays were set down, Bond recalled his conversation with Murik the previous day: about the condemned man eating a hearty breakfast.

The hoods disappeared and Caber backed into the doorway. "And ye'll no try coming for us wi' them knives and forks when we collect the trays. All of us have got the wee shooters. Naebody's gonna get away this time," he said and slammed the door home.

The trays contained steaming plates of bacon, eggs, sausages, two large silver pots of coffee, plenty of toast, butter and marmalade— laid out under ornate covers on the laird's personal china.

Lavender pushed her tray away. "It's no good, James. I just can't swallow it."

Bond went over, catching her by the shoulders. "Dilly, where's your faith, girl? We'll find a way out—*I'll* find a way out. Murik'll be only too happy if you show your fear. You have to fight. Come on." He had no idea how they could possibly escape, or even stop the events which were now, he knew, rolling inevitably towards what could be a holocaust. Yet all Bond's experience told him Murik would only be beaten by some show of character.

Lavender swallowed. "Of course, James. I've come a long way with Anton as well. Let's try and get the bastard."

Bond set an example, even though he too found it hard to eat. The bacon and eggs stuck in his throat, but he managed to wash it down with cup after cup of sweet coffee. At least his body would be provided with some extra energy. Lavender did her best, nibbling on toast and sipping coffee.

There was no way of telling the time, but Bond guessed they had been allowed to sleep late. It must now be after midday, French time. The deadline here was one in the afternoon. They would not have to wait much longer.

Five minutes later Caber and the other men reappeared. The two prisoners were taken from the cell at gunpoint, through silent passages, narrow corridors and finally up some steps which led to a metal fire door—Caber waving them through.

Bond heard Lavender gasp behind him. They stood in the hangar he had seen on their arrival—a vast structure, huge and echoing, smelling of oil and rubber. An aircraft stood in the centre, a yellow tractor already hooked to the nose.

Bond recognized it at once. It was the massive Lockheed-George C-141—the Starlifter: the great American strategic transport aircraft with a wing span of over forty-eight yards and a length of over forty-four yards. Even the hangar seemed dwarfed by this magnificent brute, with the blue, white, red and yellow insignia of the French Armée de l'Air. Towards the rear of the wide fuselage the words Aldan Aerospace had been added.

Murik could get everything he needed into this beast—from technicians to all the electronic equipment necessary for his shielded radio beams.

"Yes, Mr. Bond, the Starlifter." Murik stood at his elbow, dressed casually in jacket and slacks. "Specially modified, of course . . . . Now it's time to go aboard."

From the front of the hangar came the sound of the towering roller doors starting to move. Caber prodded Bond with his pistol, and they began to climb the steps up to the forward doorway. Murik led the way, and Bond caught sight of the crew through the flight deck window, going through the pre-takeoff check.

Inside, the fuselage had obviously been altered to Murik's own specifications. The doorway took them into a bright canteen with a bar, small round tables and seating for a dozen people. Two men were already at work in a galley.

"I'm afraid you'll not be eating here, with the rest of us," said Murik, looking from Bond to Lavender. "However, I shall see you do not go hungry or thirsty." He pointed towards the sliding hatchway leading to the rear of the fuselage. "I should be grateful if you would take care when passing through the next section. It contains the intestines of my electronic labours, and is, perhaps, the most important part of the whole project."

The section on the far side of this hatchway ran back down the fuselage for about forty feet, its sides crammed from deck to the upper bulkheads with banks of electronic equipment. Towards the centre there was a recess on either side, with two men in clean white overalls sitting in each, in front of complex control consoles.

At the end of this electronic cave there was another sliding hatchway, which was, to Bond's experienced eye, bullet and fireproof. Murik paused, his hand on the sliding latch. "My personal preserve," he announced, tugging the door to one side. They stepped into a circular area lit by shaded lights. Murik gave a smug look around him as the door closed with an automatic hiss. "This is where I shall control Meltdown."

On either side of the door was a pair of wide curved desks, each backed by another complicated array of electronic wizardry. Three body-moulded swivel seats were bolted to the deck in front of each of the desk consoles. Leading aft, there was another hatchway. In large letters on this door had been stencilled: DO NOT ENTER IF RED LIGHT IS ON. Near this exit yet another, smaller, passage was visible to the right. Murik gestured towards it. "The usual offices, as the estate agents say," he said, smiling. "We have everything on board for a pleasant day trip over the sea. Now, if you'll just take your seats . . ."

Bond felt Caber's arms gripping him, and at the same time he saw the two other men close in on Lavender. Bond was manhandled into a chair in front of one of the consoles and a seatbelt fastened around him.

"We have made certain modifications to the safety harness for you and my ward." Murik slid into the seat to Bond's right, and as he did so his jacket rode back slightly, revealing a holster behind his hip and the curved butt of a small, deadly Colt Python.

Bond's hopes of reaching the weapon were dashed seconds later when Caber hissed, "Put yer arms behind yer back, Bond." He felt his hands being pressed together as the big Scot pulled a short webbing strap tightly round his wrists. Two further webbing belts, anchored to the underside of the seat, were now crossed over Bond's chest and shoulders and pulled hard. He felt them being locked somewhere underneath the seat, holding him immobile.

Murik had clipped on a seatbelt, and was adjusting the console in front of them, his hands moving with professional precision as pinlights started to glow. Rising like a snake's head from the centre of the desk was a microphone.

Bond studied the row of digital clocks, each marked with a time zone, covering all six locations of the targets. British time showed at ten minutes to noon. He glanced over to the other console, where Lavender had been fastened in exactly the same way as himself between two of Murik's men, who were now concentrating on the equipment facing them. These, Bond realized, were not just heavies, but trained technicians. At that moment he felt the deck beneath his feet tremble. The yellow tractor was moving, giving the aircraft a push-back from the hangar.

Murik looked up. "I promised you a ringside seat, Bond," he said, grinning, "and here it is. Everything."

Bond turned to see Caber disappearing through the hatchway to their rear. He asked where it led, and Murik gave a mocking laugh. "The exit," he almost shouted. "There's a ramp, you know. Everybody's seen pictures of parachute troops hurling themselves down that ramp, in the more conventional Starlifter. I had thought of hurling you down it. Then a better idea came to mind."

"You didn't say what . . . ?" Bond began, and then the first of the four powerful turbofans began to throb. The Starlifter was coming alive.

"No, I didn't say." Murik glanced at the instruments in front of him. "But all in good time."

Caber returned and nodded to Murik, as though passing a message. "Good," said Murik in acknowledgement. Then, pointing to the seat on his right, he commented that Mary-Jane should have been sitting in it. "She's here in spirit, though." He did not smile.

The engines surged, one after another, and the aircraft swayed along the taxiway. A metallic click from somewhere in the roof signalled contact being made from the flight deck. "Captain to all crew and passengers of Aldan Five-Six." The voice was English, with a drawl. "Please fasten your seatbelts and extinguish cigarettes. We shall be taking off shortly."

The British-time digital clock clicked towards 11:54 as the engines settled and then rose into a blasting roar. The thrust pushed the crew and two captives back into their seats, but soon the aircraft ceased bumping along the runway and tipped smoothly into its natural element.

Murik leaned over, placing a pair of headphones over Bond's head. "You will hear everything; and I shall also be able to speak to you through these."

British time showed two minutes before noon. "The witching hour," Murik chuckled again. "Very soon you'll hear the terrorist squads making their reports."

LESS THAN FIVE MINUTES before the Starlifter rose from the runway at Perpignan, events were taking their course the world over. M, having now received information regarding the location of Bond's call, had checked all possible connections with Anton Murik. His investigation led naturally to Aldan Aerospace (France), Inc. and their headquarters at Perpignan. There had been rapid telephone calls, and a van carrying members of the French Secret Service,

together with a squad of armed police, was now tearing towards the airport.

They had received further encouraging news at the Regent's Park headquarters. A Mary-Jane Mashkin, close friend of Dr. Anton Murik, had died of a heart attack in the middle of a fashion show in Perpignan; while the body of a man had just been identified as the much-wanted terrorist known as Franco.

"007's work, sir?" Bill Tanner was not really asking.

"Could be. Two of 'em out of it, anyway."

"Then there's a very good chance . . ." Tanner began.

"Don't count your chickens, Chief-of-Staff. Never do that. We could still be too late, fiddling around half the night waiting for information. Time's not with us."

NEAR THE FRENCH CITY of Orléans, deep under the complex which makes up the nuclear power stations known as Saint-Laurent-des-Eaux One, Two and Three, certain people were quietly going through a well-rehearsed routine.

Two men tending the large turbine of Plant Two left their posts at just before twelve fifty. A maintenance man excused himself from the duty room where he had been playing cards. The security man at the entrance to the main control room waited anxiously while the other three made their way along the pipe-lined, stark passages, picking up pieces of cached equipment as they went. They met up in the gallery immediately outside the plant's control room. It was one minute to one, French time.

Inside the control room, the six men who watched the dials and controlled the flow of power went about their work normally. One of them turned, shouting irritably at the security man as he opened the large main door. "Claude, what are you doing? You know you're not allowed . . ." He stopped, seeing the automatic pistol pointing at him, and a second man with a submachine gun, its barrel sweeping the room.

The security man called Claude spoke: "Hands on your heads. Stand away from all equipment. Now. Move, or you will be killed. We mean it." The tone of his voice convinced the six men. Flustered, they dropped clipboards and pens, clamped their hands to their heads and stepped clear of the equipment. So hypnotized were they by the weapons that it is doubtful if they even saw the other two men slip past their comrades, and move quickly to two points in the room. In a matter of seconds they had cut off all links with the outside world by severing the communications cables and pulling the external control override switches. The reactor operating at Saint-Laurent-des-Eaux Two could now be handled only from this room.

The gunmen ordered the technicians to line up, facing the door. A series of images flashed through the minds of these half dozen unfortunates—pictures of their wives and families crossing bleakly with incidents they had seen on television newsreels: hostages held in terrible conditions, hostages shot as a warning to others. It was with a sense of great surprise and relief that they heard the gunmen tell them to leave quietly through the main door and get up the stairs.

"It would not be advisable for anyone to take panic action," the gunman called Claude told them. "Just report to the authorities that a message with certain demands will be coming through within a few minutes. Any sudden move before that and we shut down the cooling system. We cause a China Syndrome. Tell them that, OK?"

The six men nodded shakily. The heavy door to the control room slammed behind them and the two gunmen clamped on the interior safety locks. Meanwhile the other two men had been busy removing their most essential piece of equipment, the small, box-like transceiver, from a canvas haversack. The security guard, Claude, switched it on. Pressing the transmit button he said loudly and distinctly, "Number Three. War."

Similar scenes to these were being enacted in five other nuclear power stations, in Europe and the United States.

JAMES BOND HEARD the words clearly through the headphones: "Number Three. War."

"That's the French one," Murik said, his voice interrupted by another quick message: "Number One. War."

Then "Number Four. War." "Number Five. War." "Number Two. War."

They came in quickly, tumbling into the earphones. Then a long pause. Bond saw Murik's hand clench and unclench. Then after what seemed an eternity: "Number Six. War."

"All in." Murik grabbed Bond's arm excitedly. "Now," he said, his voice strange, almost out of control, "now for *my* message. In a moment I shall activate the ultimatum. Throughout Europe and the United States we have a series of hidden micro-transmitters controlled by a signal from this aircraft. The transmitters will relay a translated message to every European country, and a number of Asian countries too. The transmission is locked into the normal broadcasting frequencies of the countries concerned and will cut in on any programme already going out."

Murik leaned forward, threw two switches and prepared to press a red button on the console. He added, "By the way, you will not recognize my voice. There is an ingenious device called in the trade the Electronic Handkerchief. By using it, you can alter your own voice beyond recognition. I have chosen the voice of a rather seductive lady. Now, listen."

Without warning, Bond heard the message in his headphones. Slowly the full impact came home to him and he felt a sickening lurch in his stomach.

ALMOST AN HOUR LATER M sat with members of the government, security services, and chiefs-of-staff who make up the secret crisis committee known as COBRA, in a room deep under Whitehall. They were listening again to a recording of that sudden, audacious and terrifying ultimatum.

The voice relaying that message was a woman's. "Stop whatever you are doing and listen. This is an emergency broadcast of extreme urgency to every man, woman and child. Stop. Stand still and listen," the voice clipped out, sharp and commanding. Then it continued, calm and deliberate. "This message concerns everyone. It is directed at the governments of Britain, France, the Federal Republic of Germany, the German Democratic Republic and the United States.

"At exactly twelve noon British Summer Time today, six nuclear power plants were seized by terrorist groups. These groups now occupy the main control rooms of the following nuclear plants." The voice listed the names of the plants and their precise locations. The tone rising, it continued, "I must make two things clear. The men who hold these nuclear power plants are dedicated to a point that some would call fanaticism. They will die if necessary. Second, all lines of communication have been cut between these groups and the outside world. They can make contact with one person only—myself. These men are under orders to do the following: if an attempt is made to assault any one of the six power plants, my men will immediately turn off the cooling system to the core of the nuclear reactor.

"This will cause immense heat to build up. Within a very short time there will be an explosion and a very large area surrounding the plant will be contaminated by radioactive material. The core of the reactor will proceed to burn its way through the earth, eventually finding an exit point where further radioactive material will be expelled. That is known, to those who have not heard of it, as the China Syndrome.

"These men are under instructions to carry out this same operation exactly twenty-four hours after I stop speaking unless certain demands are met. If my demands are not met the results will be catastrophic, and there will be no way to stop disaster. It is no exaggeration to say that it could well mean the end of the world as we know it.

"These are my instructions: I require a ransom payable only in cut gem diamonds to a value of not less than fifty billion dollars to be paid at today's rate. These diamonds are to be placed in one large-sized yellow naval flotation bag, equipped with a normal recovery hoop. The consignment is to be dropped by aircraft at the following point." The voice calmly went on to give the latitude and longitude.

"Before the diamonds are delivered, an area of fifty square miles around the dropping point is to be cleared of all shipping, and once its mission is completed the aircraft employed is to fly well out of the zone. I shall not give the order for the nuclear plants to be released until I have picked up the diamonds in safety and have been assured of the amount. This operation will take me approximately two hours:

thus the governments concerned have in reality around twenty-two hours to comply with my demands.

"I stress that this is no hoax. This broadcast is my ultimatum. There will be absolutely no other contact. I repeat that any attempt to communicate with those holding the plants can only result in tragedy. You have exactly twenty-two hours. Message ends."

The prime minister, who had been driven back to London at breakneck speed from an engagement in Hampshire, was chairing the meeting. "I have been in touch with the heads of all other governments concerned." The prime minister looked worried; but the natural poise was still there. "We are all agreed that, no matter how difficult, this is one terrorist action in which we have no choice. At this moment all the threatened countries are gathering diamonds of good quality. We have experts working on it in London, and diamonds are being flown to Paris, where a French military aircraft is standing by. As you know, the dropping zone is in the Mediterranean and at the moment we are scheduling a drop to be made at nine o'clock our time tomorrow. I am, personally, depressed by this action. It is the first time this country has given way to blackmail by terrorist groups, but our combined advisers seem to think there are no options open. Has anybody got any further points?"

M cleared his throat. "Yes, on behalf of my service, Prime Minister: we think we know who is behind this horrific act. We also think we know where this person is: in an aircraft over the Med now. With permission I am going to ask for this aircraft to be shadowed by the Armée de l'Air. I know we can take no action until the terrorists have left the nuclear power plants, but it is a lead, and we might just be able to retrieve the diamonds."

The prime minister nodded. "I read your report on my way here. You mention something about one of your agents?"

M looked solemn. "There is a possibility that one of my people is on board the aircraft."

The prime minister looked down at the documents on the table. "Do you think he might be able to do something about the situation?"

"If he can't halt this ungodly mess, Prime Minister, nobody can."

Warlock

Bond sat in front of the console, the facts fighting each other in his mind, as though trying to drag him into despair. Murik had mustered his forces through the most elusive international terrorist in the world and set up a complicated tactical operation. There was little to stop him at this stage. For his own safety, Murik would have to get rid of both Bond and Lavender. Why Murik had not already killed them was almost beyond Bond's comprehension—he could only presume it was because Murik's vanity needed to feed on the applause of doomed witnesses.

Don't let yourself go, Bond told himself. Keep alert. Try anything to combat the inevitable. He began by trying to guess the Starlifter's flight pattern. It appeared to him that the aircraft was locking into a wide, oval holding pattern, each circuit covering around fifty miles or so. That made sense: maximum altitude, with the aircraft using the minimum fuel.

He glanced towards Lavender and smiled. She returned the look with a twist of her lips, bravely struggling with the horrors that must have been going through her head.

He knew their chances of survival were slim. He must go on searching for further chinks in the armour. Bond might play on Murik's vanity for a time, yet in the end that could not affect the outcome. To do anything concrete he had to be free and mobile. After that, there was the problem of taking out Murik, Caber and the two heavies sitting with Lavender at the other console.

Bond gazed blankly at the array of electronic units before them. The earphones had been plugged into a unit bright with pin-lights, visual units and half a dozen tuning dials. He had no doubt that this was the most important piece of equipment in Murik's impressive array; in particular the microphone with its transmit button. Press that button, speak, and you would be through to the squads. What would Murik say to them once he was away and safe with the diamonds? How would Murik defuse the situation?

Vanity. Use it. Play on the vanity. "What happens to the terrorist squads?" Bond asked, casually.

Murik gave him a sly look. "What d'you mean?"

"Well, nobody can fault you on anything, Anton." Bond chanced the familiarity. "This is probably the most brilliantly organized terrorist strategy of the century. But, when you've picked up the diamonds and got safe home . . ."

Murik laughed. "Unfortunately you won't be around to see."

Bond nodded, as though the point was academic. "I realize that. But I suppose you call off the dogs. What happens to them then?"

Murik shrugged: the sly look again. "If they're ordered to abort, they simply come out with their hands up. Custody. Interrogation. Trial. And, if any of them breaks, he can only point the finger at Franco, who is dead." He paused. "I imagine they won't be in gaol for long. There will be hostages, deaths, demands."

Bond nodded slowly. "And you have to call up all six groups? Or does a blanket code cover it?"

For a second, Murik was caught off his guard. "Same code, but each group enumerated. That was the arrangement."

It was enough for Bond. He needed the defusing code word; and, having already heard each of the groups come in, it required only common sense to work out how the occupying groups could be made to stand down. At least he had a reasonable idea of what to do *if* he managed to get free. But how to accomplish that part of the trick?

If only he could release his arms. Every time Murik moved, Bond glimpsed the butt of the Python revolver under the jacket. If his arms were free and the right moment could be found . . . . There had to be a way, and there was still time. If he managed anything it would have to be late in Murik's scheme of things, some time tomorrow. A message to the terrorist squads now would only alert their suspicions. Better to wait.

Suddenly the earphones came to life. He recognized the pilot's voice: "Captain to the Laird of Murcaldy, sir. Could you send someone up here for a moment?"

Murik gave a quizzical tilt of the head and beckoned Caber. "Up to the flight deck with you. See what it's all about."

Caber left with a nod. He was gone for around ten minutes, returning with a puzzled look. He bent low and muttered in Murik's

234

ear. The laird's face underwent no change as his hand gently eased Caber away and he swivelled his chair towards the men at the console opposite. "The captain says they're picking up an intermittent trace on the flight-deck radarscope—two blips coming up every now and then, as though they were holding station with us. See what you can do."

The men bent over viewers, through which they were probably looking at radar screens. Bond knew that if aircraft were shadowing the Starlifter, M had probably succeeded, late in the day, in getting the right answers to some difficult problems.

"There it is," one of Caber's men exclaimed. "Two of them. In and out of this screen very quickly. Could be shadow aircraft. Coming for an occasional look."

"Well, it won't do them any good," snapped Murik. "They can't take action."

"Not until you've collected your diamonds and given the stand-down order," Bond said. "Then they'll blow you out of the sky. Force you down. Anything. Even shadow you to your lair."

Murik looked at him gravely for a full minute, then burst out laughing, his white hair ruffling as he threw his head back. "After all the planning, you think I've left *that* to chance? You think I would undertake this without having some radar-jamming gear on board?" Murik was still laughing. "Let them have their fun. If they really are shadow aircraft, we'll fuzz their pictures as soon as we turn in to pick up the loot."

"And if they are? They'll already know where you're going—for the diamonds, I mean."

"I'll be away long before they'll dare come near. I'll hold off on the terrorist squads until, literally, the last moment. Anyway, they may have nothing to do with us. Could be coincidence."

"Could be. But somehow . . ." Bond left the sentence unfinished.

FAR AWAY TO THE NORTH of the Starlifter, the two Armée de l'Air Super Mirage fighters turned in unison.

It was good exercise, the pilot of the first Super Mirage thought. But there must be more to it than a routine shadowing. It wouldn't be a Russian they were following; and he had not believed his squadron commandant, who had told them this was a snap defence exercise. For one thing they were armed to the gills—everything from cannon to rockets.

The pilot bent his head to look at his small radar screen. The blip came up at the expected place. The two aircraft turned away, to begin another long looping pattern high over the sea. If the blip vanished, they had orders to close until they made contact again.

Away to the south of Perpignan Airport, SEPCAT Jaguars sat, off the main runways, as though waiting to leap into the air for a kill. In the airport's operations room, senior Armée de l'Air officers were going over the flight plan filed by Aldan Aerospace for their Starlifter. So far it had not deviated from it. The aircraft was maintaining a holding pattern at almost 30,000 feet while testing Aldan's specialized equipment. The holding pattern would continue for the best part of twenty-one hours. After that Aldan planned to descend almost to sea level before turning in to return to Perpignan at just before one o'clock the following afternoon.

In the building overlooking Regent's Park, M examined the latest reports radioed to him from France. Anton Murik's Starlifter was maintaining its filed flight plan. Yes, M thought, it probably will. Right up until the last moment, when he's got the ransom aboard. Unless—M hoped—unless James Bond was on board, and could do something about it.

IT WAS A LONG and tiring evening: prelude to an even longer night of intense fatigue. Quite early on Murik told Bond that he did not expect the ransom aircraft to arrive anywhere near its dropping zone until around nine or ten the following morning. Murik had drilled his staff to perfection, so that they followed a prescribed routine.

As for Bond and Lavender, they were fed—mainly on coffee and sandwiches—where they sat, their wrists being freed only for eating, or when they were taken to the washroom by an armed man, who locked them into the closet and stood outside the door. On returning, they were carefully strapped into their chairs again, always under the wicked eye of at least one pistol. There had been no opportunity to reverse the situation, but Bond had far from given up hope. Already, in the washroom, he had begun to act.

236

On his last visit, Bond had quickly taken a large wad of tissue and rolled it into an elongated ball, a good three inches thick. Back in his seat, Bond placed both hands behind his back, ready for his wrists to be strapped. At the same time he manipulated the wedge of tissue from the palm of his hand up and between the wrists, which he held tightly together.

It was an old trick. When the ball of tissue was removed and once more in his palm, the strap was looser around his wrists. There was freedom of an inch or so for him to work the strap around with his fingers and pick away at the fastening.

Near dawn they would all be tired and at their lowest ebb. It would be then, he decided, that he would act, whatever the consequences.

At around five thirty in the morning, just after Murik had been to the forward part of the aircraft for coffee, Caber went to the canteen. Bond knew his movements would have to be both very fast and accurate. Murik seemed preoccupied with the apparatus in front of him, and the other two men were still at Lavender's console: one had his eyes closed, resting; the other was intent on watching his screen.

Gently James Bond flexed his hands, allowing the wrist strap to come free. Then he dropped the strap and moved. His right hand came up, arrowing towards the gun inside Murik's jacket, while the left swept round in a vicious chop at the laird's throat. The blow from the heel of his left hand had all Bond's strength behind it, and as it landed his right hand grabbed at the butt of the Colt Python, which came out of the holster easily as Murik crumpled onto the deck. Bond, still strapped in, swivelled his chair round with his feet, holding the Colt up firmly in a two-handed grip.

He fired almost before Murik's body had hit the ground, yelling to Lavender, "Stay quite still." Of the two men at the console, the technician at the radar screen moved first, going for his own gun a split second before his partner. As Bond squeezed the trigger it crossed his mind that this was one of the most foolhardy exploits he had ever attempted: one bullet through the metal of the fuselage and the pressurization would go. In all, he fired twice: two bursts of two—the ammunition exploding like a cannon in the confines of the

237

cabin. Four bullets reached their individual targets. Lavender screamed as the first of her captors spun to one side, a bullet lodged in his shoulder. The second bullet caught him on the side of the head, hurling him into eternity with a great spatter of blood leaping from the wound, and as he fell his trouser leg rode up to reveal a Highland dirk tucked into his woollen stocking. The man who had been resting with his eyes closed caught both rounds in the neck, the sound of his gargling emerging from the after-echo of the shots.

Then there was silence except for a cry of fright from Lavender. "It's OK, Dilly. The only way. Sorry it was so close."

She looked in horror at the bodies, then took in a breath and nodded. "It's all right, James. Sorry. How . . . ?"

"No time now. Got to do something about those bloody terrorist squads before anything else." 007 grasped the microphone on its snake-like stand. Now he would see how far logic went. He pressed the transit button and began to speak, slowly and distinctly: "Number One . . . Lock; Number Two . . . Lock; Number Three . . . Lock" right through all six of the squads—completing the word Anton Murik had used as his personal cryptonym for Meltdown—Warlock.

"Now we pray." Bond's hands went to the buckle on his belt in order to reassemble the small knife concealed in its various components—the knife he had used to strip off the section of the money belt in Perpignan. He glanced towards Lavender as he worked, smiling and giving her a few words of confidence. He was already attacking the webbing straps binding him to the seat. The small blade was sharp, but its size did not make for speed: one slip and he could slash himself badly. As he worked there were no sounds about them except for his own breathing counterpointed with that of the unconscious Laird of Murcaldy. Bond wondered how badly he had damaged Murik. If his aim had been really accurate, the man would now be dead from a shattered trachea.

The first cross-strap came clear, then the second, and then Bond was completely out of the harness, springing up and flexing his muscles to get the blood flowing again. In a second he was with Lavender, on his knees. Feeling under the chair he found the release mechanism; another couple of seconds to undo the wrist

238

strap and she too was free. "Hadn't you better stand by with that gun?" She nodded towards the other console, where Bond had left the Python. "Caber's already been gone for nearly fifteen minutes."

"Don't worry, he's not going to cause us much . . ." He stopped, seeing her eyes turn towards the sliding door, widening with fear.

Bond whirled around. Caber stood in the doorway, his eyes taking in the carnage. Both Caber and Bond were frozen for a second, looking at each other. Bond's eyes flicked towards Murik's console, and the Python; and, in that second, Caber also saw the weapon.

As Bond came up from his crouched position, so Caber let out a great roar of fury and launched himself at Bond. For the first time, Lavender expressed her pent-up fear in a long, terrified shriek.

Airstrike

The previous day M had set up his own operations room, next to his suite of offices in the building overlooking Regent's Park. He dozed fitfully on the camp bed until a familiar sound broke into his consciousness: it was the red telephone. M noted it was nearly five o'clock in the morning as he picked up the handset and answered with a throaty "Yes?"

Bill Tanner was on the line. "They've surrendered." The chief-of-staff made no attempt to disguise his excitement.

"Who've surrendered?" M snapped.

"The terrorists. All of them. Just walked out with their hands up. Said it was over."

M frowned. "Any explanation?"

"It only happened a short while ago." Tanner calmed down. "Reports are still coming in, sir. Apparently they said they'd received the message to abort the mission. They seem to think their operation's been successful. Our people up at Heysham One believe they've been given the call-off by mistake."

M grinned to himself. "I wonder," he grunted. "I wonder if it was an engineered mistake?"

"007?" the chief-of-staff asked.

"Who else? What about the Starlifter?" M was out of the camp bed now, trying to hang onto the phone and wrestle with his trousers at the same time.

"Still keeping station. The French are going in now. Two sections of fighters are on their way."

M paused. "The French fighters? They're briefed to force the Starlifter down?" His grip on the receiver tightened.

Tanner's voice became grave. "They're briefed to buzz it into surrendering, then to lead it back to Perpignan. And if that doesn't work, the orders are to blast it out of the sky."

"I see." M's voice dropped almost to a whisper. Slowly, he cradled the receiver.

BOND DID NOT STAND a chance of getting to the revolver. Murik's chief lieutenant was as dangerous as a wounded bull elephant: his roar had changed into a bloodcurdling cry as he seemed to take off through the air and catch Bond halfway across the cabin. Bond felt his breath go from his lungs as the weight of the brute landed on him with full force. Caber had Bond straddled on the floor, his legs across Bond's thighs and the enormous hands at his throat. Bond tried to cry out for Lavender's help as the red mist clouded his brain, but Caber's pressing fingers prevented him. Only a croak emerged. Then, with the same swiftness of Caber's attack, the whole situation changed.

The Starlifter's engines, which until now had been only a steady hum in the background, changed their note, rising and straining in a roar, while the deck under the struggling men lurched to one side. As he rolled, still locked with Caber, across the cabin floor, Bond caught a glimpse of Lavender being flung forward, as a great buffeting of the airframe ensued. Then the Starlifter lurched again, followed by yet another sudden and violent change of attitude, which threw Caber free.

"There are aircraft attacking us," Lavender yelled. "Fighters coming in very close."

Bond tried to get to his feet and stay upright on the unstable deck, which was now juddering and bucking like a rollercoaster. He finally managed to prop himself against the forward door and began to make for the revolver. Caber on his hands and knees near Murik's console was bracing himself for yet another attack, an arm stretched out towards the gun.

The giant leaped forward, landing unsteadily on the rolling floor, his mask of fury giving way to a smile of triumph. "I ken a bullet's too guid for ye." His hand almost hid the Python revolver, which pointed at Bond's chest, motioning his victim towards the large hatchway leading aft.

"Ye'll get over there," Caber growled, keeping his balance, even though the aircraft was descending rapidly. There was no way to avoid the order without ending up with his chest torn away by the Python's bullets, so Bond crabbed across the cabin towards the hatchway.

"Now"—Caber had managed to get close behind him—"now ye'll slide that open, and hold it until ma own hand's on it."

Bond did as he was bidden; felt the revolver barrel jab at his back as, together, they stepped through into the rear of the Starlifter. The aircraft made another fast and unexpected turn, throwing them apart momentarily.

"I'm still behind ye, Bond, with the wee shooter, so dinna do anything daft. There's a wee lever I have to pull over here."

The rear loading bay was cold: a bleak airborne hangar of metal, smelling of oil. Bond had to grip hard on a curved spar to keep his balance, for the big aeroplane seemed to be turning alternately left and right, still going down, with occasional terrifying bucketing and noise—which Bond now clearly recognized as other aircraft passing close and buzzing them.

"There we go," Caber called, and Bond heard the solid sound of a large switch going down. It was followed by the whine of hydraulics and an increased reverberation. Caber was leaning against a bulkhead just inside the hatchway, the revolver still accurately aimed, while his left hand was raised to a two-foot double knife-switch which had just been pulled down to the "on" position. Caber laughed. "The laird had some daft idea of trailing ye along with the pick-up line when we went fur the ransom. I'm gawn tae make sure o' ye, Bond."

There was a distinct decrease in temperature. Bond could feel air blowing around him. Looking back towards the tail end of the hold, he saw the rear sides of the fuselage slowly pivoting outwards, while an oblong section of the deck gently dropped away. The ramp was going down. Already he could see a section of sky. "It'll tak aboot twa minutes," Caber shouted. "Then ye'll have a nice ski slope there. Ye'll be goin' doon that, Bond. Goin' doon it tae hell."

James Bond clung onto his spar, transfixed by the quickly widening gap between metal and sky. He felt the clammy hand of death on his neck, and the cold sweat of fear closed over him. With a heavy rumble and thump, the ramp locked down, leaving a huge open hole the size of a house in the rear of the aircraft.

"This is where we say fare ye weel—for auld lang syne, Bond. Now git ye doon that ramp and practise flying wi'out wings."

"You'll have to shoot me down it," Bond shouted. He was not going without a fight. Letting go of the spar, he aimed himself at Caber just as the Starlifter dipped lower, the tail coming up at a precarious angle. Bond lurched towards Caber, losing his balance. Bond saw the smile broaden on the man's face, his gun hand coming up to point the Python straight at 007's chest.

Again the deck jerked under them and Bond staggered to one side as the aircraft dipped and the door to the hatchway slid open. For a second, Bond thought it had opened with the movement of the aircraft. Then he saw Lavender, the dirk from the dead guard's stocking firmly in her hand, raised to strike.

Caber tried to turn and bring the revolver to bear, but the instability of the deck gave him no chance. Almost with a sense of dread, Bond saw the dirk flash down as Lavender plunged it with all her strength into the big man's throat. Caber's gurgling rasp of terror echoed around the hold. The revolver fell as he scrabbled at his throat, from which blood pumped out and down his jersey. Then Caber spun round, still clamping hands to his neck, and fell.

Bond reached the door as the aircraft once more changed its attitude and started to climb. Caber rolled towards the point where the deck dipped into the long-angled ramp, and Lavender turned her head away, hanging on to Bond, as Caber tumbled like a stuffed effigy down the ramp.

As he reached the far end, the big man's body seemed to correct

itself. For a second his eyes locked with Bond's, and even though
Caber's already held the glaze of death, they also contained a deep,
dark hatred. Then Murik's giant lieutenant slid over the edge, into
the air beneath the Starlifter.

"I killed him," Lavender murmured.

"An obvious statement, Dilly darling. What matters to me is that
you saved my life." He reached up the big knife-switch, grasping
the wooden handle and pulling it up, into the "off" position. The
hydraulic whine began again, and the ramp started to move. Then,
as Bond turned, he saw Lavender looking towards the closing gap.
In the sky still visible, a pair of Super Mirages could be seen
hurtling in towards the Starlifter. As they watched, Bond and
Lavender saw the bright flashes at the nose of each aircraft. The
Mirage jets had passed before the Starlifter felt any effect from the
short bursts of fire.

There followed a series of massive thuds, small explosions and the
rip of metal, and the deck under their feet began a long wave-like
dance. Then the engines roared again, and the deck steadied.
Bond's nose twitched at the acrid smell of smoke. Pushing Lavender
to one side, he slid open the hatchway to be met by a billow of
smoke. Two or three of the small-calibre shells from the Mirages
had passed through the roof, slamming into the main console, from
which the flames flicked upwards.

Bond yelled at Lavender to keep out of the way and grabbed one
of the two large fire extinguishers on either side of the hatchway. He
smashed the activating plunger against a metal spar, slid back the
door and pointed the jet of foam into the control room.

Coughing and spluttering from the fumes, Bond returned for the
second cylinder. It took both the extinguishers at full pressure
before the fire was out. Then, keeping Lavender close on the hold
side of the door, Bond waited for the smoke to clear. He was
conscious of the Starlifter settling into a more natural flying pattern.
Then came the heavy grind as its landing gear locked into place. The
one burst of fire from the French fighters had done the trick, he
thought. The international symbol for an aircraft's surrender was the
lowering of its landing gear.

Inside the control cabin, the air was less foul. Lavender went straight towards one of the oval windows and reported that they seemed to be losing height. "There's a pair of fighter aircraft on this side," she called.

Bond made for the other window. Below, the coastline was coming up, and on his side two Mirages kept station. He peered down and saw the familiar shape of the Canigou. They were making an escorted final approach to Perpignan.

Bond looked around. The bodies of the two technicians had been thrown across the cabin, but of Anton Murik there was no sign. The Laird of Murcaldy had disappeared.

In the briefing that followed when they landed at Perpignan, one of the Mirage pilots reported seeing a man fall from the rear ramp: undoubtedly Caber. Another thought that a crew member may have baled out after the fighters had fired their shells, but in the general mêlée he could not be certain.

It was, then, with a certain number of unanswered questions that Bond reported to M that evening at the Regent's Park headquarters.

Warlock's Castle

"You ran it a bit too close for comfort, 007." M sat at his desk, facing Bond.

"For whose comfort, sir?" James Bond was weary after the long debriefing. Since his arrival back in London, Bond had gone over the story a number of times. One of the senior female officers was looking after Lavender—and, no doubt, grilling her as well, thought Bond.

"Even then you let him get away." M sounded irritated.

"Too close for whose comfort, sir?" Bond repeated.

M waved the question to one side. "Everybody's. What concerns me now is the whereabouts of Anton Murik, so-called Laird of Murcaldy."

The white phone bleeped on M's desk. Following a brief exchange, M turned to his chief-of-staff. "There's a signal in from Perpignan. Bring it up, will you?"

The news at least solved part of the mystery: the French

authorities had now been over the Starlifter from stem to stern and had discovered a small hold, accessible from under one of the tables in the canteen. It was large enough to conceal one man and was kitted out with sufficient rations for a few days. There were signs that it had been used; and the exit, through movable plates on the underside of the fuselage, had been opened.

"That settles it," M snapped, picking up his phone. "Better get this report typed up and signed, Bond. I'll have to alert Duggan and Ross. The fellow's still at large."

Bond held up a hand as though appealing for M to put down the phone. "With respect, sir, can I ask some questions? Then, maybe, make a couple of requests?"

M put down the telephone. "Ask away. I can promise nothing, but be quick. We haven't got all night."

"Are Duggan's men still prowling around Murik Castle?"

"Moved out this afternoon. They'd been over the castle and Murcaldy village with the proverbial fine-tooth comb."

"Did they find anything? Legal documents, mainly concerning Miss Peacock? Well-hidden?"

"Haven't a clue, 007. Hidden documents?"

"Can you find out, sir? Without mentioning when my report'll be going to Sir Richard Duggan and Special Branch?"

M raised his eyebrows. "This had better be good, 007." He stabbed at the telephone. Within minutes, Bond was listening to one side of a conversation between M and Sir Richard. At last M put down the phone, shaking his head. "They took away all stray papers. But no legal documents concerning Miss Peacock. Duggan says they'll be going over the castle again in a day or so."

"And, in the meantime, it's unguarded?"

M nodded. "Now the requests, eh, Bond?"

Bond swallowed. "Sir, can you hold my report for about forty-eight hours?"

"Why?"

"Because I don't want Special Branch thumping around there. If Murik's escaped I believe he'll be on his way back there now."

"Then Special Branch should be waiting for him . . ."

"No, sir. Anton Murik will be heading for the castle. He'll know

245

the time's come to destroy the evidence of Miss Peacock's claim to the title and estates of Murcaldy. I want to catch him in the act, alive if possible."

"You're asking me to bend the rules, 007. That's Duggan's territory, and I've no right . . ." He trailed into silent thought. "What exactly were you thinking of?"

"That the chief-of-staff comes with me, sir. That you give us forty-eight hours' freedom, and the use of a helicopter."

"Helicopter?"

"To get us up there quickly. Oh yes, and just before we go in, I'd like some kind of overflight. Just to make certain the coast is clear, that Murik hasn't arrived first."

"Overflight," M came near to shouting. "Overflight? Who do you think I am, 007? President of the United States?"

Bond tried to look sheepish. Bill Tanner was grinning. "Well, sir, haven't you got a couple of old Chipmunks and the odd Gazelle helicopter under your command?"

M fiddled with his pipe. "You sure you wouldn't like a squadron of fighter-bombers to strafe the place?"

Bond grinned. "I don't think that'll be necessary, sir."

There was a long pause before M spoke. "On one condition, Bond—providing, of course, the chief-of-staff agrees to this foolhardiness." He looked towards Bill Tanner, who nodded. "You do *not* go armed. I cannot allow you to move into Duggan's area of operations carrying arms. I know nothing about any of this, James," M said, with a sly smile. "But good luck." Then sarcastically, he added, "nothing else?"

"Well . . ." Bond looked away. "I wonder if Sir Richard's people could let us have the keys to the castle for a while? So that I can recover clothes left there, or some such excuse."

M sighed, made a grumbling noise, and reached for the telephone again.

IT WAS ALMOST four o'clock in the morning when the Gazelle helicopter carrying James Bond and Bill Tanner reached Glen Murcaldy. Bond had already been through the landing pattern with the young pilot. He wanted to be put down on the track near to the point where the Saab had gone into the large ditch. Most of all, he was concerned that the Gazelle should be kept well out of sight.

Exactly five minutes before reaching touchdown, they heard the code word "Excelsior" through their headphones. The Chipmunk had overflown the castle, giving them the all-clear. There was no sign of any vehicle or other helicopter in the vicinity.

The rotor blades of the Gazelle had not stopped turning by the time Bond and Tanner were making their way through the gorse and bracken towards the grim mass of Murik Castle. They carried no weapons, as instructed, though Bill Tanner had got hold of a pair of powerful torches. It took over half an hour for the pair to get as far as the Great Lawn. Bond, silently making signals, took Tanner alongside the rear of the castle, the old keep rising above them like a dark brooding warning against the skyline. If Bond was right it would be from the helicopter pad behind the keep that Anton Murik would make his final visit to his castle.

In spite of the place having been empty only for a short time, the air smelled musty and damp once they got inside the small tradesmen's door. Bond had to find his way down to the laird's control room and collection of weapons; for Bond was certainly not going to face Murik without some kind of defence. For a while they blundered around by torchlight, until Bond finally led the way down to the long weapon-adorned room in the cellars.

Outside, dawn would just be breaking. If Murik was going to make his dash for freedom he would either arrive soon, or wait for the cover of nightfall. Bond was running his torch over the weapons when Tanner suddenly clutched at his arm. They stood, motionless, ears straining for a moment. From a long way off, they could both hear the faint buzz of an engine.

"He's arrived." Bond grabbed at the first thing he could lay hands on: a sporting crossbow, with a thick taut cord bound securely to a metal bow, the well-oiled mechanism including a *cranequin* to pull back and latch the cord into place. Taking this and three sharp bolts which were next to it, Bond motioned Tanner out of the room.

"Up to the hall," he whispered. "The light's not in his favour. He'll want to get hold of the stuff and be away fast. Pray God we can catch the bastard outside."

There would be more chance in the open. Bond was sure of that. They reached the hall, and the noise of the helicopter became louder as it fluttered down behind the keep.

Somewhere towards the back of the house, there was the scratch and squeak of a door. Murik, too, was entering by the tradesmen's door. Thank heaven Tanner had locked it behind them. There was a click and then the sound of footsteps moving surely, as a man will move in complete darkness when he knows his house with the deep intimacy of years. The steps were short and quick: unmistakable to Bond. Murik—Warlock—was home again.

From far away outside came the gentle buzz of the chopper's engine, which meant the pilot was almost certainly waiting in his cockpit. Bond signalled with the crossbow, and they set off silently in the direction of the door through which the laird had returned. Outside it was almost fully light now, with only faint traces of cloud, pink from the reflected rising sun. The noise of the helicopter came from behind the keep, to which Bond now pointed. Side by side, Tanner and Bond sought the edge of the old stone tower, and sheltered behind one angled corner, from which they had a view of the castle's rear.

Bond bent to the task of turning the heavy *cranequin*, panting as the steel bow drew back and its cord finally clicked into place. Raising the weapon skywards for safety, Bond slid one of the bolts into place. He had no idea of its accuracy, though there was no doubt of its being a lethal weapon.

The seven or eight minutes' wait seemed like a couple of hours. Then they heard footsteps fast on the gravel. Lifting the crossbow to his shoulder, Bond stepped from his cover. Anton Murik was running hard, heading for the far side of the keep. In his left hand he carried a bulky oilskin package, while in his right he clutched at something Bond could not quite see. Squinting down the primitive crossbow sights, Bond shouted, "Far enough, Murik. It's over now."

The Laird of Murcaldy hardly paused, seeming to turn slightly towards Bond's voice, his right hand rising. There was a sharp crack followed by a high-pitched screaming hiss. A long spurt of fire streaked from Murik's hand, passing so close between Bond and

Tanner that they felt the heat from the projectile which hit the side of the keep with the thud of a sledgehammer. A whole block of the old stone cracked and splattered away, sending great shards flying. Tanner gave a little cry, clutching his cheek, where a section of sharp stone had sliced him.

Bond knew immediately what Murik was using: a collector's item now, the MBA Gyrojet Rocket pistol, whose 13mm bullets were capable of penetrating thick steel plates.

Bond did not hesitate. Before Murik—still running—could hurl another rocket from his Gyrojet, he squeezed the trigger of the crossbow. The mechanism slammed forward, its power taking Bond by surprise. Any hiss the bolt might have made through the air was blotted out by Murik's cry as the heavy bolt speared the upper part of his chest.

Murik continued to run, as both Bond and Tanner started after him. Then he staggered and the Gyrojet pistol dropped onto the gravel. Still clutching at the oilskin package, Murik doggedly ran towards the rising ground above the helicopter pad.

Bond ran hard, pausing only to sweep up the Gyrojet, and checking that there was a rocket in place. Grunting with pain, Anton Murik was gasping his way up the bank as Bond shouted to him for the second time. "Stop, Anton. I don't want to kill you; but I'll fire if you don't stop now."

Murik continued, as though he could hear nothing, until he reached the top of the mound.

Bond shouted "Stop" once more, but for Murik there was no turning back. Carefully Bond levelled the Gyrojet pistol and squeezed the trigger. There was a crack, then he felt the butt push back into his hand as the rocket left the barrel—a long trace of fire moving faster and faster until it struck Murik's back.

It was as though someone had taken a blowlamp to the back of a cardboard cut-out target; for the centre of Murik's back disintegrated, and his body was lifted a good six feet above the ground before falling forwards out of sight.

Tanner was beside Bond, his face streaked scarlet with blood, as they paced each other up the bank. Below, the pilot was revving his motor for takeoff. One glance towards Bond and the levelled

Gyrojet pistol changed his mind. The pilot shut down the engine and slowly climbed from the cockpit, placing his hands over his head.

Bond handed the weapon to Bill Tanner and descended towards the mangled remains of Anton Murik. He hardly looked at the body. What he wanted lay a short way off—a heavy, thick oilskin package, which he picked up before turning to walk slowly up the rise towards the old keep. There Bond stood for a good two minutes, taking a final look at the castle. Warlock's Castle.

Quite a Lady

James Bond stood on the station platform, looking up into Lavender Peacock's bright eyes. It had been one of the best summers of his life, but he knew that all good things must end some time. Now, the moment had come.

The packet recovered at Murik's death contained a whole folio of interesting items. Most important of all was the documentation concerning Murik's real parenthood and Lavender's claim to the estates and title. These documents were placed in the hands of solicitors in Scotland, and Bond was optimistic that there would be a quick ruling on the matter. In a few months Lavender would gain her inheritance.

In the meantime, Bond had been given a long leave to recuperate; though Bill Tanner had stayed on duty, his cheek decorated with sticking plaster for over a month.

A few days after his return from Murcaldy, Bond had left with Lavender, by car, for the French Riviera. To begin with, things had gone according to plan. Thinking it would be a great treat, Bond had taken the girl to the best hotels; but she was unsettled, and did not like the fuss. So they decided on more simple pleasures—motoring into the mountains, staying in small villages far away from the crowded resorts, or at little-known seaside places, basking in the sun, lazing, eating, talking and loving.

Bond explained the new responsibilities that would soon be thrust upon her, and Lavender slowly became more serious and withdrawn. They were still having fun, but, as the weeks passed, Bond noticed she was spending more time writing letters, making telephone calls. Then one morning, out of the blue, she announced that they must return to England.

So it turned out that, a week after their return to London, Lavender visited a solicitor in Gray's Inn, who was acting for a firm in Edinburgh, to be told that the Scottish courts had upheld her claim to the Murik estates and title.

Two days later, Lavender visited Bond with the news that she had obtained a place at one of the major agricultural colleges, where she was going to study estate management. She would be leaving on the sleeper that night to tie up matters in Edinburgh. "I want to get the place running properly again," she told him. "It needs a new broom and a blast of cold air blowing through it."

Bond would not have tried to stop her. She was right, and he felt proud of having had some part in what looked like a glowing future. He took her out to dinner, then drove her to the station.

"You'll come and stay, James, won't you? When I've got it all going again, I mean." She leaned down out of the train window, the last-minute bustle going on around them.

"You try and stop me," he said with a smile. "Just try. But you might have to hold my hand at night—to lay the ghosts."

"The ghosts? Really? It'll be a pleasure, James." Lady Murik leaned forward and kissed him just as the train started to move. "Goodbye, my dear James. See you again soon."

"Yes, Dilly, you'll see me again soon." He stepped back, raising a hand.

Quite a Lady, thought James Bond, as the train snaked from the platform. Quite a Lady.

John Gardner

When John Gardner was asked to revive Ian Fleming's incomparable hero, James Bond, he jumped at the chance; he had long admired Fleming's books and was thrilled to be given the opportunity to carry on the tradition. Indeed, Gardner's own early books, featuring agent Boysie Oakes, had established something of a tradition themselves—as spoofs of the Bond adventures!

Times have changed since those first Boysie Oakes novels and Gardner has branched out into other areas—writing straight novels and suspense thrillers such as *The Garden of Weapons*, *The Nostradamus Traitor* and *The Werewolf Trace*. He is a master storyteller in his own right, and his books have sold a staggering three million copies throughout the world.

John Gardner was born in a small mining village in the north of England the day after the seven month miners' strike of 1926 ended. His father, the local vicar, had to forage for coal on the slag heaps to heat the bedroom during the birth. "I've loathed cold weather ever since," Gardner comments.

By the time he was a teenager, there were only two things he wanted to do—go on the stage or write. The war came, and Gardner served with the Royal Marines in the Far and Middle East, returning home with the same ambitions he had had before.

None of the right opportunities came his way so his parents persuaded him to enter the Church. About a year after his ordination, however—to use his own words—"A little voice inside me said 'WRONG'." There followed the most traumatic period of his life—a struggle with conscience and belief; then a struggle with the authorities as he took the final decision to relinquish Holy Orders.

Eventually he got a job as drama critic with the *Stratford Herald*, and for the next eight years he covered plays and films for that paper. It was at this time he wrote *The Liquidator*, the first of the Boysie Oakes adventures, which launched his successful career as an author.

John Gardner now lives in the peaceful seclusion of the Wicklow mountains, where he is currently at work on his second James Bond novel.

THE
CRADLE
WILL
FALL

a condensation of the book by

Mary
Higgins Clark

ILLUSTRATED BY DAVID BLOSSOM
PUBLISHED BY COLLINS

Katie DeMaio's life was in deadly
peril—but she didn't know it. As Valley
County's assistant prosecutor,
she was busy investigating the mysterious
deaths of Vangie Lewis, a pretty,
young, expectant mother, and Edna Burns,
receptionist at the maternity clinic at Westlake Hospital.
It was there that the esteemed Dr. Edgar Highley
was making medical history by helping
previously barren women achieve motherhood.
Vangie Lewis, for instance, had been
desperate to have a baby. Why, then, had she taken
her own life? It seemed unfathomable
until Westlake's maternity clinic gave up,
one by one, its horrifying secrets.

CHAPTER ONE

IF HER mind had not been on the case she had won, Katie might not have taken the curve so fast, but the intense satisfaction of the guilty verdict was still absorbing her. It had been a close one. Roy O'Connor was one of the top attorneys in New Jersey. The defendant's confession had been suppressed by the court, a major blow for the prosecution. But still she had convinced the jury that Teddy Copeland had viciously murdered eighty-year-old Abigail Rawlings during a robbery.

Miss Rawlings' sister, Margaret, was in court to hear the verdict. "You were wonderful, Mrs. DeMaio," she'd said to Katie afterward. "You look like a young college girl. I never would have thought you could do it. But you *proved* every point; you made them *feel* what he did to Abby." Her eyes filled with tears. "I keep thinking how frightened Abby must have been. It would have been awful if he'd gotten away with it."

"*He didn't get away with it!*" Katie said. The memory of that reassurance distracted her now, made her press her foot harder on the accelerator. As she rounded the curve, the car fishtailed on the sleet-covered road.

"Oh . . . no!" She gripped the wheel frantically. The car raced across the divider and spun completely around. She could see headlights approaching.

She turned the wheel into the skid, but the car careened onto the shoulder of the road, poised for an instant at the edge and slammed down the embankment into the woods. Katie felt the sickening crunch as metal tore into bark. Her body was flung forward against the wheel, then backward. She raised her arms to protect her face from the glass that exploded from the windshield. Biting pain attacked her wrists and knees. Velvety blackness was closing over her as she heard a siren in the distance.

The car door opening; a blast of cold air. "It's Katie DeMaio!" A voice she knew. Tom Coughlin, that nice young cop. He had testified at a trial last week. "She's unconscious."

She tried to protest, but her lips wouldn't form words. She couldn't open her eyes.

"Looks like she's cut an artery."

Something tight was being pressed against her arm.

A different voice: "She may have internal injuries. Westlake's right down the road. I'll call for an ambulance."

Hands lifting her onto a stretcher, a blanket covering her, sleet pelting her face. She was being carried. An ambulance. Doors opening and closing. If only she could make them understand. I can hear you. I'm not unconscious.

Tom was giving her name. "Kathleen DeMaio, lives in Abbington. She's an assistant prosecutor. Judge DeMaio's widow."

John's widow. A terrible sense of aloneness. The blackness was starting to recede. A light was shining in her eyes. "She's coming around. How old are you, Mrs. DeMaio?"

The question, so practical, so easy to answer. "Twenty-eight."

The tourniquet Tom had wrapped around her arm was being removed. Her arm was being stitched. Needles of pain.

X rays. The emergency-room doctor. "You're fortunate, Mrs. DeMaio. Some severe bruises but no fractures. I've ordered a transfusion. Your blood count is very low. Don't be frightened."

"It's just—" She bit her lip, managed to stop herself before she blurted out that terrible, childish fear of hospitals.

Tom asking, "Do you want us to call your sister?"

"No. Molly's just over the flu. They've all had it." Her voice was so weak that Tom had to bend over to hear her.

"All right. Don't worry, Katie. I'll have your car hauled out."

She was wheeled into a curtained-off section of the emergency room. Blood began dripping through a tube inserted into her right arm. A nurse was smoothing her hair back from her forehead. "You're going to be fine, Mrs. DeMaio. Why are you crying?"

"I'm *not* crying." But she was.

She was wheeled into a room. The nurse handed her a paper cup of water and a pill. "This will help you rest, Mrs. DeMaio." It must be a sleeping pill. Katie was sure it would give her nightmares. The nurse turned off the light as she left.

Katie slid into sleep knowing a nightmare was inevitable. This time it took a different form. She was on a roller coaster and she couldn't control it. It kept climbing higher and higher, and then it went off the tracks and it was falling. She woke up trembling just before it hit the ground.

Sleet rapped on the window. She sat up. The window was open a crack and the shade, which was pulled halfway down, was rattling. She'd close the window and raise the shade. Then maybe she'd be able to sleep.

Unsteadily she walked over to the window. The hospital gown they'd given her barely came to her knees. Her legs were cold. She leaned against the windowsill, looked out. Sleet was mixed with rain now. The parking lot was running with streams of water.

Katie gripped the shade and stared down into the lot one story below. The trunk lid of a car was going up slowly. She was so dizzy now. She let go of the shade. It snapped up. Was something white floating down into the trunk? A blanket? A large bundle?

She must be dreaming, she thought. Then she pushed her hand over her mouth to muffle the shriek that tore at her throat. The trunk light was on. Through the waves of sleet-filled rain that slapped against the window, she watched the white substance part. As the trunk closed, she saw a face—the face of a woman grotesque in the uncaring abandon of death.

THE alarm had awakened him promptly at two o'clock. He was instantly alert. Getting up, he went over to the examining-room sink, splashed cold water on his face, pulled his tie into a smooth knot, combed his hair and put on his steel-rimmed glasses. His socks were still wet when he took them off the radiator. Grimacing, he pulled them on and slipped into his shoes. He reached for his overcoat. It was soaked through.

He'd wear the old Burberry raincoat he kept in the closet. It was unlined. He'd freeze, but it was the only thing to do. Besides, it was so ordinary that if anyone saw him, there was less chance of being recognized.

He hurried to the closet, put on the raincoat and hung up the heavy wet chesterfield. He went over to the window and pulled the shade back an inch. There were still enough cars in the parking lot so that the absence of his own would hardly be noticed. He bit his lip as he realized that the back of his car was silhouetted by the light at the far side of the lot. He would have to walk in the shadows of the other cars and get the body into the trunk as quickly as possible.

It was time. Unlocking the medical supply closet, he bent down and picked up the body. She had once weighed around one hundred ten pounds, but she had gained a lot of weight during her pregnancy. His muscles felt every ounce as he carried her to the examining table. There he wrapped a blanket around her. Noiselessly he opened the door to the parking lot. Grasping the trunk key in two fingers, he moved to the table and picked up the dead woman. Now for the twenty seconds that could destroy him.

Eighteen seconds later he was at the car. Sleet pelted his cheek; the blanket-covered burden strained his arms. Shifting the weight, he inserted his key into the trunk lock. The lid rose slowly. He glanced up at the hospital windows. From the center room on the second floor a shade snapped up. Was anyone looking out? Impatient to have the blanketed figure out of his arms, he moved too quickly. The instant his left hand let go of the blanket, the wind blew it open, revealing her face. Wincing, he dropped the body and slammed the trunk closed.

The trunk light had been on the face. Had anyone seen? He looked up again at the window where the shade had been raised. Was someone there? He couldn't be sure. Later he would have to find out who was in that room.

Driving swiftly from the lot, he kept the headlights off until he was well along the road. Incredible that this was his second trip to Chapin River tonight. Suppose he hadn't been leaving the hospital when Vangie Lewis burst out of Dr. Fukhito's office and hailed him. Vangie had been close to hysteria as she limped down the covered portico to him. "Doctor, I'm going to Minneapolis tomorrow. I'm going to see the doctor I used to have, Dr. Emmet Salem. Maybe I'll even stay there and let him deliver the baby."

If he had missed her, everything would have been ruined.

Instead he had persuaded her to come into the office with him, talked to her, calmed her down, offered her a glass of water. At the last minute she'd suspected. That beautiful, petulant face had filled with fear.

And then the horror of knowing that even though he'd managed to silence her, the chance of discovery was still so great. He had locked her body in the medical supply closet and tried to think.

Her bright red Lincoln Continental had been the immediate danger. It would surely have been noticed in the hospital parking lot after visiting hours.

He knew she lived on Winding Brook Lane in Chapin River. She'd told him that her husband, a United Airlines pilot, wasn't due home until tomorrow. He'd leave her body in the closet while he took her car and handbag to the house, to make it seem as though she'd driven home. He'd dispose of the body later.

It had been unexpectedly easy. The houses in Chapin River were placed far back from the road and reached by winding driveways. He'd parked the car inside her garage.

The door from the garage to the den was unlocked. There were lamps on throughout the house, probably on a timing device. He'd hurried through the den and down the hall. The master bedroom was the last one on the right. There were two other bedrooms, one a nursery, with colorful elves and lambs on the wallpaper and an obviously new crib and chest.

That was when he realized he might be able to make her death look like a suicide. If she'd begun to furnish the nursery three months before the baby was expected, the threatened loss of that baby would provide a powerful motive. He would have to get her body back here, put it on top of her own bed! It was dangerous, but not as dangerous as dumping her body in the woods some-where. That would have meant an intensive police investigation.

He had left her handbag on the chaise longue in the master bedroom and then walked the four miles back to the hospital. There he skirted the main entrance and let himself into his office through the door from the parking lot. It was just ten o'clock.

His coat and shoes and socks were soaked. He was shivering. He realized it would be too dangerous to carry the body out until there was a minimal chance of encountering anyone. He'd set the alarm for two o'clock, then lain down on the examining table and managed to sleep until the alarm went off.

Now for the second time that night he was pulling into Vangie's driveway. Turn off the headlights; back the car up to the garage; put on surgical gloves; open the garage door; open the trunk; carry the wrapped form past the storage shelves to the inside door. He stepped into the den. In a few minutes he'd be safe.

He hurried down the hall to the master bedroom and placed the body on the bed, pulling the blanket free. In the adjoining bathroom, he shook crystals of cyanide into the flowered blue tumbler, added water and poured most of the contents down the sink. He rinsed the sink carefully and returned to the bedroom. Placing the glass next to the dead woman's hand, he allowed the last drops of the mixture to spill on the spread. He folded the white blanket carefully.

The body was sprawled face up on the bed, eyes staring, lips contorted in an agony of protest. That was all right. Most suicides changed their minds when it was too late.

Had he missed anything? No. Her handbag, with the keys, was on the chaise; there was a residue of the cyanide in the glass. Coat on or off? He'd leave it on. The less he handled her the better. Shoes off or on? Would she have kicked them off?

He lifted the long caftan she was wearing and felt the blood drain from his face. The swollen right foot wore a battered moc-casin. Her left foot was covered only by her stocking. The other moccasin must have fallen off. Where? He ran from the bedroom, searching, retracing his steps. The shoe was not in the house or garage. Frantic, he ran out to his car and looked in the trunk. The shoe was not there. It had probably come off when he was carrying her in the parking lot.

Because of her swollen foot, she'd been wearing the moccasins recently. He'd heard the receptionist joke with her about them.

He would have to go back and search the parking lot. Suppose someone said, "Why, I saw her moccasin lying in the parking lot. She must have lost it on her way home Monday night"? But if she had walked even a few feet off the portico without a shoe, the sole of her stocking would be badly soiled. The police would notice that it was not.

Rushing back to the bedroom, he opened the door of the walk-in closet. A jumble of women's shoes were scattered on the floor. Most of them had impossibly high heels for a woman in her condition to wear. Then he saw a pair of sensible low-heeled shoes, the kind most pregnant women wore. They looked fairly new. Relieved, he grabbed them. Hurrying to the bed, he pulled the one moccasin from the dead woman's foot and placed the shoes on her feet. The right one was tight, but he managed to lace it. Jamming the moccasin into the wide, loose pocket of his raincoat, he picked up the white blanket and strode quickly to the garage.

At the hospital parking lot, he drove to a far corner and parked the car. Then he hurried to retrace his steps from the space where he'd kept the car to the door of the office. The shoe might have fallen off when he'd shifted the body to open the trunk. Bending forward, he searched the ground, working his way closer to the hospital.

Headlights came around the bend into the parking lot. A car screeched to a halt. The driver, probably looking for the emergency entrance, made a U-turn and raced out of the lot.

He had to get out of here. He fell forward as he tried to straighten up. His hand slid across the slippery macadam. And then he felt leather under his fingers. He had found the shoe.

Fifteen minutes later he was turning the key in the lock of his home. Peeling off the raincoat, he hung it in the foyer closet. The full-length mirror on the door reflected his image. Shocked, he realized that his trouser knees were wet and dirty. His hair was badly disheveled. His cheeks were flushed, and his eyes were bulging and dilated. He looked like a caricature of himself. Rushing upstairs, he undressed, bathed, got into pajamas and a robe. He was too keyed up to sleep, and savagely hungry.

The housekeeper had left slices of lamb on a plate. Crisp, tart apples were in the fruit bin of the refrigerator. Carefully he prepared a tray and carried it into the library. From the bar he poured a generous whiskey and sat at his desk. As he ate, he reviewed the night's happenings. If he had not stopped to check his calendar, he would have missed her, been unable to stop her.

Unlocking his desk, he opened the large center drawer and slid back the false bottom, where he kept his current special file. He took out a single manila folder. Then he reached for a fresh sheet of paper and made a final entry:

February 15

At 8:40 p.m. this physician was locking the rear door of his office. Subject patient had just left Fukhito. She approached this physician and said she was going home to Minneapolis and would have her former doctor, Emmet Salem, deliver her baby. Hysterical patient was persuaded to come inside. Obviously patient could not be allowed to leave. Getting her a glass of water, this physician dissolved cyanide crystals into the glass and forced patient to swallow the poison. Patient expired at 8:51 p.m. Fetus was 26 weeks old. Had it been born it might have been viable.

Laying down the pen, he slipped the final entry into the manila folder, then walked over to a panel on the bookcase. Reaching behind a book, he touched a button, and the panel swung open, revealing a wall safe. Quickly he opened the safe and inserted the file, subconsciously noting the growing number of folders. He could have recited the names on them by heart. Elizabeth Berkeley, Anna Horan, Maureen Crowley, Linda Evans—over six dozen of them: the successes and failures of his medical genius.

He closed the safe, snapped the panel back into place, then went upstairs and got into bed. Had he overlooked anything? He'd put the vial of cyanide in the safe. He'd get rid of the moccasins tomorrow night. The events of the last hours whirled furiously through his mind.

He'd drop his suit at the cleaners on the way to the hospital. He'd find out what patient was in the center room on the second floor of the hospital's east wing, what that patient could have seen. Now he must sleep.

"IF YOU don't mind, we'd like you to leave through the rear entrance," the nurse told Katie. "The front driveway froze over terribly, and the workmen are trying to clear it. The cab will be waiting in back."

"I don't care if I climb out the window, just as long as I can get home," Katie said fervently. "And the misery is that I have to come back here Friday. I'm having minor surgery on Saturday."

"Oh." The nurse looked at her chart. "What's wrong?"

"I seem to have inherited a problem my mother used to have. I practically hemorrhage every month during my period."

"That must be why your blood count was so low when you came in. Who's your doctor?"

"Dr. Highley."

"Oh, he's the best. He's top man in this place, you know." She helped Katie with her coat.

The morning was cloudy and bitterly cold. Katie shivered as she stepped out into the parking lot. In her nightmare, this was the area she had been looking at from her room. A cab pulled up. Gratefully she got in, wincing at the pain in her knees. "Where to, lady?" the driver asked, and pressed the accelerator.

From the window of the room that Katie had just left, a man was observing her departure. Her chart was in his hand. It read: "Kathleen N. DeMaio, 10 Woodfield Way, Abbington. Place of Business: prosecutor's office, Valley County, New Jersey."

He felt a thrill of fear go through him. *Katie DeMaio.*

There was a note on the chart that the night nurse had found her sitting on the edge of the bed at two eight a.m. in an agitated state and complaining about nightmares. The chart also showed she had been given a sleeping pill, so she would have been pretty groggy. But how much had she seen? Even if she thought she'd been dreaming, her professional training would nag at her. She was a risk, an unacceptable one.

CHAPTER TWO

SHOULDERS touching, Chris Lewis and Joan Moore sat in the end booth of the Eighty-seventh Street drugstore, sipping coffee. Her left arm rested on the gold braid on his right sleeve. Their fingers were entwined.

"I've missed you," he said carefully.

"I've missed you too, Chris. That's why I'm sorry you met me this morning. It just makes it worse."

"Joan, give me a little time. I swear we'll work this out."

She shook her head. He saw how unhappy she looked. Her hazel eyes were cloudy. Her light brown hair, pulled back in a chignon, emphasized the paleness of her smooth, clear skin.

For the thousandth time he asked himself why he hadn't made a clean break with Vangie when he was transferred to New York last year. Why had he given in to her plea to try a little longer to make a go of their marriage when ten years of trying hadn't done it? And now a baby coming. He thought of the ugly quarrel he'd had with Vangie before he left. Should he tell Joan about that? No, it wouldn't do any good.

Joan was a flight attendant with Pan American. She was based in New York and shared an apartment with two other Pan Am attendants. Chris had met her six months ago at a party in Hawaii.

Incredible how right some people are together from the first minute. He'd told her he was married, but was able to say honestly that he had wanted to break with his wife when he transferred from Minneapolis to New York. But he hadn't.

Joan was saying, "You got in last night?"

"Yes. We had engine trouble in Chicago, and the rest of the flight was canceled. Got back around six and stayed in town."

"Why didn't you go home?"

"Because I wanted to see you. Vangie doesn't expect me till later this morning. So don't worry."

"Chris, I told you I applied for a transfer to the Latin American division. It's been approved. I'm moving to Miami next week."

"Joan, no!"

"I'm sorry, but it's not my nature to be an available lady for a man who is not only married but whose wife is finally expecting the baby she's prayed for for ten years. I'm not a home wrecker."

"Our relationship has been totally innocent."

"In today's world who would believe that?" She finished her coffee. "No matter what you say, Chris, I still feel that if I'm not around, there's a chance that you and your wife will grow closer. A baby has a way of creating a bond between people." Gently she withdrew her fingers from his. "I'd better get home. It was a long flight and I'm tired. You'd better go home too."

They looked at each other. Chris tried to smile. "I'm not giving up, Joan. I'm coming to Miami for you, and when I get there, I'll be free."

THE cab dropped Katie off. She hurried painfully up the porch steps, thrust her key into the lock, opened the door and murmured, "Thank God I'm home." She felt that she'd been away weeks rather than overnight and with fresh eyes appreciated the soothing earth tones of the foyer and living room, the hanging plants.

Katie hung up her coat and sank down on the living-room couch. She looked at her husband's portrait over the mantel. John Anthony DeMaio, the youngest judge in Essex County. She could remember so clearly the first time she'd seen him. He'd come to lecture to her class at Seton Hall Law School.

When the class ended, the students clustered around him. Katie said, "Judge, I have to tell you I don't agree with your decision in the *Kipling* case."

John had smiled. "That obviously is your privilege, Miss . . ."

"Katie . . . Kathleen Callahan."

She never understood why at that moment she'd dragged up the Kathleen, but he'd always called her that.

They'd gone out for coffee that day. The next night he'd taken her to dinner in New York. Later, when he'd dropped her off, he said, "You have the loveliest blue eyes I've ever had the pleasure of looking into. I don't think a twelve-year age difference is too much, do you, Kathleen?"

Three months later, when she was graduated, they were married and came to live in the house John had inherited from his parents. "I'm pretty attached to it, Kathleen, but maybe you want something smaller."

"John, I was raised in a three-room apartment in Queens. I slept on a daybed in the living room. I *love* this house."

Besides being so much in love, they were good friends. She'd told him about her recurring nightmare. "It started when I was eight years old. My father had been in the hospital recovering from a heart attack and then he had a second attack. The old man in the room with him kept buzzing for the nurse, but no one came. By the time someone finally got there, it was too late. In my nightmare I'm in a hospital going from bed to bed, looking for Daddy. I keep seeing people I know asleep in the beds. Finally I see a nurse and run up to her and ask her where Daddy is. She smiles and says, 'Oh, he's dead. All these people are dead. You're going to die in here too.'"

"You poor kid."

"Oh, John, I missed him so much. I was always such a daddy's girl. All through school I kept thinking what fun it would be if he were at the plays and the graduations."

"Kathleen, darling, I'm going to uproot that sadness in you."

"You already have, Judge."

They'd spent their honeymoon traveling through Italy. John's pain had begun on that trip. He'd had a checkup a month after they got home. The overnight stay at Mount Sinai Hospital stretched into three days of additional tests. Then one evening he'd been waiting for her at the elevator, a wan smile on his face. He said, "We've got trouble, darling."

Back in his room, he'd told her. "It's a malignant tumor. Both lungs, apparently."

It seemed incredible. Judge DeMaio, not thirty-eight years old, had been condemned to an indeterminate sentence of six months to life. For him there would be no parole, no appeal.

Knowing their time was slipping away, they made every minute count. But the cancer spread, and the pain got steadily worse. He'd go to the hospital for chemotherapy. Her nightmare began again; it came regularly.

Toward the end, he said, "I'm glad Molly and Bill live nearby. They'll look out for you. And you enjoy the children."

They'd both been silent then. Bill Kennedy was an orthopedic surgeon. He and Molly lived two towns away in Chapin River and had six kids. John had bragged that he and Katie would beat Bill and Molly's record. "We'll have seven," he'd declared.

The last time he went in for chemotherapy, he was so weak they had him stay overnight. He was talking to her when he slipped into a coma. He died that night.

The next week Katie applied to the prosecutor's office for a job and was accepted. The office was chronically shorthanded, and she always had more cases than she could reasonably handle. It was good therapy. There was no time for introspection.

She'd kept the house, although it seemed silly for a young woman to own a large home surrounded by five acres.

"You'll never put your life with John behind you until you sell it," Bill had told her. He was probably right.

Now Katie shook herself and got up from the couch. She'd better call Molly and tell her about the accident. Maybe Molly would come over for lunch and cheer her up. Glancing into the mirror over the couch, Katie saw that a bruise under her right eye was turning a brilliant purple. Her olive complexion was a sickly yellow. Her collar-length dark brown hair, which usually bounced full and luxuriant in a natural wave, was matted against her face and neck. After she talked to Molly, she'd bathe and change.

Before she could pick up the phone, it began to ring. It was Richard Carroll, the medical examiner. "Katie, how are you? Just heard that you were in some kind of accident last night."

"Nothing much. I took a little detour off the road. The trouble is there was a tree in the way."

"Why the blazes didn't you call me?"

Richard's concern was both flattering and threatening. He and Molly's husband were good friends. Several times Molly had pointedly invited Katie and Richard to small dinner parties. But Katie wasn't looking to get involved, especially with someone she worked with. "Next time I run into a tree I'll remember," she said.

"You're going to take a couple of days off, aren't you?"

"Oh, no. I'm going to see if Molly's free for lunch; then I'll go in to the office. I'm trying a case on Friday."

"There's no use telling you you're crazy. Okay. Gotta go. I'll poke my head in your office around five thirty and catch you for a drink. Then dinner." He hung up before she could reply.

Katie dialed Molly's number. When her sister answered, her voice was shaken. "Katie, I guess you've heard about it. People from your office are just getting there."

"Heard about what? Getting where?"

"Next door. The Lewises. That couple who moved in last summer. That poor man; he came home and found his wife, Vangie. She's killed herself. Katie, she was six months pregnant!"

The Lewises. Katie had met them at Molly and Bill's New Year's Day open house. Vangie, a very pretty blonde. Chris, an airline pilot. Numbly she heard Molly's shocked voice: "Katie, why would a girl who wanted a baby so desperately kill herself?"

The question hung in the air. Cold chills washed over Katie. Last night's nightmare. The face she'd glimpsed through the hospital window was Vangie Lewis'.

RICHARD Carroll parked his car within the police lines on Winding Brook Lane. He was shocked to realize that the Lewises lived next door to Bill and Molly Kennedy. Bill had been a resident when Richard interned at St. Vincent's. Later he'd specialized in forensic medicine, Bill in orthopedics. They had bumped into each other in the Valley County courthouse when Bill was appearing as a witness in a malpractice trial, and their friendship was revived. Now they golfed together frequently, and Richard often stopped at the Kennedy house for a drink.

He'd met Molly's sister, Katie DeMaio, in the prosecutor's office and had been immediately attracted to the dedicated young attorney, with her dark hair and intense blue eyes. Katie had subtly discouraged him, and he'd tried to dismiss her from his thoughts. But in the past few months he'd seen her at a couple of parties at Bill and Molly's and had found that he was far more intrigued by Katie DeMaio than he wanted to be.

Richard shrugged. He was here on business. It was his job to look for any medical signs that might indicate Vangie Lewis had not taken her own life. Later in the day he'd perform an autopsy.

A young cop from Chapin River let him in. A man in an airline captain's uniform was sitting in the living room, clasping and unclasping his hands. He was pale and trembling. Richard felt a twinge of sympathy. Some brutal kick to come home and find your wife a suicide. "Which way?" he asked the cop.

"Back here." He nodded to the rear of the house. "She's in the master bedroom."

In death Vangie Lewis was not a pretty sight. The long blond hair seemed a muddy brown now; her face was contorted. Her coat was buttoned, and the soles of her shoes were barely showing under a long flowered caftan. Richard pulled the caftan up past her ankles; the sides of her right shoe bit into the flesh of her swollen foot. Expertly he picked up one arm, held it for an instant, let it drop. He studied the mottled discoloration where the poison had burned her mouth.

Charley Nugent, the detective in charge of the Homicide Squad, was beside him. "How long you figure?"

"Anywhere from twelve to fifteen hours. She's pretty rigid." Richard's voice was noncommittal, but his sense of harmony was disturbed. Coat on. Shoes on. Had she just come home, or had she been planning to go out? The tumbler was beside her on the bed. Bending down, he sniffed it—the unmistakable bitter-almond scent of cyanide. He straightened up. "Did she leave a note?"

Charley shook his head. "No letters; no nothing. Been married ten years to the pilot. He seems pretty broken up. They're from Minneapolis; moved east less than a year ago. She always wanted to have a baby. Finally got pregnant and was in heaven. Starts decorating a nursery; talks baby morning, noon and night."

"Then she kills it and herself?"

"Her husband says lately she's been afraid she was going to lose the baby. Other times she'd act scared about giving birth. Apparently she was showing signs of a toxic pregnancy."

"And rather than give birth or face losing the baby, she kills herself?" Richard's tone was skeptical. He could tell Charley wasn't buying it either. "Who found her?" he asked.

"The husband. He just got in from a flight."

Richard stared at the burn marks around Vangie Lewis' mouth. "She must have really splashed that in," he said, "or maybe tried to spit it out. Can we bring the husband in here?"

"Sure." Charley nodded to the young cop at the bedroom door.

When Christopher Lewis came in, he looked sick. His complexion was now green; perspiration beaded his forehead. He had pulled open his shirt and tie. Richard studied him appraisingly. Lewis looked distraught, nervous. But not like a man whose life has just been shattered.

Charley questioned him. "Captain, this is tough for you, but we won't be long. When was the last time you saw your wife?"

"Two nights ago. I was on a run to the Coast."

"And you arrived home at what time?"

"About an hour ago."

"Did you speak with your wife in those two days?"

"No."

"What was your wife's mental state when you left?"

"I told you. Vangie was worried that she might miscarry. She'd become quite heavy, and she was retaining fluid."

"Did you call her obstetrician to discuss this with him?"

"No."

"All right. Captain Lewis, will you look around this room and see if you notice anything amiss? It isn't easy, but will you study your wife's body carefully and see if there's anything that in some way is different."

Chris obeyed, his face going white as he looked at every detail of his dead wife's appearance.

Through narrowed eyes, Charley and Richard watched him.

"No," he whispered finally. "Nothing."

Charley's manner became brisk. "Okay. As soon as we take some pictures, we'll remove your wife's body for an autopsy."

"I have some calls to make," Lewis said. "Vangie's father and mother. They'll be heartbroken. I'll phone them from the den."

After he'd left, Richard and Charley exchanged glances.

"He saw something we missed," Charley said flatly.

Richard nodded grimly. "I know."

272

CHAPTER THREE

Before she'd hung up, Katie had told Molly about the accident and invited her over for lunch. But Molly's twelve-year-old, Jennifer, and her six-year-old twin boys were home from school recovering from flu. She would pick up Katie and bring her back to her own house.

While she waited, Katie bathed quickly, then put on a red wool sweater and tweed slacks. As she got herself ready, she tried to rationalize last night's hallucination.

Had she even *been* at the window? Or was that part of the dream? It had seemed so real: the trunk light had shone directly on the staring eyes, the long hair, the high-arched eyebrows. What frightened her was the clarity of the image.

Would she tell Molly about it? Of course not. Molly had been worried about her lately. "Katie, you're too pale. You work too hard. You're getting too quiet." Molly had bullied her into the operation scheduled for Saturday. "You can't let that hemorrhaging condition go on indefinitely. It can be dangerous."

From outside, a horn blew loudly as Molly pulled up in her battered station wagon. Katie struggled into a warm beaver jacket and hurried out as fast as her swollen knees would allow. Molly pushed open the car door and eyed her critically. "You're not exactly blooming. How badly *were* you hurt?"

"It could have been a lot worse."

The car smelled vaguely of peanut butter and bubble gum. It was a comforting, familiar smell, and Katie felt her spirits lift. But the mood was broken when Molly said, "Our block is some mess. Your people have the Lewis place blocked off, and some detective from your office is going around asking questions. Big guy. Beefy face. Nice."

"Phil Cunningham. He's a good man. What kind of questions?"

"Pretty routine. Had we noticed what time she left or got back— that kind of thing. We hadn't, of course."

They were approaching the turn to Winding Brook Lane. Katie bit her lip. "Molly, drop me off at the Lewis house, won't you?"

Molly looked at her, astonished. "Why?"

Katie tried to smile. "Well, I'm an assistant prosecutor and adviser to the Chapin River Police Department. As long as I'm here, I think I should go in."

The hearse from the medical examiner's office was just backing into the driveway of the Lewis home. Richard stood in the doorway, watching. He came over to the car when Molly pulled up. Quickly Molly explained. "Katie's having lunch with me and thought she should stop by here. Why don't you come over with her, if you can?"

He agreed, and helped Katie out of the car. "I'm glad you're here," he said. "There's something about this setup I don't like."

Now that she was about to see the dead woman, Katie felt her mouth go dry. She remembered the face in her dream.

"The husband is in the den," Richard said.

In the bedroom, Katie forced herself to look at the face. She recognized it instantly. She shuddered and closed her eyes.

"You all right, Katie?" Richard asked sharply.

"I'm fine. I'd like to talk to Captain Lewis now."

When they got to the den, the door was closed. Without knocking, Richard opened it quietly. Chris Lewis was on the phone, his back to them. His voice was low but distinct. "I know it's incredible, but I swear to you, Joan, she didn't know about us."

Richard closed the door noiselessly. He and Katie stared at each other. Katie said, "I'm going to recommend that we launch a full investigation."

"I'll do the autopsy as soon as they bring her in," Richard said. "Come on, let's make the stop at Molly's a quick one."

Molly's house, like her car, was a haven of normality. The smell of good food cooking, the blare of the television set, the kids shouting. When Katie went there, it was like reentering the real world, especially after a day of dealing with murderers, muggers, vandals and crooks.

The twins came whooping up to greet them. "Did you see all the cop cars, Katie? Something happened next door!" Peter, older than his twin by ten minutes, was always the spokesman.

"Next door!" John echoed. Molly called them Pete and Repeat.

"Get lost, you two," she ordered.

"Where's Jennifer?" Katie asked.

"She's in bed. Poor kid still feels lousy."

They settled at the kitchen table. Molly produced corned beef sandwiches and poured coffee. But when Katie tried to eat, she found her throat was closed. She glanced at Richard. He was eating with obvious pleasure. She envied him his detachment. On one level, he could enjoy a good sandwich. On the other, she was sure that he was concentrating on the Lewis case. His forehead was knitted; his thatch of brown hair looked ruffled; his blue-gray eyes were thoughtful. She'd have bet they were both pondering the same question: Who had been on the phone with Chris Lewis?

She remembered the only conversation she'd had with the airline captain. It had been at Molly's New Year's party, and he'd been interesting, intelligent, pleasant. With his rugged good looks, he was very appealing. She also remembered that he'd been unenthused when she congratulated him on the coming baby.

"Molly, what was your impression of the Lewises' marriage?" she asked.

Molly looked troubled. "I think it was on the rocks. Whenever they were here, she kept yanking the conversation back to babies, and he was upset about it. Since I had a hand in the pregnancy, it was a real worry for me."

Richard looked up. "You had *what?*"

"I mean, well, you know me, Katie. The day they moved in, last summer, I went rushing over and invited them to dinner. Right away Vangie told me how much she wanted a baby, and I told her about Liz Berkeley. She never was able to conceive until she went to a gynecologist who's something of a fertility expert. Liz had just given birth to a little girl. So I told Vangie about Dr. Highley. She went to him, and a few months later she conceived."

"Dr. Highley?" Katie looked startled.

Molly nodded. "Yes, the one who's going to . . ."

Katie shook her head, and Molly's voice trailed off.

EDNA Burns liked her job. She was receptionist-bookkeeper for the two doctors on the Westlake Maternity Concept team.

Dr. Edgar Highley was a gynecologist-obstetrician. As Edna

told her friends, "It's a riot to see the way his patients act when they finally get pregnant; so happy you'd think they invented kids. He charges plenty, but he's a miracle worker. On the other hand, Highley is also the man to see if you've got an internal problem that you *don't* want to grow. If you know what I mean."

Dr. Jiro Fukhito was the psychiatrist on the team. The Westlake Maternity Concept was one of holistic medicine. It was based on the idea that mind and body must be in harmony to achieve a successful pregnancy.

Edna enjoyed telling her friends that the Westlake concept had been dreamed up by old Dr. Westlake, who had died before he could act on it. Then, eight years ago, his daughter Winifred had married Dr. Highley, bought the River Falls Clinic, renamed it for her father and set up her husband there. "She and the doctor were crazy about each other," Edna would sigh. "She was ten years older than he and nothing to look at, but they were real lovers. It was some shock when she died. No one ever knew her heart was that bad.

"But," she'd say philosophically, "he keeps busy. I've seen women who never were able to conceive become pregnant two and three times. Of course, a lot of them don't carry the babies to term, but at least they know there's a chance. You can read about it yourself," she'd add. "*Newsmaker* magazine is doing an article about him. They photographed him last week in his office, and if you think we're busy now, wait till that article comes out."

Edna was a born bookkeeper. Dr. Highley always complimented her on the excellent records she maintained. The only time he gave her the rough side of his tongue was once when he overheard her talking to one patient about another's problems. He had finished by saying, "Any more talking and you're through."

Edna sighed. She was tired. Last night both doctors had had evening hours, and it had been hectic. Now, while it was quiet, she'd check the calendar to make sure she'd made all the necessary future appointments. She had been told by Dr. Highley that she was to make follow-up appointments with people as they left. Frowning, she leaned her broad, freckled face on a thick hand.

She was an overweight woman of forty-four who looked ten

years older. Her youth had been spent taking care of aging parents. When Edna looked back at pictures of herself from secretarial school, she was always surprised at what a pretty girl she'd once been. A mite too heavy, but pretty nevertheless.

Her mind was only half on the page she was reading. Then something triggered her full attention. Last night. The eight-o'clock appointment Vangie Lewis had with Dr. Fukhito.

Vangie had come in early and sat talking with Edna. She was sure upset. Vangie had put on a lot of weight during the pregnancy; she really wasn't well. Last month she'd started wearing moccasins because her other shoes didn't fit anymore. She'd shown them to Edna. "Look at this. My right foot is so swollen, I can only wear these clodhoppers my cleaning woman left behind. The left one is always falling off."

Edna had tried to kid her. "Well, with those glass slippers, I'll just have to start calling you Cinderella. We'll call your husband Prince Charming." Vangie was nuts about her husband.

But Vangie had just pouted and said impatiently, "Prince Charming was Sleeping Beauty's boy friend, not Cinderella's."

Edna had just laughed. "Never mind—before you know it, you'll have your baby and be back in pretty shoes again."

Last night Vangie had pulled up that long caftan she'd started wearing to hide her swollen leg. "Edna," she'd said, "now I can hardly even get this clodhopper on. And for what? For what?" She'd been almost crying.

"Oh, you're just down in the dumps," Edna had said. "Good thing you came in to talk to Dr. Fukhito. He'll relax you."

Just then Dr. Fukhito had buzzed and asked her to send in Mrs. Lewis. As Vangie started down the corridor to his office, she stumbled. She'd walked right out of that loose left shoe.

"Oh, to hell with it!" she cried, and just kept going. Edna had picked up the moccasin, figuring Vangie would come back for it when she finished with Dr. Fukhito.

But when Edna was ready to go home around nine o'clock, Vangie still hadn't come back. Edna decided to ring Dr. Fukhito and tell him she had the shoe, but there was no answer. Vangie must have left by the door that led directly to the parking lot.

That was crazy. She'd catch her death of cold getting her foot wet.

Irresolutely Edna had held the moccasin in her hand and locked up. She went out to the parking lot toward her own car just in time to see Vangie's big red Lincoln Continental pull out with Dr. Highley at the wheel. She'd run a few steps to wave to him, but it was no use. So she'd just gone home.

Now, checking her calendar, she wondered if Dr. Highley had already made a new appointment with Vangie. She decided to phone her just to be sure. She dialed the number. The Lewis phone rang once, twice.

A man answered. "Lewises' residence."

"Mrs. Lewis, please. This is Dr. Highley's office. We want to set up Mrs. Lewis' next appointment."

"Hold on."

She heard muffled voices talking. What could be going on? The voice returned. "This is Detective Cunningham of the Valley County prosecutor's office. I'm sorry, but Mrs. Lewis has died suddenly. You can tell her doctor that someone on our staff will contact him tomorrow."

"Mrs. Lewis died!" Edna's voice was a howl of dismay. "Oh, what happened?"

"It seems she took her own life." The connection was broken.

Slowly Edna lowered the receiver. It just wasn't possible.

The two-o'clock appointments arrived together: Mrs. Volmer for Dr. Highley, Mrs. Lashley for Dr. Fukhito.

"Are you all right, Edna?" Mrs. Volmer asked curiously.

Edna knew Mrs. Volmer had sometimes talked to Vangie in the waiting room. It was on the tip of her tongue to tell her she was dead. But some instinct warned her to tell Dr. Highley first.

His one-thirty appointment came out. He was on the intercom. "Send Mrs. Volmer in, Edna."

"Doctor, may I step into your office for a moment, please? I'd like to have a word with you."

"Certainly." He didn't sound very happy about it.

She hurried down the hall to his office, then timidly stepped inside. "Doctor," she began, "you'll want to know. I just phoned Vangie Lewis to make an appointment. A detective answered and said she killed herself. They're coming to see you tomorrow."

"Mrs. Lewis did what?"

Now that she could talk about it, Edna's words came tumbling out in a torrent. "She was so upset last night, wasn't she, Doctor? She acted like she didn't care about anything. But you must know that; I thought it was the nicest thing when I saw you drive her home. I waved to you, but you didn't see me. So I guess of all people you know how bad she was."

"Edna, how many people have you discussed this with?"

There was something in his tone that made her nervous. Flustered, she replied, "Why, nobody, sir. I just heard this minute."

"You did not discuss Mrs. Lewis with Mrs. Volmer or with the detective on the phone?"

"No, sir."

"Edna, tomorrow when the police come, you and I will tell them everything we know about Mrs. Lewis' frame of mind. But listen to me now." He pointed his finger at her and leaned forward. "I don't want Mrs. Lewis' name mentioned by you to any-one—*anyone*, do you hear? Her suicide reflects very badly on our hospital. How do you think it's going to look if it comes out that she was a patient of mine? If I hear you have so much as mentioned the Lewis case, you're finished here. Is that clear?"

"Yes, sir."

"Are you going out with friends tonight? You know how you get when you drink."

Edna was close to tears. "I'm going home tonight. I want to have my wits about me tomorrow when the police talk to me. Poor little Cinderella." Tears came to her eyes, but then she saw the expression on his face. Angry. Disgusted.

Edna straightened up, dabbed at her eyes. "I'll send Mrs. Volmer in, Doctor. And you don't have to worry," she added with dignity. "I value our hospital. I know how much your work means to you and to our patients. I'm not going to say one single word."

The afternoon was busy. She managed to push the thought of Vangie to the back of her mind. Finally at five o'clock she could leave. Warmly wrapped in a leopard-spotted fake fur coat, she drove home to her apartment in Edgeriver, six miles away.

CHAPTER FOUR

IN THE autopsy room of the Valley County Morgue, Richard Carroll gently removed the fetus from the corpse of Vangie Lewis. It was a boy, and he judged that it weighed about two and a half pounds. He noted that the amniotic fluid had begun to leak. Vangie Lewis could not have carried this baby much longer; she had been in an advanced state of toxemia. It was incredible that any doctor had allowed her to progress so far in this condition.

Richard had no doubt that it was the cyanide that had killed the woman. She'd swallowed a huge gulp of it, and her throat and mouth were badly burned. The burns on the outside of her mouth? Richard tried to visualize the moment she'd drunk the poison. She'd started to swallow, felt the burning, changed her mind, tried to spit it out. It had run over her lips and chin.

To him it didn't make sense.

There were fine white fibers clinging to her black coat. They looked as though they'd come from a blanket. He was having them analyzed, but, of course, they might have been picked up at any time.

Her body had become so bloated that it looked as though she had just put on any clothes she could find that would cover her.

Except for the shoes. They were an incongruous note. They were well cut, expensive and looked quite new. It was unlikely that Vangie could have been outdoors on Monday in those shoes. There were no water spots on them, even though the ankles of her panty hose were spattered. Which suggested that she must have been out, come in, decided to leave again, changed her shoes and then committed suicide. That didn't make sense either.

Another thing. Those shoes were awfully tight. Particularly on the right foot. Considering the way she was dressed, why bother to put on shoes that will kill you?

Richard straightened up. He was just about finished. Once more he turned to study the fetus. Suddenly something struck him. Was it possible? It was a hunch he had to check out. Dave Broad was the man for him. Dave was in charge of prenatal research at

Mount Sinai. He'd send this fetus to him and ask for an opinion.

If what he believed was true, there was a good reason why Chris Lewis would have been upset about his wife's pregnancy.

Maybe upset enough to kill her!

Scott Myerson, the Valley County prosecutor, had scheduled a five-o'clock meeting in his office for Katie, Richard and the two Homicide Squad detectives assigned to the Lewis suicide.

Katie arrived first. As she eased herself into a chair, Scott looked at her with a hint of a smile. He was a small man with a surprisingly deep voice. Large-rimmed glasses, a dark, neat mustache and meticulously tailored conservative suit made him look more like a banker than a law enforcer. Now he observed Katie's bandaged arm and the bruise under her eye.

"Thanks for coming in, Katie," he said. "If you start feeling rotten, you'd better go home." Then he became businesslike. "The Lewis case. What have we got on it?"

While she was talking, Richard came in with Charley Nugent and Phil Cunningham. Silently they settled in the remaining chairs.

Scott listened to Katie, then turned to the detectives. "What did you come up with?"

Phil Cunningham pulled out his notebook. "That place was no honeymoon cottage. The neighbors liked Chris Lewis, but they thought Vangie was a pain in the neck. At parties she was always hanging on him; got upset if he talked more than five minutes to another woman. Then when she got pregnant she was really insufferable. Talked baby all the time."

Charley opened his notebook. "Her obstetrician's office called to make an appointment. I said we'd talk to her doctor tomorrow."

Richard spoke quietly. "There are a few questions I'd like to ask that doctor about Vangie Lewis' condition."

Scott looked at Richard. "You've finished the autopsy?"

"Yes. It was definitely cyanide. She died instantly. Which leads to the crucial point."

There were some paper cups and a water pitcher on top of the file cabinet. Walking over to the file, Richard poured a generous amount of water into a cup. "Suppose this is filled with dissolved cyanide," he said. "I take a large gulp." Quickly he swallowed. He held up the paper cup. It was still nearly half full. "In my judgment, Vangie Lewis must have drunk at least the approximately three ounces I just swallowed in order to have the amount of cyanide we found in her system. But here's the problem. The outside of her lips and chin and even her neck were burned. The only way that could have happened would have been if she spit a lot of the stuff out. But would she then take another mouthful? No way. The reaction is instantaneous."

Richard went on to explain his belief that Vangie Lewis could not have walked comfortably in the shoes that had been laced on her feet. While Katie listened, she visualized Vangie's face. The face she had seen in the dream and the face she'd seen on the bed slid back and forth in her mind. She forced her attention back to the room. Charley was saying, "Richard and I feel the husband noticed something about the body that he didn't tell us."

"I think it was the shoes," Richard said.

Katie turned to Scott. "I told you about the phone call Chris Lewis made."

"You did." Scott Myerson leaned back in his chair. "All right. You two"—he pointed to Charley and Phil—"find out everything you can about Lewis. See who this Joan is. Find out what time his plane came in this morning. Check on phone calls Vangie Lewis made the last few days. Katie, try to see Mrs. Lewis' doctor and get his opinion of her mental and physical condition."

"I can tell you about her physical condition," Richard said. "If she hadn't delivered that baby soon, she could have saved her cyanide."

"There's another thing. Where did she get the cyanide?"

"No trace of it in the house," Charley reported. "Not a drop."

"Anything else?" Scott asked.

"There may be," Richard said. "But it's so far out. Give me another twenty-four hours. Then I may have something."

Scott stood up. "I believe we all agree. We're not closing this as a suicide." He looked at Richard. "Is there any chance that she died somewhere else and was put back on her bed?"

Richard frowned. "It's possible."

Katie started to get up. "I know it's insane, but—" She felt Richard's arm steadying her.

"You sure look stiff," he interrupted.

She'd been about to describe the crazy dream she'd had in the hospital. His voice snapped her back to reality. What a fool she'd have appeared to them. Gratefully she smiled at Richard. "Stiff in the head mostly, I think," she commented.

HE COULD not let Edna destroy everything he'd worked for. His hands gripped the wheel. He could feel them trembling. He had to calm down.

It was ironic that she of all people had seen him drive the Lincoln out of the parking lot. Obviously she'd assumed that Vangie was with him. The minute she told her story to the police, everything would be over.

Edna had to be silenced. His medical bag was on the seat next to him. In it he had put the paperweight from his office desk. He didn't usually carry a bag anymore, but he'd taken it out this morning, planning to put the moccasins in it. He'd intended to drive into New York for dinner and leave them in separate litter cans.

But this morning his housekeeper, Hilda, had come in early. She'd stood talking to him while he put on his tweed overcoat. He'd had no chance to transfer the moccasins from his Burberry to the bag. No matter. He'd get rid of the shoes tomorrow night.

It was a stroke of luck that Edna lived quite near the hospital. Several times he'd dropped off work for her when she was laid up with sciatica. That was why he knew her apartment. He'd make it look like a murder committed during a felony; take her wallet, grab any bits of jewelry she had. Once, when he'd left some work at her place, she'd shown him a butterfly-shaped pin with a minuscule ruby, and her mother's engagement ring with a dot of a diamond in it. She kept them in a plastic jewelry box in the night-table drawer.

He thought about the apartment. How would he get in? Did he dare ring the bell? Suppose she wasn't alone?

But she would be alone. He was sure of it. She was going home to drink. He could tell. That's why he waited a few hours before coming. So that she'd be drunk. Watching her from the corridor, he'd seen how agitated she was, obviously filled with the stories she wanted to tell to the police tomorrow.

He was driving into her apartment area. She lived on the ground floor at the end of her building. Thick bushes and a rusting chain link fence separated the complex from a steep ravine that dropped down a dozen feet and terminated in railroad tracks.

Edna's bedroom window backed onto the parking lot. By now she must be very drunk. He could go in and out by the window. That would lend credence to a burglary.

He parked his car, then pulled on his surgical gloves. He put the paperweight in his coat pocket and slid cautiously out, closing the door noiselessly.

Edna's bedroom shade was pulled down most of the way, but she had a plant in the window. The shade rested on the top of the plant, and he could see in clearly. The room was partially lighted by a fixture in the hall. The window was open a crack. She must be in the living room. He could hear the faint sound of a television program.

Glancing about to make sure that the area was deserted, he raised the window, pulled up the shade, carefully lifted the plant out onto the ground. He hoisted himself up to the sill.

He was inside. In the dim light he observed the virginal tidiness, the crucifix over the bed, the lace runner on the dresser. Now for the part he detested. He felt for the paperweight in his pocket and began to tiptoe down the short hall, past the bathroom, to the living room. Cautiously he peered in. The television set was on, but the room was empty. He heard the sound of a chair creaking. She must be at the table in the dinette. With infinite care he moved into the living room. This was the moment. If she saw him and screamed . . .

But her back was to him. Wearing a woolly blue robe, she sat slumped at the table, one hand next to a cocktail glass, the other in her lap. A tall pitcher was almost empty. Her head was on her chest. She must be asleep.

Quickly he appraised the situation. His eye fell on the hissing radiator to the right of the door. It was the old-fashioned kind

284

with sharp, exposed pipes. Was it possible he didn't need the paperweight after all? Maybe . . .

"Edna," he whispered softly as he came around the table.

"Wha . . ." She looked up at him with bleary eyes. Confused, she began to rise, twisting in her chair. "Doctor . . ."

A mighty shove sent her smashing backward. Her head cracked against the radiator. Blinding lights exploded in her brain. Oh, the pain, the pain! Edna sighed, floated into darkness.

He jumped clear of the spattered blood. As he watched, the pulse in her throat flickered and stopped. He bent over her carefully. She had stopped breathing. He slipped the paperweight back into his pocket. He wouldn't need it now. He wouldn't have to bother robbing her. It would look as though she'd fallen.

Quickly retracing his steps, he went back into the bedroom. He scanned the parking area, then stepped out the window, replaced the plant, pulled down the shade and closed the window to the exact place where Edna had had it. As he did, he heard the persistent chiming of a doorbell—*her doorbell!* Frantically he ran back to his car. He started the engine and drove out of the apartment complex, not turning on his headlights until he approached Route 4.

Who was standing on Edna's doorstep? It had been close, so terribly close. Adrenaline pounded through his veins. Now there was only one threat left: Katie DeMaio. He would begin to remove that threat at once. Her accident had given him the excuse he needed to start medication.

It was a matter of hospital record that her blood count was low. He would order another transfusion for her on the pretense of building her up for the operation. He would give her large doses of Coumadin pills to short-circuit her blood-clotting mechanism and negate the benefits of the transfusion. By Friday, when she came to the hospital for surgery, she'd be on the verge of hemorrhaging. The surgery would then be very dangerous, and he would make it even worse by giving her heparin, another anticoagulant. The initial low blood count, the Coumadin and the heparin would be as effective on Katie DeMaio as the cyanide had been on Vangie Lewis.

286

AFTER THE MEETING IN SCOTT MYERSON's office, Richard drove Katie to a rustic restaurant perched precariously on the Palisades. The small dining room was warmed by a blazing fire and lighted by candles. The proprietor obviously knew Richard well. "Dr. Carroll, a pleasure," he said as he guided them to the table in front of the fireplace.

Richard ordered a bottle of wine; a waiter produced hot garlic bread. They sat in companionable silence, sipping and nibbling.

Richard was a big man with a wholesome look, a thick crop of dark brown hair, strong, even features and broad, rangy shoulders. "Do you know I've been wanting to ask you out for months?" he said. "But you release a do-not-disturb signal. Why?"

"I don't believe in going out with anyone I work with."

"I can understand that. But that's not what we're talking about. We enjoy each other's company. We both know it. And you're having none of it. Here's the menu."

His manner changed, became brisk. "*L'entrecôte* and steak *au poivre* are the specialties here," he told her. When she hesitated, he suggested, "Try the steak *au poivre*. It's fantastic." He ordered salads and baked potatoes, then leaned back and studied her.

"Are you having none of it, Katie?"

"The salad? The steak?"

"All right, I'm not being fair. I'm trying to pin you down and you're a captive audience. But tell me what you do when you're not at the office or your sister's. I know you ski."

"Yes. I rent a condominium in Vermont with some friends."

"Maybe you'll invite me up sometime with you." He did not wait for an answer. "Sailing is my sport. I took my boat to the Caribbean last spring. . . . Here's your steak."

They lingered over coffee. By then Richard had told her about himself. "I was engaged during med school to the girl next door."

"What happened?" Katie asked.

"We kept postponing the wedding. Jean was a very nice girl. But there was something missing."

"No regrets; no second thoughts?" Katie asked.

"Not really. That was seven years ago. I'm a little surprised that the 'something missing' didn't turn up long before now."

He did not seem to expect her to comment. Instead he began to talk about the Lewis case. "It makes me so angry, the waste of life. Vangie Lewis had a lot of years ahead of her."

"You're convinced it wasn't a suicide?"

"I'll need much more information before I pass judgment."

"I don't see Chris Lewis as a murderer. It's too easy to get a divorce today if you want to be free."

"There's another angle to that." Richard pressed his lips together. "Let's hold off talking about it."

It was nearly ten thirty when they turned into Katie's driveway. Richard looked quizzically at the handsome fieldstone house. "How big is this place?" he asked. "How many rooms?"

"Twelve," Katie said reluctantly. "It was John's house."

Richard did not give her the chance to say good night at the door. Taking the key from her hand, he unlocked it and followed her in. "I'm not going to stay, but I do admit to an overwhelming curiosity as to where you keep yourself."

She turned on some lights and watched somewhat resentfully as he looked over the foyer, then the living room. He whistled. "Very nice." He studied John's portrait. "I hear he was quite a guy."

"Yes, he was."

"How long were you married, Katie?"

"One year."

He watched as a look of pain flickered over her face. "When did you find out that he was sick?"

"Shortly after we got back from our honeymoon."

"And ever since, it's been a deathwatch. Sorry, Katie; my job makes me too blunt for my own good. I'll take off now." He hesitated. "Don't you draw these drapes when you're alone here?"

She shrugged. "Why? No one's going to come barging in on me."

"You, of all people, should be aware of the number of home burglaries. Do you mind?" He went to the window and pulled the draperies shut. "See you tomorrow. How will you get to work?"

"The service-station people are going to lend me a car. They'll drop it off in the morning."

"Okay." For a moment he stood with his hand on the knob of the door, then in a highly credible brogue said, "I'll be leavin' ye,

288

Katie Scarlett. Lock your door now. I wouldn't want anyone tryin' to break into Tara." He bent down, kissed her cheek and was gone.

Smiling, Katie closed the door. The clock chimed musically. After Richard's bear-warm presence, the room seemed hollow. Quickly she turned out the lights and went upstairs.

The phone rang just as she got into bed.

"Mrs. DeMaio?" It was a man's voice.

"Yes."

"This is Dr. Highley. I hope I'm not calling too late, but I've tried several times to reach you this evening. The fact that you were in an accident and were in our hospital overnight has come to my attention. How are you feeling?"

"Quite well, Doctor. How nice of you to call."

"How is the bleeding problem?"

"I'm afraid it's about the same."

"Well, it will all be behind you by this time next week. But I do want you to have another transfusion to build you up for the surgery, and I also want you to start in on some pills. Can you come to the hospital tomorrow afternoon?"

"Yes. As a matter of fact, I was planning to come anyhow. You've heard about Mrs. Lewis?"

"I have. A terrible situation."

"I'd like to discuss her emotional and physical states with you."

"Fine. Call in the morning to arrange a time."

"Thank you, Doctor," Katie said. As she hung up, she reflected that Dr. Highley hadn't really appealed to her at first because of his aloof attitude.

It shows how you can misjudge people, she decided.

CHAPTER FIVE

BILL Kennedy rang the bell of the Lewis house. Tall, prematurely white, and scholarly, Bill was an orthopedic surgeon at Lenox Hill Hospital. He had not heard about Vangie Lewis' death until he returned home.

Briefly Molly had told him about it. "I called and asked Chris to come to dinner. He doesn't want to, but you go drag him here."

As he walked between the houses, Bill considered what a shock it would be to come home and find he had lost Molly. But no one in his right mind could think that the Lewises' marriage had been anything like his and Molly's. Bill had never told Molly that one morning when he was having coffee at a drugstore in Manhattan he'd seen Chris with a very pretty girl in her early twenties.

Chris Lewis opened the door, and Bill saw the sadness in his eyes. He gripped the younger man's arm. "I'm terribly sorry."

Chris nodded woodenly. The meaning of the day was sinking in on him. Vangie was dead. Had their quarrel driven her to kill herself? He felt lonely, frightened and guilty. He allowed Bill to persuade him to come to dinner. Numbly reaching for a jacket, he followed Bill down the street.

Bill poured him a double Scotch. Chris gulped it. Calm down, he thought, calm down. Be careful.

The Kennedy kids came into the den to say good night. Nice kids, all of them. Well behaved too. Chris had always wanted children. But not Vangie's. Now his unborn child had died. Another guilt. His child, and he hadn't wanted it. And Vangie had known it. What had, *who* had driven her to kill herself? Who? That was the question. Because Vangie hadn't been alone last night.

He hadn't told the police. They would start an investigation. And where would that lead? To Joan. To him.

The motel clerk in New York had seen him leave last night. He'd gone home to have it out with Vangie. Let me go, please. I can't spend any more of my life with you. It's destroying both of us.

He'd arrived at the house sometime after midnight. He'd driven in, and the minute he opened the garage door he knew something was up. Because she'd parked the Lincoln in his space. No, someone else had parked her car in *his* space. Vangie always used the wider side of the garage. And she needed every inch. She was a lousy driver. But last night the Lincoln had been expertly parked in his spot on the narrower side.

He'd gone in and found the house empty. Vangie's handbag was on the chaise in their room. He'd been puzzled but not alarmed. Obviously she'd gone off with a girl friend to stay overnight, taking a suitcase and leaving her heavy purse behind.

The house had depressed Chris. He'd decided to go back to the motel. And then this morning he'd found Vangie dead. Somebody had parked the car for her before midnight. Somebody had driven her home after midnight. And those shoes. The one day she'd worn them she'd complained endlessly about how the right shoe dug into her ankle.

For weeks now she'd worn nothing but those dirty moccasins. Where were they? Chris had searched the house thoroughly. Whoever had driven her home might know.

He hadn't told the police any of this. He hadn't wanted to involve Joan. Besides, maybe the shoes really weren't that important. Vangie might have wanted to be fully dressed when she was found. That swollen leg embarrassed her.

But he should have told the cops about his having been here, about the way the car was parked.

"Chris, come into the dining room. You'll feel better if you eat something." Molly's voice was gentle.

Wearily Chris brushed a hand over burning eyes. "I'll have something, Molly," he said. "But I'll have to leave pretty quickly. The funeral director is coming to the house for Vangie's clothes."

"When is the funeral?" Bill asked.

"The coffin will be flown to Minneapolis tomorrow afternoon, and the service will be the next day." The words hammered in his ears. Coffin. Funeral. Oh, Vangie, he thought, I wanted to be free of you, but I didn't want you to die.

At eight he went back to his house. At eight thirty, when the funeral director came, he had a suitcase ready with underwear and the flowing caftan Vangie's parents had sent her for Christmas.

The funeral director was quietly sympathetic. He requested the necessary information quickly. Born April 15. He jotted down the year. Died February 15—just two months short of her thirty-first birthday, he commented.

Chris rubbed the ache between his eyes. Something was wrong. "No," he said. "Today's the sixteenth, not the fifteenth."

"The death certificate clearly states that Mrs. Lewis died between eight and ten last night, February fifteenth," the man said. "You're thinking the sixteenth because you *found* her this morning. But the medical examiner pinpointed the time of death."

Chris stared at him. Waves of shock swept over him. He had been home at midnight and the car and Vangie's purse had been here. He'd assumed that Vangie had come in and killed herself sometime after he drove back to New York.

But at midnight she'd been dead two to four hours. That meant that after he'd left, someone had brought her body here, put it on the bed and laid the empty glass beside it. Someone had wanted to make it seem that Vangie had committed suicide.

"Oh, Lord," Chris whispered. At the last moment Vangie must have known. Someone had forced that poison into her, viciously killed her and the baby she was carrying.

He had to tell the police. And there was one person they would inevitably accuse. As the funeral director stared at him, Chris said aloud, "They're going to blame it on me."

DR. HIGHLEY hung up the phone slowly. Katie DeMaio suspected nothing. Her office apparently wanted nothing more of him than to discuss Vangie Lewis' emotional state. Unless, of course, someone had questioned Vangie's apparent suicide, perhaps raised the possibility that her body had been moved. The danger was still great.

He was in the library of the Westlake home—his home now. The house was a manorlike Tudor with archways, marble fireplaces and Tiffany stained-glass windows. The Westlake house. The Westlake Hospital. The Westlake Maternity Concept. The name had given him immediate entrée, socially and professionally. Marrying Winifred Westlake and coming to America to carry on her father's work had been a perfect excuse for leaving England. No one, including Winifred, knew about the years before Liverpool, the years at Christ Hospital in Devon.

Toward the end she had started to ask questions.

It was nearly eleven o'clock and he hadn't had dinner yet. Knowing what he was going to do to Edna had robbed him of the desire to eat. But now that it was over, he craved food. He went into the kitchen. Hilda had left dinner for him in the microwave oven—a Cornish hen with wild rice. He just needed to heat it up.

Because he needed the freedom of the house, the privacy of his library, he'd gotten rid of Winifred's live-in housekeeper. She had looked at him with sour, sullen eyes, swollen with weeping. "Miss Winifred was almost never sick until . . ." She was going to say "until she married you," but she didn't finish.

Winifred's cousin resented him too. He had tried to make trouble after Winifred's death, but couldn't prove anything. They'd dismissed the cousin as a disgruntled ex-heir.

Selecting a chilled bottle of wine from the refrigerator, Highley sat down to eat in the breakfast room. As he ate, his mind ran over the exact dosage he would give Katie DeMaio. Traces of the heparin and the Coumadin might show in her bloodstream if there were a thorough autopsy. But he could circumvent that.

Before going to bed, he went out to the foyer closet. He'd get those moccasins safely into his bag now. Reaching into one pocket of the Burberry, he pulled out a misshapen moccasin. Expectantly he put his free hand in the other pocket—first matter-of-factly, then rummaging frantically. Finally he pawed through the overshoes stacked on the closet floor.

At last he stood up, staring at the battered moccasin he was holding. The *right* one. The one he had tugged off Vangie's right foot. Hysterically he began to laugh.

Somehow in the dark the moccasin had fallen out of his pocket. The one he'd *found* after crawling around in the parking lot like a dog was the one he'd already *had*. Somewhere the left moccasin that Vangie Lewis had been wearing was waiting to trace her footsteps back to him.

KATIE had set the clock radio for six a.m., but she was wide awake long before. Her sleep had been troubled; several times she'd almost started to jump up, frightened by a vague, worrisome dream. Shivering, she adjusted the thermostat, then ran to the kitchen, quickly made coffee and took a cup back upstairs to bed.

Propped against the pillows, the comforter wrapped around her, she eagerly sipped as the heat of the cup warmed her fingers. "That's better," she murmured. "Now, what's the matter with me?"

She glanced into the mirror of the antique mahogany dresser

opposite the bed. Her hair was tousled. The bruise under her eye was now purple tinged with yellow. Her eyes were swollen with sleep. I look like something the cat dragged in, she reflected.

But it was more than the way she looked. It was a heavy feeling of apprehension. Had she dreamed that queer, frightening nightmare again? She couldn't be sure.

Vangie Lewis. It seemed impossible that anyone would choose to kill her by forcing cyanide down her throat. She simply didn't believe Chris Lewis was capable of that kind of violence.

She thought of Dr. Highley's call. That damn operation. Well, at least she was getting it over with. Check in Friday night. Operation Saturday, home Sunday. At work Monday. No big deal.

As she sipped her coffee, she glanced instinctively at John's picture. A handsome, grave-looking man with gentle, penetrating eyes. Maybe Richard was right. Maybe she was keeping a deathwatch. John would be the first one to blast her for that.

A hot shower picked up her spirits. She had a plea-bargaining session scheduled for nine, a sentencing at ten and Friday's trial to prepare for. I'd better get a move on, she thought.

She dressed quickly, selecting a soft brown wool skirt and a turquoise silk shirt with long sleeves that covered the bandage on her arm. The car from the service station arrived as she finished a second coffee. She took the driver back and drove to the office.

It had been a busy night in the county. There had been a drunken-driving accident resulting in four deaths, and two armed robberies.

Scott Myerson was just coming out of his office. "Lovely night," Katie observed.

He nodded. "Look, I'm interested in the psychiatrist Vangie Lewis was going to. I'd like his opinion of her mental state. I can send Phil, but a woman would be less noticeable over there."

Katie hesitated. "Maybe I can help out. Dr. Highley is my gynecologist. I actually have an appointment with him today. Perhaps I could see Dr. Fukhito before or after."

Scott's eyebrows shot up in surprise. "What do you think of Highley? Richard made some crack yesterday about Vangie's condition; seemed to think that he was taking chances with her."

Katie shook her head. "I don't agree. Highley's specialty is difficult pregnancies. That's the point. He tries to save the babies other doctors lose." She thought of his phone call to her. "I can vouch for the fact that he's a very concerned doctor."

Scott frowned. "How long have you known him?"

"Not long. My sister, Molly, has a friend who raves about Dr. Highley, so I went to see him last month." She remembered his words. "You're quite right to have come," he'd said. "I think of the womb as a cradle that must always be kept in good repair." The one thing that had surprised her was that he did not have a nurse in attendance during the examination, unlike other gynecologists.

"All right," Scott said. "Talk to Highley. And the shrink too. Find out whether or not they think she was capable of suicide. See if she talked about her husband. Charley and Phil are checking on Chris Lewis now. Talk to the nurses too."

"Not the nurses." Katie smiled. "The receptionist, Edna. She knows everybody's business. I wasn't in the waiting room two minutes before I found myself giving her my life history."

Katie went into her office for her files, then rushed to her appointment with a defense attorney about an indicted defendant. From there she hurried to a second-floor courtroom to hear the sentencing of a youth she had prosecuted for armed robbery.

When she returned, she had two messages to call Dr. Carroll. She tried to reach him, but he was out on a case.

She phoned Dr. Highley's office fully expecting to hear the nasal warmth of Edna's voice. But whoever answered was a stranger. "Doctors' offices."

Katie decided to ask for Edna. "Is Miss Burns there?"

"She called in sick today. I'm Mrs. Fitzgerald."

Katie realized then how much she had counted on talking to Edna. Briefly she explained that Dr. Highley expected her to call for an appointment and that she'd also like to see Dr. Fukhito. Mrs. Fitzgerald put her on hold a few minutes, and then said, "Dr. Fukhito is free at a quarter to four. Dr. Highley would prefer three o'clock if it is convenient."

Katie confirmed the appointments, then turned to the work on her desk. At lunchtime Maureen Crowley, one of the office secretaries, popped her head in and offered to bring Katie a sandwich. Deep in preparation for Friday's trial, Katie nodded.

"Ham on rye with mustard and lettuce," Maureen said.

Katie looked up, surprised. "Am I that predictable?"

The girl was about nineteen, with a mane of red-gold hair, emerald-green eyes and a lovely pale complexion. "Katie, about food you're in a rut." The door closed behind her.

You're on a deathwatch. You're in a rut. Katie was astonished to realize she was close to tears. I *must* be sick if I'm getting this thin-skinned, she thought.

When the lunch arrived she ate it, only vaguely aware of what she was having. Vangie Lewis' face was constantly before her. But why had she seen it in a nightmare?

CHAPTER SIX

RICHARD Carroll was in his office just after nine. Twice he tried phoning Katie, hoping to catch her between court sessions. He wanted to hear the sound of her voice. For some reason he'd felt edgy about leaving her alone in that big house last night. Why did he have a hunch that something was troubling her?

He went out on a case. When he returned to his office at four thirty, he was absurdly pleased to see that Katie had returned his calls. Quickly he phoned her, but the switchboard operator said that she had left for the day.

That meant he wouldn't get to talk to her today. He was having dinner in New York with Clovis Simmons, a TV actress. Clovis was fun, but the signs were that she was getting serious.

Richard made a resolve. This was the last time he'd take Clovis out. It wasn't fair to her. Refusing to consider the reason for that sudden decision, he turned his thoughts again to the Lewis case.

He had not been exaggerating when he'd said that if Vangie Lewis had not delivered her baby soon, she wouldn't have needed cyanide. How many women got into that same condition under the Westlake Maternity Concept? Had there been anything unusual about the ratio of deaths among Westlake's patients? Richard asked his secretary to come in.

Marge was in her mid-fifties, an excellent secretary who thoroughly enjoyed the drama of the department.

"Marge," he said, "I want to do some unofficial investigating of Westlake Hospital's maternity section. I'd like to know how many patients died either in childbirth or from complications during pregnancy. I also want to know the ratio of deaths to the number of patients treated there. Do you know anybody at Westlake who might look at the hospital records for you on the quiet?"

His secretary frowned. "Let me work on it."

"Good. And check into any malpractice suits that have been filed against either of the doctors."

Satisfied at getting the investigation under way, Richard dashed home to shower and change. Seconds after he left his office a call came for him from Dr. David Broad at Mount Sinai Hospital. Marge took the message asking Richard to contact Dr. Broad in the morning. The matter was urgent.

KATIE was a few minutes early for her appointment with Dr. Highley. The other receptionist, Mrs. Fitzgerald, was coolly pleasant, but when Katie asked about Edna's illness, the woman seemed nervous. "It's just a virus," she replied stiffly.

A buzzer sounded. The receptionist picked up the phone. "Mrs. DeMaio, Dr. Highley will see you now," she said.

Katie walked quickly down the corridor to Dr. Highley's office. She knocked, then opened the door and stepped inside. The office had the air of a comfortable study. Bookshelves lined one wall; pictures of mothers with babies nearly covered another. A club chair was placed near the doctor's elaborately carved desk. The doctor stood up to greet her. "Mrs. DeMaio." His tone was courteous, the faint British accent barely perceptible. His face was round and smooth-skinned. Thinning sandy hair, streaked with gray, was carefully combed in a side part. Eyebrows and lashes, the same sandy shade, accentuated protruding steel-gray eyes. Not an attractive man, but authoritative.

As they sat down, Katie thanked him for the phone call.

He dismissed her gratitude. "If you had told the emergency-room doctor that you were my patient, he would have given you a room in the west wing. Far more comfortable, I assure you. And about the same view."

Katie fished in her shoulder bag and took out her notebook and pen. She looked up quickly. "Anything would be better than the view I thought I had the other night. . . ." She stopped. She was here on official business, not to talk about her nightmares. "Doctor, if you don't mind, let's talk about Vangie Lewis." She smiled. "I guess our roles are reversed for a few minutes. I get to ask the questions."

His expression became somber. "That poor girl. I've thought of little else since I heard the news."

Katie nodded. "When was the last time you saw her?"

He leaned back in the chair. His fingers interlocked under his chin. "It was last Thursday evening. I'd been having Mrs. Lewis come in weekly since the halfway point of her pregnancy."

"How was she," Katie asked, "physically and emotionally?"

"Her physical condition was a worry. There was danger of toxic pregnancy, which I was watching very closely. But every additional day she carried increased the baby's chance of survival."

"Could she have carried the baby to full term?"

"Impossible. In fact, I warned Mrs. Lewis last Thursday that we'd have to bring her in soon and induce labor."

"How did she respond to that news?"

He frowned. "I expected her to be concerned for the baby's life. But the closer she came to delivery, the more it seemed to me that she was morbidly fearful of giving birth."

"Did she show any specific depression?"

Dr. Highley shook his head. "I did not see it. But Dr. Fukhito should answer that. He saw her on Monday night, and he's better trained than I to recognize the symptoms."

"A last question," Katie said. "Your office is right next to Dr. Fukhito's. Did you see Mrs. Lewis at any time Monday night?"

"I did not."

"Thank you. You've been very helpful." She slipped her notebook back into her bag. "Now it's your turn to ask questions."

"You answered them last night. Now, when you've finished talking with Dr. Fukhito, please go to room 101. You'll be given a transfusion. Wait about half an hour before driving after you've received it. Also . . ." He reached into the side drawer of his desk and selected a bottle containing a number of pills. "Take one of these tonight. Then one every four hours tomorrow; the same on Friday. I must stress that this is very important. If this operation does not cure your problem, we must consider more radical surgery, perhaps a hysterectomy."

"I'll take the pills," Katie said.

"Good. You'll be checking in around six o'clock Friday evening. I'll look in on you." He opened the door for her. "Till Friday, then, Mrs. DeMaio," he said softly.

THE investigative team of Phil Cunningham and Charley Nugent returned to the prosecutor's office at four p.m. exuding the excitement of hounds who have treed their quarry. Rushing into Scott's office, they proceeded to lay their findings before him.

"The husband's a liar," Phil said crisply. "He wasn't due back till yesterday morning, but his plane developed engine trouble. The passengers were off-loaded in Chicago, and he and the crew deadheaded back to New York. He got in Monday evening."

"Monday evening!" Scott exploded.

"Yeah. We talked to his crew on the Monday flight. Lewis gave the purser a ride into Manhattan. Told him his wife was away and he was going to stay in the city overnight and take in a show. He parked the car and checked in at the Holiday Inn on West Fifty-seventh Street; then he and the purser had dinner together. The purser left him at seven twenty. After that, Lewis got his car. The garage records show he brought it back at ten. And get this. He took off again at midnight and came back at two."

Scott whistled. "He lied to us about his flight. He lied to the purser about his wife. He was somewhere in his car between eight and ten and between midnight and two a.m. And Vangie Lewis died between eight and ten."

"There's more," Charley Nugent said. "Lewis has a girl friend, a Pan Am stewardess. Name's Joan Moore. Lives on East Eighty-seventh Street. Her doorman told us that Captain Lewis drove her home from the airport yesterday morning. She left her bag with him and they went for coffee in the drugstore across the street."

"It's four o'clock," Scott said crisply. "The judges will be leaving soon. Phil, get one of them on the phone and ask him to wait around for fifteen minutes. Tell him we'll need a search warrant. Charley, you find out what funeral director picked up Vangie Lewis' body in Minneapolis. Get to him. The body is not to be interred. Did Lewis say when he was coming back?"

Charley nodded. "Tomorrow, after the service."

"Find out what plane he's on and invite him here for questioning. And I want to talk to Miss Moore. What do you know about her?"

"She shares an apartment with two other stewardesses. She's planning to switch to Pan Am's Latin American division and fly out of Miami. She's down there now, signing a lease on an apartment. She'll be back Friday afternoon."

"Meet her plane too," Scott said. "Bring her here for a few questions. Where was she Monday night?"

"In flight on her way to New York."

"All right." He paused. "Something else. I want the phone records from the Lewis house, particularly from the last week. See if they had an answering service, since he's with an airline. And look again for cyanide. We've got to find out fast where Vangie Lewis got the stuff that killed her. Or where Captain Lewis got it."

Dr. Fukhito's office was spacious and bright. There was a long writing table, graceful cane-backed chairs with upholstered seats, and a matching chaise. A series of exquisite Japanese woodcuts decorated the walls.

Dr. Fukhito was conservatively dressed: pin-striped suit, light blue shirt, blue silk tie. His jet-black hair and small, neat mustache complemented pale gold skin and brown eyes. He was a strikingly handsome man, Katie thought as she reached for her notebook. "Doctor, you saw Vangie Lewis at about eight o'clock Monday night. How long did she stay?"

"About forty minutes. She phoned Monday afternoon and asked for an appointment. She sounded quite distressed. I told her to come in at eight."

"Why was she so distressed, Doctor?"

300

He chose his words carefully. "She had quarreled with her husband. She was convinced he did not love her or want the baby. And, physically, the strain of the pregnancy was beginning to tell on her. She was quite immature, really—an only child who had been inordinately spoiled and fussed over. The physical discomfort was appalling to her, and the prospect of the birth had become frightening."

His eyes shifted away. This man was nervous, Katie thought. What advice had he given Vangie that had sent her rushing home to kill herself? Or had sent her to a killer?

Leaning forward, Katie said, "Doctor, I realize that Mrs. Lewis' discussions with you are confidential, but we need to know all you can tell us about the quarrel she had with her husband."

He looked at Katie. "Mrs. Lewis told me that she believed her husband was in love with someone else. She'd accused him of that. She'd warned him that when she found out who the woman was, she'd make her life hell. She was angry, bitter and frightened."

"What did you tell her?"

"I told her that the baby might be the instrument to give her marriage more time. She began to calm down. But then I felt it necessary to warn her that if her marriage did not improve, she should consider the possibility of divorce. She became furious. She swore that she would never let her husband leave her, that I was on his side, like everyone else. She got up, grabbed her coat and left. She used my private entrance to go out the back way."

"And you never heard from her again?"

"No."

"I see." Katie got up and walked over to the wall with the pictures. Dr. Fukhito was holding something back. "I was a patient here myself Monday night, Doctor," she said. "I had a minor automobile accident and was brought here around ten o'clock. Can you tell me, is there any chance that Vangie Lewis did not leave the hospital shortly after eight thirty? That after I was brought in, semiconscious, I might have seen her?"

Dr. Fukhito stared at Katie. "I don't see how," he said. But Katie noticed that his knuckles were clenched and white, and something—was it fury or fear?—flashed in his eyes.

CHAPTER SEVEN

AT FIVE o'clock Gertrude Fitzgerald turned the phone over to the answering service and locked the reception desk. Nervously she dialed Edna's number. Again there was no answer. There was no doubt. Edna had been drinking more and more lately. She was such a good person. They had both worked for Dr. Highley for several years and often had lunch together. Sometimes Edna would want to go to a pub for a manhattan. Gertrude understood her need to drink, understood that hollow feeling when all you do is go to work and then go home and stare at four walls.

Gertrude was a widow, but at least she had the children and grandchildren to care about her. She had her own lonely times, but it wasn't the same as it was for Edna. She'd *lived*. She had something to look back on.

She could swear Dr. Highley had known she was lying when she said Edna had called in sick. But suppose Edna *hadn't* been drinking? Suppose she was sick or something? She'd have to find out. She'd drive over to her house right now.

Her mind settled, Gertrude left the office briskly and drove the six miles to Edna's apartment. She parked in the visitors' area and walked around to the front. As she neared Edna's door, she heard the faint sound of voices. The television set, of course.

Gertrude rang the bell and waited. There was no familiar voice calling "Right with you." Gertrude firmly pushed the bell again. Maybe Edna was sleeping it off.

By the time she'd rung the bell four times, Gertrude was thoroughly alarmed. Something was wrong. The superintendent, Mr. Krupshak, lived across the court. Hurrying over, Gertrude told her story. The super was eating dinner and looked annoyed, but his wife, Gana, reached for the keys. "I'll go with you," she said.

The two women hurried across the courtyard together. "Edna's a real friend," Gana Krupshak volunteered. "Sometimes in the evening I pop in on her. Just last night I stopped over at about eight. I had a manhattan with her, and she told me that one of her favorite patients had killed herself. Well, here we are."

They were on the small porch leading to Edna's apartment. The superintendent's wife inserted the key into the lock, twisted it and pushed open the door.

The two women saw Edna at the same moment: lying on the floor, her legs crumpled under her, her graying hair plastered around her face, her eyes staring, crusted blood making a crimson crown on the top of her head.

"No. No." Gertrude's voice rose, high and shrill. She pressed her knuckles to her mouth.

In a dazed voice Gana Krupshak said, "It's just last night I was sitting here with her. And she was talking about a patient who killed herself. And then she phoned the woman's husband." Gana began to sob. "And now poor Edna is dead too!"

CHRIS Lewis stood next to Vangie's parents at the right of the coffin, numbly acknowledging the sympathetic utterances of friends. When he'd phoned her parents about her death, they had agreed that they would view her body privately and have a memorial service the next morning followed by a private interment.

Instead, when he'd arrived in Minneapolis, he found that they had arranged for a public viewing that night.

"So many friends will want to say good-by to our little girl," her mother sobbed.

Our little girl. If only you had let her grow up, Chris thought, it might all have been so different.

Vangie's parents looked old and tired and shattered with grief. They were plain, hardworking people who had brought up their unexpectedly beautiful child to believe her wish was law.

Would it be easier for them when it was revealed that someone had taken Vangie's life? Or did he owe it to them to say nothing, to keep that final horror from them? He wanted badly to talk to Joan. She'd been so upset when she heard about Vangie. "Did she know about us?" He'd finally had to admit to her that Vangie suspected he was interested in someone else.

Joan would be back from Florida on Friday, two days away. He was going to return to New Jersey tomorrow right after the funeral. He would say nothing to the police until he had warned

Joan that she might be dragged into this. The police would be looking for a motive for him to kill Vangie. In their eyes, Joan would be the motive.

Chris glanced over at the coffin, at Vangie's now peaceful face, the quietly folded hands. He and Vangie had scarcely lived as man and wife in the past few years. They'd lain side by side like strangers, he emotionally drained from the endless quarreling, she wanting to be cajoled, babied.

A suspicion that had been sitting somewhere in his subconscious sprang to life. Was it possible that Vangie had become involved with another man, a man who did not want to take responsibility for her and a baby? Had she confronted that other man, hurled hysterical threats at him?

He realized that he was shaking hands, murmuring thanks to a man in his mid-sixties. He was slightly built but sturdily attractive, with gray hair and bushy brows over keen, penetrating eyes. "I'm Dr. Salem," he said. "Emmet Salem. I delivered Vangie and was her first gynecologist. She was one of the prettiest things I ever brought into this world, and she never changed. I only wish I hadn't been away when she phoned my office Monday."

Chris stared at him. "Vangie phoned you Monday?"

"Yes. My nurse said she was quite upset. Wanted to see me immediately. I was teaching a seminar in Detroit, but the nurse made an appointment for her for today. She was planning to fly out yesterday. Maybe I could have helped her."

Why had Vangie called this man? Chris tried to think. What would make her go back to a doctor she hadn't seen in years? A doctor thirteen hundred miles away?

"Had Vangie been ill?" Dr. Salem was looking at him curiously.

"No, not ill," Chris said. "As you probably know, she was expecting a baby, and it was a difficult pregnancy."

"*Vangie was pregnant?*" The doctor stared in astonishment.

"I know. She had just about given up hope. But in New Jersey she started the Westlake Maternity Concept. You may have heard of it, or of Dr. Highley—Dr. Edgar Highley."

"Captain Lewis, may I speak with you privately?" The funeral director had a hand under his arm.

304

"Excuse me," Chris said to the doctor. He allowed the funeral director to guide him into the office.

The director closed the door. "I've just received a call from the prosecutor's office in Valley County, New Jersey," he said. "Written confirmation is on the way. We are forbidden to inter your wife's body. It is to be flown back to the medical examiner's office in Valley County immediately after the service tomorrow."

They know it wasn't suicide, Chris thought. Without answering the funeral director, he turned and left. He wanted to see Dr. Salem, find out what Vangie had said to the nurse on the phone.

But Dr. Salem was already gone. Vangie's mother rubbed swollen eyes with a crumpled handkerchief. "What did you say to Dr. Salem that made him leave like that?" she asked. "Why did you upset him so terribly?"

WEDNESDAY evening Edgar Highley arrived home at six o'clock. Hilda was just leaving. He knew she liked this job. Why not? A house that stayed neat; no mistress to constantly give orders; no children to clutter it.

No children. He went into the library, poured a Scotch and watched from the window as Hilda disappeared down the street.

He had gone into medicine because his own mother had died in childbirth. His birth. "Your mother wanted you so much," his father had told him again and again. "She knew she was risking her life, but she didn't care."

Sitting in the chemist's shop in Brighton, watching his father prepare prescriptions, asking questions: "What is that? What will that pill do? Why do you put caution labels on those bottles?"

He'd gone to medical school, finished in the top ten percent of his class. He'd interned at Christ Hospital in Devon, with its magnificent research laboratory. He'd become a member of the staff;

305

his reputation as an obstetrician had grown rapidly. But his project had been held back by his inability to test it.

At twenty-seven he'd married Claire, a distant cousin of the earl of Sussex. She was infinitely superior to him in social background, but his growing reputation had been the leveler. And what incredible ignominy. He who dealt in birth and fertility had married a barren woman.

When had he started to hate Claire? It took a long time—seven years. It was when he realized that her disappointment was faked; that she'd *known* all along that she could not conceive.

Impatiently he turned from the window. It would be another cold, wind-filled night. When all this was over, he'd take a vacation. He was losing his grip on his nerves. He had nearly given himself away this morning when Gertrude told him that Edna had phoned in sick. He'd grasped the desk, watched his knuckles whiten. Then he'd realized: Gertrude was covering for her friend.

The missing shoe. This morning he'd gone to the hospital soon after dawn and once again searched the parking lot and the office. Had Vangie been wearing it when she came into his office Monday night? He couldn't be sure. The other shoe, the right one, was still in his bag in the trunk of the car.

Even if the police started an investigation into Vangie's death, there was no evidence against him. Her file in the office could bear intensive scrutiny. All the true records of the special cases were here in the wall safe, and he defied anyone to locate that safe. It wasn't even in the original plans of the house.

Anyway, no one had any reason to suspect him—no one except Katie DeMaio.

Fukhito had come in to see him just as he was locking up tonight. He'd said, "Mrs. DeMaio was asking a lot of questions. Is it possible that they don't believe Mrs. Lewis committed suicide?"

"I really don't know." He'd enjoyed Fukhito's nervousness.

"The interview you gave to that magazine comes out tomorrow?"

"Yes. But I gave them the impression I use a number of psychiatric consultants. Your name will not appear in the article."

"Still, it's going to put the spotlight on us."

"On *yourself*. Isn't that what you're saying, Doctor?"

He'd almost laughed aloud at the troubled, guilty look on Fukhito's face. Now, finishing his Scotch, he realized that he had been overlooking another avenue of escape. If the police concluded that Vangie had been murdered, if they *did* investigate Westlake, he could reluctantly suggest that they interrogate Dr. Fukhito. Especially in view of his past. After all, Fukhito was the last person known to have seen Vangie Lewis alive.

CHAPTER EIGHT

AFTER leaving Dr. Fukhito, Katie went to the east wing of the hospital for the transfusion. She had a long wait, and didn't leave the hospital until nearly six o'clock. She was hungry, and the idea of going home did not appeal to her. She thought she had learned to cope with loneliness. The feeling of emptiness that had been coming over her lately was something new.

She passed the restaurant where she and Richard had eaten the night before, and on impulse swung into the parking area. Maybe in the warm, intimate atmosphere she'd be able to think.

The proprietor recognized her, beamed with pleasure and led her to a table near the one she had shared with Richard.

Nodding at the suggestion of a glass of Burgundy, Katie leaned back. Now if she could just sort out the impressions she'd received talking with Dr. Highley and Dr. Fukhito.

Taking out her notebook, she began to scan what she had jotted down during the interviews. Dr. Highley. He'd explained that Vangie Lewis was in serious trouble with her pregnancy. What he told Katie was completely reasonable. What then? What more did she want of Dr. Highley? He'd expressed regret over Vangie's death, but certainly not sorrow. Of course, a doctor had to stay objective, as she'd heard both Bill and Richard say.

Richard. Her eyes slid over to the table where they'd sat together. Was it possible that it could happen twice in a lifetime, that from the very beginning you *know* someone is right?

When she and Richard were leaving Molly's after lunch yesterday, Molly had asked them both to dinner Thursday night—tomorrow—to meet Liz and Jim Berkeley. "She's the one who

307

thinks Dr. Highley is God," Molly had said. Katie realized how much she was looking forward to that dinner.

Again she looked down at her notes. Dr. Fukhito. Something was wrong there, the way he'd weighed every word when he'd discussed Vangie's Monday-night visit. It had been like watching someone walk step by step through a minefield. What was he afraid of? He had said Vangie left by his private entrance.

No one had seen her go.

Suppose she *hadn't* left? Suppose he'd gone with her or followed her home. Suppose he'd realized that she was suicidal, that he was responsible in some way. . . .

The waiter arrived to take her order. She made one final entry in her notebook: "Investigate Fukhito's background."

EVEN before he crossed the George Washington Bridge, Richard knew that he should have canceled the date with Clovis. He was preoccupied with Vangie Lewis' death. He had missed something in the autopsy. What was it?

And he was worried about Katie. She had looked so thin and pale last night. She wasn't well. That accident. Was it possible that she'd been hurt more than anyone realized? The thought haunted Richard as he turned into East Fifty-fourth Street and headed for Clovis' apartment.

Clovis had a pitcher of martinis waiting, and a plate of crab-meat puffs fresh from the oven. With her flawless skin and Viking coloring, she reminded Richard of a young Ingrid Bergman. Until recently he'd thought they might end up together. But as he returned her kiss, he was acutely aware that he'd never worry about Clovis the way he was now worrying about Katie.

He realized Clovis was talking to him as she filled two glasses. ". . . and I just got home. So I fixed the drinks and figured you could relax while I get dressed. Hey, are you listening to me?"

Richard accepted the drink and smiled apologetically. "I'm sorry. Do you mind if I make some calls while you get ready?"

"Go ahead and dial away." She picked up her glass and started toward the hall that led into the bedroom and bath.

Richard took out his credit card and dialed the operator. He gave his account number and the call went through. The phone rang a dozen times before he gave up. Katie wasn't home.

Next he tried Molly's house. But Molly had not spoken to Katie today. "She'll probably call me later. But I wish she was home by now. She should take it easy."

It was the opening he needed. "Molly, what's the matter with Katie? There is something wrong physically, isn't there? Besides the accident, I mean?"

Molly hesitated. "You'd better talk to Katie about that."

Cold fear washed over him. *"What's the matter with her?"*

"Oh, not much. I promise you that. But it's nothing she wants discussed. See you tomorrow night. Don't forget."

The connection broke. Richard frowned into the dead receiver. Then he called the prosecutor. "Anything going on?"

Scott did not waste time on preliminaries. "The body of a woman was found in an apartment in Edgeriver. She was the receptionist Katie wanted to talk to at Westlake. Name's Edna Burns. We're heading over there, and we need you."

"Give me the address," Richard said.

He wrote it quickly and hung up the phone. Vangie Lewis and now Edna Burns. He knocked on Clovis' bedroom door. Wrapped in a terry-cloth robe, she opened it. "Hey, what's the hurry?"

"Clo, I'm sorry." Quickly he explained. He was frantic to get away.

She was clearly disappointed. "Oh, of course I understand. Go, but let's have dinner tomorrow night. Promise?"

Richard temporized. "Well, very soon."

ON THE way home from the restaurant, Katie thought about the conversation she'd had with Edna Burns on her first visit to Dr. Highley. Edna was a born listener. How much had Vangie told her? And how much did Edna know about Dr. Fukhito?

Katie pulled up in front of her house and decided not to put the car away yet. Suppose she phoned Edna and suggested driving over to see her? If Katie was any judge, Edna Burns would love a chance to have a cup of tea and gossip about Vangie Lewis.

Inside, Katie looked up Edna's number in the telephone book

and quickly dialed it. The phone rang once and was picked up.

A man said, "Yes." The short word was delivered in a clipped, familiar voice. It belonged to Charley Nugent from the prosecutor's office.

"Charley? It's Katie. What are you doing in Edna's apartment?"

"She's dead. Fell—or was pushed—into the radiator. Split her head open." His voice became a whisper. "Get this, Katie. She was last seen alive around eight o'clock last night. A neighbor was with her. The neighbor heard her on the phone with Chris Lewis. Edna Burns told Lewis that she was going to talk to the police about Vangie's death. You better come right down."

AFTER he finished a second Scotch, Highley went into the kitchen and opened the refrigerator. He had told Hilda not to prepare anything for him tonight, but had given her a shopping list: lamb chops, fresh asparagus, and watercress for a salad.

Emotional exhaustion always compelled him to eat. After Winifred's death, he'd left her relatives and friends at the grave site, refusing invitations to join them for dinner. "No. No. I need to be alone." Then he'd driven to the Carlyle Hotel in New York. There he had requested a quiet table and ordered dinner. Halfway through the meal he looked up and saw Winifred's cousin, Glenn Nickerson, seated at a table across the room. He was dressed in the dark blue suit and black tie he'd worn to the funeral. It was obvious that he had followed Highley to the Carlyle. Nickerson had lifted his glass in a toast, a mocking smile on his face. He might as well have shouted, "To the grieving widower."

A week later Alan Levine, the doctor who'd treated Winifred, indignantly told him that Glenn Nickerson had asked to see Winifred's medical records. "I told him that Winifred had developed classic angina symptoms. Even then, he had the gall to speak to the police. I had a call from a fellow in the prosecutor's office asking if a heart ailment could be induced. I told him that being alive today was enough to induce heart trouble. They backed off, said it was obviously a disinherited relative trying to cause problems."

But you *can* induce heart trouble, Dr. Levine. You can prepare intimate little dinners for your dear wife. You can use her sus-

310

ceptibility to gastroenteritis to bring on attacks that register as heart seizures on her cardiogram. After enough of these, the lady has a fatal seizure. No one suggests an autopsy. And even if someone had, there would have been little risk.

But if they had thought to delve into Claire's death . . .

The chops were nearly cooked. He expertly seasoned the watercress, removed the asparagus from the steamer and took a half bottle of Beaujolais from the wine rack in the pantry.

He had just begun to eat when the phone rang. He hurried to the extension in the kitchen. "Dr. Highley," he said curtly.

A sob sounded over the phone. "Oh, Doctor, it's Gertrude Fitzgerald. I decided to go see Edna on my way home."

He tightened his grip on the receiver.

"Doctor, Edna is dead. The police are here. She fell. Doctor, could you come right away? They're talking about performing an autopsy. She hated autopsies. She used to say how terrible it was to cut up dead people. Doctor, oh, please come here and convince them that she fell and that they don't have to cut her up."

KATIE made a cup of tea and took it with her in the car. She'd planned to have tea with Edna. And now Edna was dead.

How could a person she'd met only once have made such an impression on her? In that one conversation they'd had, Edna had understood perfectly about John. She'd said, "I know what it is to watch someone die. You want the misery to be over for them, but you don't want to let them go. When Mom and Dad died, all my friends said, 'Now you're free, Edna.' And I said, 'Free for what?' I bet you felt that way too."

Edna had reassured her about Dr. Highley. "You couldn't find a better doctor. That's why it makes me so mad when I hear him criticized. And those people who file malpractice suits! I could shoot them. I tell you, when a doctor loses a patient today, he has to worry. I guess nobody's supposed to die anymore."

What had Charley meant by saying that Edna had phoned Chris Lewis last night? Was Charley suggesting that Edna might in some way have *threatened* him?

As she drove into the parking lot of Edna's apartment complex, she slowed down; a black medium-size car was pulling in ahead of her. The driver chose the first spot available on the right. Katie found a space directly behind the building, parked and got out of the car. Suddenly she heard footsteps and turned quickly. A figure loomed near her, a silhouette accentuated by the dim light from a solitary lamppost. "Excuse me. I hope I didn't startle you." The cultured voice had a faint English accent.

"Dr. Highley! Did my office call you?"

"Mrs. DeMaio. We didn't expect to see each other so soon and under such tragic circumstances. Here. Let's take this footpath around the building." Lightly touching her elbow, he followed her on the path. "Mrs. Fitzgerald called me. Evidently she was the one who found Edna."

They were turning the corner to the front of the building when Richard appeared. She was very glad to see him. He grasped both her shoulders and pulled her to him. Then his hands dropped. "Scott reached you?"

"No. I happened to call Edna myself. Oh, Richard, this is Dr. Edgar Highley." The two men shook hands.

Charley let them into the apartment. He said to Richard, "We've got pictures, but I'd like you to have a look too."

Katie was used to death. She often studied gory pictures of crime victims. But it was a different matter to see Edna crumpled against the radiator, to see the solid evidence of loneliness—the slices of canned ham, the empty cocktail glass.

Gertrude Fitzgerald was sitting on a couch, sobbing softly. Katie and Dr. Highley sat down beside her as Richard went into the dinette to examine the dead woman.

Gertrude tried to talk to them. "Oh, Dr. Highley, Mrs. DeMaio, isn't this just terrible?" The words brought a fresh burst of sobs. "She was always such fun. She always made me laugh. Maybe she had that little weakness, but she never bothered anyone with it. Oh, Dr. Highley, you'll miss her too."

"I surely will, Mrs. Fitzgerald."

"Doctor," Gertrude blurted out, "I told them you've been here, that you knew about Edna's little problem. It's just silly to say she didn't fall. Why would anyone want to hurt her?"

Dr. Highley looked at Katie. "Edna suffered from sciatica, and a few times when she was laid up I dropped off work for her to do at home. On one occasion I came unexpectedly. It was then I realized that she had a drinking problem."

Katie nodded, looking past him. Richard had completed examining the body. Getting up, she walked over to him and asked what he had found.

He shrugged. "I'll have to see how bad the fracture is. Certainly it was a hell of a smash. But she might have stumbled when she tried to get up."

"Any sign of forced entry?" Katie asked Charley.

"None. But you could spring these locks with a credit card. If she was as drunk as we think, anyone could have walked in."

"What were you telling me on the phone about Chris Lewis?"

"The superintendent's wife—name's Gana Krupshak—was a buddy of Edna Burns. She was with Mrs. Fitzgerald when the body was found. We let her go to her own apartment just before you came. She's shook up bad. Anyhow, last night she came over here around eight o'clock. She said Edna already had a bag on. She stayed till eight thirty, then put out the ham, hoping Edna would eat something and sober up. Edna told her about Vangie's suicide. Then, when Mrs. Krupshak went into the kitchen, she heard Edna on the phone. She swears Edna called whoever she was talking to 'Captain Lewis,' and told him she had to talk to the police tomorrow. And get this. Krupshak swears she heard Edna give Lewis directions for driving here. Then Edna said something about Prince Charming."

"Prince Charming?"

Charley shrugged. "Your guess is as good as mine."

Richard said, "Obviously we'll treat this as a potential homicide. I know Scott has a hunch about Lewis. I can see why."

Katie thought, I do not believe Chris Lewis could have done this to Edna; I don't believe he killed his wife. She looked around. "Are you *sure* there's nothing valuable missing?"

Charley shrugged. "Her wallet's in her pocketbook; eighteen dollars there. Credit cards. The usual. No sign of anything being disturbed, let alone ransacked."

"All right." Katie returned to Dr. Highley and Gertrude. "Mrs. Fitzgerald, I think it would be best if we have you driven home."

Dr. Highley reached into his pocket. "I brought these sedatives along in case you needed them. Here, take one now."

"I'll get a glass of water," Katie said. She went down the hall to the bathroom, then came back to Gertrude and sat beside her. "Mrs. Fitzgerald, do you know whether Edna kept any valuables here—any jewelry, perhaps?"

"She had a ring and a pin she wore on special occasions. I wouldn't know where she kept them. Oh, wait a minute. Doctor, I remember that Edna said she showed you her ring and pin when you were here. Perhaps you can help Mrs. DeMaio."

Katie looked into the cold gray eyes. He hates this, she thought. He's angry about being here.

"One time Edna did show me a pin and ring that were in a box in her night-table drawer."

"Would you show me, Doctor?" Katie asked.

Together they walked down the hall into the bedroom.

"It was in there," Dr. Highley told her, pointing to the night table on the right side of the bed.

Using only the tips of her fingers, Katie opened the drawer. She knew that the fingerprint experts would be called in.

The drawer was deep. Reaching in, Katie pulled out a blue plastic jewelry case. She raised the lid to find a small butterfly-shaped brooch and a thin old diamond ring nestled against cotton velvet.

"That eliminates the robbery theory, I guess," Katie said. She started to close the drawer, then stopped. "Oh, Doctor, look." Setting the jewelry box on the bed, she reached back into the drawer. "My mother kept her mother's old black hat for sentimental reasons. Edna must have done the same thing."

She was holding up an object for him to see. It was a scuffed brown moccasin, shaped for the left foot.

As Dr. Highley stared at the shoe, Katie said, "This was probably her mother's and she considered it such a treasure she kept it with that pathetic jewelry. Oh, Doctor, if memorabilia could talk, we'd hear a lot of stories, wouldn't we?"

314

EDGAR HIGHLEY STARED AT KATIE DEMAIO as she stood there holding that shoe in her hand. Was she mocking him? No. She believed that the shoe had had some sentimental meaning for Edna. Suppose she showed it to the detectives? Or to Gertrude? She'd been at the desk many times when Vangie came in.

He *had* to have that shoe.

Katie put it back, closed the drawer and walked out of the bedroom, the jewelry box tucked under her arm. He followed her, desperate to hear what she would say. But she simply handed the jewelry box to the detective. "The ring and pin are here, Charley," she said. "I guess that shoots any possibility of burglary."

There was a rap at the door, and Katie opened it to admit two men carrying a stretcher. Edgar Highley said to Gertrude, "I'll get you more water, Mrs. Fitzgerald." The others were watching the attendants as they lifted the body. It was his chance. He had to risk taking the shoe.

He walked rapidly to the bathroom, turned on the tap, then slipped across the hall to the bedroom. Using his handkerchief to avoid fingerprints, he opened the night-table drawer. He was reaching for the shoe when he heard footsteps coming down the hall. Quickly he pushed the drawer shut, stuffed his handkerchief into his pocket, and was standing at the door of the bedroom when Richard Carroll appeared. "Dr. Highley," he said coldly, "I'd like to ask you a few questions about Edna Burns."

"Certainly." Then, in what he hoped was a casual tone, Highley said, "Excuse me. I'm letting the tap run. I want to get Mrs. Fitzgerald a glass of cold water. The poor woman's terribly distressed."

Richard Carroll stood aside to let him pass. Highley filled the glass and took it to Gertrude. The attendants had left with the body, and Katie DeMaio was not in the room.

"Has Mrs. DeMaio left?" he asked the detective.

"She's talking to the super's wife. She'll be right back."

He could not leave until he was sure that Katie did not talk about the shoe. When she came back a few minutes later, she did not mention it.

They left the apartment together. Deliberately he stayed with Katie as she walked to her car, but then Richard Carroll joined them. "Let's get some coffee at the Golden Valley diner, Katie," he said, and Highley watched them drive off.

On his way home, Edgar Highley decided there must be a personal relationship between Katie DeMaio and Richard Carroll. When Katie bled to death, Carroll would be both professionally and emotionally interested in the cause of death. He would have to be very careful.

He drove into his garage, then entered the house. The cold lamb chops were on the plate; the asparagus had wilted; the salad was limp and warm. He would reheat the food in the microwave oven, prepare a fresh salad.

As he set to work, he found himself becoming calm. He was so near to being safe. And soon it would be possible to share his genius with the world. He already had his success. He could prove it beyond doubt. He had accurate records, pictures, X rays, the step-by-step accounts of how he had dealt with all the problems that had arisen. All in the files in his secret safe.

When the proper time came, he would burn the files on the failures and claim the recognition that was due him. By then there would surely be more triumphs. He sat down at the table and slowly ate his dinner. As always, food restored his sense of well-being. Tomorrow the *Newsmaker* article would appear. It would enhance his social as well as his medical prestige.

"My patients are not allowed to drink or smoke during their pregnancies," he had told the *Newsmaker* interviewer. "They are required to follow a specific diet. I will not accept a patient who will not cooperate with my methods. I can show you dozens of women I have treated who have had a history of several miscarriages but now have children. Many more could experience that same joy, *if* they were willing to change their habits, particularly their eating and drinking habits."

The *Newsmaker* reporter had been impressed. But her next question was a loaded one. "Doctor, isn't it true that a large number of women have miscarried, even *after* following your schedule rigidly—and paying you ten thousand dollars?"

"It would be insane for me to claim that I bring every difficult pregnancy to term. Yes. There have been occasions where a de-

316

sired pregnancy was spontaneously aborted. After several of these occurrences, I suggest that my patient adopt a child, and I help to arrange a suitable adoption."

"For a fee."

"Young woman, I assume you are being paid to interview me. Why don't *you* use your time for volunteer work?"

It had been foolish to antagonize her, foolish to give her any reason to want to discredit him or to delve into his background.

The interviewer's next question had been meant to entrap him.

"Doctor, you also perform abortions. Isn't it incongruous to try to save one fetus and to eliminate another?"

"I refer to the womb as a cradle. I despise abortion. But I also deplore the grief I witness when women come to me who cannot conceive because their wombs have been damaged during abortions. It is my wish that all women carry their babies to term. For those who do not want to, at least I can make sure that when they do want a child, they will still be able to have one."

That point had been well received.

He finished eating, leaned back in the chair and poured himself more wine. He was feeling expansive. Tomorrow morning he had a cesarean section scheduled—another difficult case that would add to his reputation. The mother was from the socially prominent Payne family. The father, Delano Aldrich, was an officer of a prestigious foundation. This was the sort of family whose championship he needed.

Only one obstacle left. He had brought Katie DeMaio's file home from the office. He would begin now to prepare the substitute file that he would show to the police after her death.

Instead of the history she'd given him of prolonged periods of bleeding, he would write, "Patient complains of frequent hemorrhaging, unrelated to monthly cycles." Instead of sponginess of uterine walls, a condition that could be remedied by a simple operation, he would note signs of vascular breakdown. Instead of a slightly low hemoglobin, he would indicate that the hemoglobin was chronically in the danger zone.

He went into the library. Her official file was on top of his desk. From the drawer he extracted a new folder, put Katie's name on it and set down her previous medical history. This was the folder he would take to the hospital. He added several paragraphs to the file he would put in the wall safe when completed.

Patient was in minor automobile accident on Monday night, February 15. At 2:00 a.m. sedated patient observed the transferal of the remains of Vangie Lewis by this physician. Patient still does not understand that what she observed was a true event rather than a hallucination, but inevitably she will. She cannot be permitted to remain as a threat to this physician. On pretense of preparation for Saturday surgery, this physician prescribed anticoagulant medication to be taken on regular basis until Friday night.

He laid down his pen. It was easy to imagine how he would complete this report.

Patient entered the hospital at 6:00 p.m. Friday, February 19, complaining of dizziness and general weakness. At 9:00 p.m. this physician, accompanied by Nurse Renge, found the patient hemorrhaging. Blood pressure was falling rapidly. Emergency surgery was performed at 9:45 p.m. The patient expired at 10:00 p.m.

He smiled in anticipation. Every detail was perfectly planned, even to assigning Nurse Renge to floor duty Friday night. She was young, inexperienced and terrified of him. Putting the file in the temporary hiding place in the top desk drawer, he went upstairs to bed and slept soundly until six in the morning.

Three hours later he delivered a healthy baby boy by cesarean section to Mrs. Delano Aldrich and accepted as his due the tearful gratitude of the patient and her husband.

CHAPTER NINE

AT EIGHT a.m. Thursday morning the Investigative Squad of the Homicide Division of Valley County pulled up to the Lewis home. The six-man team was headed by Phil Cunningham and Charley Nugent. The detectives in charge of fingerprinting were told to concentrate on the master bedroom and bath and the kitchen.

According to the lab report, Vangie's fingerprints had been found on the tumbler that had been lying next to her. She had been right-handed. When she poured the cyanide crystals into the glass, it would have been natural for her to hold the glass with her left hand and pour with her right. Yet only her right prints were on the tumbler. This further discredited the suicide theory.

Every bottle in the medicine chest was opened, sniffed. But the bitter-almond scent they were looking for was not to be found.

The bedroom was carefully vacuumed in the hope of finding human hair. As Phil put it: "Any house can have hairs from delivery people, neighbors, anybody. We're all shedding hair all the time. But most people don't bring even good friends into the bedroom. So if you find human hair that doesn't belong to the people who sleep in the bedroom, you might have something."

Close attention was given to the shelves in the garage. The usual garden tools, hoses, insecticides and weed killer were there in abundance. Phil grunted in annoyance as a prong of a gardening fork pulled at his jacket. The prongs had been protruding over the edge of the shelf, the handle wedged in by a heavy paint can. Bending to free his sleeve, he noticed a sliver of printed cotton hooked on the prong.

That flowered print. He'd seen it recently. It was the dress Vangie Lewis was wearing when she died.

He called the police photographer out to the garage. "Get a picture of that," he said, pointing to the tool. When the picture was taken, he removed the material and sealed it in an envelope.

In the house, Charley was going through the desk. When Phil came in, Charley said, "We've come up with a big zero. Wait a minute. They had an answering service. We'd better check it for messages."

He got the number of the answering service from a file in the desk, then dialed and identified himself. "Give me any messages left for either Captain or Mrs. Lewis starting with Monday."

Taking out his pen, he began to write: "Monday, February 15, 4:00 p.m. Northwest Orient reservations phoned. Mrs. Lewis is confirmed on Flight 235 at 4:10 p.m. from La Guardia Airport to Minneapolis/St. Paul on Tuesday, February 16."

Charley asked, "Did Mrs. Lewis receive that message?"

"Oh, yes," the operator said. "I gave it to her myself at about seven thirty Monday evening. She sounded very relieved."

"All right," Charley said. "What else have you got?"

"Also on Monday a Miss Edna Burns called at ten p.m. She wanted Mrs. Lewis to phone her no matter how late it was. But Mrs. Lewis never contacted us again that night."

There were no further messages on the service, but the operator knew a call had come through Tuesday evening and had been picked up by Captain Lewis. "I was just starting to answer when he came on," she explained. "I got right off."

Charley thanked the operator, then hung up the receiver and looked at Phil. "Let's go. Scott's going to want to hear about this."

"How do you read it?" Phil asked.

Charley snorted. "How else can I read it? As of seven thirty Monday evening Vangie Lewis was planning to go to Minneapolis. A couple of hours later she's dead. As of ten o'clock Monday night, Edna Burns had an important message for Vangie. The next night Edna's dead, and the last person who saw her alive heard her telling Chris Lewis she had information for the police."

For Katie, Wednesday night had seemed endless. She'd gone to bed as soon as she returned from Edna's apartment, first taking one of the pills Dr. Highley had given her. She'd awakened feeling vaguely troubled. Her grandmother's old black hat. Why was she thinking about that hat? Of course. Because of that shabby old shoe Edna obviously prized. But why just *one* shoe?

Grimacing, she got out of bed. The soreness throughout her body had intensified during the night. Hoping that a hot bath might soak some of the achiness away, she went into the bathroom and turned on the taps in the tub. A wave of dizziness made her sway, and she grabbed the side of the tub to keep from falling. The bathroom mirror revealed the deathly pallor of her skin. It's this bleeding, she thought. If I weren't going into the hospital tomorrow night, I'd probably end up being carried in.

The bath did reduce some of the stiffness, and foundation make-up minimized the paleness. With her orange juice Katie swallowed another of Dr. Highley's pills. Then she grabbed a coat and her handbag and went out to the car.

Charley and Phil were searching the Lewis house this morning. Scott was drawing a web around Chris Lewis. If only she could find another avenue to explore before Chris was indicted.

She arrived at the office just before eight and found Maureen Crowley already there. "Maureen," Katie said, "I've got a job. Could you come in when you have a minute?"

The girl got up quickly. She had a narrow-waisted, graceful young body. The green sweater she was wearing accentuated the vivid green of her eyes. "How about coffee, Katie?"

"Great. But no ham on rye—at least not yet."

Maureen looked embarrassed. "I'm sorry I said that yesterday. You, of all people, are not in a rut."

"I'm not sure about that." Katie hung up her coat and settled down with her notebook. Maureen brought in the coffee, pulled up a chair and waited silently, her steno pad on her lap.

Katie said slowly, "We're not satisfied that the Vangie Lewis death is a suicide. Yesterday I talked with her doctors, Dr. Highley and Dr. Fukhito, at Westlake Hospital."

She heard a sharp intake of breath and looked up quickly. The girl's face had gone dead white.

"Maureen, is anything the matter?"

"No. No. I'm sorry."

Unconvinced, Katie looked back at her notes. "As far as we know, Dr. Fukhito was the last person to see Vangie Lewis alive. I want to find out as much as I can about him. Find out where he came from, where he went to school, other hospitals he's been connected with, his personal background."

"You don't want me to talk to anyone at Westlake Hospital?"

"No. I don't want them to know we're checking on him."

For some reason the younger woman seemed relieved. "I'll get right on it."

"You'd be a good lawyer," Katie said, meaning it. "I'm surprised you didn't go to college."

"I was insane enough to get engaged the summer I finished high school. My folks persuaded me to take a secretarial course before I got married so at least I'd have some kind of skill. How right they were. The engagement didn't stand the year's wait."

She looked unhappy, and Katie decided she must have been pretty hurt about the breakup.

Maureen went out of the room. The telephone rang. It was Richard. "Katie, I've just been talking to Dave Broad, the head of prenatal research at Mount Sinai. On a hunch, I sent him the fetus Vangie Lewis was carrying. My hunch was right. Vangie *was not pregnant with Lewis' child. The baby was distinctly Oriental!*"

CHAPTER TEN

THE funeral service for Vangie Lewis was held on Thursday morning in the chapel of a Minneapolis funeral home. Chris stood beside Vangie's parents, their muffled sobs assaulting him like hammerblows. They had been outraged to hear that Vangie could not be buried, that her body was to be shipped back east, then returned later for burial. "Why?"

"I simply don't know." There was no use saying more—not now. He thought of Edna's call. Could she throw some light on Vangie's death? Before he left Minneapolis, he had to call Dr. Salem. What did he know about Vangie that had made him react with such shock last night? Why had Vangie wanted to see him?

There had been someone else in Vangie's life. He was sure of it now. Suppose Vangie had killed herself in front of someone and that person had brought her home?

The minister was saying the final prayer. "When every tear shall be dried . . ." Chris led Vangie's parents into the anteroom to accept the sympathy of their friends.

When he was able to get away to a phone, Chris called Dr. Salem's office. "This is Vangie Lewis' husband," he said. "It's urgent I speak with the doctor immediately."

"I'm sorry," the nurse told him. "Dr. Salem left a short time ago for the American Medical Association convention in New York. He will not be back until next week."

"New York! Can you tell me where he's staying, please?"

The nurse hesitated. "I suppose it's all right. I know Dr. Salem intends to get in touch with you. He took your wife's medical records with him. You can reach him at the Essex House Hotel on Central Park South."

Scott Myerson had called a noon meeting to discuss Vangie Lewis' death. When Katie arrived, Maureen was there with a pen and paper.

"We're bringing sandwiches in," Scott said. "I'm due in court again at one thirty. We've got to move fast on Captain Lewis."

As Katie had expected, Scott was zeroing in on Chris. She looked at Maureen. The girl had an aura of nervousness around her. "Any results on Dr. Fukhito?"

"So far not much. He's not a member of the AMA or the Valley County Medical Society. But I have a call in to the University of Massachusetts. He attended medical school there."

"Who told you that?" Katie asked.

"I remember hearing it somewhere."

Katie sensed that Maureen was being evasive.

At that moment Richard, Charley and Phil came into the office. Quickly they gave Maureen their lunch choices. Scott began to speak. "By now you all know that the Lewis baby had Oriental characteristics. So that opens two possibilities. One: with the birth imminent, Vangie panicked and killed herself because she knew she could never pass the baby off as her husband's. Two: Chris Lewis found out that his wife had been having an affair and killed her. She could have been rushing home to Minneapolis because she was afraid of him. From what Katie tells us, the psychiatrist claims she ran out of his office nearly hysterical."

"The *Japanese* psychiatrist," Katie said.

"Are you suggesting there was something between him and Vangie?"

"I'm not suggesting anything yet. Vangie could have known another Oriental man. But he was nervous when I spoke with him yesterday. He carefully chose every word he said to me, and I certainly did not get the whole truth from him."

"Which brings us to Edna Burns," Scott said. "What about it, Richard? Did she fall, or was she pushed?"

"It's possible that she fell. The alcohol level in her blood was point two five. She was blotto."

"But it is possible she was murdered?" Scott persisted.

"Absolutely."

"And Edna was heard talking to Chris Lewis about Prince Charming." Katie thought of the handsome psychiatrist. Would Edna refer to *him* as Prince Charming?

"Maybe Vangie told her something Monday night," Charley suggested. "Maybe she knew Chris and Vangie had quarreled and why they'd quarreled. Maybe she was putting the arm on Lewis. She did threaten to go to the police."

"She said she had something to tell the police," Katie objected. "That's the way the super's wife put it."

"All right," Scott said. "What turned up at the Lewis house?"

"Not much," said Charley. "There's a phone number with a 612 area code scribbled on the pad beside the kitchen phone. We thought we'd call it from here. The other thing is that she tore her dress on a prong sticking out from a shelf in the garage."

Scott picked up the message pad Charley had handed him and tossed it to Katie. "Why don't you try this number now?"

Katie dialed the number and waited while the phone rang.

"Dr. Salem's office."

"Perhaps you can help me. I'm Kathleen DeMaio from the Valley County, New Jersey, prosecutor's office. We're conducting an inquiry into the death of Vangie Lewis last Monday. She had Dr. Salem's phone number on her pad."

"Oh, that is a coincidence. I was just about to call your medical examiner. Dr. Salem wants to talk with him. The doctor is on his way to New York right now for the AMA convention. Can your medical examiner phone him around five p.m. at the Essex House Hotel on Central Park South?"

"Yes. I'll give him the message." Then, on a chance, Katie added, "Do you know anything about Mrs. Lewis' call? Did she speak with the doctor?"

"No. She spoke to me. She called Monday and was so disappointed that he wasn't going to be back till Wednesday. I made an emergency appointment for her for Wednesday."

324

"One last question. What kind of doctor is Dr. Salem?"

"Oh, he's a prominent obstetrician and gynecologist."

"I see. Thank you. You've been very helpful." Katie hung up the phone and reported the conversation to the others.

There was a knock at the door and Maureen came in with coffee and sandwiches. "Katie," she said, "that call from Massachusetts about Dr. Fukhito is just coming in. Want to take it?"

Katie nodded and picked up the phone. As she waited for the call to be switched, she became aware of a slow, persistent headache. I'm not operating on all cylinders, she thought. So many things were teasing her mind. What was she trying to recall?

The personnel director at the University of Massachusetts Medical School answered guardedly. "Yes, Dr. Fukhito graduated from U. Mass. He interned at Massachusetts General and later became affiliated with the hospital. He also had a private practice. He left the hospital seven years ago."

"Why did he leave?" Katie asked. "You must understand this is a police investigation. All information will be kept confidential."

There was a pause. "Dr. Fukhito was asked to resign. He was found guilty of unethical behavior after he unsuccessfully defended a malpractice suit."

"What was the cause of the suit?" Katie asked.

"A patient sued Dr. Fukhito for inducing her to have a personal relationship with him. She bore Dr. Fukhito's child."

MOLLY bustled around her kitchen, rejoicing in the fact that all the children were back in school. Bill was not going into New York for another half hour. They were enjoying a rare chance to chat in peace, as Bill sat at the table sipping coffee and Molly sliced vegetables. "I'm sure Katie and Richard and the Berkeleys will enjoy each other," Molly was saying. "Now if Liz just doesn't spend the whole evening talking about the baby . . . When I phoned to invite her, she spent the first twenty minutes on Maryanne's latest trick . . . which is to blow her oatmeal all over the place. Isn't that cute?"

"It is if it's your first baby and you waited fifteen years to have one," Bill commented.

325

"Anyhow, even if Liz does rave about the baby tonight, maybe a little of it will sink in on Katie and Richard."

Bill's eyebrows rose. "Molly, you're not very subtle. You'd better watch out or they'll start avoiding each other."

"Haven't you noticed the way they act together? There's something smoldering there. And Richard called me last night and wanted to know if there was something the matter with Katie."

"Did you tell him about the operation?"

"No. Katie doesn't want me to. But the poor guy is so worried about her. I don't think it's fair to him."

Bill got up and put his cup and saucer in the dishwasher. "If Katie doesn't want to tell Richard about this operation, don't fill him in. That's not fair to her. You've gotten them together. Now—"

"Now bug off." Molly sighed.

"Something like that. And tomorrow night when Katie goes into the hospital, you and I are going to the opera. You can be at the recovery room Saturday morning, but it won't hurt to have her wish she had someone with her Friday evening. Maybe she'll do a little thinking."

"Let her go into the hospital by herself?" Molly protested.

"By herself," Bill said firmly. "She's a big girl."

The telephone rang. Molly picked it up. "Hello. . . . Liz, hi." She listened. "Oh, for heaven's sake, bring her along. She can sleep up in our room. . . . Great. See you at seven. By."

She hung up. "Liz Berkeley's regular baby-sitter had to cancel, so she's bringing the baby along."

"Fine." Bill looked at the clock. "I'd better go." He kissed Molly's cheek. "Will you quit worrying about your little sister?"

Molly bit her lip. "I can't. I've got this creepy feeling about Katie, like something might happen to her."

CHAPTER ELEVEN

WHEN Richard returned to his office after the meeting with Scott and the others, he stood for a long time staring out the window. In the pocket-size park in front of the courthouse a flurry of snow pelted the already frozen grass.

He glanced up at the sky. Vangie Lewis' body was being flown to Newark from Minneapolis on a two-thirty flight. It would be brought to the morgue, and tomorrow morning he'd reexamine it. There was something about her left foot or leg that he had noticed and dismissed as irrelevant. He pushed that thought aside. It was useless to speculate until he could reexamine the body. Sighing, he snapped on the intercom and asked Marge to bring in his phone messages.

She hurried in with a sheaf of slips in her hand. "None of these are too important," she said. "But I got the statistics on the West-lake obstetrical patients. In the eight years of the Westlake Maternity Concept, sixteen patients have died either in childbirth or of toxic pregnancies."

"*Sixteen?*"

"*Sixteen,*" Marge repeated with emphasis. "However, the practice is huge. And all the women who died had been warned by other doctors that they were high pregnancy risks."

"I'll study the fatalities," Richard said. "Anything else?"

"Maybe. Two people filed malpractice suits against Dr. Highley. Both were dismissed. And a cousin of his wife's claimed that he didn't believe she'd died of a heart attack. The prosecutor's office contacted her physician, Dr. Alan Levine, and he said the cousin was crazy. The cousin had been the sole heir before Winifred Westlake married Dr. Highley."

"I'll have a talk with Dr. Levine."

"And these are the people who filed the malpractice suits."

Richard looked down at the two names on the sheet of paper Marge handed him. Anthony Caldwell, Old Country Lane, Peapack, New Jersey, and Anna Horan, 415 Walnut Street, Ridgefield Park, New Jersey. "You do nice work, Marge," he said.

She nodded. "I know."

He phoned Dr. Levine and caught him as he was leaving his office. They agreed to meet at the Parkwood Country Club.

Alan Levine was a Jimmy Stewart look-alike, which endeared him to his older patients. He and Richard enjoyed the easy cordiality of professionals who respected each other. At the club, Richard came directly to the point. "Winifred Westlake was your patient. Her cousin suggested that she did not die of a heart attack. What can you tell me about it?"

Levine sipped his martini and glanced out the picture window at the snow-covered fairway. "I have to answer that question on a couple of levels. First: Winifred for years had all the classic symptoms of a duodenal ulcer, except it never showed up on X ray. When she'd experience pain, I'd prescribe an ulcer diet and she'd feel relief almost immediately. No great problem.

"Then the year before she married Highley she had a severe attack of gastroenteritis, which actually altered her cardiogram. I put her in the hospital for a suspected heart attack. But after two days the cardiogram was well within the normal range."

"So there might or might not have been a heart problem?"

"I didn't think there was. But her mother died of a heart attack at fifty-eight, and Winifred was nearly fifty-two when she died. She was older than Highley by some ten years. Several years after her marriage she began to complain of frequent chest pains. The tests produced nothing significant. I told her to watch her diet."

"And then she had a fatal attack?" Richard asked.

The other doctor nodded. "One evening, during dinner, she had a seizure. Highley had his service call me. When I got there, he was still trying to revive her. But it was hopeless. She died a few minutes after I arrived."

"And you're satisfied it was heart failure?"

There was a hint of hesitation. "I was satisfied at the time."

"*At the time*." Richard underscored the words.

"I suppose the cousin's absolute conviction that something was wrong about her death has troubled me these three years. I practically threw Glenn Nickerson out of my office when he came in and as much as accused me of falsifying records. But he is a family man, active in his church, on the town council; certainly not the kind to go off half-cocked at being disinherited. And he must have known that Winifred would leave her estate to her husband. She was crazy about Highley. Why, I never could see. But I've got to hand it to him. He's an excellent doctor."

"Excellent enough to have chemically induced a heart attack in his wife?"

328

Dr. Levine looked directly at Richard. "Frankly, I've often wished I'd insisted on an autopsy."

They parted at the entrance to the bar. Richard fished in his pocket for change, went over to the public telephone and dialed the Essex House in New York. "Dr. Emmet Salem, please."

There was the repeated sound of a phone ringing. The operator broke in. "I'm sorry, but there's no answer."

"Are you sure Dr. Salem has checked in?" Richard asked.

"Yes, sir. He called specifically to say that he was expecting an important call and he wanted to be sure to get it. That was only twenty minutes ago. But I guess he changed his mind. Because we are definitely ringing his room and there's no answer."

CHAPTER TWELVE

THE *Newsmaker* article was on the stands Thursday morning. The phone calls had begun as soon as Highley went to his office after delivering the Aldrich baby. The response was beyond his expectations. The Dartmouth Medical School phoned. Would he consider a guest lecture? A writer for *Ladies' Home Journal* wanted an interview. Would Dr. Highley appear on *Eyewitness News?*

Smiling, he signaled for his first patient to come in. She was an interesting case: her womb was so tipped that she'd never conceive without intervention. She would be his next Vangie.

The phone call came at noon, just as he was leaving for lunch. The nurse covering the reception desk was apologetic. "It's long distance from a Dr. Emmet Salem in Minneapolis."

Emmet Salem! He picked up the phone. "Edgar Highley here."

"Dr. Highley. From Christ Hospital in Devon?"

"Yes." He felt a chill, sickening fear.

"Doctor, I learned last night that you treated my former patient Vangie Lewis. I'm leaving for New York immediately. In fact, I'm at the airport now. I am planning to consult with the medical examiner in New Jersey about Mrs. Lewis' death. I have her records with me. In fairness to you, I suggest we discuss her case first."

"Doctor, I'm troubled by your tone and insinuations."

"I'll be checking into room 3219 at the Essex House shortly

329

before five. You can call me there." The connection was broken.

Highley was waiting at the hotel when Emmet Salem emerged from the cab. Swiftly he took an elevator to the thirty-second floor, walked past room 3219 and around a corner. Another elevator stopped at the floor. He listened as a key clicked and a bellman said, "Here we are, Doctor." A minute later the bellman emerged from the room. "Thank you, sir." Highley waited until the corridors were silent. Quickly he opened his bag and took out the paperweight. He slipped it into his coat pocket, put on his gloves, grasped the bag firmly in his left hand and knocked on the door.

Emmet Salem pulled the door open. He had just removed his suit coat.

"Dr. Salem!" Highley reached for Salem's hand, walking forward, backing the older man into the room, closing the door behind him. "I'm Edgar Highley. It's good to see you again. You got off the phone so abruptly that I couldn't tell you I was coming into town for dinner. I have only a few minutes, but I'm sure we can clear up any questions." He was still walking forward, forcing the other man to retreat. The window behind Salem was wide open. He'd probably had the bellman open it because the room was very hot. The sill was low. "I tried to phone you, but your extension is out of order."

"Impossible. I just spoke to the operator." Salem stiffened.

"Then I do apologize. But I'm so anxious to go over the Lewis file with you. I have it right here." He put his bag down and reached for the paperweight in his pocket, then cried, "Doctor, behind you, watch out!"

The other man spun around. Highley crashed the paperweight on Salem's skull. Emmet Salem slumped against the windowsill.

Jamming the paperweight back into his pocket, Edgar Highley cupped his palms around Salem's foot and shoved up and out.

"No. No. Please!" The half-conscious man slid out the window and landed on the roof of the extension some fifteen floors below. The body made a muffled thud.

From Salem's suit coat on the bed Highley pulled out a key ring. The smallest key fitted the attaché case on the luggage rack. The Vangie Lewis file was on top. Grabbing it, he shoved it into

330

his own bag, relocked Salem's bag, returned the keys to the suit-coat pocket. He placed the bloodstained paperweight in his bag, then glanced around. The room was in perfect order.

He opened the door and looked along the corridor. It was empty. As he stepped out, the phone in Salem's room began to ring. An elevator was just stopping. He got on, his eyes scanning the passengers. No one he knew.

At the lobby, he walked rapidly to the Fifty-eighth Street exit. Ten minutes later he reclaimed his car from a park-and-lock garage, tossed his bag into the trunk and drove away.

WHEN she left Scott's office, Katie called in Rita Castile, one of the investigators, and together they went over the material Katie would need for upcoming trials. "That armed robbery on the twenty-eighth, where the defendant had his hair cut the morning after the crime. We'll need the barber to testify. It's no wonder the witnesses couldn't make a positive identification. Even though we made him wear a wig in the lineup, he didn't look the same."

Rita jotted down the barber's address.

"That's about all I have for you now," Katie said, "but I won't be coming in over the weekend, so next week will really be a mess. Be prepared."

"You won't be coming in?" Rita raised her eyebrows. "Well, it's about time. You haven't taken a full weekend in a couple of months. I hope you're planning to have some fun."

Katie grinned. "I don't know how much fun it will be. Oh, Rita, I have a hunch that Maureen is upset about something. Is it the breakup with her fiancé?"

Rita shook her head. "No, that was just kid stuff, and she knew it. The problem is, just about the time they broke up she realized she was pregnant and had an abortion. She's weighted down with guilt about it. She told me that she keeps dreaming about the baby, that she'd do anything to have had it, even though she would have given it out for adoption."

Katie remembered how much she had hoped to conceive John's child. "That does explain it. Thanks for telling me. I was afraid I'd said something to hurt her."

After Rita left, Katie called Westlake Hospital. She wanted to talk again with the receptionist, Gertrude Fitzgerald. Then she would call Gana Krupshak.

The hospital told her that Mrs. Fitzgerald was home ill, and gave Katie her home phone number. When the woman answered, her voice was weak and shaking. "I have one of my migraines," she said, "and no wonder. Every time I think of poor Edna . . ."

"I would like to ask you something," Katie said. "Did Edna ever call either of the doctors she worked for Prince Charming?"

"*Prince Charming?* Dr. Highley or Dr. Fukhito? Why would she call either of them Prince Charming? My heavens, no."

"All right. It was just a thought." Katie said good-by and dialed Mrs. Krupshak. The superintendent answered. His wife was out, he explained. She'd be back around five.

Katie glanced at the clock. It was four thirty. "Do you think she'd mind if I stopped to talk to her for a few minutes?"

"Suit yourself," the man answered shortly.

MRS. Krupshak was home when Katie rang her bell. "Now, isn't that timing!" she exclaimed. For her, the shock of discovering Edna's body had worn off and she was enjoying the excitement.

"This is my bingo afternoon," she explained. "When I told my friends what happened they could hardly keep their cards straight."

She ushered Katie into an L-shaped living room, and they both sat down on an imitation-leather couch.

"Mrs. Krupshak," Katie said, "I wonder if you would go over with me very carefully what happened Tuesday night: how long you were with Edna; what you talked about. When she spoke to Captain Lewis, did you get the impression that she made an appointment with him?"

Gana Krupshak leaned back. "Now, let's see. I went over to Edna's right at eight o'clock, because Gus started to watch the basketball game and I thought I'd go have a beer with Edna. The thing is, Edna had made a pitcher of manhattans and they were about half gone and she was pretty rocky. She talked in a sort of rambly way about this patient who had died, how

332

beautiful she'd been, how sick she'd been getting and how she—Edna, I mean—could tell the cops a lot about her."

"Then what happened?" Katie asked.

"Well, I had a manhattan, or two, with her and then figured I'd better get home. But I hated to see Edna drink much more, so I got out that nice canned ham for her."

"And that was when she made the call to Captain Lewis and mentioned Prince Charming?"

"As God is my witness."

"All right, but one last thing, Mrs. Krupshak. Do you know if Edna kept any articles of clothing of her mother's as a sentimental keepsake? I noticed a shabby old moccasin in Edna's nighttable drawer. Did she ever show it to you or mention it?"

Gana Krupshak looked directly at Katie. "Absolutely not," she said flatly.

CHRIS Lewis arrived at the Twin Cities airport at one thirty. He had an hour to wait before his plane left for Newark. Vangie's body would be on that plane. At Newark the medical examiner's office would be waiting for it.

And the prosecutor's office would be waiting for him. Of course. If they were suspicious in any way about Vangie's death, they were going to look to him for answers. If they'd investigated at all, they knew by now that he'd returned to the New Jersey area Monday night. He had to see Dr. Salem, find out why he had been so upset. If Chris were detained for questioning, he might not be able to talk to him.

He also had to talk to Joan. He had the number of the stewardess, Kay Corrigan, with whom she was staying in Florida. Not knowing what he would say, he put through the call.

Kay answered. "It's Chris, Kay. Is Joan there?"

"Chris, the Valley County prosecutor's office has been calling here asking questions about you two. Joan is frantic!"

"Is she there?"

"No. She won't be here till about eight tonight."

"Tell her to stay in till I call her. Tell her—" He broke the connection, leaned against the phone and pushed back a sob. It was

333

all too much. He didn't know what to do. In a few hours he'd be in custody, suspected of killing Vangie.

No. There was another way. He'd get the flight into La Guardia. He could still make it. Then he'd be able to see Dr. Salem at almost the same time he reached the hotel. Maybe Dr. Salem could help him somehow.

He barely made the La Guardia flight. On the plane, he listlessly thumbed through *Newsmaker* magazine. His eye caught the headline WESTLAKE MATERNITY CONCEPT OFFERS NEW HOPE TO CHILDLESS COUPLES. *Westlake.* He read the first paragraph. "For the past eight years, a private clinic in New Jersey has been making it possible for childless women to become pregnant. The program is carried on by Dr. Edgar Highley. . . ."

Highley. Vangie's doctor. Funny she never talked very much about him. It was always the psychiatrist, Fukhito.

The plane landed at four thirty. Chris hurried through the terminal and hailed a cab. It was five when he reached the Essex House. He headed for a lobby telephone, asked the operator for Dr. Salem's room number and dialed it. The phone rang . . . again . . . again. After six rings he hung up. He dialed the operator and asked her to try it for him.

The operator hesitated. "Sir, when Dr. Salem checked in, he told me that he expected an important call. But apparently he's stepped out. Why don't you try again in a few minutes?"

"I'll do that." Chris hung up the phone, walked over to a lobby chair facing an elevator bank and sat down. The elevators opened, dislodged passengers, filled again, disappeared.

One elevator caught his attention. There was something vaguely familiar about someone on it; a middle-aged man with a turned-up coat collar. Dr. Salem? No. Not Salem.

At five thirty Chris tried again. And at quarter to six. At five past six he heard the whispers that ran through the lobby like a flash fire. "Someone jumped out a window." From outside came the wail of an ambulance and the yip-yip of police cars.

Chris went to the bell captain's desk. "Who was it?" he asked.

"Dr. Emmet Salem. A big shot in the AMA. Room 3219."

Walking like an automaton, Chris pushed through the revolving door to Fifty-eighth Street. He hailed a cab and got in. "La Guardia, please," he said.

There was a seven-o'clock flight to Miami. He had to get to Joan, try to make her understand before he was arrested.

CHAPTER THIRTEEN

TWELVE-year-old Jennifer threw open the door for Katie. "Katie, hi." The two smiled at each other. With her intense blue eyes, dark hair and olive skin, Jennifer was a young Katie.

"Hi, Jennie. Anybody here yet?"

"Everybody. The Berkeleys brought their baby. Richard is here too. His first question was 'Is Katie here yet?' He's got a case on you, Katie."

"Jennifer!" Half laughing, half irritated, Katie walked inside.

In the den, Liz and Jim Berkeley were seated on the couch. Molly was passing hors d'oeuvres. Richard was standing by the window, talking to Bill. He turned and saw her. "Katie." He came hurrying over. "I've been listening for the doorbell."

So often since John's death she'd entered a room where she was the outsider, the loner, amid couples. Tonight, Richard had been waiting for her, listening for her. Before she had time to consider her feelings, everyone was saying hello.

On the way to the dining room she asked Richard if he'd reached Dr. Salem. He said, "I just missed him at five. I left this number with the hotel operator and with my answering service."

At dinner Liz Berkeley said, "I'm holding my breath hoping Maryanne won't wake up. Poor kid, her gums are swollen."

Jim Berkeley laughed. He was darkly handsome, with brown eyes and thick black eyebrows. "When Maryanne was born, Liz used to wake her up every fifteen minutes to make sure she was okay. Now it's always, 'Quiet, don't wake up the baby.'"

Liz, who was a slender woman with flashing brown eyes, made a face at her husband. "I'm calming down, but she *is* a miracle to us. I'd just about given up hope. Dr. Highley's a genius."

Richard's eyes narrowed. "You really think so?"

"Positively. He isn't the warmest person," Liz began.

"But he knows his business," her husband interrupted. "He put Liz to bed in the hospital almost two months before the delivery and personally checked on her three or four times a day."

"Listen, I pray for that man every night," Liz said. "The difference that baby has made in our lives! Don't let Jim fool you. He's up ten times a night to make sure that Maryanne is covered."

As the others chatted, Katie only half listened. She felt tired and light-headed, but she did not want to break up the party.

Her chance came as they headed for the living room for a nightcap. "I'm going to say good night," Katie said. "I'm bushed."

Molly did not protest. Richard said, "I'll take you to your car."

The night air was cold, and she shivered as they started down the walk. "Katie, I'm worried about you," Richard said. "I know you're not feeling up to par. You don't seem to want to talk about it, but at least let's have dinner tomorrow night."

"Richard, I'm sorry. I can't. I'm going away this weekend."

"You're *what?* With all that's happening at the office?"

"I . . . I'm committed." What a lame thing to say, Katie thought. This is ridiculous. She would tell Richard that she'd be in the hospital. . . .

Suddenly the front door was thrown open. "Richard," Jennifer shouted. "Clovis Simmons is on the phone."

"Clovis Simmons!" Katie said. "The actress?"

"Yes. Oh, hell, I was supposed to call her."

"I'll see you in the morning." Katie got into the car and closed the door. Richard hesitated, then hurried into the house as Katie drove away. His "Hello, Clovis" was brusque.

"Well, Doctor, it's a shame I have to track you down, but we did discuss dinner, didn't we?"

"I'm *sorry.* Clovis, let me call you tomorrow. I can't talk now."

There was a sharp click in his ear. Richard hung up the phone slowly. Tomorrow he must call and apologize and tell her that there was someone else. For now he'd make his excuses and go home. Maybe try Dr. Salem again.

He went into the living room. Molly, Bill and the Berkeleys were there. And swathed in blankets, sitting on Liz's lap, was a baby girl.

"Maryanne decided to join the party," Liz said. "What do you think of her?" Proudly she turned the baby to face him.

It might have been a magazine cover: the smiling parents, the beautiful offspring. The mother and father olive-skinned, brown-eyed, square-featured; the baby fair-complexioned, red blond, with a heart-shaped face and brilliant green eyes.

Richard stared at the family group. Who do they think they're kidding? he thought. That child has to be adopted.

PHIL Cunningham and Charley Nugent watched in disgust as the final stragglers came through Newark airport's gate 11.

"That's it." Charley shrugged. "Lewis must have figured we'd be waiting for him. Let's go."

From a nearby pay phone he dialed Scott. "You can go home, boss," he said. "The captain didn't feel like flying tonight."

"He wasn't on board? How about the coffin?"

"That came in. Richard's guys are picking it up. Want us to hang around? There are a couple of other flights he might be on."

"Forget it. If he doesn't contact us tomorrow, I'm issuing a pickup order for him as a material witness. And first thing in the morning you two go through Edna Burns's apartment again."

Charley hung up. He turned to Phil. "If I know the boss, I'd say that by tomorrow night at this time there'll be a warrant out for Lewis' arrest."

RICHARD phoned the Essex House as soon as he got home from the Kennedys'. Again there was no answer in Dr. Salem's room. The operator came back on the line. "Operator, did Dr. Salem receive the message to phone me? I'm Dr. Carroll."

The woman's voice was hesitant. "I'll check, sir."

While he waited, Richard flipped on the television to *Eyewitness News*. The camera was focusing on Central Park South. He watched as the marquee of the Essex House appeared on the screen. Even as the telephone operator said, "I'm connecting you with our supervisor," the television reporter was saying, "This evening in the prestigious Essex House Hotel, Dr. Emmet Salem of Minneapolis, Minnesota, fell or jumped to his death. . . ."

338

JOAN MOORE SAT DISTRACTEDLY BY THE phone in Miami. "Kay, what time did he say he'd phone?" she asked, her voice trembling.

"I told you," said the other young woman. "He said he'd be in touch with you tonight and that you should wait for his call. He sounded upset."

The doorbell rang insistently, making them both jump from their chairs. Joan ran to the door and yanked it open.

"Chris—oh, Chris!" She threw her arms around him. He was ghastly white; he swayed as she held him. "Chris, what is it?"

His voice was nearly a sob. "I don't know what's happening. There's something wrong about Vangie's death, and now the only man who might have told us about it is dead too."

HE HAD planned to go directly home from the Essex House, but after he drove out of the garage, he changed his mind. He was very hungry. He needed to correct the terrible depletion of energy now that the business with Salem was over. He'd go to the Carlyle for dinner.

After tomorrow he'd be safe. Inevitably there'd be an investigation when Kathleen DeMaio died. But her former gynecologist had moved away. No old medical records would loom up from the past. Right now, at the AMA convention, doctors were probably discussing the *Newsmaker* article and the Westlake Maternity Concept. He was on the path to fame, and Salem, who might have stopped him, was out of the way. He was anxious to go through Vangie's medical history in Salem's file. It would be invaluable in his future research.

He parked on the street in front of the Carlyle. His bag was locked in the trunk. Salem's file on Vangie, the paperweight and the moccasin were in it. He could dispose of the shoe and the paperweight in one of the city's trash baskets. They'd be lost among the decaying food and discarded newspapers. He'd do it on the way home, under cover of darkness.

He got out of the car and carefully locked it. He walked to the entrance of the Carlyle, his dark blue suit covered by a blue cashmere coat, his shoes shined to a soft luster.

The doorman held the door open for him. "Good evening, Dr.

339

Highley." In the dining room, the maître d' led him to the corner table he preferred.

Wine warmed and soothed him. The dinner restored him, as he had anticipated. He was just signing his check when the maître d' came hurrying over. "Dr. Highley, I'm afraid there's a problem."

His fingers tightened on the pen. He looked up.

"It's just, sir, that a young man was observed prying the trunk of your car. The doorman saw him just as he got it open. Before he could be stopped, he had stolen a bag from the trunk. The police are outside. They believe it was a drug addict who chose your car because of the MD license plates."

When Highley spoke, his voice was surprisingly steady. "Do the police believe that my bag will be recovered?"

"I'm afraid they don't know, sir. It might be discarded a few blocks from here after he's taken what he wants from it, or it might never show up again. Only time will tell."

BEFORE she went to bed, Katie packed an overnight bag for her stay in the hospital. She realized how glad she'd be to get the operation over with. The sense of being physically out of tune was wearing her down. She felt depleted, exhausted, depressed. It was all physical, wasn't it? Or was part of it the thought that Richard might be involved with someone else?

By Monday she'd be feeling better. Wearily she showered, brushed her teeth and got into bed. A minute later she pulled herself up on one elbow, reached for her handbag and fished out the small bottle Dr. Highley had given her. Almost forgot to take this, she thought as she swallowed the pill with water from the glass on her night table.

GERTRUDE Fitzgerald opened the prescription bottle. The migraine was letting up. This last pill should do it.

Something was bothering her . . . something over and beyond Edna's death. It had to do with Mrs. DeMaio's call. *Prince Charming.* Edna *had* mentioned him in the last couple of weeks. If she could only remember. It was eluding her, the exact circumstance.

When this headache was gone she'd be able to think. She

swallowed the pill, got into bed, closed her eyes. Edna's voice sounded in her ears. "And I said that Prince Charming won't . . ." She couldn't remember the rest.

AT FOUR a.m. Richard gave up trying to sleep. He had phoned Scott Myerson about Emmet Salem's death, and Scott had informed the New York police of their interest. More than that had been impossible to accomplish. Mrs. Salem was not at home in Minneapolis. Nor could he reach the doctor's nurse.

Richard got up and began making notes. "1. Why did Salem want to talk to him? 2. Why did Vangie want to see Salem? 3. The Berkeley baby."

The baby was the key. Was the Westlake Maternity Concept as successful as had been touted? Or was it a cover-up for secret adoptions? Were the women being put to bed in the hospital two months before the supposed delivery to hide the fact that they were not pregnant?

But Vangie Lewis had been pregnant. So she didn't fit into the adoptive pattern. She was desperate to have a child, but how did she expect to pass off an Oriental baby on her husband?

The malpractice suits. He had to find out the reason those people sued Highley. And Emmet Salem's office would have Vangie's medical records. That would be a place to start.

Vangie's body was back in the lab now. First thing in the morning he'd review the autopsy findings, go over the body again. There was something. . . .

At five thirty Richard set the alarm for seven and turned out the light. When sleep came at last, he dreamed of Katie. She was standing looking in the rear window of Edna Burns's apartment, and Dr. Edgar Highley was watching her.

CHAPTER FOURTEEN

EDNA Burns had kept meticulous records. When the search team headed by Phil Cunningham and Charley Nugent descended on her apartment on Friday morning, they found a statement in the old-fashioned breakfront.

I leave my worldly goods to my friends, Gertrude Fitzgerald and Gana Krupshak. Mrs. Fitzgerald is to receive my diamond ring and whatever household possessions she cares to have. Mrs. Krupshak is to receive my ruby pin, my imitation fur coat and whatever household possessions Mrs. Fitzgerald does not wish to have. My $10,000 insurance policy less funeral expenses is assigned to the nursing home which took such fine care of my parents.

Methodically the team dusted for fingerprints, vacuumed for hair and fibers, searched for signs of forced entry. As the final step, they asked the neighbors if anyone had noticed any strangers in the vicinity on Tuesday night. At the last apartment they had a break. An eleven-year-old boy had just come home from school for lunch. He heard the question asked of his mother.

"Oh, I told a man in a car which apartment Miss Burns lived in," he reported. "You remember, Ma, when you made me walk Porgy just before I went to bed."

"That was about nine thirty," the boy's mother said.

"What did the man look like?" Charley asked.

"He had sort of dark hair. *His car was neat.* It was a Corvette."

Charley looked at Phil. "Chris Lewis drives a Corvette," he said flatly.

THROUGH the long, sleepless night, Edgar Highley rationalized the problem of the stolen bag. The odds were it would be abandoned after the thief went through it. Few people would take the trouble to return it.

Suppose the New York police recovered the bag intact? His name and address were inside it. If they phoned and asked him for a list of the contents, he'd simply mention some standard drugs and a few patients' files. They would assume that Vangie Lewis' file was his. If they asked about the shoe and the bloodstained paperweight, he'd say that the thief must have put them there.

It would be all right. And tonight the last risk would be removed. At five a.m. he gave up trying to sleep, showered and went downstairs. He was not going in to the office until noon. Meanwhile he'd go over his research notes. Yesterday's patient would be his new experiment. But he hadn't yet chosen the donor.

342

ON FRIDAY MORNING KATIE GOT IN TO the office by seven o'clock and began a review of the case she was trying. The defendants were teenage brothers accused of setting fires in two schools.

Maureen came in at eight thirty, and immediately made fresh coffee. Katie looked up. "Boy, I'm going all out to nail those two," she said. "They did it *for kicks*. It's sickening."

Maureen reached for Katie's coffee cup and filled it. "Katie . . ."

Katie looked into troubled green eyes. "Yes?"

"Rita told me that she told you about . . . about the baby."

"Yes, she did. I'm terribly sorry, Maureen."

"The thing is I can't seem to get over it. I've been trying to forget, and now this Vangie Lewis case brings it back."

Katie nodded. "Maureen, I'd have given anything to have had a baby when John died. That year I prayed I'd get pregnant so I'd have something of him. When I think of all the friends I have who elect never to have children, I wonder about the way life works out. But we'll both have children someday, and we'll appreciate them because of not having the ones we wanted before."

Maureen's eyes were filled with tears. "I know. But the thing about the Vangie Lewis case is—"

The telephone rang. Katie reached for it. It was Scott Myerson. "Glad you're in, Katie. Can you run over here for a minute?"

"Of course." Katie got up. "Scott wants me now. We'll talk later, Maureen." Impulsively she hugged the girl.

Scott was standing by the window staring out. He turned when she came in. "You're on trial today—the Odendall brothers?"

"Yes. We have a good case. We'll get them."

"You usually do, Katie. Have you heard about Dr. Salem?"

"The doctor from Minneapolis? No, I haven't spoken to anyone this morning. I went straight to my office."

"He fell—or was pushed—out a window in the Essex House a few minutes after he checked in. We're working with the New York police on it. Incidentally, Vangie Lewis' body arrived from Minneapolis yesterday. Lewis wasn't on the flight."

Katie stared at Scott. "What are you saying?"

"I'm saying that he probably took the flight that went into La Guardia. It would have gotten him into New York about the time

343

Salem checked in. I'm saying that if we find he was anywhere in the vicinity of that hotel, we may be able to wrap this case up."

"I don't believe Chris Lewis is a murderer," Katie said flatly. "Where do you think he is now?"

Scott shrugged. "I think his girl friend will lead us to him. She's due in from Florida tonight. Can you hang around?"

Katie hesitated. "This is one weekend I have to be away. But I'll be honest, Scott. I feel so lousy that I'm not thinking straight. I'll get through this trial, but then I will leave."

Scott studied her. "You should have a checkup. You look paler than you did right after your accident. All right, get the trial over with and clear out of here. We'll go over everything Monday morning."

Katie went back to her own office. It was nearly nine, and she was due in the courtroom. Mentally she reviewed the schedule of the pills Dr. Highley had given her. She'd taken one last night, one early this morning. She swallowed another, washing it down with the last sip of coffee from the cup on her desk, then gathered her file. The sharp edge of the top page of the brief slit her finger. She gasped at the quick thrust of pain and, wrapping a tissue around it, hurried from the room.

Half an hour later, as she rose with the rest of the people in the courtroom to acknowledge the entrance of the judge, the tissue was still wet with blood.

EDNA Burns was buried on Friday morning after a Mass at St. Francis Xavier Church. Gana Krupshak and Gertrude Fitzgerald followed the coffin to the nearby cemetery and watched Edna placed in the grave beside her parents. After the ceremony, the priest, Father Durkin, escorted them back to their cars.

"Will you ladies join me for a cup of coffee?" he asked.

Gertrude dabbed at her eyes and shook her head. "I really have to get to work," she said.

Mrs. Krupshak also declined. Then, turning to Gertrude, she said, "Why don't you come by for dinner tonight?"

Gertrude quickly accepted. It would be good to talk about Edna, and about what a shame it was that neither of the doctors

344

had come to the Mass, although at least Dr. Fukhito had sent flowers. Maybe talking with Gana would help her get a handle on the thought that kept buzzing around inside her head—about something that Edna had said to her.

She said good-by to Gana and the priest, got into her car, turned on the ignition. Dr. Highley's face loomed in her mind: those big, fishlike, cold eyes. There'd been something funny about him Wednesday night. Like when he went to get her a drink of water, she'd started to follow him. He'd turned on the tap, then gone into the bedroom. From the hall she'd seen him take out his handkerchief and start to open Edna's night-table drawer.

Then that nice Dr. Carroll had started to come down the hall and Dr. Highley had closed the drawer. Gertrude had let Dr. Carroll pass her, then slipped back into the living room. She didn't want them to think she was trying to eavesdrop. But if Dr. Highley wanted something from that drawer, why didn't he just say so and get it? And why on earth would he open the drawer holding a handkerchief over his fingers? Why, Edna's apartment was immaculate!

THE lifeless body of Vangie Lewis was placed on the slab in the autopsy room of the Valley County medical examiner. Richard watched as his assistant removed the silk caftan that was to have been Vangie's burial robe. He had missed something on Tuesday afternoon—something to do with her legs or feet.

Minutes later he found what he was seeking: a fresh two-inch scratch on Vangie's left foot. That was what had bothered him. Vangie's foot had been scratched shortly after her death, and Charley had found a piece of the dress she was wearing when she died, dangling from a sharp implement in the garage.

Richard turned to his assistant. "Dress Mrs. Lewis in the clothes she had on Monday night. Call me when she's ready."

Back in his office, he scribbled on a pad: "Shoes she was wearing were cut fairly high. Could not have been wearing them when foot was scratched."

He began to examine the notes he'd made during the night. The Berkeley baby. He was going to talk to Jim Berkeley, get him to admit that the baby was adopted. Once that admission was made, the whole Westlake Maternity Concept would be exposed as a fraud. Would someone kill to prevent that fraud from being exposed?

He needed to see Dr. Salem's medical records on Vangie. Quickly he dialed Scott. "Have you spoken to Salem's nurse?"

"Yes, and also to his wife. They're terribly broken up. Both swear he had no history of high blood pressure or dizziness. No personal problems, no money problems. I say forget both the suicide and the accidental-fall angles."

"How about Vangie Lewis? What did the nurse know?"

"Dr. Salem asked her to get out Vangie's file yesterday morning. She saw him put it in his attaché case. That case was found in his hotel room. But the Lewis file wasn't in it. And get this: after Dr. Salem left his office, Chris Lewis phoned. Said he had to talk to Salem. The nurse told him where Salem would be staying in New York. I'll tell you something, Richard: by the end of the day I expect to be swearing out a warrant for Lewis' arrest."

"You mean you think there was something in that file that Chris Lewis would kill to get? I find that hard to believe."

"Someone wanted that file," Scott said.

Richard hung up the phone. Who would know what was in a medical file that might be threatening? A doctor.

Was Katie right in her suspicions about the psychiatrist? And what about Edgar Highley? Impatiently Richard searched on his desk for the slip of paper Marge had given him with the names of the two patients who had filed malpractice suits against Edgar Highley: Anthony Caldwell of Peapack, Anna Horan of Ridgefield Park. Over the intercom he asked Marge to phone them both. And to try to reach Jim Berkeley.

She came in a few minutes later. "Berkeley wasn't in. I left a message. Anthony Caldwell moved to Michigan last year. I got one of his former neighbors on the phone. She told me that his wife died of a tubal pregnancy. Mrs. Caldwell had been told by two other doctors that she'd never conceive, but as soon as she started at Westlake she became pregnant. She was terribly sick all the time, however, and died in her fourth month."

"That gives me what I need," Richard said. "We're going to subpoena the hospital records. What about Mrs. Horan?"

"I caught her husband home. Says she works as a computer programmer. Here's her office number."

Richard dialed it. "Mrs. Horan," he said.

"Yes."

Richard introduced himself. "Mrs. Horan, you filed a malpractice suit last year against Dr. Highley. I wonder if I might ask you some questions about that case. Are you free to talk?"

Her voice became agitated. "No . . . not here." She had an accent he could not place.

"I understand. But it's urgent. Would it be possible for you to stop by the prosecutor's office after work today and talk with me?"

"Yes . . . all right. I know where it is. I'll be there by five thirty." The connection was broken.

It was nearly noon. Richard decided to go to the courtroom where Katie was trying her case and see if she'd have lunch with him. He wanted to ask her about Highley. Would she agree that maybe something was wrong at Westlake—a baby ring, or a doctor who took criminal chances with his patients' lives?

The courtroom was deserted except for Katie, who still sat at the prosecutor's table. Preoccupied with her notes, she shook her head when he came over and asked her to lunch.

"Richard, those skunks are trying to say someone else set the fires, and I swear the jury is falling for it."

Richard studied her. Her skin was deadly pale. He noticed the tissue wrapped around her finger. Gently he unwound it.

"That darn thing," Katie said. "It must be deep. It's been bleeding off and on all morning."

Richard studied the cut. Released from the tissue, it began to bleed rapidly. Pressing the tissue over the cut, he picked up a rubber band and wound it above the cut. "This should stop it. Have you been having any clotting problems, Katie?"

"Yes, some. But I can't talk about it now. This case is running away from me and I feel so lousy." Her voice broke.

Richard reached down and hugged her head against his chest. "Katie, I'm going to clear out of here. But wherever you go this

weekend, do some thinking. Because I'm throwing my hat in the ring. I want you. I want to take care of you."

He straightened up. "Now go and win your case. You can do it. And please, take it easy this weekend. Monday I'm going to need your input on an angle I see in the Lewis case."

All morning she'd felt so cold—so desperately, icy cold. Even the long-sleeved wool dress hadn't helped. Now, close to Richard, she felt the warmth of his body. As he turned to leave, she impulsively grasped his hand and held it against her face. "Monday," she said.

"Monday," he agreed, and left the courtroom.

BEFORE they left Edna's apartment complex, Charley and Phil rang the Krupshaks' doorbell.

"We're finished with our examination," Charley told Gana. "You're free to enter the apartment." He showed her Edna's note. "You and Mrs. Fitzgerald can look the stuff over and divide it between yourselves, but don't remove anything yet."

The two investigators returned to the office and went directly to the lab, where they turned in the contents of the vacuum bag. "Run this through right away," Phil directed.

Scott was waiting for them in his office. At the news that Chris had been in the vicinity of Edna's apartment on Tuesday night, he grunted with satisfaction. "Lewis seems to have been all over the map this week," he said, "and wherever he's been someone has died. Two bellmen positively identify him as being in the lobby of the Essex House around five o'clock."

The phone rang. Impatiently he answered it. Then his expression changed. "Put her on," he said quickly. Holding his hand over the mouthpiece, he said, "Chris Lewis' girl friend is calling from Florida. . . . Hello, yes, this is the prosecutor. . . . Yes, we are looking for Captain Lewis. Do you know where he is?"

Scott's forehead furrowed as he listened. "Newark at seven? Very well. I'm glad he's surrendering voluntarily. If he wishes a lawyer, he may want to have one here." He hung up the phone. "Lewis is coming in," he said. "We'll crack this case open tonight. Now let's see what Richard's got."

349

The three men went to the autopsy room; with Richard they studied the body of Vangie Lewis, now dressed in the clothes in which she had died. The scrap of flowered material that had been found on the prong in the garage exactly fitted the tear near the hem of her dress. The panty hose on her left foot showed a two-inch slash directly over the fresh cut.

"No blood on the hosiery," Richard said. "She was already dead when her foot caught on the prong."

"How high was the shelf that prong was on?" Scott asked.

"About three feet from the floor," Phil answered.

"So someone carried her in through the garage, laid her on her bed and tried to make it look like suicide," Scott said.

"Without question," Richard agreed. A few moments later he left the autopsy room and returned to his office.

At four thirty Jim Berkeley called. "I understand you've been trying to reach me." His voice was guarded.

"It's important. Can you stop in my office on your way home?"

"Yes, I can." Now Jim's voice became resigned. "And I think I know what you want to talk about."

EDGAR Highley turned from the girl on the examining table. "You may get dressed now."

She had claimed to be twenty, but he was sure she wasn't more than sixteen or seventeen. "Am I—"

"Yes, my dear. You are very definitely pregnant. About five weeks. I want you to return tomorrow morning and we will terminate the pregnancy."

"I was wondering: Do you think I should maybe have the baby and have it adopted?"

"Have you told your parents about this?"

"No. They'd be so upset."

"Then I suggest you postpone motherhood for several years at least. Ten o'clock tomorrow."

He left the room, went into his office and looked up the phone number of the new patient he had chosen yesterday. "Mrs. Englehart, this is Dr. Highley. I want to begin your treatment. Kindly come to the hospital tomorrow morning at eight thirty."

CHAPTER FIFTEEN

WHILE the jury was deliberating, Katie went into the courthouse cafeteria and sat at a table with her back to the room. She did not want anyone to join her. She felt fatigued and weak, but not hungry. Just a cup of tea, she thought. Mama always said that a cup of tea would cure the ills of the world.

She sat for nearly an hour, sipping the tea, reviewing the proceedings. The Odendall boys were blaming the fires on a friend who was killed in a motorcycle accident last November. Had she convinced the jury that they were lying?

At five o'clock she returned to the courtroom. Five minutes later the jury came in and the foreman announced the verdict: Robert and Jonathan Odendall were "not guilty on all counts."

"I don't believe it." Katie wasn't sure if she had spoken aloud.

The judge dismissed the jury curtly and told the defendants to stand up. "You are very lucky," he snapped, "luckier than I hope you'll ever be again. Now clear out of my courtroom, and if you're smart, you'll never appear before me again."

Katie stood up. No matter if the judge clearly felt the verdict was erroneous, she had lost the case. She saw the victorious smile the defense attorney shot at her. She stuffed her notes into her file. Maybe if she hadn't felt so lousy all week she'd have conducted a better case. She should have had this hemorrhaging problem taken care of a year ago instead of putting it off because of her childish fear of hospitals.

"Will the State please approach the bench?"

She walked over to the judge. "Your Honor." Katie managed to keep her voice steady.

The judge leaned forward and whispered to her, "Don't let it get you down, Katie. You proved that case. They'll be back here in two months on other charges. Next time you'll nail them."

Katie tried to smile. "Thanks, Judge."

She left the courtroom and went back to her office. Maureen looked up hopefully, but Katie shook her head.

Maureen's expression changed to sympathy. "Katie, I'm sorry about the Odendall verdict, but try not to take it too hard. You

351

really look sick. Are you all right to drive? You're not dizzy or anything?"

"No, really. I'm not going far. Then I won't budge till Sunday."

JIM Berkeley parked his car in the courthouse lot, went into the main lobby and checked the directory for the medical examiner's office. He had seen the expression on Richard Carroll's face last night when he'd looked at the baby. Angered, he'd wanted to say, "So the baby doesn't look like us. So what?"

After several wrong turns, he found Richard's office. The door was open and Richard came out immediately. "Jim, it's good of you to come." Jim's own greeting was reserved and cautious.

As they went inside, Richard's manner became businesslike. "Jim, we're investigating Vangie Lewis' death. She was a patient at Westlake's maternity clinic. Where your wife had the baby."

Jim nodded.

Richard chose his words carefully. "Our investigation is turning up some disturbing problems. Now I want to ask you a few questions, and I swear to you that your answers will remain in this room. But you can be of tremendous help to us if—"

"*If* I tell you that Maryanne is adopted. Is that it?"

"Yes."

Jim thought of Maryanne. Whatever the cost, she was worth having. "No, she is not adopted. I was present at her birth. I filmed it."

"It is quite unlikely for two brown-eyed parents to have a green-eyed child," Richard said flatly. Then he stopped. "Are you the baby's father?" he asked quietly.

"If you mean did Liz have an affair with another man? No. I'd stake my life on that."

"How about artificial insemination?" Richard asked.

"Liz and I rejected that possibility years ago."

"Might Liz have changed her mind and not told you?"

Jim looked away a moment and then said, "I've often wondered about Maryanne's coloring, but I haven't let it bother me. That baby is everything to us." He looked at Richard. "My wife is the most honest person I've ever known. Last month I decided to make it easy for her. I said that I'd been wrong about artificial insemination, that I could see why people went ahead with it."

"What did she say?" Richard asked.

"She said that if I thought she could make a decision like that and not tell me, I didn't understand our relationship. I swore I didn't mean that; went through hell trying to reassure her. Finally she believed me. But, of course, I know she did have artificial insemination. She was lying."

"Or else she wasn't aware of what Highley did to her," Richard said flatly.

AT THE hospital, the admitting clerk was briskly bright. "You certainly rate, Mrs. DeMaio. Dr. Highley has given you suite one on the third floor of the west wing. That's like going on a vacation. You'll never dream you're in a hospital."

"He said something about that," Katie murmured. She was not about to confide her fear of hospitals to this woman.

"You may be a bit lonesome up there. The other two suites on that floor are empty. And Dr. Highley is having the living room of your suite redecorated. Why, I don't know. It was done less than a year ago. Anyhow, if you want anything, all you have to do is press the buzzer. Now here's your wheelchair. We'll just whisk you upstairs."

Katie stared. "I have to use a wheelchair?"

"Hospital regulations," the admitting clerk said firmly.

John in a wheelchair going up for chemotherapy. John's body shrinking as she watched him die. The antiseptic hospital smell.

Katie sat down in the chair and closed her eyes. There was no turning back. The attendant, a middle-aged volunteer, pushed the chair down the corridor to the elevator.

"You're lucky to have Dr. Highley," she informed Katie. "His patients get the best care in the hospital."

They got off the elevator at the third floor. The corridor was carpeted in soft green. Reproductions of Monet and Matisse paintings hung on the walls. In spite of herself, Katie was reassured. The corridor turned to the right. "You're in the end suite," the volunteer explained. "It's kind of far off."

353

She wheeled Katie into a bedroom. The walls were ivory, the carpet the same soft green as in the corridor. The furniture was antique white. Printed draperies in shades of ivory and green matched the bedspread. "Oh, this is nice!" Katie exclaimed.

"I thought you'd like it. The nurse will be in in a few minutes. Why don't you just make yourself comfortable?"

She was gone. Katie undressed, put on a nightgown and warm robe. She put her toilet articles in the bathroom and hung her clothes in the closet. Suddenly she was swaying. She held on to the dresser until the light-headed feeling passed. It was probably just the rushing and the aftermath of the trial and, let's face it, she thought—apprehension. She was in a hospital. Daddy. John. The two people she'd loved best in the world had gone into the hospital and died. No matter how she tried, she could not lose that terrible feeling of panic.

There were four doors in the room. The closet door, the bathroom door, the one leading to the corridor. The other one must go into the living room. She opened it and glanced in. As the admitting clerk had said, it was pulled apart. The furniture was in the middle of the room, covered with painter's drop cloths.

She closed the door and walked over to the window. The hospital was U-shaped, with the two side wings facing each other across the parking lot. On Monday night she'd been exactly opposite where she was now. Where was the parking stall she'd dreamed about? Oh, of course—that one, over to the side, directly under the last light post. There was a car parked there now, a black car, just as in her dream. Those wire spokes on the wheels; the way they glinted in the light.

"How are you feeling, Mrs. DeMaio?"

She spun around. Dr. Highley was standing in the room. A young nurse was hovering at his elbow.

"Oh, you startled me. I'm fine, Doctor."

He came over to the window and drew the draperies. "These windows are drafty. Suppose you sit on the bed and let me check your pressure. We'll want blood samples too."

The nurse followed him. Katie noticed that the girl's hands were trembling. She was obviously in awe of Dr. Highley.

354

The doctor wrapped the pressure cuff around Katie's arm. A wave of dizziness made her feel as though the walls of the room were receding. She clutched at the mattress.

"Is there anything wrong?" The doctor's voice was gentle.

"No, not really. I'm just a touch faint."

He began to pump the bulb. "Nurse Renge, kindly get a cold cloth for Mrs. DeMaio's forehead." He studied the pressure gauge. "You're low. Frankly, if you hadn't scheduled this operation, I'm sure you'd have had it on an emergency basis."

The nurse came out of the bathroom with a neatly folded cloth. She was biting her lower lip to keep it from quivering. Katie felt a rush of sympathy for her. She neither wanted nor needed a cold compress, but she let the nurse put it on her forehead. The cloth was soaking, and freezing water ran down her hairline. A flash of humor raised her spirits. She could just see telling Richard about this poor, scared kid who'd practically drowned her.

Richard. She should have told him she was coming here. She wanted him with her now.

Dr. Highley drew blood from a vein in her right arm and put the blood-filled tubes on the tray the nurse held out to him.

"I want these run through immediately," he said brusquely.

"Yes, Doctor." The nurse scurried out.

Dr. Highley sighed. "I'm afraid that timid young woman is on desk duty tonight. But you won't require anything special, I'm sure. Did you take all the pills I gave you?"

Katie realized that she had not taken the three-o'clock pill and it was now nearly seven. "I'm overdue for the last one. They're in my handbag." She glanced at the dresser.

"Don't get up. I'll hand it to you."

When she took the bag from him, she unzipped it, fished inside and brought out the small bottle, which she held out to him. There were just two pills in it. Dr. Highley poured a glass of water from the carafe on the night table. "Take these," he said. He handed her the glass and dropped the empty bottle into his pocket.

Obediently she swallowed the pills, feeling his eyes on her. His steel-rimmed glasses glinted under the overhead light. The glint. The spokes of the car glinting. There was a blur of red on

355

the glass as she laid it down. He noticed it, reached for her hand and examined her finger. The tissue had become damp again.

"What's this?" he asked.

"Oh, nothing. Just a paper cut. But it keeps bleeding."

"I see." He stood up. "I've ordered a sleeping pill for later."

"I really prefer not to take sleeping pills, Doctor."

"I'm afraid I insist. I want you well rested in the morning. Oh, here's your dinner now."

A thin, sixtyish woman carrying a tray came into the room and glanced nervously at the doctor. They're all petrified of him, Katie thought. Unlike the usual plastic or metal hospital tray, this one was made of white wicker and had a side basket that held the evening newspaper. A single red rose stood in a slender vase. Double loin lamb chops were carefully arranged on the dinner plate. The china was delicate. The attendant turned to go.

"Wait," Dr. Highley commanded. He said to Katie, "As you will see, all my patients are served fare that compares favorably with the food in a first-class restaurant." He frowned, then added, "However, I would prefer if you did not eat dinner tonight. I've come to believe that the longer a patient fasts before surgery, the less likelihood she will experience discomfort after it."

"I'm not at all hungry," Katie said.

"Fine." He nodded to the attendant. She picked up the tray and hurried out.

"I'll leave you now," Dr. Highley told Katie.

At the door he paused. "Oh, I regret, your phone apparently isn't working. The repairman will take care of it in the morning. Is there anyone you expect to call you here tonight? Any visitors?"

"No. My sister is the only one who knows I'm here, and she's at the opera tonight."

He smiled. "I see. Well, good night, Mrs. DeMaio, and please relax. You can trust me to take care of you."

"I'm sure I can."

He was gone. She leaned back on the pillow, closing her eyes. She was floating somewhere; her body was drifting like . . .

"Mrs. DeMaio." The young voice was apologetic. Katie opened her eyes. It was Nurse Renge carrying a tray with a pill in a small paper cup. "You're to take this now. It's the sleeping pill. Dr. Highley said I was to stay and be sure you took it."

"Oh." Katie put the pill in her mouth, swallowed water from her carafe. Then she pulled herself up and went into the bathroom while the nurse turned down the covers. In the bathroom, she removed the sleeping pill from under her tongue. No way, she thought. I'd rather be awake than have nightmares. She splashed water on her face, brushed her teeth and returned to the bedroom. She felt so weak, so vague.

The nurse helped her into bed. "You really are tired, aren't you? Just push the buzzer if you need me for anything."

"Thank you." Her head was so heavy.

Nurse Renge went to pull down the shade. "Open the drapes and raise the window about an inch, won't you?" Katie murmured. "I like fresh air in my bedroom."

"Certainly. Shall I turn off the light now, Mrs. DeMaio?"

"Please." She didn't want to do anything except sleep.

The nurse left. Katie closed her eyes. Minutes passed. Her breathing became even. She was not aware of the faint sound when the door from the living room began to open.

CHAPTER SIXTEEN

AFTER Gana Krupshak's excellent pot-roast dinner, Gertrude gratefully accepted a generous slice of homemade chocolate cake.

"I don't usually eat this much," she apologized, "but I haven't swallowed a morsel since we found poor Edna."

Gana nodded soberly. Her husband picked up his coffee cup. "I'm gonna watch the Knicks," he announced, not ungraciously. He settled himself in the living room in front of the television.

Gana sighed. "The Knicks . . . the Mets . . . the Giants. . . . But at least he's *here*. When I come home from bingo, I know I'm not going into an empty place, like poor Edna always had to."

"I know." Gertrude thought of her own solitary home, then reflected on Nan, her oldest granddaughter. "Gran, why not come to dinner?" or "Gran, are you going to be home Sunday? We thought we'd drop in to say hello." She could have it a lot worse.

"Maybe we should go take a look at Edna's place," Gana said.

"I kind of hate to do it, but it's something you can't avoid."

"I'll get the key."

As they hurried across the courtyard, Gana thought of Edna's lovely imitation-leopard coat. Maybe she could take it home tonight. It was hers.

Inside the apartment, they became quiet. Inadvertently they both stared at the spot where Edna's crumpled body had lain.

"There's still blood on the radiator," Gana muttered.

"Yes." Gertrude shook herself. Get this over with.

Gana went to the closet and removed the leopard coat. It did not take them long to finish sharing the contents of the apartment. Gana had little interest in the furniture; what Gertrude did not want Gana was giving to the Salvation Army, but she was delighted when Gertrude suggested she take the silver plate and good china. "I guess that's it." Gana sighed. "Except for the jewelry, and the police will give that back to us pretty soon."

The jewelry in the night-table drawer. Gertrude thought of Dr. Highley. He had started to open that drawer.

"That reminds me," she said, "we never did look there. Let's make sure we didn't forget anything." She pulled it open. The police had removed the jewelry box. But the deep drawer was not empty. A scuffed moccasin lay at the bottom of it.

"Now why would Edna save that thing?" Gana said. She held it up. It was stained and out of shape.

"That's it!" Gertrude cried. "That's what had me mixed up."

Gana looked mystified, and Gertrude tried to explain. "Mrs. DeMaio asked me if Edna called one of the doctors Prince Charming. She didn't, of course. But Edna did tell me how Mrs. Lewis wore terrible old moccasins for her appointments. The left shoe was too loose, and Mrs. Lewis was always walking out of it. Edna used to tease her that she must be expecting Prince Charming to pick up her glass slipper."

Gertrude reflected. "I wonder. Could Mrs. Lewis' shoe be what Dr. Highley wanted from this drawer? You know, I've half a mind to go to Mrs. DeMaio's office and talk to her, or at least leave a message. Somehow I feel I shouldn't wait till Monday."

Gana thought of Gus, who wouldn't have his eyes off the set until midnight. Her desire for excitement surged. "Tell you what: I'll drive over there with you. Gus'll never know I'm gone."

DANNYBOY Duke zigzagged across Third Avenue, racing toward Fifty-fifth and Second, where he had the car parked. The woman had missed her wallet just as he got on the escalator. He'd heard her scream, "That man robbed me."

She had come rushing down the escalator after him, shouting and pointing as he went out the door. The security guard would probably chase him.

If he could just get to the car. He couldn't ditch the wallet. It was stuffed with bills. He'd seen them, and he needed a fix.

Was he being followed? He didn't dare look back. He'd call too much attention to himself. In a minute he'd be in the car. He'd drive home to Jackson Heights and get his fix.

He looked back. No one running. No cops. Last night had been so lousy. The doorman had almost grabbed him when he broke into that doctor's car. And what did he get for his risk? No drugs in the bag. A medical file, a messy paperweight and an old shoe. He'd have to get rid of it all.

He was at the car. He opened it, slipped in. He put the key into the ignition, turned on the engine, then heard the siren as the police car came racing the wrong way up the block. He tried to pull out, but the squad car cut him off. A cop, his hand on the butt of his pistol, jumped out.

The cop yanked open the door, reached in and pulled out the ignition key. "Well, Dannyboy," he said. "You're still at it, right? Don't you never learn any new tricks?"

THE plane circled over Newark. The descent was bumpy. Chris glanced at Joan. She was holding his hand tightly, but he knew it had nothing to do with flying. Her face was composed.

"Chris," she'd said, "I can't bear thinking that Vangie committed suicide because of me. Don't worry about dragging me into this. Tell the truth; don't hold anything back."

If they ever got through this, they'd have a good life together.

Joan was a woman. He still had so much to learn about her. He hadn't even realized he could trust her with the simple truth. Maybe because he'd gotten so used to shielding Vangie.

They were silent as the plane taxied to the gate. Inside, Chris was not surprised to see two detectives waiting for him—the same two who had been at the house after he found Vangie.

MOLLY settled back as the orchestra began the overture to *Otello*. Bill was already totally absorbed, but she couldn't relax. She glanced around. The Met was packed as usual. Overhead the twinkling chandeliers began to fade into darkness.

At the first intermission she'd phone Katie. She should have insisted on going to see her in the hospital tonight. But she'd be there in the morning before the operation and make sure Katie wasn't too nervous.

The first act seemed interminable. Finally intermission came, and Molly hurried to a phone.

A few minutes later, white-lipped, she rushed to Bill. Half sobbing, she grabbed his arm. "Something's wrong. The hospital wouldn't put the call through to Katie's room. They said the doctor forbade calls. I got the desk and insisted the nurse check on Katie. She just came back. She's a kid, she's hysterical. Katie's not in her room. Katie's missing."

CHAPTER SEVENTEEN

EDGAR Highley had left Katie's room with a smile of satisfaction on his face. The pills were working. The cut on her finger proved that her blood was no longer clotting.

He went down to the second floor and stopped in to see Mrs. Aldrich. The baby was in a crib by her bed. Her husband was with her. Dr. Highley smiled, then bent over the child. "A handsome specimen," he proclaimed. "I don't think we'll trade him in."

He knew his humor was heavy-handed, but sometimes it was necessary. These people were important. Delano Aldrich could direct thousands of dollars of research funds to Westlake.

Delano Aldrich was staring at his son, his face a study in awe and admiration. "Doctor, we still can't believe it. Everyone else said we'd never have a child."

"Everyone else was obviously wrong." Her anxiety had been the main problem. Fukhito had spotted that. Muscular dystrophy in her father's family. She knew she might be a carrier. And she had some fibroid cysts. He'd taken care of the cysts and she'd become pregnant. Then he'd done an early test of the amniotic fluid and had been able to reassure her on the dystrophy question. Still, she was highly emotional. She'd had two miscarriages over ten years ago, so he'd put her to bed two months before the birth. And it had worked.

"I'll stop by in the morning." These people would be witnesses for him if there were any questions about Katie DeMaio's death.

But there shouldn't be any questions. The dropping blood pressure was a matter of hospital record. The emergency operation would take place in the presence of the top nurses on the staff. He'd ask the emergency-room surgeon to assist. They'd tell the family that it had been impossible to stop the hemorrhaging.

Leaving the Aldriches, he went to the nurses' desk.

"Nurse Renge."

She stood up quickly, her hands fluttering nervously.

"I am quite concerned about Mrs. DeMaio. I will be back right after dinner to see the lab report on her blood count. I would not be surprised if we have to operate tonight."

He had made a point of speaking to several people in the lobby and then gone to the restaurant adjacent to the hospital grounds for dinner. He wanted to be able later to present the image of a conscientious doctor: Instead of going home, I had dinner next door and went back to the hospital to check on Mrs. DeMaio. At least we *tried*.

At a quarter to eight he was in the restaurant ordering a steak. Katie had been given the sleeping pill at seven thirty. By eight thirty it would be safe to take the last necessary step. While he waited for his coffee to be served, he'd go up the back fire stairs of the hospital to the third floor. He'd give her a shot of heparin, the powerful anticoagulant that, combined with the pills, would send her blood pressure and blood count plummeting.

He'd come back here and have his coffee, pay the bill and then return to the hospital. He'd take Nurse Renge up with him to check on Katie. Ten minutes later Katie would be in surgery.

That would be the end of the danger. His bag had not shown up. It probably never would. He had eliminated the Salem threat. Edna had been buried this morning. The moccasin in her drawer would mean nothing to whoever disposed of her belongings.

A terrible week. And so unnecessary if he'd been allowed to pursue his work openly. But now nothing would stand in his way. Someday he would receive the Nobel Prize. For contributions to medicine not imagined possible. Single-handedly he had solved the abortion problem and the sterility problem.

"Did you enjoy your dinner, Doctor?" the waitress asked.

"Very much indeed. I'd like cappuccino, please."

"Certainly, Doctor, but that will take about ten minutes."

"While you're getting it, I'll make some phone calls." He'd be gone less than ten minutes. The waitress wouldn't miss him.

Slipping out the side door near the hallway with the telephones and rest rooms, he hurried across the parking lot. He kept in the shadows. He had his key to the fire exit at the rear of the maternity wing. No one ever used those stairs. He let himself in.

The stairway was brightly lighted. He turned off the switch. He could find his way through this hospital blindfolded. At the third floor he opened the door and listened. There was no sound. Noiselessly he stepped into the hall. An instant later he was in the living room of Katie's suite.

That had been another problem he'd anticipated. Suppose someone had accompanied her to the hospital—her sister, a friend? Suppose that person had asked to stay overnight on the sofa bed in the living room? By ordering the room repainted, he'd blocked that possibility. Planning. Planning. It was everything.

That afternoon he had left the needle with the heparin in a drawer of an end table under the painter's drop cloth. A light from the parking lot filtered through the window, giving him enough visibility to find the table. He reached for the needle.

Now for the most important moment of all. He was in the room, bending over her. The drapery was open. Faint light was

362

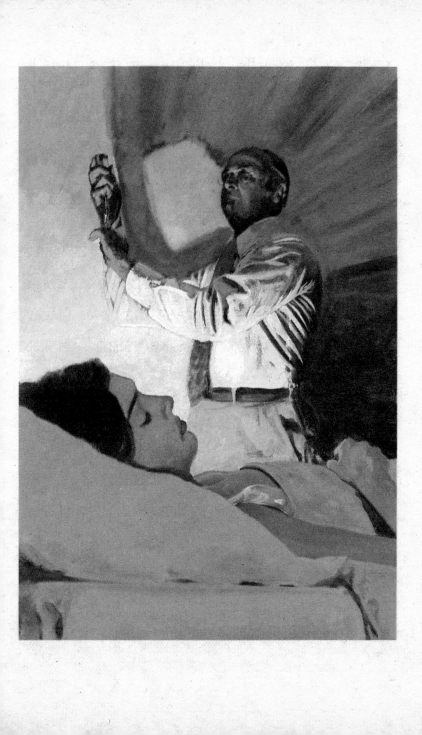

coming into the room. Her breathing was uneven. She must be dreaming. He took her arm, slipped the needle in, squeezed. She winced and sighed. Her eyes, cloudy with sleep, opened as she turned her head. She looked up at him, puzzled. "Dr. Highley," she murmured, "why did you kill Vangie Lewis?"

SCOTT Myerson was more tired than angry. Since Vangie Lewis' body had been found Tuesday morning, two other people had died. Two very decent people—a hardworking receptionist who deserved a few years of freedom after caring for her aged parents, and a doctor who was making a real contribution to medicine.

They had died because he had not moved fast enough. If only he had brought Chris Lewis in for questioning immediately, Edna Burns and Emmet Salem would be alive now.

Scott couldn't wait for the chance to get to Lewis. He and his girl friend had landed at seven. They should be here by eight. Lewis was cool all right. Knew better than to run. Thought he could brazen it out. Knows it's all circumstantial. But circumstantial evidence can be a lot better than eyewitness testimony when properly presented in court.

At seven fifty Richard walked into Scott's office. "I think we've uncovered a cesspool," he said, "and it's called the Westlake Maternity Concept."

"If you're saying that the shrink was probably playing around with Vangie Lewis, I agree," Scott said.

"That's not what I'm talking about," said Richard. "It's Highley I'm after. I think he's experimenting with his patients. I just spoke to the husband of one of them. He's been thinking that his wife agreed to artificial insemination without his permission. I think it goes beyond that. I think Highley is performing artificial insemination without his patients' *knowledge.*"

Scott snorted. "You think Highley would inject Vangie Lewis with the semen of an Oriental and expect to get away with it?"

"Maybe he made a mistake."

"Doctors don't make mistakes like that. Even allowing your theory to be true—and frankly, I don't buy it—that doesn't make him Vangie's murderer. Look, we'll investigate Westlake's ma-

364

ternity clinic. If we find any kind of violation there, we'll prosecute. But right now Chris Lewis is my first order of business."

"Do this," Richard persisted. "Go back further with the check on Highley. I'm already looking into the malpractice suits against him. But *Newsmaker* said he was in Liverpool, in England, before he came here. Let's phone there and see what we can find."

Scott shrugged. "Sure, go ahead." The buzzer on his desk sounded. He switched on the intercom. "Bring him in," he said. Leaning back in his chair, he looked at Richard. "The bereaved widower, Captain Lewis, is here with his paramour."

DANNYBOY Duke sat in the precinct house miserably hunched forward in a chair. He was trembling and perspiring. In another thirty seconds he'd have gotten away. He'd be in his apartment now, feeling the blissful release of the fix. Instead, this steamy hell. "Give me a break," he whispered.

The cops weren't impressed. "You give *us* a break, Danny. There's blood on this paperweight. Who'd you hit with it?"

"I don't know what you're talking about," Danny said.

"Sure you do. The doctor's bag was in your car. We know you stole it last night. The doorman at the Carlyle Hotel can identify you. But who'd you hit with that paperweight, Danny? And what about that shoe? Since when do you save beat-up shoes?"

"It was in the bag," Danny said.

The two detectives looked at each other. The younger one shrugged and turned to the newspaper on the desk behind him The other dropped the file he had been examining back into the bag. "All right, Danny. We're calling Dr. Salem to find out just what he had in this bag. That'll settle it."

The younger detective looked up from the paper. "Dr. Salem?"

"Yeah. That's the name on the file. Oh, I see. The nameplate on the bag says Dr. Edgar Highley. Guess he had some other doctor's file."

The younger detective came over to the table carrying the *Daily News*. He pointed to page three. "Salem's the doctor whose body was found at the Essex House last night."

The police officers looked at Dannyboy with renewed interest.

HE WATCHED KATIE'S EYES CLOSE, HER breathing become even.
She'd fallen asleep again. The question about Vangie had come
from her subconscious, triggered perhaps by a duplication of her
mental state of Monday night. Suppose she asked it again in the
operating room before they anesthetized her?

He had to kill her before Nurse Renge made her check, in less
than an hour. After the Coumadin pills she had taken, the heparin
shot would further act to anticoagulate her blood. He had planned
on several hours to complete the procedure. Now he couldn't
wait. He had to give her a second shot immediately.

He had heparin in his office. He'd have to go down the fire
stairs to the parking lot, use the private door to his office, refill
the hypodermic and come back up here. It would take at least five
minutes. The waitress would question his absence from the table,
but there was no help for that. Satisfied that Katie was asleep, he
hurried from the room.

THE technician in the Valley County forensic lab worked over-
time on Friday evening. Dr. Carroll had asked him to compare
all microscopic samples from the home of the presumed suicide
Vangie Lewis with all microscopic samples from the home of the
presumed accident victim Edna Burns.

The technician had a superb instinct for microscopic evidence,
a hunch factor that rarely failed him. He was particularly interested in loose hair, and he was fond of saying, "It's astonishing
how much hair we are constantly shedding."

Sifting the vacuum-bag contents from the Lewis home, he
found many strands of the ash-blond hair of the victim. And he'd
discovered a fair quantity of medium brown hair—undoubtedly
the husband's. But there were also a number of silverish sandy
hairs in the victim's bedroom. The length suggested that the hair
was a man's. Some of the same strands were on the coat the victim
had been wearing.

And then the technician found the connection Richard Carroll
had been seeking. Several sandy hairs with silver roots were
clinging to the faded blue bathrobe of Edna Burns.

The technician reached for the phone to call Dr. Carroll.

366

SHE tried to wake up. There was a click; a door had closed. Someone had just been here. Her arm hurt. Dr. Highley. She dropped
off. . . . What had she said to Dr. Highley? Katie woke up a few
minutes later and remembered. The black car and the shiny
spokes and the light on his glasses. She'd seen him put Vangie
Lewis in his trunk Monday night. Dr. Highley had killed Vangie.
And now he knew she knew about him. Why had she asked him
that question? He'd be back. She had to get out of here. He was
going to kill her too.

Help. She needed help. Why was she so weak? Her finger was
bleeding. The pills he had given her. Since she'd been taking
them she'd been so sick. The pills were making her bleed.

Oh, God, help me, please. The phone! Katie fumbled for it,
knocked it over. She pulled it up by the cord, put the receiver to
her ear. The line was dead.

Highley had said the phone was being repaired. She pushed
the bell for the nurse. The nurse would help her. But there was
no click to indicate that the light was on outside her door. She
was sure the signal wasn't lighting the nurse's panel either.

She had to get out of here before Highley came back. Fighting
waves of dizziness, she stood up. She'd go down to the second
floor. There were people there—other patients, nurses.

From nearby, a door closed. *He was coming back.* Frantically
Katie looked at the open door to the corridor. He'd see her if she
went out there. Stumbling to the living-room door, she opened
it, got inside, closed it before he came into the bedroom.

Where could she go? She couldn't stay here. She heard a door
open inside. He was in the bathroom looking for her. Hide under
the drop cloth? No. He'd find her, drag her out. Dizziness clawed
at the space behind her eyes. Her legs were rubbery.

She stumbled to the door that led to the hall. There was a fire
exit there. She'd seen it when she was wheeled in. She'd go down
that way to the second floor. She'd get help.

The door to the fire stairs was heavy. She tugged at it . . .
tugged again. Reluctantly it gave way. She stepped inside. It

closed so slowly. Would he see it closing? The stairs. It was so dark here, terribly dark. She grabbed the banister. The stairs were steep. There was a landing after eight steps. Another short flight, then she was at the door. She tried the handle. It was locked. It could be opened only from the other side.

Then she heard the third-floor door open and heavy footsteps coming down the stairs.

CHRIS refused to call a lawyer. He sat opposite the prosecutor; he looked at the two detectives who had met him at the airport. "I have nothing to hide," he said.

Scott was unimpressed. A young man carrying a stenographer's pad came into the room, sat down and took out a pen. Scott looked directly at Chris. "Captain Lewis, it is my duty to inform you that you are a suspect in the deaths of Vangie Lewis, Edna Burns and Dr. Emmet Salem. You may remain silent. You are not required to answer any questions. You are entitled to the services of a lawyer. Any statement that you make can be used against you. Is that perfectly clear?"

"Yes."

Scott shoved a paper across the desk. "This is a copy of the *Miranda* warning you have just heard. Please read it carefully. Be sure you understand it. If you are so disposed, sign it."

Chris read the statement, signed it and handed it back. He braced himself for Scott's question. "Did you murder your wife, Vangie Lewis?"

Chris looked directly at him. "I did not murder my wife. I do not know if she was murdered. But I do know this. If she died before midnight Monday, she did not kill herself in our home."

Scott, Charley and Phil were astonished as Chris calmly said, "I was there a short time after midnight Monday. Vangie was not home. I returned to New York. At eleven the next morning I found her on the bed. It wasn't until the funeral director told me the time of death that I realized her body must have been returned to our house. But even before that I knew something was wrong. My wife would never have worn the shoes she was wearing when she was found. Her right leg and foot were badly swollen, and the only shoes she could wear were a pair of battered moccasins."

It was easier than he had expected. The questions came at him. "You left the motel at eight Monday night and returned at ten. Where did you go?"

"To a movie in Greenwich Village. After I got back to the motel, I couldn't sleep. I decided to drive home and talk to Vangie. That was shortly before midnight."

Then the hammerblow. "Did you know your wife was carrying an Oriental fetus?"

"Oh, my God!" Horror mingled with a sense of release flooded over Chris. *It hadn't been his baby.* An Oriental fetus. That psychiatrist. Oh, the poor kid. That must have been why she had called Dr. Salem. She wanted to hide.

"You didn't know she was involved with another man?"

"No. No."

"Why did you go to Edna Burns's apartment Tuesday night?"

"Wait, please—can we take this just the way it happened?" Coffee was brought in, and he began to sip it. It helped. "Edna Burns called me Tuesday night, just after I realized that Vangie must have died before she was brought home. Miss Burns was almost incoherent. She rambled on about Cinderella and Prince Charming, said she had something for me and that she had a story for the police. I thought she might know who Vangie had been with. I drove to her apartment complex. Some kid pointed out where she lived. I rang the bell and knocked. The television was on, the light was on, but she didn't answer. I figured she'd passed out and there was no use trying to talk to her. I went home."

"What time was that?"

"About nine thirty."

"All right. What did you do then?"

More questions, one after another; he drank more coffee. Truth. The simple truth. It was so much easier than evasion. He took a deep breath. They were asking about Dr. Salem.

RICHARD sat at Katie's desk as he waited for the head of personnel of Christ Hospital in Devon, England, to answer his phone. Only by emphasizing his need to talk to someone who had been in authority at the hospital for more than ten years had he been given the man's private number.

"Yes." An angry, sleepy voice had answered.

Richard introduced himself and went directly to the point. "Sir, I apologize for calling you at this hour, but the matter is vital. This is a transatlantic call. I must have information about Dr. Edgar Highley."

The man's voice became wary. "What do you want to know?"

"I have just spoken with Queen Mary Clinic in Liverpool and was surprised to learn that Dr. Highley had been on staff there a relatively short time. We had been led to believe otherwise. However, I was told that Dr. Highley was a member of the Christ Hospital staff for at least nine years. Is that accurate?"

"Edgar Highley interned with us after his graduation from Cambridge, then became staff. He is a brilliant doctor."

"Why did he leave?"

"After his wife's death, he relocated in Liverpool. Then we heard that he had emigrated to the United States."

"Sir, I can't waste time being discreet. I believe that Dr. Highley may be experimenting with his pregnant patients. Is there any information you can offer to support that possibility?"

The words that came next were slow and deliberate. "While he was with us, Dr. Highley was deeply involved in prenatal research. He did quite brilliant experiments on embryos of frogs and mammals. Then a fellow doctor began to suspect that he was experimenting with aborted human fetuses—which is, of course, illegal."

"What was done about it?"

"He was watched very carefully. Then a tragedy occurred. Dr. Highley's wife died suddenly. There was the suspicion that he had implanted her with an aborted fetus. Dr. Highley was asked to resign. This is absolutely confidential. There is no proof."

Richard absorbed what he had heard. His hunch had been right. A question came into his mind—a long shot. "Sir, do you by any chance know a Dr. Emmet Salem?"

The voice warmed. "Of course. A good friend. Dr. Salem was visiting staff here at the time of the Highley scandal."

Silently Katie ran down the stairs to the main floor. Desperately she grasped the knob, tried to open the door. But it was locked. Upstairs the footsteps had paused. He was trying the second-floor knob, making sure that she had not escaped him. The footsteps started again. He was coming down. Through these heavy doors no one would hear her if she screamed.

She felt dull pain in her pelvic area. Whatever he had given her had started the hemorrhaging. She was dizzy. But she had to get away. Wildly she began rushing down the staircase. One more flight. It probably led to the basement. He'd have to explain how and why she'd gotten there. The farther she got, the more questions would be asked. She stumbled on the last stair. Don't fall. Don't make it look like an accident.

But she'd be trapped down here. Another door. This one would be locked too. She tried the knob. He was coming. Dark as it was, she could sense a presence rushing down at her.

The door opened. The corridor was dimly lighted. She was in the basement. She saw rooms ahead. The door snapped closed behind her. Could she hide somewhere? Help me. Help me. There was a switch on the wall. She turned it off. The corridor disappeared into blackness. Then, a few feet behind her, the door from the stairwell burst open.

Highley was suspected of causing his first wife's death. Winifred Westlake's cousin believed he had caused Winifred's death. Highley was a brilliant researcher. Highley may have been experimenting on some of his patients. Highley may have injected Vangie Lewis with the semen of an Oriental male. But why? Would he try to accuse Fukhito? Or had Vangie been involved with Fukhito? Was Highley's possible experimentation only incidental to Vangie's pregnancy?

Richard could not find the answers. He sat at Katie's desk twirling her pen. He wished he knew where she was. He wanted to talk to her.

There was a soft knock on the door and Maureen looked in. Her eyes were emerald green, large and oval. Beautiful eyes.

"Dr. Carroll."

"Maureen, I'm sorry I asked you to stay. I thought Mrs. Horan would be here long ago."

"She phoned. She's on her way. Something came up at work and they needed her. But there are two women here. They're friends of Edna Burns. They wanted to see Katie. One of them, Mrs. Fitzgerald, said she met you the other night at the Burns apartment."

"Right. Tell them to come on in. If it's anything much, we'll make them wait to talk to Scott."

They entered the office together, Gana's eyes snapping with excitement. Gertrude was carrying the moccasin in a paper bag. Her gray hair was neatly in place. She leaned forward, shook the bag, and the shabby moccasin fell onto Katie's desk. Primly she began to explain. "That shoe is the reason we are here."

SHE zigzagged down the corridor. Would he know where the light switch was? He knew this hospital. Where would she go? There had been a door at the end of the hall. If she ran straight, she'd get to it. Maybe she could lock herself in there somehow. Maybe he'd try the other doors first.

He was standing still. He was listening for her. Her outstretched hand touched a cold wall, then a doorframe. Her hand found a knob. She turned it. A heavy formaldehyde smell filled her nostrils. From behind her she heard rushing feet. She stepped inside and tried to push the door closed, but she was so dizzy. She stumbled and fell. She reached out. Her hand touched a pant leg.

"It's all over, Katie," Dr. Highley said.

"ARE you sure this is your wife's shoe?" Scott demanded.

Wearily Chris nodded. "I am absolutely certain. This is the one that was so loose on her . . . the left one."

"When Edna Burns phoned you, did she tell you she had this?"

"No. She said she had something to tell the police and that she wanted to talk to me."

"All right. Your statement will be typed immediately. Read it carefully, sign it if you find it accurate, and then you can go home. We'll want to talk with you again tomorrow morning."

For the first time Chris felt as though the prosecutor had begun to believe him. He got up to go. "Where is Joan?"

"She's completed a statement. She can go with you. Oh, one thing. What impression do you have of Dr. Highley?"

"I never met him."

"Did you read this article?" Scott held up a copy of *Newsmaker* magazine.

Chris looked at the picture of Dr. Highley. "I saw this yesterday on the plane into New York." Memory jogged. "That's it. That's what I couldn't place. He's the man who got off the elevator at the Essex House last night when I was trying to reach Dr. Salem."

HE SWITCHED on a light and stood staring down at her, his sandy hair falling untidily on his forehead.

She managed to stumble to her feet. She was in a small area like a waiting room. It was so cold. A thick steel door was behind her. She shrank back against it.

"You've made it so easy for me, Mrs. DeMaio." Now he was smiling at her. "Everyone knows about your fear of hospitals. When Nurse Renge and I make rounds in a few minutes, we'll assume you left the hospital. Certainly no one will dream of looking for you in the morgue.

"An old man died in the emergency room tonight. He's in one of those vaults. Tomorrow, when the undertaker comes for his body, you'll be found on the floor. What happened will be obvious. You were hemorrhaging; you became disoriented. Tragically, you wandered down here and bled to death."

"No." His face was blurring. She was dizzy, swaying.

He opened the steel door, pushed her through it, held her as she slid down. She had fainted. Kneeling beside her, he injected the last shot of heparin. She probably wouldn't regain consciousness. Even if she did, she couldn't get out. From this side the door was locked. He closed it and turned out the light. At last he was finished with Katie DeMaio.

Cautiously he opened the door into the corridor and hurried out into the parking lot by the fire exit through which he'd entered fifteen minutes before.

Moments later he was drinking lukewarm cappuccino, waving away the offer of the waitress to bring him a hot cup. "My calls took a bit longer than I expected," he explained. "And now I must hurry back to the hospital. There's a patient there about whom I'm quite concerned."

CHAPTER NINETEEN

"Good night, Dr. Fukhito. I feel much better. Thank you." The boy managed a smile.

"I'm glad. Sleep well tonight, Tom." Jiro Fukhito got up slowly from his desk at the Valley Pines Psychiatric Clinic, where he did volunteer work. This young man had been in deep depression for weeks, nearly suicidal. He'd been doing eighty miles an hour in a car that crashed. His younger brother had been killed.

Fukhito knew he had helped the boy get through it. The work he did here with disturbed children was so satisfying, he reflected, as he walked toward the elevator. And now he'd been asked to join the staff. He wanted to accept that offer.

Should he start the investigation that would destroy him? Edgar Highley would instantly reveal the Massachusetts case if he found that Fukhito had taken his suspicions to the police.

He got into his car, sat there thinking. Vangie Lewis did not commit suicide. She absolutely did not willingly drink cyanide. She had gotten on the subject of the Jones cult during one of their sessions. "Those cults, they're all crazy. Remember all those people who killed themselves because they were told to? Did you hear the tape of them screaming after they drank that stuff? I had nightmares about it. And they looked so *ugly*."

Pain. Ugliness. Vangie Lewis? Never!

Jiro Fukhito sighed. He knew that he had to tell the police about Vangie. She had run out of his office toward the parking lot. But when he left, fifteen minutes later, her Lincoln Continental was still there. There was no longer any doubt in Fukhito's mind. Vangie had gone into Edgar Highley's office.

He drove out of the clinic's parking lot and turned in the direction of the Valley County prosecutor's office.

374

Scott held the moccasin. Richard, Charley and Phil sat around his desk. "Let's try to put this together," Scott said. "The last known place Vangie Lewis visited was Dr. Fukhito's office. She was wearing the moccasins. Somewhere in the hospital she lost one of them, and Edna Burns found it. Whoever brought her home put other shoes on her to try to cover up for the missing one. Edna Burns found the missing shoe. And Edna Burns died.

"Emmet Salem wanted to talk to Richard about Vangie's death. He fell or was pushed to his death, and the file he was carrying on Vangie Lewis disappeared."

"And Chris Lewis swears that he saw Edgar Highley in the Essex House," Richard interjected.

"Which may or may not be true," Scott reminded him.

"But Dr. Salem knew about the scandal in Christ Hospital," Richard said. "Highley wouldn't want that to come out."

"That's no motive to kill," Scott said.

"How about Highley trying to get the shoe?" Charley asked.

"We don't *know* that. The woman from his office claimed he was opening the drawer. He didn't touch anything." Scott frowned. "We're dealing with a prominent doctor. We can't go off half-cocked. The big problem is motive. Highley had no motive to kill Vangie Lewis."

The intercom buzzed. Scott switched it on. "Mrs. Horan is here to see Dr. Carroll," Maureen said.

"All right, bring her into my office," Scott directed. "And I want you to take down her statement."

Richard leaned forward. This was the woman who had filed the malpractice suit against Edgar Highley.

The door opened and a young Japanese woman preceded Maureen into the room. Her hair fell loosely on her shoulders. Her delicate, graceful carriage gave a floating effect even to the inexpensive pantsuit she was wearing.

Scott stood up. "Won't you sit down, Mrs. Horan?"

She nodded. Clearly nervous, she deliberately folded her hands in her lap. Maureen sat behind her with her steno pad.

"Mrs. Horan, you were Dr. Highley's patient?" Scott asked.

Richard turned suddenly as he heard Maureen gasp. But the girl

375

quickly recovered and, bending forward, resumed taking her notes.

Anna Horan's face hardened. "Yes, I was that murderer's patient."

"*That murderer?*" Scott said.

Now her words came in a torrent. "I went to him five months ago. I was pregnant. My husband is a law student. We live on my salary. I didn't want to, but I decided I had to have an abortion."

Scott sighed. "And now you're blaming Dr. Highley?"

"No. He told me to come back the next day. And I did. He brought me to an operating room. He left me, and I knew—I *knew*—that no matter how we managed, I wanted my baby. Dr. Highley came back; I was sitting up. I told him I'd changed my mind. He said, 'Lie down.' He pushed me down on the table."

"Was anyone else in the room? The nurse?"

"No. Just the doctor and me."

"And you allowed him to persuade you?"

"No. No. I don't know what happened. He jabbed me with a needle while I was trying to get up. When I woke up, I was lying on a stretcher. The nurse said it was all over."

"You don't remember the procedure?"

"Nothing. The last I remember is trying to get away. Trying to save my baby. Dr. Highley took my baby from me."

A harsh cry echoed Anna Horan's heartbroken sobs. Maureen's voice was a wail. "That's exactly what he did to me."

Richard stared at the weeping women: the Japanese girl; Maureen, with her red-gold hair and emerald-green eyes. And with absolute certainty he knew where he had seen those eyes before.

WHEN Edgar Highley reached the second floor of the hospital, he instantly felt the tension in the air. Frightened-looking nurses scurried in the hall. A man and woman in evening dress were standing by the nurses' desk. Quickly he walked over. His voice was brittle. "Nurse Renge, is there something wrong?"

"Doctor, it's Mrs. DeMaio. *She's missing.*"

The woman in evening clothes must be Katie DeMaio's sister. What had made her come to the hospital?

"I'm Dr. Highley," he said to her. "What does this mean?"

376

Molly found it hard to talk. "Katie—" Her voice broke.

Her husband interrupted. "I'm Dr. Kennedy," he said. "My wife is Mrs. DeMaio's sister. When did you see Mrs. DeMaio, Doctor, and what was her condition?"

This was not a man to be easily deceived. "I saw Mrs. DeMaio earlier this evening and her condition was not good. As you probably know, she's had two units of whole blood this week. The laboratory is analyzing her blood now. I expect the count to be low, so I plan to perform surgery tonight. I think Mrs. DeMaio has been concealing the extent of her hemorrhaging."

"Oh, God, then where is she?" Molly cried.

He looked at her. "Your sister has an almost pathological fear of hospitals. Is it possible that she would simply leave?"

"It's possible," Bill said slowly.

"Doctor." Nurse Renge spoke up. "That sleeping pill should have put her to sleep. It was the strongest one I've ever seen."

He glowered at her. "I ordered it because I understood Mrs. DeMaio's anxiety. You were told to see that she took it."

"I saw her put it in her mouth."

"Did you watch her swallow it?"

"No . . . not really."

He turned his back on the nurse and spoke to Molly and Bill, his voice reflective, concerned. "I hardly think Mrs. DeMaio is wandering around the hospital. Do you agree that she might simply have walked out among the visitors?"

"Yes. Yes. I do." Molly prayed, Please let it be that way.

"I want to see if her car is in the parking lot," Bill said.

The car. He hadn't thought about her car. If they started looking for her in the hospital now . . .

Bill frowned. "Oh, hell, she's still got that loan car. Molly, what make is it? I don't think I've even seen it."

"I . . . I don't know," Molly said.

Edgar Highley sighed. "I suggest that you phone her home. If she's not there, go and wait for her to come in. She's scarcely been gone an hour now. When you do find her, please insist she return to the hospital. Mrs. DeMaio is a very sick girl."

Molly bit her lip. "I see. Thank you, Doctor. Bill, let's just go to her house. She could be there and not answering the telephone."

They believed him. They would not suggest searching the hospital for several hours. And that was all he needed.

He turned to the nurse. "I am sure that we'll be hearing from Mrs. DeMaio shortly. Call me immediately when you do. I'll be at my home." He smiled. "I have some records to complete."

"WE MUST seize Dr. Highley's records before he has a chance to destroy them. Does he keep all his records in his office?"

Jiro Fukhito stared at Richard. He had gone to the prosecutor's office to make a statement. They had listened to him almost impatiently, and then Dr. Carroll had outlined his incredible theory. Was it possible? Fukhito reviewed the times when suspicions had formed in his mind. Yes, *it was possible*.

Records. They had asked him about records. "Highley frequently takes files to his home," he said.

"Have search warrants sworn out immediately," Scott told Charley. "I'll take the squad to the house. Richard, you come with me. Charley, you and Phil take the office. Pick up Highley as a material witness. If he's not there, we'll nab him as soon as he gets home."

"What worries me is that he may be experimenting on someone now," Richard said. He wished Katie were here. She'd be relieved to know that Chris Lewis had been eliminated as a suspect.

Dr. Fukhito stood up. "Do you need me any longer?"

"Not right now, Doctor," Scott said. "We'll be in touch with you. If by any chance you happen to hear from Dr. Highley before we arrest him, please do not discuss this investigation with him."

Dr. Fukhito smiled wearily. "Edgar Highley and I are not friends. He would have no reason to call me at home. He hired me because he knew he'd have a hold over me. How right he was."

He left the room. As he walked down the corridor, he saw a nameplate on a door: MRS. K. DEMAIO. Katie DeMaio. Wasn't she supposed to have gone into the hospital tonight? But, of course, she never would go through with her operation while Edgar Highley was under investigation.

Jiro Fukhito went home.

378

SHE WAS DRIFTING DOWN A DARK CORRIDOR. At the very end there was a light. It would be warm when she got there. Warm and safe. But something was holding her back. Before she died, she had to make them know what Dr. Highley was. Her finger was dripping blood; she could feel it. She'd smear Highley's name on the floor. He was insane. He had to be stopped. Slowly, painfully, Katie moved her finger. Down, across, down again. H . . .

HE GOT home at quarter past nine. Having at last eliminated the final threat, he was feeling buoyant. He had finished eating less than an hour ago, but somehow could not even remember the meal. Perhaps Hilda had left something for a snack.

It was better than he had hoped. Fondue. Hilda made remarkably good fondue. He lit the Sterno can under the pot, adjusted it to a low flame. A crisp loaf of French bread was in a basket, covered by a damask napkin. He'd make a salad.

While the fondue heated, he would complete Katie DeMaio's file. He was anxious to be finished with it. He wanted to think about tomorrow's two patients: the donor and the recipient. He was confident that he could duplicate his success.

He went into the library, opened the desk drawer and withdrew Katie DeMaio's file from its compartment. He made a final entry:

> Patient entered hospital at 6:00 p.m. with blood pressure 100/60, hemoglobin no more than 10 grams. This physician administered the final two Coumadin pills at 7:00 p.m. At 8:30 this physician returned to Mrs. DeMaio's room and administered 5-ml heparin injection. Mrs. DeMaio awakened briefly. In a near comatose state she asked, "Why did you kill Vangie Lewis?"
>
> This physician left to obtain more heparin. When this physician returned, patient had left room in attempt to escape. Patient was apprehended and another 5 ml of heparin was administered. Patient will hemorrhage to death tonight in Westlake Hospital. This file is now closed.

He put down his pen, stretched, walked over to the wall safe and opened it. Bathed in light from the crystal sconces, the buff-colored files inside took on an almost golden sheen.

They *were* golden: the records of his genius. Expansively he lifted them all out and laid them on his desk, savoring his great successes: Berkeley and Lewis. Then his face darkened at the sight of the failures: Appleton, Carey, Drake, Elliot . . . Over eighty of them. But not really failures. He had learned so much, and they had all contributed. Those who had died, those who had aborted.

From somewhere in the distance a sound was beginning to penetrate the library: the wail of a siren. He hurried to the window, snatched back the drapery and glanced out. A police car had pulled into the driveway.

Had Katie been found? Had she been able to talk? Running to the desk, he stacked the files, replaced them in the safe, closed it and pushed back the panel. Calm. He must be calm.

If Katie had talked, it was all over.

All the possibilities and consequences were exploding in his mind. And then it came. The icy calm, the sense of power, the godlike omniscience that never failed him during difficult surgery.

There was a sharp rap at the door. Slowly, deliberately he smoothed his hair, then tightened the knot in his tie. He walked to the front door and opened it.

CHAPTER TWENTY

IN HIGHLEY's driveway, the two detectives who were in the front seat of the squad car jumped out. As he and Scott followed, Richard noticed the movement of a drapery in a window at the far right of the house.

They had parked behind a black car with MD plates. Scott touched the hood. "It's still warm. He hasn't been here long."

The younger detective rapped sharply on the front door. They waited. The door opened. Edgar Highley was standing in the foyer. Scott spoke first. "Dr. Highley?"

"Yes?" The tone was cold and questioning.

"Dr. Highley, I'm Scott Myerson, the Valley County prosecutor. We have a search warrant for these premises, and it is my duty to inform you that you have become a suspect in the deaths of Vangie Lewis, Edna Burns and Dr. Emmet Salem. You have the right to consult a lawyer. You can refuse to answer questions. Anything you say may be used against you."

Suspect. They weren't sure. They hadn't found Katie. With controlled fury he said, "Come in, gentlemen. I will answer any questions you have, and you are welcome to search my home. However, when I consult a lawyer, it will be to bring suit against Valley County and against each one of you personally."

He led them into the library. He knew he looked imposing sitting behind the massive Jacobean desk. It was vital that he unnerve them, make them afraid to question too closely. With a gesture of contempt, he waved them to the leather couch and chairs. Scott Myerson handed him the printed *Miranda* warning. Scornfully he signed it. Myerson and Dr. Carroll sat down; the other two did not.

"We'll proceed with the search," the older detective said politely. "Where do you keep your medical records, Dr. Highley?"

"At my office, of course," he snapped. "However, please satisfy yourselves." He stood up, walked to the bar and poured Scotch and water into a crystal tumbler. Then he sat down in the high-backed striped velvet chair near the fireplace, sipped the Scotch and eyed them coldly.

The questions began. "Did Mrs. Lewis enter your office after leaving Dr. Fukhito last Monday night?"

"As I told Mrs. DeMaio . . ." They had absolutely no proof.

"Where were you that night, Doctor?"

"Home. I came home directly after my office hours."

"Were you in Edna Burns's apartment on Tuesday night?"

His smile, contemptuous. "Hardly."

"We'll want some hair samples from you."

Hair samples. Had some been found in Edna's apartment? But he'd been there with the police on Wednesday night. And Vangie always wore that black coat to the office. If strands of his hair had been found near the dead women, they could be explained.

"Were you in the Essex House last night after five o'clock?"

"Absolutely not."

"We have a witness who is prepared to swear that he saw you get off the elevator there at approximately five thirty."

Who had seen him? He had glanced around the lobby as he got off the elevator. He was certain that no one he knew was there. Maybe they were bluffing.

"I was *not* in the Essex House last night. I was at the Carlyle! I dine there frequently; in fact, my medical bag was stolen while I was dining there."

He'd make it seem that he was cooperating.

"What was in your bag?" The question seemed perfunctory.

"A basic emergency kit, a few drugs. Hardly worth a thief's effort." Should he mention that it contained files? No.

The prosecutor beckoned to the younger investigator. "Get that package out of the car."

What package? Highley gripped the glass.

They sat in silence, waiting. The detective returned and handed Scott a small parcel. He pulled off the wrapping paper. "Do you recognize this moccasin, Doctor?"

Careful. Careful. He leaned over, examined it. The *left* shoe, the one from Edna's apartment. *They had not found his bag.*

"Certainly not. Should I recognize it?"

"Your patient Vangie Lewis wore this shoe for weeks. Didn't you ever notice?"

"Mrs. Lewis wore a pair of rather shabby shoes. I certainly would not recognize one particular shoe."

"Did you ever hear of a Dr. Emmet Salem?"

"The name seems familiar. I'd have to check my records."

"Wasn't he on staff with you at Christ Hospital in Devon?"

"Of course. Yes. He was visiting staff. Indeed, I do remember him." How much did they know about Christ Hospital?

"Were you aware Mrs. Lewis was carrying an Oriental baby?"

So that was it. He said, "That explains why Mrs. Lewis was becoming terrified of giving birth. She knew that she could never make anyone believe her husband was the father."

Now they were asking about Anna Horan and Maureen Crowley. They were coming close, too close.

"Those two young women are typical of many who demand abortions and then blame the physician when they experience emotional reactions."

Richard listened bleakly. Highley was so composed, so sure. Unless they could prove wrongful death in the maternity cases, it would be impossible to charge him with anything and make it stick. He felt certain they'd never find anything incriminating in Highley's records. He was far too clever for that.

Scott was asking about the Berkeley baby. "Doctor, you are aware that Elizabeth Berkeley gave birth to a baby who has green eyes. Isn't that a medical improbability when both parents and all four grandparents have brown eyes?"

"Clearly Mr. Berkeley is not the baby's father," Highley said.

Neither Scott nor Richard had expected the admission. "I don't know who the father is," Highley continued smoothly, "but it is hardly the obstetrician's business to delve into such matters."

A shame, he thought. He would have to defer fame a little longer. He'd never be able to admit the success of the Berkeley baby now.

Scott looked at Richard, sighed and stood up. "Dr. Highley, when you go to your office, you will learn that we have seized your records. We are concerned at the number of maternity deaths at Westlake, and that matter is under intensive investigation."

He was on safe ground. "I invite minute scrutiny of my patients' records. I can assure you that the death ratio is remarkably low in consideration of the kinds of cases we handle."

The smell of the fondue was filling the house. Unless it was stirred, it would surely burn. Just a few minutes more.

The phone rang. Undoubtedly it would be the hospital saying that Mrs. DeMaio had not yet returned home and her sister was frantic. He picked up the phone. "Dr. Highley here."

"Doctor, this is Lieutenant Weingarden of the Seventeenth Precinct in New York. We've just arrested a man who answers the description of the person who stole a bag from the trunk of your car last night."

The bag. "Has it been recovered?" Something in his voice was giving him away. Scott Myerson stalked over to the desk and reached for the extension.

"Yes. And several items in it may lead to far more serious charges than theft. Doctor, will you describe the contents of your bag?"

"Some medicine—a few basic drugs. An emergency kit."

"What about a patient's file from the office of a Dr. Emmet Salem, a bloodstained paperweight and an old shoe?"

Highley closed his eyes. When he spoke, his voice was remarkably controlled. "Are you joking?"

"I thought you'd say that, sir. We're cooperating with the Valley County prosecutor's office concerning the suspicious death of Dr. Salem. I'll call the prosecutor now. It looks as though the suspect might have killed Dr. Salem during a theft. Thank you, sir."

He heard Scott Myerson say on the extension, "Don't hang up!"

Slowly Highley replaced the receiver. It was all over.

Dr. Carroll was looking at him curiously. Somehow Edgar Highley was sure that Richard Carroll was the man who had become suspicious of him. But he had his revenge. Katie DeMaio's death was his revenge on Richard Carroll. Highley smiled. "I have just remembered that I do have some medical records that might interest you," he said. He walked over to the bookcase, released the spring. The panel swung out. Mechanically he opened the wall safe. Let them know his genius. Let them mourn it.

He lifted out the files, stacked them on the desk. The prosecutor had hung up the phone. They were all staring at him now.

"Oh, there is another case you'll want to have." He reached for his drink and sipped it casually as he walked over to the safe. The vial was there, right in the back. He'd put it away Monday night for possible future use. The future was now.

At the safe, he quickly flipped the vial open and dumped the cyanide crystals into his glass. As understanding swept over Richard's face, Highley held up the glass in a mocking toast.

Richard leaped across the room as Highley raised the glass to his lips and gulped down the contents. Richard knocked the glass away as Highley fell, but it was too late. The four men watched helplessly as Highley's screams and groans died into silence.

The younger detective bolted from the room, his face green.

Richard bent over the body. Highley's face was contorted; the protruding gray eyes were open and staring.

"Why'd he do it?" the other detective asked.

"He knew he couldn't murder his way out anymore," Scott said.

384

Straightening up, Richard went over to the desk and scanned the names on the files. Berkeley. Lewis. "These are the records we're looking for." He opened the Berkeley file. The first page began, "Elizabeth Berkeley, age 39, became my patient today. She will never conceive her own child. I have decided that she will be the next extraordinary patient."

"There's medical history here," Richard said quietly, and thought, He could have done so much good.

Scott was standing over the body. "And when you think that this nut was Katie's doctor," he muttered.

Richard looked up. "What? Highley was treating Katie?"

"She happened to mention it when—" The phone interrupted him. Scott picked it up. "Yes," he said, then, "I'm sorry, this is not Dr. Highley. Who is calling?" His expression changed. "Molly! This is Scott Myerson. What's the matter?" He listened, then covered the mouthpiece with his hand. "Highley admitted Katie to Westlake tonight and she's missing."

Richard yanked the phone from him. "Molly, what do you mean she's missing?" He listened. "Come on, Molly. Katie would never walk out of a hospital. You know that. Wait."

Dropping the phone, he frantically scattered the files on the desk. Near the bottom of the pile he found the one he dreaded: DeMaio, Kathleen. He raced through it, his face paling as he read. He came to the last paragraph. He picked up the phone. "Molly, put Bill on," he ordered. "Bill, Katie is hemorrhaging somewhere in Westlake Hospital. Call the lab. We'll need to hang a bottle of O negative the minute we find her. Have them ready to analyze a blood sample and cross-match for four units of whole blood. Tell them to have an operating room ready. I'll meet you there." He broke the connection and turned to the detective at the desk. "Call the hospital and have them start looking for Katie. Tell them to look everywhere—every room, every closet. Get all available hospital personnel to help. Every second counts."

"Come on, Richard," Scott snapped.

Richard grabbed Katie's file. "We have to know what he's done to her." They'd been seconds too late preventing Edgar Highley's death. Would they be too late for Katie?

With Scott, he hunched in the back of the squad car as it raced through the night. Katie, he thought, why didn't you tell me? If you'd only trusted me, *told* me you were seeing Highley. I'd never have let you go near him. Katie, don't die. Let me find you. Katie, *hang on.* . . .

They were at the hospital. Squad cars were roaring into the parking lot. Scott and Richard dashed up the stairs into the lobby. Phil, his face drawn, was commanding the search.

Bill and Molly came running in. Molly was sobbing. Bill was deadly calm. "They've got a reasonable supply of whole blood on hand here. Have you found her?"

"Not yet," Phil answered.

The door to the fire stairs, partly ajar, burst open. A young policeman ran out. "She's on the floor in the morgue. I think she's gone."

Seconds later Richard was cradling her in his arms. Her skin and lips were ashen. He could not get a pulse. "Katie. Katie."

Bill gripped his shoulder. "Let's get her upstairs. We'll have to work fast if there's any chance at all."

SHE was in a tunnel. At the end there was a light. It was warm at the end of the tunnel. It would be so easy to drift there.

But someone was keeping her from going. Someone was holding her. A voice. Richard's voice. "Hang on, Katie, hang on."

She wanted so not to turn back. It was so hard, so dark. It would be so much easier to slip away.

"Hang on, Katie."

Sighing, she turned and began to make her way back.

ON MONDAY evening Richard tiptoed into Katie's room, a dozen roses in his hand. She'd been out of danger since Sunday morning, but hadn't stayed awake long enough to say anything. Her eyes were closed. He decided to go out and ask the nurse for a vase.

"Just lay them across my chest."

He spun around. "Katie. How do you feel?"

She grimaced at the transfusion apparatus. "I hear the vampires are picketing. I'm putting them out of business."

387

"You're better." He pulled up a chair. He hoped the sudden moisture in his eyes wasn't noticeable.

She had noticed. She gently reached up and brushed a finger across his eyelids. "Before I fall asleep again, please tell me what happened. Why did Dr. Highley kill Vangie?"

"He was experimenting on his patients, taking fetuses from women who had abortions and implanting them in the wombs of sterile women. In these past eight years he learned how to immunize a host mother to prevent her from rejecting an alien fetus, at least for a few months. Most cases eventually ended in spontaneous abortion, but he did have one complete success.

"After that one success, he wanted to break more new ground. An Oriental woman named Anna Horan, who's married to a Caucasian, claims he knocked her out and took her fetus when she was unconscious. She was right. He had Vangie Lewis in the next room waiting for the implant. Vangie thought she was simply having some treatment to help her become pregnant. Highley never expected Vangie to retain the Oriental fetus so long. When her body did not reject the developing fetus, he decided to bring it to term. Who would blame him if Vangie had a partly Oriental child?"

"He was able to suppress the immune system?"

"Yes, and without harm to the developing fetus. But the danger to the mother was great. He's killed sixteen women. Vangie was getting terribly sick. Unfortunately for her, she ran into Highley last Monday evening just as she left Fukhito. She told him she was going to consult her former doctor in Minneapolis. That would have been a risk because her gynecologist would know that a natural pregnancy for Vangie was a million-to-one shot. And when she mentioned Emmet Salem's name, she was finished. Highley knew that Dr. Salem would guess what had happened. Salem was in England when Highley's first wife died. He knew about the scandal.

"And now," Richard said, "that's enough of that. All the rest can wait. Your eyes are closing again."

"No . . . You said Highley had *one* success."

"Yes. And if you had stayed five minutes longer at Molly's last

388

Thursday night and seen the Berkeley baby, you could guess who it is. Liz Berkeley carried Maureen Crowley's baby to term."

"Maureen's baby." Katie tried to pull herself up.

"Easy, you'll pull that needle out." Gently he touched her shoulder, holding her until she leaned back.

"Does Maureen know?" she asked.

"It was only right to tell her and the Berkeleys. Jim has been living with the belief that his wife lied to him about artificial insemination. You know how Maureen felt about that abortion. It's been destroying her. She went to see her baby. She's one happy girl, Katie. She would have given it out for adoption if she had delivered it naturally. Now that she's seen Maryanne, sees how crazy the Berkeleys are about her, she's in seventh heaven."

"What about the mother of Vangie's baby?"

"Anna Horan is heartbroken enough about the abortion. We saw no point in telling her what Highley did with her baby. She'll have other children."

Katie bit her lip. "Richard, tell me the truth. When they found me, how far did they have to go to stop the bleeding?"

"You're okay. You can still have a dozen kids if you want them."

His hand reached over to cover hers. That hand had been there, had pulled her back when she was so near to death. That voice had made her want to come back.

For a long, quiet moment she looked up at Richard. Oh, how I love you, she thought. How very much I love you.

His troubled expression changed suddenly into a broad smile. Obviously he was satisfied at what he saw in her face.

Katie grinned back at him. "Pretty sure of yourself, aren't you, Doctor?" she asked him crisply.

LIFE WITH MOTHER

by David Clark

A typical morning of my childhood: It's seven a.m. I walk down the stairs to the familiar sound of tapping typewriter keys. In the kitchen is Mother. She happily announces, "Five pages done, ten more planned, and the French toast is almost ready." Within an hour all five children are off to school, and Mother is still intently planning the ending of her latest short story.

I don't think we realized, when we were growing up, what fine mysteries were plotted and written at our kitchen table. But we all knew Mother was a good writer. After all, who else could proofread a homework paper, spruce up a college application essay, and help write an entertaining "What I Did on My Summer Vacation" report all in one evening?

Perhaps the greatest strength she brings to her family and to her writing is her confidence and persistence. That confidence faced its greatest challenge in 1964, when our father died of a heart attack. My sister Marilyn was thirteen, my brother Warren was twelve, I was ten, Carol eight, and Patty just five.

Shortly after my father's death, Mother took a job writing scripts for a radio promotion firm. Soon she became involved in production and sales, and began a daily commute from our home in New Jersey to New York City. In 1970, to meet our family's growing financial needs, she and a co-worker boldly established their own company to produce syndicated radio programmes.

The same economic considerations encouraged her to play for higher stakes at the typewriter. The early morning hours formerly spent writing short stories she now devoted to her first suspense novel, *Where Are the Children?* Despite occasional setbacks in business, a family tendency to broken arms, and the difficult transition to writing novels, her Irish optimism refused to be shaken. There was never a problem so serious that it couldn't be handled with her comment, "Someday we'll all look back on this and laugh."

It is impossible to forget the feeling of celebration when *Where Are the Children?* sold for the huge advance of three thousand dollars. The party Mother threw must have greatly diminished the profits.

As if five children, a full-time job, and a new career as a novelist were not enough to keep her busy, Mother announced several years ago that she had no intention of being the only non-college graduate in the Clark family. The same dogged determination that powered her as a writer served her well in the classroom. For her children, the most memorable aspects of her college

Mary Higgins Clark weds Ray Ploetz in August 1978. Her five children are grouped in the middle. David Clark is standing fourth from right.

days were the courses that gave her difficulty. When a midterm exam in logic produced a failing grade, we saw an opportunity to return past favours and introduced drastic measures to help her. I confiscated the car keys. My sisters placed severe restrictions on Mother's social life. My brother lectured her on the difficult job market she would face if her grades did not improve. Our "parental" concern paid off and Mother graduated with honours.

Luckily, part of her drive has proved genetic. My sister Marilyn is an assistant prosecutor in Bergen County, New Jersey. In fact, she served as role model for Katie DeMaio. My brother Warren recently opened his own law firm. Carol is an aspiring actress, Patty is a senior at Boston College, and I am in publishing.

In 1978 Mother married Ray Ploetz, an attorney. Now Ray's four children are enjoying her help with homework and waking up in the morning to the clatter of typewriter keys.

A
VERY
PRIVATE
WAR

a condensation of the book by

Jon Cleary

ILLUSTRATED BY GEORGE JONES
PUBLISHED BY COLLINS

To American planter Cornelius Mullane, the South Pacific island of New Britain was supposed to be a peaceful haven, a place where he could put the past behind him. But now it is August 1942. Japanese troops have occupied the island. Fleeing into the jungle, Mullane and his fellow Coastwatcher Frank Vokes find themselves leading a ragtag band of natives—and a beautiful young doctor—on a mission of vital importance to the Allied cause. What the others don't know is that Con Mullane is a man with an old but bitter wrong to avenge, a man fighting his own very private war.

This is a harrowing adventure about a little-known theatre of World War II, and about the renewal of love and hope in a man who had given up believing in either.

CHAPTER ONE

Cornelius Mullane was playing catch with his native overseer, Buka, the latter's strong right arm thumping the ball into Mullane's battered old baseball mitt, when Frank Vokes came chugging across the bay in his launch to say that the Japanese were coming at last.

"It's more than a patrol this time, Con! A supply boat and four barges—they've just passed Murota, so they should be here in an hour at the outside."

Frank Vokes had an excess of energy; he was never still. He had the long angular face Mullane had come to think of as Australian, but unlike the wary, prove-it-to-me-mate countenances of most Australians Mullane knew, Vokes's was wide open with curiosity. He was twenty-two years old, the assistant manager of Tanga, the Burns Philp plantation across the bay, and he was the last person Mullane would have chosen as company for the weeks ahead.

"You all ready, Con? Geez, I'm raring to go. All these months sitting on our bums—"

Mullane turned around to give an order to Buka, then jumped as a shot went off right behind him. "What the—"

"Sorry, mate." Vokes picked up his .303 Lee-Enfield from where it had fallen by his foot. A bullet had scored a mark across the toe of his boot. "I dropped it. I suppose I'd better warn you—I think I'm accident-prone. I must be the only bloke in the world who's ever been attacked by a *dove*."

Mullane restrained himself from asking about the vicious dove. He feared he was going to learn more about Vokes than he really wanted to know about any man. They had both been Coast-watchers for the past six months, but every time they had had to flee their plantations when a Japanese patrol appeared, each of them had gone to his own hideout. Now orders had come in on their radios that they were to operate as a team.

Mullane sighed. "Okay, Buka. Get the boys rounded up," he said. He was always glad that Buka understood English. The infant talk of pidgin irritated him. "Tell Bingiti to hide Mr. Vokes's boat with mine—and who, may I ask, is *that*?"

Vokes looked back down the beach. "Oh, that's Ruth Riddle. She's the Native Medical Practitioner from Malapio. They had a visit from a Jap patrol and she thought she'd be safer with us—"

"With *us*? She's not coming with us!"

"Con—we can't leave her here! You know what the Nips would do to her."

"She's not coming with us," said Mullane adamantly.

Vokes shrugged. "Right, you tell her, then."

Ruth Riddle stood and waited with her medical case as the tall American came down to the beach with Vokes and stared angrily at her. "Miss Riddle, I don't want you to think this is personal—"

She laughed. "Mr. Mullane, I've been hearing that preface ever since I came back from my medical training in Fiji two years ago. It's always personal, so please don't beat about the bush."

"Ruthie—" Vokes had an Australian habit of adding *ie* to everyone's name. "I haven't had time to tell Con that you're going to be a great help up there in the hills. Who knows when we're going to need medical attention?"

Mullane held up a silencing hand. He was surprised at how good-looking Ruth Riddle was. She was of mixed blood, but not all the locals, as the white islanders called them, looked as she did, like Dorothy Lamour. She stood very straight, and he wondered if her carriage had some defiance in it, a challenge to the white men and women who would never accept her as an equal.

"Where we are going is no place for a woman," he said.

She let out something that was half sigh, half snarl. "Do you think *this* is going to be a safe place for a woman like me?"

In exasperation Mullane pulled at the black beard he had grown in the past three months, when he had spent some time in the hills avoiding a Japanese patrol. He was a handsome man, with a certain sadness and cynicism in his dark blue eyes.

"Just a minute, Con." Vokes was standing still, arms akimbo. "So far there's been no argument about who's going to be boss on this job. But I got word the night before last—"

"I was tuned in, too. You're now a sublieutenant in the Royal Australian Navy. You want me to salute?"

Vokes started waving his arms. "No, I don't! But a naval bloke outranks a civilian. Especially a *foreign* civilian. Though I don't suppose a Yank ever thinks of himself as a foreigner."

"Occasionally," said Mullane, thinking of Tokyo and how foreign he had always felt there, even in the dark alone with Mieko. But that had been five years ago and now this was August 1942. And here on this South Pacific island called New Britain he had lost any sense of being a foreigner. Of course, till last December and Pearl Harbor, he had also lost a good deal of the sense of being an American.

"Well," said Vokes, "I say she comes with us."

Mullane looked out across the bay to the point where the Japanese would soon appear. The sea and the sky always suggested the peace he had come seeking here. And had found, up until last February, when the first Japanese patrols came prying their way down the coast. He had always known the Japanese would come back here to Kiogo, and come to stay.

Blomfield, the Royal Australian Navy lieutenant, had told him as much when he had flown over just before the Japanese had appeared. "We can't hold New Britain, Mullane," he'd said. "They took Rabaul as if we'd handed it to them on a plate. That's why we're advising everyone who wants to leave the island to do so now. But if you want to stay, we can't *order* you out—"

"I do want to stay."

Roger Blomfield believed in the blunt approach. "I'm looking for volunteers. For the Coastwatchers. It's a bit unfortunate you're an American—"

"I'm sorry about that." Mullane wondered if Australia had ever produced any diplomats.

"I only meant that we could commission you if you were an Aussie. Might help. If the Nips should capture you as a civilian, they could shoot you as a spy."

"Couldn't the US Navy commission me?" He thought of his brother Liam at his desk in the Navy Department in Washington.

"I suppose so. Don't know how the USN works. Well, are you willing? I mean, if you're staying here."

"I'm willing," Mullane said after a long moment.

He already knew of the Islands Coastwatching Service, which had been developed as part of the intelligence arm of the Australian navy. Manned by volunteers like himself—planters, traders and missionaries—the network of stations stretched in a twenty-five-hundred-mile arc from New Guinea down to the New Hebrides, with headquarters at Townsville in northern Australia.

The Coastwatchers were under strict orders not to fight unless absolutely necessary to save their own lives; they were to avoid contact with the enemy at all times. They were the eyes of the forces defending Australia and the islands to the north and northeast of the continent. Small though their ranks were and meagre their resources, they had become invaluable in the desperate campaign now being fought by the Allies. They were spies, possibly the loneliest spies, subjected to the most uncomfortable conditions of anyone working behind enemy lines in the worldwide war. Mullane felt a sardonic amusement that he should be volunteering to spy again. But he did not mention that to Blomfield.

Committing himself, he had felt a sudden fierceness, which he managed to hide. He did not want to explain to Blomfield why he felt more a sense of vengeance than of patriotism.

And now the Japanese were coming here to Kiogo, to Mullane's copra plantation, and he would have to accept Ruth Riddle's presence whether he liked it or not.

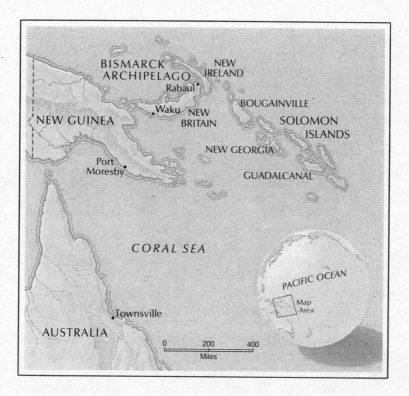

"Okay," he said to her. "But you're Frank's responsibility, not mine."

"I'm nobody's responsibility but my own, Mr. Mullane. You learn that when you're a local."

He took her medical case firmly from her. "Frank, get an extra boy. I've got a couple standing by as reserves."

Vokes took the case and went up through the coconut groves to where Buka had marshalled the natives who were to act as carriers. Ruth Riddle looked after him, then up at Mullane.

"He must have forgotten that he outranked you."

"Let's say he bows to my age. Thirty-eight is very elderly to someone Frank's age."

"Mine, too. Lead on, Dad."

A mocking woman; just what he needed. Then he heard Vokes shout: "Con! They're just off the point now!"

Mullane had only time to glimpse the boats appearing around the distant point when there was another shout and immediately following it the roar of an approaching plane. He swung around and saw a Zero coming in low above the mangrove swamps at the southern end of the bay. He shouted, "Down!" and dropped flat. Vokes and Ruth Riddle fell down, but most of the natives, some bewildered, some excited, remained standing. The bullets came smashing through the trees and found their targets.

The plane was gone as swiftly as it had come. Mullane stood up, saw it curve out over the bay in a beautiful arc, waggle its wings at the oncoming boats, then head for the Burns Philp plantation. Vokes's natives were going to get the same treatment.

Then he heard the moaning and weeping and the solitary scream of anguish. A young woman was crouched over a child, hugging it to her bosom; an elderly man and two women lay still, in attitudes of sleep. Mullane moved quickly, but Ruth Riddle was ahead of him, shouting for someone to bring her medical case. The villagers, stunned by the abrupt appearance of the plane, moved slowly and stiffly, like clockwork figures whose springs had run down. Then suddenly they came to life, converged on the wounded and dead, began to wail and shout.

"Get back!" Mullane bellowed, trying to impose some order. Trembling with anger at this needless strafing of the natives, he was like a psychopath trying to control an asylum.

But his rough methods worked; the natives quieted, stood back. Ruth was on her knees beside the young woman and child. She looked up at Mullane and shook her head. The woman began to wail again. Mullane looked for Vokes, saw him getting the carriers back into line.

"We're moving out, Con." Vokes looked shaken. "You coming?"

Mullane glanced back at Ruth, who was working on the other fallen villagers. "You get going," he said. "Leave me one carrier. We'll catch up."

Buka shouted an order for the carriers to pick up the packs and gear. Twelve of the natives were needed to carry the various

400

parts of the radio transmitter and receiver and the equipment required to operate it. The radio itself was packed in three metal boxes, but there were car batteries to power it, a charger for the batteries and a seventy-pound gas engine used to run the charger. Mullane wondered if the Japanese had developed something lighter and easier to carry than this Type 3BZ that he and Vokes would have to cart around the hills. The remaining six natives would be bearing bedding, tents, food and other trappings.

But the carriers stood irresolute, with their heads turned towards the villagers congregated around those who had been hit. Then one of them broke from the line and ran towards the group; immediately the others followed him.

Mullane wanted to shout at the boys, but he couldn't. This wasn't their war; he had no right of command now. If they wanted to stay here on the plantation and take their chances with the Japanese, he could not blame them. The white man had brought enough misery and exploitation to this part of the Pacific.

Buka, anger coming out of him in a sheen of sweat, loomed up beside Mullane. The natives on this part of the coast were not a handsome lot and Buka was less handsome than most. His face could have been a relief map of the district where he came from: a mountain of a nose jutted out from deep ravines furrowing his cheeks, a crater of a mouth showed betel-stained teeth. An ex-police sergeant, he believed in simple methods of authority. "I break their bloody heads, Boss—"

"No, Buka." Mullane crossed to Bingiti, the village headman, who was trying to comfort the young woman who had lost her child. "Bingiti, I need your help!"

The old man's face had a look of reproach that Mullane had never seen before. "Is this what you are going to bring to my people? Why should we help you now?"

"Con—one of the barges is coming across the bay!" Vokes's shout had a note of panic.

Mullane glanced quickly out at the bay, then back at Bingiti. "We didn't bring this to you," he said in dialect, trying to sound convincing but knowing he was lying. "The white man didn't start this war—"

"The men in that boat—" Bingiti nodded out at the barge, now only a mile away. "They don't have skins like ours."

There was no argument to that. Europeans and Japanese were lumped together in the eyes of this old man.

"Bingiti, those men will treat you worse than we ever did. We'll come back, but we'll need your help. Then things will be like they used to be—"

The old man just stared at him, but the answer was there in the sad, cataract-scarred eyes. Things would never be like they used to be, not as they were before the white men came.

"Con! Let's go."

Mullane pointed down at the gear still lying where the carriers had dropped it. "Bingiti, if the Japanese see all those boxes and packs, they will know that white men have been here. And they will punish you till you tell them where we can be found."

The old man looked out towards the bay; the barge was clearly visible. Suddenly he shouted to the carriers. The young men looked at him, some bewildered, others resentful. But he was their headman. They moved to the baggage and picked it up.

Mullane gathered his own gear and his Thompson submachine gun. It had been left by a fleeing Australian soldier, with just enough ammunition for Mullane to have to use it sparingly. He put out his hand, but Bingiti ignored it; instead he turned to Ruth.

"If we need you, will you come back and help us?"

Ruth did not look at Mullane. "I'll come back, old man."

"YOU WANT US to move *closer* to King's Cross?"

"If it's possible. We need earlier warning. We have lost contact with Charlie Edward Charlie and Don Robert May."

Mullane sat back, switching off the crackling receiver. CEC and DRM were stations down in Bougainville, in the Solomon Islands. King's Cross was the code name for Rabaul, a major port on the northeast coast of New Britain. Headquarters at Townsville was asking him to move closer to the town, where there could be as many as fifty thousand Japanese in occupation.

"They're out of their flaming heads," said Vokes. "Who do they think we are, the Invisible Man?"

For months Mullane had charted the conquests and aims of the Japanese here in the southwest Pacific. His work in Japan had given him an appreciation of strategy, and it had not been difficult to guess at their intentions. The Solomon Islands—Bougainville, New Georgia, Guadalcanal and more than a dozen others—stretched for some seven hundred miles to the south of New Britain. The chain, if occupied, could be used to throttle the supply line from the United States down to New Guinea and Australia. The Solomons had to be held.

What neither Mullane nor Vokes knew was that a major task force of American ships and marines was on its way to Guadalcanal. The Japanese, already in force on that island, were building an airstrip near a place called Lunga. The airstrip was to become the keystone of the defences of whichever side held the island. In the next twenty-four hours the American invasion was to succeed; but that would be only the beginning of the Guadalcanal campaign, one of the most bitter of the Pacific war. Within hours of the American landing, the Japanese would be regrouping for a major counterattack. The base for the counterattack, for its planning, its supplies, the marshalling of its ships and troops, its squadrons of bombers, would be Rabaul, hundreds of miles from the soon-to-be-besieged Guadalcanal, but only sixty miles or so east of where Mullane and Vokes were now camped.

There had been a rain shower, and water still dripped from the trees. The campsite, a wide ledge backed by a cave, was just a mat of muddy grass. Clouds had come in to obscure the bay, five miles away and below them; up the slope behind them the mountain seemed to have slid down below its cloud cover to threaten them. Mullane had the feeling that their world had suddenly become small and fragile.

"We have to find out first if we're going to be able to move on at all." He looked pensively at the radio. He was one thousand miles from headquarters in Townsville; he could only deal with them by way of the relay station at Port Moresby in New Guinea. Maximum range of the 3BZ radio was four hundred miles on voice and six hundred miles on Morse key, and contact had to be kept to a minimum so that the enemy could not get a bearing on their whereabouts. The conditions were anything but ideal for debate.

"Frank, those boys still aren't enthusiastic," Mullane said, watching the carriers. Some were sitting, others standing; but none was lying down. They were all too tense to rest properly. It had been a fast, backbreaking climb up from Mullane's plantation. Mullane himself had been constantly looking back for the pursuing Japanese. But either Bingiti had convinced the invaders that there had been no Europeans at Kiogo for months, or the Japanese were content to take their time, confident they had Mullane and Vokes trapped. In the meantime the safest course was to move on.

"I'd leave the boys to Buka," said Vokes. "He'll belt them into line."

"That's not going to do it. How much money do you have?"

"About two quid. I paid off all my blokes just before I came across to your place. What about you?"

Mullane shook his head and raindrops fell from the peak of the faded baseball cap he wore. It was one of the few clues to his past that he ever showed in public, but no one, not even Vokes, had ever asked him what the interlocked letters NY stood for. If anyone had ever guessed that the cap was that of a New York Yankee, the fact had never been mentioned.

"I've got about a fiver," he said. "The cheque for my last copra shipment is probably still in the post office at Rabaul. Seven pounds between us. That won't last long. Not if we have to keep some in reserve for further bribery."

"You reckon we're going to have to do much bribing?"

"I think we'll be buying votes like politicians. There's no reason why the natives should show any loyalty to us. And they may find they can live very easily with the Japs."

"Not from what I've heard."

"How would you know?" Mullane said sharply. "You don't know anything about the Japanese."

"How do you know so much, then?"

"I once lived in Japan," he said, giving away more than he had intended, but having to defend the ghost of Mieko and all the decent Japanese he had known.

He got up and went along to the main group. Ruth Riddle, sitting on her medical case, looked at him but said nothing as he passed. She had kept up with the fast pace of their climb, but now she was exhausted.

"How do the boys feel, Buka?" Mullane asked the big man.

Buka looked contemptuously at his fellow workers. "They say they go no farther, Boss. They worried about what happening back at Kiogo."

Mullane walked across to one of the young men. "What's the matter, Mariba?"

The young man looked up from under sullen brows. Normally he would have sprung to his feet when the boss spoke to him, but this afternoon he sat stolidly.

"We go back," he said in pidgin. "This new feller just come, he might be killing our families."

Mullane knew that could be true. "If I send someone to see what's happening, will you stay till he comes back?"

Mariba glanced at the other carriers, then looked up insolently at Mullane. "Maybe."

Suddenly Mullane wanted to boot him. He came of an intolerant family and he had had to learn tolerance, almost as he had learned pidgin and six other languages. Now it seemed he was dropping back to being a natural McArdle. He had discarded his family name when he had come to the islands, taking his mother's maiden name, but he had not been able to discard his family influences.

He started on the first recruiting speech he had ever made. "Listen, Mariba, those men down in Kiogo won't treat you as well as the white man has. You must help us drive them out. I looked after you well, didn't I?"

"You know the boss looked after you!" Buka bellowed, and Mullane waved a restraining hand in his direction.

Mariba shot them a surly look, then moved away to the other natives, and they congealed into a muttering huddle. Only then did Mullane turn towards Ruth Riddle, who had been listening. For the first time she smiled at him. It was a beautiful smile, altering the character of her face; the cautious defiance that spoiled it had disappeared.

Mariba came stalking back. He said, "We go with you, Boss,

405

if two of us can go back to Kiogo to see if our families are safe. If they are, we come back and carry your things for you."

"You and Rama can go. But do not let the Japanese see you."

"One more thing, Boss. We want more pay."

Mullane felt rather than saw Vokes come up beside him. He could also feel Vokes's shock at this new phase of rebellion, and out of the corner of his eye he saw Buka swelling up with temper.

"How much do you want, Mariba?"

Mariba held up two fingers. "Two times what you pay us down on the plantation."

Vokes was incredulous. "Con, I think you've got to jump on these beggars right from the start. Tell 'em where they get off—" He was winding himself up, arms flailing.

Mullane turned back to Mariba. "You'll get double pay, but only at the end of our journey and only if you give me no more trouble."

Mariba was new to rebellion, not sure how far he could go. At last he nodded. "Now Rama and I will go down to Kiogo."

"No." Buka stepped forward. "I go with Rama, Boss."

Mullane was about to say no when he recognized that Buka was trying to tell him something: *Mariba could not be trusted.* He nodded. Buka and Rama, a boy of eighteen, went off immediately. Mullane went back to the radio, followed by Vokes and Ruth.

"How are you going to pay them double, Mr. Mullane?" Ruth asked. "I heard you say how much money you had."

"I'll have to write IOUs."

"Which you may or may not honour, depending on whether you survive. The natives get the dirty end of the stick, don't they?"

"Not while you're around, I'm sure," he said as she walked away. What to do with such a woman? He remembered Mieko, who had been content as a good Japanese wife to accept his decisions.

It was two and a half hours before Buka and Rama came back. "We watch careful, Boss." Buka was exhausted, but he stood at attention. He is the only one of us with enthusiasm for this, Mullane thought. "They treat our families well. Some of our men smile at them," he said with contempt.

"Don't be too harsh on them, Buka. They have to live with the enemy. We don't." He could feel Ruth standing in judgment behind him, but he did not look at her. Instead he glanced at Mariba, who was close by. "Do you come with us now, Mariba?"

"We go with you, Boss. For two times money."

"Okay. You will be paid double when we return to Kiogo."

"When that going to be, Boss?"

"Not long," said Mullane, and turned to Buka. "We move off in ten minutes, as soon as I've spoken to headquarters."

Mullane sat down beside the radio, waited for the hiss that said the set was working. The Port Moresby relay station came in almost immediately, but it seemed to him that he had had to wait several minutes. He was becoming edgy, something foreign to him. "Message to Townsville," he radioed. "We'll move on as ordered."

The answer came, sounding too laconic for his sensitive ear: "Jolly good. Good luck. Keep in touch."

"I could hear them sipping their pink gins as they said that," Vokes said with quiet venom.

Mullane began to repack the radio. All at once he was aching for the opportunity to strike at the Japanese. There was still a debt to be repaid. . . . "Which is the best track for Rabaul?"

CHAPTER TWO

They camped that night on a ridge above a river. The natives made some shelters from huge taro leaves; Mullane and Vokes had their own tents. Mullane, after some ungallant hesitation, approached Ruth. "You may use my tent if you like."

"No, thanks. I've slept out in the open before this."

He didn't argue. "Do you have a mosquito net?"

"Yes. Did you bring your Atabrine with you?" She sounded like a starched hospital matron.

"I have three months' supply," Mullane said. "I think I may be safer from the mosquito's bite than from yours. Have you any antidote for your bite?"

"A little understanding helps. Good night."

There was no door to her taro-leaf shelter, but he felt as though something had been shut in his face.

In the morning he went down to the riverbank to wash. He

had just stripped off his shirt when, farther along, he saw that Ruth, naked above her trousers, was also bathing. She looked up and saw him but made no attempt to cover herself. She picked up a towel and began to dry off. "I came down early, before the boys were awake. The mission where I grew up taught me to be modest. It's a handicap at times."

He decided to be casual. "You really should be more careful of the crocodiles."

"Don't worry, Mr. Mullane. I can take care of myself."

Then he heard the low-flying aircraft. The natives came running out from beneath their shelters and he yelled at them to get back under cover. He dropped down beneath a bush, saw Ruth pull on her shirt and do the same farther along the bank. She lay on her back and it seemed to him even at a distance that she looked relaxed. Or anyway resigned.

The plane, a slow observation aircraft, came over the ridge; it made several circles, then suddenly swung down towards the river. For a moment Mullane thought he had been spotted, but the plane went on to the sea. Mullane and Ruth stood up.

"You reckon he saw us?" Vokes shouted, coming out from cover.

"He could have seen us and not let on," Mullane called back. He walked up the bank and joined Vokes. "We'll have breakfast, then get going. I'll get on the radio to Moresby. We're going to need an airdrop for more supplies."

Port Moresby came in at once. "We'll want a month's food supplies," he told them. He looked at his map, chose a spot and gave the coded coordinates and time for the requested drop. "We'll also want some money. Two hundred pounds, if the war effort can afford it."

"We'll do what we can. We'll have to ask paymaster."

"Tell him I'll send a personal cheque. Over and out."

Half an hour later he led the party down towards the river. Twice they heard planes and they all stopped abruptly, standing like tree stumps among the tall trunks of the trees themselves; but these were fast-moving aircraft and their sound died away almost immediately, leaving Mullane wondering who was going to be bombed or shot up in the next hour or so.

They stopped at the edge of the narrow, swift-flowing river. Lawyer vines and red D'Albertis creeper hung down like frayed fishermen's nets from the trees. On the opposite bank half a dozen herons walked in single file, like first communicants, towards the altar of a fallen tree. The image was Mullane's and he wondered why he should all at once be thinking of the church he had left long ago; maybe he was going to start praying again.

"We'll cross here. Try and find us a safe spot, Buka."

Buka strode into the water without bothering to remove either his shirt or his lap-lap. He was a strong swimmer with no fear of water, but the current caught him at once. He was swept fifty yards downstream before he struggled ashore and came back, shaking water from himself like a huge dog.

"No good, Boss. Better go farther up."

"Wait!" Vokes grabbed Mullane's arm. "There's someone coming down on the other side!"

They were trapped on the few yards of bank between the river and the wall of jungle behind them and there was no time to hide.

The track on the opposite side of the river ran behind a tall screen of wild sugarcane. Mullane could see movement through the tangle of stalks. Then the newcomers came out into the open.

"Stone the crows!" said Vokes. "Where have *they* come from? There's no mission within miles of us."

The small procession halted and looked across at Mullane's party in equal surprise. An elderly priest, in a white cassock and carrying a white umbrella, led the group. Behind him was a nun, in a black habit and coif, and three young native boys, each with a bundle on his head.

"Have you just crossed the river?" Mullane yelled.

The priest gestured upstream. He said something, then turned to the nun. Her shout was even louder than Mullane's. "About a hundred yards up—there are some stones you can't miss!"

Ten minutes later Mullane and the others joined the small mission group on the other side of the river.

"Good morning, sir," said the priest, in a formal manner out of place in the circumstances. He spoke with a heavy German accent. "I am the bishop of Waku, Bishop von Scheer. This is Sister Brigid from the Talio mission, and these three rather weary little boys are Matthew, Mark and Luke."

Mullane introduced himself and Vokes and Ruth. "You've come all the way from Waku?" The town was two hundred miles to the west. "I thought everyone had been evacuated from there."

"The good sister and I decided to stay. We thought the church could be neutral. Then . . ." His soft guttural voice withered away.

"We left before the Japanese got to us," said Sister Brigid; her Irish brogue was as thick as Kerry cream. "His Reverence has some ideas that, begging his forgiveness, he should be forgetting. I've been arguing with him all these months—"

"You've spent months wandering around the island?"

"Glory be to God, no!" It was difficult to tell how old Sister Brigid was, to know whether it was age or the rigours of life in the tropics that had marked her face. She had shrewd, faded blue eyes and a wide mouth that Mullane saw, with growing disquiet, was as mobile as Vokes's. "We found ourselves a nice village back along the coast. We hid every time the Japanese would be coming down, going into the jungle while the bishop would be making up his mind about what's troubling him—"

Mullane had to dam the flood. "Frank, move everyone on. I'd like a word with the bishop."

When the others had moved ahead along the bank he said to Scheer, "Would you care to tell me about those ideas of yours that Sister Brigid spoke of? I have reasons for asking."

"I am debating whether I should return to Germany. I am at the moment an enemy alien. Do you wish to arrest me?"

"I don't think I have any powers of arrest. You're a long way from Germany. How do you propose to return there?"

"God, give me guidance," Scheer said in German.

"Maybe God is like the church," Mullane said, also in German. "Trying to be neutral."

"You speak German well." Then the bishop reverted to English, as if that made him less of an enemy alien. "I am thinking of surrendering to the Japanese in Rabaul. From there I hope they may repatriate me to Germany."

"Are you a Nazi sympathizer, Bishop?"

411

"I know nothing of Nazism other than what I've read. I have not been home for fourteen years."

"How did you get this far east?" asked Mullane as they began moving towards the others.

"We had a small motor launch. But last night it ran aground on a reef at the entrance to this river and sank. I'm afraid we shall have to walk the rest of the way to Rabaul."

"Are you planning to take Sister Brigid and those kids into Rabaul with you?"

"I'm hoping the Japanese will repatriate her, too. The Irish are neutral—or are supposed to be. But one finds it difficult to imagine the Irish being neutral about anything," Scheer added ruefully as they rejoined the party.

"We're heading towards Rabaul, Bishop," said Mullane. "I think you'd better join us."

There was a note in the American's voice that made the German look at him sharply. "That sounded like an order."

"I've just decided I do have the power to arrest you, at least till my headquarters tells me what to do with you."

"Arrest His Reverence! Glory be to God, what will you be doing next?" said Sister Brigid.

"Mr. Vokes and I have a job to do, and we don't want it fouled up by someone who may be more committed to the other side than he thinks he is. Let's get going."

They started walking in single file along the narrow overgrown track beside the river, Ruth behind Mullane. She gazed at his back as he walked ahead of her; he was well made, every inch of him. She was a physical woman who responded to the physical side of men. But she had gone against the grain of her nature because she had not wanted to be thought of as easy. Too many white men took it for granted that all mixed-blood women were easy.

She had never known her father. He had been the skipper of a trading schooner and he had left the islands and gone back to Sydney as soon as he learned he was to become a father. She was six when her mother, half Chinese, half Polynesian, died of blackwater fever. Ruth had been reared by a Methodist missionary couple, who later sent her to Fiji for medical training. She gradu-

412

ated as an NMP, a Native Medical Practitioner; professionally it was as high as anyone of her class could expect to go in the islands.

Intent on her thoughts, she walked straight into Mullane's back as he pulled up sharply, arm in the air.

"Watch it!" His voice was low; he didn't turn around. "Pass the word to be quiet!"

They had come to a fork in the track; one path continued on along the riverbank, the other swung left up a slope. Mullane stood tense, ears strained; he had heard a sound that brought back memories. Then he heard it clearly, a cheerful whistling; he recognized the merry beat of *"Aikoku Koshin Kyoku,"* a Japanese marching tune. He pointed up the left-hand track, waving the rest of the party to hurry on ahead of him. The Europeans stumbled up the track; the natives slipped easily into the bush on either side.

"One of the little kids fell behind. He's still back there!" Vokes said.

Mullane swore softly, then pushed Vokes ahead of him. "Let's hope he has the sense to stay in the bushes. Move!"

He unslung his Thompson gun as he slid down beneath a bush. He had no intention of ambushing the Japanese patrol. That would only provoke a search-and-kill operation by the enemy. The best spies were the unsuspected ones: that had been his guiding principle in Japan.

The patrol came into view less than fifty yards away, five men walking jauntily along the bank, all whistling, sure that they were in safe territory. Then abruptly the leader, a corporal, stopped whistling; the other whistles died away in discord behind him. The patrol halted, guns falling off their shoulders into the firing position. Oh, no, Mullane thought, don't shoot the kid!

The boy (Matthew? Mark? Luke?) came along the bank, bent beneath the weight of his oilcloth-wrapped bundle. He was only fifteen yards from the Japanese before he saw them. He pulled up sharply; the bundle wobbled, then fell from his head. He looked about wildly and Mullane could imagine the whimper of fear that came from the small open mouth.

Sister Brigid stirred, rising on one knee; but Mullane, lying beside her, roughly pulled her down. The patrol had fanned out

413

and two of the soldiers were now at the bottom of the path that came up the slope.

The corporal was interrogating the frightened boy, but Mullane was too far away to hear. All he could see was that the boy was giving no answer. The corporal slapped the boy; it took all Mullane's strength to hold Sister Brigid down. Suddenly one of the soldiers pointed at his feet, then gestured excitedly up the slope. He had seen the boot marks of the Europeans in the mud.

Mullane was out of the bushes on the run, the Thompson held tightly against his ribs. He plunged down the track towards the Japanese, the gun pumping. The two soldiers at the bottom of the slope went down without firing a shot. The corporal and the other two soldiers on the riverbank got off some shots, but they went over Mullane's head. Then his own burst of fire hit them; they fell against each other. And behind them the native boy stared at Mullane, then slowly slumped face forward in the mud.

There was a scream and Sister Brigid, habit flapping, came flying down the track like a huge berserk bird. She grabbed the boy and cradled him to her, moaning—*just like the native woman back at Kiogo,* Mullane thought. Then she looked up at him and he was shocked at the hatred in the face dedicated to charity.

"You murderer!"

Everyone had now come down to the riverbank. Vokes, Ruth and the bishop crowded forward.

"Let me look at him." Ruth had to pry the boy out of Sister Brigid's arms. "Which one is it?"

"It's Matthew." The nun shook her head, the tears coursing down her cheeks. "Murdered!"

Mullane exploded. "I didn't murder him! It was an accident. I had to kill the Japs before they killed us!"

"Why would they have killed us?" the bishop asked quietly.

"Bishop—" Mullane tried to make his own voice as quiet as that of the German. "Mr. Vokes and I are, technically speaking, spies."

"They'd have killed us all right," said Vokes. "They've already done it to a couple of other Coastwatchers."

Sister Brigid stood up. There was no forgiveness in her face as she looked at Mullane.

414

"Sister—" Mullane was just realizing what he had done. For the first time in his life he had killed a man. Five men and a small boy: a massacre. He didn't look down at the bodies, but he would always remember the look on Matthew's face in the moment before the boy died. Suddenly he wanted to weep.

Then Buka stepped forward. "Better move, Boss. What you want me to do with them dead fellers?"

"Tie rocks to them and drop them in the river," said Vokes. "The crocs will take care of them."

There was a gasp from Sister Brigid. Even Mullane was surprised at the callous practicality of the Australian; but what he had suggested was common sense. No evidence must be left that the patrol had been ambushed.

"Do that, Buka. Collect their guns and ammunition first."

But Sister Brigid stood over the corpse of the dead boy. "You're not going to put Matthew in the river like that!"

Mullane looked at the tense, belligerent nun. "Okay, take him up the hill and bury him. He'll have a Christian burial, if that's what's worrying you. Frank, take some of the boys and bury him in the bush, where the Japs can't find the grave. Buka and I will catch up."

Vokes at once marshalled the carriers into line, picked up the dead boy himself and started up the slope. Sister Brigid fell in behind him; Scheer and Ruth were the last to move off.

"You must forgive Sister Brigid," said Scheer. "She has very narrow standards."

"They'll have to broaden if she wants to stay with us." Mullane had to forgive himself for the death of Matthew before he could make concessions to the nun.

"Then I'd appreciate it, Mr. Mullane," said the bishop stiffly, "if you would contact your headquarters and have us evacuated. I should prefer to be interned rather than continue as we are." He snapped open his umbrella, turned around and went stalking up the slope. It seemed to Mullane that under the mud-stained white cassock the feet were moving with a hint of goose step.

Ruth said, "If it's any consolation, I think you did the only thing possible."

Mullane glanced at her in surprise, but had enough grace left to nod his head in thanks.

Buka and the four carriers helping him, one of them Mariba, worked quickly. Rocks were tied to the feet of the dead men and they were rolled into the river, sinking at once beneath the swiftly running water. Suddenly Mullane felt a nostalgia for the land that had given him Mieko, felt sorry for the dead men who would not be returning there. He had killed them, but somehow the killing had not satisfied his need for vengeance.

"What about the guns, Boss?"

Mullane hesitated. He could see Mariba and the carriers eyeing the weapons expectantly, but he could not trust them with fire-arms. He picked up the four grenades that had been taken from the soldiers' belts and shoved them into his pack.

"Keep a rifle for yourself, Buka, and all the ammunition. Throw the rest into the river."

Buka almost danced with delight; he now had all the status he wanted. He scooped up four of the guns, hurled them, one by one, out into the river. Mariba and the other carriers watched him enviously. Then he slung the last rifle over his shoulder.

They walked up the track to a flat spot where the rest of the party was gathered. Vokes came out of the bush with Sister Brigid and two of the carriers, one of the latter carrying a spade.

"Where's the boy buried?"

Mullane followed Vokes into the bush, saw the small mound covered with leaves. And above it a cross made of two twigs tied together. He pulled out the cross and tossed it away.

Behind him Sister Brigid said with quiet savagery, "You promised him a Christian burial!"

"Did you bury him with prayers?"

"The bishop said them."

"Then he's had his Christian burial." Mullane leaned tiredly against a tree. "Sister Brigid, in other circumstances I'd see that Matthew had a proper funeral and a decent grave. I'd pay for a headstone—I owe him that. But I'm afraid that here Matthew has to be buried unmarked. I don't think dead souls come back to see what monuments have been erected to their memory. And I have

416

a lot of live souls I still have to care for. You should be applying yourself to them."

"Don't expect me to pray for yours, Mr. Mullane."

They marched for another hour, climbing away from the river, the coast and the Japanese. At last Mullane called a halt and he and Vokes assembled the radio. So far they had been of no use to the Coastwatching Service; they had reported nothing. Even now he was only making a further request.

He knew he was beyond voice range of Port Moresby; the signal had been weak this morning. He encoded a message for Morse key, then tapped it out: "Have German bishop Irish nun local medical girl. Wish evacuation urgentest. Advise."

The reply came in: "No ship or aircraft immediately available. Suggest you co-opt guests. Other rendezvous as arranged."

"Co-opt our guests! What do they think we're doing here, holding a prayer meeting?" Vokes bounced up and down.

"Well, we're stuck with them for a while. But at least the supply drop is on."

Mullane leaned back against the tree beneath which he sat. He was still a civilian and Vokes had the service rank; but Vokes hadn't mentioned it again and seemed content to let him assume all the responsibility. Mullane had, in effect, been preparing for this war for years, far longer than any of those with him, and now he was unprepared for what was being asked of him.

How the hell did I get here? he asked himself.

IT HAD BEEN a long roundabout journey, begun in the big house on East Avenue in Rochester, New York. That had been another age, another world. Women wore shirtwaisters and straw boaters in summer; automobiles were beginning to take over from horses and the McArdle family owned a Peerless.

In 1921 Con had gone to Yale planning to study law; it had been taken for granted that he would eventually go into the family law firm. But he had lost interest in legal technicalities and started to learn languages, finding that he had an almost perfect ear and the ability to think in any language he took up. He also found that he was a better baseball pitcher than anyone else in

Ivy League competition. When he told his parents on graduation day that he was going to accept an offer from the New York Yankees, his mother had fainted and his father had looked as if he were about to have a stroke.

He had gone to Japan for the first time in 1934 with the Exhibition All Stars. . . .

"Con! Aircraft!"

He sat up, coming back to the present. A dark ragged cloud of planes was moving across the sky. He grabbed his binoculars. "Get on the radio! I'll give you the number in a moment."

Vokes sent it out in Morse: "42 bombers heading south." Acknowledgment came in from Port Moresby at once. The message would now go through its relay; Vokes's warning would start a chain reaction. Somewhere down south the US Navy ships and planes would start preparing for the Japanese bombers.

"What do you do now?" asked Ruth.

"Wait and count them again when they come back. Then we let headquarters know how many are missing."

"The profit and loss of war," said Scheer. "It is so simple when one has to count only airplanes. I remember . . ." The quiet voice trailed off. The bishop's thoughts and voice did not seem able to keep pace with each other. Mullane wondered how inconclusive his sermons were. Scheer had the look and sound of a man who no longer had any confidence in his own evangelism.

Mullane pressed him. "You remember what?"

Scheer, beneath his white umbrella, blinked—against the sun or against a too bright memory?

"I was at Verdun in the last war. I've read since that a million men died there. How does one count so many dead?"

Vokes stood up, looking uncomfortable. Talk of the dead disturbed him. "I think we better get going, Con."

But when Mullane went to sign off, Moresby held him, relaying a message from Townsville: "Imperative you move into King's Cross area. Detailed information troopships urgently needed."

Mullane sat back on his haunches. He and Vokes were alone now; the others had moved away.

"I think things are going to get much tougher, Frank. I think only one of us should go into Rabaul. You can take Ruth and the others down to the coast and wait for a sub to come in."

"No." Vokes shook his head stubbornly.

"Frank, you said yourself we can't dump Ruth—"

"I don't care about her and the others."

Mullane knew that was untrue, but he wondered at the bitterness in Vokes's voice. "What's eating you?"

Vokes said, "My old man fought in the last war. He wouldn't talk to me because I didn't join up when this war first broke out. In the last letter I had, just before the Nips took Rabaul, he asked me how long I was going to keep running away."

"Frank, how is he going to know what you're doing up here?"

"I'll tell him myself at the end of the war. If you go into Rabaul, I'm going with you."

They started off again, still climbing. At the first bend in the track the bishop approached Mullane. "Did you mention to your headquarters my request to surrender?" he asked.

"They don't want you to yet, Bishop."

Scheer looked up the track that wound through the thick rain forest. The mountains lay ahead of them like barricades. "If I refused to move on, just lay down to die, would that be suicide?"

Mullane smiled. "All I ask you to do is stay alive and not be a pain in the neck to me."

"I'll pray for the strength," said the bishop.

Five hours later they were on another tree-clad ridge. There was a stillness to the jungle-covered hills that made Mullane feel ill at ease. In his younger days he had gone shooting in the Maine woods once the ball season was finished; there among the birch, spruce and pines he had unwound. But not here, in these tree-tangled hills.

Everyone, including the carriers, was exhausted by the long climb. Mullane allowed a fifteen-minute rest, then set them to work building the observation post. He had kept the party on the march till they found this spot. It was on a narrow ridge that ended in a sheer cliff. The view was magnificent; they could see ten miles of coastline in either direction. If he and Vokes got out of Rabaul alive, this would be an ideal haven to return to.

He was giving orders as to what he wanted done when he stopped in midsentence, listened and raised his binoculars. He found the returning bombers with his first scanning.

"How many?" said Vokes beside him.

"Thirty-eight. That means they lost only four," he said, disappointed. "I'll set up the radio. And I'll ask if the drop is still on for tomorrow night."

"Are we far from the drop zone?"

Mullane took out a map. The maps they had were based on old German charts and they were more guesswork than proper surveys. He had given headquarters some coordinates, but they were no more than a rough guide. "It's somewhere up beyond that rock outcrop. We can light our guide fire behind those trees and maybe they won't see it down on the coast."

By late afternoon the camp was complete. Two natives had been sent out foraging and returned with the news that they had found an abandoned garden where there were yams and taro roots. It had been a surprise to Mullane, when he had first arrived on the island, to find that the jungle provided very little in the way of food. Game was scarce and edible plants were so few that even the natives relied on cultivated food.

Mullane hoped fervently that tomorrow night's plane would have no trouble finding the drop zone.

IN THE TOWNSVILLE headquarters of the Coastwatchers, Roger Blomfield stared at the map of New Britain tacked on the wall. His office was papered with maps freckled with coloured pins, and he felt some guilt that men whose lives were in constant danger should be represented by no more than a pin with a coloured head.

Lieutenant Commander David Lowell appeared in the doorway. "Anything new on Mullane and Vokes?"

Blomfield gestured at a copy of Mullane's message. "They've got company. A German bishop, a nun and some local girl, a medic."

Lowell came into the office and sat down heavily. He was the US Navy liaison officer with the Coastwatchers. "That complicates things. Does AIB know?"

AIB was Allied Intelligence Bureau, a General Headquarters

420

group that was only a few months old and still feeling its way.

"They wouldn't be interested. All they want is for Mullane and Vokes to walk into Rabaul, pinch the Japs' order of battle and walk out. It must sound easy to them," Blomfield said.

"What's aerial reconnaissance been showing?"

"Joe Parnell up on New Ireland reported a week ago that there was some ship movement at night, but he couldn't be precise on how much. We haven't heard from him since."

"How long before you take *his* pin down?"

"We give them two weeks." Blomfield opened a drawer in his desk, took out an old tobacco tin. Five pins rattled loosely in it. "Those are blokes we've lost contact with. Charlie Helidon, for instance. We haven't heard from him for over three months."

Lowell sucked on an empty pipe. "Let's hope you don't have to take down Mullane's and Vokes's pins. In the meantime, what are you going to do about those people they're stuck with?"

"I'm hoping you can dig up a spare sub to bring them out."

"Fat chance. I couldn't even get you a sub to go in and bring out Mullane and Vokes."

Blomfield put the tin of pins back in his desk, slammed the drawer shut. "I wonder what it's like to lose a war."

THE NEXT DAY seemed interminable to Mullane and he found himself unable to relax. Finally, at five o'clock, he went on the air. Port Moresby confirmed that the supply drop would take place, then tapped out a long message. Vokes decoded it, then sat back and looked at Mullane. "They're still on our backs about Rabaul."

For the moment Ruth and the others, who had congregated around to listen, might not have been there; Mullane saw only himself and Vokes and the carriers they would need to take with them. It was Ruth who intruded.

"What do they want you to do?"

"Go right into Rabaul, inside the Jap perimeter, and come back with a report of what's going on there. Something big is happening, but they're not quite sure what."

"Can't you send a couple of the boys?" Sister Brigid was unable to stay out of any conversation within her hearing. "They wouldn't be noticed."

"How would a boy know what's going on?" said Vokes. "He wouldn't know one sort of plane or ship from another. He can't count beyond ten. What would he come back with? Lots of machines that fly, lots of big canoes, lots of men. We could make up that sort of useless information without going near Rabaul."

The bishop said quietly, "I take it, Mr. Mullane, that you *are* going in?"

Mullane glanced at Vokes, saw no hesitation, and nodded.

"Then what happens to us?"

"If they don't send a submarine in the next day or two, I'm afraid we're going to have to leave all of you."

"You'll just abandon us?" said Sister Brigid.

"I didn't say that. We'll make some provision for you." Mullane wished he sounded more convincing.

Sister Brigid abruptly walked away. "I'll be getting supper."

"You should treat her more gently," said Ruth. Then she, too, went off, leaving Mullane feeling that he had been cruel.

"The last six months have not been kind to Sister Brigid," Scheer said. "I think she is at the end of her strength. Spiritually as well as physically. One doubts God's goodness at times."

Leaving Vokes to close up the radio, Mullane and Scheer walked out to the ledge of rock that formed the lip of the cliff. The sun had gone down behind the mountains; sun-shot clouds flared up like the tail of some golden bird of paradise.

"So the generals want you to take more risks." Scheer took out a pipe, began to fill it from a leather pouch. "You don't smoke?"

Mullane shook his head. Then abruptly he turned, walked quickly to his hut and came back with a bottle of whisky and two mugs. He held up the bottle and the bishop nodded.

"Splendid stuff. My father's favourite drink." Scheer raised his mug in salute, then said, "My father was a general."

Mullane recognized that the German was feeling a need to talk. "If he is still alive, he must be pleased with the way things have gone," he said in German.

Scheer was grateful for the use of his own language. "He died in the year Herr Hitler became Chancellor. Perhaps it was just as well. Like all generals, my father had no respect for politicians."

"What did he say when you lost the last war?"

"Oh, he would never admit that the generals lost. They were stabbed in the back by the rest of the country. Your generals will say the same when you lose this war."

"You think we're going to lose?" Mullane suddenly resented the German's arrogance.

But Scheer was not arrogant; he had left all that at home years ago. "Mr. Mullane," he said in English, "the war is almost three years old. We Germans and the Japanese have been preparing for it for years. Your side is still not prepared."

True, thought Mullane, but could not admit it. He wondered what the generals thought, sitting before their maps in Australia.

Darkness fell an hour later and the supply plane, a Hudson bomber, came two hours later, on time. Mullane, Vokes and all the carriers had been up in the drop zone for an hour.

"Light the fire!" Mullane called when he heard the plane.

The heap of firewood, soaked with precious paraffin from their meagre supply, burst into flame at once. And at that moment it started to rain in a deluge. The fire began to sputter and die; Mullane could no longer hear the plane. He yelled at Vokes for another can of paraffin.

Vokes came running, can in hand. Then he stumbled over a protruding root and the opened can shot out of his hand, spilling the paraffin. Mullane rushed forward, picked up the can and ran towards the dying fire. There was still some fuel left. He upended the can and the tiny flickering flames flared up. He yelled for more wood. The type of aircraft that flew slowly enough to make these supply drops was not always available; it could be a week or even a month before another trip could be arranged.

Just as abruptly as it had started, the rain stopped. The flames of the struggling fire crackled weakly, then blazed again, lighting the clearing. Mullane heard the plane coming back, engines growing louder. "Run!" he shouted. "Get under the trees!"

If the plane crew started dropping supplies, there was no way he and the others could see them tumbling through the low clouds.

A bag of rice or sugar falling on one's head from several hundred feet was just as lethal as any bomb.

Vokes was last under the trees and the first sack landed almost at his heels. Four more bags came crashing down before the Hudson roared up and away, the pilot climbing steeply to avoid running into the mountain.

"Stay where you are!" Mullane shouted. "There's more to come!"

The plane came twice more, sending sacks hurtling down out of the darkness into the trees and, once, into the drop zone. Then it came back for what Mullane guessed must be its final run. The plane roared overhead and out of the clouds five parachutes appeared, looking like giant pink puffballs in the glow of the fire. Four of the parachutes held food containers; the fifth carried a leather gladstone bag. It floated gently across the drop zone and straight into the fire. The bag burst open at once and pieces of paper sprayed out, caught fire and added to the blaze.

By the time Mullane realized what had been in the bag, the money, all two hundred pounds of it, was ashes.

CHAPTER THREE

It took them four hours to bring everything down to the camp. It had not been easy working in the darkness, carting the crates through the heavy brush. But Mullane had wanted everything cleaned up before daylight. The fire at the drop zone had been put out, earth and leafy branches strewn over it. The few trees that had been chopped down had been dragged into the jungle and their stumps smeared with mud to make them look like old rotting trunks. It was a rough camouflage, but Mullane hoped that from the air the zone would look like an abandoned native garden. He might need to use it again.

Now it was seven o'clock on a morning clear and shining as new glass. Mullane and Vokes sat down in front of the radio. It began to hum and crackle as it warmed up. A scramble of voices came and went as if they were being pumped through bellows; they were American voices, probably pilots talking to their aircraft carriers. They would be somewhere north of the Solomons,

424

part of the defence force that wanted to know what major threat there was for them in Rabaul.

Mullane's first message to Port Moresby reported the safe drop of the supplies but mentioned the fate of the money. The reply was quick: "Bad luck about money. Go over to Champion."

"I haven't had any practice on that one," said Vokes, taking out a code book. Playfair was the normal code used by the Coast-watchers: easy to send and to receive, it was also easy to break. But Champion was a new and much more difficult code.

The message, when finally decoded, was emphatic: "Suspect major activity soon regarding Guadalcanal. Urgent you deliver troop information on Rabaul within 48 hours."

Mullane coded a message, handed it to Vokes: "Will need money first. Carriers restless. Advise availability."

Vokes grinned. "That'll upset them."

But someone must have anticipated them; the answer came back immediately: "600 pounds in safe half mile upriver from Noku plantation. In bush east bank. Leave chit in safe." Noku was another Burns Philp holding, several miles up the coast.

"Funny buggers," said Vokes. "Leave chit in safe!"

"In bush on east bank—we could spend hours looking for it! And Noku's probably occupied by the Japs now."

Mullane looked out across the green spill of jungle to the placid sea. Sunlight played on the small waves. The party was compara-tively safe here. He felt a strong temptation to stay put. But he said, "Okay, we'll start off tomorrow for Rabaul. First we've got to get that money down at Noku, though; otherwise the boys are going to walk off. Would that safe be a combination job?"

"No, it's probably an old-fashioned key job. The manager at Noku might still have it. It used to be Jack Kayser, but he had to get out. A Chinese, Lee Chin, is running the place now."

"Whose side would he be on?"

Vokes shrugged. "Anyone's. He was born on the island. He'd be like the natives, I guess. Go with the winning side. What do we do—go right into Noku and ask him for that key?"

Mullane smiled. "I think that's exactly what we'll have to do. I may as well get started now."

Vokes said, "I think I'd better go, Con."

"No, you're the senior man. You stay here and run the post."

"Bull." Vokes grinned. "Let's toss."

Mullane took a silver dollar out of his wallet. "My lucky coin. Heads I go, tails you go."

But it had not been his lucky coin last time he'd tossed it.

"I KNOW WE'RE asking a lot," his brother Liam had said. "But you could be in a better position than our own men in the embassy in Tokyo."

They were in Liam's office in the navy building in Washington. Mullane still had his old identity: Cornelius McArdle. It was January of 1936. He had played his last baseball season with the Yankees and had signed up to coach the Tokyo Athletics, where he was due to report March 1.

He had been surprised when his brother had called and asked him to come down to Washington. He had been even more surprised when Liam had told him why. "You want me to *spy?*" Con had said.

"I haven't used that word, old chap." Liam had always been something of a stuffed shirt. "Intelligence is what we're after and our problem is Japan. The President is worried about how things are going over there. The Japanese walked out of the naval conference in London last week when we suggested a five-five-three ratio in naval power for Britain, us and them. They're going to build up their navy. We need to find out what sort of ships they're planning, what training they are giving their personnel."

"But why ask me? An amateur."

"Because the professionals, our attachés at the embassy, are watched day and night by the *kempei*, the Jap secret police. They won't be watching you, a baseball hero."

"You're asking an awful lot, Liam. I don't think I've ever given a thought to *My country, 'tis of thee. . . .*"

"It's time you did." There was real concern in Liam's face. "Some of us in this town feel that the way Japan is going, we'll be at war with her eventually. And we should be prepared."

"I wouldn't know what to look for."

426

"Our intelligence men will give you a crash course."

"How long do I have to make up my mind?"

"Until tomorrow." Liam smiled at Con's look of amazement. "Come on, let's go home."

Next morning Liam came into the guest room of the large house he rented in Georgetown. "Well, old chap?"

Con was sitting up in bed tossing a silver dollar. "Babe Ruth gave me this. Said it was his lucky coin. I found out later he had dozens of them." He spun the coin idly. "Tell you what. I'll toss you for it. Heads I work for you in Japan, tails I don't."

"It's a hell of a way to decide to serve your country."

"Well, that's the way it's going to be, Liam. I don't know what they do to spies in peacetime. They may chop off my head, slap me into gaol, or just kick me out of the country."

He spun the coin, caught it, slapped it on his wrist, looked at it ruefully. "Heads. Maybe it's not lucky any more."

VOKES SAID, "Well, what is it? Heads or tails?"

"Heads," said Mullane. "I go."

Then Buka came running up, panting, to where the two Coast-watchers still sat before the radio. "Boss—Japs down on track!"

"They must have heard the plane last night!"

Mullane grabbed his Thompson gun and followed Buka along the ridge to the main track. When they reached it Buka turned east, then pulled up abruptly on a narrow ledge. The trees here thinned out, giving way to a tumble of huge limestone rocks that must have slid down the mountain centuries ago.

Buka pointed. "There, Boss. I come along here look for gardens, maybe. Then I hear dogs barking—"

"Dogs?" Then Mullane heard the barking and a chill ran through him. There was something terrifying about being hunted by dogs.

"They coming up here, Boss. How we going to stop them?"

Mullane could catch only occasional glimpses of the Japanese as they moved up the jungle track from the river. Once they came out into the open and he made a quick count: there were at least twenty. Too many for just three guns to ambush. And they would be up on this ridge in less than half an hour at the rate they were moving. He leaned back against the boulder behind him; his heels slipped in the mud and he sat down with a thump. Buka started to help him up, but Mullane waved him away. He looked in under the boulder, then scrambled to his feet.

"Get back to camp—quick! Bring the shovels and some of the boys. Tell Boss Vokes to get packed—we're moving on!"

Mullane began to move among the boulders, picking out the ones which would be easiest to shift. Buka and two of the carriers were back in a few minutes and Mullane at once pointed to two of the largest rocks, one behind the other.

The two natives looked puzzled; then Buka thumped one of them across the shoulders with the barrel of his rifle. They began digging furiously into the muddy soil on the downward side of the lower boulder. Once or twice they looked up anxiously at the huge mass looming over them, but Buka kept them at their task. Then Mullane set them to digging beneath the higher rock.

Vokes came running along the track. "We're ready to go, Con."

"Bring everyone up, but keep them out of the way. I'll need another half dozen boys with axes."

Vokes ran back towards the camp. And from down the steep slope of the narrow valley there came shouts as the Japanese caught sight of Mullane.

He dropped to one knee, making a smaller target of himself in case they started shooting. The baying of dogs increased and the Japanese began to run up the track. In another five minutes they would be beyond the line through which the boulders would fall.

Vokes and half a dozen of the carriers, all with axes or machetes, were back in a minute. Mullane set them to work chopping down thick poles. When the first batch were cut and ready he yelled for them to be shoved under the upper boulder.

"Heave!"

Four of the natives lifted their shoulders to the poles. Muscles straining, they pushed against the huge boulder. It teetered on its base, then settled back. Vokes swore at the natives, jumping in among them with a pole of his own.

Mullane saw the odds going against his party. He dropped his gun, picked up a spade and started furiously shovelling mud away from beneath the boulder. Then a chip flew off the rock beside him. A moment later another bullet slapped into the mud beside him, and another and another.

"Look out, Con!" Vokes's yell of warning was more a scream.

Mullane slipped in the treacherous mud, fell on his back, looked up and saw the huge mass of rock begin to totter. He heard the whine of a ricocheting bullet; knew he was going to be either shot or crushed to death. Desperately he tried to crawl away. Then a big brown hand reached out, grabbed him by the back of his shirt; Buka hauled him to safety as the boulder rolled past within inches of his legs. It hit the huge boulder in front of it. The two massive rocks, each weighing several tons, fell over the tip of the ridge and went crashing down the slope.

Mullane, still lying in the mud, trembling from his narrow escape, looked over the rim of the ledge. The effect he had hoped for was happening. The boulders had hit two of the largest trees, hundred-and-fifty-foot *erimas*, snapping them off close to their bases. A chain reaction started at once. A huge green surf of trees and undergrowth began to cascade down the steep slope. The Japanese suddenly stopped, then started to run—straight down the path of the avalanche. Terrible in its unstoppable fury, it swept over the target point Mullane had marked, taking everything with it: trees, dogs, the Japanese. There was a flash of bright splinters of light as it hit the river, and then silence.

Mullane hauled himself to his feet. He nodded to Buka. "Thanks, Buka. You saved my life."

The big man showed a flash of teeth. "Not want to see you squashed flat, Boss. You be no use that way."

The rest of the party had now come up the track. Ruth said, "What about all those supplies? Do we have to leave them?"

"I'm afraid so. How much did you manage to get packed?"

"Not much. The boys hid most of it in the bush. I brought this." She handed him his remaining bottle of whisky.

He took it, decided a nip would do him good and had one. "Thank you, Miss Riddle. You're an understanding woman."

Sister Brigid had gone to the rim of the ledge, looked over and then blessed herself. Now she turned back and made a conscious effort to sound businesslike. "You need so many boys to carry your radio and that engine. If you are going to abandon us, why not leave us here with the supplies? At least we shouldn't starve."

"More Japs will be up here in a day at the outside. I'm not *abandoning* you to them. We'll leave you in a safer place."

Sister Brigid picked up her skirts and went off down the track. She could feel herself at the end of her tether. Prayer was all she had left to sustain her and lately she had, to her horror, begun to wonder at the efficacy of it.

The party moved off until Vokes, who was leading, called an abrupt halt. The line shrank, everyone bumping into the man in front of him. One native fell over and his companions laughed at him. It struck Mullane that there was less tension among the natives than among the whites. They were still not fully committed; they could walk off at any moment. His sudden fear was confirmed as soon as he reached Vokes to find out why he had stopped. "It's Mariba, Con. He's dumped his load and wants to know when they're going to be paid."

Mariba stood sullenly beside his pack, which contained part of the radio. Mullane said to him in pidgin, "I told you you'd get your pay at the end of the journey."

"We want it now, Boss. No pay, we finish, go home."

Behind the defiant native Mullane could see the growing rebellion in the other dark faces. Mariba seemed to have most of the natives on his side.

Mullane sighed. "All right, Mariba. You will be paid tomorrow."

"Where you get the money, Boss?"

"I'll get the money tonight." Mullane wondered what would happen to Vokes and the others if he did not return from Noku.

THEY TREKKED for another four hours. Mariba and his fellow unionists, as Vokes called them, had had a short conference and decided to continue. But they left no doubt that if they were not paid tomorrow, they would turn around and go back to Kiogo.

For the last three hours the party walked through a thin grey mist that chilled everyone as soon as they halted. At last they came

to a ridge above another river. Mullane could hear the roar of a waterfall.

"That *should* be the Noku River, but I'm not sure. I'll follow it down to the coast and hope I come to Noku. We'll camp here."

"How far do you reckon we are from Rabaul?" Vokes asked.

Mullane consulted his map. "If this is correct, about fifty miles. But we're not going to get in there and out again in forty-eight hours. I still have to get that money and find a place where we can leave Miss Riddle and the others."

The camp was set up. The mist thickened and the air was like a cold damp rag against the cheek. The bishop sat huddled in his cassock, and Sister Brigid, looking like a waterlogged crow, sat beneath a leaf shelter with Luke and Mark.

Ruth was doling out food to the cook-boy, having taken charge of the rations. "I'm putting a bit extra in the pot."

"Can we spare it?" Mullane pushed back the peak of his baseball cap and looked at her.

"Everyone's pretty cold and down-in-the-mouth. And I think it might have a soothing effect on your rebels. There's a lot of truth in that saying about the way to a man's heart."

In the late afternoon it began to rain steadily. No one was in the mood for talk and there was no sound but the drum-drum of rain on the tents, the shelters and the soupy mud.

Then they heard the plane. It was somewhere immediately above them, flying low but invisible in the thick clouds. It flew over the camp, engines roaring; then the engines took on a louder, more desperate note as the pilot gunned them. The sound rose to a crescendo; the sudden booming crash was an unexpected climax.

Vokes said, "He went down pretty close—"

The camp had come alive with the sound of the crash. Everyone ran out from under his shelter and stood listening.

"That was a Japanese plane, wasn't it?" said the bishop.

"Probably one of their bombers trying to find its way home. Frank and I will take a look when the rain lifts," Mullane said.

"There may be some injured." Sister Brigid spoke directly to Mullane. "Miss Riddle and I had better come with you. The bishop, too. He was a doctor once, you know."

Mullane looked hard at Scheer. "You didn't tell me that."

"There was no reason to. I gave it all up when I joined the church. I am too out of practice to be of any use to you."

Mullane said to the group, "None of you will come with us. If there are any survivors, there could be some shooting."

As soon as the rain stopped, Mullane and Vokes set off up the mountain towards where they thought the crash had occurred, taking with them three of the natives. The little party climbed for almost an hour but covered less than a mile in the thick undergrowth. Then Vokes, in the lead, gave a yell.

Below them, in a dip, the trees had been snapped off; jagged yellow stumps stuck out of the mud. A twisted mass of metal, hardly recognizable as a plane, had plunged into the mountain.

"It's a Kawanishi—a flying boat," said Vokes. "Let's see who was aboard."

There was no sign of any movement in or around the plane. They slid down the side of the dip and Mullane peered through the gathering gloom into the wreckage. He saw the four broken bodies (or what had been bodies) wrapped in the tangle of metal. Through the wreckage he glimpsed Vokes on the other side.

"Four dead. You found any more?"

"I've got one here in the mud. A live one."

Mullane scrambled up to where Vokes stood. Lying with one arm trapped under some wreckage, the other lying awkwardly and uselessly beside him, was a Japanese. He stared at Mullane and Vokes, moved his body desperately, but could not grasp the pistol in his holster. He lay back and waited.

"We might as well put him out of his misery," said Vokes.

"I think we'd do better to keep him alive," said Mullane. "He outranks even you, Frank. He's a lieutenant general."

CHAPTER FOUR

Mullane took the pistol from the holster. Then he said in Japanese, "I want your name, rank and number, sir."

There was the faintest flicker of surprise in the eyes of General Nara Kijomi at being addressed in his own language. He moved, felt an agonizing pain in his shattered arm, but did his best to keep his face expressionless. "I do not answer to civilians."

"My friend here is a navy officer."

"He has no uniform. I refuse to recognize him."

Mullane searched in the Japanese's pockets and straightened up with some papers in his hand.

"Meet Lieutenant General Nara, Frank."

"What are we going to do with him?"

As they stood in the last silver-green light of day, the rain began to fall again, promising a chill night. "We'd never get him down the mountain in the dark. Tell the boys to put up some sort of shelter. I'll try and pull him out from under this mess."

General Nara watched the American take the gold watch from his broken and bloody wrist. Mullane smiled and slipped the watch into the Japanese's pocket. "I'm not a looter, General."

Nara was not grateful for the care with which Mullane extricated him from the wreckage and put him in an improvised shelter. He wished he were dead; he knew he was dead anyway in the eyes of those back in Tokyo. He would have blown his brains out an hour ago if he had been able to reach his pistol. Now he saw nothing but ignominy ahead of him.

After a while the injured Japanese dropped off into a troubled sleep. Mullane sat beside him in the shelter. He himself slept only fitfully. Leeches came up out of the mud, and three times he had to light matches and burn them off his body.

At first light the carriers made a rough stretcher for the now unconscious Nara. The descent was so steep that they had to bind him to the stretcher with vines. When they finally reached the camp the bearers looked almost as exhausted as the general.

"He's all yours," Mullane said to Sister Brigid. "I want him kept alive. If he comes around, don't put a knife or anything like that near him. He'll commit suicide at the first opportunity."

While Mullane was eating his breakfast of rice and powdered milk, Ruth came up and squatted beside him, native fashion.

"You'd better let me clean up those scratches of yours."

He hesitated, then peeled off his shirt. She began to dab at the small wounds. He was aware of her closeness, of the smell of a

434

woman, something he had almost forgotten and which she was bringing back with disturbing regularity. She, too, was very aware of him, but she had something more immediately important on her mind.

"That Jap's arm is in a bad way. The bishop and I have been arguing about it. I think it should come off."

"Do you have the equipment? Any sort of anaesthetic?"

"A small bottle of ether, that's all. It might not be enough if the operation proved a long one."

He stood up, pulled on his shirt. He felt stiff and weary, in spirit as much as body. "It's your decision and the bishop's," he said. "Just keep the general alive until I can get him off my hands."

Ruth gazed at him, wondering what made him tick. Frank Vokes's dedication to the war seemed simple: he just wanted to be on the winning side. But something else was firing this American. It seemed that he *wanted* to go into Rabaul, that he had to throw himself against as many Japanese as he could find.

"If you have to wait to have him taken off the island, what happens about you going into Rabaul?"

"It will have to be delayed, I guess."

"Good," she said, and went off.

He was surprised at the hint of concern in her voice. But he could not let himself think of that.

The morning was fine. At the mouth of the river a plantation was clearly visible. They were in sight of Noku. But he knew they could not stay here. Within hours patrols would be combing the area for the downed plane. He ordered everything packed for immediate moving. But first he had to report their catch.

While Vokes set up the radio Mullane worked on coding the message. He used the Champion code, but he did not use Nara's name or rank. "The Japs might have cracked the code," he said to Vokes, "in which case they'd know he's still alive and we have him. What's an alternative to lieutenant general that they'd understand down in Townsville?"

"How about top jockey? Do they have horse racing in Japan?"

"Not much at all, as far as I can remember."

So the message went out that they were entertaining a top

jockey from another racecourse, who might be able to give some hints on current track form. The reply came back and it seemed to Mullane that the Morse key at the other end was stuttering with disbelief: "Hope we understand you correctly. Visiting jockey most welcome. When pick him up?"

They had not been able to promise any evacuation means for Ruth and the others; a Japanese general was another matter. But it did mean he could send the other three and Mark and Luke off with Nara.

"Con," said Vokes, staring down towards the coast, "I think we're going to have visitors before we can get rid of the general."

Mullane picked up his binoculars. A light destroyer had appeared around the eastern point of the shallow bay; two patrol boats and three landing barges followed it. While he was still looking at the small flotilla he heard the drone of aircraft. Automatically he yelled for everyone to take cover; then he looked up and saw two slow-flying scout planes and another Kawanishi flying boat come over the mountain and start cruising low.

It was only a short time before the crashed aircraft was discovered. Through his glasses Mullane saw one of the scout planes come speeding from the mountain to the coast. It flew out towards the destroyer, waggled its wings, then headed back through the gorge and straight up the mountain, where the flying boat and the other plane were circling above the wreck. Mullane could imagine some officer on the destroyer taking a bearing on the scout plane's line of flight.

Down at Noku the landing barges were already nosing into the beach; it was impossible to count the soldiers scrambling ashore, but there must have been a hundred and fifty of them.

Mullane moved cautiously back to the rest of the party. "We're going to sit tight and hope the Japs don't come near us. It means no moving around, maybe for a few hours."

"Boss?" Mariba didn't stand up. "When we going to be paid? It's tomorrow now. You promised."

Confound it, he's testing my patience more than the Japs. "I have to go and get the money, Mariba. I can't do that till the Japanese have gone."

Mariba looked up at him, then turned insolently to his fellow carriers. Mullane heard a growl behind him and looked around. Buka, eyes wild with anger, was ready to jump on the rebel.

"We wait," Mariba said at last.

You bet you will. Mullane knew now that Mariba and those siding with him were not yet ready to join the Japanese.

He moved past Buka and looked down at the man who could be the top Japanese on the island. "How are you feeling, General?"

Nara, exhausted by pain and loss of blood, made no reply. He wished they would leave him alone to die. He had been on his way to Rabaul to take command of the force that was to land in the Solomons within the week. Even if he were rescued today, he would be in no state to take command. The war was over for him and life itself might as well be finished.

Mullane went back to join Vokes, who was watching the river mouth. "They're coming up on the other side of the river, Con. What happens when they find his nibs isn't up in that wreck? They're going to spread out all over this mountain like a rash."

Mullane, scanning the gorge, said, "There's a track goes up from the river on the other side. It's under cover most of the way. Those scout planes could miss it. Get everybody ready to move. We'll go down in small groups, no more than four at a time. Take two of the strongest boys to carry the general's stretcher."

"Where are we heading for?"

"I don't know—just somewhere the other side of the river. I'll find us a place to ford. When we cross the Japs' tracks on the other side everyone has to take his boots off, the women included. Then get Buka and the boys to cover our tracks."

It took half an hour of slipping, sliding descent to reach the level of the river. Once there, they had to cross the river gorge by way of a rough vine bridge, each end tied to a large tree. A waterfall, a tumbling white column that never left the perpendicular, fell straight down a cliff only a few yards from the bridge. The rope span trembled in a shimmering mist of spray, looking as insubstantial as the strands of a spiderweb. There was no other way across the river and it had to be risked.

Twenty minutes were lost getting everyone across. The roar

of the waterfall ruled out conversation; Mullane could only tell them what he had in mind by gestures. Vokes and one of the carriers were the last to come, the engine for recharging the radio batteries slung on poles between them. Mullane watched anxiously as the two men appeared out of the mist.

No more than fifteen feet from the end, Vokes missed his footing. On the swaying bridge he and the carrier could get no purchase against the heavy weight; they were forced to drop the engine in order to save themselves. As it fell into the water below, Mullane felt a sickening loss, knew their position had become even more desperate. Without the engine to recharge the batteries they would soon be out of touch with Port Moresby and Townsville.

Vokes and the carrier groped their way along the rope bridge to the other side, stood bent over in attitudes of utter dejection as they gasped for breath. Then slowly they climbed to the rest of the group and the party moved on.

The path away from the river led along the gorge, then began to drop. Soon it became a narrow aisle that wound beneath a thick overhang of trees. Despite the urgency of their position, the party could only move slowly along the narrow track. It was after midday before Mullane called a halt. They were getting into swamp country. Everyone's legs were covered with leeches; the only one who had escaped was General Nara, high and safe on his stretcher. Mullane, passing around two boxes of matches, ordered everyone to cleanse himself of the leeches by burning them off.

"Then we'll see about food. No fires, so it'll have to be something cold. You dole it out, Miss Riddle. Where are you going, Sister Brigid?"

The nun, her face strained, gave him a look full of resentment. "I am going into the bushes, Mr. Mullane. There are leeches on my legs. I will not expose them to anyone's gaze."

Mullane recognized the despair in the nun's voice, realized with a sense of shock that she was on the verge of tears. He did his best to sound kindly. "Take your time, Sister."

She looked at him in surprise, then turned and crept into the bushes, her eyes blinded by tears.

Mullane sat down beside Vokes. "We're in a mess," he said.

"I know. I'm sorry about the engine, Con. I told you before I was accident-prone, bloody bumblefooted."

"Forget it, Frank." Mullane rolled up his trousers and began to burn off the leeches. "But in the future don't try to do so much. You don't have to prove anything to me."

"Who was trying to prove anything? You make me sick, Con. You're so bloody superior—"

Mullane turned on him in sudden fury. "Do you realize what you've done? Coastwatchers are supposed to gather information. But a lot of use we'll be if we can't get our messages out!"

Then he became aware of Nara, lying on his stretcher nearby. His eyes showed his satisfaction at dissension in the enemy camp.

Vokes, too, had remarked the Japanese's interest in their argument. "What are you staring at, you Nip bastard?"

"Not a bastard, Mr. Vokes," said Nara in slightly lisping English. "I think my ancestry might prove much more honourable and legitimate than yours."

"Where did you learn to speak English?" Mullane asked.

"At Sandhurst and West Point. I studied there as a young man."

Vokes spat in disgust. "You Yanks and the bloody Poms taught those Nips how to fight this war!"

Suddenly Ruth appeared. "Where's Sister Brigid?"

On that instant they heard the scream for help. Despite their weariness Mullane and Vokes were on their feet at once. They ran back along the narrow path, plunged off into the scrub and found themselves stumbling through water. Mangrove trees stretched ahead of them, a grotesque corps de ballet with arms raised in attitudes both mocking and threatening.

Mullane shouted, "Sister Brigid!"

Then they heard the cry again and, swinging around, saw the nun. She was backed up into a clump of sugarcane, held by the tight, thick wall of stalks. Moving steadily towards her, its grey-green scaly back just showing above the surface, was one of the largest crocodiles Mullane had ever seen.

Mullane had forgotten his gun, but Vokes had the Lee-Enfield. It went off right behind Mullane's ear, deafening him; but if the bullet hit the crocodile, there was no sign that the huge saurian had felt it. Sister Brigid was trying to claw her way into the sugar-cane, but it continued to push her back.

Mullane snatched up a dead branch and stumbled through the water. The crocodile's tail slashed at him and he fell rather than jumped to the side. The beast was enormous, close to twenty feet. But Mullane knew that it could move faster than a man.

Vokes's rifle went off again and again, and at last the crocodile seemed to shudder. Mullane almost fell on it, hitting it across the snout with the heavy branch. But he was too late.

He would hear for ever the scream of Sister Brigid as the croco-dile's jaws closed on her leg. She turned her head towards Mullane and under the black coif he saw the pain and terror in her con-torted white face. The last sound she uttered was a primaeval scream, rather than a prayer, as the crocodile pulled her down into the brown waters already brightened by her blood.

Mullane beat frenziedly on the hard-scaled hide, but he might just as well have beaten at a rock. The iron jaws would not release their catch. The tail gave one last thrash, then was still. The crocodile sank beneath the water, taking Sister Brigid with it.

The nun's black-clad arm stuck up out of the water. In her hand, like a final offering, were her rosary beads. Mullane reached down, took the beads and, without thinking, put them in his pocket.

THEY DID NOT BURY Sister Brigid, but left her there among the mangroves with the dead crocodile. Both Bishop Scheer and Ruth protested, but Mullane was adamant.

"Frank let off a whole magazine—the Japs could have heard those shots. I'm sorry, Bishop, but you'll have to say your prayers for Sister Brigid on the run. Please include mine with yours. I mean that."

Scheer was in shock. The two small boys, Luke and Mark, were weeping and he held them against his bony hips, trying to com-fort them. Ruth's face was strained from the effort of keeping back her own tears. Mullane cursed himself for having allowed the nun to go off alone in this swampy coastal tract.

Vokes, even more shaken than Mullane, was marshalling the car-riers into line again. "Where are we heading, Con?"

440

"Back to the hills. I feel safer there, and not just from the Japs."

Buka had been sent off to look for a path leading up into the hills, and he came back saying there was a rough track some distance along. Within five minutes the party was moving up through thick pandanus palms, sometimes having to cut their way through creepers that had grown across the path. An hour's climbing brought them to a narrow mountain ridge.

Mullane's first task was to check on where the enemy search parties now were. Through his binoculars he caught sight of movement through the trees; the Japanese were going back down to the beach at Noku. For the time being, he and his party were safe.

Ruth organized a meal: bully beef, dry army biscuits and a small piece of chocolate. Mullane did not talk to anyone during the meal; he had a lot on his mind, as the others tacitly recognized. But when he stood up and walked out to the main vantage point on the ridge, Vokes went across to join him. His ankle had swollen slightly from his stumble on the bridge and he favoured it.

"You all right?" Mullane looked at him as he limped up.

"Yes. What's going on?"

"What do you say we make this our permanent camp? If we can get Mariba and the boys on our side again, we can send them back to the drop site for our supplies."

"*If* you get them on our side— We still have to pay them."

"If the Japs move out, I'll go into Noku for the money tonight."

Mullane and Vokes spent the rest of the afternoon taking turns watching the plantation at Noku. Buka put the natives to work erecting huts. Mullane set up the radio and tried to transmit, but the batteries were flat.

At four o'clock Vokes called to him. "Con, they're pulling out!"

Through his binoculars Mullane saw the Japanese boats moving out from the beach below. In twenty minutes the small convoy had disappeared around the eastern headland.

"What do you reckon, Con? They all gone?"

"I won't know till I go down there. I may as well start now. I'll wait in the bush till it's dark, then go and see Lee Chin."

"I go with you, Boss." Buka had followed Mullane out to the end of the ridge.

"No, there's no point in risking two of us—"

"I think he should go with you," Vokes said quietly. "That gives us a fifty-fifty chance of one of you getting back to tell us what's happened if something goes wrong."

Mullane acknowledged the wisdom of Vokes's advice. He went back along the ridge to Ruth, asking for rations for himself and Buka. She searched his face for some hint of what he felt about this danger he was going into.

She had seen panic when the whites had fled New Britain last January. The men had looked as calm, as they boarded the evacuation ship, as if they were going out fishing. Then the ship's captain had tried to stop some of them, saying the vessel was overloaded. In that moment all the calm masks crumbled. The men had stormed the small ship, and in the end it had departed packed like a cattle barge. She knew it would hurt her to see even a hint of that ugly fear on Mullane's face.

"Good luck." She put frank pressure into her handshake. "If Lee Chin has any spare supplies, ask him if we can have some."

"Do you know Lee Chin?"

"I delivered his wife's last baby." Then she said, "Don't blame yourself for what happened to Sister Brigid."

He put out a hand, touched hers; it was the first intimate approach he had made towards her. Then he left her abruptly and went along to the bishop.

"I'm going down to Noku. Say a prayer or two for me."

"I shall do that. It is always better to pray for the living than for the dead. Even Sister Brigid believed that." He sighed. "I'll miss her, even her complaints."

"She may be happier where she is," Mullane said. "It was just a miserable way to die."

"She probably is happier. She had no doubts at all that there is a heaven. But I should have insisted that she leave with Father Holtz and the other sisters. Father Holtz was my assistant in Waku. He didn't want to go, either. But he was a very sick man and he had no choice. Unfortunately Sister Brigid insisted she had a choice and she stayed. Even bishops are powerless against a nun's determination."

The old bishop sighed again, then he changed the subject. "I have had another look at our Japanese guest. I agree with Miss Riddle now. I think his arm should be amputated. But it is twenty-four years since I last touched a scalpel." He held out his hands. Mullane was surprised to see they were shaking.

"Wait till I come back to camp in the morning," he said. "Just one thing—if your patient asks you to let him die, remember whose side you're on. The church won't allow euthanasia. Neither will I, in this case."

Mullane and Buka left the camp as the sun was going down. Vokes went partway along the track with them, one hand in his pocket. When they came to where a branch track led down the slope through the jungle he took his hand from his pocket.

"My badges of rank, Con. They came in one of the airdrop packages. You want to put them on, just in case?"

Mullane shook his head, touched by the gesture. "Thanks, Frank. But I don't think I could ever pass for a sublieutenant in the Australian navy, not even with this sailor's beard."

"Well, please yourself. Just don't get caught. Oh, and if you see Lee Chin, ask him if he has a spare engine." Then, sober-faced: "Good luck, Con. You, too, Buka."

IN TOWNSVILLE headquarters, Roger Blomfield looked at the two coloured pins stuck close together on his map of New Britain. One day's silence didn't mean that Mullane and Vokes were lost, he told himself.

David Lowell, the American, came in looking worried.

"GHQ on your back again?" Blomfield asked him.

"There's a bird colonel keeps calling me every hour. What's the holdup on Rabaul? Says he knows more about the situation in North Africa than he does about Rabaul, so I asked him why he didn't go and fight in North Africa. I could be out of a job tomorrow. What's your good news?"

"None. Mullane and Vokes didn't come on the air today."

"Would they have already started for Rabaul?"

"Not without telling us. What would they have done with this Jap they've got? No, if he is top ranked, they wouldn't just dump

444

him and take off. Have you got something that can pick him up?"

"They've promised me a sub, but they'll only hold it for forty-eight hours—it has to patrol in the Solomons. But until we hear from Mullane or Vokes, where in blazes do we send it?"

CHAPTER FIVE

"Some Japs still there, Boss. Couldn't count 'em myself. Boy tell me six, eight, he dunno."

Wrapped in his lap-lap, looking like any other native on the plantation, Buka had left Mullane in the bush and gone quietly into Noku. He had been away less than twenty minutes.

"The boy you saw won't give us away to the Japs, will he?"

"He come from my village, Boss. He knows I break his bloody neck he tells the Japs about us."

The moon would not be up for another hour and the darkness here beneath the trees was that of a windowless dungeon.

"Where are the Japs? In the house?"

"Lee Chin and his family in house. Japs down on beach, sitting by fire. One feller walking up and down, he on guard."

"Okay, we wait till everyone's settled for the night."

"Boss, you go to sleep. You pretty tired."

Just then Mullane loved the brown man. He pressed Buka's arm. "Wake me when the moon comes up."

It seemed that he had barely shut his eyes when Buka was shaking him. For a moment he was disoriented. He would have to sharpen his reflexes if he was to survive. He might once have been a natural athlete, but he was not a natural animal, alert on the instant to his surroundings.

The moon was up, a yellow rheumy eye growing whiter as it climbed. Mullane and Buka moved cautiously towards the plantation. They paused on the edge of the jungle, beside a picket fence that protected the vegetable garden from marauding pigs.

"I'll go into the house," Mullane said to Buka. "You stay outside and watch the Japs down on the beach. *Don't shoot.*"

Mullane and Buka ran silently between the trees until they came to a shed with open sides and a corrugated-iron roof. Mullane saw the shape, like an angular beast, of the large petrol engine in the shed. It was too big to cart into the hills. But if the Japanese left, he might be able to bring the radio's batteries to Noku.

He gestured for Buka to move around the corner of the house and watch the beach. The house was like all island dwellings, raised on pilings for coolness and to alleviate the dampness. He went up the back steps, opened the screen door and stepped onto the veranda that encircled the house. Now he had to find Lee Chin.

He crept along the veranda towards the front of the house, then stopped abruptly, bringing the Thompson gun into position. A Japanese sentry was sitting on the front steps.

A child began to cry and an oil lamp was turned up just inside the window by which Mullane stood. The sentry rose, moved to the top step; but Mullane had already slipped to one side. He dropped on one knee and held his gun ready to shoot as soon as the Japanese came around the corner. He could feel himself sweating, knowing he was going to kill another man.

Then he heard the scrape of boots on the steps and a moment later the cough of the sentry as he moved away, down towards the beach. Mullane eased himself upright, feeling his joints creak; tension had frozen him like a cold wind.

He returned to the rear of the house, tried the back door. It was locked, something he had not expected; locked doors were rare in island houses. Lee Chin must have no trust in the Japanese. At least it hinted that he might still be neutral.

Mullane knocked gently on the door. "Lee Chin," he whispered through the keyhole. "This is Mullane, from Kiogo. Let me in."

The door swung open, a dim hand beckoned him in and he slipped into the house. He could see nothing in the blackness, then a hand groped for his arm and he was led along a short passage and into the front room. He saw the dark silhouette of a man.

"Lee Chin?"

"Yes. You are Mr. Mullane? I wouldn't have recognized you."

Mullane was puzzled. "You know me?"

"I saw you once up in Rabaul, at Burns Philp's store. You had no beard then. What do you want, Mr. Mullane?"

Then there was a yellow glow in the doorway of the room lead-

446

ing off this main room. A woman in a shift stood there, one arm cradling a baby, the other holding an oil lamp. Lee Chin stood revealed as a middle-aged man, bald and gaunt-faced; he wore only a long white undershirt that barely covered his loins. He hissed to his wife to put out the light.

"What do you want?" he repeated. "The Japanese will kill us all if they know you are here."

"I want the key to the company's safe. I'm authorized to take money from it to pay my boys."

He wondered how much he could tell Lee Chin. The Chinese in the islands never attempted to mix with the Europeans or the natives. Most were traders, running their own stores; but some, like Lee Chin, had taken jobs with the plantation companies.

He had to take the risk. "Lee, I'm up in the hills with Mr. Vokes, from Tanga. We're Coastwatchers."

"I know Mr. Vokes. He also works for Burns Philp, like me."

"The Japs have taken over Tanga. What's happened here?"

"I am on parole. They come down every two weeks from Rabaul to check on me. Those men down there—" Lee Chin nodded through the window. "They came looking for a plane that crashed in the hills. I hope they go soon. My wife is very afraid. So am I," he added. "If I give you the money, please go quickly."

"What did you say? *Give* me the money?"

"I have it in the bedroom. When I assumed responsibility here I found the safe and opened it. Some day Burns Philp may ask me about the money."

"I shall bear witness to your honesty and loyalty, Lee. Now may I borrow the money and get out of here?"

Lee Chin went into the bedroom. There was the sound of something being scraped on the wooden floor; Mullane guessed that a box was being pulled out from under the bed. He looked out of the window; the sentry was beginning to walk back towards the house.

Lee Chin returned with a paper bag. "Six hundred and eight pounds. Sign a receipt, please."

Mullane put a hand in the bag and felt the rolls of notes. Then in the dark he signed the receipt that Lee Chin held for him.

"Thank you, Lee. I'll tell Burns Philp—" Then he remembered

he could not tell Burns Philp anything at all. "Do you have a small engine I could send my boys down to get? I need it to recharge the batteries for our radio set."

"No. The Japanese took the small engine when they took my wireless. They left the big engine."

"I saw it." Mullane could hear the sentry whistling softly out in front. "What about the plantations farther up the coast?"

"I don't know. I think the Japanese would have taken their wirelesses, and their engines, too. But there is a small engine up in the mountains. It belongs to a native named Kutari who has his own village. He has what they call a cargo cult."

Mullane had never seen any evidence of a cargo cult in New Britain, but he knew that it brought a false promise of prosperity to the natives. They believed that their ancestors would return bringing supplies of modern goods to make them rich and free. The tragedy was that almost invariably the primitive people lost even what they already possessed to the nefarious cult leaders.

"Kutari has a petrol engine," Lee went on. "He uses it to run his picture machine. He shows films to the people. They believe him when he says he will bring them a world like they see."

In the bedroom the baby began to cry again. Out in the garden the sentry's whistling had stopped.

"Please go now, Mr. Mullane!"

Mullane stuffed the paper bag into his pack and began to move towards the rear hall. "I won't be back. I don't want to endanger you and your family. You do the same for me and Mr. Vokes."

"Of course."

Mullane hurried out of the house, almost fell down the back steps and stumbled into a large metal dustbin. It went over with a loud clang. He dived into the blackness under the house as the sentry, rifle at the ready, came around the corner. Mullane heard him say in Japanese, "Who's there? Stop!"

Mullane lay perfectly still, in agony: he was lying on top of broken coconut shells, their jagged edges pressing into him like broad-bladed knives. Then beyond the sentry he saw Buka move out from behind a coconut palm and take aim with his rifle. Mullane wanted to cry, *Don't, Buka, don't!*

There was the creak of the screen door and Lee Chin came down the steps, picked up the dustbin and put the lid back on. "Wild pig," he commented.

The sentry laughed, slung his rifle over his shoulder and went back towards the beach.

Mullane eased himself off the coconut shells, feeling the blood running where he had been cut. Painfully he went in a crouching run up through the plantation groves. Buka followed.

After a while he slowed to a walk, now and again putting his hand to his wounds. Most of them seemed no more than deep scratches; but there were two savage gougings, one above his knee, the other between his lower ribs.

They found the track that led up the mountain and began to climb, stumbling through the darkness. At last Mullane could go no farther. He sat down abruptly in the mud. Almost at once the mosquitoes arrived for the feast.

DAYLIGHT FILTERED DOWN through the thick overhang, like an upside-down tide. Then there was the sound of engines as a flock of bombers headed south. Mullane, coming out of a fitful sleep, hoped that some Coastwatcher in the Solomons would spot the planes and be able to warn the Americans on Guadalcanal.

He felt the dressings, made of strips of their clothing, that Buka had applied in the dark to his two major wounds. The bleeding seemed to have stopped during the night, but his leg wound started up again after only ten minutes' walking. By the time they reached the camp, the pad on his leg was a sodden mess. Vokes and the others gathered around him.

"Geez, Con—" Vokes was full of concern. "Were you shot?"

Mullane sat down and Ruth unwrapped the bandage. "I was attacked by a pile of coconut shells," he said. "You wouldn't—"

"Shut up," said Ruth curtly. "Frank, get some hot water. And tell one of the boys to bring my medical case." After she had dressed his wounds she said, "You're not starting out for Rabaul— I'll chop your other leg from underneath you if you try."

"We'll come to that. In the meantime I have another call to make." He told her and the others about Kutari and his cargo cult up in the mountains. "I don't know where it is, but maybe one of the boys does."

In the background one of the carriers, a man named Silas, coughed. "I know the place, Boss. Plenty long climb."

Silas was the next senior native to Buka, a wiry man, loyal and hardworking. He was in his late thirties but had the face of an older man.

"All right, we'll go first thing in the morning." Mullane held up a hand as Ruth was about to speak. "I'll rest up all day today. You can pamper me."

"We'll be too busy for any of that. The bishop is going to operate on the general."

Mullane had forgotten all about Nara. It was a measure of his own exhaustion that he should have done so.

"Do you have everything you need?" he said.

Scheer smiled. "Not quite. We have no antiseptic."

Vokes said, "Let 'em have your bottle of whisky, Con."

"All right. Just don't be profligate with it, Bishop. When we pay the boys we can send them to the drop site for more supplies."

Later, when Mullane was resting in his hut, Vokes came to him. "Did you see those bombers this morning? Forty-four of them. This is a good spot, Con. We should come back after Rabaul."

"Since we're off the air, I guess Townsville thinks we're already on our way in there. Have you paid the boys?"

"I gave them double time, like you promised. Mariba wanted another week in advance, but I told him off."

"You better go back with the boys for the supplies. If we send them on their own, they could just keep on going all the way down to Kiogo. Especially now that they have their money."

"Or you could stay here, Con, and I could go up and see that bloke about the engine. We could send Buka back with the boys to get the supplies. He'd keep 'em in line."

The proposition had its points, but one major drawback. From what Mullane had read and heard, a cargo cult leader had to be treated with the utmost diplomacy. Vokes did not seem the man to deal with Kutari.

"I think you'd better go back with the boys for the supplies."

"What about the general? And the bishop? Those two are going to make trouble, don't you reckon?"

"Not until Nara gets over his operation. How is that coming?"

"They're nearly ready to start."

Mullane eased himself to his feet. "They may need me."

"I wish I could be more help, Con—but I know I'd pass out. All I could do was make some clamps for them out of the spring clips for the battery leads."

Mullane marvelled at him. "You're full of surprises, Frank."

Vokes grinned with embarrassment. "Us Aussies are the greatest improvisers you'll ever find."

Ruth met them when they were halfway to the hut where the operation was to take place. "I want blood," she said flatly. "Group O, according to the general's tags. What group are you, Frank?"

He shifted his feet uncomfortably. "Group O. Geez, how much do you want?"

"As much as you can stand to lose." She looked at Mullane. "You've lost enough, otherwise I'd want some of yours, too."

"I'm coming to stand by in case you need help."

She hesitated, then nodded. "You can be the anaesthetist."

The operation began an hour later. Scheer had spoken to Nara earlier, preparing him for the amputation. Now, outside the hut, two cooking pots boiled above a fire, sterilizing the instruments. Inside, Nara's stretcher had been raised onto two makeshift horses. Ruth had mixed a saline solution and it was in a bottle hung from a crossbeam; from another beam hung a bottle of blood. Scheer looked at his operating theatre and shook his head.

Mullane sat on a stool at the head of the rough operating table. Ruth had supplied him with a rubber mask ("It's mainly been used on native women in childbirth"). Holding the mask over Nara's face, he slowly dripped ether through a cotton pad attached to the mask's tube.

A tight tourniquet had been tied around Nara's upper arm; even so, blood spurted when Scheer severed the brachial artery. Ruth snapped on one of Vokes's homemade clamps, and the flow of blood was cut off at once. Scheer worked clumsily at first on the mangled arm, but Ruth was cool, brisk and efficient.

451

Buka stood at the bottom end of the table, supervising the slow drip of blood from the transfusion bottle. Sweat was running on him like rainwater.

Scheer's hands began to take on sureness, helped by Ruth's confidence in him. Then it was time to cut the humerus bone.

Ruth looked at Mullane. "This isn't going to sound too nice. Better try not to listen."

"How does one do that?" Mullane saw Buka's eyes open wide in trepidation as Scheer picked up the butcher's hacksaw that had been borrowed from the cook-boy.

"You could sing."

He saw the laughter in her eyes and thought she was joking, then he saw the sense of it. In a good loud baritone he began to sing "The Riff Song" from *The Desert Song*. Outside the hut the natives looked at each other, wondering what madness had taken hold of the boss. One chorus, sung at full volume, was enough; Scheer was through the bone.

The bishop had been too intent on what he was doing to be distracted by the singing. Now he was sewing up the flap he had cut, turning the arm into a stump. At last he stepped back.

"Would you clean up for me, Miss Riddle?"

"With pleasure, Bishop. Congratulations." Ruth looked at their patient, thin, shrunken, pale. "Now let's hope he survives."

THEY HAD A HOT MEAL that night: tinned meat and vegetables, and watered-down condensed milk. It seemed to improve everyone's mood. But occasionally Mullane wondered what was happening up in Rabaul. For all he knew, preparations might be building for the decisive battle of the Pacific war. He had to get their radio working and he had to get Nara off his hands.

"I used to go on trips like this up into the Blue Mountains," Vokes was saying. "That's about seventy or eighty miles inland from Sydney. I remember once I got lost in the Grose Valley. I was about seventeen, and I thought I must be in the wildest country in the world. If someone had told me I'd be stuck up here—"

Then the mosquitoes, more regular than the bombers, came up out of the mud, and the nightly tattoo of slapping hands began.

452

Ruth made everyone take his Atabrine tablets; she did not want the extra chore of caring for malaria victims. They had all been sitting on logs out in the open; now they got up and started to move back towards their huts.

Mullane, still favouring his leg, touched Ruth's arm. "Would you walk me home, Miss Riddle?"

She moved close to him and he put his arm on her shoulder. After a few steps she said, "I hope you're not still thinking of going anywhere on that leg."

"I am, actually. I wanted to talk to you about it. Can you use a pistol?"

"I think I could if I had to."

"I'm sure you could. You're a very competent girl."

She looked around her. "Saturday night, moonlight, tropic breezes—and all he wants to do is tell me I'm competent."

"No, I have a proposition to put to you. I'd like you, with Buka to back you up, to take charge of the camp while Frank and I are away tomorrow. Frank will be gone a couple of days at least, but I'll be back tomorrow evening."

"I don't think you should go on that leg."

"Miss Riddle—"

"I don't think you'd be compromised if you called me Ruth."

He smiled. "Ruth, I'm going up the mountain tomorrow to look for Kutari. I'll need someone to keep an eye on the camp."

"What would you expect me to do—use your gun on the bishop or the general?" She shook her head. "I wouldn't do it—Con. You forget—this isn't my war."

"I wouldn't expect you to shoot Bishop Scheer. I couldn't cold-bloodedly shoot him myself—I like him too much. But so long as he's thinking of giving himself up to the Japs, he's a danger to us. And if they came up here and found you, you'd be raped by the soldiers or sent to an officers' brothel in Rabaul."

"I'd use the gun on myself before I'd let that happen."

"Well, let's hope you don't have to use the gun on either the bishop or yourself. Will you do it?"

She was silent for a while. Down on the coast she could see the glow of a fire on the beach at Noku, the red eye of the enemy.

At last she said, "I'll do it. But if you come back tomorrow evening and find the bishop gone, you'll know why I let him go."

"I'll understand." He was studying her, looking at her now as a woman and not as a prospective camp guard.

"You're a beautiful girl." He spoke cautiously, afraid of himself as much as of her. "I'm surprised you're not married."

"I could have been. Thanks—for the compliment, I mean. I think you'd be good-looking yourself without that beard."

"When this is all over, maybe I'll show you the real Mullane."

Then, unwittingly, she killed whatever chance there might have been of their going further. "Were you ever married?"

It was his turn to be silent. Then at last he said quietly, "Yes. I was married to a Japanese girl."

HE HAD MET MIEKO within two weeks of arriving in Japan to take over as coach of the Tokyo Athletics. It was early spring of 1936, at a reception at the American embassy. She was taller than most of the girls he had seen since his arrival. Her hair was cut Western-style, in a bob with a fringe across her eyebrows, and she wore a pale blue kimono. She was beautiful, with a natural beauty that owed nothing to the artificiality of the geisha tradition.

She bowed her head when they were introduced. Later he would learn that her deference to men was out of respect for her father, a professor of art at the Imperial University who, despite modern Western sympathies, still believed in certain of the old traditions.

Professor Tanaka did not object when McArdle asked if he might call on Mieko. She spoke English, but they had no subject in common other than an interest in each other. So they talked about themselves and, with no distractions, fell in love.

They were married six months to the day after they had met. They rented a house on a quiet street in Shibuya with a *kare sansui* garden. McArdle, who had never so much as watered an indoor plant when he had lived in New York, now learned, under the tutelage of a gardener, to rake the sand and white gravel into patterns around the moss-covered rocks, creating images of islands in a white sea or of mountains soaring above a cloud floor.

Each day during spring and summer he went to the ball park and put the Athletics through their paces. As head coach he had several assistants; but he was not left much free time. Everyone in Japan, it seemed, was working at full pace and to a purpose, though the purpose was never publicly stated.

His first attempts at espionage were bumbling ones and he was fortunate to escape detection. He paid visits to the neighbourhood of various shipyards and surreptitiously took photographs that, to his inexpert eye, were virtually useless. But he sent them off anyhow, through his contact, Kister, the naval attaché at the embassy. They met in parks and temples or in the Tokyo Club, where the Europeans congregated. It was at the club that McArdle met an American free-lance journalist named Johnson.

"I'd stay away from Johnson, Con," Kister warned him. "He's not American, he's German, and the *kempei* may be watching him."

From then on McArdle stayed away from the Tokyo Club. He was happy to spend all his nonworking hours with Mieko. Their relationship was almost perfect; each found in the other the peace and comfort that is the basis of a happy marriage.

Still, he began to wonder how Mieko would fare when he took her back to the States. By now he knew that they would have to return to America. Japan, he was convinced, was headed for war. The Japanese were constructing too many ships, building too many planes, for a nation intent only on defence.

In the winter of 1936–37 he took her home to Rochester for Christmas. Liam and his wife, Margaret, had come up from Washington, and the house on East Avenue was bright with lights and goodwill. The family, contrary to Con's expectations, welcomed Mieko warmly.

But after Christmas dinner Liam had taken Con aside. "There's going to be a war, you know," he said. "Not soon but eventually."

"I'm glad you agree. I'd hate to think all my reports were being ignored."

"You've changed. You're more—*serious*. I suppose you still have an interest in baseball, though?"

"It's a living. And it gives me a reason for staying on in Japan. But I only have a two-year contract."

"What will you do when it is up? I could find you a job in Washington, if you wanted it. Except—"

"Except for Mieko?" Goodwill towards all men: except possible future enemies. "No, I'll find something to do in New York."

He and Mieko went back to Japan after two months' travelling by car around the States. She loved America and had not demurred when he told her he could not live permanently in Japan, that when his contract with the Athletics was finished he would have to return to his own country to make a living. She was content to be wherever he wanted to be.

They had been back in Japan a month when she told him she was pregnant. It was the first day of spring training; in the garden the first blossoms hung like faint pink explosions in the air. He kissed her, held her to him.

Then, on a Friday night after a training session, he stopped in at the Tokyo Club looking for Kister. Johnson, appearing a little the worse for drink, was sitting at the bar.

"My dear friend the baseballer. I'm surprised to see you here. I thought you would be at home consoling your wife."

"My wife? What about her?"

"They took her in for questioning this afternoon."

"*They?* Who?"

"The *kempei*, the secret police. Major Yorida is in charge of the investigation, I believe."

McArdle left the other man without further word and drove home at a reckless pace. There was a police guard in the yard, a short, burly man who introduced himself as Lieutenant Fujisawa.

"You will remain here," he said. "Your wife will be returned to you in due course."

McArdle had to restrain himself from hitting the policeman. "You are mistaken, Lieutenant. I am not staying here. I am going to your headquarters. You can come with me, or you can try to stop me and I'll knock your head off!"

Lieutenant Fujisawa evidently did not carry a gun. He looked McArdle up and down, decided he was outweighed and bowed his head. "As you wish."

The bulky Japanese sat impassive beside McArdle as the latter drove through the dusk to the secret-police headquarters. It was almost dark when they reached the building. A guard stopped them, but Fujisawa waved him aside and they passed on.

McArdle was taken into a room and Fujisawa left him. In five minutes that seemed to stretch interminably in McArdle's frantic mind, the door opened and a tall thin man, almost as tall as McArdle himself, came in.

"I am Major Yorida. I have some distressing news." It struck McArdle that neither Fujisawa nor this man had bothered to ask him if he spoke Japanese; they took it for granted that he would understand them. "Your wife, unfortunately, is dead."

CHAPTER SIX

In the morning, Vokes, told to be as quick as possible, set off to walk back to the supply cache, taking Mariba and eleven carriers with him. Before leaving with Silas and the other carriers for the cargo cult village, Mullane went to see Nara. Propped up in a rough bed, the general still looked pale and drawn, almost fragile. Someone had put his gold watch on his remaining wrist.

"I'm leaving you in Miss Riddle's care, General. She has my permission to shoot you if you try to escape."

Nara looked at Ruth, who sat on a paraffin tin at the foot of his bed. "If I had the strength to get up, I'd give you every opportunity to do just that."

"How's your arm?" asked Mullane.

Nara shrugged the shoulder above his stump, winced a little.

"It is going to be all right," said Ruth. "The bishop did an excellent job."

"Console yourself, General," Mullane said. "When Japan has lost the war, there'll be others more to blame than you."

"Your optimism is admirable but foolish," Nara said.

But Nara wondered about his own optimism. He saw merit in Japan's objective of expansion into Southeast Asia and the East Indies. Those lands were rich in rubber and oil, and they offered room for colonists from the overcrowded homeland. Everything had gone well as far as the East Indies; but there, he felt, they

457

should have stopped. He was not convinced there was much to be gained by the conquest of the South Pacific islands and Australia.

Ruth and Mullane left the hut together. She said, "You be careful of that leg. It's not as good as you're trying to make out."

He put a hand on her shoulder and squeezed it; it was almost as if he had kissed her, and she blinked at the sudden intimacy. "I'll take care, Ruth. You do the same."

Then he called to Silas and the other carriers and they left the camp. They climbed for an hour before they came to the vegetable gardens outside Kutari's village. Nearly naked women were at work there among the taro, yam and cabbage plantings. As Mullane and his carriers stepped into the clearing the women rushed together in silent terror. Mullane told Silas to tell them not to be afraid, then led his party to the edge of the village.

Suddenly Mullane found himself facing a battery of men carrying spears. He held up his hands. He was carrying his Thompson gun, but these natives would not know what it was.

"Tell them we come in peace, Silas."

Silas spoke nervously in dialect. The villagers did not lower their spears, just continued to look threatening. Then behind them Mullane saw Kutari. He was barefoot, but dressed in white shirt and shorts, his thick hennaed hair bright in the sun. He came forward with an arrogant dignity that reminded Mullane of certain upstart colonial administrators, small kings in tiny domains.

"Sir? What brings you here?"

Mullane thought, I've heard this voice before, but where?

"I am Mullane. From Kiogo."

"I know it. I worked there when I was a very young man. Won't you come into my village?" He said something in dialect and the villagers lowered their spears.

Mullane followed Kutari up between two lines of huts to a larger one, more like a house, built on stilts. The two men went up the rickety steps to the narrow veranda and Kutari gestured to Mullane to sit down. The American lowered himself into a canvas chair, rested the Thompson gun across his knees. The villagers congregated around the foot of the steps; Silas and the carriers, all apprehensive, pushed to the front.

The cult leader shouted an order and two women brought some wild oranges split into quarters. "I am sorry I cannot offer you gin and bitters, Mr. Mullane."

The cultured voice was farcical coming out of the betel-stained mouth. "You speak English very well," Mullane remarked.

"I was seven years in Brisbane with my late master, Mr. Benjamin. He liked moving pictures very much and he used to take me with him. I also have my own moving pictures with talkies. Mr. Ronald Colman's *A Tale of Two Cities.*"

Mullane knew that anything was possible in this part of the world. But he had never expected to be sitting in a wild mountain village listening to a henna-haired brown man talk to him with the voice of Ronald Colman. "Do you run your movie very often?"

"Every night. My people love it. It is very old, of course."

"Is that how you keep your hold on your people?"

The brown man's face hardened into suspicion. He stared at Mullane, then barked an order at the villagers and they drifted back towards their huts. Silas and the carriers looked at Mullane.

"Get the things out, Silas," he said. They had brought a bag of salt, half a dozen knives and some beads for trading. Mullane also had money in his pocket, but he did not want to waste it here, where all trade might be in barter.

"What have you come to trade?" Kutari asked.

Mullane eased himself out of his chair. "I want to buy your engine, Kutari."

Now the cult leader's face bore a look of open belligerence. "My engine is not for buying. You better go quick, Mr. Mullane. My people do not like white men."

"I want that engine, Kutari. I'll give you a bag of salt and six knives for it. And some beads."

"No. The engine is no good any more. It will work again when the aeroplanes bring the water in tins."

"You mean you have no petrol?" Mullane did not ask where he had got the petrol in the past, probably in Rabaul. "Kutari, when did you last show your moving pictures?"

"You go quick or I call my people!" Ronald Colman had faded away completely and the voice was rough with primitive hatred.

Mullane went down the steps and looked around. He saw a bundle of wild sugarcane stacked against one of the stilts that held up the veranda. He took aim with the Thompson, then fired a short burst. The sugarcane flew apart. There was a yell of terror from the villagers and they ran away to huddle together at the end of the village.

Mullane looked up at Kutari. "Your people don't know what this is. But you have seen a gun before. You know it can kill."

"Kill me and my people will kill you."

"Let me see your engine." The brown man shook his head and Mullane brought his gun up. "Let me see it! I won't kill you, but I could shoot your leg off. People don't like one-legged kings."

Kutari hesitated, then he nodded, and Mullane went back up the steps and followed him into the house. Here, behind the rough walls, there was no attempt to ape the white administrator. This was a native's hut: the bed mat, the smooth log pillow, the bow and arrows. Only in one corner was the white man's magic: a rusted movie projector, two corroded batteries, a battered amplifier, several film cans. And the petrol engine.

Mullane brushed past Kutari and inspected the engine. It was still functional; all that was missing was the petrol to drive it. Then he looked at the projector, the sound equipment and the batteries. The latter were useless; Kutari's magic was finished.

Mullane picked up the cans of film. There were five reels of *A Tale of Two Cities;* from what he remembered there were usually more reels in a full-length movie. He wondered what parts of the story of Sydney Carton had been lost.

"Kutari, all this is no good and you know it. Sell me the engine. I'll give you the bag of salt and the knives."

"It is not enough."

Reluctantly Mullane took the roll of pound notes from his pocket. "I'll give you ten pounds."

Kutari snorted. "It is too little. Give me one hundred pounds."

Mullane swore under his breath. "I have only—" He counted the money quickly; back at the campsite he had stuffed the roll into his pocket without looking at it. "Seventy pounds. Take it or—" He held up the Thompson. "Or I take the engine and pay nothing."

Kutari reached for the money and counted it. "Seventy, seventy-one—there is too much." He handed back a one-pound note, making a display of his magnanimity and Mullane's poor arithmetic. "I am an honest man. You may have the engine."

Five minutes later, with the engine slung on poles borne by his carriers, Mullane was ready to leave. There was muttering among the villagers as they saw the engine being carried away; the sunlight shone on nervous spear tips. Mullane wondered how Kutari would placate them, what other magic he would call on.

"Don't promise them too much, Kutari," he called back.

BY THE TIME he walked into camp Mullane's leg was bleeding again. Ruth came in the hut to attend to him. He had taken off his trousers and was sitting in his shirt, unwrapping the bandage.

"We can't go on meeting like this."

"I saw you limping into camp," she said. "You'd better stay off your leg today."

"I'll do that tomorrow," he promised. "I've got to get that engine going. I want to be on the air this evening. Did you have any trouble with the general?"

She shook her head. "The bishop has been with him all day. They're like old friends now."

"Both ends of the Axis—that's what I've been afraid of."

While he worked on the engine he thought about Ruth. She in no way resembled Mieko, but he was beginning to feel the ease with her that he had felt with his wife. But, he chided himself, this was no place to be thinking of any sort of alliance.

It was dusk before he finished with the engine. He called to Buka to bring him some gas. Ruth and the bishop came to watch as he primed the machine, spun the flywheel with a length of string and hoped for the best. Nothing happened.

"A few prayers, Bishop. Don't just stand there."

Scheer took a safety pin from his cassock and pricked the carburettor. "God helps those who help themselves, Mr. Mullane."

"You see?" Mullane said to Ruth. "That's how they produced the Zeppelin and the Mercedes-Benz, with a safety pin."

He spun the wheel again and the engine roared into life. Every-

462

one admired it as if it were a newborn baby. In the last of the light Mullane connected it to the charger and the radio's batteries. Then they all went to supper while the engine hummed away.

Mullane was about to sit down when he saw Scheer, with two plates, going into the hut where Nara lay on his rough bed. Taking up his own plate, Mullane followed the German. "You don't mind if I join you, gentlemen?"

Scheer and Nara exchanged glances as Mullane lowered himself to a small log; the German sat down on the ground.

"I have to watch you two," Mullane said amiably. "After all, you are the enemy."

They ate their dinner, the tension between the three men stretching like a cable that threatens to snap.

By nine o'clock the batteries were charged. Mullane set up the radio by flashlight and started tapping on the Morse key. Port Moresby answered at once, asking the question he had expected.

"Are you on way to King's Cross?"

That meant Rabaul; and he was certainly closer to it than he had been when he was last on the air. "Yes. But still saddled with top jockey and other baggage. Are we expected to take them into King's Cross? Appreciate contribution your end."

The reply came: "Still seeking evacuation means. Expected means now delayed by engine trouble."

That meant a submarine or Catalina flying boat. But how long before it would arrive? Mullane swore softly and behind him Ruth said, "I came at the wrong time. Sorry."

He apologized, handing her the flashlight. "Hold this, please. They never allow any leeway in a code for four-letter words."

The Morse key was a good brake on one's temper and language. "GHQ better accept quid pro quo. Cannot enter King's Cross carrying top jockey. Put that in GOC's corncob."

There was silence for a long time—perhaps due to shock. Ruth switched off the flashlight and the two of them sat on his camp bed in the darkness.

Mullane was glad for her company. He rubbed citronella on his face and hands, a deterrent to romance as well as mosquitoes. But he said, "I'm glad you came along with us."

"I'm glad I let you persuade me."

He smiled, put out his hand, then changed its direction as the key began to stutter again. Ruth relaxed. She was not afraid of his touch, but wondered what would follow. She switched on the flashlight, relieved and yet irritated by Moresby's interruption.

"Quid pro quo accepted. Evacuation soon as possible."

"So we just sit and wait some more?" Ruth said.

He repacked the radio, then took the flashlight from her and snapped it off. He pulled her to her feet. They stood close together in the darkness, each of them alertly aware of the other's body. It seemed a long moment before he pulled her to him and kissed her. She kissed him without restraint and both were trembling.

Then he said reluctantly, "I don't think we'd better."

"You're probably right. I'd best go back to my hut."

He lifted her hand and kissed her fingers. "I'm sorry, Ruth. Some other time, some other place, maybe."

"Maybe. Good night."

In the morning she came over to see him in his hut. He was washing, stripped to the waist, in the canvas basin Silas had brought him. "I had a bad night," she said.

"Me, too." He splashed water on his face.

"I think we'd better not even shake hands from now on."

He dried his face, combed his beard and hair. "What about my leg? Do I do my dressings from now on?"

"I can do that for you. But . . ." She hesitated. "If we start anything, Con, I'm not interested in one-night flings."

"I must tell you something," he said carefully. "I hope to get word tonight on when you and the others can be taken off."

She had known she would be evacuated and had not minded. But now, somehow, it was as if he'd said he did not want her around. And that hurt, now that she was falling in love with him.

In love: it was something she had lain awake pondering the night before. "What if I refuse to go?"

"You might not have any say."

"I could go part of the way to Rabaul with you. I could stay with the wireless while you and Frank go in—"

"No!"

Then he heard Silas shout and he hurried out of the hut. A small dark cloud of planes was heading south. Mullane adjusted his glasses and started to count: sixty-four bombers, more than he had ever seen before.

He went back into the hut, sent out the warning. Port Moresby came back: "Number of raids and planes increasing. Our photo reconnaissance unable detect source extra squadrons. Appreciate information this point when you in King's Cross."

"Will do," he replied. Then he sat back and looked at Ruth, standing in the doorway.

"I send the same message all the time," he said. "'Bombers headed your way.' All I change are the figures. Then I count them when they come back. What's happened in between I can only guess at. I've never seen a bomb dropped. I suppose thousands of people are dying every day, and I don't know as much as some little old lady sitting in a newsreel theatre in Tulsa, Oklahoma. It's a hell of a private way of being involved in a war."

"Does that disturb you?"

"Yes!" He stood up quickly, winced as the wound in his leg bit. "I'm beginning to wish I'd gone home right after Pearl Harbor. Maybe with what I knew I should have gone home earlier—"

"What did you know?"

"I knew Japan was going to war against America."

She waited for him to go on, but he brushed by her and went out of the hut. She followed, hoping he would tell her more, but he led the way into the hut where Bishop Scheer sat on the log beside the general's bed. Each time he saw the two men together now, he sensed conspiracy. "How is he, Bishop?"

"The general has remarkable powers of recovery."

"It's the story of his country. They have always recovered quickly from their disasters."

Nara had regained some of his strength during the night. He was alert now and had decided he was going to escape to Rabaul. He wouldn't be the first one-armed officer to lead an army.

"I am beginning to remember you, Mr. Mullane," he said. "Though that was not your name when you lived in Japan, was it?"

"No, it was McArdle." Mullane felt Ruth's interest quicken.

Nara nodded. "He was a famous baseball player, Bishop. He came to my country in—1934, wasn't it, Mr. McArdle?"

But Mullane had stiffened, head cocked. Then he was on his feet, at the door and yelling, "Everybody stay out of sight!"

The other two men and Ruth had heard the light single-engine sound of the scout plane. It went over not more than two hundred feet above the ridge. Nara sat up in his bed.

"Don't try anything," Mullane said, "or I'll break your other arm. You keep still, too, Bishop."

The German and the Japanese exchanged glances, then Scheer shrugged. "I was never a hero, General."

"One has to be practical, Bishop." There was no condemnation in Nara's voice, but he ached to attract the scouting pilot's attention. "Mr. McArdle is stronger than both of us."

"Mullane," said the American. "McArdle would have killed you long ago, General."

He heard the plane climbing, then it banked to return. Was the pilot suspicious because the huts showed no sign of life?

Mullane yelled again, "Silas—get outside! You and the other boys—the kids, too! Wave to the big bird!"

There was no movement in the camp; the plane was almost upon it. Then Silas and the carriers, pushing young Luke and Mark ahead of them, ventured out into an open patch among the trees. The plane swept over and Silas and the others waved frantically. The plane swung up, waggled its wings, then went on in a wide sweep across the slope of the mountain. Mullane put his binoculars on it and waited for it to swing down to Noku and the Japanese camped there on the beach; that would surely mean it would drop a message to the soldiers to come up and inspect the huts. But it disappeared north over the mountain.

He looked back at Scheer and Nara. "Bad luck, General. I think they've given up hope that you're still alive."

"Perhaps." Nara eased himself down in his bed again. "Why did you say you would have killed me if you were still McArdle?"

It surprised Mullane that Nara should pick up the conversation at the point where it had been interrupted. He said nothing for a while, then mentally shrugged. What did it matter now? Eventually all the poisonous hatred he felt over Mieko's death would have to come out. Perhaps something would be gained by letting some of it out now, to this enemy. Ruth could hear it, too; he did not think he would ever talk about it alone with her.

"On a certain day in 1937, April second to be exact, I would have killed every Japanese in uniform I could lay my hands on. I went to *kempei* headquarters and there I met a Major Yorida." He caught a flicker of interest in Nara's eyes. "You know him?"

"I knew him in Nanking."

"They sent him there after he killed my wife."

MCARDLE HAD LEANED against the cold green wall of the secret police headquarters and stared dazedly at Yorida.

"It was a most unfortunate occurrence." There was no sympathy in Yorida's voice. "We did not expect her to commit suicide."

"How?" McArdle had to force the word out.

"She fell from a window two floors up. She died instantly, that is the only consolation."

McArdle stood stock-still against the wall, gathering his strength. Then he launched himself at Yorida, his hands aimed at the throat. But three guards burst into the room and grabbed him. He struggled, but froze when a bayonet was jabbed at his back.

"Be still," said Yorida. "We do not want a double tragedy."

The bayonet was taken away from McArdle's back, and a chair was pushed towards him and he sank onto it. The guards left.

"Do not attempt to be foolish again, Mr. McArdle." Yorida went around behind a desk and sat down. "We know what you have been doing."

"Coaching a baseball team."

"You have also been spying on our military installations. We have had you and others under surveillance for some time."

He decided neither to confirm nor deny Yorida's accusations. "Why did you bring my—my wife here?"

"Because she must have connived in your activities. She had Western sympathies. Her father also has a traitor's respect for your culture."

"My wife was a Japanese patriot. So is her father. She knew

467

nothing—" Too late he realized he had said too much. "I don't believe she committed suicide. I want to see her!"

Yorida stood up. "This way," he said.

They went out of the room and down a corridor. A guard at a door saluted Yorida, let them into a harshly lit room but did not follow them. Mieko lay on a table at the far end of the room. A sheet covered the body; Yorida pulled it away. She was naked but for the silk panties she always wore. McArdle forced himself to look at the broken bloodied body.

"What are those marks on her stomach? And on her breasts?"

Yorida pulled the sheet back over the body. "That probably happened when she was being brought in. She resisted the arresting officers. They are immaterial. She died after jumping from a window. That will be our report."

McArdle put a hand on one of the small feet sticking up under the sheet; then he began to weep, grief washing out anger for the moment. Yorida stood watching, expressionless. "Here is your wife's handbag. Nothing has been taken."

McArdle took the handbag, opened it. There was very little in it: a small compact, a wallet, some keys. And his lucky silver dollar, which he had given her as a wedding present.

His hands were shaking and he dropped the coin. Yorida picked it up, looked at it, then handed it back. "American. It will be worth nothing some day."

McArdle drew himself together. "I'll take my wife with me. My car is outside."

"That is not possible. The body will be released in the morning."

"No—tonight! I deny that I'm a spy! I took the sort of photographs any tourist might take—"

Yorida actually smiled. "Tourists do not take photographs of railroad yards and warships and military airfields. You are finished here in Japan. Your baseball club will be informed that your contract is to be terminated immediately. You will be on a ship to America by the end of next week. Now you may go."

McArdle drove at once to the home of his father-in-law. In his rearview mirror he saw the small car following him; the two plainclothes policemen would stay with him till he left the next

468

Saturday. At Mieko's father's house he was shown straight into the main room. As soon as Professor Tanaka came into the room McArdle sensed that the older man knew what had happened.

"Why did they do it? Just because you are a foreigner?" the professor asked.

He had to keep lying. "They suspect me of being a spy. I told them the charges were ridiculous, but they won't believe me. I have to leave Japan."

"Our country has a poison running through it. Only the gods know where it will take us. . . ." Professor Tanaka put out a thin strong hand. "Stay here in my house till you have to go. We shall bury Mieko together."

They went next morning to collect the body. The funeral was quiet, only Tanaka and himself there as mourners, and the two policemen standing at a distance. And at the end of the week he went back to the United States, keeping to himself on the ship. From Vancouver he travelled by train to Washington, D.C., where he headed immediately for his brother's office.

"They murdered my wife!" he told him. "I want an official protest from the State Department to their Foreign Office."

"Con, no one was more distressed than I when Kister sent us the news from Tokyo." Liam showed genuine concern. "But a protest would do no good at all. There are others in the field besides you. Spies can't afford to retaliate."

McArdle left Washington that evening. Bitterness gripped him like an incurable illness; he had once been a fair-minded man, but now there was only one yardstick for value, the loss of Mieko. For weeks he drifted—to San Francisco, to Honolulu, to Sydney. Finally, in Brisbane, he idly picked up a magazine, the *Pacific Islands Monthly*, in the lobby of Lennons Hotel. One of its advertisements offered a copra plantation in New Britain for sale.

Two weeks later he was in Rabaul. A month later he bought Kiogo.

WHEN MULLANE and Ruth left the hut, Nara and Scheer looked at each other. Then Scheer asked, "Could it be true that this Major Yorida killed his wife?"

"It might be." Nara was one of those who had never accepted *kempei* officers. "They are no better than your Gestapo."

"Not mine. Those are the sort of things that trouble me—"

"You will have to make up your mind, Bishop." They were speaking in English, the language of the enemy; but it was their only common tongue. "If you are to come with me when I leave here," Nara said, "you will then have to go back to Germany. I can't allow you to stay in Rabaul."

Scheer was dubious. "I don't know if our plan will succeed. Neither of us could move far—"

"Have no fear, Bishop. We shall be carried out of here. Bribery is the second oldest form of seduction."

MULLANE passed the rest of the day quietly, giving his leg a chance to recover. He found it impossible to put out of his mind the thought of Rabaul and what might be going on there. While he sat here waiting, the end of the war in the Pacific could be starting just fifty miles north of him.

He eased himself up, feeling something rubbing against him. He reached into his hip pocket and found Sister Brigid's rosary beads. Luke or Mark, who did the laundry, must have put the beads back in the pocket after washing the trousers. He was tempted to throw them away, but his mother had been a great one for the rosary. He put the beads back in his pocket.

Ruth came to his hut again that evening when he set up the radio. Port Moresby gave him the answer he was waiting for: "US submarine will rendezvous south end Smokey Bay 2400 hours day after tomorrow. Confirm okay."

"Two more nights," he said to Ruth. "I hope Frank gets back with the supplies tomorrow morning. It's about an eight-mile hike up to Smokey Bay."

Mullane confirmed the rendezvous, then he repacked the radio. It was dark now and Ruth had lit the oil lamp. She looked up at him, but he did not return her gaze. She stood irresolute, wanting to comfort him but afraid of intruding.

He sat down heavily on his camp bed. "If you want to be alone, I'll go back to my hut," she said.

He gestured to the bed beside him. She sat down and looked sideways at him. "Tomorrow night Frank will be back in here."

"Exactly what I was thinking."

"The night after that we'll be on the beach at Smokey Bay waiting for the submarine."

"Again exactly what I was thinking."

"Well?"

"Well, I think we're both talking too much."

He turned out the oil lamp. Love was never mentioned, but it was in the minds of both of them when they fell asleep later.

CHAPTER SEVEN

Frank Vokes returned to camp the next afternoon, too late for them to start for Smokey Bay and the submarine rendezvous.

"I hoped you'd be back this morning," Mullane said.

Vokes sat down, took off his boots and socks. "I had a bit of trouble with Mariba. He wanted to go back to Kiogo—tried to take some of the other boys with him. I told him I'd follow him and blow his bloody head off. Once we get Ruthie and the others away tomorrow night, we have to do something about him."

"Those feet of yours could do with some treatment." Vokes's feet were blotched with ugly red patches of dermatitis. "How's your ankle?"

"Sore." Vokes grinned. "Twenty-two years old and I feel like a bloody old man."

He hobbled away along the ridge towards Ruth and her medical case. Mullane called Buka, told him not to unpack the supplies but to keep them ready for departure at first light in the morning. Bishop Scheer came to join him.

"I am not looking forward to internment," Scheer said. "I should rather be free to choose to go back to Germany or not."

"We all have much less free will than we think we do, Bishop."

"I should imagine you're a free man, Mr. Mullane. You're not in the army or navy. As I understand it, you could come out with us on that submarine—"

"How do you know it's going to be a submarine?"

471

The bishop shrugged. "It doesn't really matter. All I wish to be is neutral. It is the only role for the church in this war."

"Don't hide behind your cassock. You're as much a German as you are a Catholic."

"In a war, is there a place for a private conscience? I really don't know. I envy you your commitment, Mr. Mullane. You have no decisions to make."

"You don't believe that, Bishop. I could decide to be a coward and go out with you on the submarine," Mullane said.

Just then, looking back along the ridge, he saw General Nara coming out of his hut, supported by Mariba. Mullane hurried over to them. "Where do you think you're going?"

Nara stopped. "I am going into the bush to relieve myself."

"Okay." Mullane felt foolish, and also angry when he saw the barely concealed smile on Mariba's face.

Nara went on with Mariba, stumbling on his thin weak legs. Mullane watched them go into the bush. Just then he saw Ruth coming towards him.

"You've been edgy all day," she said when she reached him. "Is it because of what happened last night?"

"Of course not." In truth, she had been on his mind all day. But he was cautious about a declaration of love, even to himself.

"I'm glad. Because I have no regrets." For the first time in her life she was truly in love, that much she knew. But she could wait till he declared himself first.

He squeezed her hand; back along the ridge Vokes was watching them, but all at once Mullane didn't care.

A little later he and Vokes went on the air to reconfirm the next night's rendezvous. Moresby, in reply, relayed the message from Townsville: "GHQ still on our backs re King's Cross. Want fullest report 72 hours outside."

Mullane banged down the Morse key: "Tell GHQ if do not like our progress get off tails and take our place."

"That's telling them," said Vokes. "There goes my rank."

The reply came in. Mullane recognized the sense of humour that gave Townsville patience: "Will give GHQ your message end of war. Good luck."

After supper Mullane took his mosquito net, a blanket and his bottle of whisky to Scheer and Nara's hut. He sat on the ground with his back to the central roof pole and poured three glasses.

"A nightcap, gentlemen. You're both going to sleep early tonight because you have a long day ahead of you tomorrow."

"Are you going to spend the night with us?" Scheer savoured the first sip of his whisky. "We'll be a little crowded."

"It's all in the cause of seeing that you two gentlemen arrive safely and in good health in Australia."

Nara tasted his whisky appreciatively. There was something slightly odd about him, but Mullane could not pin it down.

Nara said casually, "Are you coming out with us tomorrow?"

"No. I'm going into Rabaul."

"You're a brave man." Another sip, then just as casually: "Colonel Yorida is there."

"*Colonel* Yorida?" Mullane kept his voice steady.

"He is the chief of Field Security in Rabaul. I wonder if he still thinks about what he did to your wife."

"Probably not." Mullane finished his drink, recorked the bottle. There was a fluttering in his chest but only the slightest edge to his voice. "You better go to sleep, General. You, too, Bishop."

Scheer had been watching both men closely. He knew that Nara had been baiting the American and he was shocked at the callousness of it, but he guessed that the Japanese had his reasons and he made no protest.

The three men settled down for the night. Scheer crawled in under his mosquito net and Mullane arranged the net over Nara. For a moment the eyes of the two men met in a hard gaze.

"Good night, General," Mullane said softly. "Just keep it in mind—you're not going to tempt me to kill you. You're going to Australia as a prisoner of war."

Then he sat back against the roof pole, draped his net about him and sat staring into the shadows of the hut and the past. He had to condition himself to the thought that the murderer of his wife could be no more than fifty miles away. That is, if General Nara, the tactician, was telling the truth.

MULLANE AND VOKES TOOK TURNS in three-hour watches, each of them having difficulty staying awake. The Japanese and the German appeared to sleep soundly, but behind their closed lids both were awake for a long time, each wondering about his trust in the other and in the third person Nara had enlisted.

Shortly before six o'clock Mullane woke the entire camp. "We'll be on our way in an hour. Buka, detail four boys to carry General Nara, two at a time—"

"Boss, I can't find Mariba. He look like he go home."

Mullane went striding across to where Scheer was helping Nara out of their hut. "The general wants to go to the latrine—"

"You better hang on a little longer, General." Mullane grabbed the Japanese's hand, held up the skinny wrist. He knew now what had looked odd about Nara last night. "Where's your gold watch? You scum! You've paid Mariba—where's he gone?"

Nara only stared back at the American. Mullane grabbed the bishop by the throat.

"I need him, Bishop, but I don't need you! Tell me where Mariba's gone or I'll choke you to death!"

No one else said a word; Ruth, Vokes, all the natives just stood and stared, watching Mullane's big left hand tighten on Scheer's throat. The German let go of Nara, put up both hands to pull Mullane's fingers away; Nara fell against him, slid to the ground. Still no one interfered.

"Tell me—where's he sent Mariba?"

Then Nara, still on the ground, said weakly, "Let him go. I have sent Mariba down to Noku."

Mullane let go of Scheer. It shocked him to realize how close he had come to killing the old bishop. He was learning the ways of war far quicker than he wished.

Scheer was massaging his throat, staring at Mullane as if he could not believe what the American had done. He turned and went into his hut. Mullane looked down at Nara. "Take the general to the latrine, Buka. And don't take your eyes off him."

Buka picked up the Japanese as if he were a child and half carried him into the bush. The other natives melted away to their tasks, disappointed that the drama was over. The two boys, Luke

474

and Mark, remained staring at Mullane till Ruth snapped at them and they fled away to help with the packing.

Silas came forward. "We pull the huts down, Boss?"

"Leave them. We've got to get out of here. Mariba may be back any time with the Japs."

They were ready to leave in ten minutes. Mullane went out to the end of the ridge and looked down towards Noku. Thick morning mist, like a tropical glacier, hid the narrow river valley and the plantation. There was nothing to be seen. Any sort of terror could be going on under that white cloud.

Then far away there was the drone of engines. He yelled to Vokes to set up the radio again, then ran back along the ridge. He wanted a head start on the Japanese who would soon be on their way up from Noku; but he and Vokes were Coastwatchers and their first duty lay with the American forces down in the Solomons. He sent the party on its way with Vokes leading it, keeping only the natives he needed to carry the radio.

He relayed the message: "48 bombers heading south. Am moving immediately." He gave Port Moresby no time to reply; he was repacking the set the moment he lifted his hand from the key.

There was only one track heading east, and he and his carriers soon caught up with Vokes and the others. After they had tramped for two hours, the track abruptly ran out on the edge of a beech forest, stopping dead in the undergrowth, as if the men who had made the track had suddenly been swallowed up.

"Better find another way, Boss," said Buka.

Mullane knew what he meant. Once, in the hills behind Kiogo, he had walked into a beech forest. At first the spongy ground cover was like a thick carpet. Then suddenly he had plunged through a weak spot and sunk up to his shoulders in soft rotting undergrowth. The floor of a beech forest, covered with years of fallen leaves, could be as treacherous as any swamp.

Then they heard the plane. It came in from behind them, so low that they could see the pilot and the observer looking down at them. "Into the trees!" Mullane yelled.

There was momentary confusion as everyone made his own way into the forest. Fifty yards into the trees Mullane called a halt.

They could still hear the plane as it went over, climbed steeply and came back. But this time it was at least a hundred yards away. Mullane knew the Japanese had lost sight of them.

The air down on the forest floor was hot and thick with the smell of decay; sweat streamed down into their eyes. A soft green-gold light filtered through the foliage; vines shimmered in it like reeds in water. But Mullane and the others, blinded by sweat, saw no beauty; they stumbled on, dragging their feet out of the green trap.

They could not see the plane, but for the next hour, as they moved on through the beech forest, they could hear it.

Vokes said, "It's a Kawanishi. He can fly for bloody hours!"

Then abruptly the forest ended. Buka found a track and they started down it, the party well spaced out. The trees here were a mixed lot: the *erima* and the eucalyptus-like *kamerere*, both of them tall trees with their foliage right at the top, obscuring little of the sky. Mullane knew the safest policy would be not to move at all, but he had no idea how rugged the country was that lay between them and Smokey Bay, and he had to be within sight of the bay before darkness fell.

He looked back over his shoulder and at once let out a yell. "Bishop, put down that umbrella!"

He stormed back along the track, grabbed the white umbrella from the startled Scheer, and was about to snap it in two when the German, recovering, grabbed at it.

"No!" The mud-stained, frayed sunshade had become important to him; he had no other bishop's staff than this.

Mullane, taken aback by the fierceness of the bishop's attack, let go of the umbrella. Scheer closed it with shaking hands. "I put it up without thinking—the sun was so hot—"

The elderly German was on the very edge of his nerves. Mullane gently touched his shoulder. "I believe you, Bishop. Just don't do it again. Because if those fellows in that plane see us and start shooting, they're not going to be selective."

On his way back to the head of the line Mullane stopped by Nara's stretcher. "I thought for a moment you'd put the bishop up to that little trick."

476

"You're too suspicious, Mr. Mullane. I do wish you'd give up. You must know you'll be caught eventually."

"Maybe not, General. Your men from Noku don't know where we're going to be picked up, and there are a dozen bays between here and Rabaul."

The plane went by overhead, its shadow flitting down between the trees. "Your optimism is pathetic, Mr. Mullane," said Nara.

It was late in the afternoon when they reached the final ridge above the sea. The Kawanishi scout plane was still with them, but they knew it would soon have to return to its base. It came up along the coast as Mullane led the party to the top of the ridge. Then it continued north, heading towards Rabaul.

Smokey Bay lay below, the small volcano at its northern point sending up a thin drift of smoke that gave the inlet its name. A shallow curve of sand ran around to the steep southern headland. At the northern end was a small abandoned plantation. It took them almost an hour to make their way down to the beach.

"I hope that bloody volcano doesn't take it into its head to blow up," said Vokes.

They came into the plantation, under the scraggly coconut palms and past neglected cacao trees. Some of the trees were black and scarred and there was other evidence of the last eruption of the volcano. The plantation house had collapsed under the weight of ash and the vegetation that had grown over it. A sense of death hung over the place.

"A bloke named Wagner, a German, lived here," said Vokes. "He and his wife and kids all died when the volcano blew up, oh, ten or fifteen years ago. Nobody would ever take it over again. They said it's loaded down with bad luck."

"Someone back in Townsville has a macabre sense of humour," said Mullane. "They picked this rendezvous."

The cook-boy lit a fire behind the house and a meal was prepared. In the meantime Mullane and Vokes had some of the natives stack firewood in two heaps at opposite ends of the beach. The submarine would need beacons to guide it into the bay.

"I don't like the look of those breakers," said Vokes.

He and Mullane had taken off their boots and socks before

477

they had come onto the sand, and now they stood at the water's edge, cooling their chafed and sweating feet. A breeze was blowing up from the south; long ranks of white combers broke on the black sand. If the wind kept up, the boats coming ashore from the submarine would have difficulty putting out again.

When they went back to the plantation, amid the wild crotons and hibiscus, Ruth brought Mullane his meal. She sat beside him, uncaring now whether the others noticed. She had the aching thought that she might not see him again after tonight.

"Do you have to stay on here, Con? Why can't your people back in Townsville get what they want from the general?"

"He'd never talk. I know him and his kind too well."

"They could get it out of him—torture him if they had to—"

Mullane was shocked at her practical callousness.

"I think she's got something," said Vokes, who was nearby.

"Frank, they'd never get a word out of Nara. People like him aren't afraid of death—"

"Everyone's afraid of it," Vokes said stubbornly, deathly afraid of it himself. "All I'm thinking about is my own neck."

Mullane stood up abruptly. "I'm going into Rabaul. If you're so concerned for your neck, Frank, you can go out on the sub tonight. Maybe they'll let you help interrogate the general!"

He left them, walked around the house and down to the beach. And saw the Japanese patrol boat come around the point.

HE RAN BACK behind the house, yelling for the natives to throw earth and palm fronds on the cooking fire. In less than a minute there was no sign of it. All of their gear was gathered up, and Mullane herded the party up through the coconut groves towards the jungle at the rear of the plantation. He kept both Nara and Scheer close to him.

"No tricks, General," he said.

The Japanese made no reply, just trotted on unsteady legs through the long grass.

Two hundred yards behind the plantation Mullane signalled a halt and everyone sank down in the undergrowth. Mullane adjusted his binoculars and saw the boat turn in towards the beach.

478

It stopped about a hundred yards offshore and he saw the soldiers, about twenty of them, lining the rail on the narrow deck.

Mullane checked back over his shoulder. General Nara caught his eye and smiled. "Why don't you surrender? I shall personally guarantee that no harm will come to you."

"Don't be stupid, General." Ruth's voice was quiet, but there was acid in it. "He's like you—he's never going to surrender."

Then Buka said, "Boss—"

Two rubber rafts were coming in from the patrol boat, each carrying half a dozen men. The rafts hit the beach, one of them turning over.

"Con!" Vokes said. "They'll know we've been here! We forgot— our footprints are all up and down the beach!"

"Relax," said Mullane, but he was more worried than he sounded. "You and I had our boots off. It could have been some boys from up in the hills."

"What about the firewood we've set?"

Mullane had forgotten about the heaps of wood at either end of the beach, obvious clues that a rendezvous had been arranged.

"The general and I—let us go down to the beach," said Scheer. "You and the others can escape back into the hills—"

Mullane looked at Nara. "Would you strike such a bargain?"

"No," said Nara quietly. "Your work with Mr. Vokes is too valuable to be allowed to continue. I'm sorry, but you have to be stopped. Either by surrendering or being killed."

Scheer looked at him, frowning in puzzlement, as if Nara had all at once turned into a stranger. "General, you promised—"

"Bishop, forgive me." He held out his only hand. "When one is at war, promises are just another weapon."

Mullane snapped, "Okay, that's it. Get moving, everyone!"

Vokes led off and everyone fell in behind him. But Scheer grabbed Mullane's arm. "Please let me go down there—I can tell the Japanese you're in the hills, heading for the north coast."

"I can't afford to trust you."

"I can't go on—I'm worn out—"

"You could go down there and the Japs could kill you and still come after us. I don't want that to happen to you."

He pushed Scheer ahead of him and turned for a last look down at the beach. The Japanese were still in the surf, trying to bring ashore the capsized raft. Then he heard a crashing in the bushes and spun around.

The bishop was running towards the plantation, stumbling on his old legs, falling but picking himself up again, running, Mullane thought, with the crazed faith of a martyr.

SCHEER STAGGERED into the plantation and leaned against a coconut palm. His breath came in long searing gasps. Blood was running from a cut on his cheek, and his right ankle, which he had turned as he had fallen, was swelling painfully.

"God, please help me—"

He stared down between the long lines of trees, waiting for the Japanese to come around the ruined house and open fire on him at sight. But they were still on the beach, out of his view. He straightened up, looked at the umbrella he still held. Then he opened it, and with the spreading of the small white canopy he seemed to gather strength.

He marched down through the plantation, something of the soldier in the straightness of his spine. The Japanese, both rafts now beached, looked up as Scheer walked towards them. A battery of guns came up and he waited for the bullets to thud into him. Then someone barked an order. The soldiers, guns still aimed at him, moved closer.

The bishop paused only a few yards from them and took a deep breath to stop the trembling that shook him.

"*Sprechen Sie Deutsch?*"

Two officers, one middle-aged and the other little more than a boy, stepped forward. The older officer said, "I speak German, not very well. Who are you?"

"I am the Roman Catholic bishop of Waku, Friedrich von Scheer." He clicked his heels and bowed. "I am German and I wish to give myself up and be taken to your commander."

The officer looked up towards the ruins of the house. "You are alone? Where are the Australian spies? And General Nara?"

So Mariba had got down to Noku with Nara's message. "They

480

have gone over the mountains, they are to be picked up by submarine tonight at midnight on the north coast, at Open Bay. I escaped last night—General Nara helped me. He was too ill to come with me—he asked me to try to get to Rabaul for help." He was surprised at how easily the lies were coming.

"I am Colonel Yorida," the officer said. "How am I to know you are telling the truth?"

The shock of the name unnerved Scheer. What was this man doing here? Had General Nara somehow managed to get his message across that Yorida was to be told that his old enemy, the American named McArdle, was here on New Britain?

"I am a priest—" The umbrella shivered above him.

Yorida took out his pistol, held it at the German's head. "Everyone can tell lies, even priests. Do you swear by your God that what you say is the truth?"

Lord, forgive me. . . . "I swear it is the truth."

ON A RIDGE behind the plantation Mullane, glasses to his eyes, peered through the dusk at the tiny figures on the beach.

"We should've gone after him," said Vokes. "He's on their side—he'll do us in, I'll bet—"

"No!" said Mullane. "They're leaving!" He felt his hands shake as he held the binoculars. All at once he was full of admiration for the bishop. The old German had sacrificed himself.

The two rafts put out into the surf, noses high, as if they were going to be flung back on the sand. But the rafts rode the breakers and a moment later Mullane saw them moving steadily towards the waiting patrol boat. The bishop had closed his umbrella and Mullane could not pick him out among the soldiers.

That night the party congregated at the edge of the sand where it merged into the long grass that had once been the front lawn of the plantation house. The breeze had dropped and the surf had flattened out. The scent of frangipani was a mocking perfume, too romantically sweet for the occasion.

"Another half hour," said Vokes. "I'd better send Buka and Silas along to the fires. You think the sub will come?"

Mullane looked up at the moon. It was too late now for doubts;

the submarine was probably already standing offshore, its periscope scanning the black coast for the beacon fires.

"It'll come." Mullane felt for Ruth's hand in the darkness.

"I wish you'd leave with us," she said. "If the Japs catch you, you'll be here for ever. Buried."

"Don't talk like that, Ruthie." Vokes stirred uncomfortably in the grass. "We'll be all right."

"I thought you were coming out with me."

"I thought about it," Vokes said, "but I couldn't leave Con to go into Rabaul on his own. . . . You know what I mean, Con." He couldn't bring himself to say anything about duty.

General Nara listened to the conversation but without any real interest. Despair had taken hold of him. He had placed so much faith in the certainty of his rescue that he had not even allowed himself to think what would happen if everything failed.

Then Vokes, who had been staring at the dark sea, shouted, "There it is! Off the southern point!"

Everyone was on his feet at once. Vokes sprinted to the southern end of the beach; Luke and Mark, on an order from Mullane, raced to the northern end to tell Silas to light his fire.

Suddenly Nara fell onto the sand and grabbed the rifle lying there; it was Vokes's .303. The Australian, in his haste to get the fire lighted, had run off without it. Now Nara, whimpering with pain, brought up his stump to steady the gun, aimed at Mullane.

"It is not going to end your way, Mr. Mullane."

"You'll never get away, General. They'll be ashore here in a few minutes—they'll hunt you down—"

"I'll be dead before then. So will you—and Mr. Vokes, too. When he comes back I am going to shoot you both."

Mullane let out a nervous sigh. He wanted to curse Vokes for his carelessness; but how could he blame the Australian? He had been just as careless for not having noticed the rifle.

Then there was a shot and Nara suddenly crumpled; the .303 went off, but the bullet went wide of Mullane. Ruth looked at the pistol in her hand, Nara's own gun, then she dropped it in the sand. At that moment, at both ends of the beach, the fires flared up.

Mullane stepped forward, leaned over the dead Japanese. He took the rifle and straightened up.

"I had to do it, Con. He would have killed you—"

"It's all right." He put his arm around her.

Vokes came running back along the beach, followed by Buka, Silas and the others.

"I heard the shots—" Then Vokes looked down at Nara's body. "Did he shoot himself? Where'd he get the gun—. Oh, no!"

Grimly Mullane handed him the .303. "Take better care of it from now on, Frank. Ruth shot him. He was going to kill us."

Vokes slammed a fist savagely against his hip. "I'm sorry, Con. I'm so bloody stupid—"

Buka said, "Boss, here come the boats!"

The two canvas pinnaces from the submarine came gliding in through the surf, onto the beach. Mullane went to meet them. There were two men in each boat, one of the four a lieutenant.

"I'm Joe Pilowski. Lieutenant Commander Berry sends his compliments, says he'd like to get us out of here as quickly as possible. How many passengers do we have?"

"A woman and two native kids."

"We were supposed to be coming in here for a German bishop and some Jap colonel or something—"

"He was a general—he's up there, dead. And the Japs took the bishop away this afternoon. Here's my report." Mullane handed over the six-page summary he had scribbled out earlier in the evening. "It's all in there, except about the general being shot. Miss Riddle will explain everything."

"Well, okay." Pilowski sounded disappointed, put out. "We brought you some supplies. Can your fellers unload them?"

The three sailors who had come in with Pilowski were already lifting boxes out of the boats. Mullane had a sudden feeling of comfort at the sound of the American voices. All at once he wanted to go home.

He turned and walked back up the beach to Ruth. "Would you post these letters for me?"

He had written them the day before, including one to Liam. In Liam's letter he had enclosed the last will and testament of

484

Cornelius James McArdle, in which everything he owned or might inherit was bequeathed to one Ruth Riddle.

She took the letters. "I hope some day you'll write to me."

"I will, I promise." He held her by the arms, kissed her gently on the lips. "I'll take care, Ruth. I love you."

She said nothing, just clung to him with a fierce passion that did not need words, then she broke from him and went down to the water's edge. He followed and helped her into the forward boat. He gave it a shove and it rose up over a small wave, then glided out towards the dim shape of the submarine.

Ruth looked back at the beach. But it was soon indistinguishable from the black bulk of the mountains behind it. She looked in vain for a last sight of the man she loved and hoped she had not lost. But all she saw was the dark silhouette of the mountains, the wild hills where Mullane and Frank Vokes would continue to fight their small and very private war.

CHAPTER EIGHT

In the morning Mullane paid off all the natives but Buka. "Silas," he said, "take the boys back to Kiogo. Tell the Japanese, if they are still there, that Boss Vokes and I went off last night in the boat that goes under the sea. I trust you, Silas. Tell the boys I trust them, too. Tell them not to be like Mariba."

"If Mariba come back, I kill him," said Silas matter-of-factly.

When Silas and the carriers had gone, Mullane, Vokes and Buka took the radio and the supplies up into the bush and hid them. After that they gathered their packs, guns and the four grenades they had taken from the Japanese Mullane had shot their second day out of Kiogo. Then the little party started off. Their first stop would be Taluka, some eight miles south of Rabaul. A reconnaissance of the Japanese airstrip there was the initial task Mullane had set for himself.

Moving up the slope, they headed almost due north so as to be out of sight of the coast. A mile inland they heard the Kawanishi scout plane coming up behind them from the direction of Smokey Bay.

"It looks as if it's heading for the north coast," Vokes said. "I wonder what the bishop told them?"

"I'm not even guessing. I just hope he's still alive."

"Yeah." Vokes was abruptly sober. "He wasn't a bad sort. Do you think they might try working him over?"

"I hope not." But he feared for the bishop if he should be interrogated by Yorida.

They covered only ten miles that day and camped for the night on a high, quiet ridge, light-years away from any war; it was difficult to conjure up what lay ahead of them in Rabaul. Mullane, lying awake, saw the flying foxes scrape a dark line across the moon, heard the call of a night bird. He felt a strong urge to stay here and let the war take care of itself.

At noon the next day they caught sight of the first village, a small collection of grass huts. "We in Baining land, Boss," said Buka. "They bad. People say they still eat long pig." Long pig was the native term for human flesh.

"You better find us another track, Buka."

Buka led them around the base of the ridge and below the village. They saw three other villages in the next four hours and skirted those, too. In the late afternoon, they were coming through a thick stand of *erima* trees when they heard the sound of a motorcycle, then of trucks. They moved on cautiously, came out behind a pile of huge limestone boulders. Ahead of them was a dirt road. The motorcycle and two trucks were bowling along it, spinning out a thick train of dust. Then half a dozen more trucks went by, each separated from the one in front of it by fifty yards and each trailing its wake of dust.

When the air cleared, Mullane saw the Japanese guard post two hundred yards down the road to the left. He crept out to the edge of the timber and raised his glasses. A hundred yards away in the other direction were three soldiers, so coated in dust that they looked like mummies. Past the three soldiers he could see a small trading store with some trucks pulled up outside it and several Japanese standing around. In the other direction, beyond the guard post, was a small bridge with sentries at either end.

Vokes and Buka came forward and crouched beside him in the

486

long grass. Vokes said, "We're not going to get to Taluka before dark if we have to make a detour."

"We'll wait till the next convoy passes," Mullane replied. "Then we'll cross the road, one by one, through the dust each truck kicks up."

It was twenty minutes before a convoy of six petrol tankers came over the bridge beyond the guard post.

"This is it. You go behind the first tanker, Frank. Then you take the next one, Buka. I'll meet you in that timber on the other side."

The first truck rumbled by, raising a thick grey murk. Vokes sprinted blindly through the choking dust, came out on the other side and plunged into the thick bush. The second tanker came by and Buka went through the dust like a brown spirit. Then it was Mullane's turn. He heard the third truck coming, saw the dust thicken and launched himself into the road. He almost hit the back of the tanker, going by its tail with inches to spare. The pack on his back slipped, pulling him sideways, and he went down on his knees. He heard the next truck coming and flung himself forward. The tanker went by, its front wheel brushing the heel of his boot. Mullane picked himself up and ran into the forest, where Vokes and Buka waited.

They could not be more than two or three miles from Taluka.

IT HAD STARTED TO RAIN heavily when they were no more than a quarter of an hour into the forest. The rain had slowed their pace, but in such a downpour few Japanese or natives were likely to be moving around. Ahead of them lay a field of tall kunai grass, then a hill dotted with trees and scrub and, at its crest, a thick wall of banyan-like ficus trees.

Then they saw the small scout plane come over the hill and go wobbling down beyond the field of kunai.

"That's it!" Vokes said. "That's Taluka!"

"When it's dark we'll head for that hill," Mullane said. "We'll hide in those trees at the top."

They stayed in the forest till darkness fell, then they moved off to the long line of ficus trees, a huge wall of timber that loomed over them like the battlements of a castle. The roots and trunks of the trees were interlinked and the foliage thick and massive, an ideal hiding place.

It was not easy climbing, but at last they were high among the top branches, under a canopy of thick leaves. Suddenly there was a commotion above them and Vokes almost fell out of the tree in fright. Dozens of flying foxes streamed away in a cloud, a black mass against the stars that were now beginning to appear. "Geez," Vokes said, "if I don't get the Victoria Cross for this trip . . ."

"Better try for some sleep," Mullane advised. "Wedge yourself in somewhere and tie yourself to a branch."

When Mullane woke at first light he was shivering and he wondered if he were coming down with malaria. He took an extra Atabrine tablet, then ate some cold spam and biscuits.

"This is a great spot," Vokes said. "We can see everything."

The landing strip was evident, a misty white swath cut through the kunai grass. Parking bays covered with camouflage netting were at either side of the runway and several low buildings stood on the western side of the strip. A hundred yards to the east of it was a coconut plantation.

"Twelve planes," said Vokes. "There should be twice or three times that. Where have all those bombers been coming from?"

"I don't know. They must be flying at least another four or five squadrons out of somewhere in this area."

"You want me to go down, look around, Boss?" Buka, the one who could merge with the landscape, was eager to prove he had not come along just for the walk.

"All right, but be careful, Buka. Try talking to some of the villagers, find out if anything special is going on."

Buka, leaving his Japanese rifle and his pack, disappeared down into the depths of the tree. It was now broad daylight, and as the mist lifted, Mullane saw the airfield come alive. Trucks started up, aircraft were pushed out to the sides of the runway to be fuelled by the tankers.

Then Vokes let out a yelp. "Over to the right! The plantation!"

Mullane swung his glasses. The plantation was an estate of mature coconut palms. But as he focused he saw several of the boundary trees being *drawn aside*.

488

"The whole bloody plantation is camouflage!" said Vokes.

Mullane gazed carefully at what was being exposed, amazed by the Japanese ingenuity. Actual trees had been left standing at intervals of a hundred feet, wide enough for a bomber to be manoeuvred between them. Strung between the trees were wires from which hung netting painted with matching tree trunks. The top of the plantation, hundreds of palm fronds spread out like umbrellas, was nothing more than one huge camouflage net. From the air the estate would look like a working operation.

As Mullane watched, the first bomber took off, racing down the strip towards the trees where he and Vokes were hidden. The noise was deafening as, one by one, thirty-two planes passed over their heads. These planes would link up with bombers from the other strips and the mass of them would head south for another raid. Mullane could only hope that the Coastwatchers down in the Solomons were able to alert the fighters waiting to take off from Guadalcanal. He itched to get to a Morse key.

For the rest of the day the two men dozed in turn, knowing that there would be little sleep for them that night, when they moved on to Rabaul.

Buka came back in the late afternoon, an hour after the last bomber had returned. There had been no missing planes, a bad sign; it suggested that the Coastwatchers were not on the air. Mullane wondered if the posts had been overrun and the men captured, or whether, like himself and Vokes, they had lost the use of their radios.

Buka came up out of the twisted depths of the tree as if he were emerging from the bowels of the earth.

"I found a police boy worked with me one time. He work for Jap now. He say plenty things going on, lots more Jap come here. Plenty ships in harbour. But he dunno where they going or when."

As soon as darkness fell they climbed down out of the tree. The sky was clear and Mullane set a course by the stars.

They made good progress, and it was not yet midnight when they came out on top of the cliffs above the road that skirted Simpson Harbour at Rabaul. They had passed several Japanese guard posts, but these were in cleared areas and easily visible. Once, when they passed close to a native garden, a dog barked at them, but no one came out to see what had disturbed the animal. Mullane was grateful for the Japanese complacency.

On the cliff top, early German settlers had planted a thick stand of ficus trees as windbreaks for their plantations. Now Mullane and the others climbed into one and looked down at Rabaul.

The moon was still high, a bomber's moon, and Mullane was able to pick out landmarks. Immediately to their right was the six-hundred-foot Mount Vulcan, the volcano that had erupted in 1937. The harbour itself was the flooded crater of what had been another huge volcano. On the far side of the palely shining stretch of water was Rabaul township, yellow diamonds of light in the darkness below black hills.

"I wonder if the bishop is over there?" Vokes whispered.

"Maybe we can find out tomorrow." Mullane was restless now, wanting to gather all the information they could and be gone. "You willing to go into town tomorrow, Buka?"

"Okay, Boss."

"There's a storekeeper in Chinatown named Charlie Hong—you remember him. We used to buy some of our stuff from him."

"Charlie Hong good feller. What you want me to ask him?"

"Ask him where Jap headquarters are. If we can pinpoint it, our planes can bomb it. And find out where Field Security is."

"You're not thinking of going after that bloke Yorida, are you?" said Vokes.

Mullane was glad of the darkness. "No. But a bomb on *him* would be some satisfaction."

Just before dawn Buka set off again, armed only with the colour of his skin. Day came up grey and drab, and the harbour and the town were soon clearly visible to the two Coastwatchers. In the harbour there were dozens of ships: tankers, supply ships, transports, destroyers; out at sea on the edge of the big bay were warships, an aircraft carrier and several large cruisers.

From his pack Mullane withdrew some yellowed pages from *Jane's Fighting Ships*. He had taken them to Japan to identify ships in Tokyo Bay and other harbours. Now he called out the types of ships before him as Vokes wrote down the information.

"At least seventy ships this area, tell them," he said. "Two Nati first-class cruisers, two Kako first-class cruisers, two Mogami second-class cruisers, one Kuma second-class cruiser, one Tenryu second-class cruiser, three sloops, thirty destroyers, two passenger liners—all those off Blanche Bay. In Simpson Harbour four more destroyers, sixteen freighters, six tankers, one submarine mother ship. And eight Kawanishi flying boats."

"When do you reckon the fleet's going to move out?"

"They're not going to keep a buildup like that waiting around to get bombed. They'll be on their way tomorrow at the outside."

"They must be heading for Guadalcanal." Vokes was doing some quick calculations. "That's about seven hundred miles from here— two and a half days' steaming. If we wait till they leave, we're really going to have to turn on the speed to get back to the wireless in time."

"You better get going right after dark, then."

"Why me? What are you planning to do?"

"I'm going back to Taluka." The plan, wild though it seemed, had taken hold in Mullane's restless mind. "I'm resigning from the Coastwatchers for a few days. I'll rejoin when I meet you back at Smokey Bay."

Vokes looked at him carefully. "You still got that Yorida on your mind. How are you going to settle anything with him? Unless you're thinking of something stupid, like a suicide mission."

"No, nothing like that. I'm going to try and do something about that camouflaged hangar."

"You're out of your bloody head."

Mullane looked across the harbour again, as conscious of Yorida's presence as if the man were standing in full view a hundred yards away, down in the plantation between the road and the water's edge. Then he said, "I'll take your .303 and the telescopic sight. You can have the tommy gun."

Vokes was not sure what Mullane had in mind and he preferred not to know. He had developed an affection for the American that he would not have believed possible in the time they had been together. Con Mullane was a friend, one whom he would miss terribly if something happened to him.

"I'll be okay, Frank. Really." Mullane sensed the other's concern for him and was touched by it.

"Hey!" Vokes said suddenly. "Look along there!"

Less than two hundred yards away was an anti-aircraft gun emplacement, its crew going about their morning ablutions, cooking breakfast, dragging a camouflage net over the gun pit.

Mullane studied them. "We'll be all right if we just sit tight." He had observed that men in war were rarely, if ever, concerned with anything beyond their immediate task.

The day dragged on. They saw fighters and small planes come and go on the airstrip south of the town. Barges moved between the ships in the harbour and the shore. Later a fleet of barges packed with troops moved out to the transports in the harbour.

Buka came back with the darkness. "Jap going out, some tonight, some tomorrow night," he reported. "Charlie not know where, but he think Bougainville, Guadalcanal, somewhere down there."

"It's on, then," said Vokes.

"Jap headquarters, it up in New Guinea Club, Charlie say. I couldn't get up that street, they got guards all around it. But Charlie say there is big hole in ground, covered up—"

"A bunker?"

"Yeah, that what he call it. It where the Jap big boss is. It just across the road from the New Guinea Club."

"What about Field Security, Buka?"

"Their headquarters in police station. Charlie say feller, Colonel Yorida, he very tough on all Chinamen."

"You hear that, Frank? When you get back to Smokey Bay, tell them I'd like a bomb right on the police station. With a bit of luck you'll be back there the day after tomorrow."

"I'll never make it in these rotting boots. They're falling off my feet after all this mucking around. I'm going by boat."

"How do you think you're going to do that?"

"Con, look out there. There are boats coming and going all the time—it's like a regatta in Sydney harbour. I've been watching that plantation on the water there. It's got five or six launches and a petrol dump at the end of the jetty. All I'll need is a four-gallon drum and one of those boats."

"How are you going to get down there to swipe them?"

"I've just got to be careful, that's all. The boat's my only hope. Once I'm on my way, you two can start off for Taluka. You keep Buka with you."

Buka nodded. Mullane saw there was no point in further argument. And the possibility of Vokes's reaching the radio in a few hours had given him another idea. "If you do get away, you should be down at Smokey Bay in—what—four hours? Send the main message, that's the important one. Then tell them I'd like some air force cooperation. This is what I'm planning to do. . . ."

Vokes listened to Mullane in silence, then said, "You *are* committing suicide, Con."

"Just tell the RAAF—it has to be Hudsons coming in at night—that I want them over the target area at twenty minutes after midnight."

"Righto, I'll tell them. But there's going to be hell to pay when Townsville finds out what you're up to."

"I'm still a civilian, remember? The worst they can do is send me to Australia."

"Well, that'd please Ruthie, if no one else." Vokes fumbled 'in his pack. "You've just reminded me. I'm putting my tabs on, just in case. There. A bloody sublieutenant." He picked up his gear. "Well, time I was going. See you back at Smokey Bay."

"I'll come down to the road with you, make sure you get started. Stay here, Buka."

Mullane went ahead of Vokes, not wanting any argument. He left his pack and the .303 Lee-Enfield in the tree; he also left his Yankees baseball cap, but he did not notice its absence.

They found a path and started off, clinging to rocks and shrubs to keep from sliding down the almost vertical track. When they reached the road Mullane stopped. He clasped Vokes's hand. "Take care, Frank."

"You, too, Con."

For a moment Vokes wondered if he would ever see Mullane again; but there was no time for the emotion he felt well up in him. He ran in a crouch across the road and towards the jetty. The plantation, he now saw, was some sort of workshop area; there was a row of five trucks and behind them three tin sheds that he had not seen from their treetop observation post. Vokes suddenly lost heart, knew he had done the wrong thing in attempting to steal a boat; but there was no turning back.

He almost ran into the Japanese sentry before seeing him. He dropped down behind a pile of petrol drums just in time. Then luck, the element the generals say should not be trusted in war, struck. There was the drone of engines high in the moonlit sky as four Royal Australian Air Force Hudsons came in. Suddenly the night exploded with noise and red light. Out on the harbour, fans of blue-white water opened up in a ghastly sort of beauty; there was a brilliant mixture of red, yellow and black as a ship blew up. Vokes could not have wished for a better distraction.

Behind him he saw a truck swing in off the road. A dozen soldiers came tumbling out of it, fell into the ground and disappeared from sight. There must be slit trenches all around the area. He was lucky he hadn't fallen into one, but that seemed to be the limit of his luck. He wasn't going to get out of here, not before the bombers had gone.

Mullane, who was hidden in the trees on the other side of the road, saw the soldiers fall out of the truck and dive into the ground. He could not see Vokes, but he knew it was only a matter of minutes before the Australian would be discovered. He'd never get away unless there was another diversion.

Mullane sighed and patted his right-hand breast pocket: the silver dollar's luck had at last run out. Then his hand strayed to his hip pocket and he took out the rosary beads.

He held them while an idea formed in his mind: he had to remember a name. Then he remembered: it was Holtz, Father Holtz.

Mullane crossed the road on the run and stood by the now empty truck. Anti-aircraft guns along the cliff barked and thundered; out in the harbour, ships were adding their bit to the barrage as the Hudsons made their bombing runs. Standing there in the open, Mullane saw a head come up out of a slit trench and remain fixed, as if its owner could not believe what he saw; then the soldier came upright, his rifle pointed straight at Mullane. The latter flung his hands in the air.

The other soldiers sprang out of their trenches. Arms still above his head, the rosary beads dangling from one hand, Mullane looked around at the puzzled, threatening Japanese.

"I am Father Holtz," he said in German. "A German missionary, from Waku." He straightened his right arm. *"Heil Hitler!"*

The Japanese hesitated; then one of them, a corporal, jabbed his rifle at Mullane and pushed him towards the truck.

Behind the petrol drums at the jetty, Vokes saw Mullane being bundled into the truck. The sentry who had been lying in a trench nearby had run up the road towards a blazing shed. Sick at the thought of what was going to happen to his friend, Vokes ripped back a tarpaulin and grabbed two drums. Then, staggering under his load, he stumbled to the launches on the beach.

Hurriedly he inspected the first, the second, then the third boat: no oars in any of them. He gave a yelp of relief when he saw the oars in the fourth launch. He dumped the petrol drums and his gear into the boat, pushed it into the water and sculled out past the end of the small jetty, keeping low in his seat. When he rounded the narrow point at the end of the beach he fumbled with the starter of the engine. There was a cough, then silence. On the third attempt the motor caught. He settled back against the tiller and headed the launch at the shadow thrown by the tall cone of Mount Vulcan ahead of him. He had a long, still dangerous way to go, but he knew he was going to make it back to Smokey Bay.

CHAPTER NINE

By the time the Japanese truck was two hundred yards along the road to town, the RAAF Hudsons were on their way home. Mullane wondered if Vokes had managed to get away; if he hadn't, then Mullane had done the wrong thing in giving himself up. He should have sacrificed Vokes, climbed back up the cliff and set off for Smokey Bay with Buka to send the information they had gathered. He had acted on a personal level, been concerned only for Vokes, not for the larger, more important issue. He wondered about Buka, waiting for him on the cliff top, and hoped he would have the sense to give up and go back to Kiogo.

The truck pulled up at the police station, and it struck Mullane that he was about to come face to face with Yorida. Would the Japanese recognize him? He touched his beard, then felt the hair curling around his ears. *I wouldn't have recognized you,* Lee Chin had said. But perhaps Yorida, the professional investigator, would be sharper-eyed.

Mullane was roughly bundled down from the truck and marched inside. He remained impassive, doing his best to hide that he understood what was being said, while the corporal explained to the sergeant where he had picked up the newcomer. "He must be German; he saluted Hitler. He has those beads—what are they?"

"Rosary beads. He could be a missionary. Leave him here."

There were two other men in the office besides the sergeant. "Do you speak German?" Mullane said. "I am Father Holtz—"

The sergeant shook his head. "You speak Japanese?" he asked. Then in English: "Do you speak English?"

Just in time Mullane stopped himself from shaking his head. With an effort he looked blank. "I am German—"

"Try him with pidgin," said one of the clerks.

"That's no good for interrogating anyone—it's baby talk. No, you'd better go and get Colonel Yorida. He speaks German."

Oh, no, thought Mullane. Would he have an ear for accent? Scheer had complimented Mullane on his fluency in German, but had not commented on his accent.

It was fifteen minutes before Yorida arrived. In five years he had changed. He was even thinner and he looked unhealthy. He wore horn-rimmed glasses and they seemed to accentuate the gauntness of his face.

Yorida looked Mullane up and down. Mullane smiled at him. After all, he was supposed to be a missionary, a man of charity. But he could feel the old anger and hatred welling up inside him like a sickness. Five years fell away in an instant and the two of them were back in the harshly lit room with Mieko's body lying on the table between them.

"You are German?" Yorida's German was strongly accented. "You are a Christian missionary? What is your name?"

"Father Gottfried Holtz." He didn't know where the Gottfried came from; it just fell onto his tongue. "I am from Waku, west of here, near Gasmata."

Yorida stared at him and for a moment Mullane thought he saw the dawning of recognition in his face. Then the Japanese nodded and led the way into an inner room. He lit the lamp on his desk, gestured to Mullane to sit down on a chair opposite him. Mullane hoped the light did not fall directly on his face.

"Tell me your story, Father Holtz."

Mullane looked down at the beads in his hands, wondered why he was still holding them (they seemed such a simple, futile disguise), then applied himself to his story.

"My bishop, Bishop von Scheer—" He paused, but there was no expression on Yorida's face. Was Scheer already dead? "My bishop ordered me to leave last March. But I disobeyed him—I went to see some sick natives. When I got back, the boat had gone. Since then I have been living with the natives in the mountains."

"Why have you come into Rabaul now?"

"My conscience has been worrying me. I want to go home to the fatherland, where I feel I can perhaps do more good."

"Waku is a long way from here. Why did you not go to Gasmata to give yourself up?"

"I did not want some junior officer at Gasmata deciding my fate. I decided to come to Rabaul, to the top, as it were."

"The senior officer at Gasmata is of superior rank to myself," said Yorida. "But I'm the one who will decide your fate here."

"With due respect, Colonel Yorida, I demand that I be taken before the general in command."

Yorida smiled. "You will have to be satisfied with me, Father Holtz. Your story needs to be checked. We seem to be overrun with priests wanting to go home to save their fatherland." Then he called out in Japanese: "Sergeant, bring the German bishop here. But don't tell him why we want him."

When the sergeant had gone, Yorida looked back at Mullane. "Do you have family in Germany?"

"No." The less history one had, the less one had to remember. "They are all dead."

"Killed in the war?"

"No. My parents and my brother died before the war." He could not resist asking, "Do you have a family in Japan, Colonel? A wife perhaps?"

"No." Mullane was surprised when Yorida offered more information than he had expected: "My wife and children were killed in a bombing raid by the Americans on Tokyo last April."

Mullane could feel no satisfaction at the other man's tragedy, but he could not bring himself to offer sympathy. He sat there on the uncomfortable chair, thinking about Scheer now, wondering how he was going to enlist the bishop on his side.

Yorida looked exhausted, and he seemed to have difficulty in getting his breath. He's dying, thought Mullane; and wondered what disease had got to him. TB, malaria, typhus: any of them might have attacked him. He could not believe that Yorida was dying from grief.

The sergeant brought Bishop Scheer into the room. Mullane stood up at once, grabbed Scheer's hand and said in German, "Your Reverence, how glad I am to see you still alive! When you said to me, 'Father Holtz, you must leave the island,' I should have listened to you."

"That's enough," snapped Yorida. He leaned forward. "Bishop Scheer, do you know this man?"

Scheer was silent. He's going to give me away, Mullane thought; he's chosen his side. The German no longer wore his tattered cassock; he had been issued new cotton twill trousers and shirt and rubber-cleated boots.

At last Scheer spoke. "You always were a stubborn man, Father Holtz. Yes, Colonel, I know this man. He was one of my assistants down at Waku. His name is Father Willy Holtz."

Yorida straightened up. "Father *Willy* Holtz? That was not the name he gave me."

Mullane said, almost too quickly, "Willy was my nickname. The natives had trouble saying Father Gottfried."

Yorida said, "Father Holtz is like you, Bishop. He wants to go home and fight the war for Herr Hitler. You can both sail on the ship leaving tomorrow morning for Singapore. How you get from there to Germany will be someone else's problem. Good night."

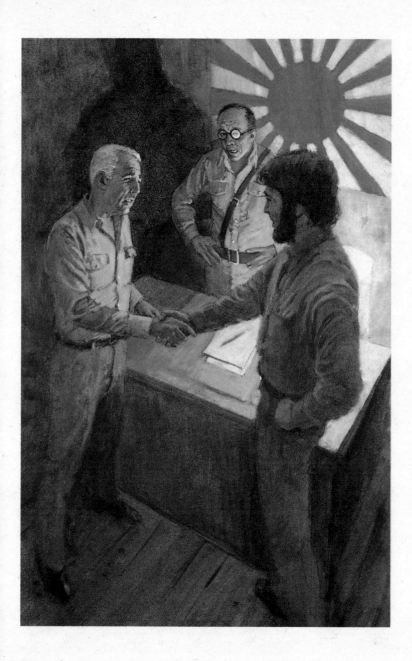

I can't believe it, Mullane thought. After all these years it can't end like this. A formal bow, a polite good night: you don't say goodbye to your wife's killer like this.

Scheer took Mullane's arm. "Let us go, Willy. You look in need of a rest." His grip was strong; Scheer was going to get Mullane out of the room before he did something stupid.

Outside the police station, the sergeant turned Mullane and the bishop over to two soldiers, said good night to the prisoners and went back inside.

"We have some distance to walk," said Scheer. "They have no transport for a couple of unwanted priests. What are you doing in Rabaul?" He saw Mullane glance inquiringly at the two soldiers close behind them. "Don't worry, they don't speak German."

Mullane, knowing now that the German could be trusted, told him everything. "But I don't know if Vokes got away," he finished. "I just hope so."

"What about Buka?"

"If he had any sense, he headed back to Kiogo."

"What made you decide to pose as Father Holtz?"

Mullane grinned, took out the rosary beads. "Inspiration, I guess. Sister Brigid must have put a ghostly hand on my shoulder."

It was a good twenty-minute walk to the house on the beach where Scheer was being held. In the harbour, ships were still burning from the RAAF raid. But the seagoing traffic had started up again and barges were chugging from the wharves towards the transports and supply ships. As they neared the beach, Mullane saw four Japanese soldiers pull an outboard launch up on the sand and quickly disappear into a waiting truck.

Scheer and Mullane arrived at the house and went in, leaving their two guards on the veranda. Scheer led the way into a bedroom containing a single iron-framed bed and a wardrobe.

"You had better sleep here," said Scheer. "My room is opposite. They are calling us early. Our ship sails at six o'clock in the morning."

"Bishop, I'm not going anywhere on that ship!"

"Mr. Mullane, what's the alternative? Suicide? I don't think that is in your nature, any more than it is in mine."

"How long do you think I can keep up this pretence of being a German?"

The bishop sighed. "Who knows? But so long as you can, you will remain alive. We may never even reach Germany. We may spend the rest of the war together as guests of the Japanese. The prospect doesn't appeal to me. . . ."

"Nor to me, Bishop. If you hear any sort of disturbance during the night, just stay in your room."

"If you get away, what shall I tell Colonel Yorida? That you had changed your mind about fighting for Herr Hitler?" Scheer went to the window, looked out through the rattan blind. "There are two guards out there. I was flattered that Colonel Yorida thought I was worthy of such surveillance." The old bishop laughed softly, but only for a moment. "They will shoot you as soon as you make a move, Con. I am concerned for you." It was the first time Scheer had used the name.

"I'm concerned for you, too, Bishop. If I do get away, it will make things awkward for you—Yorida may not believe that you did not help me. But I have to try. I may be too young for suicide, but I'm not old enough for surrender."

It seemed that Scheer winced. "You did not have to say that, even if it's true. Well, I suppose it is goodbye again." Scheer put out his hand. "I'll pray for you."

The bishop went quickly out of the room, afraid that emotion would crumble him. Mullane felt the same weakness in himself.

He lay down on the bed, tried to get his mind in some sort of order. He put aside the thought of what would happen to Scheer if he escaped: that would have to be left to God's grace, and he hoped the bishop's faith would not let him down.

But what about the soldiers guarding the house? Mullane had no weapons but his bare hands. The guards were not going to present themselves individually so that he could strangle them.

Then he heard one of the soldiers on the veranda say something and move away. He eased himself off the bed and looked out through the blind. The soldier went around the house and the second man stood up, stretched and uttered a loud yawn.

Several minutes passed, then the soldier out front looked around, walked to the corner of the house. Mullane heard him call to his companion: "Adachi?"

A dark blur hurtled out of the shadows and the soldier went down with a loud gasp. Mullane ran out of the bedroom and onto the veranda as Buka straightened up above the body of the soldier, a knife in his hand. He grinned at his boss.

"Boat down on beach, Boss. Quick!"

"Hold it a moment, Buka."

He turned to go back into the house, but Scheer was blocking the doorway. "I've changed my mind. May I come with you?"

Mullane didn't know whether to feel relief or annoyance. His conscience would be appeased, but would Scheer be able to stand up to the long trek back to Smokey Bay? But all he said was, "You're welcome. Go down with Buka to that launch. I've got something to do first. Do you have pencil and paper?"

"In my room. I'll get it—"

"No." Mullane pushed him across the veranda and down the steps. He went into the bishop's bedroom, turned up the oil lamp on the table beside the bed, where Scheer had been writing a letter. He grabbed a clean sheet of paper, wrote his name and a date in bold Japanese characters: McArdle, April 2, 1937. He went back to his own room, laid the note on the bed. As he was about to turn away he had another thought. He took the silver dollar from his pocket and laid it on the note as a weight.

Mullane left the house at a run, sped over the beach and jumped into the launch as Buka pushed it out. He started the engine, handed over the tiller to Buka and lay down beside Scheer in the bottom of the boat. "Better that we stay out of sight." Then he pushed the umbrella towards Scheer. "I grabbed that as I came out of your room. Somehow you're not you without it."

Scheer lay on the uncomfortable boards, his back in a pool of water. "Are you wondering why I asked to come with you?"

"Not really, Bishop. I think it's a case of the devil you know and the devil you don't. . . . At least you'll be more comfortable in Australia than in Germany."

They made their way across the harbour unchallenged, while Buka explained how he had seen Mullane captured.

502

"I run into town, Boss. Long way. I guess they take you to police station. Then I see them bring you out and take you to house. Was easy, then."

Was easy, then: two men knifed to death, his own life risked, all just to save his boss, the man who was going to desert him in a day or two.

But all Mullane said was, "Thanks, Buka."

Twice they passed close to barges heavily laden with supplies, but no one seemed to query why a lone native should be moving across the harbour in a launch in the middle of the night. It was obvious that the Japanese had bigger things on their minds.

Buka took the launch into the western shore. He whispered to Mullane, "Nobody here, Boss. But we got to walk half a mile back along road to trees on cliff. Our guns and packs still up tree."

Mullane said to Scheer, "We have something to do on the way to Smokey Bay. There may be some risk. Do you want to go on alone and we'll meet up with you?"

"If you don't mind, I'll stay with you. I may be of help."

THEY BEACHED the launch and went back to the steep path that led up to the cliff overlooking the harbour at Rabaul. The bishop found the going hard; once Mullane had to grab him to prevent him from falling backwards. But they reached the top, and Mullane and Scheer waited while Buka retrieved the guns and packs.

The brown man pushed something at Mullane in the darkness. "You want this, Boss?"

It was the New York Yankees cap. Mullane put it on, and it was almost like slipping on an old identity. If he got back to Townsville, he would present himself to Ruth as Con McArdle. . . .

It was an hour before daylight when they reached the stand of ficus trees from which they had watched the Taluka airstrip. They climbed into the same tree they had occupied before, with Scheer needing help from both Mullane and Buka. He was exhausted by the march, but he made no complaint.

They made themselves as comfortable as possible and settled down. When the three men woke, cramped and stiff but at least refreshed by their sleep, it was broad daylight. Clouds began to build up in the afternoon and by dusk were thick and low. Mullane suddenly felt pessimistic. There had always been only a slight chance that the bombers would come at his request, but now his scheme seemed hopeless.

He had told Buka what he had in mind and there had been some small satisfaction when the big native did not question or scoff at the idea.

But Scheer had said, "Your fire should start in the palm fronds at the top. How are you going to get up there?"

Buka said, "Maybe we use arrows. I see it in a fillum, one time in Rabaul. Fellers shoot arrows with fire on them—"

"Can you make a bow and some arrows?"

"I can find 'em, Boss. I'll be back."

So in midafternoon Buka had slipped down out of the tree and disappeared. He came back just after dark with a bow about five feet long and a bark quiver full of arrows.

"Took me long time, Boss. I found that police boy I know. He took me to feller who buy bow and arrows from Baining tribe, sell 'em to Japs for—what they call 'em?"

"Souvenirs." He and Buka would give the Japs a souvenir tonight that they would remember for a long time.

Just before dusk, twenty Mitsubishi Bettys had come in from the north, landed and parked along both sides of the strip. Mullane guessed that there must now be over fifty bombers on the strip and in the camouflaged hangar: sitting ducks waiting to be bombed. The Allied planes *had* to come tonight.

But the night remained black and unpromising. Mullane became cramped, hungry and miserable. At last he looked at his watch in the shaded glow of his flashlight. "Time to go. You stay here, Bishop. If Buka and I don't come back, here's my map. I've marked the route to Smokey Bay. It won't be easy, but you should make it."

"Good luck, Con. I'll give you two hours."

"We'll be back before then—I hope."

He and Buka left their rifles and packs stacked in a cleft in the tree, taking with them only the bow and arrows, their knives, one grenade and Mullane's spare shirt.

They moved in towards the southern end of the strip and found their way to where the petrol tankers were parked. They saw the two Japanese sentries, standing beside a tanker, when they were less than thirty yards away. Buka touched Mullane's arm and held up his knife. Mullane took out his own knife, feeling squeamish. I'm not a killer, he thought. But of course he was; given the opportunity, he would kill Yorida without a qualm.

He and Buka crept towards the two Japanese, and in a moment one slumped forward, with Buka's knife deep in his back. Mullane took the other man, grabbing him around the throat and pulling him backwards to drive the knife home.

Then he and Buka moved quickly. It took Mullane a minute or two to find the drainage cock on the first petrol tanker. He fumbled with it, managed at last to unscrew it. Petrol spilled out and the air reeked with the fumes. He raced to the second tanker; then the third; in five minutes he had unscrewed the cocks on all five tankers. He pulled the spare shirt from where he had stuck it in his belt, soaked it under the spilling cock of the last tanker. By the time he had finished, Buka was beside him with a jerrican he had snatched from the nearby dump. They filled the can, then raced up the strip, past the parked bombers, towards the first track that led towards the plantation. They could hear the voices of other sentries farther up the strip, and Mullane wondered if they would smell the petrol fumes.

Most of the plantation was in darkness, but in the huge hangar ahead of them there was a light. They could see three or four mechanics working on an aircraft. They could also see the dim shapes of planes parked wing tip to wing tip. Coconut palms stood among the planes, supporting the camouflage roof of netting and palm fronds.

They moved deeper into the kunai grass to give Buka a better angle for shooting the bow. In the darkness Mullane ripped the shirt into strips, tied each strip to an arrow, then doused the pieces of cloth in petrol from the can. At last he straightened up, stood waiting and listening and hoping.

He had no idea how long it was before he heard the faint drone of an aircraft engine. When it came it was too far to the west. Then he heard the others: five, six, he couldn't guess how many. And these were closer.

"Ready!"

He splashed the arrows once again with petrol and handed the first to Buka, who fitted it into the bow.

"Right, Boss!"

Mullane struck a match and held it to the arrow tip. The cloth flared up at once and, with a twang of the bowstring, shot towards the roof of the plantation hangar. A second and a third arrow followed. In seconds the netting and dead palm fronds were in flames. The last three arrows were shot straight into the front wall of netting; it, too, flared up. Then it was time to run.

They rushed back to the track down which they had come and had almost reached the end of it when they heard trucks racing along the strip. They plunged into the kunai and emerged only a few yards from the petrol tankers. Mullane abruptly stopped. He wrenched the grenade from his pocket, pulled the pin.

"Run, Buka!"

Then he hurled the grenade. It was a toss rather than a pitch, but he had never thrown a ball with as much satisfaction as he did that grenade. He dropped flat as it went off, then he was on his feet, running after Buka. The big native was looking back over his shoulder, grinning broadly in the glare of the huge blaze behind them. He did not see the sentry who rose up right in front of him and fired at him point-blank.

Buka ran straight into the soldier who had shot him and the two went down in a tumbling heap. Mullane, following on fast, drove his knife into the chest of the Japanese as he tried to get up. Then he crawled towards Buka, who lay face down, arms spread wide.

One look was enough: Buka was dead. Mullane let out a terrible cry of anguish, but it was lost in the roar of the first bomb as it struck. He saw the plantation, a mass of flames, heave outward as the bomb landed dead centre among the hidden Japanese aeroplanes. Mullane turned Buka's head, but the big dark eyes saw nothing of the destruction he had helped cause.

Sobbing with grief, Mullane got to his feet and started running again.

"I JUST WISH I COULD HAVE BURIED him, that's all."

Mullane had got back to the ficus tree, but it had taken him several minutes to recover enough to tell Scheer what had happened. The German at first had been almost youthful in his excitement, but had quickly subsided when he learned Buka was dead. He did his best to comfort the grieving Mullane.

"I think we should leave now, Con," he said. "You can't stay here and watch all that. . . ." The Allied bombers had gone, but the airstrip and plantation were still a blazing wreck. "It's not going to compensate for Buka's death or make you feel any better."

"I'm not leaving yet. I have something to do." He didn't explain. "Here's my compass. Keep heading west till you cross the main Jap supply road." He closed his eyes, tried to remember the countryside he, Vokes and Buka had passed through. "You'll come to a small limestone escarpment. Wait for me there. If I don't come by midmorning, head for Smokey Bay. Tell Frank everything went off as planned. Well, nearly everything."

Scheer said nothing, just slung Buka's pack onto his back and grasped his umbrella. Then he disappeared down into the darkness, and Mullane was left alone to stare at the blazing night and the memory of Buka's last big smile before he died.

COLONEL YORIDA knew he should not have trusted the bishop. The German had lied when he had said the Australian spies were to be picked up on the north coast. Constant patrols of planes and boats had sighted nothing: no submarine, no flying boat coming in at night. The party, with General Nara held prisoner, must still be on the island.

The bishop should never have been allowed to get away with his second lie, that the American McArdle was Father Holtz. Yorida stiffened with fury each time he thought how easily he had been fooled. He could not believe it when he had been wakened and told by his sergeant that the German priests had escaped; his disbelief had increased when the sergeant had produced the piece of paper with the pencilled characters on it and the American silver dollar. Now he took the coin out of his pocket. Was it some sort of unlucky charm?

How could he have not recognized the American, even with his beard and long hair? He knew he himself was not the man he had once been; he had advanced tuberculosis and he was to be repatriated as soon as the impending big campaign got under way. He was not as alert as he had been, but he should have remembered the American. If he had, last night's sabotage at Taluka would not have occurred. Now, in his staff car, he was on his way to inspect that disaster.

Yorida stiffened again with fury when he thought of how the American had got his revenge for what had happened in Tokyo five years ago. The death of the woman had been a mistake, the result of too much zeal on the part of his men. She had obviously known nothing of her husband's espionage work.

It was seven o'clock when Yorida reached the airstrip at Taluka. As the car drove down beside the long strip he could see the havoc that had been caused. Work gangs were trying to clear the strip for the few undamaged aircraft to take off. Some military cars were parked near the black wrecks of the petrol tankers. A group of officers was standing beside them and he instructed his driver to take him over to them.

He got out of the car, walked across to the commanding officer and saluted. It was not a crisp salute; he had forgotten the silver dollar still clutched in his hand.

"A bad business, Colonel Yorida. I cannot believe it was the work of natives."

"No, Colonel Toyama." He looked up and down the strip, then south to the hill some distance away, where he could see a line of thick trees. "I'm sure it was not the work of natives."

In the tree Mullane was firmly settled, the .303 Lee-Enfield with its telescopic sight resting on a thick branch. Through his binoculars he had seen the staff car coming down the strip and he had known Yorida would be in it. There had been no surprise when he saw the tall thin figure step out of the car. No security chief would send out a subordinate to report on such a major disaster as last night's.

He drew a deep breath and steadied himself. He put out of his mind how long he had waited for this moment. In the centre of his telescopic sight he saw Yorida face him. He allowed for the rifle's slight pull to the right, then squeezed the trigger.

Yorida had a moment of bewilderment before he died. The first bullet hit him in the chest, the second in the top of the head as he bent over. His hand tightened on the silver dollar, then opened, and the coin fell to the ground. He knew he was going to die, and he knew who had shot him.

MULLANE, RIFLE SLUNG over his shoulder, slid down the tangled trunk of the tree at a dangerous speed and hit the ground running. He figured it would take a few minutes for the men on the airstrip to determine where the shots had come from. He was in fairly good condition, but he had not run half a mile in more years than he could remember; certainly he had not run it with a pack and rifle bouncing on his back.

Suddenly he was under the blessed, sheltering screen of trees. He fell against a trunk, let it support him while he tried to mend his bursting lungs and turn the water in his legs back into bone and muscle. Then he drew himself together and moved on, no longer running but walking fast, feeling luck was with him.

He should catch up with the bishop long before midmorning.

RUTH SAT ON THE VERANDA of the house outside Townsville where she was billeted with Luke and Mark, and watched the big man in the white shirt and shorts, his navy officer's cap pushed back on his head, come up the street. She knew he was bringing bad news and she wondered how she was going to accept it.

Lieutenant Blomfield had come up four days ago to tell her they had word from Frank Vokes. Blomfield had said that Vokes had made no mention of Con Mullane, but she had had the feeling he was lying. She had gone down each morning and afternoon to Coastwatchers headquarters, and each time Blomfield, who had appointed himself her protector, had told her there had been no further news from Vokes.

Now she stood up, steeling herself. Then she saw that Blomfield was smiling. "We've heard," he said. "They came on the air this afternoon."

"Both of them? Con Mullane, too?"

"Both of them."

She wanted to weep and to laugh; but succeeded in doing neither. In a dry voice that hurt her throat she said, "Is he all right?"

"Con? I gather so. But he's asked us to bring them out and so we're sending a Catalina in tonight. The German bishop is with them. They should be here by tomorrow."

"Did they get all the information you wanted?"

"More than we expected. Marvellous stuff. I shouldn't tell you this, but you were part of the operation in a way. It'll be released to the press soon anyway. There's been a big battle in the Solomons and the Japs have been pushed back. Con's and Frank's information, plus what we got from our chaps at the top end of the Solomons when they got on the air—all that info had the Yanks waiting when the Japs arrived. I gather it was one hell of a battle," he said wistfully, wishing he had been at sea.

"Will Con and the others be mentioned in the press reports?"

"Afraid not. Nobody is supposed to know we exist. We just run our own private little war."

"Will you want them to go back?"

"Afraid so. The chief has said they can have two weeks' leave, then he wants them back on New Britain. The war is a long way from over, girl. We're just at the corner; we haven't turned it yet. What will you do?"

"Wait for Con. After that . . ."

But she wouldn't think about it. She could not think about anything but tomorrow.

Jon Cleary

"I never write about a place I haven't visited," says Jon Cleary, who knows at first hand the mountain jungles that provide the setting for *A Very Private War*. Although he did not belong to the Coastwatchers, Cleary did see action in New Britain during World War II, when he served in the Australian army. When he went back recently for a second look, he was amazed to discover that the island countryside had changed hardly at all in the intervening years.

Jon Cleary was born in Sydney, Australia, in 1917, the eldest of seven children. He left school at fifteen, during the depths of the Depression, to help support his family, and for the next few years he held a variety of jobs—from laundryman to film cartoonist. Then came the war and his army service. It was during this period that he began writing. After sharpening his skills on short stories, he finally published his first novel in 1947, and he has been a full-time writer ever since.

"I enjoy writing," Cleary says. "I look on myself as primarily a storyteller, but I do labour over my style. My recurring themes are of people set against action in remote regions."

Cleary is today acclaimed as one of Australia's leading authors. Several of his stories have been made into films, including the very popular *The Sundowners*. He is not one to linger over past triumphs, however. When asked which of his books is his favourite, he invariably replies, "My next one."

Jon Cleary is married to the former Joy Lucas, a Melbourne girl whom he met on a ship going to England in 1946 and married two weeks after disembarking. The couple, who have two daughters, have lived in a number of European capitals and continue to travel widely. But today they make their home in Sydney, where they have a breathtaking view of Sydney harbour from their living room.